LEVEN THUMPS

BOOK ONE:
THE GATEWAY TO FOO

BOOK TWO:
THE WHISPERED SECRET

◆

Don't miss these other
unFOOgettable adventures by Obert Skye:

LEVEN THUMPS
AND THE
EYES OF THE WANT

LEVEN THUMPS
AND THE
WRATH OF EZRA

LEVEN THUMPS

BOOK ONE: THE GATEWAY TO FOO
BOOK TWO: THE WHISPERED SECRET

OBERT SKYE

ILLUSTRATED BY BEN SOWARDS

Aladdin Paperbacks
New York   London   Toronto   Sydney

FOR THOSE OF YOU WHO SAW ME SLIP THROUGH
AND HELD THEIR TONGUES—
YOUR PART IN THIS IS JUST BEGINNING

❧ ALADDIN PAPERBACKS
An imprint of Simon & Schuster Children's Publishing Division
1230 Avenue of the Americas, New York, NY 10020
Leven Thumps and the Gateway to Foo text copyright © 2005 by Obert Skye
Leven Thumps and the Gateway to Foo illustrations copyright © 2005 by Ben Sowards
Leven Thumps and the Whispered Secret text copyright © 2006 by Obert Skye
Leven Thumps and the Whispered Secret illustrations copyright © 2006 by Ben Sowards
All rights reserved, including the right of reproduction in whole or in part in any form.
ALADDIN PAPERBACKS and related logo are registered trademarks
of Simon & Schuster, Inc.
Leven Thumps and the Gateway to Foo published in arrangement with Deseret Books.
The text of this book was set in Adobe Garamond.
Manufactured in the United States of America
This Aladdin Paperbacks edition May 2009
10 9 8 7 6 5 4 3 2 1
Library of Congress Control Number 2008943587
ISBN: 978-1-4169-6824-5

These titles were previously published individually by Aladdin Paperbacks.

CONTENTS

Contents

CONTENTS

———◆———

". . . it is a place where possibility is eternal; where scenery can change as effortlessly as dreams. There a being's view is shaded not by obstacle or travail, and *impossible* is a whisper spoken only by the souls who have just accidentally stepped in. It is a place where young children play in the shadows of Morfit, their voices a familiar melody, singing low in the wind, 'Step on a crack and Foo will snatch you back . . .'"

———◆———

THE BEGINNING

It was at least forty degrees above warm. The day felt like a windowless kitchen where the oven had been left on high for an entire afternoon. Heat beat down from above and sizzled up from the dirt as the earth let off some much-needed steam. The sky had decided it had had quite enough, thank you, and had vacated the scene, leaving the air empty except for heat. No matter how wide a person opened his mouth that afternoon or how deep a breath was taken, there just wasn't enough oxygen in the air to breathe. The few remaining plants in people's gardens didn't droop, they passed out. And the flags that only days before had hung majestically on the top of local flagpoles no longer looked majestic, they looked like multicolored pieces of cloth that had climbed up and tragically hung themselves.

All this in and of itself was not too terribly unusual, but as the heavy sun started to melt away an odd, wild, uncoordinated wind began to pick up. Not a northerly wind or an easterly breeze, it was a wind with no direction or balance. It was as if the four corners of earth and heaven all decided to simultaneously blow, creating what the local weather personalities in Tin Culvert, Oklahoma, called "beyond frightening." Sure, people could breathe, but now they were getting blown away.

Trees bent and writhed, whirling like pinwheels as the atmosphere pinched and pulled at them. Rooftops buckled and nature picked up huge handfuls of dirt and spastically flung them everywhere. Cats learned how to fly that evening, and any loose article weighing less than a car was taken up in the rapture of the moment. People locked themselves in their homes, radios on, waiting for someone to tell them everything was going to be okay, or for nature to do them in.

As dusk matured into night and just when those cowering in fear could stand no more, a darkness, the likes of which had never before been seen, began to ooze up from the ground and ink in the gray of evening. The hot windy sky quickly became a thick sticky trap. Animals that had foolishly taken shelter in trees or ditches began to suffocate as the heavy, plastic-like blackness folded over them. The wild wind swooped in from all directions to steal their last breaths and leave them dead where they once whined.

The blackness weighed down on everything. Porch lights burst under the weight of it. If the wind had been absent, a person could have clearly heard the explosion of almost every light and window in Tin Culvert as the fat, dark atmosphere let its full bulk rest upon anything glowing. Homes came alive with screams as front windows buckled and blew inward. Cars and mobile homes creaked under the force of darkness upon their backs. People cowered under tables and beds trying to escape the advancing crush.

Just when it looked like the end of the world had officially begun, the lightning started. Jagged stripes of blinding light flashed continually against the black sky. Anyone foolish enough to be standing outside would have been able to watch as the lightning moved with calculating accuracy, deliberately touching anything above ground level and quickly setting it ablaze. It moved sideways and upward. The sky became a giant blackboard with heaven scratching out its apocalyptic messages with lightning bolts.

Tin Culvert was dying, and this was the first night of the end of its life. Fate had set its course and was making certain to carry it out.

Even amongst the complete destruction and panic, a person would have had to be dead not to hear and feel the thunder that struck at exactly 10:15 that fateful night. The boom was felt as far as fifty miles away, and the entire sky fractured from light, scribbling one final message—"It is over!"

Lightning bled down on everything, touching and igniting any structure Tin Culvert had ever dared raise. People finally figured out that hiding was no longer a sensible option. Folks set out into the open, desperate to get away from it all.

In the chaos nobody noticed Antsel, a thin, aged man running across the ground at a terrific speed. Electrical static buzzed around him as he flew across the earth. The odd little man had traveled half the world to get to this spot and now, as the moment grew closer, his heart and soul surged. Fire raged up around him as he moved. His long beard curled and began to singe at the edges.

Lightning flashed in the tumultuous sky.

Antsel's stride became uneven, his face red with sweat and heat. He ran in a pattern, away from the fire and as if he were trying to throw somebody off his trail. The thick gray robe he wore flapped in all directions as the wind became aware of him and started to work him over.

Lightning flashed again.

Antsel stumbled and fell as he looked toward the sky. His knees plowed into the earth as he ground to a halting stop.

Lightning flashed yet again.

Kneeling, he reached with aged hands into his robe and pulled out Clover, a small cat-like creature—the tiny being wriggled and spat angrily.

"Be calm," Antsel ordered, wiping sweat from his own forehead.

Instantly the small furry being relaxed. Clover's tiny body was covered with gray hair. He had leaf-like ears that were thick and wide, and his knees and elbows were as bare as any palm. He had on a tiny cloak that was the color of his fur but shimmered slightly under the light of fires.

"This is it," Antsel whispered with severity. "The shadows will soon be here. You know what you must do. It'll be some time from now, but he will be here, and the girl as well. Be patient."

"Only if you tell me to be."

"Be patient," Antsel insisted.

"I won't leave you," Clover whimpered.

"You *will* leave me," Antsel commanded.

"I will leave you," he answered.

"Now run!" Antsel shouted, setting the furry creature down. "Run!"

Clover looked at Antsel. "You will be proud of me?"

"Of course. Now run."

Clover spat and smiled. He jumped, shivered violently, and ran off on two feet, bucking oddly as he leapt, and was lost almost instantly in the dark. Antsel gazed after him. He knew the risk he took in putting so much trust in such a mischievous creature, but he had no choice. He turned and ran the opposite direction.

Lightning flashed.

Antsel slowed his pace, feeling his age and marveling over the fact that his heart had not yet given out. He reached into his robe and withdrew an object more important than any soul within a million miles could comprehend. Sweat poured from his neck and wrists, and he could feel his heart beginning to crumble. Antsel held the tiny seed up to the light of the surrounding fires and glanced at it one last time.

Lightning flashed again.

He placed the seed back in his robe and kneeled. He pressed his face to the ground and used his ability to see everything beneath the soil. Every insect, every particle. This was the perfect spot. He lifted his head and brushed the sweat from his eyes. He then began to dig. His old hands bled and trembled as he plunged them deeper into the dark, rich earth. Lightning struck continuously as fire after fire ignited. The atmosphere began to relax, drawing in more oxygen to feed the flames.

Antsel paid no attention.

He had something to finish. He pulled the seed out again and pressed it down into the earth, then worked madly to fill the hole with the soil he had scraped out.

Lightning flashed, thunder crashed, and the howling of the wind increased.

He looked over his shoulder and shuddered. They were here, he could feel it in the wind. Antsel glanced at the ground, knowing that the fate of a thousand generations rested beneath only a foot of soil.

"Grow, Geth," he whispered. "Grow." Antsel patted the ground and dusted his palms. His job was done, and he stood with purpose.

Lightning flashed again, while simultaneously a sickened soul in another realm breathed a small dark army of shadows out over Tin Culvert. Sabine sat impatiently in Foo, breathing heavily and yet with control, letting his shadows twist down through the dark dreams of men and into reality. His castoffs were darker than the night, black. Like a perverted wind they swirled and billowed as they rushed across the fiery earth, laughing and screeching. Their white eyes and shrill voices gave their two-dimensional forms an eerie depth. Invisible to mankind, they swept the fiery landscape. They were not here to sightsee, however; they were here for a purpose.

Antsel knew the shadows had arrived. He couldn't let them find the spot. Running deeper into the night and far away from what he had planted, he wiped at his forehead with his heavy cloak and clutched his chest in agony. He would not last the night. He accepted this; after all, his mission was accomplished. The only thing he could do now was to run as far as possible away from the ground he had just touched. He pushed himself, darting to the right and turning a sharp left. His legs screamed in pain, and he could feel his heart pulsing up inside him like some sort of red-hot inflammation.

The moans of the shadows roared as they circled the burning town. Like a cyclone they twisted in tighter and mightier, their hollow eyes searching the firelight for the withered form of the old man they had been sent to find. The wind shifted and all together they lifted their heads and looked to the east. Nothing but flames and beyond that, darkness.

The winds shifted again.

Light from the fires reflected off a small hint of silver in the distance. The reflection vanished for a second only to spark up again even farther away. The shadows took notice. Something was running from them. Their restless forms turned toward the dark and flew.

Antsel ran. He could feel them coming toward him now and in a brief moment they were hovering over him, hissing and screeching. His old heart was making his stride short and almost pointless. Sabine's shadows swooped down and wrapped themselves around him, smothering his progress and slowing his gait even further. He pushed with his arms, waving the night away and struggling to go on.

It was no use: they had him surrounded and were pressing their hideous forms against him, moaning and gnashing their teeth. They circled him like a ring of plague. Antsel's purple eyes could faintly make out their inky outlines as they whispered wickedly.

He moved to the east but was stopped by the billowing of a shadow. He moved to the north and received a blow to the side.

Antsel was trapped.

"Where is it?" the shadows hissed. "Give us the seed."

His heart struggling to keep beating, Antsel wiped his eyes, put his palms to his knees, and tried to draw in breath. He straightened and lit an amber stick and lifted the firebrand to just below his eyes. The light from the stick glowed in a sphere around the gathering.

Antsel could see nothing but dripping darkness and thousands of shadows wildly circling him. They moaned, their white eyes even dimmer in the light of the amber stick. Nowhere in the sea of muted eyes could Antsel detect even a hint of mercy. He knew that somewhere in Foo, Sabine looked on with pleasure—his former friend no longer having any thought or feeling for anyone but himself.

Antsel's breathing was shallow and his heartbeat weak. The insistence of the surrounding shadows and the roaring of the fire in the distance seemed fitting to what he knew would be his end.

"Give us the seed," they hissed. "The seed."

"It is in Foo," Antsel gasped at them.

"You lie," they whispered back. "You lie."

"I—"

The shadows had no patience. Screaming, they leapt onto the old man. They clawed at him, searching for the object. Their hands ripped at his robe and body. Their mouths screamed and moaned as they tossed Antsel around like a rag doll. Antsel tried to fight back, but there were too many, and his strength and will were gone. The shadows thrust his face into the soil. Antsel could see everything. He watched the seed, though far from where he now lay, already begin to grow.

The shadows spun him once more and then withdrew with nothing.

Antsel lay on the ground moving only his lips. He murmured weakly, committing his soul to rest and waiting for fate to tell him it was over. He stared up and could see the false face of

Sabine in the thousands of shadows. His soul relaxed and his life slipped away.

The shadows began to moan. The seed had not been found. They knew too well that Sabine, the being who had cast them, would not be happy Antsel was dead. The shadows berated themselves. A few of them began to hiss, "Burn everything. Burn it!"

Antsel might have deposited the seed on earth. Sabine knew this, and even the remotest possibility of that couldn't be ignored. Most of the landscape was on fire, but a few pieces and parts were still void of flame.

"Burn it all," the shadows were now whispering fiercely. They all began to rise and laugh and dance, happy in their fury to carry out such a horrific thing. They swirled and scattered in a thousand directions to do Sabine's bidding. Some twisting together in a massive funnel cloud, they sucked up fire and dripped it down upon everything.

In the distance, far away from the heat and light, Clover stopped running so as to better cry. He stood to his full twelve inches and shivered. The fur over his body bristled in waves. His wet eyes viewed the flames as they devoured the entire landscape.

"Antsel," he whispered, his thin leathery mouth quivering. He wiped his blue eyes with the hem of his small robe, his leaf-like ears twitching to listen to the wind. He turned and continued running. Clover saw no reason to go back. Antsel was gone, and the journey had begun.

CHAPTER ONE

A RELATIVE OF FOO
THE BIRTH OF LEVEN

W ho can say for sure what constitutes the perfect birth? Perhaps a mother, while playing cards and sipping lemonade, might simply hiccup, pat her stomach, and there in her arms would be a beautiful child, already diapered and pink-cheeked, looking up at her and emitting a soft coo. That wouldn't be too bad.

Or perhaps, while taking a nice ride up the coastline on a golden afternoon, a woman might tap her husband on the shoulder and say, "Look what I found."

Together they would peer into the backseat and there would be their lovely newborn buckled in a car seat and sleeping blissfully. A person could argue that that scenario would be perfect to a lot of people.

Well, Leven Thumps experienced nothing of the sort. He

came into the world like a delivery that no one knew what to do with and nobody wanted to sign for. His father had passed away in a tragic car accident only a week before his arrival, sending his mother spiraling down into a deep pit of grief and mourning. Her only hope was in knowing that the husband she had lost would live on in the son she was about to give birth to. Two days before the delivery her health suddenly began to deteriorate. She couldn't stand, she couldn't sleep, and she found it difficult to even breathe.

On October fifteenth, at 2:30 in the morning, Maria Thumps knew she was not long for this world. She called her neighbor, who came immediately and quickly drove Maria to the hospital. Maria had been inside the hospital for only five minutes when her son was born. The child had a head of thick dark hair and wise open eyes.

The doctor placed the baby in her hands, and for the first time in a while Maria smiled. "Leven," she whispered.

Maria's smile began to fade. Her face paled to a new shade of white. She clenched her eyes shut and began to struggle for breath. Her hands twitched and Leven rolled from her arms and into her lap. Every machine in the room with a voice immediately began to wail and frantically beep, and the lights suddenly dimmed. Doctors and nurses huddled over Maria, trying desperately to work a miracle. It was no use. A tall doctor picked up Leven and handed him to one of the attending nurses. She stepped quickly out of the room with the child, saving him from the scene and pulling him away from the last person on earth who would love him for some time. Two minutes later Maria Thumps closed her eyes, ceased her labored breathing, and passed away.

Leven lay alone in the hospital nursery for days. Every morning at 10:00 and each afternoon at 3:15, a different nurse would come in, pick him up, and hold him for exactly four and a half minutes. Other than that he was touched only when being fed or changed. The hospital staff whispered about what to do with him, waiting for the state to decide, but the wheels of compassion were slow to get moving. Everyone was holding out hope that a kindly relative or family member might be found and the little orphan would be taken away and off their hands. The hospital was already short-staffed and money was hard to come by, thanks in part to a dozen or so recent malpractice law suits the administrators had been forced to settle.

On the fourth day following Leven's birth, the prayers in his behalf were answered. Well, sort of. Contact had been made with a half sister of Leven's mom. Her name was Addy Graph, and at this very moment, she was on her way to the hospital from one state over and two states up.

She arrived that evening, bringing with her a violent rainstorm that battered the hospital. Addy pulled up in a dull-looking black car with only one headlight and a mismatched door. The car shuddered to a stop in the spot reserved for ambulances and Addy Graph got out. Addy was not a pleasant-looking woman. She was heavy-set and had a high forehead and no lips. Her flesh was pasty white, and the veins beneath her chalky skin were not only visible, they were bulging, as if there were too much thick blood coursing through them. She had a protruding stomach and skinny legs you felt sorry for due to the big ball of weight they were called upon to support.

She slammed the mismatched car door and held a newspaper over her frizzy hair as she cursed the weather and moved toward the entrance to the hospital.

As she walked away from her car, a little security guard with a whistle around his neck hollered out at her. "This is for emergency personnel only," he chirped. "You'll have to move your car."

Addy glared at him. "Excuse me?" she sneered, her neck veins bulging.

The short man cleared his throat. "No unauthorized vehicles allowed." He made a large circle with his arm, indicating the area. "Your car must be moved."

"Then move it," Addy snapped. She pushed past him and into the hospital.

The young woman at the reception desk did her best to welcome Addy, but her pleasant greeting was met with total disgust.

"I drive all day and then when I get here some Neanderthal with a whistle tries to tell me where to park," Addy growled.

"I'm sorry . . ." the young girl tried. "But we—"

"Stow it. I'm here to pick up a kid," Addy interrupted, dismissing whatever the girl was about to say. "His mother died, so I'm saddled with him."

"Saddled?" the girl asked, confused.

"Stuck with him," she snarled.

"So you want the nursery?"

"What I want and what I'm about to get are two different things, Sweety. I've already spent too much money coming to fetch this brat."

"I'm sure someday he'll be grateful," the girl said, trying to be kind.

"I'd take that bet, if I thought you were good for it," Addy sniffed. "Now where's the nursery?"

For a moment, the young girl considered pointing in the wrong direction—thinking that might buy her some time to race up the stairs and rescue the poor baby that was going to be stuck with this piece of work. But she had to stay and answer the phone, so she simply pointed to the stairs and said, "The nursery's on the fourth floor, east wing."

"There had better be an elevator," Addy huffed.

"There is, just past the stairs."

Addy stormed off, mumbling and criticizing everything she passed. The elevator took too long to come. The inside of it smelled funny. The person at the reception desk for the nursery was curt. The nursery was cold. The floor was dirty. The staff was unfriendly.

By the time she finally laid eyes on the child she was completely out of sorts.

"That's him?" she almost laughed. "He's so small."

Leven squinted at her.

"He's just about the right size," the nurse on duty said.

"For what?" Addy sniffed.

"He'll be old before you know it," the nurse tried. "Babies grow so—"

"Thank you," Addy snipped. "I'm perfectly aware that babies grow. Do I need to sign something?"

The nurse was dumbfounded. Sure, all of the years she had worked there had made her a bit callused and bored. Babies were born every day, and it had long since ceased to be a miracle to her. She had seen everything. She once saw a baby born with two heads. She had even seen newborns come out laughing. She had also seen a dozen or so children be born and pronounced dead only to come alive again minutes later. She had seen a lot, but this loud, vicious lady was uglier and meaner than anything she could remember.

"I'll get the doctor," the nurse said, biting her lip. She stepped away, leaving Addy alone with her new responsibility.

Addy eyed Leven coldly. She sniffed again and looked away. When she looked back he was still there. She lifted up one of his legs and looked at it. She touched Leven's head. She scowled. She put her hand on the baby's arm and gingerly lifted it as if it might be diseased.

She dropped the tiny arm, screaming.

A huge, hairy, gray ball scurried out from under Leven, circled over his stomach, and rolled back under him.

Addy screamed hysterically as she pushed back and away, knocking over an empty cart and sending diapers and baby shampoo everywhere. The shampoo bottles exploded all over the floor, causing Addy to lose her footing and fall hard onto her rear. Her rump seemed to pop as a loud rush of air escaped her screaming, lipless mouth. A small team of nurses and a couple of doctors rushed through the door wondering what could possibly be going on to generate so much noise.

Addy just sat there, screaming and pointing. The nurse, who had had the pleasure of talking with her just moments before, filled a cup with water and happily threw it in Addy's face.

Sputtering, Addy said, "A rat. There's a giant rat on that child."

The medical staff all looked at the baby. No rat. Leven was simply lying there with his eyes wide open and a serious look on his face.

"That's impossible," one of the doctors said. "There are no rats here. Besides, it wouldn't be able to climb into the cart."

"Maybe it fell from the ceiling," Addy offered.

Everyone looked at the ceiling. It looked okay, no holes or possible way for a rat to fall from it.

Two nurses tried to help Addy to her feet, but thanks to the soapy floor, they lost their footing and also went down. Their flailing limbs knocked the legs out from under one of the doctors, and he fell, taking two more nurses with him. Everyone scrambled across the slippery floor, reaching for something to pull themselves to their feet with. It took a number of tries, but eventually everyone was standing again.

Once up they all carefully worked their way over to the baby. One of the nurses picked him up and inspected him.

"I don't see a rat," she said.

"It's there," Addy cried. "I saw it with my own two eyes. He was huge."

One of the doctors loosened the diaper and made sure the supposed rat had not hidden in there.

"No rat," he declared. "I've worked here for twenty years, and I have never seen a rat."

"Well, I've been here for a little over twenty minutes and already I've seen one," Addy said meanly. "Give me the child so I can take him somewhere safe."

"There are a few papers we need you to fill out," the doctor informed her. "And we have some questions and information for you."

"Fine, just hurry. I have a long drive back."

Everyone left the room except for one nurse who was on her hands and knees trying to clean up the soapy mess while the baby slept. Neither she nor Leven noticed Clover as he once again slipped up over him and scurried back underneath. Smiling.

CHAPTER TWO

A COLD WIND BLOWS IN
THE ARRIVAL OF WINTER

Amelia sat silently across the hall from the delivery room. She looked down at the baby in her arms, held her finger to the infant's thin lips, and softly quieted her. Amelia's meshing cloak hid them both from view and helped them blend nicely into the wall of vending machines on the fourth floor of the hospital. To anyone passing by, Amelia's head would have looked like a bag of chips, her body an assortment of candy bars and sodas. Amelia smiled at the baby in her arms.

"You're going to do great," Amelia whispered. "Remember, this is for Foo."

The child's green eyes widened at the mention of Foo as Amelia shifted and stood just a bit so as to have a better look into the delivery room. It appeared for a moment as though the

vending machine were stretching. Amelia could clearly see everything in the birthing room.

Unfortunately, things didn't look wonderful. As far as births
go it looked rather sad. No father around—he had left months
ago—and the mother of the impending child was not terribly
happy about what she had gotten herself into. Amelia could see
her embittered face.

Janet Frore was a square woman with an oval mouth and
thick, wild eyebrows. Thanks to the research she had recently completed, Amelia knew the whole history of Janet's pathetic life. She
knew Janet was a bitter person who saw nothing good in the world
around her. It had been documented that Janet had smiled only
twice in her life and certainly today's events would not elicit a
third. Normally a stern and quiet person, Janet was at present ranting and screaming as a small army of masked doctors and nurses
scurried around, performing their duties and trying to act calm.

"Push," Amelia heard the doctor order. "Push!"

Two pushes later, Janet's own screaming was drowned out by
the wailing of a brand new voice ushered into this very old world.

The new child screeched as if it had been sent to earth to do
just that. It put her mother's hollering to shame. Lights rattled
and windows shuddered in the face of the unworldly wailing.

The new mother pinched up her cheeks and squinted as
sweat cascaded down her face. The doctor tried to hand her baby
to her, but Janet was plugging her own ears. Nurses scurried
about acting busy, none of them wanting to be handed the wailing infant.

Amelia watched the doctor through the open door. He was begging the mother to hold her own child.

"I'm not holding her," Janet said, pushing back and waving the child away. "I don't want to hold her."

"Mrs. Frore," the doctor pleaded, "this is your daughter."

Janet looked at the small helpless child, her eyebrows wild. She twitched and rubbed her own forehead. "Maybe so, but I'm in no frame of mind to hold her. Take her away," she ordered.

Amelia tsked, she and the blond baby hidden beneath her cloak still blending in with the vending machines. Amelia could see the frustrated doctor wipe his brow. She figured he was probably wondering why someone had not helped him think through the decision to become an obstetrician.

Dr. Scott handed the child to a fat, happy-looking nurse named Pipa, who was the only nongrimacing person in the room. Nurse Pipa gently placed the child on a rolling table with high plastic sides. She clucked her tongue in disgust loudly enough to be heard and walked out of the room and down the hallway right past Amelia and the infant she was holding.

Amelia followed Pipa, the meshing cloak she was under making it look as though the wall was rolling in a wave behind the fat nurse. She slipped into the nursery after Pipa and moved into a far corner to wait.

Pipa bathed the newborn, gave her a couple of shots, and left the infant lying naked under the heat lamp. When she waddled out of the room, Amelia glided over to the newborn. She pulled back the meshing cloak to reveal her own face and the blond child she was holding in her arms. The cloak made the back half of her look like medical cabinets and a sink, while her exposed face had a lumpy nose. She wore thick glasses that made her piercing eyes look huge. She glanced over her thin shoulders and around the room. She was not a pretty woman, but her countenance was bright, and she had a strong, determined look about her, like a mother protecting her child from bullies. Amelia leaned forward, put the blond child under the heat lamp, and picked up the baby Janet Frore had just given birth to.

"Come, child," she whispered to the Frore baby. "You'll be much better off where I'm taking you."

Amelia turned from the baby she held and looked down at the one she had placed. "Good luck, and remember," she whispered ominously, "don't touch him."

She glanced at the blond child one last time, pulled the cloak back over her face, and stepped out of the nursery—unseen, with the once-screaming newborn resting calmly in her arms.

Nurse Pipa returned and stared curiously at the little blond baby who was now lying there.

"I don't remember wrapping you up like that," she muttered. "I've got to stop working two shifts in a row," she said, shaking her head. She moved to the adjoining room to attend to her other duties.

The child lay there in the still room. She was a cute baby, with thick, white-blond hair, a pink face, and brilliant evergreen-colored eyes. She smiled and laughed softly as the clock on the wall ticked. She rocked her body, flexed, and sat straight up on her hind end. She wriggled out of the tightly wrapped baby blanket and touched the sides of her cradle. She looked about the room and smiled. Sure, she wouldn't exactly be loved in the home where she'd be living, and yes, what she needed to accomplish in her life would take many long years. But none of that mattered at the moment. She was here, and the journey for her had begun. She took in the room. She couldn't believe how differently things looked here. The realm she had just left seemed like a dream. The fighting and the desperation she had escaped in Foo felt more like a story she had heard than a situation she had lived through. The thought of Sabine's eyes and his hatred for her burned in her mind, but even now she could feel the memories dissolving and fading away. She knew her knowledge of where she had just come from would soon be gone. Somehow that didn't frighten her. What she was here to accomplish made any risk worth taking. She lay back down and gazed up at the fluorescent lights on the ceiling.

Nurse Pipa stepped into the nursery with a skinny nurse named Elizabeth. They stood together and let their eyes rest on the unwrapped child. The baby looked back at them, her green eyes seeming to focus on their faces.

"How'd you unwrap yourself?" Pipa questioned. "That's odd." She picked the child up, rewrapped her, and laid her back down.

"Oh, look at the smile on her," Elizabeth said with wonder. "That's sort of unsettling—she looks all grown up."

"All grown up," Pipa gently scolded, "don't be silly. She's got a little gas, that's all." Pipa rubbed the baby's belly and told her she was beautiful, gas and all.

"Look at those eyes," Elizabeth said. "I've never seen such a color. And they look so . . . knowing."

Pipa touched the baby's cheek and noted, "She feels a bit cold." The fat nurse turned up the heat lamp above the baby.

The baby frowned. In a few hours she would no longer know anything about her former self, and she was hot. She frowned again, the reality of who she really was beginning to slip farther away.

"Pity she's stuck with such an awful mother," Pipa whispered to Elizabeth as they continued to look at her. "I have never seen such a bitter person."

"The woman just had a baby," Elizabeth defended. "Maybe she'll mellow a bit."

"Let's hope so." Pipa touched the baby's nose and smiled. "Will you be okay?" she asked in a soft voice.

"I'll be fine," the newborn answered.

Both nurses' jaws fell. Elizabeth dropped the towels and rolls of bandages she was holding.

"Did you hear that?" Pipa whispered in awe.

"I think I did," Elizabeth squeaked. "Ask her again."

Pipa touched the baby's nose again and with more interest than last time asked, "Will you be okay?"

The baby smiled, closed her green eyes, and slept.

CHAPTER THREE

WHERE MONSTERS LIVE

The Rolling Greens Deluxe Mobile Home Park was situated on fifty-five acres of Burnt Culvert's finest burnt soil. The town, once named Tin Culvert, had rebuilt itself following a devastating fire that had burned most of it down a few years earlier. No one really wanted to build over the actual charred parts, but Mr. Hornbackle, an Irishman with a bad knee and a soft heart, bought fifty-five acres of blackened land. He put in a couple of wells, laid out a few roads, and called it Rolling Greens Deluxe Mobile Home Park. Now it housed over one hundred and twenty mobile homes. Thirty-two of them were double-wides, and all the rest were singles, except for two RVs that had been allotted the tiniest of space to reside near the north end of the park, by the east leech field.

As soon as the park opened people began to move in and either upgrade or downgrade the area. Some residents planted trees. Some put in lawns. A few built sheds or outbuildings. Some paved tiny slabs of concrete so as to have somewhere to put a picnic table and a barbecue. Others added awnings and outdoor carpeting.

Some, of course, did nothing.

Despite what residents did and didn't do, almost the entire park had sold out. Folks in the area were happy to live somewhere cheap. They were willing to put up with the surrounding scorched earth and the constant smell of smoke in the air. They didn't even mind that after a rainstorm their streets would run with what looked like tar. If a person could make his mortgage payment and still have money for food and entertainment, that was all that seemed to matter. To heck with the condition of the soil your home rested on if you could still afford to go to the movies every once in a while.

Strangely though, one lot in the Rolling Greens Deluxe Mobile Home Park had never sold. Near the far back at the edge where the park skirted up against a shallow creek bed there sat empty a single plot of land, and as hard as Mr. Hornbackle had tried to sell it, nobody wanted to buy it. That was somewhat surprising, seeing how it was situated in a relatively quiet area and had the only mature tree in the park growing on it.

People were interested, but something always came up to squelch the sale. For instance, while walking around the lot, potential buyers would stumble into deep sinkholes that peppered the ground. Or they would be put off by an odd smell that wasn't evident just one space over. Unusual weeds also grew on the land—weeds with sharp ends that seemed to have angry or defensive spirits. There had been a number of people poked or stabbed by the wild growth that spot of soil produced.

A ladies' auxiliary group that focused on community beautifi-cation had come and spent a day trying to clean up the area. One of the women ended up in the hospital with serious, weed-related injuries. The foliage was so fearsome that no one had since attempted to yank anything up.

It was simply bad land.

Mr. Hornbackle had lowered the price of the lot until it was almost free, but land that comes with a foul smell, hundreds of sink holes, and weeds with an attitude is not all that desirable, even at a cut-rate price. So the lot had remained unoccupied, watched over by the lone tree, which grew quite well despite the seemingly poor earth in which it was planted. The tree produced huge leaves in the summer, and in the winter its thick gray bark was striking. It had hundreds of gnarled limbs that lifted and twisted in the most unusual manner and directions. It had come a long way from the seed it once was.

A true thing about seeds is that they don't always stay seeds. In addition, most seeds grow up to be something. Some become plants or trees that then go about producing more seeds. Some seeds get popped and eaten and . . . well, you probably have a pretty good idea of what happens to things after they get eaten.

Some seeds are dried, some are pressed for oil, and some simply end up in bean bags or as the rattle in a baby's toy. It's probably fair to say that the life and times of a seed isn't necessar-ily the most exciting thing in the world, but what the seed lacks in excitement, it makes up for in miracles.

It's a miracle that a tiny seed can change from a dot in your palm into a towering tree whose wood can be made into the home you live in or the paper books are printed on.

But the seed that Antsel had slipped from his robe and deposited in the rich soil all those years before was not an ordinary seed. It was a transplant from the realm of Foo, a fantrum seed that contained the exiled soul of a great lithen named Geth.

The plot of ground in which Geth was planted might very well have remained unsold forever if it had not been for Addy and Terry Graph. They drifted into town like an unpleasant odor. She was loud and self-righteous, with a head full of perpetually bad hair. He was loud and usually soused. When they inquired about buying a lot at the Rolling Greens Deluxe Mobile Home Park, they were told by Mr. Hornbackle that the place was full up.

"Full up?" Terry snapped, obviously used to people finding or making excuses to keep him out of their neighborhood.

"No vacancies," Mr. Hornbackle insisted. "Except . . ."

"Except?" Terry questioned, suspiciously.

"There is one open lot, but I'm not sure it would suit you and your lovely family." Mr. Hornbackle looked at Addy Graph as she held an almost two-year-old Leven on her lap.

"That's not my family," Terry insisted. "I'm married to the woman, but the kid belongs to my wife's half sister who died. He doesn't even have our last name."

"I'm sorry to hear that," Mr. Hornbackle said sincerely.

"We've been tried heavier than most folks," Terry offered. "Now where's this lot?"

"It's unlivable," Mr. Hornbackle insisted.

"We'll see about that," Terry snorted, his lumpy nose and forehead growing red.

Mr. Hornbackle instructed the Graphs and their young burden to get into the cab of his pickup truck. He then drove them to the one open spot he had never been able to sell.

"It's not perfect," Mr. Hornbackle primed them as he drove. "The ground's not very good, and it's a bit overgrown with weeds."

"Oh, great," Terry whined, turning his bloodshot eyes to Addy. "I'm not spending my days pulling weeds someone else let grow."

"There's also a tree," Mr. Hornbackle pointed out.

"A tree," Addy sniffed sarcastically. "Did you hear that, Terry, a tree?" She rolled her puffy eyes.

Terry laughed, making an annoying gurgle in his throat as he did so. "Are there any other mobile home parks around here?" he asked. "My wife's employment is just up the street."

"I'm afraid not," Mr. Hornbackle said sadly, wishing he had never met these two. "The town is slowly rebuilding from a huge fire that came through here a few years ago. There are a couple of mobile home parks about fifty miles west."

"I'm not driving fifty miles to work each day," Addy declared. "You'll pull weeds before I submit myself to that."

"I'm not pulling any weeds," Terry whined. "Where's this lot?"

"Right around this bend," Mr. Hornbackle answered. "I'm sure you'll find it—"

Mr. Hornbackle's jaw dropped as he turned the corner and

saw the lot. There at the end of the road sat 1712 Andorra Court, a spectacularly beautiful piece of land. The tree was lush and full. Around its base, the ground was covered with an array of dainty white and purple flowers. Chirping birds flitted in and about the leafy tree, which was illuminated beautifully by a shaft of brilliant sunlight.

"That's it?" Addy asked in amazement. "That's the unlivable lot?"

Mr. Hornbackle was too busy gawking in disbelief to respond.

"Just as I thought," Terry bit, wiping his lumpy nose on his sleeve. "Holding out on us, huh? Well, it's not going to work. We'll take it."

"I don't—" Mr. Hornbackle tried to say.

"I said, we'll take it." Terry reached into his wallet and fished out enough for a down payment. "We'll be back next week with our home."

Mr. Hornbackle took the money, still gaping at the serene and beautiful lot that lay in front of him. Just yesterday the place had been nothing but weeds and darkness. Today it was a section of land he could have easily charged double or triple price for.

Mr. Hornbackle turned the pickup around and slowly drove back to the office. Once there he stayed in the truck as Terry, Addy, and the small child got out.

"Don't even think of leasing that out to anyone else," Terry warned. "We'll have you in court. Unlivable my eye." He turned and spat on the ground.

Mr. Hornbackle just stared, his mouth still hanging open.

CHAPTER FOUR

GETH

Fate was working splendidly. Geth stood tall, shading with his branches the newly parked trailer house of Leven. He stretched his trunk, creaking as he took on inches. Geth peeked with the tips of his limbs through the windows of the single-wide, looking for Leven. Terry and Addy had finally settled in, but there would now be some wait for the child to grow into his role.

Geth twisted the tips of his branches inward to look at himself. He was a long way from what he had been in Foo. Geth, you see, was a member of the First Order of Wonder. He was also a lithen, a rare species that travels and lives by fate. Lithens know little of fear or confusion because they let fate move them. A true lithen would think nothing of walking off a four-hundred-foot cliff because he would know that if it were his time, he would hit the ground and die. But if it were not meant to be, he would simply be picked up by the wind or rescued by a giant eagle.

Lithens were fearless and honest to a fault. They were also the original inhabitants of Foo, given a sacred charge to guard the realm that gives humans the privilege of dreaming.

Geth had grown well where he was planted. At first a tiny shoot, he had emerged through the soil and into the blue sky knowing that there was plenty of time to grow as he waited to accomplish what needed to be done. But by the time he had grown two stories tall, Geth had discovered the power of his limbs. It had happened quite by accident. A family of birds had made themselves happy in his top branches, and he had simply *thought* about shooing them away. Well, no sooner had he thought it than his branches began whipping around, waving the birds off.

He also had the remarkable ability to see from every tip of his branches. He could see in front, in back, and on all sides continually. There was not a creature or person who could approach without him knowing.

By simply willing it, Geth could also extend his roots hundreds of feet underground, boring effortlessly into the earth to fill it with holes and pock marks. He could collect rainwater in these underground channels and use that water to produce wicked sprouts that sprang out of the earth like angry weeds. Geth knew all of these tools would be necessary for what was coming.

Antsel had known there was no way for Geth to return to Foo without help. He had been well aware that in order for hope to continue, Geth would need a bit of assistance on his return. Antsel also understood that there was only one person who could both bring Geth back and thwart Sabine's evil plan.

It was that person Geth was now watching over—Leven Thumps. It was only a matter of time before Leven would be old enough to complete the task at hand.

Geth stood tall in the Oklahoma soil, growing stronger each moment, and behaving like the lithen he was. He had no worries, no concerns, and no panic. Fate had put him where he was, and if he did his part, fate would get him back home.

Geth uncurled the tips of his branches and gazed into eternity. The waiting had begun.

CHAPTER FIVE

FOURTEEN YEARS OLD

Terry and Addy Graph couldn't stand to hear Leven talk or fuss, so from the time he was a little child, they insisted he sleep in an old twin bed on the screened-in back porch of their trailer house.

Leven didn't mind. He liked sleeping outside by himself. He would listen to Terry snore or the neighbors argue and count stars and trace the long swaying branches of the huge tree in his yard.

His life was not charmed. He had no friends, no cousins, no grandparents, not even a single kindly neighbor who looked out for him or waved as he walked by. Terry wouldn't let him get a pet, and Addy insisted he stay away from other kids for fear that Leven would form some unhealthy attachment to some hoodlum who would only grow up and steal her good jewelry when he came by to visit Leven. So, for the bulk of his childhood, Leven had been alone.

All that changed one night in the middle of summer and during a low moaning wind storm. Leven got a surprise. He was fourteen now and so tall that his feet hung off the end of his small bed by a good six inches. His long dark hair was the color of rich mud and on the right side of his head there was a streak of brilliant white hair. According to Addy something had happened to him when he was four that had scared the pigment out of him. Addy claimed the incident had occurred when she wasn't around and that she had no idea what had transpired. "What business is it of mine?" she would always say. Leven couldn't remember any incident. He had tried to color the streak, but no matter what he did it remained bright white.

Beyond that, he had clear brown eyes, a straight nose, ears that protruded slightly more than most people's, and a large mouth that made him look a bit like a boy who had not completely grown into himself yet, which is what he was.

Normally, Leven wasn't scared of sleeping alone on the porch, but tonight he was a little spooked by the strange wind and the low noise it was emitting. As he lay in his bed he stared out through the screened porch. Leven was looking toward the home next door when he saw a thick patch of black swoosh behind the neighbor's place. It glided and seemed to be whispering something.

Leven sat up rail straight, his heart pounding, the back of his neck burning.

He squinted his brown eyes and tried to make out whatever it had been. His eyesight was awful, and his aunt refused to buy him glasses on the grounds that she thought it would make her look silly to be walking around with a bespectacled boy.

Another swath of black slid across the ground and brushed over the screen, whispering. The shadow turned, and tiny pinpoints of white stared at Leven from a dark, rat-like face as it glided by.

Leven scooted as far as he could away from the screen and back in his bed, willing whatever it was to go away. The black shape circled back, pressing up against the screen, its white eyes glowing.

"Find him," it whispered. "Him."

The shadow pushed against the screen and began to work itself in. Like black spaghetti it oozed through the mesh. That was enough. Leven leaped out of bed and began pounding on the door to the trailer house.

"Let me in!" he insisted. "Aunt Addy! Terry!"

The black shadow moaned and oozed some more.

"Aunt Addy!" Leven yelled. "Aunt Addy!"

Leven could hear movement and grumbling inside.

"What is it?" she hollered through the door.

"There's something out here!"

Terry and Addy kept the door locked at night so as to keep out burglars and prevent Leven from waking them up by using the bathroom or coming in too early. Those locks now turned as she unlocked the door to open up.

"This better be good," Addy threatened through the door. "I was applying my mask."

Over his shoulder, Leven could see the blackness seeping into the porch, hanging there like a stringy rag. It drooped, dripped, and then began to quickly retract.

The door opened. Leven turned to look at his aunt, his face white and his eyes frantic. He glanced back at the screen. The black swath was gone, but now Leven had his aunt to contend with. He half wished the blackness was back.

"Something was coming through the screen," Leven pleaded. "It was—"

"Where is it now?" she barked. Her face was green, thanks to a nighttime mud mask she was wearing, and her hair was sticking up all over the place, making her head look like a honeydew melon sprouting kinky hay.

"It's gone," Leven said sheepishly, his eyes foggy.

"I have a job," Addy hissed. "Do you think I can go to work tired and still keep my job? Do you?"

"No," Leven said. "I'm sorry; maybe I should sleep inside tonight."

Addy laughed. "I should say not. You're fourteen. Besides, this night air will do your imagination some good." Small flecks of dried green mud showered from her face as she spoke.

"Really," Leven begged. "It was coming in."

"Monsters don't come in through doors," Addy said impatiently. "They live under beds like that one," Addy added, pointing to the small, used bed that Leven slept on. "But don't worry, if there was one under yours it would have eaten you already," she said coldly.

"Aunt—"

"How many times have I told you, don't call me *aunt*. I am your mother's half sister." She slammed the door and locked it.

The wind moaned.

Leven looked at his bed. He looked at the screen door and quickly bounded across the porch and jumped back onto his mattress. He pulled the blankets up over himself and tried to think of something safe and comfortable. His short blanket was a clear symbol that his life had not been full of too many safe and comfortable things, so it took great imagination to conjure up something pleasant. He thought about his parents, whom he had never known. He thought about his mother, who had died giving him birth. He thought about his futile life and wished he could just fly away from it. Not on a plane or in a helicopter, but just by himself. He wanted to stand in the open prairie and lift off, up to the moon to soar between clouds and above houses. He had almost forgotten about the blackness that had visited him earlier when he heard a scratching from beneath his bed.

He stopped breathing so as to better panic.

Skritch, skritch.

Leven's heart stopped. Something was under the bed. He could feel the light vibration as it scraped away.

"Just go to sleep," he told himself. "Just go to sleep." He closed his eyes as tightly as he could. The back of his eyelids burned and white dots danced in the blackness.

Skritch, skritch.

It was still there. Leven thought about jumping off of his bed, but there was nowhere for him to go. The door to the inside of his home was locked, and the screen door leading outside had just been occupied by oozing black. He thought about trying to fall asleep, but he couldn't bear the thought of that happening now for fear that whatever was scratching would feast upon him as he slept.

Skritch, skritch.

"Who's there?" Leven whispered. The noise stopped. With the rest of his body pressed tightly against the wall, Leven moved his head to the edge of the bed and peered over. He could see nothing but floor. He pulled his head back onto his pillow and breathed deeply. Then he inched back to the edge and leaned over a bit farther so he could see under the bed. Nothing. He pushed his head down even more, the ends of his shaggy brown hair hanging and touching the cold floor. He gazed under the bed.

He was not alone.

Two big glowing blue eyes stared back at him. Leven pulled back so quickly he pushed the bed away from the wall and fell into the space onto the floor. Scuttling like a crab he backed into the corner of the porch, searching for anything he might use to protect himself. He grabbed a couple of rocks out of the bucket Addy kept by the back door for throwing at noisy dogs or cats. He crouched against the wall, facing his bed, ready to throw them at whatever was there.

The blue eyes under the bed blinked.

Whatever it was, it was clinging to the bottom of the mattress, its head hanging beneath it with its eyes staring out. It looked no larger than a small cat, but its shape was inconsistent with any animal Leven had ever seen. He thought about hollering, but he knew Addy would never come out now that he had already cried wolf once. The creature blinked and smiled.

"Hello, Lev," it said kindly.

"Excuse me?" Leven said in disbelief, amazed that whatever it was, was now talking to him.

"Sorry, for the scare and all." The creature's nose twitched. "Antsel told me to not do that."

"Antsel?" Leven asked.

"He was my burn before you."

"Your *burn?*"

"My assignment. We sycophants burn only for those we are assigned. It has always been our lot. I desired nothing but to serve him at that time."

Am I dreaming? Leven questioned himself, wondering if he had perhaps fallen asleep.

"Not likely," the little creature laughed. "Dreams are pretty and usually involve horses or rainbows or castles, or big—"

"I know about dreams," Leven interrupted. "Then who are you?"

"I am Clover. Clover Ernest." His blue eyes blinked. He let go of the bottom of the bed and twisted to land on two of the littlest feet Leven had ever seen. He strode out from under the bed with confidence. He stood like a human but with a body more like a cat. He had no tail and was about twelve inches tall and covered in gray hair everywhere except for his face and his knees and elbows. He had leaf-like ears, a wide, crooked smile, and wet, blinking blue eyes. His nose was straight but pointed to his right just a bit. He wore what looked to be a little silvery dress with a hood on the back. His fingers were as thin as twigs and as knotty as any pine a person might encounter. He was like no monkey, bear, raccoon, cat, or any other animal Leven had ever seen. The long hair directly above his eyes stood and wiggled whenever he spoke.

"What are you?" Leven asked.

"That all depends upon you," Clover smiled. "What do you want me to be?"

Leven looked closely at Clover; there was an aura about him that wasn't threatening and Leven wasn't afraid. He felt comfortable and relaxed just a bit. "How about being honest?" Leven said.

Clover sighed, his eyelids contracting. He motioned to a small stepstool Terry used to change light bulbs. "Do you mind?" he asked, wanting permission to sit.

Leven nodded.

"I can't believe they keep you out here," Clover said, hopping up onto the stool.

"It's not too bad," Leven shrugged.

"It's better than where you lived when you were first born. I'll give you that. That place was awful," Clover complained.

"You know where I used to live?" Leven said in amazement.

"Of course," Clover seemed to brag. "I was there, too."

"Under my bed?"

"Under your bed, in your dresser, your car, your yard, your bathroom—you name it, and I was there." Clover shook his head and smiled as if reliving a pleasant memory.

Leven stared at the creature in amazement. "Why?" he finally asked.

"I'm guessing you're a nit. Although I haven't seen your gift surface yet."

"A nit?"

"They're fairly common in . . . well, that's not important. What matters is that Antsel told me to stick by you."

"And you do whatever this Antsel says?"

"Of course; I'm a sycophant. That's what we do," he said nonchalantly. "But now, I'm *your* burn."

"I don't understand," Leven said. "I don't know any Antsel." He stood and looked at the locked door leading inside. He gazed at his bed. "I must still be asleep," he reasoned.

"Do you want me to agree with you about that?" Clover asked nicely.

"Only if it's true."

"You're not asleep. Nope, in fact, this is probably the beginning of a long sleepless night. It's actually the beginning of much more than that. But, for now, all that's important is that I'm Clover, or Cloe, or whatever. I answer to any of those. Of course, I would be fine with you labeling me something else entirely." Clover paused to see if Leven was going to say something.

Leven didn't.

"I was assigned to Antsel hundreds of years ago," Clover went on. "He wasn't much older than you are now. A little shorter, though."

"Hundreds of years ago," Leven said skeptically. "How old are you?"

"I can't remember," he waved. "We sycophants live forever. There's only one way for us to die."

"How's that?" Leven asked.

"It wouldn't be very prudent of us to go telling folks that, now would it?" Clover grinned, and his blue eyes slanted as the corners of his mouth pushed up on them.

"I suppose not," Leven smiled, beginning to like the small creature. "So why are you here?"

Clover shook a bit and said, "I've been with you since birth. There have been few moments of your life when I have not been around. I slept in late a couple of years ago and you made it to school without me, but aside from that . . . "

"How is that possible?" Leven asked, more in wonder than in doubt. "How could you have been there for any of that? I've never seen you."

Clover smiled and looked around. "You want me to show you?"

"Sure," Leven answered, his brown eyes blinking.

Clover got up off his stool and brushed his forearms. He walked right up to Leven and asked him to hold out his hand. "Can you feel this?" he asked, touching Leven's right thumb.

Leven nodded.

Clover stepped back. His robe shimmering slightly in the

moonlight, he looked like a doll designed for trolls to play with. Then he pulled his hood up over his head and touched Leven's hand again. Leven felt nothing. Not only that, he could no longer see Clover. Leven looked around the porch and glanced under the bed and into the corners.

"Clover?" he whispered, surprised to find himself hoping it had not all been just a dream. "Clover?"

Suddenly there he was again, sitting in Leven's lap. Leven jumped just a bit.

"How'd you do that?"

"I'm a sycophant," Clover said again. "It's what we do. Technically, I am a part of you, and I want nothing but to make you happy."

"I don't believe it," Leven said sadly. "Why would anyone . . . or anything . . . want to make *me* happy?"

"Ah, Antsel said you would be slow to believe," Clover smiled. "Leven Thumps, you are incredibly more than you believe yourself to be. I wouldn't be here otherwise."

"I've got to be dreaming," Leven said honestly. It was harder for him to believe that he was of value than it was to believe that there was a furry creature named Clover Ernest.

"You're not dreaming," Clover insisted, brushing his own ankles with his hands. "I've been here and I will be here for the duration."

"The duration of what?"

"Of our time," Clover said sharply.

"Why have I never seen you before?"

"Because you weren't supposed to see me."

"Why now?" Leven asked, flexing his shoulders as he leaned closer to Clover.

"Because time is running out and they are getting near."

"Who's getting near?" Leven said, looking around.

"I wasn't the first to show myself tonight, was I?" Clover asked, cocking his head to one side.

"You mean the blackness?"

"That blackness was one of Sabine's shadows. They have been looking for you for many years."

"Why?" Leven asked, as if he had just been told a joke. "Why would they be looking for me?"

"I can't tell you everything," Clover insisted.

"But I thought you had to tell me everything."

"I desire nothing but," he bowed.

"So tell me," Leven asked kindly.

"I was bound to Antsel first," Clover replied. "His wishes are still of importance to me."

"So what will happen if *they*, whoever they are, find me?"

"Nothing good," Clover whispered. "That's why we have to get going soon."

"Going where?"

"That's for Geth to explain." Clover jumped up onto the bed and made himself comfortable on Leven's pillow.

"Geth?"

"Yep," Clover said. "Pretty much the fate of the entire world is depending on it though." Clover yawned, and his small face scrunched up as he did so. He blinked and closed his eyes. "No pressure, though."

Leven simply sat there staring at him, with his wide mouth hanging open. A few moments ago he was an unwanted child sleeping on the porch of his cold-hearted aunt's . . . his mother's half sister's . . . house. Now, he was a confused boy, talking with a stuffed animal that seemed to think Leven held the future of the world in his hands.

"You're kidding about all this, right?"

Clover opened his blue eyes.

"Do you want me to be?"

"I'm not sure," Leven answered honestly.

"Well, then neither am I."

Leven got up onto the bed next to Clover. His mind was racing a million thoughts per second. He couldn't focus his brain on any one thing. He wanted to fall asleep so that he could wake up and realize that all this was just a dream. On the other hand, he was afraid to close his eyes for fear of discovering that he wasn't what Clover was saying he was.

"Good night," Clover said softly.

"So I should call you Clover?" Leven asked in reply.

"Whatever you wish."

"Good night, Clover."

The leaves on the giant tree in Leven's yard rustled softly in the night breeze. Leven lay next to the furry, cat-like thing named Clover, trying to mentally digest everything he had just seen and heard. His head kept filling with self-doubts and odd pictures.

For some reason his mind began to play images of a girl. She wasn't familiar to him, but no matter how he tried he could not get her face out of his head.

Clover complained about Leven's fidgeting.

"Sorry," Leven said. "By any chance is the person we're waiting for a girl?"

Clover laughed. "Geth, a girl?"

"Well?" Leven asked.

"No."

"I keep seeing a girl in my head," Leven said.

"Is she pretty?" Clover asked sweetly.

"No . . . I don't know. She's just there."

"Pay attention to her face," Clover yawned. "She might be important."

Leven didn't sleep a wink.

CHAPTER SIX

HAIRY SITUATION

Winter Frore had a hard life. Her mother, Janet, was not a good person. If you had a mom who continually taunted you, tripped you, talked poorly about you behind your back and negatively in front of you, drew mean pictures of you, the kind of pictures where your head looked small and your rear looked big, told lies about you, pointed at you in public places and ridiculed you, stole your things and broke your favorite possession by stomping violently on it, well, you'd call it a hard life, too. And that's the kind of life Winter had been dealt.

Winter had long, wild, blond hair and wide-set, green eyes. She had a small nose and rounded cheeks that made her look as though she were always about to blow out a candle or begin whistling. She had no friends and spent most of her time at the library, in the back corner, reading books about people with

families and friends, or at the very least, pets. She had felt alone for as long as she could remember.

The only positive in her life was a kindly family who lived in a yellow house with missing shutters and a red front door two blocks down from her and her mother. The house was home to Tim and Wendy Tuttle—a fun-loving, extremely brainy couple that loved having Winter around. Wendy Tuttle was a kind woman with big hips and long black hair that she always wore in a braid tied off with a yellow ribbon. Her husband, Tim, was a garbage man with a weak chin and big ears. His job, although not one esteemed by society, seemed desirable to Winter because he always came home with interesting finds—lamps that sort of worked, bikes with no seats or missing spokes, and furniture that didn't look half bad once it was repaired and painted. The Tuttles had two young boys named Darcy and Rochester. Darcy was eight and Rochester was six. Winter loved the Tuttles and their boys. They were an island in the sea of disdain and sadness in which she lived.

Winter's mother, Janet, did not like the positive influence the Tuttles had over her child.

"The world is not a happy place," her mother would always insist. "The Tuttles are giving you false hopes."

Janet forbade Winter from visiting them, but it was an order that Winter refused to obey. Whenever possible, Winter would sneak away from home to be with a family that loved her and was so completely different from her own.

Winter's mother, Janet, knew nothing about "love," unless you were talking about the love of self. She placed mirrors everywhere around the house, so she could catch frequent glimpses of herself. Janet would stare into the mirrors for hours, fascinated for some perverse reason with her pinched, sour reflection and her bushy eyebrows and homely oval mouth, which she could never completely close.

Janet didn't talk unless she had something mean to say, and she thought only of the negative even if life was treating her fairly. The worry and bitterness she carried around had turned her into a sour, disgruntled person. She was a wrinkled prune of a woman with a heart no bigger than a raisin.

She had never caught on to the fact that the child she was "raising" was not the actual child she had given birth to. In all honesty, she had never looked at Winter long enough to realize how completely different from each other they were. The only good thing Janet saw in Winter was that the girl provided her with a huge, never-ending something to complain about.

The only time they ever spent with each other was at dinner. Janet insisted the two of them eat together, sitting at a table in front of the window so that any neighbors driving by could spot them being a family. Of course, when Winter and her mother did sit down to eat, Janet would do nothing but mumble and slobber over her heaping plates of food. As Janet would stuff her face, Winter would sit there with nothing but her usual dinner: a half dozen peas, which Janet had usually picked from her meal, a single crust of bread, and a spoonful of sugar-free strawberry jam—sugar-free because Janet had read once how bad sugar was for children.

Winter hated peas. She stared at them with her green eyes, wishing they were something else. They never were. She was equally unimpressed by the crust of bread, and she thought the jam always tasted funny. So she would usually roll her peas into the jam and sop them up with the stale crust, all the while pretending it was something other than what it actually was.

Today, however, Winter was more disappointed than usual.

It was her thirteenth birthday, and she had been hoping that tonight she might get a full piece of bread or maybe a bit of broccoli. It seems strange that a teenager would want broccoli, but when you're hungry and sick of peas, odd things sound surprisingly good.

Winter considered her half dozen peas and sighed. She thought about the thirteen years she had been alive and hoped the next thirteen might be different. It had taken the doctors a lot of coaxing to get Janet to even take Winter home from the hospital. Janet had not wanted her, and she had been frightened to death of the responsibility. She felt as though Winter would ruin the lazy lifestyle she had done so little to achieve. So Janet had named her Judy—after the patron saint of desperate cases—in hopes that the child might grow up to serve her and make something good from what she thought was a *very* desperate case.

No sooner had Janet brought Winter home than odd things began to happen. For one thing, Winter was always cold. Janet could put her under a blanket with a heating pad for hours and the baby would still feel cool to the touch when she unwrapped her. Janet would also find Winter's bottle in the mornings, frozen over. And even though the first days of Winter's life were warm, on two separate occasions Janet had witnessed frosty breath coming from the child's mouth; it was as if she were standing out in the cold in the dead of winter, exhaling.

Resenting her daughter's demands on her, Janet referred to her as "a bad bit of winter." Over time, Janet was simply too lazy to say the whole thing, so she shortened it to Winter, and the name stuck. It was almost as if fate desired her to be named that.

In the weeks leading up to Winter's thirteenth birthday, a strange, new feeling had begun to come over her. She couldn't quite figure it out, but it seemed as if she could feel the future coming toward her. She had no clear idea of what lay ahead, but she felt there must be someplace she needed to be, other than the spot where she now was. It was almost as if her life might have a purpose she had never discovered. She would have visions while wide awake—images of people and places she did not remember ever having seen before. There was a reason she was here, she just couldn't remember it yet. The thought both delighted and frightened her.

Winter stared at her peas while her mother slurped up her bountiful meal. Winter wished for plates filled with food and friends to share it with. She thought back to a daydream she had had just yesterday and the boy who had been in it. She thought of her neighbors the Tuttles and imagined them gathered around their table, eating and laughing. More than anything Winter wanted that for herself. She wanted desperately for the future that was coming to involve a real family.

Winter was so deep in thought she didn't realize her mother wasn't feverishly consuming food any longer. Winter looked up and found Janet staring at her. The silence was deafening, and the expression on Janet's face was one of complete horror. Winter hurriedly began to eat her small portion, figuring her mother was simply disgusted with her for not joyfully eating what she had sacrificed to provide her. It took Winter only a second to finish, seeing how a half dozen peas, a crust of bread, and a spoonful of sugar-free jam go down pretty fast if eaten frantically. Winter looked up again, hoping her repentance would be enough to satisfy her mother. Janet looked even more horrified.

"I ate—" Winter tried.

"What is that?" Janet asked, pointing at Winter. "What's happening to your hair?"

Winter could hear clicking now.

Her mother jumped up from her chair and hollered. "Whatever trick you are trying to pull, knock it off this instant!"

Winter could not have been more confused. She looked around the room, wondering if perhaps her mother was speaking to someone other than her. Nobody else was there—just her horrified mother, and a strange clicking noise.

Winter lifted her hands to her hair and was shocked to feel movement and ice. She stood quickly and turned to the mirror that hung on the wall next to the table, the same mirror Janet had forbidden Winter to use for fear of her image ruining it. Winter didn't care about that at the moment. She looked into the mirror with her green eyes and gasped. Her long, wild, blond hair was

LEVEN THUMPS AND THE GATEWAY TO FOO

floating and spinning everywhere. And even more astonishing, the mass of hair looked to be completely frozen, each strand clicking against the next as they moved in a pulsating motion. The light from the overhead lamp reflected off the frozen strands, throwing flecks of light all over the walls and ceiling like an uncoordinated disco ball. Winter turned to her mother, stunned and confused.

"What are you doing?" Janet whimpered, her wide-open mouth a perfect oval. "Stop it!"

"I'm not doing anything," Winter insisted. "I was—"

"Stop it immediately!" Janet ordered.

"I can't stop it," Winter pleaded. "I don't know how I started it."

Winter's icy hair spun wildly, the frozen strands lashing out and striking Janet on the forearm and face. Red welts instantly began to appear.

"Ahhh!" Janet screamed, scooting herself as far away from the table as possible. "Stop it!" she yelled. "Stop it!"

Winter looked at her wild-eyed mother. Janet was holding a fork and knife out as if to defend herself. Her wrinkly face was covered in food she hadn't had time to wipe off. Her bushy eyebrows were wet and stringy. Her hair was sweaty, and she shivered as if this were the end of the world and she were being personally invited to burn. The red welts upon Janet's face formed the backwards letters, D, A, B.

Winter's green eyes smiled. Her entire life she had been picked on and pushed around by her mother. This was the first time she could remember ever having the upper hand. But then the movement of her hair began to slow, finally settling in large, icy sweeps upon her head. The frozen strands began to melt and drip. A few strands, still swirling, flung water around the room, but in a few more seconds it was all over. Winter sat, her face dripping wet.

Janet wiped at the food on her face and dabbed at her greasy lips. She glanced out the window to see if anyone had witnessed what had happened, then stood and looked closely at Winter's hair, cautiously reaching out to touch it. Upon feeling the wet mess she jerked back her hand and made a disgusted face.

"Are you done?" Janet asked, her anger growing. Her dinner had been interrupted, and the portion she had been able to previously inhale would be difficult to digest, what with all the discomfort and commotion Winter had just caused.

"Was that some sort of prank?" she demanded. "Because if it is, it's not the least bit funny."

"It's my birthday," was all Winter could think to say.

Janet glared at her. "Your *birthday*," she ridiculed, her nasty composure returning in full. "That's what this is? I give birth to you, keep you in this house for thirteen years, and you repay me with a childish prank?"

Her greasy mouth twitched angrily. "This food you ruined cost good money," she complained. "Do you think I love working at the post office so much that it doesn't bother me to throw away the hard-earned money I make?"

Knowing there was no right answer to the impossible question her cruel mother had asked, Winter sat without responding.

"Too clever to answer me?" Janet demanded, her mean, wrinkled face scrunched up into a sneer. "Well, let me tell you this. You will clean up this mess. You will wipe down every spot in this room twice. You will polish this table and make the floor sparkle. Or I will turn you over to the state to be dealt with properly."

Winter clenched her fists under the table, willing her hair to act up again. She thought of everything cold she had ever experienced. She thought of the vicious delight she had experienced just moments before as her mother had sat, shaking in awe.

Nothing happened.

"I should take the strap to you," Janet snarled, "but my television show starts in three minutes." She stood up and looked at herself in the mirror. She studied the red welts on her face and could see what they spelled out. "I will deal with you later," she huffed, too angry to say more. She brushed up her brows, smoothed her cheeks, and stormed out of the room.

Winter sat there alone, her hair now hanging in wet ringlets from her head. She reached over to her mother's abandoned plate and stabbed a big piece of roast beef. She swirled it in the gravy and lifted it to her mouth, juice dripping across the table as she did so. Chewing, she closed her eyes and reveled in the flavor. She had never tasted anything so delicious. She helped herself to a few more bites, then lifted her glass and was astonished to find the water in it completely frozen.

"Odd," Winter said to herself, looking closely at her glass.

Defiantly, she grabbed one of her mother's drinks. Janet always insisted on having three full glasses of soda with her meals, and two of them had not been touched.

Winter drank one of the sodas down.

She smiled, stabbed another piece of roast beef, and contemplated what a wonderful birthday she was having after all. She was obviously much more unique and extraordinary than anyone had ever told her she was. Savoring every bite, Winter finished her meal and made her way over to the Tuttles, where Wendy was waiting with a small cake that was topped with a ring of thirteen burning candles.

Winter didn't hesitate at all before making her wish.

CHAPTER SEVEN

LIGHTNING STRIKES TWICE

L even's male guardian, Terry Graph, was a short man with
  long arms and little education. He was mean and always
looking for someone to blame for all his problems. He had deep-
set eyes, a spongy nose, and a tiny, tight mouth that framed his
crooked, yellow, rotting teeth.

Terry was a little man with no compassion or concern for
others. Not much interested him aside from giving Leven a hard
time. He didn't just holler and taunt Leven on occasion; Terry
made tormenting Leven his full-time occupation. Terry particularly enjoyed verbally assaulting Leven when he came home from
school, berating him for dawdling, failing to do his chores, or for
anything else that might be bugging Terry at the moment. He
also enjoyed hiding behind the door and jumping out at Leven
when the boy walked unsuspecting into a room. If Leven made a
friend or had an interest, Terry made certain to squelch it.

In Terry's view, Leven was his greatest burden. He had never gotten over the resentment he felt the day Addy announced there would be another mouth to feed. From then on, he saw Leven only as a nuisance and a pest, and he had literally never said a single kind word to the boy. Leven was not a son, he was just an additional expense and a bother.

Terry never had steady work. He procured an odd job here and there, but what he earned was not enough to support a wife and a leftover child. He always blamed his lack of good fortune on the current president or on his seventh-grade shop teacher who told him he would never amount to anything—or, more easily, on Leven.

Terry's laziness meant Addy had to work to support the family. Her job was folding napkins for a small, posh napkin company called Wonder Wipes. The shop was located about five miles away from the mobile home park, and one of the selling points of the napkins was that they were hand-folded. The owners of the company made a big point of this, as though the fold of the napkin enhanced its capacity for absorbing spills or wiping a face. Fortunately for the company and for Addy, the Wonder Wipe napkin had become a real status symbol for those who could afford them. There was enough work to keep Addy away from home and busily folding napkins day in and day out.

Addy would get up, go off to fold, and come home too tired and worn out to prevent her husband from making Leven's life miserable. Once in a while she would pretend to stick up for Leven, but for the most part she ignored him and his needs.

Leven's impression was that she was annoyed that he was still even there. She was a worthless advocate who always had tired hands and the weight of her world on her shoulders. Leven felt she and Terry wouldn't mind if he were to simply run off and disappear out of their lives. On those rare occasions where she would defend or say something concerning Leven, it only made things worse.

"Leave the boy alone," she would yell while Terry was picking on him. "He ain't all there."

Terry would throw up his hands. "The boy needs discipline, Addy," he would slur, "and he's certainly not going to get it from the likes of you. Always working and away. Folding, folding, folding. Making me cook my own meals and live in a filthy house while you're folding some piece of cloth so that some uppity rich people can properly wipe their pampered faces."

Terry and Addy would argue until one was too tired to carry on or until Terry went out for some night air, which the three of them knew meant air that was at least ninety proof. Addy would then turn the TV up so loud Leven wouldn't dare speak, and he would wander off to bed on the porch or go outside to sit beneath the huge tree and wonder what he could do to make things better.

This was Leven. He was a tall, surprisingly strong, fourteen-year-old who saw things in a way that most kids his age didn't. He had not had a pretty life, and yet for some reason he didn't understand, he always felt there had to be something better. Things couldn't possibly be this bad forever. Sometimes, if Leven squinted his brown eyes and really concentrated, he could almost see, or at least pretend, that the existence he was living was only a prelude to something much more important. It was a feeling that continued to burn inside him, even as Terry tore him apart or as the rest of his life crumbled around him.

Understandably, Leven didn't smile much; but when he did he was a rather handsome kid. Older folks could easily pat him on the head and know that a couple of decent kids still existed in this world. He always wore Levi's and one of the free T-shirts Addy would occasionally get at work. As if making friends wasn't hard enough, imagine being a fourteen-year-old boy trying to impress his peers while wearing a shirt that says "Wonder Wipes."

To avoid ridicule, Leven would always wear the T-shirts inside out so the decal wasn't as noticeable. Of course this infuriated Addy, who thought it was a slap in the face to all the hard work she put in to support the family. So Leven had to remember to always turn his shirt inside out before arriving at school and reverse it before he got home at night.

Thanks to Clover, in the last few days Leven's life had changed dramatically. In Clover, Leven had found both friendship and an affirmation that something more was out there. Leven had learned a few things about Clover and where he had come from, but for the most part the furry little guy remained tight-lipped whenever it came to discussing the task and future that lay ahead of them.

"You have to tell me what's going to happen," Leven said as they climbed down through the rocks that lined the steep ditch

at the edge of the prairie. "And if you're not from here, then where? Another planet?"

"Don't do this," Clover said, rubbing his own bare left elbow. "I am bound to keep the secret."

"How do I know that you're not just some made-up part of my imagination?"

Clover stopped climbing. His leaf-like ears fluttered. He looked at Leven as if he had been wounded.

"I'm sorry," Leven said. "I shouldn't say things like that."

"I would love to tell you everything I know," Clover explained again, "but I am bound. I can tell you this, though," Clover said, looking carefully around, "it's getting close."

Leven picked up a small rock and looked at it. "You've said that already. What's getting close?" he asked.

"I've been with you for fourteen years. Of course, I had to wait a while before you were born for you to get here. But I can tell now that the time is close," Clover affirmed, taking the rock from Leven's hand and looking at it. "During all those years I have known that someday we would go. And now I know that someday is near."

Clover reached into the front pocket of his robe. Leven was pretty amazed by Clover. He was, after all, a twelve-inch-tall furry creature with wet eyes and a huge smile who was supposed to serve him, but was usually too busy telling stories or marveling over rocks and leaves to attend to Leven's immediate needs. As interesting as Clover was, it was the pocket on the robe he wore that fascinated Leven most. Clover called it a void.

"My mother stitched it on when I was seventy-two," he had explained.

Void was a perfect name for the pocket, seeing how there appeared to be an endless capacity to it. Clover was constantly pulling things out of it. Books, small toys, an array of useful tools, and even a kite. And those were just the things Leven recognized. Clover had pulled out many things Leven had never heard of or could never have imagined even if he had tried. The pocket also held an unlimited store of food and candy. Clover was always chewing or sucking on some kind of weird treat he had apparently stocked enough of to last over all the years he had been here.

"Mupe?" Clover asked, holding out to Leven what looked to be a purple rock.

"What's mupe?" Leven asked.

"Just try it," Clover smiled. "Back home it's very popular candy."

Leven stuck the purple thing in his mouth and bit down. It tasted like honeyed, cooked wheat. It wasn't awful, but it wasn't candy. "This stuff is popular?" Leven asked in amazement.

"It's kind of fun," Clover said, skipping.

"What's fun about—?" Leven's mouth started to feel sticky. He tried to open it wide, but it felt as if his tongue were glued to both the roof and bottom of his mouth. At the same time his vision went weird. He could see in what seemed to be two different directions and an unpleasant odor filled his nostrils.

Clover was looking at him and laughing. "Wow! That was a strong piece of mupe."

"What do you mean?" Leven asked, talking out of the side of

his head. He threw his hands up to his face and realized that his mouth was not where it had been. He touched his face frantically. He found his mouth on the side of his head where his right ear used to be. One eye was where the other ear used to be, and the other eye was underneath his chin. He yelled, and almost broke the eardrum of the ear that was in the hair right above his mouth. His streak of white hair had moved to the top of his right hand.

"Best I've ever had was an ear on my elbow," Clover said enviously. He looked at the wrapper. "Oh, this pack has 'Extra Feature Fission.'"

"What do I do?" Leven hollered.

"It'll wear off in a moment," Clover said, as if disappointed.

"What's that smell?" Leven asked. "Where's my nose?" Leven began to touch his arms and stomach trying to find his nose. He sniffed. "Oh, great," he complained. He sat down and hurriedly untied his left shoelace. He threw the shoe off and pulled off the sock. Leven's nose was sticking out from between his big toe and the next in line.

Clover was quite amused. "I wish I had a camera," he said, as if he were a parent, wanting to capture the image of a well-groomed son going off for the first day of school.

Leven was happy Clover didn't have one. He could only imagine how odd he must look. In a few moments, the effect of the candy slowly began to wear off. Leven could see his nose sliding up his leg and over his body as it migrated north. His ears sprang back into their places, and his eyes circled around his mouth and returned to their rightful spots.

"Am I normal?" Leven asked, feeling around to know for himself.

"Yes," Clover said sadly.

"Don't give me anything like that ever again," Leven said seriously.

Clover looked hurt. "I'm not the best sycophant," he admitted.

Leven couldn't stand to see Clover feel sad. "It's all right," Leven sighed, patting Clover on the head. "Besides, I'm glad you're around."

Clover smiled. "Me, too," he added sincerely, happy to move on to other subjects. He stopped, looked at his little right foot, pulled out a pebble from between his toes, and smiled.

"I'm sure whatever happens next, we'll be fine," Leven said.

"Let's hope so."

"I mean, I shouldn't worry with you around," Leven said, setting Clover up. He wanted to see if he could trick Clover into telling him more.

"I'm glad you feel that way," Clover sniffed proudly. "It'll be fun."

"So where are we going again?" Leven asked, so casually that Clover fell for it.

"To Foo, of course. . . ." Clover caught himself, his eyes wide and frightened. "I mean, to wherever it is we will be going."

"Foo?" Leven asked. "Did you say Foo?"

"I didn't say anything," Clover denied. "I was just muttering."

"What's Foo?"

"Foo's nothing," Clover insisted. "I was talking about food."

"We'll go to *food* someday?" Leven said sarcastically.

"Right," Clover tried to say with conviction. "We'll get some food someday."

"Foo," Leven said to himself as he slid down a big rock and stepped across the shallow stream, avoiding the water. "Is it a building?"

"No," Clover adamantly answered, placing his small furry feet into the stream. The current was almost strong enough to pull him down. He braced himself and smiled, proud to still be standing.

"But is it—"

"I'll disappear," Clover warned, lifting his hood as if to put it on.

"Forget it, then," Leven quickly said. Leven couldn't stand it when Clover just disappeared. It was impossible to see or find him once he was gone. "Maybe you're not such a good sycophant after all. I thought you were supposed to do my bidding," Leven joked.

"I try, but whatever I do I just can't help thinking of myself a little."

"I don't see why you can't just tell me what's coming," Leven sighed. "You make it sound urgent, and then we spend our days doing nothing. I promise I won't tell anyone. It's not like I have anyone to talk—"

Leven stopped speaking due to the sudden appearance of Brick, the official school, neighborhood, and all-around-town bully. Standing next to Brick in the stream bed was Brick's pale, rich friend, Glen. The two of them had been out shooting cans and prairie dogs with their BB guns.

"Who you talking to, Skunk?" Brick laughed at Leven, making fun of the white streak in his hair. "Playing make-believe?"

Leven looked quickly to see if Clover was still in sight. He was gone. "I wasn't talking to anyone," Leven insisted, looking Brick in the eye.

Leven tried to move past the two of them.

"Not so fast," Brick sneered, holding out his arm to prevent Leven from passing. "This is our field. Me and Glen don't like it when others trespass. Isn't that right, Glen?" Brick asked.

"Can't stand it," Glen said meanly, pumping the lever on his BB gun. "I mean, what's the world coming to when just anyone can come onto our field?"

Brick pumped his gun, smiling cruelly.

Leven tried to keep going, but Brick jabbed Leven's shoulder with the barrel of his BB gun.

Leven grabbed his shoulder in pain. "It's not your field," he protested, a strange, confident feeling beginning to creep over him.

Brick jabbed Leven even harder. This time Leven stumbled, slipping on a rock and sprawling on his back in the water.

For as long as he could remember, Leven had been uneasy around water. He frequently dreamed of drowning and often woke up in the middle of the night choking and gasping for breath. Now here he was, soaking in a stream after being pushed down by the barrel of a BB gun.

Brick and Glen laughed like they had never seen anything funnier.

Leven scrambled up out of the water. He was surprised. He wasn't mad, and he wasn't scared. In fact, he was remarkably calm. As he watched Brick laughing, thoughts formed in his mind. They weren't thoughts such as *I wonder what I'll have for lunch,* or *I think green is my favorite color.* They were thoughts so strong and so focused it was almost as if he could see the future. He pictured lightning coming down from the darkened, cloudy sky. And there, suddenly, was a bolt of it, striking the ground no more than a hundred feet away. The flash was blinding and the sound deafening, and Brick and Glen screamed and fell over on their backs in the stream bed.

Leven steadied himself. He looked at Brick and Glen cowering in fear and was amazed.

He envisioned another bolt of lightning, and once more a brilliant scratch of light shimmered and crackled just beyond Glen and Brick.

The sound shook the earth.

Their previous screams were nothing compared to the ones Brick and Glen were now emitting as they began scrambling on their stomachs up the bank and away from Leven and back toward the mobile home park. Leven envisioned lightning chasing them all the way home and, amazingly, that was exactly what happened. One after another, lightning bolts struck the earth directly behind them as they scuttled on their stomachs, crying hysterically and trying to cover their heads with their hands. They had both abandoned their BB guns and were scraping their knees and hands something fierce as they crawled frantically across the dry prairie.

Leven watched them squirm under the mobile home park fence. Astounded by what he had been able to do, he gaped after them in awe. He looked to the far distance, beyond the park and past the town water tower. He pictured a bolt of lightning and watched in wonder as it flashed out of the cloudy sky. "Unbelievable," he whispered to himself as the echo of it died down.

"Pretty neat," Clover said, suddenly sitting on his left shoulder.

"Thanks for leaving me," Leven half-joked.

"I knew you'd be okay."

"Did you know I could do that?"

"I didn't know *what* you could do," Clover said, climbing onto the top of Leven's head to get a better look at the now-vanished Brick and Glen. "They're not so tough." Clover shook a tiny fist in their direction.

"What do you mean you didn't know what I could do?" Leven asked, still in awe over what had happened.

"All nits have a gift. You know, fire, flying, burrowing. Some sort of freaky talent that sets you apart from everyone else—weird breed." Clover brushed the thick hair on his calves and sniffed, his leaf-like ears wiggling as he did so.

"Nits?" Leven asked, finding it odd that Clover would consider anyone else to be a weird breed.

"To be honest with you," Clover said, ignoring Leven's inquiry and climbing down off his head, "I had my doubts about you being the right one. I like you and all, but I was beginning to wonder."

"The right one for what?"

Clover stared at him and smiled. "Do you think every boy here gets a sycophant?"

"No."

"You have a purpose beyond any of these people out here. In fact, if you fail they're all pretty much toast." Clover picked up a rock that was about half his size and heaved it into the stream. He smiled at the splash it made.

"This is crazy," Leven said, frowning and brushing his dark bangs back. "I am just a kid who lives in Oklahoma and is bad at math. I can't save anyone or make lightning strike."

"You just did."

"That was a coincidence."

"Stop it!" Clover said forcefully. "Don't use those kinds of words around me." His ears twisted and shook.

"What kinds of words?"

Clover looked around. "There are no coincidences," he said sternly. "Sabine and his shadows would love you to believe that every small miracle you witness throughout the day is nothing more than a chance happening. But I know better. You should, too." Clover looked wounded.

"I don't know what I know anymore," Leven said honestly.

The two of them waded out of the shallow stream. Leven

climbed up the rocky bank onto the flat prairie and gazed off to the north. Nothing but horizon and sky. He walked toward the Rolling Greens Deluxe Mobile Home Park and picked up one of the BB guns that Brick and Glen had dropped. He held it to his shoulder and pointed the barrel into the empty distance. He pulled the trigger and a weak puff of air shot out. Clover found the other gun and ran it back to Leven. Leven waved it away, and Clover happily aimed it toward the sky and pulled the trigger. A little puff of air shot out and into the sky.

"Weird," Clover said. "Is that supposed to scare someone?"

"They're just toys," Leven answered, his thoughts elsewhere. "So, do these nits have only one gift?"

"Usually."

"And mine is to make lightning?"

"I guess," Clover replied, smoothing down his little dress-like robe.

Leven looked to the north again and tried to envision lightning striking.

Nothing happened. He turned and thought of it coming down to the south.

Nothing.

He could feel his thoughts were different this time. They weren't as clear or as focused as they had been before, when Brick and Glen were laughing at him. His mind wandered for a bit and then suddenly things solidified. He envisioned a huge hawk dropping from the sky, its talons extended, aimed right at Clover.

He quickly turned.

A huge raptor *was* swooping down right above Clover. Leven yelled at Clover to disappear and Clover did just that. The confused bird almost flew into the ground. Its talons brushed the earth as it pulled up and returned to the sky, turning its head to find any sign of the furry feast it had viewed just moments before.

"Clover?" Leven yelled.

"I'm right here," he replied, materializing on Leven's right shoulder.

Leven jumped. "I've told you not to do that."

"Sorry," he said casually. "How'd you know that bird was there?"

"I saw it before it happened," Leven answered, confused.

"Unbelievable," Clover whispered. "Your gift isn't *just* lightning."

"What is it then?"

"You're not a nit, you're an offing," Clover said almost reverently.

"What's an offing? Is that bad?"

"Oh, I wish Antsel was around to see this," Clover lamented.

"See what?" Leven asked almost desperately.

"I can't believe my burn is an offing," he said with excitement.

"What does that mean?" Leven asked, frustrated.

"You can see the future," Clover said enviously. "You have it in you to manipulate fate a bit. Offings can not only see the future, they can help make it turn out to their advantage. Your safety and dislike for those boys probably helped you pick that lightning's striking point. You have a great gift, Lev, an extremely rare gift. I know of only one other who has it."

"Who?"

"I can't say."

"I just saved your life," Leven pointed out.

Clover waved. "That bird couldn't have killed me," he said confidently. "I told you there's only one way for us sycophants to die."

"How?" Leven tried.

"I'm not falling for that." Clover smiled, his blue eyes squinting.

Leven smiled back.

"Imagine, little old Clover working for an offing," he went on. "I wish I was somewhere where people could be envious." Clover jumped off of Leven's shoulder and skipped along the ground.

Leven picked up both guns and put them over his shoulder. He followed Clover back across the field toward home. In the far distance he could see the tree that shaded his house. He thought of Terry and Addy and Clover. He thought of the turns his life had taken recently. He tried to draw his thoughts in, but it was no use; some gift, he couldn't see his own future.

Clover turned to Leven and smiled. "What are you thinking?" he asked merrily.

"I think it's time for us to leave," Leven replied, surprised to hear the words coming from his mouth. "We should think about getting out of this place."

"Good." Clover hopped. "I was thinking you'd never say that."

"So do you have any more of that candy?" Leven asked sheepishly, admitting that the stuff wasn't half bad.

"I told you it's popular," Clover smiled, taking another piece of mupe from his pocket.

CHAPTER EIGHT

EVERYBODY PLEASE REMAIN SEATED

Winter's life was by no means going any more smoothly. She came home from school one day to discover that her mother had been fired from her job at the post office for throwing away a bag of mail she was too tired to sort. Since then Janet had decided she didn't want to do anything but watch TV for the rest of her life. So she lay on their worn orange couch, eating and eating and eating while watching shows about thin people doing things she was never going to do anymore: things like walking, reading books, or getting up for the remote themselves.

She was also done with being a parent. From that moment on, the most extensive parenting Janet provided was to yell loudly at Winter whenever she blocked her view of the TV set. Janet moved the refrigerator closer to the couch and fed the yard hose in through the window so she could get a drink of water whenever she felt like it.

It cannot be stressed enough: Winter was not in a happy place.

Things at school were no better. It seemed that no one wanted to be friends with an unusual-looking girl who had wild blond hair, wore tattered clothes, and was so introverted. Most kids saw Winter as nothing more than the perfect test case for their clever put-downs.

"Garbage-heap head."

"Frostbite."

Even the teachers were cruel.

"Now class," Mr. Bentwonder, her homeroom teacher, would say, "leave that skinny white thing alone. Only heaven knows the last time soap and water touched her."

Mr. Bentwonder was a big fat meanie. Sorry, but there's really no better way of saying it. His puffy face was as round as a melon, and his fleshy lips were always wet. He couldn't say a single thing without having to wipe them afterwards. He had eyes the color of dung and a nose that was pushed up so drastically at the end that students from across the room could tell that he needed to use a tissue even before he knew himself. He taught math by trade, and hate and ignorance by example. Unable to find a woman who was actually attracted to a homely man who couldn't say a kind thing and never did a kind deed, he had never married. True, there are people who are married to individuals who can't say or do anything kind. But in most cases, those individuals are not married to someone unkind who also has a giant mushy melon head, breath that always smells of liver, and perpetually has to have his mouth wiped by an elected student.

Mr. Bentwonder had been good for something, however—that one good thing being a comment he made that finally set Winter to thinking about getting away from the life she had been dealt.

It was during the middle of math class at Samuel Tolerance Junior High when Wendell Prattlemelt, the school kiss-up, raised his hand and told Mr. Bentwonder that he was sure there had never been another teacher as inspired and brilliant as he. Mr. Bentwonder had responded by expressing his conviction that there were few people who could match Wendell's intellect and stating how if every child were as perceptive as Wendell, he, Mr. Perry Bentwonder, might very well be the president of the United States, and the country would be much better off for it.

Then he boasted, "I am who I am, class, because I have made myself so." Mr. Bentwonder failed to mention that he had been born into a wealthy and privileged family and had been pampered his entire life. Nor did he explain to the class that he had gotten the job he now held only because his uncle was the principal of Samuel Tolerance Junior High. No, he left all of that out and smugly repeated, "I am who I am because I have made myself so."

His words triggered something in Winter's mind. It was suddenly clear. She would never be anything if she kept waiting for someone else to change things for her. The thought made her feel as though someone had flipped a switch and finally activated her soul. She sat still, listening to Mr. Bentwonder go on and on about poetry, and how it took a rare and sensitive mind such as his to actually understand it.

"What's in a name?" he drooled. "That which we call a rose by any other name would smell as sweet." He turned his mushy head so that young Patty Foote could dab his mouth. She did so and smiled. "You don't just read poetry, you breeeeeathe it," he instructed.

"No one breathes it as well as you," Wendell Prattlemelt gushed. Mr. Bentwonder nodded and bowed slightly.

"Again, Wendell, what a *joy* you must be to your parents," he cooed.

Winter snickered. She just couldn't help it. Wendell a joy? Mr. Bentwonder breathing poetry? It struck her as funny, and she couldn't keep from laughing.

Mr. Bentwonder looked up and over his spectacles toward her.

"Excuse me?" he said indignantly. "Does something strike you as funny, Miss Frore?" Flecks of spittle flew from his fleshy lips, and the ever-accommodating Patty Foote reached to blot his mouth.

"No, sir," Winter replied, her green eyes unable to hide her mirth. "I just . . ."

Winter laughed again.

The class went silent. No one had ever laughed at Mr. Bentwonder, unless he had made it clear they were supposed to. Now here was Winter, laughing at him, twice. His forehead reddened and Patty went in for another dab. He brushed her away and heaved himself to his feet.

"I have never," he huffed. "Never, never," he puffed. "Never have I been burdened with such an insolent and disrespectful pupil."

Wendell smiled as he watched Mr. Bentwonder work his ponderous way through the desks and toward Winter. Winter just sat there, her gaze locked on the floor.

"Poverty is one thing," he went on, gesturing to Winter's old clothes and disheveled appearance, "but even in poverty one ought to show respect to those who are attempting to help her." The desks were positioned too close together for Mr. Bentwonder to fit through. He began pushing and shoving students out of the way. Some students frantically moved to get away from him as he waded closer to his prey.

His voice was menacing. "I have given you my time and my attention, and you have returned to me spite and ingratitude . . ."

Winter tried to control her feelings, but as she sat there in her desk, with her classmates scurrying out of the path of the threatening Mr. Bentwonder, a powerful feeling came over her. Her body burned, and she was afraid to look up for fear of losing the sensation. She would have kept her eyes averted from her oncoming teacher if it had not been for the screams and cries of her classmates.

She looked up and marveled at what was happening. An expanding circle of silvery ice was flowing out from where she sat and filling the room. As from the epicenter of a frozen earthquake, waves of ice rippled out and away from her, arresting and suspending everything in their way.

Winter smiled and the avalanche of cold increased.

She watched as Wendell turned to run. The silvery frost

caught his left foot, keeping him right where he stood. Wendell screamed and cried as ice crept up his leg and over his body, eventually immobilizing him completely. Suddenly fearful, Mr. Bentwonder turned to lumber for the door, but cold tapped him on his big, cowardly back. He turned to look, and in an instant he was one of the fattest and least aesthetically pleasing sculptures Winter had ever seen.

Those who had not yet been frozen tried to wriggle out of their desks and escape from the room, but Winter wouldn't have it. She simply shook her head, and at once, the entire rest of the room was frozen solid. Students had their arms out and in midstride, motionless in place. Desks and walls glistened and shined. The fish tank at the front of the room was a solid block of ice. No clock was ticking, no computers were humming, nor was Mr. Bentwonder prattling. The frost-filled room was completely quiet.

Winter was amazed. The only things unfrozen were herself and her desk. She stood, gathered her books and put them into her backpack, then walked to the front of the room, stopping only twice: once to snap Mr. Bentwonder's tie in two, and once to touch the fish tank. When she did, the water in the aquarium melted instantly, and the fish resumed swimming. Winter felt better. The fish had never done anything cruel to her.

She walked to the frozen door and touched it, and it warmed. She pulled it open and walked out. Now suddenly seemed like as good a time as any for her to escape her unhappy life. She had been contemplating running away, and she was smart enough to know it would be wise for her to be gone by the time Mr. Bentwonder and her class thawed. She knew they would defrost soon, and when they did they would be cold but none the worse for wear.

It was time for Winter to go.

"Excuse me?" a strong male voice said, interrupting Winter's flight down the hall. Winter jumped and put her hand to her heart. She had been so deep in thought that she had not noticed Principal Helt walking toward her.

"Why aren't you in class?" he demanded.

"I'm running an errand for my teacher, Mr. Bentwonder," Winter lied.

"Mr. Bentwonder?" the principal questioned. "My nephew? I would think a man of his intellect and breeding would be sufficiently prepared not to need children scurrying about for him."

Principal Helt took Winter by the arm and pulled her back toward her classroom. It was not a smart move on his part. Winter closed her eyes and let the feelings she had experienced only moments before return.

"We can't allow—"

Mr. Helt was stopped cold. Winter opened her eyes to see him open-mouthed and frozen solid. She looked up and down the empty hall and then opened a janitor's closet door right behind him. She slid him inside, taking care not to break off an arm or finger, closed the door, and continued down the hall and out into the open. She had walked out these doors hundreds of times, but today it felt different.

She was free.

"I am who I am because I made myself so," she said aloud, looking toward the east and feeling as if she had been this strong once before but just couldn't remember where or when.

It was a good feeling.

When Winter reached her house she climbed into her room through the window so as to not bother her mother, who was watching TV. She collected some money she had been saving and packed a couple of outfits. She wanted to stop and tell the Tuttles she was leaving, but she knew they would try to talk her out of it. She also knew that it would be too heartbreaking for her to have to say good-bye. She felt better after telling herself she would be back to see them again someday. It wasn't all that believable. Winter pushed those thoughts aside. She had something to do, and whatever it was, she couldn't let anything stop her. She climbed out her window one last time.

Winter walked straight to the bus station and up to the ticket counter. She looked at the schedule and tried to determine which destination would be the best. After some time her eyes fell upon a place that felt perfect! It was the next step and she knew it. She gave the big lady behind the glass forty-two dollars and bought a bus ticket to someplace away from where she now was.

"Are you traveling with your parents?" the ticket lady asked suspiciously.

"Alone," Winter answered. "I'm going to see my grandmother," she lied. "Those are my parents over there." Winter pointed to a couple sitting on a bench, two ordinary people with their noses buried in magazines. "They've come to see me off."

The large lady realized she had invested enough of her time in this funny-looking girl's business as it was. "Here's your ticket. The bus leaves in forty minutes." She pointed. "It will pull up right there at that rear door."

Winter thanked the woman and walked off in the direction of the couple she had pointed at. Just to be safe she stopped in front of the man and woman and asked them the time. The woman smiled at Winter and gave it to her.

"Thank you," Winter said, her evergreen eyes shining for the first time in a while. "Is this seat taken?" she asked, pointing to an empty place on the bench beside them. The woman shook her head and Winter sat.

"Traveling alone?" the woman asked.

"For the moment," Winter replied. "I'm going to visit my grandmother," she lied.

"How nice," the thin lovely woman said. "And how brave of you."

Winter shrugged.

"When I was your age I would have never traveled on a bus alone," the woman tisked. "I clung to my mother until I was out of high school. Your parents must think you're really responsible."

Again Winter shrugged.

"And modest," the woman added, referring to Winter's quiet nature.

Winter stifled a laugh. Her mother didn't even know she was missing, much less care about her. Her entire life she had been confused and lost. It was as if she didn't know who she was, and she had constantly felt as though she didn't belong where she was. Sometimes she would have memories or see things that seemed so unusual they scared her. Now this morning she had turned her whole class into ice cubes and it had felt normal. It had felt like something she was expected to do—like something she had done before.

She thought about how rude it had been of her to just walk away from her house without telling her mother where she was going. Winter wondered if she could freeze things she couldn't directly see. Now felt like a good time to find that out. In her mind she pictured Janet's water hose frozen solid. Although she couldn't see it, Winter could feel it work. She smiled. It would be a small reminder to Janet of her child.

"Well, you just stay by us," the lovely woman said to her, pulling Winter out of her thoughts. "Our bus doesn't leave for an hour. How about yours?"

"Thirty-five minutes," Winter reported.

"There, then," the woman smiled. "You won't be alone."

Winter smiled back, knowing that "alone" was exactly where she was headed. For some reason, however, that didn't frighten her. It just seemed as if she had been there before. Winter glanced at her ticket and whispered the destination.

"Oklahoma."

She had never wanted to go there before. She was both determined and incredibly uneasy. Something bigger and scarier than she could clearly understand had begun.

CHAPTER NINE

SABINE'S RANT

Foo was changing. As the history of mankind had advanced, the dreams and desires of those on earth had become darker and more selfish. This darkness had changed Foo. In the beginning Foo was a secret location the heavens had created to give imagination and dreams their own place to flourish without restraint. It was a world that existed within the minds of all men and women, made possible by the boundless potential that lies within each of us. But over time the beauty and magic of Foo had begun to erode, as some of its inhabitants became poisoned by the increasingly selfish and perverted dreams of humans and the destructive idea that the dreams of those in reality were not their concern.

Sabine had grown powerful by the rank wishes and sordid desires of men gone wrong, and he wanted out of Foo. He knew the time was finally coming. The skies in Foo dimmed dramatically as the dreams of man grew ever darker. He had selfishness on his side. He had done very well to stir up the inhabitants of Foo. Now it was crucial for him to find the gateway out. Foo and reality could never be one if there was no way to move between them and bring the two together.

Sabine thought of little else besides this gateway. The Council of Whisps still fought against him, but as soon as they were properly dealt with his only resistance would be in not knowing the direction to lead his followers out of Foo.

Sabine was not a happy being, but he knew of two things that would bring him great joy. One was discovering the gateway, and the other was locating the only one who could stop him: the missing link and the only person alive who could destroy the gateway before Sabine could find it and bring his dark legions through it into reality.

Sabine's to-do list was short, but difficult.

He stood by the window, shifting and creating shadow after shadow, each instantly trying to flee his dark presence, only to realize it couldn't completely operate on its own. As each new shadow materialized, Sabine would blow, sending it through incoming dreams into reality. He would feel the shadows as they floated above the earth, undetected by all those living. He would call them in from time to time and berate them for not being able to accomplish such a simple task as finding the single human on earth who could destroy everything.

Through the window Sabine could see Jamoon thundering closer. Jamoon was a rant and one of Sabine's most loyal confederates. Sabine withdrew from his position to welcome his visitor.

Jamoon entered Sabine's lair like a swirling storm—blowing through the doors and down the long corridor into the grand hall. His thick black robe billowed as he strode across the room. Sabine was seated at the far end of the room in a chair made from the hide of a large roven.

Jamoon bowed and Sabine nodded.

Rants were a strange breed; often only a half of each one was ever recognizable. They were beings in constant change, one half human and stable, the other half whatever someone in reality was currently dreaming. As a breed, rants were typically easy to control. The main cause of their condition was that they were easily influenced and manipulated. They were offspring of nits who didn't have the character and fortitude to just enhance the dreams and imaginations of those on earth and then move on. Instead the dreams overcame the rants and stole half of their personality and individualism.

Rants were not happy or stable beings.

At times being half a dream can come in handy. For example, if your right arm is injured and your left arm is currently that of a surgeon. Or if you just don't have the strength to open a new jar of potch, and one half of you becomes a weight lifter with an iron grip. But say you are down at the Dripping Trough, trying to enjoy a guys' night out, and suddenly your entire south side becomes a beautiful ballerina that some child on earth is dreaming of becoming. That would make things a bit awkward. Because of just such a scenario, most rants wore long black cloaks that covered their entire unstable bodies and hid the truth of whatever half of them might be at the moment.

"Remove your cloak," Sabine demanded. He liked to see exactly what he was dealing with.

Jamoon dropped his cloak to the floor. He was tall and strong, with a right arm and leg in top physical condition and cloaked in a smaller robe. The other half of him at the moment looked to be an astronaut.

Sabine didn't smile. To a rant a smile was the most insulting thing you could show them. They felt certain all smiles were aimed at their ever-changing second halves.

"News?" Sabine asked.

"You have our support," Jamoon said solemnly. "We stand waiting in the shadows to flee Foo."

"Excellent." Sabine twitched. "And what of the gateway?"

Jamoon's left side spoke out of turn. "Houston, we have a problem." Jamoon then began to tremble . . . not out of fear, but due to the transformation he was suddenly undergoing. The astronaut part of him began to pucker and boil, then the image ran together and dripped slowly to the floor. Obviously little Bobby back in reality no longer wanted to be a spaceman. As the image dripped away it was filled in with that of a seven-foot-tall basketball player. Half of Jamoon instantly began to dribble a ball and sweat. It was easier for a rant to become half of something that was close to his same size. But since Jamoon's right half was only 5'10" and his left half was now seven feet tall, it looked particularly odd. The dribbling and the height were distracting, but Sabine, ever the evil diplomat, refrained from smiling.

Jamoon ignored the gyrations of his left side and continued as if nothing was happening. "We have found no indication or clue as to the location. We are searching as fast as we can for the gateway, but we have so little to go on."

"Intensify your search," Sabine insisted, ignoring Jamoon's left half. "Your very happiness is dependent upon it."

"Pass it here, I'm open!" Jamoon's new left side hollered.

"I understand," his stable half replied. "What of the whisps?"

"*I* will take care of them," Sabine said. "Soon they will no longer be a problem for us."

Jamoon bowed and Sabine waved him away. Jamoon slipped his cloak back on and ran quickly from the room as if driving down a basketball court and going in for a dunk.

CHAPTER TEN

A MARKED TARGET

With every mile Winter traveled away from her home, she began to feel more and more at peace with her decision to leave. It was as if she were doing exactly what she was destined to do. As she rode the bus toward Oklahoma, the image of a boy she didn't know began playing in her mind. For some reason Winter had never experienced dreams while sleeping. She figured that was because of her awful life. She did occasionally have visions during the day. Her eyes would glaze over and she would see things. Lately, she had seen a lot of Leven Thumps. She had no idea who he was or what purpose he might have in her life, but she knew she needed to find him. Each time his face would flash into her mind, a voice within her head would whisper, "Don't touch him."

The warning was so troubling and confusing, that the first time Winter heard it she had been unable to sleep the next night, but now as the images of Leven came more and more frequently, the familiar whisper seemed more a warning to be cautious than a threat. She found it perplexing that the very person she seemed to be pursuing was someone she should not touch.

Winter arrived in Oklahoma early in the morning, unsure of just what to do next. Her wonder was answered by a poster on the wall of the bus station. It read: "Visit Burnt Culvert: Site of the State's Worst Lightning Fire." Winter thought two things: one, Burnt Culvert could use a new ad campaign, and two, that was where she needed to go. She was happy to learn that Burnt Culvert was only an hour away. She found a taxi and asked the driver to take her there.

"Site of the state's worst lightning fire," the driver said, confirming what the sign had proclaimed.

"Is it a big town?" Winter asked.

"Depends on what you think is big," he smiled. "It's bigger than where I come from, but that's not saying much."

"Do you know if it has a junior high school?" Winter asked.

"It does," he replied. "If I remember right, it's the home of the Fighting Ashes."

"Can you take me to the school?" she asked.

"Sure," he smiled. "Are you starting there?" he asked, having no problem prying into her business.

"No," Winter replied. "I just need to pick something up."

The driver dropped the flag on the meter and pulled out.

Winter knew what she was looking for was there in Burnt Culvert, but as they drove she heard the voice whisper again in her head, "Don't touch him." Still puzzled, she looked to see if someone else might be in the backseat with her.

Winter was very much alone.

ii

The softball hit Leven squarely in the back of his head. The pain was immediate, and he could see stars and hear laughter. Leven was not a big fan of lunch break.

"What's a matter, Skunk?" Brick called out. "Can't catch with the back of your head?"

Leven turned and saw Brick laughing. Brick's long skinny face was scrunched up, nearly pinching his little pea-sized eyes shut. His fat knees stuck out from under his shorts and were knocking together as he and Glen laughed it up. Brick had the personality of a pit bull—he picked on and chewed up anyone who got in his way or was a threat to his ego. And since he had the smarts of a week-old doughnut, almost anyone qualified as a threat to his intelligence. Brick was a large child who in reality should have been in a class two grades up, though his intellect best qualified him to attend classes two grades down.

Leven pointed to the sky and said, "Lightning."

Both Brick and Glen immediately stopped laughing.

"Ahh, forget about him," Brick said, momentarily scared. "He's not worth it."

Leven just stared at them, wondering why they took so much pleasure in picking on him. He had never said an unkind word to them or hurt them in any way, but from the moment he had started middle school, Brick and Glen had singled him out and made him the target of their animosity and hatred.

Leven looked around the field. Students were everywhere—peers of all shapes and sizes, yet for some reason Leven was Brick's favorite person to pick on. Leven wasn't the heaviest, or the shortest, or the tallest, and his brown eyes were as average as his grades. Maybe it was the bright white streak in his hair that had drawn their attention. Something like that was hard to hide. He kept his hair a little longer in hopes of it helping, but that only made the streak more prominent. To most of his school he was "Skunk." Leven got no credit for what he didn't do: he didn't pick his nose or laugh like a mule or cry when picked on. And he was always careful to wear his Wonder Wipes T-shirts inside out. None of that mattered; Leven stood out and probably always would. Imagine the attention he might have gotten if people knew he had Clover always clinging to him.

Brick picked up the ball he had just thrown at the back of Leven's head and turned—he and Glen laughing it up as they left.

"They're just a couple of bullies," a voice from behind Leven said. "Not tough enough to fight their way out of a cobweb."

Leven turned to see who was speaking to him. It had to be someone with no knowledge of what Brick could do, to say something so bold. A girl with messy blond hair and an angry expression on her face was staring back at him. She had her hands behind her back. Though Leven knew they had never met, he thought he recognized her. She gazed at him with her deep green eyes.

"Excuse me?" Leven asked.

"They're bullies," she sniffed, pulling back her wild hair.

"You might want to keep your voice down," Leven whispered. "Brick would be plenty happy to verify what you're saying." Leven looked closely at her. "Do I know you?" he asked.

"I don't think so. My name's Winter."

"I'm Leven," he replied, reaching casually to cover his white streak with his hand.

"Lev," Winter said reflectively, shortening his name, like Clover often did. "That sounds right," she added. "And don't ask me how, but I think I already know you."

Leven stared at her, his mind trying to make sense of what he was saying. She was a different-looking girl. Her strong features would have made her easy to pick on at his school. He half hoped she had come to enroll so that he would drop to second in the pecking order. She had on faded jeans with flared bottoms and a thin blue shirt with a pocket in the front and long loose sleeves. She was either really cutting edge and wearing hip retro clothes, or she was poor and wearing clothes so outdated they were in style again. Her eyes stood out against her light-colored skin and long wild blond hair—they were large and looked like wells of deep green water. She was about four inches shorter than Leven, but the shoes she was wearing made her look no more than three.

"I think I know you, too," Leven finally spoke.

"Weird, isn't it?" Winter responded, appearing relieved to know she wasn't alone in her thoughts. "Us seeming to know each other and never having met, I mean."

"Do you go here?" he asked, nodding toward the school.

"No," she answered.

Leven was captivated by Winter's green eyes, and he gazed at them as he might have looked at a treasured object. As he studied her face, his head cleared and his brown eyes burned gold. Leven had tried many times since that day in the field to see the future again, but had never succeeded. Now all of a sudden it was working again. In his head he saw himself and Winter running. He blinked his eyes and shook his head, puzzled by what he had seen.

"So you're here because . . ." Leven let his question hang, hoping she would complete it for him.

Winter laughed just a bit and shrugged her shoulders. "I think I'm looking for you," she said shyly. "Is that odd?"

Leven smiled. "It would have been a few weeks ago, but it's no odder than some of the things that I've been through lately."

They were silent for a moment.

Winter could hear the voice in her head whispering fiercely. "Don't touch him." She looked at Leven, noticing his straight nose and strong brown eyes. She could see a cautious determination buried deep beneath his somewhat insecure exterior. He seemed to be fighting himself to stand tall and slouch at the same time. His shirt was on inside out, and he had an unusual streak of white hair on the right side of his head. "Don't touch him," the voice warned again.

Normally Winter would have had no problem obeying the warning, but for some odd reason she was drawn toward Leven, as though he were a piece of home or an emotional oasis.

"So what do we do now?" Leven asked, the two of them continuing to look at each other.

"I was hoping you could tell me."

"I can't tell you anything except that I knew something was coming," Leven said. "I think that something is you."

"And I think I've been looking for you."

Leven laughed. "Disappointed?" There was a brief awkward silence.

"I don't think so," Winter said, dipping her head shyly and keeping her hands behind her.

"I guess—" Leven started to say, but he was interrupted.

"Hey, who's the broom with hair?" Brick sneered, breaking into their conversation. He and Glen had grown bored of playing ball, and in their boredom they had spotted their favorite victim, Leven, talking to a skinny girl with wild hair. It was too good to pass up.

"New girlfriend, Skunk?"

"Knock it off," Leven warned.

"Oh, Skunky's unhappy," Brick teased. "Maybe we should help cheer him up."

Leven looked around for someone to help—no one was there. No teacher was *ever* there. The schoolyard was full of kids running and screaming, but as usual, no teacher was on duty. There never was. A big kid with a bat was chasing after a smaller boy. Two girls were playing in the mud and getting dirtier than any student should ever be allowed to get, and the entire seventh grade was taking turns drawing chalk outlines around the bodies of students who were posing as dead and sprawled out on the asphalt.

Sterling Thoughts Middle School was not exactly the best school to send your child to. It was a forgotten school where teachers with no backbone or gumption were sent to teach. Its principal was a noodle of a man who hid out in his office, making occasional announcements over the speaker system and hoping the students would leave his car alone.

Leven's eighth grade teacher was a tall woman who had experienced a nervous breakdown at a different school, so she had been transferred here to bide her time until retirement. All she did was sit behind her desk, begging the students to stop hitting each other and pleading with them to please open their books. Discipline was a rarity and, unlike so many of the other kids, Leven couldn't stand it. He craved order in his life and yet he couldn't find it at any point. Now here were Brick and Glen, threatening to rough him up once again, and there was not a single adult around to intervene.

Leven thought of lightning—nothing. He tried to kick his gift into gear and still nothing.

"No one's going to help you, loser," Brick sneered. "The sky's clear."

Leven looked to the sky for a brief second, and in that instant Brick swung and punched him squarely in the gut. The air whooshed out of Leven, and he bent forward, holding his stomach. Brick grinned.

"Leave him alone," Winter snapped, stepping up next to Leven, her arms by her sides. "Are you all right?" she asked, looking at Leven over her shoulder.

"I'm fine," he wheezed, embarrassed, his eyes now on Brick.

"That didn't look like a very strong hit," Winter said firmly, making fun of Brick's punch. She stepped closer to the bully.

Glen "Ohhhhed" seriously.

Only one person had ever stood up to Brick, and that person was Nervous Todd. He had been just plain Todd previously, but ever since the lesson Brick had taught him he had been nicknamed "Nervous." He spent his days sneaking around, hiding in corners, and trying to make himself inconspicuous, for fear of saying or doing anything to ever upset Brick again.

"What did you say, you smelly piece of trash?" Brick asked, stepping closer to Winter and smacking his right fist into his left palm. A small crowd gathered, hoping to witness something exciting.

Winter leaned close to Leven. "Want to see something cool I can do?" she whispered.

Leven looked at her, wondering if she was crazy. Before he could think further of it, Brick lunged out to attack. He got about a foot from Winter before he was stopped in his tracks by his feet turning to solid ice.

"What the—?" he yelled, looking down at his feet. The ice rose slowly, like quicksand in reverse, climbing up his legs and toward his waist. He reached down and tried to pull his legs up but they wouldn't budge. Glen stepped back, eyes wide and mouth hanging open in wonder.

"Help me!" Brick ordered. "Give me your hand!"

Glen inched farther away. Winter looked at Glen and blinked. Glen was suddenly a solid ice sculpture.

Winter turned back to Brick. He was staring at Glen and whimpering. The ice inched up his legs and frosted his fat bottom.

He pounded at it, screaming, trying to break it apart. Leven looked on in both astonishment and fear.

"Make it stop!" Brick yelled at Leven. "Help me!"

Leven moved toward Brick as if to help, but Winter motioned him back. The ice continued to migrate north, covering Brick's chest and neck and inching toward his head. The students who had gathered to see a fight were in shock over what was happening and from seeing Brick cry.

"Help me," he sobbed. His arms were now frozen stiff. "Help!" he cried. "H——" the ice covered his mouth, silencing him as it crept over his nose, past his panicked eyes, and then capped him off completely.

Everyone stood there with open mouths, in disbelief. Leven gaped at Winter.

"Did you do that?" he whispered.

"I can't stand bullies," she said.

"Will he be okay?"

"Sure," Winter said, seemingly not overly concerned.

Some of the students had run back into the school and retrieved a few teachers to come and see what had happened. You couldn't retrieve just one or two teachers at Sterling Thoughts Middle School, you had to get five or six before they would have the nerve to come out and investigate. A handful of them crept cautiously out of the building, looking scared. A few students pointed in the direction of Leven and Winter.

"Let's get out of here," Leven said nervously, his brown eyes alive.

"I was just waiting for you to say the word," Winter said,

smiling. It is amazing, the amount of confidence a person can have when blessed with the ability to freeze things.

Leven reached to grab Winter's arm and guide her back around the school.

"Don't touch me!" she said sharply, drawing back.

Leven pulled his hand away, looking confused.

"Just don't touch me," Winter said again, this time a bit softer.

The teachers running toward them hollered and ordered them not to move. Leven and Winter did just the opposite, sprinting away, running around behind some portable classrooms, skirting the pond, and topping the small hill where students often met to fight with one another at the end of the school day.

"Where are we going now?" she asked.

"I'll tell you when I know," he yelled back.

Winter smiled, happy to finally have someone besides her calling the shots. They turned a street corner and worked their way back behind a record shop and a shoe store.

"How did you do that?" Leven asked. He was out of breath and stopped to catch it.

"I don't know how," Winter answered, breathing hard and brushing her stringy hair back out of her face.

"She's a nit," Clover said, unseen but not unheard.

"Who said that?" Winter asked, confused.

Clover materialized and smiled. Winter stepped back just a bit, her green eyes wide.

"It's okay," Leven said. "It's just Clover."

Clover leaped from Leven's head onto Winter's shoulder, smiling. "You don't know this, but I think I might know you," he said happily. Winter smiled back. "If so, you were taller before," he added.

"Really?" Winter said, tentatively touching Clover on the back of his head. She slowly began to pet him as if he were a cat. Her smile made it obvious just how delighted she was.

"Sure," Clover purred, his eyes closing slightly. "But we can reminisce later. I think the time has come for us to go," he said, suddenly serious and shrugging Winter's hand off of him.

Leven looked at Winter. Something was finally happening in his life. He felt different than he had felt only moments before. It was time for him to step away from his past and walk into his future.

"I just need to get a few things from my house before we go," Leven replied.

"Well, hurry," Clover insisted. "I've been waiting years for this to begin."

"I can't wait till I know what we're even talking about," Winter laughed.

"Me, too," Leven said seriously, looking at Clover.

"I'd tell you if I could," Clover smiled. "But I was told specifically not to be the one to break the news."

"So tell Winter, and she can tell me," Leven tried.

"I would still be telling Winter." Clover disappeared.

"So, you could—" Leven was stopped by the school gym teacher, Coach Tally. He had been out having lunch when he spotted Leven and Winter running off. A lover of the hunt, he had hidden behind the shoe store and jumped out, and he was now holding Leven by the ear.

"Where are we off to, Thumps?" he asked, his crew cut bristling in the sun. "You should be on campus." Coach Tally was heavy, kept his hair cropped short, and had a perpetually red face. His breath always smelled of garlic.

"Nowhere," Leven said in pain, his ear being stretched to its limit.

"Nowhere's the other direction," Coach Tally yanked.

Winter was just about to turn the belligerent man to ice when Clover came up with an idea. He materialized, sprang from Leven's head, and like lightning hurled himself into the face of Coach Tally, cramming himself into his open mouth. Coach Tally let go of Leven, gagging and choking as Clover began to slip down his throat. He threw his hands to his neck and tried to squeeze Clover out. His eyes bulged, and his face was the color of fire. As Clover meshed into his body, becoming one with the coach, Tally emitted a loud belch and looked desperate and confused. Clover twisted the big body and stood up straight. The coach stared, bug-eyed, at Winter and Leven. They in turn stared back, not knowing what to make of him or what had just happened.

"Now where was I?" Coach Tally said, sounding like himself but with the inflections of Clover. "Oh, yes, Foo."

Under the influence of Clover, Coach Tally pulled a piece of chalk out of his pocket. The coach kept it there to draw circles on pavement, in which he made students stand until they, as he said, "developed character." Coach Clover began to draw on the outside wall of the shoe store.

Leven and Winter were dumbfounded.

"Listen closely because I am only going to say this once and even then I am going to deny having said it." Coach Clover looked around as if to make sure nobody was near. "There is a space between the possible and the impossible—a very real place called Foo." He drew a big circle. "It is a place your mind enjoys keeping from you, yet it is as real as a thick patch of goose bumps or as any strong nagging notion. It exists within the minds of everyone, because without it there would be no room to dream or hope. It was created at the beginning of time so mankind could aspire and imagine. It is an entire realm hidden in the folds of your mind."

Coach Clover was talking with great excitement. Spit was flinging everywhere. He again looked around to make sure no one could overhear what he was saying.

"As real as Foo is, however, it is not easy for someone to get there," he went on. "You can't plan a trip and call your travel agent. Most people who enter Foo do so by accident."

Leven looked around as if confused.

"Pay attention," Coach Clover insisted, tipping a bit. He was having a hard time balancing such a big body. "Now, someone interested in things other than themselves might have, at one point in their lives, noticed that all sidewalks and street corners and roads are not the same. Some are wide, some are narrow. Some are made of concrete while some are brick or stone. The world is covered with thin, dirt lanes and wide, expansive stretches of asphalt, all of them designed to lead someone somewhere and most of them connecting and crossing evenly, straight, and just as they were planned. There are, however, roads and lanes that are not quite so uniform—street corners and crossings that don't match up as they should. Whether they were designed poorly or constructed by people too lazy to do a perfect job, it doesn't make a difference."

Leven and Winter looked down at the ground they were standing on. It looked all right.

"If you stand between two connecting lanes that don't match up quite right, while the temperature is divisible by seven, and the universe sees fit to fire off a couple of shooting stars, you will get quite a surprise—quite a surprise indeed." Coach Clover spat. It wasn't an impressive spit. The saliva just barely cleared his lips, then sort of drizzled down onto Coach Tally's chin. The big body began to sway back and forth. "The mind will snatch you up instantly and take you to Foo." From the way Coach Clover was teetering, it was obvious that Clover was having a hard time managing such a heavy body. He leaned up against the shoe store to keep his balance.

"How does—" Leven tried to ask.

"Save all questions to the end. Take Gladys Welch, for example." Coach Clover used his chalk to draw a stick figure of a woman on the side of the building. "She was an innocent woman who was simply walking her child on a hot August night when she unknowingly stepped upon the very spot where East Willow Road and Juniper Way haphazardly meet. Who knew that twenty years earlier, when John Packer and Timmy Lance were pouring that sidewalk, that they were unknowingly creating an entrance to Foo? John was in a hurry to meet up with his girlfriend, and Timmy wanted the day to end so he could play a little pool before going home. They had rushed through the job, ignoring the plans and doing a halfway job. Their sloppiness resulted in a less-than-perfect street corner and a potential portal to Foo.

"It wasn't Gladys's fault she stopped to calm her fussy child right there on that particular corner. Likewise, it could be argued that she was simply going about her business when she looked up at the dark sky and spotted a shooting star streaking across the black, like chalk across a newly inked blackboard. Before she could make a wish, however, she was gone, swept into Foo."

Leven and Winter remained silent and amazed.

"Nobody ever saw Gladys Welch again. The papers went on and on about how tragic it was—her disappearance, that is. A young mother taking her child for a walk just up and disappears, the helpless baby left on the corner of a public street alone and scared. Some speculated that Gladys Welch had been murdered; others assumed she had simply abandoned the child; a few suggested she had been abducted by aliens. But no one knew the truth, which is that Gladys had been taken to Foo."

Leven and Winter stood there with open mouths.

"These are the evidences and thumbprints of a place and force nobody knows to worry over or actually even wonder about. No one knows to be careful or to step lightly, but their lack of knowledge doesn't change the fact that all over the world there are street corners and intersections that don't quite match up or evenly meet. And if the heavens have you in their sight, they just might take you before your time and send you, in interim, to a place called Foo."

Coach Clover drew on the wall what looked to be a big raisin and a square sun, when in reality it was supposed to be a brain and a gateway.

"There is no place on earth that even begins to compare with the realm of Foo. In the beginning it was a perfect place set up so there would be room for all those who were born on earth to dream, an area the brain created to hatch the dreams and imaginations the logical, physical world would deem impossible."

"Amazing," Leven whispered.

Clover just couldn't manage the big body any longer, so he decided to wrap it up.

"In conclusion, sycophants are a blessing to us all."

Coach Tally began to quake and teeter. His body was doing the wave. A large lump rose in his throat, and he suddenly expelled through his open mouth the agitated Clover, who landed in Leven's hands. Coach Tally crumpled into a big pile of human on the ground.

Leven and Winter stared at Clover.

"What was that all about?" Leven asked.

"Is that true?" Winter asked in awe.

"I don't know what you're talking about," Clover sniffed. "I didn't say anything."

"Unbelievable," Leven whispered, his brown eyes glowing. "Foo's a real place?"

"My lips are sealed," Clover declared.

Coach Tally began to twitch and groan. Leven led Winter at a quick pace to Leven's house. Addy was at work at the napkin factory, and Terry wasn't at home. He was most likely down at the corner bar telling the waitress his troubles. Leven had planned on gathering a few things to take with him, but he soon realized he had little to gather. He threw on a thin hooded sweatshirt and shoved some extra socks into his pocket.

As he exited the house the wind was blowing fiercely, causing the huge tree in his yard to sway and violently bend. Small branches were breaking off the limbs, and it looked as if the gigantic trunk might be wrenched out of the ground. Leven gazed at the wind-whipped tree, realizing he might never see it again, and was surprised to experience a feeling of sadness.

He said good-bye to the writhing tree and empty house and he and Winter walked away. As they did so, the wind ceased.

"So you can freeze things?" Leven asked Winter as they headed toward town.

Winter nodded.

"Anything?" Leven asked.

"I think so," she smiled.

"Well, Lev can see the future," Clover bragged, materializing in the hood of the sweatshirt Leven was wearing. "He's an offing."

"You can see the future?" Winter asked, amazed.

"Sort of," Leven answered.

"And," Clover went on, "he can change the future."

"Really?" Winter said as if she didn't exactly believe it.

"I think so," Leven said. "If the timing's right, or if it's necessary, I can make things turn out in a way different than they might have."

"That's pretty cool," Winter smiled.

"Pretty unpredictable," Leven smiled back. "I think I'd

rather be able to freeze things whenever I wanted."

"We all have our strengths," Clover said, trying to sound wise.

Winter and Leven looked at him and laughed.

"So where should we go?" Winter asked. "How do we get to this Foo place?"

"I say we head downtown," Leven answered. "Let's find someplace to practice your freezing and my manipulations while we figure out where we're going."

Both Leven and Winter looked at Clover as if to prompt him to speak.

"All right, I think I can let you in on one more thing," Clover said, looking around nervously.

Leven and Winter stared at him.

"We're looking for a person named Geth," he whispered. "He knows the way."

"Geth?" Winter questioned.

"Yes," Clover answered seriously. "He's the only one who knows what's next. He'll find us."

"That's all you can tell us?" Leven asked. "Geth? Can't you take over Winter and tell me more?"

"No way!" Winter gasped, covering her mouth with her hands.

"I think I've said enough for one day," Clover said, then disappeared.

Leven and Winter walked at a fast pace toward town. Leven wished he had a better idea of what his future really was to be. At the moment all he sensed was a new purpose, mixed with equal amounts of panic and uncertainty.

CHAPTER ELEVEN

TAKING AN AX FOR THE HOME TEAM

The morning was different from usual on Andorra Court. Yes, the sun rose and the night faded. Sure, the paper boy came by flinging papers. A few automatic sprinklers turned on and off, and Mrs. Pendle stuck her ratty morning head out of her front door. She looked around to see if anyone else was out, then waddled quickly out to get her paper, wearing nothing but the tattered robe her husband had begged her for years to throw away.

As usual nobody saw her.

Actually, that's not completely true. The giant fantrum tree, which possessed the soul of Geth and stood in front of Leven's house, saw her—just as he had seen her every morning for so many years. He had seen everything that had happened there at 1712 Andorra Court—the ends of his branches gazing at all times in hundreds of directions and places.

Geth breathed and shook his leaves as if the wind were pushing through him. He shivered again, knowing the time had finally come. He was strong enough and Leven was gone. He had tried to stop Leven from leaving, or at least get his attention, but the boy had walked off.

At first Addy and Terry had made no mention of Leven not coming home that afternoon. But eventually Terry began to complain about what a stubborn and careless child Leven was to stay away when there were chores to be done. Addy took an hour off of work to both grocery shop and circle around Leven's school to see if he was there. Exhausted, she finally gave up the search and went home and argued with her husband about him finding a job, so she could take a break from folding.

Geth saw it all.

It was not a coincidence that in the afternoon, three quarters of Leven's house was shaded by Geth. Fate had put the Graphs' mobile home right where it sat, and now fate was going to take the next step. As Mrs. Pendle read her horoscope and drank her prune juice, the giant tree in her neighbor's yard was implementing a plan.

Geth would have preferred fate to have matched him up with Leven before the boy left, but what was done was done. Fate needed a little help, and it was now up to Geth to get to Leven. Of course, it's not easy for a tree to just walk down the street and get on its way. Trees have rules they are bound to obey simply because the earth feeds them. There are, however, ways to accomplish things when the need gets desperate, and Geth had been preparing and practicing for just such a situation.

The morning got brighter. Addy's alarm clock rang, and she rolled over and hit the poor thing harder than was necessary. It fell from the nightstand and softly bounced on the shag carpet. Addy sat up and moaned. All that folding had given her carpal tunnel syndrome, and her wrists were hurting like crazy. She felt cheated out of a life of luxury and resented the necessity of having to work. She was sick of it. She picked up the clock and looked at the numbers. Her face was pale green from her dried mask, and her hair, as usual, was a mess.

"A woman of leisure shouldn't have to get up before ten," she grumped to herself, her tongue feeling thick in her dry morning mouth. "Look at him," she added spitefully, glancing at Terry as he lay next to her, unshaven, mouth agape, snoring loudly. He had his knees pulled up to his chest and one arm hanging off the opposite side of the bed—every fifteen seconds or so his left leg would quiver.

Addy had finally had enough. "Get up!" she said, suddenly angry and whacking him on the chest with one of her sore arms. "Get up. I'm sick of it. You need to find a job." The mask on Addy's face cracked.

Terry grimaced and motioned for her to leave him alone.

"Get up!" Addy snarled. "Now!"

"I'm tired," Terry complained. "There's no work out there for me."

"Paul Brogan got a job last week. A good job with benefits," Addy informed him. "That job could have been yours."

"No use talking about it now," Terry whined. "He got the job and I didn't."

"You weren't looking," Addy snapped at him. "Now get up and go look."

"I will this afternoon," Terry said, closing his eyes.

Addy got up and moved around the bed to the closet, making as much noise as possible. She opened the closet door and pushed the hanging items to the side.

Addy's actions got Terry's attention. His right eye popped open; it was sunken and red like a pitted cherry.

Addy pulled out the two brown boxes that sat on the floor of the closet.

Terry's left eye opened; it matched the right.

Addy pulled back the carpet and lifted up the loose board that was hiding Terry's secret drinking money. She had known it was there for years, but figured it was easier to let him have his secret than to have him constantly begging her for money.

Terry's mouth opened. "Hey!" he hollered, jumping out of bed and grabbing for the money she had just snatched. "How'd you know? . . . that's my money."

"Wrong," Addy smirked. "It's *my* money. I earned it and I'll keep it." She stuffed the entire wad deep down the front of her nightgown.

"All right," Terry panicked. "I'll go look for work as soon as I can. I promise." His eyes were opened wide and his mouth sagging. His mushy nose glowed.

"You'll look *now*!" Addy screeched, the veins in her neck bulging.

"Now?" Terry repeated sadly. "But it's early. I can't just be expected to—"

Addy stamped her foot and glared.

"I can't believe I'm treated this way in my own house," Terry complained.

Addy pushed her hair back behind her square head and smiled coldly. "I'll give you the money back as soon as you've found a job."

Terry gaped at her helplessly. Addy smiled even wider.

"Fine." Terry stamped off to the bathroom to pretend he was getting ready for the day. He sat down on the toilet and began to think. This was not the morning he had planned. He rubbed his stubble of beard with his hand and tried to think harder. Sure, he could have spent his mental energy wondering how to find a job, or where the best place to begin looking for work was. Instead, however, every thought was directed toward simply getting that money back so he could blow it as soon as possible at the local bar. Just thinking about looking for work was making him thirsty.

Terry might very well have gone on for hours thinking about the money and growing even thirstier if it had not been for the unexpected tapping on his backside as he sat on the toilet.

He sprang immediately off the seat, screaming and slapping blindly at whatever had touched him.

He yanked his pajama bottoms up and turned to look at the toilet. There, wriggling out of the bowl, like some giant bark snake, was one of Geth's humongous tree roots. It pushed up out of the bowl like a huge serpent, writhing in the air. Terry's jaw dropped. He rubbed his red bloated eyes in complete disbelief. Then, as if to prove it was really happening, the root swelled and the toilet burst, sending water and shards of porcelain everywhere. Terry threw his hands up to cover his face as he cowered against the bathroom door, still not believing what he was seeing.

"What's going on in there!?" Addy yelled from outside the door. "What was that noise!?"

Roots came slithering out of the faucet and drain in the sink, reaching out toward Terry, stopping him from saying anything besides, "Heeeelp!"

The bathroom floor creaked and buckled upward as a huge root pushed up from below the trailer house. Terry fumbled for the door, screaming, wanting nothing more than to get away. He pulled open the door and came face to face with Addy. She was staring at him, her puffy eyes and green face creating a sight almost as frightening as the surreal scene behind him.

"Just what do you think you're doing?" she scolded. "If you've made a mess in—"

Before Addy could finish her sentence, Terry whipped past her. A thick wet root sprang up from beneath the floor, caught him by the ankle, flipped him across the bed, and slammed him

into the wall. The whole house began to lift and sway. Addy stumbled. She was horrified and screaming at the top of her lungs. Had Mrs. Pendle stuck her ratty head out her front door at that moment she would have seen the giant fantrum tree surging and pushing the entire house up from beneath, its roots writhing and thrashing like the tentacles of a crazed octopus.

Terry ran for the window. Addy ran for the door. Both were stopped by thousands of tiny hairy roots that latched onto their feet and lifted them into the air and began whipping them around on the mattress.

Trees don't normally smile, but at that moment anyone could have seen the grin on that tree from miles away. The mattress whipping wasn't actually necessary, but Geth felt they deserved some payback for the way they had treated Leven.

After Geth had had his fun, his tiny roots pulled Terry and Addy off the bed by their ankles and dragged them screaming out through the back window. They were whipped about, spun in the air, and dropped with a thump at the base of the tree. Roots were sticking out of every window and door of the trailer house, waving madly.

Before Terry could free himself and run for help, the roots stopped wiggling and began to quickly withdraw, slithering back through the windows and doors and down through the floor of the trailer home. The entire place creaked as it settled back into a crooked, slightly-off-the-foundation position. In a few moments all the roots had disappeared.

Breathing hard, Terry looked at Addy.

"Did you see . . . ?"

"I did," she said, breathing just as hard and fanning her green face. She pushed her frizzy hair out of her face, wailing. It was at that moment she first noticed the bright red ax lying on the ground near her. She hadn't realized they owned an ax. She wiped at her tears. "I don't want you looking for work today," she finally managed to say.

"I told you I shouldn't—"

"I want you to get rid of this tree," she interrupted. "And do it now. It's never been right. Chop it up, sell the wood, and then you'll have the money." Addy worked herself up off the ground and stepped over to the ax. She picked it up, examined its blade, and carried it over to her husband.

"Now?" Terry whined.

"Now!" she almost screamed, thrusting the tool at him.

Terry stood up and tested his knees. He looked back at the house. Through the bathroom window he could see one root still sticking up out of the broken toilet. Suddenly it shivered and water flung off of it as it quickly retracted.

"I don't think my drain snake could fix that," he mumbled to himself.

Terry hefted the ax and moved toward the trunk of the tree. He was really thirsty. He drew the ax back and swung. The blade cut deep into the trunk, as if the tree had relaxed to let the ax slice deeper. Addy was almost impressed with Terry's strength; Terry actually was. He pulled the ax back and whacked again. A chunk the size of a football flew out and landed at Addy's feet. At this rate Terry would have the thing down and chopped up by early afternoon.

Terry smiled.

Geth stood there, taking every blow.

Trees don't really enjoy being cut to pieces. Some recognize their place in the world and accept it bravely, but few would actually provoke a human into chopping it up. Geth had done just that.

Whack!

Geth closed his leaves as darkness began to push upward into his trunk and through his branches. Geth could feel his bark pulling away and beginning to separate from the body of wood. His foliage trembled with each blow. The air was becoming black and only bits and pieces of the surrounding scenery were clear anymore. The sky smeared and started to slide to the ground as pain made his thoughts dark.

Terry went at the tree with all his force.

Geth swayed. He was dizzy. Standing tall was quickly not becoming an option.

"Timber!!!" Terry shouted, taking one last swing. The ax sliced deep into the remaining trunk and got lodged. Terry began to violently jerk and wiggle it. As it pulled free, Geth, tipsy from destruction, leaned to the east and toppled, his remaining strand of trunk snapping loudly. The huge tree crashed down next to the rear corner of the trailer house, cracking the roof and crumpling a section of wall. It settled with a whump.

Terry looked at the tree lying there. His house was damaged, but still livable. "Stupid tree," he spat. Addy turned and went back inside. She had napkins to go fold.

The giant tree was no more.

CHAPTER TWELVE

DIVIDE AND CONQUER

It is a grand thing to be a stately fantrum tree that stands tall and oversees the world around it. With its massive structure and lush foliage, such a tree can be justifiably proud. Oh, there are a few drawbacks to being a tree. Birds give you no rest with all their constant flittering, chirping, and nesting; kids love to shoot at you with BB guns; and lovers invade your space and wreak indignities on you by gouging their initials into your bark. But those disadvantages are bearable.

There are the more serious drawbacks like, say, death. For example, when a tree is turned into firewood for burning or used to make furniture for sitting. Trees in our world know nothing else. They are born, they live, and then they die. The most they can hope for is to be transformed into the front page of a really historic newspaper edition, or to be shaped into a cane for an important person, or to be made into a polished banister of some huge mansion.

The giant fantrum tree that Terry chopped down and dismembered had aspired to be something much greater than a chair or an ottoman. Geth knew very well what he was doing when he permitted Terry to take him down. Now it was up to fate to take Geth to the next step.

Terry loaded up the wood and hauled it to a lumberyard two miles from the mobile home park. He drove it there in his beat-up old truck, licking his lips the whole time.

Terry was thirsty. Very, very thirsty.

The owner of the lumberyard, Frank Welt, at first had no interest in acquiring such green wood, but when Terry explained how thirsty he was and said how little he was asking for the load, Frank gave him twenty dollars, and Terry was on his way.

Frank sorted the wood, pulling out the largest pieces and piling them under a tin-roofed shelter. He tossed the twigs and smaller limbs onto a heap of scrap he had drying.

Normally there's not much need to be concerned about what happens to a tree once it's been downed. It's a sad thing to lose a tree, but the loss is generally only temporarily mourned. A chunk of this tree, however, was worth tracking. Six inches beneath its bark, in its trunk, next to its lowest branch, was the heart and soul of Geth. And whereas the ax might have killed the limbs and body of the tree, the heart was still faintly beating in this piece. Geth was not done for yet.

"Lousy drunk," Frank said to himself. "Destroy a beautiful tree so that you can wet your tongue. Pathetic." Frank ran his gloved hand over the wood he had just bought and moved to go.

"Frank," Geth whispered, amazed that his reduced size

allowed him to vibrate enough to actually make a noise.

Frank wheeled around, looking for whoever had spoken to him. He saw only open sky and his empty lumberyard.

"Frank," he heard again, this time more loudly and a bit deeper.

"Hello?" Frank yelled.

"Frank," the wood whispered back.

"Who's there?" Frank said, bewildered, knowing nobody was around but him.

"Frank . . ." Geth's voice faded.

Frank looked at the pile of green wood Terry had just delivered. He stepped closer and pushed aside a few of the large pieces, half expecting to find someone buried in the pile. No one was there.

"I must be crazy," he whispered. "I'm the one who needs the drink."

He looked more closely at a section of the tree's trunk. It was a piece about a foot and a half in diameter and two feet long. Protruding from it was a two-inch stump of a thick branch, and almost all the bark had been scraped off it. As he studied it, the chunk of wood appeared to inflate then deflate itself, almost as though it had inhaled then exhaled.

Frank rubbed his eyes, then picked up the piece of wood and held it in his hands. It was warm, and when he squeezed it, his fingers made an impression, as though it were made of clay. The wood reshaped itself as soon as he let go.

"Whoa," Frank whispered. "Odd."

A large truck pulled into the lot and honked, and Frank motioned the driver over.

"I'm here for the Tatum load," the driver hollered.

"I've got it all ready for you around back," Frank replied, nodding toward another shed.

The driver pulled ahead, and as it passed him, Frank tossed the whispering piece of wood into the open bed of the truck.

"One less thing for me to worry about," Frank said, dusting his hands and heading toward the office to get the forms the Tatum driver would need to sign.

ii

Tatum, Inc. was a manufacturer of a variety of products. The company had its hand in plastics, wooden toys, and handles for yard tools. They also had a division that produced indoor fans and one that molded outdoor chairs. Their best-selling item at the moment was a portable grill that flipped the meat for you. They also made rugs, manufactured doll body parts, and were the North American manufacturer of seven types of garden hoses.

They were diversified; a small arm of their business even manufactured wooden paint stirring paddles, popsicle sticks, and toothpicks.

It was into this division of the company that the driver brought the heart of Geth and the rest of the wood from Frank's lumberyard. He backed the truck up to a large metal vat and dumped the load.

Geth buzzed. In order to complete his mission, his heart had to stay intact. He was concerned about being reduced to pulp and made into paper. But he was powerless to resist what was happening. It would be up to fate to take it from here and work him into a position where he could find Leven.

A man with big arms picked up the section of Geth's trunk and heaved it into a rotating bin. Geth tried to call out, but things were moving so fast and there was too much noise. The bin tilted, and its contents were spilled into a vat of liquid chemicals. Geth bobbed around in the smelly mix until he was hooked with a long stick and dragged into an oven. Everything was black and the grinding of loud motors vibrated the building.

The chemical solution Geth had been thrown into was cold, and the heat of the oven was at first welcome, but it soon became unbearably hot. Geth felt as though at any moment he might spontaneously burst into flame. Just as he was ready to give up and turn to ash, he was hauled out of the oven and dumped onto a speeding conveyer belt. Machines whirred, clanked, and screamed around him in the darkness, and he heard the ominous sound of wood going through a grinder. The conveyor belt abruptly ended, and the heart of Geth plummeted down into the grinder. In an instant he was devoured by the blades. The lights in the factory surged and dimmed a bit. One of the workers commented on how that had never happened before and then simply went on with his job.

The rest of the day played out routinely for the workers at the Tatum toothpick factory. The new toothpicks were boxed up and stacked onto pallets and put onto trucks that would deliver them to surrounding states. For the workers, it was an ordinary day. Life just went on.

But Geth was down.

CHAPTER THIRTEEN

REALIZING YOU HAVE NOTHING

Y ou may wonder what a messy-haired girl, an obscure boy, and a chopped up fantrum tree have to do with one another, and in doing so you would be justified. Typically a person wouldn't associate one with the others. A psychiatrist might grow concerned if he or she were to show you an ink blot shaped like a tree and you were to respond, "Young boy," or "Messy girl." But thanks to fate, these three were about to become entwined. Weaved together like a rug that humanity was about to unknowingly wipe its feet on.

It's difficult to know where you belong when the soul isn't even aware of what its options are. You can easily picture yourself behind the wheel of a fast car or lying on a sandy beach because you have seen pictures of or witnessed such things. But how can a person see himself somewhere his mind has refused to show him?

This was the situation Leven was in.

His entire life he had been told where to go, where to sit, where to stand, what to say, how to act, who he was, and who he was not. Now, fate was finished keeping Leven in complete darkness, but the boy still couldn't picture his future. Clover had hinted at Foo, but it seemed like a fable being told by a pretend friend. And Leven had a bigger problem that he was even less aware of.

Sabine was searching for him.

Sabine didn't clearly know it was Leven he was after, but he lusted to find the one who alone had the power to destroy his plan. He couldn't leave Foo to find that person himself, but he had an army to help, thanks to the dark shadows he cast. Sabine's horrid thoughts and evil desires consumed him. In his hatred and greed he had become completely dark in the head, sicker than any being had ever been in Foo, which is quite an awful accomplishment, since over time some pretty foul people had accidentally stumbled into Foo. In fact, a *number* of notable criminals and thugs had made their way into the realm. But even the worst of them paled in comparison to Sabine, who knew nothing but wickedness and rage thanks to an unknown force that controlled him. So profound was the evil within him that the very shadows he cast loathed him and desired to escape his presence.

Of course they could never do so—a shadow cannot exist without a master to cast it. These shadows were a legion of diverse, inky images—short, tall, fat, and thin—desperate, dark, whispering images of Sabine, frantic to escape him, but destined to remain captive to his will. And day by day, minute by minute, Sabine's shadows multiplied, an army of darkness that was ever growing.

Sabine's shadows could do things no other being had ever been able to do. Most remarkably, they could slip in and out of Foo effortlessly and at any time. Because they were shadows, they were able to insinuate themselves into the dark dreams of men and emerge in reality. Sabine simply had to exhale, and his slavish minions would swoop over the earth, penetrating the minds of any who entertained selfish or conspiring thoughts. A quick intake of breath, and the dark images of Sabine would come back with a swoosh to the being who cast them. So invasive were Sabine's shadowy legions they had the power to affect both those in Foo and those in reality, whomever Sabine sought to harm.

Every morning when he awoke, Sabine would step to his balcony, which looked out over the Fundrals of Foo. He would gaze down with evil satisfaction upon the gathering of his shadows, a gathering that stretched endlessly across the base of Ardion, awaiting his directions. Then he would exhale, sending his envoys out of Foo and into the dark dreams of mankind.

His shadows swept the earth, spiraling down through the dreams of mankind, searching for the one soul who had the power to ruin Sabine's plan—the one soul who could destroy the gateway before Sabine could find it and go through it himself into reality.

Of course, his shadows had been looking for the wrong thing. Sabine had figured that the descendant of the gatemaker would be a grown man—a strong, wise being who could single-handedly step into Foo and destroy Sabine and his evil intentions.

You may doubt their existence, for the shadows of Sabine are not easy to spot, unless you are connected to Foo. But even for those who know nothing of Foo, it is possible to catch a glimpse of them. You can see the shadows searching even now. Watch when a car goes by. See how the light flashes off the chrome, reflecting things so quickly that the normal eye can't take it in? If you are perceptive enough you'll see the shadows in those flashes.

Observe when someone waves her arm and her silver watch glistens. The shadows are there. If someone flips a coin, you'll see how it catches the light in its rotations but how quickly darkness extinguishes the glimmer. It is in these twinklings that the shadows of Sabine can be observed in their earthly flights. These are the fleeting evidences to those who know that the battle continues—the battle in which Leven and Winter were now very much involved.

The two of them had escaped their horrid lives and now were on a quest, searching for a person or thing named Geth. They had spent an entire day down by the river, hidden behind a thin line of trees, experimenting with their gifts. Winter had her ability down. She was able to freeze anything she chose: water, trees, even an abandoned car. Once the object was frozen, she needed only to touch it and it would thaw.

Whereas Winter had full control of her ability, Leven was struggling to manage his. He felt as if fate kept intervening, keeping him from manipulating the future. If he concentrated really hard he could get his brown eyes to burn gold, but unless the timing was just right, he couldn't clearly see what was coming. The best he achieved was envisioning an older boy crossing the street and being struck by a bicyclist. Leven had concentrated like mad, causing the cyclist to look up at the last moment, swerve around the boy and run instead into a parked car. It was a neat trick that left the boy intact but the cyclist shaken.

After spending a full day practicing, they slept that night under a bridge and woke up cold, hungry, and miserable. They arose and began searching the streets for Geth, a search that seemed futile since they had no idea what this Geth looked like or where he could possibly be.

Clover was of no help. All he did was repeat over and over, "Fate will work it out. We'll find Geth."

Clover's repetitive mantra got old fast and, out of patience, both Leven and Winter finally told him to keep his thoughts to himself. He responded by pulling his cloak over his head and disappearing. In all likelihood, however, he was probably perched on top of Leven's head.

The town of Burnt Culvert wasn't much to look at. There was an older downtown section where the burned-out shells of a number of buildings still leaned or rested. A giant charred wall stood all by itself. It was scorched and covered with spray-painted messages and drawings. There was a park in the center of town that had green grass and a small Chat-n-Chew Snak Shack near the playground. Some of the buildings on Main Street had survived the fire and been cleaned up years before to give the town an all-American feel. It was really the only stretch of Burnt Culvert that looked put together. The city had installed some antique lampposts and, depending on the season, a variety of colorful flags were hung from them. At the moment all the flags on Main Street were black with orange jack-o'-lanterns stenciled on them. Surrounding the business district on Main Street were the residential areas.

Leven, Winter, and Clover would have been able to live for a while off the money Winter had brought with her. But for some reason that was still being argued, Clover had thrown away Winter's purse. That left them broke, hungry, and homeless. Oh, and a bit fed up.

"So do we just keep walking?" Winter asked Clover as day two was coming to an end. "It's getting dark, and I thought this Geth was supposed to find us."

"Well, tonight could be the night," Clover said from the top of Leven's head.

"You said that last night," Leven pointed out.

"Fate will work it out. We'll find Geth," Clover repeated, which made Winter wonder again if she hadn't ought to freeze the little pest. She had threatened to before, but he had told her that because he was a sycophant, her gift wouldn't work on him. She wondered if that were true.

The October night was cold, and there was an ominous feeling in the air. Leven wondered if he would not have been better off staying at home and dealing with his miserable life instead of taking on the task of saving the world. At least he would have had a bed to sleep in.

"What do we do now?" Winter asked as they walked down Main Street for the four hundredth time. "Shouldn't you be telling us where to go?"

Clover shrugged. "I'm here to get you back, but I think

Antsel would be upset if I started making the decisions. I only know that fate will lead us to Geth."

"Geth, Antsel, Foo," Winter muttered. "I don't think anyone is coming for us."

"Can I bite her?" Clover asked Leven, upset that she was bad-mouthing Antsel, his last burn.

Leven shook his head.

"We've been walking all day," Winter complained. "We've gone down every street and block in this city. We haven't eaten and we're broke."

"Well, it's not my fault that you can't manage your money," Clover countered.

"You threw away my purse," Winter huffed.

"I thought it was an enemy."

Leven listened to them arguing. The night was dark, and the stars in the sky were not strong enough to shine through the orange glow of the street lamps. Leven squinted and could see the neon lights of a diner down the way. His head cleared, his brown eyes burned gold, and in an instant he could see the future. His gift was working, and as usual he had little control of it. He saw Winter and himself sitting at the counter of that diner with nothing in front of them on the counter. He saw an old man beside him and an old woman walking out. He thought for a second. Lights shot across his view and Leven could feel his thoughts physically touching the woman's mind. He suggested she hand the nice-looking children some money. Leven finished manipulating the future and shook his head, returning to the present.

"I thought I saw it breathe," Clover argued, his voice bringing Leven even farther out of his thoughts.

"Purses don't breathe." Winter sighed.

"Maybe not here," Clover said.

Leven stared at the diner down the street.

"Are you okay?" Winter asked him.

"I'm fine," Leven replied. "Let's go get something to eat."

"But—" Winter said.

"It's okay," Leven smiled. "I've worked something out."

Clover stuck his tongue out at Winter one last time and flipped his hood up.

"It freaks me out when he vanishes," Winter complained. "He's probably sitting on top of my head making faces."

"Let's eat," Leven repeated, feeling an urgency to move toward the diner. "And besides, he's my sycophant, so he's most likely on my head making faces."

"So, did you see someone feeding us?" Winter asked as they walked, sounding as if they were animals in a zoo.

"Not exactly."

"Not exactly? What does that mean?"

"It means I helped fate a little bit."

Winter looked skeptical. "That's a nice trick. When it works."

Leven nodded. "Well, if they forget to give us ice in our drinks, you can work a little of your own magic."

They entered the diner and sat at the counter where Leven had pictured them sitting. They were studying the menu when an old woman stopped on her way out of the diner and handed

Winter a twenty-dollar bill. The woman had a puzzled look on her face but said the meal was on her.

"I'm glad you're on the good side," Winter said, commenting on Leven's ability to manipulate fate, and now looking at the menu with renewed interest. "I think I would have made her give me more than twenty dollars." Winter reached to pat Leven on the shoulder but stopped herself. Leven noticed her pull back.

"So, what exactly happens if you touch me?" Leven asked. "Do I explode or something?"

"I don't know," Winter said, blushing just a bit. "But I'm pretty sure it's not good."

"How can you know that?" Leven asked. "Maybe that's what's holding us back." Leven reached over as if to touch Winter on the arm.

She drew back. "Don't!" she warned, loud enough that the man sitting next to them looked over.

Leven pulled his hand back, and Winter smiled to show that it was all in fun.

"The thing is, I don't think it's a joke," she whispered. "Something bad will happen."

Leven shrugged, too hungry to care at that moment. He turned from her to concentrate on the menu. He tried to focus, but his thoughts kept circling around the room and back to the old man sitting next to him. Once again his gift was acting up. There was nothing unusual about the old man. He probably had children and grandkids who loved him, but that didn't exactly do anything for Leven.

Leven's eyes burned gold.

The old man took a bite of sandwich.

Leven's thoughts raced and pulsated. He could see the whole diner. He could see the area outside the diner. Lights flashed and buzzed in his mind. He could see Winter, and once again his thoughts raced and settled in on the old man sitting right next to him.

"Can I take your order?" the waitress asked Leven for the third time.

"Lev," Winter prompted. "She wants to know what you want."

Leven shook off the feeling he was having and focused on the menu. "I'll have the open-faced roast turkey sandwich in butter gravy. And a large glass of milk."

"All right," the waitress said, walking off.

"What were you doing?" Winter questioned. "She asked you three times what you wanted."

Leven would have answered her, but his mind was wandering again. In his thoughts the old man was getting up. He saw him throw some money down and flick a toothpick from his mouth onto the floor.

Leven came out of his thoughts and looked at the old man sitting there. He watched him finish his sandwich and begin to pick his teeth.

"Excuse me," the old man said to Leven. "Could you please pass me another napkin?"

Leven reached for the napkin dispenser and tried to pull one out, but the napkins were packed so tightly it was a struggle to remove even one. He pushed on the dispenser and the silver napkin holder jiggled. Light reflected off of it as it moved and as the glint disappeared Leven thought he saw something in the flash. It was a face, black and hollow. He quickly pulled his hand from the dispenser and glanced to see if anyone was behind him. A thick wisp of black slipped silently out through one of the windows of the diner. Leven would have spent a few moments being frightened, but the old man interrupted him.

"Could I have a napkin?" the man asked again, nicely but still needing a napkin.

"Sure," Leven fumbled. "I'm sorry, I thought I . . . Do I know you by any chance?" Leven asked politely, confused by what he had just seen reflected in the napkin holder. He handed the man a napkin.

"Not that I know of," the old man smiled.

The waitress served Leven's and Winter's drinks and gave them place settings as the old man stood up. He put down some money, flicked the toothpick he had been using onto the floor, smiled and nodded at Leven and Winter, and left the diner.

"What was that about?" Winter whispered.

"I kept seeing him in my thoughts," Leven said, confused.

"He was sitting right next to you," Winter laughed. "Now you need visions just to know who's sitting by you?"

Leven shook his head. "It wasn't the future," he added. "It was something about the scene." Leven picked up his glass of milk and drank it down in three gulps.

There had been something about that man.

CHAPTER FOURTEEN

I CAN SEE CLEARLY NOW MY HEAD IS GNAWED

Leven was halfway right, there *had been* something about that man, but it wasn't the man himself: it was the small sliver of wood he had used to pick his teeth and then discarded on the floor.

Fate had taken Geth from being a giant tree that stood proudly in the Oklahoma soil to a toothpick that had been loaded into a tiny, clear, plastic toothpick holder on the counter of Tina's Diner. Geth, of course, couldn't see anything; his world had been dark ever since Terry had taken an ax to him. Fate had left him little to work with, only his heart.

He was okay with that. After all, he was alive. He could feel pieces of himself missing, pieces that the machine had shaved off and distributed to other toothpicks—toothpicks too dead to know what they had.

At the moment Geth was crowded into a pile of hundreds of other toothpicks who were as dead as wood could be. He shook internally and his toothpick body vibrated. The vibration caused the toothpicks around him to move slightly. He vibrated some more and made a little more room for himself. He then began to work his way downward toward where Geth hoped the opening of the toothpick dispenser would be. He felt no real urgency in getting picked next, but he knew of no other way to get out and find Leven.

As he vibrated his way down, a strong wave of understanding rippled through his thin body. Geth could *tell* that Leven was nearby. He couldn't see Leven, but he sensed his presence. He wiggled more frantically through the other toothpicks, rolling himself down toward the little plastic roller with the notch in it. He could feel the weight of the other toothpicks as he settled deeper into the pile, each shift making it harder for him to move.

He rolled again and felt the base of the container against his backside. The notch was filled with another toothpick. He wiggled his end and was able to wedge himself between the other toothpick and into the notch. He had no breath to catch or nerves to calm, but he was jittery. No sooner had he claimed the notch than the small plastic barrel rolled, and Geth popped out of the dispenser and into the fingers of someone. Geth thought for a moment it might be Leven, but he could tell almost instantly the old hands holding him did not belong to Leven Thumps.

Geth felt something pinch him on one end as his other end was jammed between two hard surfaces. He could feel moisture and a tongue.

The old man rolled the toothpick to the side of his mouth and let it rest with just the tip sticking out. Never had Geth felt more useless. It was one thing for a lithen to travel by fate while he was strong and mobile, but it was a whole other thing to trust in fate when he was the size of a sliver and had no real way of doing anything.

The old man rolled the toothpick with his tongue. He pinched the end again and pulled Geth out. He bit down on the top of Geth and turned him just a bit.

Geth's mind exploded, and pain jolted his tiny frame. He felt his mind waver and then as if he were having a vision, light began to seep in. The old man bit again and again—more pain, and even greater light.

Geth saw colors, deep rich colors, and bright lights. He could see the old man's tongue and teeth and bits of food. He was rolled over and stored in the side of the mouth again. The tip sticking out this time was the end where the teeth had perforated him, leaving a hole, and the light was almost blinding.

Geth could see! He saw the diner and the counter and the back of what looked to be a young boy's head. But from the angle he was on, Geth couldn't make out if it was Leven or not.

Roll me, Geth thought as loud as he could. *Roll me.*

The old man rolled the toothpick in his mouth and there, much to the great joy of Geth, was Leven. Sitting next to Leven was a messy-haired girl who had her face down over her plate, eating.

The old man leaned over and asked Leven something. Leven responded, looking confused and concerned. The old man took some napkins from Leven. He blew his nose, which created some terrible turbulence for Geth and was incredibly uncomfortable. Then he stood, tossed some money on the counter, and flicked Geth out of his mouth.

Geth tried to fall in such a way as to land on Leven, but he couldn't make it happen. He tumbled and fell, light flashing and swirling as he dropped. He hit the floor, bounced, and partially rolled into a crevice between the floor and the metal base of the counter. His eye was wedged into the crack and he couldn't see anything. He tried to roll himself so he could peer up and out toward Leven, but he couldn't budge. He couldn't hear and he couldn't see.

ii

Leven had never tasted anything better. The open-faced turkey sandwich had been hot and smothered with rich gravy. It had been so delicious he began to think about manipulating fate so as to get himself another one. He thought about the old man who had been sitting by him earlier. As Leven savored the deep-fried, honey battered onion rings dipped in ketchup, he wondered what the connection might be between the old man and Geth. He grabbed a napkin for himself and thought about the hollow, shadowy face he had seen earlier in the polished surface of the napkin holder. He closed his eyes and remembered the black vapors that had tried to invade his sleeping porch on the night he had first met Clover.

His mind cleared and his eyes burned gold. He could see the

diner from outside. He could see the door open and the counter he was sitting at. He could see beneath the counter and the stool he was sitting on.

Leven leaned over and looked down at the floor. Nothing. He used his toe to kick at a toothpick that lay up against the base of the counter and noticed a dime by Winter's feet. He leaned down and picked up the coin.

"Can you make wishes on dimes?" he asked Winter. "Or is that just on pennies?"

Winter hadn't said much because she too had been reveling in the meal they had been lucky enough to procure. She had ordered a roast beef sandwich with creamy horseradish sauce and thick homemade French fries. She had also ordered a big slice of chocolate cake and a foamy root beer that came in a mug shaped like a cowboy boot.

"We couldn't have wished for better food," Winter said, as she came to the end of her meal.

"Unbelievably good," Leven said, smacking his lips. "What now?"

"You're the decision maker," Winter pointed out.

They both finished eating. Leven gave the waitress the twenty dollar bill, and she gave him one dollar and seven cents back.

iii

The pain came out of nowhere. One moment Geth was lying there wedged in the crevice, then the force of Leven's kick ripped him out of the space he was in and slammed him up against the metal footing that anchored the counter to the floor. On the end of the footing was a sharp piece of metal edging. The metal tore into Geth, splintering one side of his body and causing him excruciating pain. Geth lay there wishing for death and realizing he had no chance of getting to Leven now. He tried to roll over to better see where he was and realized he was more mobile than before. He glanced down at his left side where the hurt was so strong, and saw what had happened. The strength of Leven's kick had shaved Geth an arm—a sliver he could bend and move like a real appendage. He pushed away from the footing and rolled back under Leven's stool. He could see Leven's feet and felt his soul soar at the possibility of finally connecting. He pushed off the base and put his newly formed arm to his side so as to roll more efficiently.

He stopped just under Leven's feet.

Leven's right shoelace was hanging low enough that it was almost touching the ground. Geth pushed himself up to it and lay on his backside to try and reach the dangling lace with his new arm.

He could almost touch it.

Leven shifted, and the lace dropped down even farther, touching Geth's body. But before he could catch hold of it, Leven stood up, whipping the lace away, and walked off.

Geth wanted to scream, but that's hard to do when you have no mouth. He wanted to run after Leven, but that too was impossible. He felt like crying, but as any self-respecting being knows, there is no dignity in a crying toothpick.

Geth watched Leven and the girl go through the diner doors and out into the dark and windy night.

iv

Leven stopped just outside the diner and bent down to tie his shoelace, his dark hair blowing all over in the strong wind. Of course, it was nothing compared to what the wind was doing to Winter's hair.

"So what was up with that old man?" Winter asked, trying to hold her hair down.

"I have no idea," Leven answered. "I just kept seeing a close up of him. I thought for a second he might be Geth."

Winter frowned. "I'm beginning to think we made a mistake. It's pretty hard to feel like you're making progress when you don't know where you're going."

Clover appeared, clinging to the front of Leven's shirt. "So where's my food, you guys?"

"I thought you said you'd take care of yourself," Leven said nicely, feeling sorry he hadn't even thought of saving some for Clover.

"Sure, I grazed off the plates of everyone else in there, but it still would have been a nice gesture for you to save me some of yours."

"We need to find a place to sleep," Leven pointed out, ignoring Clover.

"There's always the bridge again," Winter sighed.

"This is beginning to feel hopeless," Leven admitted.

Clover vanished, and Leven and Winter turned toward the river.

V

Geth knew what he needed to do. He was useless in the state he was currently in. Fate had given him vision, and fate had caused Leven to kick him in such a way as to create an arm. Geth knew now that in order for him to get anywhere he needed to make a few more changes to himself. Without some work, he would be dead. He lay on the floor wondering what the best way to do that would be.

He closed his eye and thought.

After a few moments he rolled to his left side and pushed off into the walkway of the restaurant, where the heavy foot traffic was. Waitresses and waiters and customers were walking back and forth, going about their business with no concern for the small sliver of wood underfoot.

It was now up to fate again.

A teenager with green hair and heavy shoes was the first to unknowingly kick Geth. He skidded across the floor and came to rest next to a booth a heavy woman was currently trying to work herself out of. The woman's high heel on her left shoe came down on the bottom end of Geth. His vision went momentarily black, as pain stronger and more massive than he had ever felt ripped through his body. He could see stars, and stars circling around those stars, and moons and lightning. He was half glad he didn't have a mouth for fear that his scream would have garnered a lot of attention. The woman moved off, leaving Geth there on the floor, writhing in pain. He looked down at his crumpled end and winced. He would have taken some time to feel sorry for himself, but the waitress who had been serving the large woman stepped up to the booth to see how much of a tip she had earned.

There was no tip.

The waitress stamped her foot in anger. "Well, thanks a lot," she muttered, hoping the stingy customer might look back and see her making a nasty face.

Geth might have been slightly interested in the entire exchange, if the waitress's stomp had not come down on the upper part of his thin body. He was now one tiny bruise. He rolled beneath the bench so he could recover a bit before going on.

"Ohhhh," he moaned.

Geth instantly stopped moaning. Noise had come out of him. "Amazing," he whispered. He couldn't hear what he was saying for lack of ears, but he could feel the sound within his head.

He lifted his left arm to the small hole beneath his eye that the stomping waitress had caused. He had a mouth. He looked to the bottom half of himself where the pain was still strong. The high heel had split his lower half perfectly. He moved his newly formed legs. Geth breathed hard.

He pulled himself up, and stood, took two steps, and smiled. Fate had worked him over pretty well. Geth wasn't done yet, however. He spotted the sharp point of a screw sticking out from the base of the bench.

"I can't stop now," he said to himself.

Geth took a deep breath, closed his eye, and smacked the side of his head into the tip of the screw. The pain was horrific, but nowhere near as bad as the high heel had been. Geth wobbled and felt lightheaded as noise rushed into him.

He could hear.

He whacked the other side of his head on the screw to make another ear and then worked on boring out a hole to smell with. It wasn't actually fun, but the results were miraculous. He could hear, he could smell, and he could walk. Geth tried to jab a hole for a second eye, but he could bang his head only hard enough to make a shallow dent—not a deep enough hole to see out of. Knowing what he had to do, he walked to the far underside of the bench, turned, and ran full speed toward the screw tip.

Now you might not think what Geth was doing too heroic or amazing. But if you had been under that bench and had watched that toothpick run valiantly across the floor and hurl himself face-first into the end of a sharp screw, you would have been quite impressed . . . or fairly mortified.

Geth was screaming in pain, but he now had two eyes, one a little lower than the other on his skinny toothpick face.

A family who had slipped into the booth above him heard the tiny screaming and assumed it was a mouse. The mother jumped up on top of the bench, and the father got the manager, who insisted they must be mistaken. The diner was rodent-free and would they like to keep their voices down and enjoy a complimentary piece of pie for their troubles? The family accepted the offer, but moved to a different booth.

Geth caught his breath and looked around. He could now see well. Even with one eye located slightly lower than the other, he had a full range of sight. He opened and closed his mouth and smiled. He bent his legs and jumped. He flexed his arm. He had only one and it was a bit stiff, but he would now be able to fend for himself. He stuck his head out from under the bench to see if the coast was clear. It had not been long since Leven left, and with any luck Geth could get out of the diner and catch up to him.

The door of the diner was closed, and Geth could see no opening around it. He watched a couple of people come in and he figured it was now or never. He bolted out from under the bench and sprang across the floor as the doors were swinging to a close. He sprinted harder and jumped just as the doors were shutting.

He didn't make it. The doors came together, closing tight with him wedged between them. All the pain and agony he had endured from being stepped on and split apart and poked and gouged were nothing compared to what he now felt. He tried to scream, but he couldn't open his mouth. Trapped as he was, he couldn't move his arm or legs or see anything. He was just a squashed toothpick caught about an inch off the ground between two gigantic, heavy metal doors.

It was a full six minutes before someone walked out of the diner and Geth was able to drop to the ground and roll out to freedom. He was in such agony he could barely move, but he knew if he stayed in the pathway he would only get beaten up further. He crawled into the grass just to the side of the door and flopped over onto his back. He looked up at the sky and wondered what in the world he was doing.

He began to laugh.

Geth was not a toothpick. Geth was the last heir of the great realm of Foo. He was a king and a leader. He was crucial to the well being and survival of all mankind. Yet here he was: a beaten up toothpick, tossed to the side of a diner, in the middle of nowhere.

He thought of those back in Foo and how they would react if they could see him now. He thought of his enemies and the joy they would have knowing the state he was in. He thought of Sabine and the satisfaction Geth's plight would give that dark figure. His body hurt. Being trapped by the door had crushed every bit of him, but it had also given him total mobility. Fate was too good to him.

Geth closed his eyes and fell asleep in the grass.

CHAPTER FIFTEEN

RUN FASTER

Leven and Winter walked toward the tree-lined river. In the darkness they made their way carefully through the woods and came to a dry rocky patch of bank. The still night air was cold and clammy.

"That old man has something to do with us," Leven insisted, still puzzled over the feelings he had experienced at the diner.

"How are we supposed to know who we are even looking for?" Winter asked in frustration.

Clover had been riding in the hood of Leven's sweatshirt. He showed himself and smiled at Winter. "You'll know." His nose wiggled.

"Why do we need him?" Winter questioned, gesturing toward Clover.

"He knows the way," Leven said.

"This is ridiculous," Winter moaned. "We've wasted—"

A rustling in the woods shut Winter up. Leven put his finger to his lips. A sudden wind blew and again there was the noise of something moving amongst the trees.

Clover disappeared.

"Hello?" Leven asked the wind.

A low moaning commenced.

"Something doesn't feel right," Winter whispered.

No sooner had she said the words than the trees around them began to bend inward over them. Dark vapors soared through the trees and swept low over their heads, whispering.

"You see us, you see us," the shadows whispered.

"Run!" Leven yelled.

It was a silly thing for him to say. Winter was already sprinting off through the woods with Leven frantically dashing after her. Branches scratched and whipped at them as they fled, while the dark shadows swarmed around them, encircling their heads and penetrating their noses and mouths.

Screaming in terror, Winter came to a sudden stop, with Leven right behind her. He looked to see what had stopped her and gasped.

The dark shadows were gathered in front of them in a tall, hissing spiral. Beneath the swirling mass, the ground suddenly erupted, heaving up a gigantic mound of rocks, dirt, and twisted foliage. Rising out of the fractured earth, a huge shape emerged. Shaking dirt and tree branches off its massive head and shoulders, it grew as big as a building—with a thick, wide body, like that of a bullfrog. It stood on four sturdy legs with thick scales covering its belly and its white eyes burning over a cavernous, wet mouth. A layer of rocks and dirt covered its back.

The beast breathed, showering mud and rocks on Winter and Leven. The blast stung Leven's bare arms, and a gob of smelly mud filled his right eye.

The beast bellowed, snorted, and moved toward Leven and Winter. The shadows laughed hideously, hissing and screaming.

Winter and Leven backed away from the beast, eyes wide, their hearts in their mouths, and their minds spinning. Leven was quaking with fear almost strong enough to cause him to simply give up and be swallowed just to be done with it.

The beast bellowed again, giving Leven the courage to move. "Get into the trees!" he yelled.

Winter and Leven ran back into the trees. The beast lumbered after them but was stopped by the heavy growth. It screamed and again spewed mud all over. Leven and Winter ran even faster as mud clods showered around them. The shadows were nowhere to be seen.

"Stop!" Winter yelled as they came into a clearing.

Leven was happy to oblige. His lungs were burning and his legs about to give out. He bent over with his hands on his knees, sucking in air.

"It can't run any farther," Winter gasped. "I think the trees stopped it."

Leven lifted his head and squinted into the darkness. He couldn't see a thing. "What *was* that?" he wheezed.

"Like I know?" Winter said. "It—" An ominous rumbling noise caused her to stop talking. "Oh, no," she whispered.

The noise was coming from the direction of the beast, and it was quickly getting louder.

Leven squinted into the darkness. A huge mound of earth was rolling toward them. The trees and foliage above it lifted and lowered as it came closer. As the burrow exited the woods, the ground broke open, and the beast they thought the trees had stopped erupted out of the earth once again. It looked much bigger and more angry than it had before.

Leven's mind spun as he tried to think of something to do. "Freeze it!" he yelled, remembering Winter's gift. "Freeze it!"

Winter trembled and closed her eyes. Ice began to build over the beast's ankles and on its scaly belly. He pitched and swung his massive head wildly, spewing clods of mud from its mouth in every direction. Ice quickly encased him, sealing his angry mouth and silencing his hideous roars.

Leven looked at Winter in awe. "Unbelievable," he breathed.

Winter was about to accept the compliment when a loud sizzling noise began to come from the huge block of ice. The beast beneath the icy cage groaned and shook violently. The ice covering him exploded with an ear-splitting crack, hurling huge chunks and shards of ice everywhere. Leven barely had time to cover his face before he was struck in the side by a heavy piece of ice that knocked the breath out of him. While trying desperately to breathe, he could see Winter lying unconscious on the ground.

The monster was now ice-free, and angrier than ever. Leven closed his eyes and tried to see the future. But he was no better at managing his gift now than before. He couldn't see anything but fear.

Hoping to manipulate fate into destroying the beast for him, he willed the beast to be gone. Nothing. The beast lumbered closer. Leven's mind cleared and he could see a possible solution. The solution involved him picking up Winter. He looked at her as she lay there and remembered her voice warning him not to touch her. He shook the warning off and bent over to pick her up.

The instant Leven touched Winter, there was an explosion that stunned him and made his ears pop. The world began to spin. The air around him appeared to melt and drip downward, and the landscape became smeared, as though a giant hand were being dragged across a still-wet portrait. Shooting stars traced crazy patterns in the sky, and big dots of burning light rose and fell on the horizon.

Then, like a spinning coin settling, things began to revolve more slowly and finally ceased moving entirely.

The beast roared again. Leven had no time to contemplate what had happened. He slid his arms under Winter and strained to lift her. Straightening, he looked into the white eyes of the approaching beast and shifted Winter in his hold. He turned and ran as fast as he could, through the trees and out onto the open prairie, praying his plan would work.

The monster stomped madly, hesitated for a moment, then plunged into the earth and began burrowing after them. Carrying Winter in his arms and trying to run was exhausting. Her weight was breaking Leven's back. His shoulders ached and the muscles in his arms were burning. Leven shifted Winter and pushed forward faster.

Winter began to stir. Still dazed, she looked up at Leven as he ran.

"What are you doing?" she moaned.

"Saving you!" Leven's heart and legs ached as his mind tried to calculate how much farther he needed to go.

Oklahoma is a relatively flat state. No Alps, no Rockies. If you rolled a ball in most places of the state it would stop eventually, due to there being no slope. There was, however, a cliff just to the east of Burnt Culvert. It was a sheer drop-off that towered over the vast prairie far below. It was a site where long ago, Native Americans used to drive huge herds of buffalo over its edge. The buffalo wouldn't see the drop until it was too late, plummeting by the hundreds to their deaths below.

It was toward that cliff that Leven was now running, his arms and shoulders screaming with pain from carrying Winter and his legs going numb. He pushed on across the prairie, listening to the rumble of the burrowing beast behind him. Leven peered into the darkness. He couldn't see, he was exhausted, and he was leading a giant dirt clod to a cliff that would more than likely kill him and Winter before it killed the beast.

The earth directly below him began to rise, and Leven struggled to keep his balance on the hurtling mound that had caught up to them. It was as if he were surfing a gigantic, speeding dirt wave. He teetered, trying to stay on top of the burrowing monster as it rushed forward. Leven peered ahead and prayed that his memory and calculations were correct.

"Get ready to fall!" he hollered to Winter as he held her, the rumbling of the earth so loud he had to yell.

"What?" Winter screamed.

Leven didn't have time to answer. He shifted Winter in his arms, closed his eyes, and leaped sideways off the mound of speeding earth. He hit the ground hard and lost his hold on Winter, who flew out of his arms and rolled away.

The giant burrowing creature was caught by surprise. Before it could adjust for Leven's departure and change its course or slow down, it hurtled through the wall of the cliff and out into space, hundreds of feet above the prairie floor below.

Leven and Winter crawled as fast as they could to the edge of the cliff and looked over. The beast traveled beautifully through the air, arching past the quarter moon and dropping to burst violently on the hard ground far below. Even with Leven's poor eyesight he could see the tremendous explosion of dirt and debris of monster.

Leven rolled over onto his back and tried to catch his breath. Winter sat up and began to assess how many injuries she had.

"Do you think that killed him?" she asked, pulling dirt and twigs from her hair.

"Let's not stick around to find out," Leven said, getting to his feet.

Clover materialized and Leven shook his head in amazement.

"Where were *you?*" Leven asked.

Clover ignored the question. "That was impressive," he glowed. "Only an offing could have pulled that off."

"Yeah, well, thanks for the help," Winter complained. "The first sign of trouble and you disappear."

"I couldn't help it," Clover explained. "If the shadows had seen me, we would have been in an even bigger mess."

"Do you know what that was all about?" Leven brushed off his knees and his backside.

"Ah," Clover waved. "It was just an avaland, and a huge one, I might add. I'm sure Sabine's shadows set it free."

"Sabine's shadows?" Leven asked. "Is that what I keep seeing? Who's Sabine?"

"I can't say," Clover insisted.

"Of course not," Leven complained.

"Let's just get out of here," Winter sighed, looking toward the black sky. "I don't like this prairie, it—" Winter stopped mid-sentence. For a moment Leven thought she had seen something else alarming, but she just stared at him.

"You touched me," Winter whispered, her eyes big with the realization.

"I had no choice," Leven apologized. "You would have been eaten, or buried, or muddied."

"Muddied?" Winter smiled slightly.

"I don't know what dirt monsters do," Leven said, flustered, the white streak in his hair bright under the partial moon. "I had to pick you up. Besides, nothing really happened. The air just—"

"Listen to him," Clover said admiringly. "Nothing happened. You shot an avaland out of a cliff," Clover bragged. "Don't sell yourself short. That was very im—"

"I was talking about touching Winter," Leven clarified.

"Oh," Clover said.

"I hope we're not in too much trouble." Winter said, looking worried.

"I guess we'll find out either way," Leven added.

Clover disappeared, and the two of them made their way past the trees down to the river and over to the bridge. They were only just beginning to understand the magnitude and danger of what was ahead. It had been quite a night.

CHAPTER SIXTEEN

PICKED OUT OF A CROWD

The shadows were not stupid. They were the castoffs of Sabine and his darkness, but they were not without wit and cunning. At the moment they were angry and desperate. They had been looking for Leven for some time and still nothing. Their problem was they were looking for a grown man with a crown and a scepter, not an obscure kid with bad eyesight and a white streak in his hair.

Okay, they were a little stupid.

Sabine had not been sleeping well. He could feel the pace of things ratcheting up. He could sense his shadows were close to capturing the prize, but he could not get a clear picture of what that prize was. He had exhaled and bidden his shadows to stop holding back. He had willed them to feel the air, the dirt, and the wind in an effort to discover who they were after.

They had assembled and descended in full force to do their master's bidding.

They had identified a few "persons of interest" whom they felt compelled to investigate—an old man in Germany who had an odd aura, a prince in Saudi Arabia with a look about him, a Canadian with a dark visage who appeared to draw the shadows in, a retired couple in Florida that might have magical powers, a woman in Mexico who was hiding something, and a young boy in Oklahoma who could see shadows. Each of these individuals had aroused Sabine's suspicions.

In his evil quest, Sabine instructed his shadows to fall upon each of these persons and observe his or her reaction. The shadows had conjured up avalands and telts as an ordeal for each. Confronted by these apparitions, the German cried, the Arabian cowered, the Canadian fainted, the Florida couple locked themselves in their double-wide and trembled, and the woman in Mexico tried to put a curse on them. Only the young boy in Oklahoma had thought his way through and escaped his ordeal.

Sabine dismissed them all except the boy. It is not easy to escape an avaland. He doubted Leven was the one only because he was so young, but upon further thought Sabine decided the boy's age might be the perfect deception. He sent his shadows once more. They spiraled out of Foo, locating the boy as he slept and invading his mind. Sabine could instantly tell that this was the heir of the Gatemaker. Someone or something from Foo had touched this child. That touch had left a mark on the dreams of Leven, which were different from the dreams of any other human. He clearly had a connection to Foo, and he had been touched by a nit.

Sabine roared. The only possible way for Leven to have been

touched by a nit was for one to have made it out of Foo through the gateway.

Sabine raged and breathed every last shadow down upon the boy as he slept, penetrating Leven's dreams. They screeched and whispered and hissed, filling Leven's head with a cavalcade of dark images calculated to convince Leven that he was worthless, without merit, and insane to take even one more step on the journey he had begun.

"Go home, go home," the shadows whispered. "Impossible. Impossible," they hissed.

Sabine's dark shadows were more powerful and dangerous than a whole herd of avalands could ever be. All night long Sabine's demons tormented Leven, filling his brain with frightening images and feelings of inferiority and hopelessness. They ceased afflicting him only when the first hint of light surfaced in the morning and Sabine inhaled, summoning his shadows out of the recesses of Leven's now-darkened brain and back to Foo.

CHAPTER SEVENTEEN

DIRTY ROTTEN

Winter awoke to the sound of Leven tossing and moaning. She had slept under the opposite side of the bridge, where there was more room. Now he was awake. She could see him crawling out from under the bridge and looking around. His hair was a mess and he had a lost and vacant look in his brown eyes—as if someone had stolen his personality as he slept. He had scratches on his arms and face and a big bruise on his left cheek. She looked at herself and observed the nicks and cuts she had suffered in their flight through the trees and in her fall from the beast.

She sat up. "Where are you going?" she hollered to Leven.

Leven squinted, looking over at her. "I'm going back." He pushed his dark bangs away from his face.

"Back where?" Winter asked, crawling out from under the bridge and assuming he was referring to the diner and the intriguing old man they had met there.

"To my house," Leven said dully.

"To get something?"

"No, I'm done, Winter." He looked ashamed. "This is not how it should be," Leven said. "We have been wandering the streets with nothing to show for it. This isn't right."

"What about last night?"

"What about last night?" Leven questioned. "Oh, yeah, we almost died," he added sarcastically. "So you can freeze things and I can see stuff. How do we know that everyone else can't do those things?" Leven rubbed his forehead and winced as he touched one of his bruises. "I'd trade my gift for the possibility of not ever getting beat up by dirt again." He shook his head. "We're fooling ourselves."

"It's different and you know it," Winter said sadly. "I can feel it, Lev. I found you. You're supposed to do this."

"Do *what?*" he asked. "I can't do *anything.* I'm nothing but an orphan who has no family and no friends. I live on a porch because those who know me can't stand to have me in the house. I got a C in math, a B in English, and a C-plus in science. I am average, unwanted, and of no use to anyone. Now I'm supposed to believe a furry ball . . . "

Clover materialized sheepishly on Leven's shoulder.

" . . . when he tells me I can save the world? Come on, Winter, this is crazy." Leven looked distressed, as if the words he was saying were painful to expel. The shadows had convinced him well. "I wish I were dreaming so I could just wake up and have it all over with. I can't make this better."

"Well, if you leave now you don't have to worry about ever

dreaming again," Clover said, brushing his forearms.

"What's that supposed to mean?" Leven said, trying not to look directly at Clover.

"If Foo falls, it's over for all of us."

"Foo?" Leven said, shaking his head. "I don't believe in Foo. I don't believe in *you*," he said, pointing toward Clover, "and I don't believe in you," he said, looking at Winter. "I'm sorry," Leven added, "I guess I don't believe in me."

"Lev . . ." Winter tried.

He waved her off. "There is no way the world could be dependent upon me. And if by some chance it is true, then we're all in big trouble." Leven turned and began to walk off. He stopped, lifted Clover from his shoulder, and set him on the ground. "Stay here."

"I can't," Clover said sadly.

"Don't you have to do what I say?" Leven asked.

"In theory," Clover shrugged.

"Then I order you or command you or whatever the strongest instruction I can give you is, to stay away from me. Stay with Winter, understand?" Leven said sadly.

Clover looked hurt and confused.

Leven was gone.

ii

Geth could not believe how bright the sun was. He opened his eyes to find it almost directly overhead, burning like a celestial bonfire. He rubbed his eyes with his left arm and sat up. He could hear birds singing and see people walking in and out of the diner he had escaped from the night before. He shifted in the grass and stood. His entire tiny body ached. His final slam in the door last night had been fate's most brilliant move. After that impact he was now flexible and much more mobile than he could have ever imagined. He could bend at the waist and even twist his top half to look around.

He gazed at his single arm and wished for fingers. They didn't appear instantly, but he felt confident that before too long, fate would hook him up with digits of his own. He also put in a silent plea for another arm.

Geth moved away from the grass and over to the gutter. An old man hosing down the sidewalk was creating a nice-sized stream of water, and a small piece of paper came floating by. It seemed too fateful for Geth to ignore. He did his part and jumped off the curb and down onto the paper raft.

He sloshed back and forth as the little scrap of paper danced over small ripples and twisted around a corner. A child crossing the street stepped into the gutter, creating a splash that showered the raft and flooded Geth's eyes. He wiped away the water and could see a culvert into which the water was flowing at the end of the street.

Geth lay back on the paper and enjoyed the ride as his little craft swirled through the culvert and bobbed along toward the river. Eventually he got caught up in a tangle of leaves and trash. Geth abandoned his raft and dove into the current, letting it carry him farther. Using his single arm to guide him and kicking his legs, his light little body was swept along in the cool water.

He imagined he looked quite impressive.

The culvert eventually emptied out onto a large cement spill-way. Geth skimmed along the bottom as the shallow stream of water thinned to a trickle. Twenty more feet and Geth could feel the cement rubbing against his belly. Five feet later the stream of water was so diminished that Geth no longer floated, he dragged. He pulled himself out of the trickle of water and looked into the sun. He shook his legs and wiped off the tip of his head.

"What now?" he asked himself. He was standing in the bottom of a huge cement cistern with sides too high for him to climb and the sun beating down. A few dark clouds in the distance drifted closer.

Geth followed the miniscule string of water as it dribbled down toward the end of the waterway.

"I could use a little help," Geth said aloud and to nobody in particular. "I mean, I'm all for doing my part, but being a tooth-pick is not exactly the greatest confidence builder."

He reached a metal grate where the trickle of water fell into a deep, dark hole. A big pile of trash had gathered at the opening. Geth climbed to the top of the heap and looked down. After a few seconds of thought he stepped through the grate and blindly jumped into the darkness, anxious to see where fate would take him. He squeezed his legs together, tucked in his arm, and held himself rigid to look more like a traditional toothpick. Down he dropped into the musky, dank-smelling darkness, landing legs first and impaling himself almost body deep in the soft mud at the bot-tom of the hole. Due to the pressure of the foul smelling muck, he couldn't move his arm or even wiggle his legs. He couldn't speak, and he could see only a little bit from his slightly higher right eye.

Geth was stuck.

iii

Winter walked slowly down the road. She had no money, no direction, and no idea what she was going to do. She knew perfectly well that Clover was sitting on her head or clinging to her back or holding onto her leg, so she didn't feel completely alone, but she did feel completely helpless. To make matters worse, the once-blue sky was quickly filling with clouds.

"What do we do?" she asked.

"I don't know," Clover answered, the direction of his voice making it obvious that he was holding onto her leg.

"You're supposed to be helping," Winter said.

"I'm only supposed to make sure Lev makes it safely to Foo."

"Well?" Winter said.

"Well, this is just a minor setback," Clover insisted.

"*Minor setback?* This is a disaster. How can you return Lev to Foo if you don't even have him?" Winter's green eyes burned.

"It's not all my fault," Clover said, still invisible but climbing higher up Winter. "You were assigned to him as well."

"What?"

"You were . . . oh nothing," Clover said quickly.

"Show yourself, Clover."

"No."

"Clover Ernest, you show yourself this instant," she demanded.

"No."

"Listen, Clover, I am in no mood to goof around," Winter insisted. She stopped and began turning as if to spot him. "I have come all this way and have had nothing but trouble. Now you're saying I'm 'assigned'?"

"I talk too much," Clover admitted. "I shouldn't have said anything."

"If we're going to get Lev back I have got to know what's going on." Winter stopped, turning in an attempt to see Clover. She was a bit dizzy.

Clover materialized on her right shoulder. "I guess it won't hurt to tell you a few things."

"Good. To start with, who am I?"

"I'm not totally sure," Clover admitted. "All I know is that Antsel said there would be another to help lead Lev back to Foo."

"And that's me?"

"I think so." Clover scratched his head. "It's obvious from that ice trick you can do that you are a nit. It seems sensible that they would send a nit to help Lev back."

"And why's that?" Winter questioned.

"Nits are extremely loyal," Clover explained. "They stay true to their purpose no matter what."

Winter was silent as she thought. Dark clouds continued to pile up in the sky.

"That's a compliment," Clover pointed out. "Of course Sabine's a nit, and, well, he didn't exactly stay loyal."

"So there are others like me?" Winter asked.

"Of course," Clover said. "Thousands."

"Thousands," Winter whispered.

"Nits are those humans who are born on earth and stumble into Foo by accident," Clover explained. "As they adapt to Foo they take on a certain and unpredictable trait. You must have liked ice. It's a popular talent."

"So I've been to Foo before? I'd think I would remember that."

"Let's just say there's way more to you than you currently know."

Winter smiled. The thought of there being more like her was a revelation. And that she had some special purpose was exciting. "We have got to get Lev back," she said strongly.

"Maybe we should find Geth first," Clover suggested.

"So who is this Geth?" Winter asked.

"Well . . . since I already blew the secret," Clover said, bending over to brush his ankle hair, "I guess it wouldn't hurt to tell you." He cleared his throat, then said, "Geth was cursed by Sabine and brought here by Antsel so he would not be destroyed. Last I heard, he was a seed."

"But, who is he?"

"He is the last heir and king to the Order of Wonder. He is also one of the few who knows where the gateway to Foo is."

"You came through. Don't you know the way there?"

"Antsel kept me hidden," Clover said. "The fewer who know, the safer it is."

"So why does Geth need Lev? Why does he need any of us? Can't he just go back himself?"

"Antsel didn't tell me everything," Clover said sadly. "I'm just a sycophant. But from what I heard while hiding out on the ceiling and eavesdropping in Antsel's room all those years ago, Lev is of some major importance as well. I think it has something to do with him being related to someone important."

"So we have to find Geth," Winter said seriously.

"I've been saying that for a week," Clover pointed out.

Winter shook her head. "Do you have any idea where he could be?"

"Well," Clover said, "he *is* a king. Are there any castles around here?"

Winter was highly discouraged.

iv

Geth struggled in the mud. It was of no use. No matter how hard he wiggled or strained he couldn't pull himself out. The foul smell of the storm drain was almost nauseating, and if he had not been a lithen he might have figured himself for dead. But, seeing how he was a lithen and had great faith in fate, he simply closed his eyes and waited.

He had been asleep no more than a couple of hours when the rumbling began. Geth could hear the thunder tearing up the sky outside and above him. In a moment the sky opened up and proceeded to squeeze every bit of moisture out of the heavy clouds. Rain fell like cats and dogs and then tigers and elephants. Water poured off roofs and down rain spouts, running into the gutters and quickly turning the streets into wide, wild rivers. A small dog was washed away, a car was spun around, and store fronts all along Main Street were flooded as the deluge increased. Storm drains were quickly filled to capacity and water surged through them like a runaway train through a tunnel.

Geth just waited.

He could hear the distant rush of water, and then all at once the hole he was in was flooded, the water crashing down on him in a thunderous wave. The muck around him loosened and he could feel his legs again. He wiggled as the torrent of water cascaded over him, and suddenly he was loose and being carried along in the flood in the darkness. Using his one arm, he tried to steer himself, but it was no use. He folded up and let the water take him.

The weight and volume of the water was tremendous. He was flying. It would have been fun had he had any control, but he was being tumbled along and banged into the walls of the culvert, and his mouth and eyes were filled with water. Just as he thought the buffeting would never end, he shot out of the culvert and floated into the middle of the flooded Washita River. The swollen river was foaming and rushing along. Geth pointed his legs and let the current carry him. Gradually the roaring water carried him near the far shore, where he bounced against some rocks and finally came to a welcome stop in a patch of long grass.

The raging river continued to churn past him—water huffing and spitting as it pursued its wild course downstream. Geth stayed there in the tangled growth, marveling once again at how effective travel by fate was.

V

Winter huddled under a storefront awning, wondering if the rain was ever going to stop. It looked like heaven had literally tipped and was spilling torrents of moisture down. She dashed to the next corner and waited beneath a shelter at a bus stop. No one was out. Here and there she could spot a face pressed against a window, gazing out in awe at the deluge, but for the most part, she was it. A huge truck roared down the street, parting the water like a great ship, hurling it up on the curb and drenching her.

Winter was miserable.

In fact, she was as ready as Leven to give up. She didn't need shadows filling her head with doubt as she dreamt. She possessed plenty of doubt all by herself. She had seen and done some amazing things in the last while, but it all seemed for naught.

They had accomplished nothing.

Clover's revelation that Winter was assigned to Lev had left her immediately uplifted, but now even that little bit of truth seemed stupid and unbelievable. Big deal. Nobody in their right mind would send a girl like her to take care of anything. She had no experience and no potential. She hated to be a baby, but there beneath the bus shelter, she began to cry. She figured the tears would camouflage well in this weather.

Her jeans and shirt were soaked. She didn't think she could possibly be more uncomfortable. It seemed as if everything she had ever endured or survived was now a big knot, pushing up inside of her, pleading to be let out.

"I can see you crying," Clover said softly, not showing himself.

Winter wiped at her eyes. "I'm not crying," she insisted.

"It's all right," he said. "Things are sort of bad."

Winter wept. The rain had nothing on her.

"Maybe I should show you something," Clover said.

Winter didn't respond; she just kept crying. Clover materialized, hanging on her arm. She was so used to him showing up in odd spots she didn't even flinch. He climbed to the top of her head and wiped his feet in her hair as if cleaning his shoes on a welcome mat.

"Watch the street," he said.

Winter looked at the street. It was filled with water up to the top of the curbs, flowing wildly. No cars were in sight. She wondered why Clover would tell her that, but before she could question him or complain about him using her head as a door-mat, he jumped from her head down into the road. He landed in the rushing water, and his body seemed to dissipate and flow outward, painting the entire street with color and images. Clover was gone, but Winter was mesmerized by what she could see. Reflected in the water, she saw a countryside with an amber sky. The water surged. A moon and a river appeared, framed by a brilliant white braided rainbow.

Winter stared.

She could see a tall woman with straight red hair and strange animals circling around her. What she saw was not Oklahoma or anyplace on earth. What she saw was a bit of Foo. The oddest thing about these scenes was that they were not peculiar to her. She recognized them. She had seen them before.

She saw a tall, dark man on a horse-like creature, surrounded by shadows. She saw the turrets of Foo and the crowds of beings gathering to fight for what she was somehow a part of.

The water rose and flowed on, the images moving down the street with it. She stared at them until they were completely gone.

"Does that help?" Clover asked. Once again he was back on her shoulder and drying his hair with a towel he had pulled from his pocket void.

"How'd you do that?" Winter asked.

"We sycophants are pretty good at a lot of things," Clover smiled. "I'm not bragging, I'm just telling the truth."

"The tall man on the horse thingy," Winter said somberly. "I recognized him."

"I thought you might," Clover whispered. "That's Sabine. I know this all seems pointless and I'm not exactly the perfect traveling companion, but what we are hoping to stop is real and terrible. I promise."

Winter was silent for a moment. The clouds thinned and the rain softened a bit.

"We've got to find this Geth," she finally said with determination.

"That's what I've been—" Clover stopped himself and smiled. "I know we do."

"We'll find Geth and take him to Lev," Winter said firmly, trying to convince herself she could do it.

"Perfect," Clover cheered.

"I just don't have any idea where to start looking," she admitted.

"Fate will help," Clover assured her.

Winter smiled at Clover. There is nothing like the joy of having a conversation with a twelve-inch-tall, furry sycophant. She was still scared and unsure of herself, but she had seen something amazing in those watery images. It made her more frightened, but also considerably more hopeful. She pictured Sabine on the horse and shivered. He was part of this, she knew that. She stepped across the street and over to the park.

With the rain letting up a bit, a few people and cars began to make their way through the streets again.

CHAPTER EIGHTEEN

A LITTLE DISAPPOINTED

In some ways Geth had simply moved from one mess to another. No matter how hard he tried, he could not free himself from the tangle of grass near the side of the river. The swollen stream was calming a bit and the sky had cleared, but his body was knotted into the growth, and he didn't have the strength to break loose.

But he didn't panic. Not Geth. He relaxed and tried to enjoy the moment. His mouth was just above the water line, but as the water moved it would splash into his eyes and ears and mouth, making things look, sound, and taste wet. He halfway wished he were still a tall tree with the ability to stretch and push his roots around. He missed being able to see from every angle and hear sound from beneath the ground and from the sky.

He missed a few things, but lithens never yearn for what was or what could have been. There's no point in it. There is no moment more precious than the exact moment they are living. And that exact moment has a lot to do with how future moments play out.

Geth bobbed up and down in his watery nest. He closed his eyes and tried to whistle with little success. A fat fish came careening down the way and pushed through the grass at the edge to scratch its belly on the growth. The weight of the fish pushed Geth all the way under. He sprang right back up. The sun touched the top of his head and felt warm.

He was almost content.

In fact, if it weren't for the entire future of mankind depending on him and Leven getting back to Foo, Geth wouldn't have minded a bit just living out his days there attached to that grass.

A young girl walking down the edge of the river stopped on the bank near Geth. She was alone and eating a piece of fruit. From where he lay, Geth couldn't see all of her, but what he could see looked familiar. As she stood there eating fruit, a small, gray sycophant materialized on her shoulder. Geth was speechless. He had seen Clover many times before while standing in Leven's yard as a tree. Geth's mouth hung open as he listened to Clover and the girl.

"So I can't even have one bite?" Clover asked Winter.

"You've already had twelve whole ones," she laughed.

"I would have had more if that farmer hadn't caught us borrowing from his tree."

Winter took a few more bites then tossed the core of the fruit toward the river. Geth could see it coming straight toward him. The core bounced off his head, leaving bits of fruit clinging to him. He looked up to see Clover disappear and Winter begin to walk farther downstream.

"I would have eaten that core," an invisible Clover said.

"Sorry," Winter smiled. "I forgot that you'll eat anything."

"What a waste," Clover complained. "There was still fruit . . ."

They were far enough down the river that Geth could no longer hear them. He wrestled with the grass, trying desperately to get free. He had to get to that girl. But the hold of the grass was too strong for his single arm to break.

A huge fly landed on Geth's head and began to nibble at the small bits of fruit stuck on him. Geth waved it away. Not intimidated by a toothpick, the fly flew back and continued to graze on the top of Geth's head. This time he didn't wave it away. He bent himself over as far as he could, pushing the top of his head toward the center of the river. The unsuspecting fly licked and bit the top of him, buzzing and spitting.

Come on, Geth thought. *Come on.*

No sooner had he thought it than a huge fish leaped from the water and engulfed the fly and the top half of Geth. The fish thrashed his head about, breaking the grass and tearing away with both the fly and Geth in his mouth. The fly buzzed madly, thrashing around in the closed mouth, desperate to get free. The poor fish couldn't properly swallow the pest because the toothpick was poking into its lip and making swallowing near impossible. Geth pulled and kicked, the fish rocked and twisted, the fly buzzed and vibrated. The large trout finally opened its mouth slightly, and Geth was freed. He skimmed across the top of the water until a wave flung him into the air and sent him flying up onto the wet, grassy shore.

He stood and cleared his eyes, marveling at the creativity fate was demonstrating. He wasn't sure if he'd been flung past Winter or if he still needed to go farther. The question was soon answered. He glanced back up the bank just in time to see a foot coming down directly on top of him. He tried to scream but there wasn't time. Winter's heel smashed him into the muddy bank as she walked right over him.

Once again Geth was stuck.

His top half was sticking out, but as he waved and hollered, his small voice was not loud enough to be heard over the sound of the still raging river. He watched Winter walk farther and farther away.

"Amazing," he said to himself. "So close."

"Amazing is right," a voice above him said.

Geth tried to look around but he could see nothing.

"A talking toothpick," the voice added. "That has to mean something."

"Who's there?" Geth asked, with no fear in his voice, only curiosity.

No one answered.

"Hello?" Geth tried.

No reply, just the sound of water rushing by. Geth looked off toward Winter. She was now almost out of sight, but suddenly she stopped. She stood still for a moment and then turned to look back in the direction she had just come. Geth couldn't tell if she was speaking or not, but in a moment she began walking back. Geth smiled. As she got nearer he could hear her voice.

"A toothpick?" she questioned loudly. "You saw a toothpick?"

"A toothpick," Clover said enthusiastically. He was still invisible. "Like one of those things you dig at your teeth with," he explained.

"I know what a toothpick is," Winter said. "But what would that have to do with us?"

"Antsel said to look for signs."

"A toothpick is a sign?" Winter said, mildly amused but also frustrated.

"It was talking," Clover insisted. "How many talking toothpicks have you ever met? It's there just beside that rock." Winter knelt down and began to carefully probe the ground with her hand.

"Hello," Geth spoke up.

Winter shifted her gaze from the spot she was searching and looked directly at Geth.

"Hello?" she said tentatively.

Clover let just his blue eyes materialize. "I was following behind looking for smooth rocks and I just heard him talking," he explained. "I thought a talking toothpick was worth investigating."

"I'm a bit stuck," Geth offered.

"Sorry," Winter apologized for not helping him out sooner. "Can I just pinch you?"

"Why not?" Geth said pleasantly. "You just stepped on me."

"I did?" Winter said surprised. "I'm so sorry."

"No problem, I'm glad you did," he replied. "Seems to be exactly what fate needed," Geth added as she placed him on her palm and studied him closely.

He was a thick wooden toothpick with light waves of grain

running vertically up and down him. He appeared to be split down the middle on the bottom half, giving him two thin legs. He had one splinter of an arm and a pointed head. His face was a pattern of randomly scattered holes. He had a large right eye and a slightly smaller and lower left eye—the right one being circular and the left having a slant. He had a tiny hole for a nose and a big notch missing for a mouth. He gave Winter a lop-sided grin.

"I'm glad the grain of the wood runs vertically," Geth joked. "Horizontal stripes make me look fat."

Winter smiled, genuinely delighted for the first time in a long while. She had no idea what she held in her hand, but it was at the very least highly intriguing.

"Weird," Clover said, his eyes gazing at Geth.

Winter took it all in—floating eyes, talking toothpicks, no big deal.

"So what are you?" she asked.

The toothpick bowed slightly. "My name is Geth. I—"

Winter snickered while Clover's blue eyeballs bulged.

"Sorry," Winter apologized, "I thought you said your name was Geth."

"That's correct," Geth stated.

"But you're not *the* Geth, are you?" she asked, a bit of panic in her voice.

"I'm not sure what you mean."

"He's not *the* Geth," Clover tried, his eyeballs looking at Winter. "Geth is a great king. He's wise and handsome with golden hair and an infectious laugh and and . . . well, he's tall."

Geth laughed. "I know I must look foolish, but I *am* Geth. I was brought here from Foo by Antsel in the condition of a seed and was buried from Sabine with the express purpose of bringing Leven back to Foo."

Neither Winter nor Clover was laughing now.

"You're a toothpick," Clover said, materializing completely. "You're supposed to help us? No offense, but I think I could do a better job than a toothpick."

"Please say you're not really who we are looking for," Winter said seriously, all laughter gone.

"I am who you're looking for," Geth affirmed. "You must be the soul who was brought here to bring Leven back. I am the heir Leven needs to succeed."

"Lev already has hair," Clover pointed out. "Besides, there have been plenty of bald people who are successful," he added. "My father—"

Geth smiled. "I mean *heir.* As in lineage and rulers."

"Oh," Clover sniffed, patting his own hairy head.

"I know my shape isn't exactly impressive, but I can get you back," Geth said confidently. "Where is the boy?"

"Well," Clover cleared his throat. "It seems that Lev gave up this morning and returned home."

"Then we've got to give him a reason to go on."

"And you propose we do that by showing him a toothpick?" Winter asked.

The toothpick straightened itself. "I am the rightful heir to Foo," he stated. "I am also a lithen of the highest Order of

Wonder, and I know there is nothing that can stop me from making it back to Foo with Leven. Fate will make it so."

"Oh, yeah," Clover said. "This has disaster written all over it."

Winter wiped her eyes and stood tall. Her clothes were still slightly wet and completely uncomfortable.

"I'm sorry if I disappoint you," Geth said softly to her. "I can only promise you that I am who I say I am and that I know how to get back to Foo."

Winter smiled at him weakly. "Then we should go," she said bravely.

"What?" Clover complained. "He's a toothpick."

"I'm tired of walking around," Winter complained. "Besides, if *I'm* a part of this then surely a toothpick could be capable enough. Let's go get Lev."

Clover shrugged. "Makes sense to me."

Winter slipped Geth into her front shirt pocket. "Is this all right?" she asked him.

"Perfect," Geth smiled, holding on to the top edge of her pocket with his one arm and gazing out.

Winter turned and headed in the direction of Leven's house.

"You might want to hurry," Geth said.

Winter looked worried.

"But don't fret about it," Geth added. "Optimism is our best ally."

Winter tried to smile. It's not that easy, however, to be optimistic, when you are taking directions from a toothpick.

CHAPTER NINETEEN

LIFT, HUCK, AND LISTEN

L even was disgusted with himself. He had turned his back on the two people—well, one person and one whatever Clover was—who believed in him. No matter how he looked at it, he had left Winter and Clover high and dry. He couldn't help it. His head was so clouded with confused thoughts and self-doubt he could hardly stand straight. And now, thanks to the rainstorm that had just ended, he was soaked. His dark bangs were matted against his forehead, covering his right eye.

"It doesn't matter," he said to himself. "There's nothing I can do about any of this." The empty words didn't make him feel any better about giving up. He tried to walk tall, but it felt like the entire world was pushing down on his shoulders.

He rounded the turn in the road and spotted his house in the distance.

The first thing he noticed was the missing tree. The stump

sat there like an ugly bone jutting out from the surface of the earth. He noticed Addy's car was not in the driveway and that the house looked askew and a bit more beat up than he remembered. One corner of the roof in the back was crumpled as if it had been crushed. And there were wood chips everywhere.

"I shouldn't be here," he whispered to himself.

Leven did not want to return home, but he had nothing else. He hated wandering the streets and having to sleep on the ground. Defeated, he sat down on the tree stump. The grass around it was long, and a few birds off to the south were chattering at each other.

His mind cleared and his eyes burned gold. His gift was flaring up. He could see Winter in his head. Lights and shadows swirled through his brain. Winter was walking swiftly and with purpose. She said something to someone and smiled. Leven couldn't remember if he had ever seen her smile that widely when he had been with her. She looked different, too: her green eyes were beautiful and her blond hair wasn't as wild as he remembered it.

Leven's thoughts suddenly darkened.

Winter appeared much happier without him. He was not surprised. Leven knew he was a problem, not an answer. That had been the pattern of his life. He had just seen the future and he now knew that Winter and Clover could get along just fine. They didn't need him. Leven rubbed his eyes and sighed loudly as if expelling air from his toes.

"Who's there?" Terry yelled from inside Leven's old house.

"It's me," Leven said with little enthusiasm.

"Where have you been?" Terry demanded. He stuck his head

out one of the trailer's open windows. It was obvious he had just gotten up.

"I got lost?" Leven tried.

"Lost? How dumb do you think I am?"

Leven prayed Terry wouldn't make him answer that.

"Your aunt spent an entire afternoon looking for you. She missed over three hours of work. Set us back something fierce."

"I'm sorry."

"We're all perfectly aware of that," Terry whined. "Now get in here and clean this place up."

Leven stood and walked up to the front door. He stepped inside and almost gasped at how messy everything was. It was as if they had done nothing but eat and litter during the two days he had been gone. A strong, unpleasant odor was coming from the kitchen, and trash was everywhere. Half-eaten plates of food littered the living room. Though he had been forced to sleep on the porch, Leven had always been the one in charge of cleaning the inside of the house. Terry pushed through the trash to stand right in front of Leven.

"See this mess?" Terry pointed, his ugly mouth drawn down into a sneer. "You did it. How do you expect us to teach you anything if we do your chores for you? Well, I'm sick of it. You have fifteen minutes to clean it up."

"Fifteen minutes?" Leven asked incredulously. The mess he saw in front of him would take a lot longer to fix than that.

"Fifteen minutes, or I'll make sure you regret showing your face around here again."

"So you cut the tree down?" Leven asked forcefully.

"Excuse me?" Terry said sarcastically. "Did I say it was special question time? Fifteen minutes! I'm going out for a drink." Terry pulled his dirty baseball cap over his greasy hair and left the trailer house, slamming the door as he went out.

ii

Leven was still cleaning two hours later when Addy came home. Terry hadn't returned yet. Addy came in the door, threw her keys and purse down, and started complaining about the weather. Then she noticed Leven.

"What are *you* doing here?"

"Just cleaning up."

"Well, hurry, the place is a mess."

That was it. No "Hello." No "We've missed you." No "Good to see you." Just, "Hurry, the place is a mess."

Addy noticed Leven was wearing his Wonder Wipe shirt inside out. She began to bark at him. "Embarrassed about what I do? Too good to promote what feeds us? Maybe you would like a shirt made of gold?"

"I don't want a gold shirt," Leven insisted. "I just put it on wrong."

"I work all day to support . . ."

Addy stopped yelling to listen to the slurred singing of Terry as he made his way home. He fumbled with the door handle and stumbled into the house. He looked around at the filth that was much less than when he had left, but still quite a mess.

"What have you been doing?" he demanded. "I can barely see the carpet."

"I'm cleaning as fast as I can," Leven defended. "It's just—"

"Well, it's not fast enough," Terry interrupted, spitting flecks of saliva into the air. "Come here," he slurred. He hadn't shaved for a few days, and with his scraggly beard and dirty clothes he looked like a bum.

"I'll keep going," Leven promised, picking up even faster.

"Don't you back talk to him," Addy snarled. "You take a vacation and come back with a smart mouth."

"I wasn't—"

"Come here," Terry stormed.

Leven had made a gigantic mistake. He should never have returned. He had been a fool to think he could just step back into the awful life he had always had. Now as Terry raged and Addy helped, Leven knew he was in trouble. He looked toward the front door, trying to gauge if he could make it out or not. Terry noticed.

"Going to make a run for it?" Terry mocked, his beady eyes red and hateful. "You'll never make it, Skuuuunk."

Addy stepped next to the back door, blocking any escape.

"Come here," Terry muttered fiercely. "I'm going to scare the rest of your hair white."

Leven began to back away.

"You should have stayed lost," Terry spat. "I think it's time to teach you the lesson your aunt never let me."

"I'm not his aunt," Addy said disgustedly.

Addy wasn't a compassionate woman, but she was less likely than

Terry to hurt someone. There had been many times during Leven's childhood when Addy had stopped Terry from striking Leven or imposing his strength on him. At the moment, however, it didn't seem as though Addy had any intention of holding Terry back. She had experienced a difficult week. The hand-folded napkin market was soft at the moment, and the company she worked for had laid off one of the fastest and most expensive folders they had, leaving Addy with over three times her normal workload. Her wrists would swell to the size of cantaloupes every afternoon from all the repetitive movement, and her carpal tunnel pain was killing her. She had come home each day a monster. She was tired of her job, tired of Terry, and tired of not being pampered and taken care of like some of those ladies she saw on TV. In short, she was spent, spoiled, and selfish, and had no more will to control Terry or feel for Leven.

"I'm his mother's half sister," she grumped.

Terry moved closer. Leven tried to clear his mind to see if by some chance he couldn't manipulate himself out of this. He couldn't see anything except the image of Winter walking and smiling.

Leven was sick about the mistake he had made in thinking he could come home.

iii

Winter was feeling better. She was still not completely confident that a toothpick was the answer to all her woes, but for the moment they had direction. That direction was north toward Leven's old house. Clover was so excited about going to get Leven that every few seconds he would materialize on a different place on Winter, shiver happily, smile, and disappear again.

Geth rested in Winter's shirt pocket as they traveled. The city wasn't huge, and they had only been five or so miles from Leven's old neighborhood, but it was slow going thanks to there being no straight shot there. They had to make their way across the river, through neighborhoods, over fences, and around businesses. Just at dusk they reached the entrance of the Rolling Greens Deluxe Mobile Home Park.

Clover materialized. "I can't wait to see Lev."

"We just saw him earlier today," Winter said.

"Seems longer," Clover sighed.

"Are all sycophants as dedicated as you?" Winter asked.

Clover smiled, shook his whole body, and disappeared again.

The Rolling Greens Deluxe Mobile Home Park had over forty-five streetlights, but only nineteen of them worked. It took time and effort to change the bulbs, so when they went out they stayed that way. That left the area pretty dark at night. A few homes were lit up, and the occasional working streetlight helped to give outlines but no real detail to the scenery.

"I'm not sure how to say this," Winter began. "But I'm not terribly confident Lev will even want to come with us."

"He'll come," Geth said confidently.

"I don't know."

"It's fate." Geth was as wide-eyed and smiley as a toothpick can get.

Winter had never met anyone so self-assured as the little

toothpick. She knew she could pick him up and snap him in half with minor effort. Or she could toss him into a fire and he would have no way to save himself. Still, he pushed forward and talked as though he had every capability and advantage at hand.

"I hope you're right," Winter said.

They turned the corner and Winter could see Leven's home. The curtains were closed and glowing over the windows. Winter had never met Leven's family, but the things Leven had said about them made it perfectly clear what kind of people they were.

As they got closer to the house they could hear yelling coming from inside. Terry was shouting at Leven. Winter hurried to the window and peeked through a gap in the curtain. Leven had his back to the opposite wall, and Terry was standing in front of him, shouting and rolling up his own sleeves. From where Geth was pocketed, he too could see clearly what was about to happen.

"We've got to stop it," Geth whispered, looking around quickly. He spotted the tree stump he had been severed from less than a week before. "If I remember Antsel right," Geth said to Winter, "he told me you were a nit."

"I think I am," Winter said, unsure.

"What's your gift?" Geth asked.

"I can freeze things."

"Perfect," Geth said. "I'm going to need your help. Set me down on that stump. I want to see if I can still work my old roots."

Winter took three giant steps and placed Geth on top of the tree stump. He lay down, face up, and oozed slowly into the wood.

Inside the house, Terry was screaming even louder.

iv

Leven had never seen Terry this bad. He was cursing and ranting and coming toward him with fire in his red-veined eyes. He spit as he spoke, rage dripping from him like sweat. All the events and tragedies and disappointment and failures of Terry's life had come to a heavy boil. He rolled his sleeves farther up, his mind focused on nothing but teaching this brat a lesson he would never forget.

Leven tried to open the window behind him, but the cheap clasp broke off in his hand. Terry smiled a wicked, lazy smile. He drew back his fist and swung, stumbling under the forward motion and missing Leven completely. He righted himself and tried again, but the house rocked, and Terry lost his balance and had to grab onto a nearby chair to keep from falling.

"What the . . ." he muttered.

The house rocked again. Leven was as frightened as Terry. Addy grabbed the kitchen bar and hung on. The house shook, tilting to the west at a steep angle, and Terry flew into the wall. Leven dropped to the floor and tried to crawl upward toward the door. The house leveled out and began rising. It twisted and shook as it rose, tossing everything inside around like bingo balls in a bin. The mess that had been there before was nothing compared to how things looked now, with cupboards and cabinets bursting open and expelling their contents all over the rooms.

The front door blew inward and a thick root shot through and toward Leven. It wrapped itself around his waist and yanked him outside, all while the home rose higher and higher. Addy wasn't just screaming anymore, she was exploding with noise. The fear on her face would have elicited mercy from Jack the Ripper. Terry was still bouncing off walls and trying to right himself somehow. Two more roots shot into the home and twisted around both his and Addy's ankles. The frantic couple clawed and scratched at the floor, fighting to keep from being pulled out, but it was no use: Geth had them.

With all three of them extracted from the trailer, Geth kept the house suspended high above its foundation. Winter looked over at the stump where Geth lay. He looked back at Winter. She wasn't certain, but she could have sworn Geth's little wood hole was smiling.

"Freeze the house!" he commanded her.

Winter looked at the house hovering high above her and panicked.

"The whole thing?"

"The whole thing!"

Winter closed her green eyes and concentrated. She saw the house as ice and it was that simple. She looked up to witness the entire mobile home as one shiny block of ice. Terry and Addy, who were still being dangled by their ankles up in the air, screamed in fear and disbelief.

Geth looked up at Winter. "You might want to plug your ears," he said, "but I happen to like the sound of breaking ice."

Geth retracted some of his roots and the entire home plummeted swiftly to the ground. A fabulous rushing noise was followed by the complete destruction of the house Leven had lived in. The

single-wide shattered into a million frozen pieces. Ice flew every-where. A few shards blew out two of the neighbor's windows, and a dog across the street got a massive surprise welt as he was sneaking up on a cat. Geth was right, the sound was spectacular, like the explosion of a blimp full of fine china. Winter reached down and touched one of the bigger chunks. The ice instantly began to thaw.

Geth lowered Terry and Addy none too gently onto the very spot where their house had once stood. He also set Leven down and retracted all the roots completely back into the earth. Then he pushed himself up and out of the tree stump and Winter put him back in her pocket.

"Amazing," Winter whispered. "Absolutely amazing."

Winter walked over to Leven, who was standing in complete shock. The house was shattered into a million tiny pieces. He scuffed some of the frozen debris with his toe.

"I think that was my bed." Leven tried to smile.

Terry and Addy cowered on the ground in fear, as neighbors cautiously approached to investigate what had happened.

Leven looked at Winter. "What are you doing here?" he asked.

"Saving you," she answered. "Are you ready to go now?"

Leven looked at Addy and Terry. She was bawling and he was sniveling. They were both trembling. Leven wanted to say some-thing nice, but all that came out was, "I'm done cleaning."

Addy glared in horror.

As Winter turned and began to walk off into the dark night, Leven paused for a moment, looking at the two people who had been most rotten to him. He wasn't quite ready to leave. He gazed at his shivering guardians and the ring of concerned neighbors who had gathered.

"What happened to your house?" Mrs. Pendle asked, holding her tattered bathrobe closed at the neck.

"The tree . . ." Addy began.

"It lifted up . . ." Terry stammered. "And then . . . my house."

They went blubbering on as Leven slipped back behind the crowd of people and off toward Winter. She was a few hundred feet ahead, whispering to the toothpick in her pocket.

"Should I introduce myself to him now?" Geth whispered to her.

"I think maybe you should wait until morning," she whispered back.

"Fine by me," Geth said, slipping down farther into her pocket.

"How did you do that?" Leven asked, as he caught up to her. "I mean with the tree and the—"

"I'll tell you later," Winter said quickly. "Right now we need to find a place to sleep. We have to leave early in the morning."

"That was amazing! I've never heard a sound like . . . leave to go where?" Leven asked.

"The gateway," Winter replied.

"Gateway to where?"

"To Foo."

"You know where it is?" Leven asked.

"Geth does," Clover said, materializing with his arms around Leven's head.

"Clover!" Leven smiled. "I can't believe you both came back for me. Especially after what I said."

"It's forgotten," Clover waved.

"Good," Leven said. "Because I am so happy to see you guys."

"Let's hope you feel that way after you get some sleep," Winter said seriously. "You have a tendency to change your mind in the night."

"So you know where Geth is?" Leven asked, remembering how awful his dreams had been and wanting to think about anything else.

"Sure, he's—" Clover tried to say.

"We'll see him tomorrow," Winter interrupted, giving Clover the eye.

"I can't believe you found him," Leven said as they exited the mobile home park. "So he's going to take us to Foo?"

"In a sense." Winter's green eyes blinked.

"Unbelievable, so Clover was right. He was waiting for us?"

"Well, not exactly. I'll tell you everything later," Winter promised.

Leven stared at her, thinking about his life and what an amazing turn it had taken. Last night he was chased by the earth, today he saw a tree lift and shatter his old house.

"Unbelievable," he said again, still wondering how a person like himself could even be involved in all of this.

"I'm glad you're back," Clover whispered to Leven.

"I only left you this morning," Leven smiled.

"Still, it wasn't the same without you."

They worked their way through town and down toward the river. The night deepened to a rich black and in the far distance a pack of coyotes yipped mournfully. Leven and Winter had a lot ahead of them, and not much time.

CHAPTER TWENTY

FURY BY DESIGN

Sabine walked swiftly down the halls of Morfit, his rat-like features twitching. Those nearby scurried to be nowhere near wherever he was actually going. Few dared question his motives or reasoning anymore. Well, a few dared, but those few were separated from their loved ones and shipped to the far borders of Foo to live out their lives harvesting gunt—a very unpleasant job, to say the least.

Sabine was darker and more powerful than ever. He had created a true division in Foo, feeding off the most troubled dreams and stirring up the hearts of any who would buy into his plan to return to reality. Thousands and thousands of beings were now sold on the idea of Foo and reality coming together. They wanted to see who they had been taken from and live the impossible in the physical world. Of course Sabine was overlooking one crucial fact—that fact being that what he was preaching would eliminate every dream on earth and ultimately cause Foo to collapse. If even a fourth of Foo were to abandon their fate, the dreams and imaginations of those in reality would cease to exist and hope would be lost to the human race. Fate took in who it needed to keep the dreams of man alive. If the population of Foo dwindled, those on earth would ultimately vanish. The wise in Foo knew this. They understood their purpose to be sacred and took their responsibility and roles seriously.

Sabine wanted none of that. He wanted to be able to slip in and out, so he could rule both reality and Foo. He foolishly believed he could have it all.

Sabine waved his hand, and the guards standing in front of the door stepped aside. He walked through and into the grand chamber. It was one of the largest caverns in Morfit. In the center of the room was a lengthy wooden table. Every seat around the table was occupied, except for the large one at the head. Sabine took his place and sat with a flourish.

"The full moon of Lant," he bowed, wishing them well, Foo-style.

Morfit was as tall as a mountain and as wide as any prairie on earth. A castle of rock, it stood next to and towered above the Lime Sea beside it. It was a work in progress, a place that constantly grew, thanks to the labors of those in Foo who sought peace in the aftermath of their own misdoings. If a person or being in Foo did something they felt was wrong or unbecoming a member of a realm of endless possibilities, they would dig up a stone wherever they stood and carry that stone to Morfit. There they would place the rock carefully and walk away without their burden. Long lines of people with stone in hand, working their way toward Morfit, were a common sight these days, stacking rocks upon rocks, building the mountain of Morfit.

Morfit had not always been so imposing. In the beginning, Morfit was only a small scar in the ground. Now, as the dreams of men on earth grew darker and the division in Foo was creating fear and jealousy, Morfit expanded hourly. The castle of rocks reached to the thick upper sky, creating an imposing mountain filled with caverns and passages. Beings of all forms and desires hid among the caves and tunnels formed by the sins of those in Foo.

Morfit, by virtue of its size, had become the center of Foo. Those who met in council did so there, as well as those who established the changing laws and sat to hear disputes. The dreams of man could not penetrate the structure, making it an off-limits area for dream enhancement and a safe ground for personal thought.

Sabine considered those around the table in the grand hall and smiled broadly.

"We hope this will go smoothly," a council member spoke, addressing him.

"*I* trust it will," Sabine humbly affirmed. "*I* have come to make amends," he announced.

The members of the council looked at each other skeptically.

"*I* have been out of line and am in need of your forgiveness," Sabine continued.

A murmur went around the table, then ceased. The council members were shocked but seemed to like the direction the discussion was going. They had gathered to rebuke Sabine and put an end to his scheme to merge Foo and reality. As much as whisps longed to be whole, they understood that were Foo and reality to merge, they, along with the dreams and imaginations of all mankind, would vanish.

"So your thoughts have changed?" the lead council spoke, his voice betraying his surprise. "You have created this division and now you feel differently?" he asked with disbelief.

Sabine nodded. "*I* was wrong. *I* see now that the path *I* was on is futile."

The room was dead quiet, which might have been expected, since all the men and women who sat on the council were pretty much dead. They were whisps, void of soul and life, a rare aberration and a unique breed in Foo.

Sometimes those on earth who step on a mismatched lane or sidewalk don't make it all the way to Foo. Or a better way of putting it is that they don't make it *completely* to Foo. Those beings only partially arrive and are robbed of only a portion of their presence: their bodies and souls remain on earth, feeling lost and confused, while Foo receives only a hollow likeness of them.

These oddities are called whisps. They have no real substance, but they can still think and react, while passing through objects as though they were ghosts. Whisps are worthless dance partners and of no help when you need to move a large object or want a push on the swings, seeing how they can't touch or react with anything physical.

Having no substance, they are valued only for their thoughts. So it is that they serve in Foo as members of governing councils and boards. They aren't indestructible, however, and Sabine was tired of those he had to answer to. He was fed up with procedures and the shifting logic and rules of Foo. Sabine thirsted for absolute power and personal glory. He wanted out of Foo so he could better control reality. If dreams and hope were the casualties of his quest for control, so be it.

"*I* thought *I* knew what was best." Sabine's voice was thick with pretended emotion and remorse. "*I* know now that *I* have been wrong," he lied.

The council members were very pleased and flattered. They were also unaware that Sabine was setting them up. The biggest weakness in a whisp was his or her inability to resist a compliment. They normally had the ability to think clearly, but the moment someone complimented them on their two-dimensional hair or their intellect or anything else, they lost their ability to reason.

"You have served Foo in a most pleasing manner," Sabine continued. "It is your example and wise decisions that have helped *me* recognize *my* misbehavior."

Everyone in the room nodded in complete agreement.

Sabine removed the hood from his cloak, signaling his shadows to come in. A number of them filtered into the room, each of them carrying a small, polished object. The shadows were of different sizes and shapes, but each was a warped and flat reflection of Sabine. Each found a place near a council member and waited.

Sabine nodded, and his shadows displayed to the council members the tiny round objects they held in their hands. Some of the whisps were reluctant to look at what the shadows held.

"Do not be concerned," Sabine smiled. "Please," he gestured broadly, "these are merely gifts from *me* to you. *My* way of saying *I* was wrong."

"What are they?" one asked skeptically.

"Soul stones," Sabine replied, casually.

There was an audible, collective gasp, then the room fell silent. Sabine could not have uttered two more powerful words.

It had been rumored since the first whisp entered Foo that somewhere in the realm of Foo there existed an object that could make a whisp whole. "Soul stones," they were called, and possessing one, a whisp would be transformed from an empty, two-dimensional image into a whole being who could touch and run and experience a complete life in Foo.

To a whisp, nothing was more sought after and wondrous than a soul stone.

"Soul stones," they whispered reverently. A few tried to touch them, but their hands went right through.

Sabine smiled amiably. "These were not easy to come by, friends. But your forgiveness of *my* misbegotten behavior seems to have merited them. It is *my* pleasure to present them to you."

The whispering intensified. The possibility of their being whole clouded their judgment and suspended all caution.

"If you would like, *my* shadows will open them for you," Sabine cordially continued. "In a mere moment you will be whole for the first time."

Ecstatic chatter and excitement filled the room. A number of whisps wobbled as if faint. Others stood trembling in front of their assigned shadows, fidgeting and wringing their hands in joy.

Sabine gestured with his right hand, and the stones split open. A deep, red glow, mesmerizing and brilliant, oozed out of each one, then tantalizingly began to withdraw. The whisps gazed in awe and wonder. They reached forward, captivated by the hope of becoming whole and unable to resist. As their ghostlike hands touched the glow, they were suddenly sucked in toward the light.

For a moment they assumed it was a part of becoming whole, but a few quickly realized what was really happening. They should have known better. It had seemed strange that Sabine would admit his wrongdoing when he had been so arrogant in the past and so close to victory at the moment. It seemed unlike him to apologize when he had for so long resented the restraints imposed on him by what he often called the *wretched* Council of Whisps. His humility and cordial behavior were entirely out of character, but the hope of becoming whole had caused the entire group to go daft. They had thrown caution to the wind, and now they were paying for it with their thin lives.

The only way to get rid of a whisp is to suck it up. That is why whisps are so horribly frightened by vacuums. Their substance is so thin that a simple sucking can draw them in. And if they are drawn into a small enough space they can be trapped. If a whisp is compacted to the size of a pea, it then has enough substance to prevent it from simply slipping through the material that is holding it captive. More than one child in Foo had tormented and teased a whisp by chasing it with a vacuum outside the steps of Morfit. Whisps weren't fond of children.

Sabine, of course, wasn't looking to simply torment and tease. Sabine wanted the whisps gone for good. His cruel genius was in creating a vacuum small enough to fit into a polished stone.

Sabine laughed scornfully as the whisps writhed and screamed while being sucked into the tiny rocks. Some cursed him and others cried, knowing they had been tricked to death. The black shiny stones glowed as they consumed the images of all the whisps.

In a few moments it was over.

The shadows closed the tiny rocks and placed them on the now-unoccupied giant table before them. Sabine looked at the pile and waved his shadows away.

Nobody could intentionally kill another being in Foo. You could hit your worst enemy in the head with a club, and it would have no effect. If someone *intentionally* pushed you off a cliff you would simply land at the bottom unharmed. If, however, someone *accidentally* bumped into you and knocked you off a cliff, you would fall to your death. That was an interesting fact of Foo that had prevailed ever since the realm had come to be.

Sabine, however, had found clever ways to kill and rid himself of those who opposed him. He had placed Geth's soul in a seed and set the crows loose on him. Now he had successfully trapped the Council of Whisps in the rocks, but he still needed some unsuspecting and innocent victims to finish the job for him.

He looked at the stones and with his power turned them into ice. Sabine too was a nit, endowed with the same gift Winter possessed. He collected the frozen rocks in a wooden box and handed

them to Jamoon, who had been standing guard outside the door.

Sabine smiled. "See that these are given to the children out in the far field," he ordered.

"Yes, Your Perfectness," Jamoon bowed.

"Let them practice stick with them," Sabine suggested. "They may use them all. *I* don't want them back."

"You are so kind and giving," Jamoon added. "So kind and giving."

Sabine turned away, knowing that in a matter of minutes the entire council would be nothing but shattered rocks strewn over a child's playing field.

He stepped into the dark musty chamber off of the hall and inhaled deeply. Shadows by the thousands rushed to him and swirled together into one dark spiral, humming and whistling vulgarly.

"We're here, we're here," they chanted. "We're here."

Sabine glanced and saw that something was not right with his minions. They were frightened and resisted his pull. Some whispered and cried as they told of Leven Thumps and how they had not been able to darken his dreams. Some reported that Leven was allied with Winter and a spirit they didn't recognize, but feared.

"What kind of spirit is with the boy?" Sabine demanded, the confidence he felt just moments before leaving him.

The shadows cowered, too frightened to speak. The shadows that surrounded Sabine were not only sinister, they were disposable. Sabine had gone through many. They couldn't escape the master who cast them, but he could will them to dissolve at any time he chose.

Sabine closed his eyes and clapped.

The dark spiral of spirits evaporated into nothing, each sending a piercing screech ringing through the chamber as it disappeared. Sabine moved in front of the tall window and drew the heavy drape back. Light flooded the chamber, casting Sabine's dark shadow onto the floor and against the far wall—a new, less intimidated shadow.

"What kind of spirit?" Sabine inquired of the newly cast dark patch. "What was the spirit like that your predecessors did not recognize?"

"It was strong," the sole shadow stated. "It was strong and familiar. It was unafraid. Royal."

"Royal?" Sabine whispered. "Did you hear mention of the name Geth?"

The shadow nodded and quaked.

"Geth is alive?" Sabine cursed.

Sabine turned and moved quickly. He walked in front of the window again, and a new, tall shadow formed to join the other. Sabine paced back and forth in front of the window, thinking, and a third appeared. By the time he had his thoughts about him, the room was filled with hundreds of new, dark forms of all sizes and lengths. They followed him out of the room, whispering eagerly, ready and willing to do his bidding.

Sabine had eliminated the Council of Whisps, but now he had Geth to worry about. He couldn't dwell on that. Those who would follow him would be much bolder, now that the council and their negative advice were gone. Sabine's followers needn't know that Geth still lived. Sabine shuddered and drew in breath like a rat. He *had* to find the gateway.

CHAPTER TWENTY-ONE

WE FELT THE EARTH SQUIRM
UNDER OUR FEET

Leven had barely fallen asleep when the shadows began their
work. As deep as the night, they moved in from beyond,
falling upon him, whispering, insinuating themselves into his
dreams.

"You're worthless. Worthless," they hissed. "Fool. Fool," they
howled.

Leven tossed and turned as they rolled over him and dived
brazenly into his mind. Leven's eyes burned behind his closed
lids, and his mouth was as dry as the entire month of July. He
cried out and moaned, thrashing around madly in his sleep.

"He did this last night," Winter whispered to Geth as she sat
beneath the bridge looking at Leven. "It looks painful."

"It is," Clover complained, appearing out of nowhere. "I can't
sleep with him any longer. He's freaking me out," Clover shivered.

"It's Sabine," Geth said. "Leven has no control. Sabine's shadows have him by the dreams."

"That can't be good," Winter said.

"It's not," Geth replied. "But there is nothing we can do. We must let fate work its course. Your touch has changed his dreams. They are now marked with traces of Foo. They can find him in his sleep. At the moment it isn't such a concern. They know where we are. In the future we'll have to be more cautious."

"We could wake him," Winter suggested boldly, her own head beginning to throb.

"That is not a solution. It would only make Leven leave us now," Geth insisted. "It would not be wise."

"So we just sit here while a bunch of ghosts work him over in his dreams?" Winter complained.

Leven rolled completely over and cried out in fear. He tucked his knees to his chest and rocked back and forth, moaning. His eyes flashed open and were burning gold. They closed and he thrashed about again.

"I'm not doing this any longer," Winter insisted. "We need to start moving anyhow." She crawled over to Leven. Geth tried to stop her, but it's incredibly hard for a toothpick with one arm to hold back a thirteen-year-old girl who is actually tall for her age. So he just rode in her pocket, curious to see how fate would work this out.

Winter knelt beside Leven and touched him. His body was as cold as snow. She felt him shivering.

"Lev," she whispered.

He moaned louder.

"Lev, wake up, it's me," she said even louder.

Leven turned and looked at her. His eyes were black and in the whites of them she could see dark images floating back and forth. Winter gasped and drew back. Leven glared at her hatefully. He was not himself.

"I'm worthless," he whispered bitterly. "Don't you understand?"

"Let him be," Geth said. He—"

The ground shook.

"What was that?" Winter asked.

Geth stood as tall as he could in her pocket and looked around. The earth hissed. Winter turned to see the end of the bridge they were under lifting upward. The structure groaned and wailed as bolts sheared off and welds began to snap. Winter could see the ground rise and recognized what was happening.

"It's back," she yelled.

"Back?" Geth hollered.

In the distance Winter could see a gigantic mound forming to the left of her and another to the right. Two more heaved up behind her. She struggled to pull Leven up. He stared blankly at her as the entire earth seemed to mound up and take shape around them.

"Wake up!" Winter yelled.

Leven blinked dumbly. Clover materialized, clinging to the front of Leven, and took a little too much pleasure in slapping Leven awake.

"Wake up," Clover screamed. "We've got to get out of here!"

The end of the bridge heaved upward and began to roll toward them. Winter took Leven by the hand and pulled him to his feet, and the two of them began running. She bolted into the trees, dragging Leven behind her, just as the avalands rose out of the earth and took full shape. There seemed to be hundreds of them this time, pushing up from the bottom of the river and covering the entire prairie like an eruption of gigantic, mutant groundhogs, beating their scaly chests and stamping their fat legs. They were spewing mud and raging.

Winter dodged trees and jumped over bushes with Leven in tow. At each step Leven became more and more conscious of his surroundings. He could see Winter pulling him and recognized clearly that they were in real trouble. The earth roared. Clover was clinging to Leven's neck and watching out behind them all as he bounced up and down. He could see great mounds of rock and earth surging from the ground and galloping toward them. There were too many avalands to count. Some stood on their back legs and roared as others lowered their heads and charged after Leven, Winter, Geth, and Clover. It looked as though the whole planet was rolling toward them.

As the avalands reached the trees some blasted through, snapping entire trees and sending splintered limbs and branches everywhere. Most of the beasts dived deep into the earth before they reached the trees and burrowed swiftly in the direction of Leven and Winter.

"Where are we going?" Geth hollered to Winter.

"I don't know for sure," she hollered back. "There's a cliff out this way. Lev used it to destroy one last night."

"Amazing," Geth commented as if this were all sort of exciting.

"I don't think I've ever met someone who's killed an avaland. To be honest with you I didn't think it was possible," he yelled.

"Great," Winter huffed, sweat pouring from her forehead. "Interesting and all," she screamed, "but we're about to be eaten by dirt!"

"Amazing," was Geth's only reply, as he tucked himself deeper into Winter's pocket.

Winter had no idea what she was doing. Her only thought was to try to do what Leven had successfully done the night before.

"Run faster," Clover yelled, still clinging to Leven's head. "They're right behind us."

Leven was now thoroughly awake. He picked up his speed, and in a few strides he passed Winter and began pulling her along.

"This isn't going to work," Leven yelled. "There are too many this time."

The world continued to mound up behind them as the avalands thundered closer, the sound of crumpling earth rumbling across the prairie. Winter and Leven could feel themselves being lifted up by the approaching avalanche of dirt.

"The cliff is just up there," Winter screamed.

Leven looked forward and could see the ridge that led to the steep drop off. He held tightly onto Winter's hand. Just before they would have plunged over the cliff they jumped to the side and rolled away from the edge, their hands and knees scraping across dirt. Winter looked up, expecting to see at least a few avalands fly past them and over the cliff. But apparently these were wiser than the one who had pursued them the night before.

Not a single beast flew off or out of the cliff. Instead, the entire herd thundered to a halt and began to circle Leven and Winter. Ring after ring of huge earthen beasts surrounded them, creating what looked to be a small, circular mountain range. The hideous beasts stamped the ground and blew mud from their mouths and nostrils, focusing their fiery eyes on the two helpless kids.

Leven held Winter's hand and the two of them faced the raging circle. Hearts racing and breathing heavily, they stared at the unbelievable sight and the impossible odds. They were ringed in.

"We're dreaming, right?" Leven exclaimed. "Please say we're dreaming." The fear inside of him was so strong it was almost paralyzing.

"I don't think so," Winter answered, her back to Leven's as they cowered in the face of the menacing ring. Her hair was all over, and she looked paler than usual under the partial moon.

"This isn't possible," Leven insisted.

"There're too many of them," Winter said.

As if on cue, the beasts all began to groan and shake. Then, one by one, domino-like, each mound began to bleed into the mound next to it, forming a gigantic ring of earth that towered over Leven and Winter.

"Is this good or bad?" Winter asked, breathing deep.

Leven would have replied, but he became distracted by the end of the coil of dirt as it took on the shape of a giant serpent's head, displaying its massive fangs. The snake was coiled in concentric circles, and the moonlight reflected dully off its scaly skin.

Rings away, the beast lifted its massive tail and rattled it. The noise was deafening.

"You've got to be joking," Leven said desperately, his brown eyes as wide open as they could be.

"What do we do?" Winter cried.

The humongous snake lifted its hideous head high and hissed. A long dusty tongue whipped out and back—Leven and Winter could feel the wind from it as it snapped inches away from them. The snake rose higher and, like lightning, thrust its massive open mouth down toward its victims. Winter and Leven leaped to one side just in time. The snake recoiled and hissed again, its monstrous tongue flicking in and out, its beady black eyes focused directly on them.

"Let's get out of here!" Leven cried.

He pulled Winter by the hand and ran directly at the coiled body of the snake. He pushed her up and onto the serpent's back, and she pulled him up after her. The snake writhed, recoiled, and struck at them again, but they had already jumped to the next coil and the beast bit into his own dirty skin. Enraged, the giant serpent thrashed to uncoil itself, flinging Leven and Winter off its back, away from the cliff and back toward Burnt Culvert.

They hit the ground running and took off like there was no tomorrow, which certainly could have been the case, seeing as how the very dirt of the earth was out to get them.

Tucked down in the hood of Leven's sweatshirt, Clover peeked out at the snake behind them. In a few moments the snake had straightened itself out and was slithering across the prairie behind them with one objective: to devour Leven and Winter.

Leven spotted a chain-link fence in the distance, the length of it glistening in the soft light of the slight moon. It was a high fence with three strands of barbed wire running along the top of it. It struck Leven that if they could get over that fence the snake might not be able to get them. It wasn't a perfect plan, but it is very hard to think up great plans when enough earth to fill ten football stadiums is slithering after you at the speed of dirt. Leven looked behind him, amazed at how close the serpent was.

"Get ready to climb," he yelled at Winter.

She, of course, was already pretty sure what Leven was thinking and was mentally ready to scale the fence as fast as possible. Leven pulled off his sweatshirt as he ran. He reached the fence and sprang up toward the top, scrambling to get higher. He frantically tossed his sweatshirt over the barbed wire and laid his body on it. He glanced down to see how close Winter was. She was not only close, she was right behind him on the fence.

"Climb up my back," he shouted. She did so and went over him and dropped to the other side of the fence. She put up her arms to catch Leven as he followed her, but he landed heavily next to her, sprawling onto the hard ground.

"Nice catch," he grunted, trying to retrieve the breath that had been knocked out of him. He wanted to lay there and moan for a few minutes, but he had his life to worry about.

They scrambled to their feet and watched through the fence as the huge snake slithered to a stop. It raised its head and hissed madly at Leven and Winter, its fiery eyes burning in the dark night. The snake tried to roll itself over the fence but the sharp barbwire sliced its stomach and gave it pause.

It hissed violently again.

Leven wiped his forehead and tried to catch his breath. He wondered why Winter was yelling in a muffled voice and was startled to turn and see that she wasn't saying anything.

"Who's saying that?" Leven asked.

"I think it's Clover," Winter said, equally out of breath.

"Clover," Leven yelled. "Where are you?"

Winter pointed toward Leven's sweatshirt that was still snagged on top of the wire. It was hanging down, and there was a wad of something in the hood, which was swinging back and forth.

"He's in there?" Leven asked, panicked.

"He must have been in your hood," Winter breathed.

The huge head of the serpent lifted and swung from left to right. It was only a few inches away from the sweatshirt.

Leven almost asked Winter what they should do, thus opening up the philosophical debate over whether they should attempt to get Clover or try to save themselves. Leven could see decent arguments on both sides. They could be snatched off the fence by the snake as they tried to untangle Clover, making their efforts in vain. Plus, one could argue that Clover was here to save Leven, and Clover himself would insist that Leven leave him and save himself. Of course, Leven had grown to sort of like the little guy, and in all honesty he couldn't bear to just leave him for dead. These are thoughts and things that almost happened. What transpired in earnest, however, was that while thoughts such as those

were racing through Leven and Winter's heads, the fat serpent shoved his huge face straight down into the ground and began tunneling under the fence. It all happened so fast Winter and Leven hardly had time to gasp.

Leven looked toward his Wonder Wipe sweatshirt as it hung there with Clover trapped inside. Before he could climb for it, the earth opened up beneath him, and the gaping mouth of the beast rose straight around Winter and him. The snake clamped its jaw shut, capturing them.

Instantly, it was pitch black and dirt filled Leven and Winter's noses and mouths. The snake writhed and moved the muscles in its throat to swallow. It felt like a tremendous vacuum trying to pull them down.

The huge serpent whipped its ugly head back and up. Then with irresistible force it shoved its face into the ground. The big head penetrated the earth, taking Leven and Winter and Geth with it. The rest of his long body followed, slithering down into the dirt as if it were a noodle being slurped up by mother earth.

In less than thirty seconds the scene was completely quiet: quiet except for the worried questioning of poor Clover trapped in the hood of a tangled sweatshirt at the top of a fence.

"Guys?" Clover laughed. "Ha, ha, I get it. Trap poor Clover."

Silence.

"Hey, is everything okay? Very funny. Guys? Winter? Lev? Toothpick?"

The moon grew fuzzy, and the night went on as if nothing unusual had happened at all.

CHAPTER TWENTY-TWO

SWALLOWED WHOLE
AND ALIVE

In the darkness of the snake's mouth, Leven couldn't see a thing, but he could feel plenty. Winter was screaming and he could feel her kicking madly. He could also feel the muscles of the great snake working to move them deeper into its belly, massaging them into its stomach. Thick mucus coating the snake's mouth and throat made it impossible to resist and they moved steadily downward. In their struggle they had created enough air pockets to still have a little oxygen to breathe. It wouldn't last long.

Everything swirled and twisted as the huge serpent continued to bore deeper into the ground.

"He's crushing me!" Winter screamed. "I can't breathe!"

"Push out!" Leven yelled.

"It's too heavy."

The muscles surged and rolled, squeezing them deeper into

the snake. Each squeeze left them with less and less of the hot air to breathe. Eventually the snake leveled out and began to slow down. At what felt like somewhere near the center of the earth it finally stopped completely. There it wriggled Leven and Winter down farther into its belly to begin digestion. Leven had a small air pocket in front of him and Winter had a slightly bigger one for her. They both were struggling to even breathe. They knew their oxygen wouldn't last much longer.

"Why'd he stop?" Winter whispered, the air deathly quiet except for their breathing. The beast's hot belly smelled of sweat and dirt and decaying flesh.

"I have no idea," Leven whispered back, scared to death.

"He's resting," Geth spoke up. "It'll lay here until we're digested."

"Who said that?" Leven asked in shock, not having yet been introduced to Geth.

"That's Geth," Winter cried.

"Geth's here?" Leven asked in amazement. "Where?"

"In my pocket," Winter choked. "He's a . . . toothpick."

There is nothing quite as painful as a truly awkward silence. If you have fallen in love and you tell the object of your affection how you feel and she simply stares at you, the air still and empty, that's awkward. Perhaps you finally get up the nerve to ask your boss for a raise and after you muster the courage to blurt out your request he lets it just hang there in the open air. That can be an awkward silence as well. But for some reason both those examples pale in comparison to the kind of uncomfortable silence a person might experience when trapped in the stomach of a colossal earth snake, miles under the ground, where there is nothing but total darkness and the sound of your own self taking your final hot breaths of musty, stale air, after you've just received news that the one person who you believe could save you because he is so big and powerful is hiding out in the pocket of a friend as a . . . toothpick.

"A toothpick?" Leven gasped.

"For the time being," Geth replied. "I won't always—"

"The Geth we were searching for is a toothpick?" Leven interrupted, still in complete shock.

"He is," Winter breathed hard.

Leven wished he could turn his head to scream, but the walls of the snake's belly held him so tightly he couldn't even wiggle his toes.

"A toothpick is going to save us?"

"Fate will figure this out," Geth said without emotion.

"Fate?" Leven came undone. "That's your plan, to wait for fate?" The claustrophobic conditions were too much to bear.

"There is wisdom in—"

"There's no air," Leven yelled. "I have got to be dreaming this," he rambled, anxiety now totally overcoming him. He began talking to himself. "It is impossible for giant dirt clods to turn into a snake and swallow me and take me to the center of the earth with a toothpick and a girl who can . . ." Leven stopped himself to think. "Winter," he whispered, "can't you freeze this thing?"

"What good would that do?" she moaned. "We would just be really cold and stuck in a frozen snake."

Leven closed his eyes, which really wasn't necessary due to the dark, and thought. Nothing came to him. He tried to manipulate the will of the snake, but no matter what he thought or concentrated on, nothing happened. Then, it hit him. His eyes jumped open.

"Freeze me!" Leven blurted.

"What?" she said in disbelief.

"Freeze me solid."

"No way, I can't see how—"

"Listen," Leven interrupted again. "You and your half-brained attempts are part of why we are in this mess and if you can't do what I ask just say so, and you and your dumb little toothpick and ratty blond hair can live happily ever after in this grave."

Leven's tactic worked.

"If you're going to be a jerk about it, I'll gladly freeze you," Winter seethed. She simply thought it and it was done.

Leven was now a block of human ice.

"I hope he knows what he's doing," Geth commented.

Winter began to cry.

"It'll be okay," Geth tried.

She was about to point out how hopeless their cause was, but she was stopped by the snake's movement. It twisted a bit and rolled its stomach. The chunk of ice inside of it was making the poor beast uncomfortable. It slithered and rocked, turning Winter upside down.

"It's working," Geth whispered. "That boy's pretty smart."

The uncomfortable snake couldn't take it. It angled its head upward and began to frantically slither its way to the top, moving at a speed that was at least double the one they had been going on the way down. The movement threw Winter against Leven, who was still frozen solid.

The serpent burst from the earth and opened its huge mouth. It rolled around and began working its muscles as if to gag itself, constricting its body from its tail forward in an attempt to eject the chunk of ice in its stomach. Winter and Leven were squeezed forward.

"I think we're going out," Geth observed needlessly.

The snake gave one last gigantic heave, and Winter and Leven were spewed out of its mouth and onto the ground. Leven's frozen body slammed up against her, remaining intact but giving her a huge bruise up her left side. The two of them were smeared with mud and mucus.

Free of its victims, the snake shook its giant head and whipped its tongue, creating small whirlwinds of dust. It glared at Winter and Leven and hissed loudly, then lifted its huge head and thrust it down into the earth, returning to where it came from.

"We're free?" Winter coughed, standing up and inhaling as deeply as she could.

"You two did it," Geth smiled. "Can you unthaw him?"

"I think you mean, *thaw* him," Winter said, flipping her hands and flinging gook around. "But not yet. I don't appreciate people calling my hair ratty."

Geth liked that.

Winter wiped some of the gunk from her face and spit more dirt from her mouth. She looked down at Leven under the quarter moon and smiled. He wasn't exactly in a very dignified position.

Thanks to being crammed in a snake's belly he had been frozen in a rather grotesque way. One leg was bent up toward his stomach and the other was sort of twisted and bent back. His hands were in front of him as if he were a very uncoordinated person about to play peek-a-boo. His facial expression was the most unflattering thing. He was bug-eyed, and his mouth looked like a goldfish's out of water, trying to suck in air.

Winter took Geth out of her pocket to give him a better look. She had never seen a toothpick laugh so hard.

"Should I thaw him now?" she asked.

"Unless you want to carry him."

Winter touched Leven on the arm, and he instantly thawed. He stretched out and moaned. In a few moments he was a limp body lying on the prairie floor. He coughed a couple of times, opened his eyes, and looked up. He blinked. Winter was leaning over him with her hands on her knees and her ratty hair hanging down toward him.

"It worked?" Leven shivered, looking around in amazement.

"It worked," Winter smiled, extending her hand and helping him up.

"Sorry about the hair comment," Leven said. "I just needed you to want to freeze me."

"Don't worry about it," Winter grinned. "I haven't given it a second thought," she lied. "So, what now?"

"Is there really a toothpick?" Leven asked.

Winter took Geth back out of her pocket and placed him in the palm of her hand. She held him out for Leven to see. Geth bowed.

"Leven Thumps," he said formally, "I am Geth."

Leven didn't know if he felt worse being in the stomach of a snake miles underground or being on top of the soil and realizing his future was dependent on a talking toothpick.

"You're so small," Leven said in shock. "You can't be Geth."

"I am," Geth reconfirmed, giving no apology for his state.

"You're a toothpick."

"At the moment."

"Clover said the fate of our world depends on you."

"In a sense that's true," Geth said humbly.

Leven looked at Winter. "I can't do this," he complained to her, his mind still under the influence of the memory of the shadows. "I barely believed in myself when I thought Geth was a great and powerful king. Now, we're supposed to save the world with the help of a sliver? What are we going to do, poke people? Clean their teeth for them?" Leven's thoughts were still black.

"Lev—" Winter tried.

"I'm sorry," he waved. "This is all wrong. Someone is playing a joke on me. Where are the cameras?" He looked around as if this were all some elaborate scam.

Leven turned back to Geth. "Aren't you supposed to be the one to take us to . . . Foo?" he said sarcastically. "I'm sorry, but I don't see you being capable of taking us anywhere. If it were up to you we would still be in the stomach of that snake, waiting for fate to figure things out."

"Fate did," Geth said strongly.

"*I* did," Leven pointed out.

"With the help of fate," Geth added.

"Fate did nothing. If fate is so great why shouldn't I just lie here on the ground and wait for it to carry me off to Foo?"

"That would be foolish," Geth said honestly.

"Arrgh!" Leven hollered, throwing up his hands, the white in his hair bristling. "I can't do this."

"Lev—" Winter tried again. "Sabine is—"

He waved her off. "I need to think." Leven looked at both of them, his brown eyes full of hurt and confusion. "I don't exactly like being chased by shadows and swallowed by snakes. I told you, I'm not the right one. I'm sorry." He shook his head sadly and walked off.

"Should we follow him?" Winter asked Geth, her head throbbing.

"No, he'll find us," Geth replied casually.

Winter put Geth in her pocket and looked out toward Leven as he slouched away. She sighed and turned to walk in the opposite direction toward town.

ii

"A toothpick?" Leven asked himself as he shuffled across the prairie. "A toothpick? Not even a stick or a log, but a *toothpick*? The world's in jeopardy," Leven mocked. "I know, let's send an orphan and a toothpick. That should take care of the problem."

The ground crunched beneath Leven's feet as he walked across the moonlit prairie. He looked up at the fuzzy moon and twisted to see if he could still spot Winter walking away from him. She was long gone. As he turned back to face forward he practically ran into the tall chain link fence they had scaled earlier. He had been so busy dwelling on his misfortunes, he hadn't even seen it coming.

"Clover," he said, remembering.

Leven followed the fence toward the east, wondering if Clover had been able to get himself out. Before long he began to hear the muffled sound of someone singing.

"Forty-seven thousand, eight hundred and ninety pretty nits on my mind. Forty-seven thousand, eight hundred and ninety. Take one out? No! Too full of self-doubt. Forty-seven thousand, eight hundred and eighty-nine pretty nits on my mind. Forty-seven thousand—"

Leven ran to the sweatshirt dangling from the barbed wire and yelled up.

"Clover!"

"Lev?" Clover said, stopping his song, his voice muffled by the sweatshirt he was tangled in. "Oh, great, now I lost count."

Leven climbed up on the fence and reached up. He tugged at the sweatshirt, but it would not come unhooked from the barbed wire.

"I'm trapped here forever," Clover lamented casually, as if he were just doing what was expected.

"I'll get you out. Hold on."

Leven held onto the shirt with one hand and jumped down. He hung there for a second until his weight caused the sweatshirt to rip away, dropping Clover and him straight to the ground.

Leven got to his knees and unwrapped Clover.

"You're supposed to be saving *me*," Leven smiled, happy to see his friend.

Clover grinned. "This makes us even." Clover bounded up as if to hug Leven, but he stopped, cleared his throat, and stuck out his hand for a shake.

Leven accommodated him.

"Besides," Clover went on. "I could have gotten myself out. I was just resting." He smiled at Leven. "Now, where are Winter and the sliver?" Clover asked.

"I left them back there," Leven said, pointing, the smile erased from his face. "I'm not going with them," he added.

"What? Are you crazy?" Clover jumped. "What else would you do?"

"I'll think of something. Something that doesn't involve dying," Leven said bitterly.

"Like what?" Clover said, interested.

"I don't know. All I'm sure of is that in the last couple of days I have almost been killed at least twice."

"Wow," Clover said, confused. "I've seen things way differently. It seems to me that in the last few days you were finally living."

Leven was silent. Clover's reasoning seemed to hit home. His head was just so full of dark thoughts and confusion. Sabine's shadows had really worked a number on him.

"I just can't do it," Leven finally said. "It's impossible."

"Exactly." Clover smiled, as if they had just had an incredible breakthrough. "It seems impossible. That, Funny Man, is why we must get you to Foo."

"Funny Man?" Leven asked.

"I'm trying to come up with an endearing nickname for you," Clover said. "Ever since Winter came and started calling you Lev. I had that first, you know."

"Well, keep trying," Leven sighed. "Funny Man doesn't work."

Clover cleared his throat. "So let's get you to Foo."

"The space between possible and impossible," Leven said, imitating Clover's voice.

"Exactly."

Leven shook his head tiredly. "You're so agreeable."

"So will you go?"

Leven sighed. "Geth is a toothpick," he complained.

"Winter is a thimble?" Clover replied hesitantly.

"What?"

"Oh, sorry. I thought we were talking in code," Clover shivered. "We have to get back. You're confused, but you will see clearly someday."

Leven sighed again. He picked up Clover and set him on his shoulder.

"So we're going?" Clover asked again, wanting to be sure.

"I guess so," Leven said unenthusiastically.

"That's the spirit," Clover cheered, his robe sparkling under the slight moon.

Leven looked at the moon, gauged where they were, and began working his way back to a girl he still barely knew, and to a talking toothpick that claimed he could save the world.

CHAPTER TWENTY-THREE

THE STRENGTH OF SHADOWS

Winter walked quickly through the trees. She had wanted to go around the grove, but Geth had assured her that they would be fine. The landscape was a mess. The ground before her was the very place where the avalands had risen out of the earth and run after them. Trees lay strewn about and dirt was heaped up in mounds all over.

"Where did they come from?" Winter asked Geth as she walked nervously through the trees. "The avalands, I mean."

"This was the work of Sabine and his shadows. Their touch brought them to life. Sabine understands earth."

Winter stepped over fallen tree limbs and made her way around the jagged holes in the ground. Moonlight filtered through the blasted trees, creating a pattern of shadows in the dark grove. She looked to the moon, and when she glanced forward again there was someone or something standing in front of her.

Winter gasped, placing her hand to her heart.

In front of her hovered a single shadow, thin and black, wearing a cloak and a hood. Though his face was dark, his evil features were visible—a long, narrow face, a nose that twitched as if smelling something foul, and deep, sunken eyes that glowed against the darkness of its hood. His stance suggested superiority.

"Hello," the shadow whispered hoarsely. As he spoke his open mouth looked like a hole right through him.

"Hello," Winter responded weakly, moving to go around him, her heart thumping wildly.

"Do not be frightened," it said coldly, his voice a hollow echo. "Stop yourself." He held up a long, thin hand with slim, crooked fingers.

Winter stopped.

"That's better," it whispered. "We know you."

Winter held her eyes down, trying to squelch the fear inside of her. She was having trouble breathing.

"You are not from here," the shadow breathed. "You are not from here."

"You're wrong," she said quickly, knowing she had been recognized.

Sabine's shadow placed its hands behind its back and drifted slowly around Winter, looking closely at her.

"You are alone?" it asked.

Winter thought about mentioning Geth, but something held her back.

"I am alone," she whispered bravely, pushing her hair back

so the shadow could see the strength of her eyes.

"Where is the boy, Leven?" it questioned.

"He gave up."

Sabine's shadow smiled. "He's smarter than we give him credit for. You would do well to follow his example," it exhaled.

"I don't know what you're talking about," Winter insisted.

"We think you do," the shadow hissed softly. "There is another."

"Another what?" Winter said harshly.

"Another spirit," it shuddered.

"There are thousands of spirits," she pointed out. "Billions." She turned to follow the eyes of the shadow as it continued to circle her.

It laughed, its laughter sounding like a cold, wicked confession that sent chills down Winter's spine all the way to the pads of her feet. She wanted to run away, but she felt as if her ankles were shackled to the ground.

"Not just any spirit," the shadow clarified. "This one is different."

"Well, I can't imagine what it would have to do with me," Winter lied. "I'm done with all this."

The shadow's eyes burned. Something in the last thing Winter had said to it caused its dark soul to churn.

"You are Winter?" it questioned in disbelief. "Winter?"

"I'm going," she said, stepping quickly away and picking up her pace.

Sabine's shadow didn't follow. But it watched her as she fled, then it slowly dissolved, leaving nothing but moonlight in the grove.

ii

Looking frantically over her shoulder, Winter splashed quickly across the river and ran toward Burnt Culvert. She wanted to be as far away from what she had just seen as possible. Her heart was thumping even harder than when she had been chased by the avalands.

She reached the edge of town and felt some relief. Winter could see a couple of people and lights and life going on. She ran up the street and stepped into the doorway of a new hotel. No one was near.

"Who was that?" she asked Geth quietly. She had still not caught her breath completely.

"Sabine's strongest shadow," Geth answered. "He's here for me and Leven. They give Sabine the chance to view us from Foo."

"We need to get back to Lev." Winter was panicked. "He's out there alone. Sabine will find him."

"We can't stop that from happening now," Geth said honestly. "It's out of our hands."

"But what if we—"

"Leven will be okay," Geth said calmly, interrupting her concern.

Winter had her doubts.

"I remember him," Winter whispered. "Sabine."

"You should," Geth said, "he tried to destroy you once. Antsel stopped him."

"How is that possible?" she asked.

"You'll understand soon."

"Now we're heading back to him?" Winter asked, sounding more panicked than she wanted to admit.

"And he's heading toward us," Geth said seriously.

Winter shivered. She had more to fear than she had thought.

iii

Leven's head was clearing, and he was beginning to feel a bit better. It just felt kind of normal for him to be with Clover, heading toward Winter. Clover was right that Leven was leaving nothing great behind. Leven had nothing to lose by following this adventure to the end. He couldn't understand why he couldn't get his mind to believe it.

"Want some gum?" Clover asked, reaching into the pouch on the front of his cloak.

"No, thanks."

"Who says no to gum?" Clover teased. "I'm worried about you."

"I don't normally say no, but I've been burned by some of your snacks before," Leven reminded him.

"How was I to know you wouldn't like the taste of roaches? This is different," Clover smiled, taking a chunk of gum out of a round tube. He tossed it in his mouth and began to chew.

"Stop it!" a voice rang out.

Startled, Leven looked around. Clover kept chewing.

"Help me. Oh, someone, please help me!"

"Is that you?" Leven asked, alarmed that he couldn't pinpoint exactly where the cries were coming from.

"Nah, that's just my gum," Clover chewed. "It'll stop complaining in a moment."

"Please, won't somebody help me?" the gum hollered. It made a gurgling sound.

"Is that normal?" Leven asked.

"It's Tarmarts's argumint flavored gum. In a second it will begin to apologize. It's a vicious cycle. It's noisier than complimint flavored, but I like it better."

"Oh, won't somebody please help me," the gum wailed. "I can't . . . I'm sorry. I'm so sorry. It won't happen again."

Clover continued to chew.

"Oh, that feels nice," the gum said.

"Would you please spit that out?" Leven asked, feeling like the whole world could hear them as they pushed through a corn field toward town.

"No one can see us," Clover pointed out.

"I still think we should be quiet."

Clover swallowed it. Leven could hear the gum screaming the whole way down Clover's throat. "I promise I'll change . . ." its yelling trailed off.

"See why I think your candy here is boring?" Clover asked.

"I'm not sure I want to go to Foo," Leven said, looking down at Clover. "I don't think I'm—"

"Good evening, Leven," a new, hollow-sounding voice spoke.

"What is that?" Leven asked, thinking Clover had put in another chunk of gum. "Creepimint flavor?"

Clover was too busy disappearing to answer. Leven looked up. Sabine's strongest shadow stood only inches away from him. Leven jumped at least a foot.

"I'm sorry. Did we startle you?" it asked, its voice seeping from its mouth and swirling around Leven's ears.

"Not really," Leven lied. "Do I know you?" His head fogged up, and his mind became stickier than it had been. Leven tried to fight it, but his mind went black.

"We're meeting for the first time," Sabine's shadow sniffed. "We think you need to know something." Sabine's shadow smiled.

"Okay," Leven said listlessly and as if drifting off into sleep.

"There are those out there who wish to harm you," the shadow whispered.

"People?" Leven questioned.

"That is correct. There are those who would lead you to believe in fables and fairy tales. We are here to make sure you understand how foolish that is—how *dangerous* that is. People who believe in fairy tales are foolish. Do you understand?"

Leven was silent, his brown eyes clouded over and dull. He couldn't fight the strength of the shadow.

"Understand?" the shadow whispered again, blowing his words into Leven's right ear.

"I don't believe in fairy tales," Leven said, as if in a trance.

"That's a good boy," the shadow approved. "We wouldn't want you trusting in foolish dreams only to end up hurt . . . or worse."

Sabine's shadow was a perfect example of uneasy. He didn't speak English, he spoke anguish. His vowels made the hair on the back of Leven's neck stand up, and his consonants sent shivers down his spine. As he spoke, the shadow's essence swirled around Leven, stealing any hope or confidence from him.

"You don't want to get hurt, do you?" it asked.

Leven looked at the glowing eyes of Sabine's shadow. Its narrow shoulders were crooked, and its wide, thin-lipped mouth was full of jagged, decayed teeth. It seemed to Leven as if he had seen this vision before—maybe in a book, or in a dream, or on a napkin holder.

"Go home, Leven," the shadow reasoned. "Forget what you have heard—before you make a mistake, before it's too late."

"But—" Leven tried.

"No!" the shadow hissed. "You can affect nothing. Remember that. You can affect nothing. We would hate to see you or someone you care for hurt because of your foolishness."

It patted Leven on the head. Its touch was empty.

"Trust no one," it whispered.

A low wind blew, and Leven brushed his bangs back from his eyes. The shadow had vanished. After a few moments Clover whispered. "Is it really gone?"

Leven continued to stand there.

"That was a strong shadow," Clover said, all the playfulness gone out of his voice. "We have to find Geth and Winter and get out of here."

Leven just stood there.

"That will involve walking," Clover pointed out, motioning for Leven to go forward.

"He was telling the truth, Clover," Leven finally spoke. "I don't belong in this. Someone could get hurt."

"Truth is so subjective," Clover waved. "Besides, we've all been hurt before. Windy Stein," Clover mocked, his ears fluttering. "Who does she think she is? She didn't even try to get to know me," Clover sniffed. "I would have made—"

Leven's stare stopped Clover.

"Right, we should get going."

"You don't understand," Leven said seriously. "I'm out. Find Winter and let her know. If she still believes in all this she can take you and that toothpick back to Foo."

"You are so fickle," Clover complained. "You're stronger than the shadows," he urged.

"I can't go," Leven replied.

"What will you do? In all honesty I'm not supposed to leave your side." Clover panicked. "I'm already going to get it for some of the things I've done here."

"Sorry," Leven said kindly. "But I didn't tell you to come."

Clover frowned. "There's no way of talking you out of this?"

"No," Leven answered, his eyes betraying his true discomfort over being himself at the moment.

"Well, I hate to do this." Clover disappeared.

"Do what?" Leven asked the air, looking around for Clover.

Clover sank his teeth into the back of Leven's neck and shook his head, releasing tiny drops of fluid that instantly knocked Leven out. A little known fact about sycophants is that they love to serve, but every once in a while, they just plain get sick of helping others. For such times and needs, nature has blessed them with a secret weapon: a venom that knocks out whomever they bite and allows the sycophants to have a little needed me-time. The truly wonderful thing about the venom is that it doesn't actually cause its victims to sleep, it just puts them in a trance where they are shown pictures and scenes of sycophants and learn how wonderful sycophants are.

Clover released his bite, and Leven dropped to the ground like a sack of potatoes.

"Sorry," Clover said, pushing on Leven to roll him behind a thick stretch of tall corn. "Pleasant viewing."

Clover jumped away in search of Winter.

iv

Winter and Geth weren't too terribly hard to find. Winter had planted herself at the main bus stop on the main road into town, hoping whenever Leven did wander back she would see him. She was sitting there wishing she had something to eat when Clover showed up. Actually, he didn't exactly show, but he drew near to her and spoke.

"Miss me?" he asked.

"Clover," Winter said with excitement, to nothing but air.

"Save the gushing," Clover smiled, his blue eyes materializing. "I have Lev."

"Where?" Geth spoke up from within her pocket.

"I sort of bit him."

"Sort of?"

"I mean, it's not like I took a chunk out of him. He's all right. Just sound asleep."

"He shouldn't sleep," Geth said with concern.

"Um," Clover hesitated. "It's not exactly sleep. He's kind of under a spell."

Confused, Winter shook her head.

"Let's go get him," Geth ordered.

Clover hopped on top of Winter's still-shaking head and gave her directions. It was dark, but they found Leven lying there on the ground, peaceful and quiet.

"He looks so young when he's resting," Clover cooed. "He's growing so fast."

"What happened?" Geth asked. "Why'd you bite him?"

"He wanted to leave again."

"Again?" Winter questioned.

"When he got me down from the fence he was ready to dash. But I talked him out of it," Clover said proudly. "But then he changed his mind."

Leven shivered and shifted. He muttered something about sycophants being great.

"Oh, I wish I had a blanket," Clover said in a motherly tone. "Silly me," he said, slapping his furry forehead. "I do." Clover reached into his void and pulled out a pretty pink blanket with lace around the edges. Winter smiled.

"It's my sister's," Clover explained defensively.

Winter smiled wider.

Clover laid the blanket on top of Leven, and the lace contracted and worked itself until Leven was wrapped snuggly. Clover continued talking.

"Anyhow, Lev and I were working our way back across the prairie, and we ran into a tall shadow with really bad teeth. I'm sorry. I think even if you're going to be sinister you can take five minutes a day to floss and brush. I had a short spell when I was a kid when I wasn't exactly the best sycophant, but I always—"

Winter cleared her throat to bring Clover back to the conversation at hand.

"Oh, yes. Anyway, this shadow was tall and spoke uneasily."

"Sabine's shadow," Geth said softly. "We saw him, too."

"He started talking junk to Lev about fairy tales and not trusting people. Lev seemed to buy into it, said he was done, and that I should tell you two to go on without him."

Winter and Geth stared at Clover.

"So I bit him," Clover added nonchalantly. He gazed dreamily at Leven. "I hope he's seeing good things."

"We have got to get him out of here," Geth said authoritatively. "I think it will help him change his mind once we are on our way. Besides, the time is getting short."

"Where are we going?" Winter asked.

"To the gateway."

"Is it far?"

"Only halfway around the world," Geth said casually.

Winter shrugged as if it were no big deal to travel halfway around the world with a toothpick, a sycophant, and an offing who didn't want to be there. I suppose if a person had been through what she had been through, they too might not see any great challenge in simply traversing thousands of miles to make their way to the mysterious gateway.

"How are we going to carry Lev?" Winter asked.

The ground began to lightly vibrate and then rumble. Winter's face turned as pale as new paper. She probably would have passed out, figuring it was a new herd of avalands coming to get them, if it had not been for the low whistle that accompanied the vibrating.

Somewhere in the distance a train was coming.

"Do you think you can drag him to the train tracks?" Geth asked Winter.

"Sure," she replied. "But there's no way we're going to be able to get him onto a moving train."

"I'll take care of that," Clover promised, evaporating into the air.

"I'd help you drag him, but . . ." Geth smiled apologetically.

"Don't worry about it," Winter said. She pulled Leven's arms out of the blanket and took hold of his wrists. She began walking backward and dragging his limp body toward the sound of the approaching train.

CHAPTER TWENTY-FOUR

ALL ABOARD

Bennett Williams was a train engineer. He had been one for just over seven years. In high school he had wanted to be a biologist who lived by himself out in the wilderness, observing the living habits of wolves. But then he met a nice girl who didn't share his dream, so he became an engineer. It wasn't a bad deal. He got to spend a lot of time by himself, watching the world fly by, and still go home to a wife and family.

At the moment Bennett was hurtling over the state of Oklahoma, pulling fifty cars and two additional engines and whistling a song he couldn't quite name but thought sounded mournful. He wasn't alone, thanks to Roy, his fireman, who was sitting in a soft chair nearby, snoring blissfully.

It was well past midnight, and Bennett was making good time. The cab of the locomotive was a bit warm, and it felt good to occasionally hold his head out the open window. He checked his gauges and routinely adjusted a couple of controls. When he looked up, there appeared to be a misshapen cat in a doll's dress hovering in the air and staring right at him. Startled, the engineer flinched, and the cat thing was gone.

Bennett looked around the cab, his adrenaline suddenly racing. He glanced over at his companion, who was still sleeping. He rubbed his eyes, and when he opened them again, the strange creature was flying right at his head.

"Ah!" Bennett threw his hands up in front of his face to protect himself, but the creature was gone again.

The noise had been enough, however, to wake Roy. Roy looked over at Bennett and blinked. Bennett was still holding his hands in front of him and frantically looking around the cab of the locomotive.

"Are you okay?" Roy asked.

"I'm not sure," Bennett breathed. "I think I saw . . . well, I was . . . oh, I'm sure it was nothing," Bennett waved, too embarrassed to explain.

Clover appeared on the top of Bennett's head, then quickly disappeared. Roy's jaw dropped as he pointed to where Clover had been.

"What was that?" Roy gasped.

"What was what?" Bennett asked, twisting to see behind him.

"It looked like—"

Clover showed up on Roy's head, and Bennett hollered. Clover was at the window. Gone. He was on Bennett's head. Gone. Flying through the air. Gone. On Roy's leg. Gone. On

Bennett's face. Gone. Clover was appearing and disappearing at such a rapid rate it looked like he was at least fifty sycophants in the air.

Bennett and Roy were swatting and screaming and brushing and stamping. Roy was having the most difficult time, crying and cursing and begging for whatever it was to go away. Bennett was swatting the air around his head and trying to catch his breath.

"Stop the train!" Roy screamed. "Stop the train!"

Both of them were too busy swinging and kicking at nothing to notice the big smile on Clover's face as Bennett frantically worked the brakes.

Clover's plan was working perfectly.

ii

Leven's wrapped-up heels created a wavy track in the dirt as Winter struggled to drag him across the prairie and toward the train tracks. In the distance, she could see the lights of the engine as it barreled closer. Winter stopped to wipe her brow, and Geth looked up at her from the inside of her pocket and grinned.

"I'm not sure why you're smiling," Winter said. "There's no way Clover can stop that thing."

A loud screeching noise screamed out into the night. It was high-pitched and sounded like a pack of howler monkeys being slowly squashed by a steamroller.

With its brakes locked, the train was slowing. Geth smiled even wider. Winter tugged on Leven's wrists and began straining backward again as the wheels of the heavy train screeched in protest at being slowed down.

Winter reached the side of the tracks just as the locomotive came to a shuddering stop. Dust and steam and the smell of burning coal filled her nose and burned her eyes. Winter stopped and dropped Leven's arms to catch her breath. Her messy blond hair was wet with perspiration. Winter was standing about in the middle of the train's length, but even in the dark she could see two men jump out of the cab of the engine up ahead, frantically swatting at the air around their heads and yelling.

"What's that all about?" Geth asked, peeking out of her pocket.

"I have no idea," Winter replied, looking down the length of the train for an open car. "There," she pointed. She picked up Leven's wrists again and dragged him behind her. The boxcar was high, with an open door that Winter herself could have easily gotten up into, but she didn't know how to work Leven up. He was a couple of inches taller and weighed at least twenty pounds more than she did.

"Hang his hands on the edge and lift him from the legs," Geth suggested, apparently trying to think of a solution as well.

Winter somehow wrestled the limp Leven to his feet and stood behind him, holding him up in her arms. She managed to lean him forward and drape his hands on the floor of the boxcar in the open doorway. But they just kept slipping off.

Frustrated, she laid Leven face down on the ground and hooked his blanketed heels on the train and lifted him from his shoulders, trying to push him up and on. It was no use; his limp body just kept folding.

"Can't we wake him up?" Winter asked as the train began making noise. "They're starting back up."

"Only Clover can wake him up from his bite."

Winter looked around, wondering where Clover was.

"You could freeze him again," Geth suggested.

Winter shrugged. She laid Leven down with his face up and his feet pointing toward the train. She pulled his arms up over his head and pictured him frozen.

In an instant he was just that.

She picked his rigid body up by the shoulders and strained to carefully lean him up against the train.

The engine whistle sounded.

Winter put her arms around his legs and lifted. It felt as if Leven weighed four hundred pounds. She lowered him back to the ground.

"I can't lift him," she cried.

"You have to," Geth yelled above the noise of the train warming up.

"He's too heavy," Winter protested. "Let's wait for the next train, or for Clover."

"No," Geth said in an unusually stern voice. "We don't have the time to waste."

Winter looked around frantically. "I could freeze him to the train," she said, half jokingly.

"Do it," Geth said, as the train began to inch ahead. Winter lugged Leven to the couplings between the boxcars. With the train beginning to move, she hoisted him up and balanced him on the hitch and pictured him frozen there. Again, her gift worked perfectly, and Leven was securely attached to the train.

Backing out of the space between the slowly moving cars, she jogged alongside the moving train, glancing at Leven's face. He looked relaxed despite the fact that he was iced. The frozen blanket wrapped around him made him appear almost cozy. Winter couldn't help but smile at her handiwork.

"Jump on," Geth shouted, reminding her that all her work would be for nothing if the train got away without her.

It was gaining speed. Winter ran as fast as she could to keep ahead of the boxcar. She grabbed the door, her feet flying and her hands gripping tightly. She counted to three, bounced her feet, and pulled herself up, rolling onto the wooden floor. Her head was spinning, but except for some sore muscles and scrapes, she was still intact. She felt her pocket to make sure Geth was still there.

"I'm here," he said as she pinched him.

She rubbed her side where she had scraped it on the train and crawled to the open door of the boxcar.

"Is he still there?" Geth asked.

"I can't see him, but I can't imagine where he would have gone," Winter smiled.

There was a pile of packing quilts in the corner of the empty car, and Winter spread them out to make a half decent bed. She folded one to create a pillow.

"Where do you think we're going?" she asked Geth as she made herself comfortable.

"East," was Geth's only reply.

"Is that good?"

"Perfect," Geth smiled. "We should run into Germany eventually.

"Germany?" Winter asked.

"Germany."

"Why?"

"That's where the gateway is," Geth said, yawning.

Winter pulled a quilt over her, thinking of Leven still frozen to the moving train. "He did say my hair was ratty," she rationalized.

Geth smiled.

"Germany," she whispered, wondering what a foreign country looked like and if they would actually make it. If Sabine was there, she half hoped they wouldn't. Exhausted, she fell asleep before she could question Geth further.

CHAPTER TWENTY-FIVE

LEAVING ON A MIDNIGHT
TRAIN TO DANGER

Winter, Geth, Leven, and Clover reached the town of Cincinnati, Ohio, a day and a half later. Clover had joined the others shortly after Winter had fallen asleep. He would have gotten to them sooner, but he had wanted to hear the conversation the train engineer and his fireman had after they had stopped the train and started it up again. Clover didn't really think staying for the conversation had been worth it, seeing how the two of them had basically just bawled and agreed to never speak about the incident to anyone ever.

As the train stopped, Winter jumped from the railroad car and carefully defrosted Leven from the train. She warmed him up to his old self. Of course he was still under Clover's spell, and she thought it might be best to tell him what was happening someplace less public and noisy than right next to the tracks.

Winter dragged him down into a ravine and into a grove of tall, leafy trees for a very pertinent powwow. At that point Clover woke Leven up.

Leven stretched and coughed and looked surprised to see Winter sitting in front of him.

"What are you doing here?" he shivered, his brown eyes clearing just a bit. "I was talking to Clover, in a cornfield at night."

"Good to see you, too," she smiled.

"We're on our way to Germany," Clover spoke up, materializing in front of Leven.

"Clover," Leven said happily, the prosycophant visions he had been shown while bitten still fresh on his mind. Clover moved closer to Leven and allowed him to scratch him behind his ears. "We're going to Germany?" Leven questioned, his face showing how odd the idea sounded.

"That's where the gateway is," Winter added. "We got this far by train."

"Really?" Leven asked, a bit of excitement in his voice now. "I've always wanted to ride in a train. I don't even remember it. Was I sleeping?"

"Well, actually . . ." Clover started to explain.

"What he means," Winter interrupted, "is that it's a pity you slept through the whole thing."

"That's not what I meant," Clover protested. "I was—"

Geth cut him off this time. He leaned out of Winter's pocket and said, "We really do need to get going."

Leven's expression changed. "I'm not going anywhere," he

said mournfully. "I don't know exactly how you talked me into getting here, but I'm not going any farther. I already told Clover I couldn't."

"Sorry, Leven, but you have to," Geth said strongly.

Winter thought that Leven would react harshly to the order Geth had given. Instead, Leven spoke earnestly.

"I can't, Geth," he replied. "I wish I were the person you think I am, but I'm not."

"Yes, you are," Geth said strongly.

"I can't put any of you in further danger," Leven sighed, brushing back his bangs. "If you knew my life you would know there is nothing remarkable about me. I can influence nothing."

"I *know* your life," Geth replied. "I have seen you every day since you were young. I have waited patiently for the time to come when you would be strong enough to enter Foo."

"You've watched me every day?" Leven questioned. "Like Clover? Where were you, in my pocket, bed . . ." he looked at Geth, "holding my sandwich together?" He tried to smile.

"No, I was the tree that stood by your home," Geth said.

Leven was shocked. "The tree? You lived in that tree?"

"I *was* that tree," Geth explained. "Your home wasn't set down there by accident. I was waiting for you."

"I don't believe it," Leven said quickly, thinking about how much he had loved that tree. "How did you . . . I mean . . ."

"As soon as you left home, I provoked Terry into chopping me down. He took me to the lumberyard. I was taken from there and cut up into a toothpick."

Leven just stared at the tiny sliver of wood.

"I know Sabine's influence on you is strong," Geth said, climbing out of Winter's pocket and leaning against a pebble by Leven. "He wants to get here so badly, and you are the only one who can prevent him from gaining access to reality." Geth shifted on his pebble. "Leven, you need to know some things about yourself."

"This ought to be good," Clover smiled, sitting down on the ground next to Leven and putting a small hand on Leven's knee.

"Your grandfather was a man by the name of Hector Thumps," Geth began. "He made candles in a small shop in upstate Ohio. He was a quiet, kind man who enjoyed what he did, and he fell in love with a girl by the name of Katie."

Clover snickered.

"One evening after a nice meal," Geth continued, "your grandfather took his Katie on a walk through the neighborhood. His plan was to ask her to marry him and make him the happiest man alive.

"Hector and Katie stopped on the corner of Elm and Twelfth to watch the sky and marvel at what an amazing world this was. There he reached into his pocket to extract a ring and ask Katie for her hand. Unfortunately, the temperature was exactly sixty-three degrees, and the sky was filled with some pretty impressive shooting stars. They were also standing over the imperfectly joined intersection of sidewalk connecting Elm and Twelfth. The situation was just right, and before your grandfather could pop the question, he disappeared from in front of Katie's eyes and was swept into Foo.

"He wasn't exactly happy. Since its creation, many souls had protested the fact that they were brought to Foo. They haven't wanted to accept their missions. Your grandfather was no exception. He simply wanted to return to the life that had been stolen from him. His talent, his home, and his love were gone. He petitioned the powers that be for some sort of escape, but they knew no possible escape existed. Were there a known exit where beings could leave, then Foo would eventually cease to exist. Almost everyone would run back to what they were snatched from, leaving Foo empty and unable to create dreams. With no Foo, those on earth could no longer dream. With no dreams there is no hope, and mankind cannot survive without hope. Ultimately everyone would perish."

"I can't dream without Foo?"

"It's impossible," Geth said kindly. "When you sleep or when you focus on what you dream to be, Foo picks that up and makes the imaginable possible. Your dream is caught by a resident of Foo, and he is responsible for bringing it to life. It is a remarkable place, but not all inhabitants want to accept being there. Your grandfather traversed the entire realm, determined to find a way out. No way existed."

"That's all true," Clover said, as if his reassurance would comfort Leven, "I've heard this story millions of times."

"So if my grandfather was stuck there," Leven asked, "how did I end up here?"

Geth held up his single arm as if motioning Leven to be patient. "After almost a year of searching and hoping, your grandfather finally discovered a way to get out of Foo."

"How?" Winter asked.

"He gave up," Geth stated plainly. "It wasn't a new idea, others in the past and since have tried, but your Grandfather Hector was the only one to ever succeed at it. Somehow he got his brain to believe he wasn't there. He refused to believe that Foo existed. He just lay on his back and closed his eyes. He wouldn't sit in a chair, because that would be admitting that chair existed. He wouldn't eat food or visit with others because in his mind they did not exist. He did not believe, and something in his brain's chemistry allowed him to fully convince himself. It took some time, weeks," Geth explained, "but eventually, after everyone had forgotten about him, his body drifted back into reality.

"Your grandfather awoke in the same spot in Ohio he had been taken from. It was almost fifteen months later, but he was thrilled. He ran to his small home only to discover it had been sold at auction some months before and now belonged to a big Italian family. He hurried to his candle-making business to find a closed sign and an empty building. He ran to Katie's house and there discovered she had married two months previously and was already expecting her first child.

"Your grandfather was devastated. He had been gone for just over a year, but in that time everything had changed. He had nothing left in reality. He knew then that he had cheated fate by leaving Foo. He had escaped his destiny and messed up the plan. He felt he had nothing in reality and began to long for the very place he had just abandoned."

"He wanted back in Foo?" Leven asked, in amazement.

"He was an interesting person," Geth answered. "His mind worked differently than most. Suddenly for him Foo seemed to be the only answer he could see. He knew the impossible was obtainable in Foo. And since he felt it was impossible for him to ever be happy without Katie, he believed he could only be well again with the help of Foo. Of course, he had no way back, and as I have mentioned before, getting to Foo is not easy. And it is almost always accidental."

"So what did he do?" Winter asked.

"He would stand on street corners that didn't match up for hours and hours, hoping the temperature would line up and the stars would cooperate. It never happened."

Geth stopped talking to scratch a small itch on his backside.

"And?" Leven asked, wanting to know more.

Geth looked at Leven and smiled. "You look so much like him," he said, "your dark eyes and the streak in your hair."

Leven touched his hair, looking confused.

"He was a brilliant man, Leven, but his confusion and desire drove him mad. He did nothing but whisper and think about Foo. It became his obsession. He wanted to return to the very magic he had once abhorred. He studied the things that made a trip to Foo possible. He built mismatched roads and learned all he could about shooting stars and how they occurred. He delved into weather and temperature and tried to determine if it is possible for a temperature to remain constant."

"Amazing," Leven whispered.

"Sad, actually," Geth added. "In his madness he discovered

that certain bodies of water had the potential to maintain exact temperatures at different depths. In chasing and detailing shooting stars he formulated a theory that it wasn't so much the stars that cause the reaction, it was the way the earth responded to them—as if the earth were in awe and humming happily. That hum, he theorized, might be possible to recreate in other ways. This was his most important discovery. He just had to make the earth as happy as it was whenever a shooting star went off.

"Then came his masterpiece. He built a large box out of stone and cement. At the base of the box he placed the dug-up portion of misaligned sidewalks from Elm and Twelfth street, the same piece he had stepped on all those years before. He extracted the pieces and inserted them at the bottom of his gateway.

"He then positioned that box deep in a certain body of water at just the right depth to achieve a correct temperature. Once it was set up, he simply swam into it and stood on the mismatched ground."

"Did it work?" Clover asked, so caught up in the story he forgot he already knew the ending.

Geth nodded.

"How do you trick the earth into being happy?" Winter asked skeptically.

"You'll see soon enough," Geth replied.

"So he made it back in?" Leven asked in wonderment.

"Unfortunately," Geth answered. "When your grandfather returned to Foo, our world went crazy. No one had believed that Hector had gotten out of Foo, but now they knew that not only had he gotten away, he had gotten back. Foo had been a place where the option of leaving didn't exist. Daily, two or three people accidentally stumbled into Foo, and they were always told there was no way out. Now, thanks to your grandfather, everyone knew it was possible to get out and to get back in. Accepting fate had been their only option. There had never been much envy and hate in Foo, until your grandfather's gateway."

Leven didn't look proud.

"It is impossible to kill another in Foo," Geth informed them, "but suddenly there were those who wanted to do just that to your grandfather. They wanted his secret. They wanted to know where the gateway was. He insisted it had been destroyed on his return into Foo, but no one believed him, not even Amelia, whom he met and married when he returned to Foo. Even after he married her he told her nothing. Antsel . . ." Geth stopped to look at Clover.

Clover smiled and blushed at the mention of his former burn.

Geth continued. ". . . Antsel, the lead token of the Council of Wonder, came forward to point out to all that even if a gateway did exist, their role was to dwell in Foo and make the dreams of mankind possible. They had a divine purpose. Sabine, on the other hand, felt the divine purpose was a myth. He believed that mankind could dream just fine without them in Foo. 'Why should we be trapped here fulfilling people's dreams when they don't even realize we exist?' he would say over and over, convincing many in Foo that any notion of a divine purpose was outdated and foolish.

"When your Grandfather Hector died everyone figured the great mystery of the location of the gateway had died with him, but they were wrong. Antsel had been given the secret by Hector before your grandfather had passed away. Hector had whispered the secret to Antsel because he wanted him to take his child and send him back to reality where he would not be persecuted and could live a life without knowing about Foo.

"The child that Antsel returned was your father."

"How did he get him back to earth?" Leven asked.

"That is the wonder of the gateway your grandfather built. It remains open in Foo as long as the occurrences are right. If people knew where the entrance on each side was, they could travel back and forth from Foo to reality quite often and fairly easy."

"Some grandfather," Clover complimented Leven.

"So we're heading to the gateway he invented?" Leven asked.

"The very same," Geth nodded. "Sabine won't stop until he has found it. He has armies of followers searching for its where-abouts. He wants into reality so that he can rule both. He doesn't care if the dreams of man cease, nor does he believe that if Foo falls he will no longer have any power."

"Why not just destroy the gateway?" Winter asked. "That way no one could ever come back." Her green eyes were dark and serious.

"Antsel tried," Geth said. "The gateway is protected. It is a law and fact of Foo that that which is truly created can only be taken apart by someone with the same blood."

"Me?" Leven asked.

"We're all hoping so," Geth answered. "You are the only blood relative of Hector Thumps left."

"And you're here because . . . ?" Leven questioned Geth.

"I was captured and put into the seed of a fantrum tree. Sabine thought it would destroy me, but I was rescued by Antsel. Antsel in his wisdom slipped into reality and placed me here, knowing that fate would someday see to it that your path and mine would cross, and you would be able to return me to my rightful position and destroy the gateway behind us."

"Wait a second," Winter said. "So we'll have no way back here once we enter Foo?"

"I hope not," Geth said solemnly. "We must keep Sabine where he is. Foo was not meant to have an exit."

Leven looked at Winter. Winter looked at Leven. They both looked at Clover.

"Listen," Clover said. "Don't worry about not being able to come back, I've lived both places, and trust me, you won't be getting the short end of the stick if you end up in Foo. I mean, candy alone . . ."

"How can Sabine not know his plan would be the death of everyone?" Leven wisely asked.

"Because he is a fool consumed by ambition," Geth answered. "His mind is not his own anymore. You will understand more once we are in Foo," Geth replied. "For now just know that the plan Sabine is selling is a lie that will bring about the end of all of us."

Everyone was silent for a few moments. Geth slid off the pebble he had been sitting on and climbed back into Winter's pocket. He looked toward the sun. "We have to go," he finally said. "I figure we have no more than five days before it's too late."

"Five days?" Leven laughed. "We're supposed to get to Germany in five days?"

"If we do our part, fate will help us," Geth said. "So, are you coming, or does Clover need to bite you again?"

Leven looked confused. "Clover bit me?"

"Only because I care," Clover explained.

"I can't see a way out of all this," Leven said, rubbing the back of his neck.

"Good," Geth replied as Winter stood. "Let's find a way to get to the eastern shore."

Winter began walking and Geth whispered to her. "We have to keep Leven awake."

"Why?" she whispered back.

"Sabine's shadows can only locate him in his dreams. Those of us from Foo don't dream here, but the shadows know Leven's dreams now. They'd find him instantly."

"Keep him awake for five days?"

"At least," Geth said seriously. "Clover can bite him again if we get desperate."

"This should be a fun trip," Winter whispered.

Leven and Clover caught up. The four of them climbed back up the side of the ravine and walked toward the railway station.

It was up to fate now. Of course, it always had been.

CHAPTER TWENTY-SIX

BOATS ARE TOO SLOW AND PLANES ARE TOO COMPLICATED

They were lucky to find a train going farther east, and fast. They climbed aboard a weathered red boxcar and rode through Pennsylvania, New York, and Massachusetts.

The landscape was beautiful, but a blur, especially for Leven and his poor eyesight. The boxcar they were in was dark and cold and it rattled uncomfortably as the train flew across the country. Any conversation they had was jittery and shaky. Geth explained to Leven the necessity of him staying awake and how Sabine's shadows could easily find them all if Leven ever slumbered. It was Leven they knew. Leven was willing to do his part in all of this, but staying awake for so many days seemed almost too much to ask, if not impossible. Thankfully, the cold, vibrating metal floor of the train car helped him remain conscious a lot easier.

In Massachusetts they got off the train they were on and

snuck into the car of another heading into Maine, a boxcar full of mattresses.

"This isn't fair," Leven complained.

"Obviously fate has a sense of humor," Geth smiled.

Leven stood up through New Hampshire and was contemplating lying down, despite the shadows, as they crossed into Maine and they all got off. From there they caught a ride in the back of a produce truck, which moved them all the way to the shore and a nice town called Cape Porpoise.

Their spirits were pretty high, what with fate helping them out so generously, but when they reached the actual coastline of Maine and looked out at the endless ocean they suddenly became more than a little discouraged. The water stretched out forever.

"It's huge," Winter gawked.

"You can't even see the other side," Clover worried.

"It's impossible," Leven said. "All that water, and, I've got to tell you, I'm tired."

"None of that," Geth chastised. "There has to be a way."

The four of them had done nothing but discuss what their options were for the last two days, that and work to keep Leven awake. They couldn't take a plane because they didn't have money. Leven suggested he try and manipulate fate so someone would give them some money, but that still left them as minors trying to buy tickets to cross the ocean. It was also true they didn't have passports or the papers and time to procure them. So flying seemed out of the question. The option of getting on a boat was considered, but that had some of the same problems as flying.

Even if they were able to stow away on a ship it would take too long to get there and, according to Geth, time was of the essence.

Leven always got just a little frustrated when Geth talked about time running out. If time were so incredibly important, why didn't the great toothpick offer suggestions that might speed things up, instead of sitting back and waiting for fate to take a hand?

"What are we going to do?" Winter moaned. "Two kids, a toothpick, and a stuffed animal against the entire Atlantic ocean."

"Maybe we should eat something," Clover suggested, ignoring the crack about him being a stuffed animal. He had been making that same suggestion for the last half of the day.

"Maybe we should sleep a bit," Leven said.

"I don't think so," Winter and Geth said together. "I wouldn't mind eating, though," Winter added.

Leven could feel the air thinning. He rubbed his eyes, hoping he might be able to see something. His mind cleared. His gift of being able to see and manipulate things was not all that dependable, and he felt he made a rather pathetic offing. At the moment, however, his gift seemed to be kicking in. His eyes burned gold. He could see lights and movement. A large picnic was in full swing. He could see Winter and him filling their plates with food from a table and sitting down to eat. He could also see a church next to a flagpole and flag.

"I know where some food is," Leven announced. "Look for a church around here with a flagpole."

They all turned from facing the ocean and wandered into Cape Porpoise. Winter spotted the steeple of a white church, and in no time Leven and Winter were helping themselves to food served by a noisy bunch of Baptists at their October-blessed celebration.

ii

Sabine was agitated, and his brain raced, and his body twitched. His shadows had lost Leven. He had called them all home to assess how their search was going, but when he sent them back out, Leven was gone. They searched the entire state of Oklahoma. Nothing. They were now working their way through the surrounding states, but so far there had been no sign of Leven's dreams.

"Where are you, Leven Thumps? You can't stay awake forever. And Geth?" Sabine seethed. "I thought I destroyed you long ago, yet here you are again." Sabine twitched. "And Winter," he slurred. "It looks as if we will meet again."

Sabine ran his thick bumpy tongue over his small teeth. He knew there was a possibility that Leven had truly given up, but he could not take that chance. Sabine also knew that if Leven had not given up he was probably heading toward the gateway. But since the gateway's location was unknown to anyone besides Geth, that information did Sabine little good.

Sabine inhaled, and like bats returning to their cave, his shadows filled the arches and open ways of his castle, cramming the halls and ceilings.

His spirits whispered, "We've failed. We've failed. Nothing." They swirled around, hissing hideously and berating themselves.

No good news. The only hope Sabine now had was to find

the gateway himself. The very idea seemed impossible, which was quite a contradiction to the spirit of Foo. But creatures and men of all breeds, under Sabine's command, had searched high and low for the opening in Foo, and nobody had ever discovered it. The search had revealed nothing. Sabine was still no closer to knowing where or even what the gateway was. He glowered, his evil mind searching for the solution. Only Leven Thumps possessed the power to destroy his dream.

A strong dark dream pushed in from reality and caught Sabine's attention. It jolted him up and backlit his features. His breathing slowed as he closed his eyes. Someone in reality was dreaming the foulest of dreams, and Sabine's soul had intercepted it. Sabine could see everything this person was dreaming. He manipulated the images to make the plot and outcome of the dream even more selfish and to satisfy his own greed. Sabine took the things he saw and twisted them into thoughts he could use. Then he opened both his hands so that his palms were facing upward, flipped his hands over, and sent the sordid dream flying back into reality.

The images Sabine had intercepted and manipulated had given him pause. A thought struck him, and his face broke into an evil smile. He stood, threw on his cloak, and stormed from his chambers. He needed to visit someone immediately.

iii

Leven had never tasted anything better than the food the First Baptist Church of Cape Porpoise had put out for their third annual October-blessed celebration. The corn on the cob was so buttery, the potato salad so tasty, and the pie so thick that Leven felt as if he had died and gone to culinary heaven. Likewise, Winter was helping herself to as much food as she could get her hands on. She had an entire half a watermelon and two of the thickest, most scrumptious burgers she had ever tasted. Clover circulated invisibly, snacking off everyone's plate. Geth pouted and complained about how fate should have given him a form that could digest food. He also went on and on about how time was growing short. Enjoying their feast, Leven and Winter ignored him.

"This isn't so bad," Winter smiled at Leven as she prepared to gnaw on a huge, butter-soaked cob of corn.

"I've never had food like this," he replied.

The folks putting on the event seemed like pretty nice people; they just kept cooking food and putting out more chips and soda. The bowery next to the church was packed. Leven felt like nobody would notice him and Winter in such a big crowd. He was wrong.

A tall woman with big hips and pushed-up hair noticed them and approached.

"Well, hello," she said. "Are you two getting enough to eat?"

Leven and Winter nodded, fearful of being discovered to be intruders.

She studied Leven's face. "You look familiar, young man, but I'm not sure I know who you are. Are you two members of our congregation?"

Leven shook his head no. "We go to the Fourth Baptists," he lied.

"Oh, I see," the woman smiled. "Well, I can't help but think how I've seen you before," she said, pursing her lips. She looked closely at the white streak in Leven's hair. She reached out to touch it and then stopped herself.

"I have a really average face," Leven tried.

"What do they call that?" she asked, ignoring his response and pointing at the stripe in his hair.

"It's a skunk spot," Leven answered. "I got it when I was four."

"I think I've seen your picture on TV," she said.

Leven began to panic. To the best of his knowledge he had never been on TV, but his knowledge was off. He didn't realize that his picture had been on a number of TV stations just recently. Apparently his house being frozen and dropped to the ground was of some interest to some people. There was even a reward being offered for finding Leven. *National Enquirer* had picked up on the story and spread it across the entire country.

The woman's tiny eyes widened. "Do you have family in Oklahoma?" she asked.

"No, ma'am," Leven lied nervously.

"Well," the woman said, retreating and wearing a strained smile, "you youngsters enjoy yourselves. There's plenty of food."

Once she was twenty paces away she took off quickly.

"I think I must have been on TV," Leven whispered to Winter, squinting and trying to see what the woman was doing now. "That lady seemed to recognize me. We'd better get out of here."

Winter looked at her remaining food and frowned.

"Take it with you," Leven insisted, watching the woman talk to a couple of men over by the church. They all looked in the direction of Leven and started to walk over.

Leven pulled Winter up and glanced around for the best way out. The men started moving faster toward them. "Let's go!"

"That's what I've been saying," Geth said.

Leven dragged Winter through the crowd and directly across the path of some children having a sack race. They jumped over a low hedge and into the church parking lot.

"Hold up!" one of the men running after them yelled.

That was their cue to stop holding back. They dashed out onto the main street and in the direction of the shore.

"Where are we going?" Winter yelled.

"I have no idea," Leven yelled back.

"That's the spirit," Geth cheered, happy that Leven was simply traveling by fate.

"Clover, are you here?" Leven hollered.

"Right on top of your head," he hollered back.

"Is anyone following us?" Leven yelled.

Clover turned to see the two men still pursuing them. Behind them a couple of other people were piling into a car.

"Yes," Clover said. "Quite a few actually."

Leven glanced back. "Run!" he hollered to himself as much as anyone.

The four of them ran—well, actually, the two of them ran and Geth held tight in the front pocket of Winter's blue shirt while Clover bounced up and down on Leven's head.

"Around there," Leven pointed, indicating a narrow, empty street to the left.

They turned the corner, hopped two fences, and crawled under a long semi-truck that was parked, delivering cheese to a tiny café. Leven stopped behind the store to catch his breath.

"What did she mean she saw you on TV?" Winter asked, fairly breathless herself.

"I have no idea," Leven huffed and puffed. "Maybe Terry and my aunt have a warrant out for me or something."

A nicely dressed young man in a red convertible pulled to the curb on the street next to where Leven and Winter were resting. He checked out his reflection in the rearview mirror, then hopped out of the car. He glanced over at Leven and Winter and sneered as if they were trash. Leven looked at himself and wondered how anyone could think anything else. His dark hair was a mess and hanging in his face, his clothes were dirty and ripped, and his hands were filthy. It's not easy trying to stay clean while on the run. Winter looked even worse than Leven. Her blond hair was always a mess, but now it was the kind of mess other hair would tell horror stories about. Her dirty shirt was also ripped in a couple of spots, and her jeans were torn at the knees.

"I can't believe what's happening to our town," the snooty young man said, loudly enough for them to hear. "It's a shame." He walked off and into a store just down the way.

"What a jerk," Winter said.

"Look at the positive," Geth spoke up. "He left his keys in the ignition."

"What good does that do us?" Leven asked, exasperated.

"I'm not sure," Geth admitted. "It just seems sort of fateful."

One of the men who had been giving chase peeked over a wall and spotted them. He hollered to those with him, and people began climbing over the wall and working their way closer to Leven and Winter.

"Do you know how to drive?" Winter asked.

"I've seen a few movies," Leven said, scared.

"Then let's get out of here!" Clover yelled.

Leven jumped into the front seat of the convertible, and Winter leapt into the back. He turned the key, and the engine started right up. He pressed on the gas but nothing happened.

"You have to put it in drive!" Winter yelled.

Leven couldn't hear her so he just kept pushing on the gas pedal and revving the engine in hopes that it would do something. Those chasing them had cleared the wall now and were just a few feet away. Winter reached over from the backseat and pulled the lever into drive. With the engine revved, the car shot forward like a bullet, tires screeching and smoking. Leven turned the wheel and barely avoided crashing into a small truck that was parked on the other side of the road. He slammed on the brakes and glanced nervously in the rearview mirror. He squinted. It looked like half the town was running after them.

"Go!" Winter yelled.

Leven pushed on the gas again and the car flew forward. He grabbed the wheel and tried to simply keep it going straight. A big bus going the same direction blocked his view and caused him to have to swing onto a side street. The sounds of sirens sang through the air.

"We're dead," Leven moaned.

"Just keep driving!" Geth ordered.

Leven flew over the road, his tires screeching and wailing. The sirens got louder as two cop cars roared up behind them.

"What do we do?" Leven hollered.

"Don't worry," Geth screamed. "It'll work out."

Leven strongly wished that Geth was lying on the road in front of the car so he could run over him. Here they were, flying down a seaside road, going eighty miles an hour, and being chased by cops, and Geth's way of helping was to suggest that he shouldn't worry.

Leven blew through an open toll booth and into the beach area. A few people hanging around the shore took notice and pointed.

"I'm running out of land," Leven said with concern, realizing he could only drive so far. "Even I can see that."

"Just keep driving," Geth hollered.

"But—"

"Keep driving!" Geth ordered.

The police cars had also entered the beach area and were breathing down Leven's tailpipe. Leven steered onto a narrow street and found himself driving onto a wooden pier.

"Seriously," Leven cried. "We're out of land!"

"Keep going!" Geth shouted.

Leven looked at the ocean in front of him. His vision wasn't the greatest, but he could clearly see where the pier ended. His heart plummeted into his shoes. He hated water, and there was nowhere else for him to go.

Clover appeared long enough to scream, "Are you crazy?"

Leven's reply was to step on the gas even harder. He closed his eyes and prepared to get wet. He couldn't imagine a worse ending. Geth looked at Winter, and she nodded. The car flew off the end of the pier and down toward the water, but there was no splash. Instead, they landed with a small bump on a long patch of ice that had suddenly appeared.

Leven opened his eyes and smiled in awe, his heart pounding and sweat dripping down his face. Winter kept the path in front of the car frozen, but the area behind she let drop off. One of the two police cars screeched to a halt on the end of the pier and the other slid into the water, lights flashing and siren wailing.

The surface of the roadway of ice was rough, not smooth, as though Winter had textured it for traction. Leven pressed on the gas and the car shot forward on the frozen highway into a bank of dense fog.

In a few moments they were miles out from shore. Leven kept his hands on the steering wheel in the ten o'clock and two o'clock positions, looking as if their very lives depended upon him holding the car straight.

"Amazing," Clover said, hanging his head over the side of the car, staring at the narrow frozen stretch they were careening along. He could see fish and other objects from the sea frozen in the trail they were traversing. He looked up ahead, seeing nothing but a thin white roadway that stretched out directly in front of them and disappeared into the fog bank.

Winter sat back in her seat, impressed with herself and smiling.

"You couldn't do this without me," she pointed out, her blond hair whipping wildly in the breeze.

"That's why I sent you," Geth added.

"You sent me?" Winter asked.

"We knew Leven couldn't get back by himself," Geth smiled. "And we didn't know just what kind of shape I would be in. So we used the dreams of those on earth to help you revert back to an infant. We then came through the gateway and switched you with another child."

"Janet's not my real mother?" Winter said with shock and glee.

"Nope," Geth said. "We didn't want to displace anyone, but we needed you to be here. So we located the worst parent we could find at the time and switched her child with you. Janet's real little girl ended up in a nice home out in the country with a pony and caring parents. Sorry for all the heartache you suffered, but we could think of no other way."

Winter didn't smile, she sighed deeply.

"You *chose* to do this," Geth added. "In fact, if I remember correctly, the child swapping was *your* idea."

"I suppose I'm happy someone else didn't get stuck with her," Winter said, the headache that had been coming finally taking hold.

"Family history is so interesting," Clover said, butting in.

Winter looked at Leven, who was still holding tightly to the wheel, his foot firmly pushing on the gas pedal. The speedometer needle was as far to the right as possible, indicating that they were going at least one hundred and twenty miles per hour.

"We're going to run out of gas eventually," Leven hollered.

"We'll worry about that when it happens," Geth said, staying true to his character.

"Just don't let the ice end," Leven begged Winter.

"Just don't fall asleep," she replied. "It's going to be a long drive."

"How wide is this ocean?" Clover asked.

"About twice the size of the Lime Sea," Geth answered.

"Wow," Clover said. He turned to Leven. "We really are going to run out of gas, Dog."

"Dog?" Leven said.

"No good?" Clover asked, referring to the nickname. "I heard someone on the radio use it. I thought it sounded important."

"Keep trying," Leven smiled.

Clover disappeared, and Leven sped like the wind farther across the surface of the Atlantic Ocean.

CHAPTER TWENTY-SEVEN

CLOSER

Sabine had to stoop to get through the crooked, old doorway. As he stepped into the ancient house, a handful of his shadows swooped in after him. It was the home of Amelia Thumps, the woman Hector Thumps had married after he returned to Foo. She was also the mother of Leven's father, whom Antsel had returned to reality shortly after Hector's death.

Amelia had been a beautiful woman in her youth, a somewhat attractive woman as an adult, and almost an eyesore as an old woman. Her hair was thin and scraggily, and the tip of her lumpy nose had for some years drooped down over her top lip. She wore thick glasses that made her eyes look huge. She was one hundred and fifty-three years old, and she planned to live at least three hundred more. People often wondered what she would look like then.

Sabine had come to visit her, hoping he might extract from her some bit of information regarding the location of the gateway.

She had been questioned many times before, but Sabine had the feeling she might be withholding something she knew. The dream he had intercepted and manipulated earlier had given him reason to visit this house again.

Amelia offered Sabine a seat but he declined to sit, choosing instead to pace as she sat uneasily on a worn velvet couch.

"How nice of you to meet with *me*," Sabine said, affecting a civility that was not natural to him.

"I don't see that I had any choice," she complained. "Your shadows kept at me until I gave in." Amelia tried to keep her voice even. She had a lot to hide.

"*I'm* so sorry," he said, trying to keep from becoming angry. "Their manners are not always the best."

"You cast them," she smiled rudely. "Now what do you want? I'm meeting friends in a short while to make splotch."

"*I* won't keep you but a moment," Sabine began. "*I* was wondering if you would mind answering a few more questions about Hector's gateway."

"Ha," she laughed. "There is nothing else to say. I've told you everything I know," she said. "Now leave."

"In a moment," Sabine snapped. "Perhaps there is something you forgot to tell *me*," he coaxed.

"I don't know where the gateway is," she lied. "I wish it had never existed. I wish he had never returned and that I had never fallen in love with him. He was trouble from the start. It took me losing my son to know that."

"Yes, your son."

"Hector couldn't bear to think his son would grow up here, never knowing life outside. Antsel snatched the baby from me after Hector's death. I should have never let him take him. At the time I didn't want the reminder. I know now I was wrong."

"Of course." Sabine tried to sound compassionate. "But certainly Hector spoke of the gateway."

"That's all he did," she said irritably, knowing she wasn't admitting anything that most in Foo didn't already know. "He was mad. He thought he had created the greatest thing since sliced splotch."

"And after he took your son back, he never used the gateway again?" Sabine asked.

"He claimed he destroyed it," she whined. "I wish he had never found a way out of Foo in the first place. Lying on the floor like a fool. Disbelieving the very place he later fought to come back to." Amelia was trying to keep her voice emotionless, but it was obvious she missed Hector.

Though he tried not to show it, Sabine was angry; the few shadows around him swirled and spit. He had one remaining question. "Is this the house in which Hector originally escaped from Foo?"

Amelia looked surprised by the question. "It is," she said, obviously bothered but trying not to show it.

"Where is the room he laid in?" Sabine asked, a wicked excitement rising in him. "The room he stopped believing in?"

"Why?" she asked, more quickly than she should have.

Sabine's shadows fluttered. "Show *me*," Sabine demanded.

Amelia got up from the couch. "You come into my house and start asking to see things. I suppose if I say no I'll wake up perched on the Cliffs of Dwell with small children playing behind me— small children who might accidentally knock me over and to my death."

"*I* suppose that's a possibility," Sabine said, confirming the threat. "Now show *me*."

Amelia looked disgusted and confused. Sabine followed her down a dark hallway into the far corner of her home. He knew he was on to something. He had heard the story many times of how when Hector had returned to reality after losing his belief in Foo, he had gone to the exact spot in Ohio he had originally been taken from. It only made sense that upon coming back to Foo, he might have reentered in the exact spot he had slipped away from. Sabine cursed himself for not putting the pieces together sooner. He had been trying to make the solution too big and too mysterious. But, if what he was now thinking were true, then that spot—in this house—was where he would find the opening to the gateway from this end.

Sabine's small, coal-like heart burned with excitement.

Amelia was frightened. She pointed to a doorway at the end of the hall. "It's just a dumb little room," she said. "He never let me even clean it. I've left it just as he left it." She stopped, hoping Sabine would just look in and then leave. "That's it," she said.

Sabine looked at the door. He breathed in deeply, drawing the hairs beneath his nose back up into his nostrils. He breathed out and they reappeared. The door opened without a sound.

The room was brightly lit, illuminated by seven large candles. In the center of the floor was a shaggy thought rug. Sitting on the rug was a table with a clear glass top with thin gold edging. There was nothing on the table, allowing a person to see the entire rug beneath it. The color and design of the thought rug shifted and changed as the thoughts of Amelia and Sabine entered the room. Part of the carpet grew dark while the other yellowed with long orange streaks.

The room was dusty and filled with books, stacked in piles on the floor and spilling out of the tall shelves against the walls. A number of the books lay open. In one corner an old clock struggled to tick, and the only window in the room was open, letting in the scent of a Foo afternoon and adding even greater light.

Sabine's shadows danced about the room. They had searched this house many times before. As Sabine moved deeper into the room, new, smaller shadows formed as he passed each candle.

"Have you read these books?" Sabine asked Amelia, wondering if perhaps there were clues in them as to the whereabouts of the gateway.

Amelia looked nervous. She pushed her heavy glasses up on the bridge of her nose and stuck out her chin, "I'm lucky to read the headlines on the *Scroll*."

"What a waste. Books are for fools," Sabine said casually. Two of the books that were lying open snapped shut and scurried off as if insulted. Sabine walked slowly around the room, touching things and looking for some indication his thoughts had been correct.

"He spent a lot of time in here?" Sabine asked.

Amelia didn't answer. She sniffed instead, the tip of her ugly nose twitching as she did.

Sabine touched the walls and listened. Nothing.

"Look all you want," Amelia said irritably. "What do I care if you take anything. Crazy fool. Just leave the candles burning so your shadows don't start knocking everything over," she added. Without excusing herself she stepped from the room, leaving Sabine alone.

"Where is it?" he said aloud, knowing he was closer to the gateway than he had ever been before. He could feel the answer was here. His black soul was sizzling. "You're here somewhere. You exist," he proclaimed. "Show yourself," he challenged, as if the gateway were a being in hiding.

Nothing.

Amelia stuck her head back into the room. "When you're

done talking to yourself, just let yourself out. I'm going to make splotch at Caroline's. Don't let the cat out."

It is hard to feel sinister when a nervous old woman with a lumpy nose is telling you not to let the cat out. But Sabine had enough sinister self-esteem for ten beings.

"All right," he sneered.

Amelia closed the door and walked to the front of the house. She knew that the cause was in big trouble.

CHAPTER TWENTY-EIGHT

BLOWN AWAY

Leven, Winter, Geth, and Clover had a lot of things working against them. For starters, they were hundreds of miles out to sea in a car, driving on ice across an ocean that was beginning to act up, *and* they were running out of gas.

The car began to buck and shiver as it choked on the final drops of gasoline. Geth and Clover had been asleep for the last couple of hours, and Winter had been telling Leven any stories she knew in an effort to keep him awake. It had been days now since he had closed his eyes, and he was beginning to show real signs of sleep deprivation.

"The car is stopping," he cried. "Please, let me sleep. Please."

"No," Winter said, pinching him on the arm to keep him awake.

The ocean around them was moving and lapping up against the bridge of ice that Winter had so ingeniously created.

"I think a storm is coming," Winter said.

The car emitted one last gasp and rolled to a stop, in the middle of the Atlantic Ocean.

"We're here," Leven tried to joke.

The ocean air blew and rocked the car.

"Should we wake up Geth?" Winter asked, looking down at the snoring toothpick in her pocket.

"Why?" Leven asked. "He'd only tell us to wait and see what happens."

"It's worked so far," Winter defended.

"This is working?" Leven asked, opening his arms to indicate the vast body of water they were now marooned in. Mist from the choppy sea began to spray them in the face, making everything wet and miserable.

"Do you think we could get this top up?" Leven wondered aloud.

"We could try."

Leven and Winter cautiously got out of the car. The ice had amazing traction. Lev inched slowly along the side of the vehicle and back to where the top was folded down. He looked at the ice and marveled. He spotted a sea turtle frozen in the path. Winter was on the opposite side of the car, pulling on the top.

"All this water," he sighed nervously. "So if you wanted to, you could make this ice go away?" Leven asked her.

"Sure," she shrugged.

"Don't you think it's weird?" he asked, looking around at the ocean.

"What do you mean?" she asked, tugging on the canvas covering the collapsed convertible top.

"Look around you," Leven motioned.

Winter gazed around at the vast and endless sea. The wind was picking up, and the blue sky was taking on massive gray clouds that looked like fat smoky marshmallows. In the distance, she could see large swells forming. A huge purple swordfish leaped from the water, arched over the ice path, and dove back down into the ocean. Winter glanced across the car at Leven and realized how completely unbelievable it was to be right where she was.

"This is a turn I never saw my life taking," she laughed. "I was in school a couple of weeks ago, wishing I were a different person." Winter twisted her long hair and wrung out some water. "I remember when I was about nine," she said, "my mother . . . well, Janet, took me to a movie. I was so surprised and happy. We had never done anything like that together. Then, we get there and she has me buy a child's ticket at a child's price and makes me go in and open a side door so she can sneak in without paying. The worst part was once we were both inside she didn't even want to sit by me, and on the way home she told me, 'Get used to opening doors for people. It's about all you're good for.'"

Winter's green eyes looked sadder and prettier than Leven had ever seen them.

"Now look at me," Winter finally said, hoping to lighten the mood. "Stranded in the middle of an ocean." Winter smiled.

"She was wrong," Leven said. "I mean, look at you now. We'll find a way out of this," Leven said confidently. "I don't know just how we—"

Leven stopped to pay attention to the image suddenly playing in his head.

His brown eyes burned gold. Lights and shadows began to fill his mind. Leven envied Winter's ability to use her talent on cue and with efficiency. He couldn't even think clearly most of the time, much less put his skill to work. Now, however, his tired head was suddenly clear, and he could see the future. Brighter lights burned within him. He saw they were driving across the ocean with the wind pushing them. They were moving slowly, and Leven let his mind tell the wind where to blow and how fast to push them. In his thoughts they were suddenly racing across the ice faster than they had been going before.

"Lev," Winter interrupted. She was still pulling on the cover. "I can't get this roof up without you."

Leven looked at the car top and thought of what he had just seen. "Kneel on the trunk," he said excitedly, climbing up on the trunk himself.

They both got on the back and started to pull the top out and up. As it extended it naturally wanted to angle forward.

"We need to bend it back," Leven shouted above the wind. The waves and the noise were quickly growing louder.

"It won't close if we bend it," Winter said, baffled.

"We don't want it to close. We can use it for a sail that will help blow us the rest of the way."

Winter instantly understood and began working to free the

top. As it came up out of its storage compartment, Leven and Winter stood up on the trunk of the car, and pulled the top back in a direction it was not designed to go. The two side bars bent, and the entire top stood straight up. The vehicle bucked and shivered from the wind.

"We need to bend it back just a bit more," Leven instructed loudly.

The waves in the ocean were beginning to splash up against the car, making the back end they were standing on slippery.

"Pull!" Leven yelled, struggling to keep his footing.

Winter pulled. Together they were able to bend the top back. It stood at an angle slanting slightly backwards.

"That should work," Leven said.

They climbed back into the front seats just as a huge wave crashed down and watered them all. Geth woke up and inquired what was going on, as casually as if he were someone asking what time it was on a lazy summer afternoon. Clover woke up complaining. Leven concentrated and could see the wind growing in large gray sheets from the west and flying toward them. Another wave rocked against the car and pushed the vehicle so close to the edge of ice the back left tire slid off.

"We're going to slide in," Clover shouted.

"Don't worry," Leven hollered back, "hold on!"

Geth popped out of Winter's pocket, looking excited. Just as Leven had seen earlier, a terrific wind came rushing across the water, from behind them. It caught the jury-rigged sail and began to move the car forward.

"It's working," Winter shouted happily, her hair flying wildly.

"Of course, at this rate it will take us a year to get there," Clover complained, the gray fur on his body wet and funny-looking. He was wringing water out of the bottom hem of his cloak.

"Don't worry," Leven said again. "The real wind is coming."

The air surged, and in a second the car was flying over the ice path.

"Impressive," Geth complimented Leven.

The wind was so strong they could feel the back wheels of the car lift off the ground. Leven kept his mind on the wind and the future to give them thrust the entire rest of the way there. Winter, in her wisdom, curled the sides of the ice so as to create a half pipe and made the path smooth. The vehicle surged ahead.

"Can you keep the wind up?" Winter yelled.

"If you can keep the ice in front of us," Leven replied, closing his eyes to better concentrate.

"You won't fall asleep, will you?" she asked, concerned that he had his eyes shut.

"I've never felt more awake," he yelled. "But when we reach the shore I might be a little exhausted."

"We'll deal with that then." Winter smiled.

Geth drifted back to sleep as Clover sang to himself until he too was sleeping. Leven looked over at Winter as she rested her head, and he glanced in the rearview mirror at Clover. The sound of the wind pushing them was noisier than the car engine had been, but amidst the noise he couldn't help but marvel at his life.

The waves bulked up and crested all around, and the sky darkened as night came on.

Still, the wind pushed them speedily across the ocean.

ii

Sabine sat, the candles burning bright, each one growing taller as it burned. The old woman had returned and since gone to bed.

Still Sabine sat.

He was more convinced than ever that he was onto something. This room held the answer and he knew it. He stared at the walls and mumbled about the wait and the value of his time. Books shifted and moved about cautiously, taking care not to come in contact with him.

As the night deepened he began to grow angry. He stared at the candles, their light filling the room. Amelia had instructed him to keep them burning, but Sabine had a sudden feeling in his thick hard heart. He wet his forefinger and thumb with his coarse tongue and reached over to the candle closest to him. He pinched the wick to extinguish the flame. There was a soft hissing sound as a thin stream of smoke drifted up. Sabine stood and did the same to another candle and another until they were all out. The room was dark except for what little moonlight was filtering in through the window. The pale light rested on the thought rug in the center of the room.

He was onto something.

Sabine lifted the glass table off the rug and pulled the rug aside. He stepped to the window and pulled the drapes closed, blocking out any trace of light.

The room was pitch black, yet there on the wood floor, a dim light shone through the cracks in the wood. Sabine dropped to the ground, his hands fluttering maniacally over the floor, his dirty long nails searching for something to grab or pull. He wedged his fingers into a thin crack and yanked. To his surprise the plank came up in a thick, long, rectangle-shaped piece. The dirt beneath the flooring glowed. Sabine's mouth went dry, his eyes on fire. The dirt was moving, smeared with blotches of red, orange, and green colors, swirling wildly around in circles.

Sabine stared at it in dark awe.

He had found the gateway.

iii

Good things come to those who wait. Patience is a virtue. In time all things are possible. You cannot rush perfection. Blah, blah, blah. Winter thought the drive across the ocean would never end. She was usually the one with the best of spirits, but this was just one long stretch of nothing. Her head hurt. Plus, the wind working at their backs was so loud, a person couldn't have a calm thought if she wanted to.

Leven had stayed conscious due to his need to stay focused on the future and the wind, but Winter was worried about how much longer he could hold out. Clover had complained and complained about how hungry he was and then they discovered him eating some actual humble pie back behind the seats. They wouldn't have caught him if they hadn't heard the extremely humble pie loudly apologizing for its flavor and promising it would taste better next time.

"You have food?" Winter scolded. "I thought you said you were hungry."

"I'm hungry for other things besides what I have," he argued back, his leafy ears twitching.

"Well, could you share some of the stuff you're sick of?"

"Here," Clover said, handing her what looked to be a square cracker.

"This is it?" she complained. "A cracker? I'm starving."

"Just eat it," Clover insisted.

Winter bit off one half and chewed. It tasted good. She stuck the second half into her mouth and did the same. "Do you have any more?" she asked.

"Trust me," Clover said, rolling his blue wet eyes. "You don't want more than that. You really shouldn't have eaten the whole thing. I thought you'd just nibble a corner."

"Why would I just . . ." Winter's stomach started to sound.

"I'd get out of her pocket before you're penned in," Clover said to Geth.

Winter suddenly looked frightened. Heeding the warning, Geth quickly clambered out and onto the dashboard. Leven had his hands on the wheel and was driving with his eyes closed, concentrating on keeping the wind coming. His arms were locked into position so that the car traveled straight down the path. He was focusing so intently on what he was doing that he didn't even hear Winter and Clover talking.

"What was that you gave me to eat?" Winter panicked.

"A Filler Crisp," Clover said, his eyes seventy percent concerned and thirty percent mischievous. Now even Geth looked frightened.

"You gave her a *whole* Filler Crisp?"

"I thought she'd nibble the corner. I didn't think she'd be so greedy."

Winter's stomach began to expand and her arms and legs started to swell. Then suddenly, as if someone were inflating her with an air pump, her whole body expanded. Even her hair got fatter. She could feel something coming up in her throat and all at once what looked like shaving cream burst from her mouth and nose, filling the front seat of the car and oozing everywhere. The foam rushed out of her with such force it knocked Clover back and flung Geth up against the front window, where he remained pinned to the glass.

Winter wanted desperately to scream, but her mouth was too busy competing with her nose to see which orifice could shoot out the most goo.

Clover screamed enough for the both of them, causing Leven to take his mind off the future for a moment and open his eyes to join in the scream-along.

Panicked by what was happening to her, Winter momentarily stopped managing the ice path. The frozen road came to a sudden end, and the car rocketed off and slammed into the water. Winter flew out of the vehicle and bounced across the water like a bloated beach ball. She finally settled on her back, bobbing, swatting, and kicking as the white goo continued to ooze out of her mouth and nose. Clover grabbed Geth from off the car's window and climbed on top of Leven, who was frantically swimming up and out of the now sinking car. In no more than a few seconds the vehicle had completely disappeared under the water, and the four of them were bobbing about on the surface of the ocean.

Even Geth looked a little concerned.

Leven splashed his way over to Winter as she bobbed up and down on the waves. She was on her back, flailing her bloated arms and legs about wildly, while white foam continued to spew from her mouth and nose, making her look like a marshmallow fountain. Her green eyes were wide with panic and disbelief. Leven grabbed onto her ankle, surprised and happy to find how buoyant she was.

"What happened?" Leven yelled.

"I didn't think she'd eat so much," Clover explained. "She'll stop doing that in a few minutes."

Leven looked at her as she continued to spout. "I sure hope so."

"I think the more important question is, what should we do now?" Clover asked.

Leven looked into the distance and wondered how they would ever get out of this. He wanted to simply hold onto Winter's ankle and go to sleep. He was so tired and too spent to go on. He wasn't sure he would even care if a shark began to nibble on his legs, as long as he could go to sleep.

Winter's mouth continued to spew white foam as she kicked

and swatted the water like mad. Leven couldn't blame her. She looked terribly uncomfortable. She kept slapping the water and oozing foam. Each time she turned toward Leven she sprayed foam in his face. Fortunately, the white goo immediately dissolved when it came in contact with the seawater.

"I think it's biodegradable," Clover said.

Winter glared at Clover, who was holding Geth in one of his hands while clinging tightly to the top of Leven's head.

"He didn't think you'd eat the whole thing," Leven said, sticking up for Clover, still slightly indoctrinated by his bite. "Besides, Clover says it will wear off before long."

"Thanks for backing me up, chief," Clover said kindly.

"Chief?"

"No good?" Clover asked.

"Keep trying," Leven insisted.

Winter splashed and kicked as if she were trying to say something. She gestured awkwardly above her head with one of her bloated hands.

"What is it?" Leven asked, treading water. He spun Winter around and pushed her up-ocean a bit. He could see instantly what she had been trying to point out. In the not-so-distant distance was a big fishing boat. Winter's swollen body had been hiding it completely from his view. Leven began to holler and wave as Winter finally began to deflate.

The ship had seen them and was heading their way.

Winter's stomach began to contract and her arms and legs hissed as they shrank back to size. She was still burping up foam and having a hard time speaking, but by the time the boat got to them she was almost back to normal—well, as normal as a person could be after having thrown up foam for half an hour.

"*Bonjour,*" a tall dark man on the bow of the boat hollered, then began jabbering in a language that sounded like French. He could tell by Leven's blank stare that he had not understood. "Can we be of assistance?" he asked in English.

"Please," Leven hollered back.

The crew helped Leven and Winter up onto the boat and asked them where their raft was.

"We don't have a raft," Leven said.

"I thought I saw you with one when I first spotted you," the captain said.

Leven smiled, knowing that what he had spotted was a bloated Winter. Winter frowned. They both, however, were amazed to discover that they were only fifty miles off the coast of France. They were questioned about how they had gotten where they were, but when they hemmed and hawed a bit with their answers, the captain simply said, "I'll make you a deal. I won't ask you what you are doing fifty miles out in the ocean if you won't ask me why I am fishing in an area I shouldn't be. *D'accord*?"

"Deal," they agreed.

The captain fed them some soup and bread that tasted marvelous to Leven. Winter didn't eat any due to her recent history, so Leven gladly had her share. Two hours later the boat docked just outside the town of Granville, and Leven and Winter set foot on the shore of France.

"So do you know any French?" Leven asked as they walked along the dock.

"No important words," Winter replied.

"How about you, Geth?"

"I've always wanted to learn," he replied.

"Clover?" Leven asked.

There was no answer.

"Clover?" both Leven and Winter asked in unison.

Nothing.

"When was the last time you saw him?" Leven asked.

"When we got on the boat," Winter said. "That's when he slipped me Geth."

"Clover!" Leven hollered, attracting stares from the waterfront crowd.

"Don't worry, he'll show up," Geth said. "We have to keep going."

"This is France," Leven pointed out needlessly. "Clover has no idea where to go."

"He's a sycophant," Geth said calmly. "They always return to their burn. We have to keep going."

"He wouldn't leave you," Winter said. "I know he'll show up."

Leven looked around hopelessly. "Clover!" he yelled one last time.

Nothing.

The three of them walked down a cobblestone street, two of them worried about Clover and all three of them waiting for fate to point out what their next ride would be.

CHAPTER TWENTY-NINE

PHYSICAL AGAIN

Sabine could not possibly have been more surprised by the sudden rush of freezing water. He had stepped into the colored dirt in Hector Thumps's room thinking he would simply walk out into the world and begin his final quest. Instead, he plunged into water so cold it took his breath away. He tried to scream, but his mouth filled with water. He pushed out of the gateway and swam toward the surface as fast as he could. His dark, wet robes were no longer just a dreary fashion statement, they were suddenly a death trap. He pushed them up over his shoulders and frantically thrashed upward.

It is true that in the eternal scheme of things, Sabine was one of the truly bad seeds. He was totally selfish and as power hungry as anyone could be. He cared not a whit for the soul or salvation of anyone other than himself. He was cruel, looked frightening, and was feared by thousands. His only concern was his own self-interest.

All that aside, he looked pathetic, frantically trying to swim to the surface, like a baby squid flailing its tentacles for the first time.

Sabine came up gasping for air but in a beautiful setting, in the middle of a large lake, surrounded by forested mountains. He looked around. The sun was shining in a perfectly clear, blue sky. In the distance he could see a small boat gliding away from him. It was a scene as picturesque as any that might be imagined. Of course, Sabine hadn't come to take photos.

He had come to take control.

He dogpaddled his way to the nearest shore, his face a perfect picture of disgust. He hauled himself out of the water and onto dry ground and shook himself like an uncoordinated dog with no rhythm. He bent over to touch again the physical world he had been snatched from many years before. His teeth were chattering so violently he couldn't fully exult in his triumph. Wet to the bone, he glanced around, trying to get an accurate idea of where he was so he could easily return to the gateway when needed.

He was a stranger here, but he felt invincible. He looked around, understanding that all he saw was real. In Foo, Sabine had control and power over the elements and beings; here he had none of that . . . yet. With access to the gateway he would be able to move freely between reality and Foo—and enjoy the ability to achieve the impossible in a world where all others had limits.

Sabine looked at his own hands. He had not been real for many years now. He was only nine when he had been snatched from reality and sent to Foo. He had been out playing with two of his friends late one autumn evening. He could still remember the sound of crickets chirping and the sweet coolness of the fall air. He could hear their mothers calling them all to come in. They had pretended not to hear, in hopes of playing just a bit longer. So they ran farther down the road, kicking a ball and talking excitedly like nine-year-old boys do. The only interruption was when the dark sky showed off a beautiful shooting star. All three boys had looked up at it in awe.

"Maybe it's a rocket," one of them said.

"I bet it's an alien spaceship," the other suggested.

They turned to get Sabine's take on it, but he was gone. There was nothing but empty space above where a sidewalk and a side street came together in an imperfect junction.

That was the last Sabine had ever seen of reality for himself. For years his shadows had scoured the planet at his direction, but their vision and reports were only two-dimensional.

This was what Sabine had longed for. He breathed in deeply, expecting his shadows to rush to him. Nothing happened. He inhaled as deeply as he could and still not a single black patch of shadow came to him. He positioned himself so he could cast a new, earthly shadow. The sun did its part, but the new shadow just lay there, two-dimensional and black. It also vanished the moment he stepped out of the sun's rays. Apparently his shadow thing didn't work in reality.

This was a concern. Sabine had anticipated being able to use his castoffs here. Now he would have to make an adjustment. He wondered where his shadows were if they were not responding to him. He worried about it for a moment, then brushed his concern aside, smiling, his tiny numerous teeth clicking against each other. The possibility of ruling everything was finally in his grasp. He could always slip back into Foo and create more shadows. Only one thing could stop him now, and that one thing was a boy by the name of Leven Thumps. Only Leven had the power to destroy the gateway leading in and out of Foo. Sabine knew what he needed to do. Leven Thumps had to die.

Sabine drew his wet robe about him and moved silently through the thick forest of trees and along the shore. He could feel Leven and Geth and Winter drawing ever closer.

ii

Leven was exhausted. He had not slept for days, and his mind was spent from the effort he had focused on conjuring the ocean wind. He could barely walk straight, and Winter constantly telling him to stay awake put them at odds with each other. So far he was not enjoying France.

Plus, they needed money, so Leven decided to try out his off-ing gift. He spotted a woman in a shop about to buy a few expensive dresses. He closed his eyes and manipulated fate to the best of his ability. Somewhat to his surprise, she actually decided not to buy the dresses, and when she walked out of the exclusive store into the street, she spotted Leven and simply handed him the money she had saved. Once again Winter was impressed. Sure, it was a neat trick, but Leven didn't exactly feel good each time he did it. Nor did he have any real accurate control over it.

In all honesty, he had really only been trying to manipulate the woman into just offering them a ride. Instead, she had handed him all her cash. He kept thinking he would someday repay the lady who had bought them food in the diner, the snotty young man whose car they had driven across the ocean, and this woman who had given up her shopping spree to provide for their needs. But he knew that would not be an easy thing, seeing how he didn't know any of them.

Leven purchased a new shirt with some of the money, one with a pocket in front for Geth to ride in and no Wonder Wipes logo. The shirt was on sale and had the words *essuie-tout* stenciled on it. Leven figured it was the name of a French rock band or something cool. Winter also got a new shirt and some pants for herself. They felt rich, pulling out all that money and paying the bill. The French clerk had been very rude to them, probably because of their appearance and the fact they couldn't speak French. But when they showed him the cash, he started treating them nicely.

After purchasing new clothes they took a few minutes to eat at a French McDonald's. It looked just like an American McDonald's except the Grimace statue was wearing a beret.

"We're in France eating at McDonald's," Winter said with astonishment, her green eyes becoming increasingly alive each mile of their journey.

"I'm still not sold on this being more than a dream," Leven replied, his eyes partly cloudy.

"I could pinch you again," Winter offered.

Leven tried to smile back.

Clover was still missing. Leven wanted to go back to the docks and search for him, but Geth had insisted there wasn't enough time. After eating, they hailed a taxi, showed the driver the money they had, and told him to drive them as fast as he could across France and into Germany. He insisted on seeing their passports. When they told him they had misplaced them, and was there any way he could get them out of France and into Germany, he asked to see their wad of money again.

He then said yes.

The ride across France seemed to take forever, even though they were speeding a hundred miles an hour across the surface of the earth.

Leven wanted more than anything to go to sleep, but Winter kept him awake by continually poking him and pulling the hair on his arms. He would beg her to let him rest, and she would pinch him in reply. To distract him, Winter constantly pointed out the villages and landscape they were flying by. On a good day Leven couldn't see very clearly, now as the taxi blew over the road he could make out even less. Everything his eyes took in at the moment was a blur.

The large, happy taxi driver seemed to be enjoying the unusual trip across his country. He laughed and smiled as he listened to French music and sang. Shortly before reaching the German border, he pulled off the road and helped Winter and Leven into the trunk of his cab. He acted as though he might have done this before.

"No talking," he said, right before he slammed the trunk closed.

"I hope this works," Leven whispered, scrunched up against Winter in the dark trunk.

"Me, too," Winter replied.

Geth was tempted to say something positive, but he wisely stopped himself.

It was incredibly warm in the trunk of the cab. It was also obvious, from the stench, that the taxi driver had carried many rank and odorous things in there before. The floor of the trunk was covered with a fuzzy material and worn in spots like knee holes in trousers. Winter hated it, but Leven couldn't help being lulled to sleep by the steady hum of the tires and the darkness. He had stayed awake as long as he could. Winter kicked and pinched him, but the trunk provided insufficient room for her to really get at him.

"Lev," she begged, "please don't go to sleep."

"Just for a second," he pleaded.

"Leven," Geth said authoritatively. "You must stay awake."

"Sleepy," Leven mumbled. "Very sleepy."

He was beginning to drift off when the taxi started to slow down just outside of Strasbourg, France.

"We're stopping," Winter hissed.

Leven opened his eyes. As tired as he was, he knew they were probably crossing the border of France into Germany. He also knew that if the border patrol opened the trunk, they were all done for.

"Be really quiet," Geth whispered.

They could hear their driver get out and slam his door. He

said something loud, in French. He laughed and another voice responded back to him. They could hear the sound of keys rattling, and suddenly the trunk popped open. Light flooded in. Leven and Winter laid there staring up at the driver. He was looking in another direction and motioning to someone to come and check the trunk if they really wanted to.

Leven and Winter stayed perfectly still.

The border guard said something, and the driver shrugged and closed the trunk. He called out something loud in French and got back into the car and slammed the door. The engine roared to life, and they pulled forward.

Leven and Winter finally breathed.

"That was too close," Leven said, his heart still racing.

"So, we're in Germany?" Winter asked, obviously short of breath herself.

"I hope so," Geth answered. "We are running out of time. In a short while the lake's temperature will change, and we will have to wait two months to return to Foo. That's the very next time the temperature will be right."

"Two months?" Leven moaned. "What do we do until then?"

"If we don't make it back now, it's over," Geth said. "Sabine's shadows are too strong. You won't last another week with them knowing about you. We have to succeed now."

"We will, won't we?" Winter asked urgently. "I mean, fate will make it happen, won't it?"

"Fate might have something else in mind for us," Geth answered honestly. "We've done our part."

"Great," Leven lamented, his right arm asleep in the cramped quarters. He was actually jealous of the sleeping limb. "Now that we are nearing the finish line, you're admitting that fate isn't the answer to everything?"

Geth was wise enough not to answer. Winter remained quiet as well. Her head throbbing, she could feel both the ending and Sabine drawing nearer.

iii

Clover was too curious for his own good. He loved looking in places he knew he shouldn't. It was a trait shared by most sycophants. So, when he saw the locked door with the big man in front of it at the bottom of the boat, he couldn't resist taking a peek.

He had waited and waited until the captain came down and unlocked the door. Clover slipped in with him. The room they had entered was small, with no windows or vents, which made it extremely stuffy. Two metal cabinets sat closed against the far wall. The captain opened one of the cabinets while singing a song in French.

Clover gasped.

The captain quickly looked around to see if someone was in the room with him. When he was satisfied he was alone, he shrugged and continued to open the cabinet doors.

Clover's gasping was called for. The cabinet shelves were piled with jewelry, coins, cups, shields, and other objects made of gold. It was clear to Clover that these men weren't fishermen afraid of being caught—they were *treasure hunters* afraid of being caught.

Clover was captivated by the glitter. He stared at it in awe, wishing he could materialize and touch it. The captain closed and locked the cabinet doors and left the room still singing. Clover could have followed, but he wanted another look at the gold.

Once he was alone in the room, Clover messed with the locks on the cabinets, but he couldn't get them to open. He pushed and pulled to no avail. With no other option, he decided it might be best to just let it be. He needed to get out and find Leven. Unfortunately, the door to the small room was locked. He banged and banged, but the walls were too thick for anyone to hear him.

Taking a page out of Geth's book, Clover just laid back and decided to let fate take care of him. After half an hour of waiting for fate to do something, Clover fell asleep, and by the time he woke up the boat had already been back out to sea for an hour.

"I bet they're just sick about me coming up missing," Clover said to himself, thinking of Leven and Winter and Geth.

A key finally sounded in the door. Clover stood invisible in the middle of the room as the captain came back in whistling. He walked to one of the cabinets and opened it up. It too was full of gold and jewels and all kinds of sparkling things that sycophants are so fond of.

Clover pulled a pout from his void and looked at it in his hand. Pouts are small, bumpy, stone-like creatures. They are the texture of wet clay, with their only real feature being a tiny, wrinkled hole on the top of them. Pouts are native to the Swollen Forest. They are shy little things that are almost impossible to find and catch unless you accidentally step on one and cause it to begin pouting. Clover had found this particular one years before when he inadvertently sat on it. He had tucked it away in his void for just such an occasion.

Clover set the pout on the floor behind the captain's back. He closed his eyes, whispered an apology, and then kicked the poor little creature as hard as he could. The pout flew up against the wall and fell down between the desk and the wall. It instantly began to pout, filling the room with the sound of sniveling.

The captain immediately turned to locate the source of the noise. As he did so, Clover slipped into the cabinet, picked out a couple of nice pieces of treasure, and shoved them into his void. Invisible, he rolled under the desk, pushed his skinny arm up behind it, and retrieved the pout. He shoved it back into his void just before the captain pulled the desk away from the wall. The sniveling immediately stopped and, finding nothing, the captain stood there scratching his head and wondering if he had gone crazy.

Clover dashed from the room and climbed the stairs to the open deck. He was surprised to not see any land. The sea was blue, and a cool wind filled his tiny nostrils with the smell of saltwater. A small boat roared up alongside the big boat Clover was on. In the little boat was a short, orange-haired man.

"I think this is the spot," the man yelled up to some crew members. "I'm getting positive readings."

"Perfect," a tall, dark man standing near Clover yelled back. "Let's get the gear and get down there."

The short man with the fiery hair left the engine of his little boat running and put his foot on a ladder, preparing to climb up to the deck of the bigger boat. At that exact moment the engine of the small boat he was still halfway balanced on suddenly roared and the craft shot ahead.

As his boat pulled away, the astonished man was dumped into the water. The crew of the bigger ship hollered as the seemingly empty little boat made a broad turn away from them and headed toward the French coastline. Their hollering did little good as the boat continued to speed farther away.

Clover smiled as he skillfully captained his first vessel. He turned and looked back at the men still hollering, then faced France and joyfully pushed the throttle down for more speed.

iv

The black French taxi stopped at a park just outside of Munich, Germany. The fat, friendly driver took all the money Leven handed him and then gave him a few bills back.

"For food," he said in broken English. "One must eat." He smiled, patted his stomach, and then drove off.

"What now?" Leven asked Geth.

"We need to get to the town of Berchtesgaden," Geth answered. "Our destination's not far from there."

"Can't I just sleep for a few minutes?" Leven begged, eyeing a large patch of grass.

"No," Winter insisted.

"What about Clover?" Leven tried. "Shouldn't we just lie here and wait for him?"

"Our time is almost up," Geth said. "We need to keep moving."

Winter took Leven's elbow and helped pull him down the street to a train depot.

The train station was large. Inside the depot, huge posters written in German hung on all the walls. Tall tiled columns and long wooden benches occupied the center of the large, open building. A short man was busy mopping the floor in front of the escalator going down to the trains.

"I can't stay awake anymore," Leven moaned. "I'm falling asleep on my feet."

"Just a little while longer," Geth begged. "This is the last place we want Sabine to know we are."

They stopped and counted the few bills they had left.

"I have no idea how much this is," Winter confessed, staring at the Euro money. "It could be ten dollars or ten thousand."

"Just go to that window," Leven pointed. "Ask the man for tickets to Berchtesgaden and see what he says. I'll be sitting right here."

Winter sighed, folded the money into her palm, and approached the ticket booth. Leven sat down on the long wooden bench and tried to keep his eyes open.

"Stay awake," Geth warned.

"I will," Leven slurred.

As she waited in line, Winter glanced back at Leven and could see him fighting to keep his eyes open. She waved to him but he was too glazed over to notice her.

"*Guten tag,*" the man at the window said, letting Winter know she was next.

Winter stepped up to the booth, trying not to look too nervous.

"Do you speak English?" she asked.

"Yes," the man replied coldly. "How may I help?"

"I would like two tickets to Berchtesgaden," she said firmly.

He punched a few buttons on his computer and tapped his fingers. Winter tried not to let her anxiety show, but she knew if the man asked to see her passport she would be caught. She was purchasing tickets to a destination within the country, but she wondered if he might ask to see her papers anyway.

Winter smiled and tried to look at ease as he typed.

"Two tickets to Berchtesgaden," he said, pulling the tickets up.

Winter felt great relief at simply seeing the tickets.

He told her the cost and held his hand out, waiting. Winter slid all the money she had through the slot at the bottom of the window.

"I'm not good with your money," she apologized.

He looked at the bills. "It is not enough," he declared.

Winter felt like crying. Her head had been aching for hours, and she was almost as tired as Leven. She wanted desperately to tell the impatient man behind the glass that she was homeless and had been chased by big clumps of land and eaten by a snake. She wanted to describe to him the fear she had felt as they had driven across the Atlantic Ocean and how uncomfortable she had been, both as a swollen girl with foam spewing out of her mouth and as a deflated girl trapped in the trunk of a taxi. She wanted to tell him about Sabine and how frightened she was. She knew once he had some idea what she had gone through he would simply hand her the tickets, and she could be on her way to the finish line.

But of course she couldn't tell him.

The German ticket master looked at her in confusion. "Are you all right?" he asked sharply.

"I'm fine," Winter lied, wiping her eyes and reaching through the slot to take her money back.

He didn't buy it. "May I see your papers?" he asked, grabbing her hand as she reached in.

"That's all right," Winter panicked. "I just need to go recount what I have."

"Your papers please," he said more firmly, squeezing her fingers tightly.

Winter was in trouble.

V

Leven simply could not stay awake any longer. His head bobbed and his eyelids felt like they weighed two hundred pounds apiece. He could barely see Winter off in the distance at the ticket window, and he wasn't sure if she was a dream or reality. He closed his brown eyes and that was it.

He was out.

Geth heard the snoring and instantly started poking Leven. Geth pulled his legs together to give him a sharper form and began jabbing Leven as quickly as he could. He climbed up Leven's face and pushed up his right eyelid. Leven gazed at him as if in a trance. He was completely checked out.

"Wake up!" Geth ordered. "Leven, wake up!"

It was no use. Leven slouched over in his seat and slid down on the bench, snoring with his face in the wood. He began to drool.

"Leven," Geth begged. "Get up." Geth thought of Winter and pulled himself up to see if he could spot her. She was still at the ticket booth, talking to a man behind the glass.

"Winter," Geth whispered, knowing his voice would never be heard above the noise of the train station. "Winter."

They were in big trouble.

VI

Sabine's shadows were confused. One moment they were under control and being driven by the very master they had desired to escape. Now, they could feel no pull. Sabine's departure into reality had cut them all off and left them to be their own beings. They were now free to do as they chose. Of course, shadows aren't the greatest free thinkers. All they knew was their command to find Leven Thumps. They flew around the earth wild and free, making whatever mischief they wished, happier than they had ever been, and still searching for Leven. Freed from Sabine, their forms became bulky, filling with air and dimension as they swirled wildly. They were no longer only two-dimensional, and they found themselves able to touch and destroy things in ways they had never been able to before. Soon after they were freed, sleep finally overtook Leven, and his location immediately became known to the shadows. Normally they would have reported back and been given instruction by Sabine. But with no master controlling them, they knew only one thing to do.

They needed to get Leven.

vii

"Your papers, Miss," the German man insisted for the last time. "I must see your papers." He was hurting her hand.

Winter panicked and turned toward Leven just in time to see thousands of shadows pulsing through the windows and doors of the train station. They looked like black waters flooding the entire place. She screamed, jerked her hand free, and ran toward Leven.

The small German behind the glass signaled two guards standing nearby and they moved toward Winter. She had already reached the bench where Leven was asleep in a pool of his own drool. She glanced over her shoulder and could see the two guards walking quickly toward her. She could also see about ten thousand black swatches of evil swooping through the station. The shadows began knocking down people and tipping over trash cans and tearing down signs. Papers were flying all over the station and people were screaming in terror.

Of course, people weren't absolutely sure what they were screaming at. With no connection to Foo, people were unable to see the shadows, only the effect they were having as they flew joyfully through the depot, discovering the thrill of having no master other than their own will. Who knew how satisfying it could be to swoop up behind an unsuspecting person and knock him off his feet? Or what about the great thrill of snatching the wig off an important-looking woman and terrorizing her poodle?

The shadows went wild, all of them swirling and working their way toward Leven.

The two guards who had been after Winter turned their attention instead to the hysterical crowd. The taller of the two guards was suddenly picked up as if riding on a horse. He was lifted to the high ceiling and dumped with precision into the large fountain in the middle of the room.

"Lev, wake up!" Winter screamed. "Get up!"

Leven stirred, mainly because the whole station was in utter chaos and sounded a bit like a bomb going off in slow motion.

"Run!" Winter yelled, grabbing him by the collar and pulling him to his feet. He had been standing for no more than a couple of seconds when a huge shadow slammed into him from behind and sent him sprawling face-first across the tile floor. Leven knocked over at least ten people before he came to a stop. He looked up to see Winter soaring across the room on the backs of two shadows, her hair flying wildly about and her eyes as big as dinner plates.

As Leven tried to stand, hundreds of shadows leaped on him and pushed him down. He kicked and hit, but they just kept piling on top of him.

"Help me, Geth!" Leven screamed in desperation.

"There's too many!" Geth yelled back, trying to work himself out of Leven's pocket.

Leven slammed his fist into a shadow and it dispersed. No

sooner had that one gone than hundreds more jumped at his wrists, pinning him to the floor. Leven kicked and bucked with his legs, but there were just too many.

Meanwhile, Winter was being bounced across a crowd of shadows, like a beach ball above a crowd of concertgoers. She flew up and down, up and down, and was becoming sick to her stomach. Tiring of the game, a cruel shadow seized Winter by the ankles, spun her around, and let go of her. She flew across the depot and might well have been seriously hurt had it not been for a group of twelve large women heading to Innsbruck for a quilting convention. Their fat bags of quilting material as well as the extra pounds they were carrying around made for a rather awkward (but soft) landing.

All over the station people were screaming and crying and covering their faces in fear. Many attempted to flee, fighting to get through the exits, but those who couldn't get out continued to be harassed by the invisible shadows.

The chaos made some sense to Leven and Winter. They could see their attackers. But those who were blind to the shadows had no explanation for the madness of the scene. They didn't know if they should bob or weave or simply drop to the floor and pray for an earthquake to cover them. If someone had just walked up to the station and looked inside through the glass doors, they probably would have been more amused than frightened. Without being able to see the shadows, it would have just looked like a bunch of Europeans practicing some extraordinarily physical mime act.

Leven was buried by shadows. They held him to the floor and jumped up and down on his stomach. He struggled, but it was no use. There were too many, and they were too strong. A few of the shadows who were holding down his arms became jealous of those who were jumping up and down on him. It just looked like so much more fun than what they were doing. They let go to have a jump on him. With less resistance Leven was able to wiggle his wrists free. His hands flew up and came together, creating a clapping noise. The shadows directly above Leven disappeared. The other shadows close by realized what had happened and began to panic. Leven clapped again, and more vanished.

"Winter!" he shouted. "Clap your hands!"

At that moment, Winter was upside down, being carried by her ankles in a circle in the air. She couldn't hear Leven, but she could see him. He was clapping, and the shadows around him were popping like soap bubbles into nothing. She clapped, and the huge black spot holding her was gone, along with about a hundred others. She landed on the floor and skidded across the tiles into a row of lockers.

A few other people in the crowd figured they would try clapping and began doing so. The shadows immediately began to vanish. Finding the chaos subsiding, others began applauding as well. Leven watched the room empty of shadows as he and the entire gathering clapped madly.

It made for a peculiar sight. It is one thing to arrive at a train station, look through the glass doors, and see people flying across the room and tripping over each other. It's another thing entirely to arrive at a train station, look through the glass doors, and see people applauding wildly, their faces panic stricken and tear stained, their mouths screaming in fear as they clap.

Winter got to her feet and went back to the ticket window. The two tickets that had been printed up for Leven and her were still lying on the counter behind the glass. She tried to reach in and grab them, but the opening was too small for her arm to reach. She looked around the room at all of the clapping people and at the few remaining shadows that were still flying around frantically and without purpose.

The ticket agent who had earlier been behind the glass, wanting to check her papers, was running to get outside when a shadow caught him by the ankles. Another shadow grabbed his wrists. The two of them flew across the room, carrying the wide-eyed man in the direction of Winter. A police officer was applauding at thin air near Winter, and his clapping caught the two shadows off guard. They disappeared, leaving the short man flying through the air. His momentum carried him toward Winter. She ducked while imagining that the glass blocking her from the tickets was ice. The man slammed into the ice, shattered it, and bounced backward onto the floor in front of his booth.

Winter reached through the opening where the glass had been and picked up the two tickets.

"Thanks," she said calmly to the dazed agent. "Fate is really depending on these."

By the time she reached Leven, only a few shadows were left. A couple of travelers in the far corner clapped and got rid of those.

"Are you okay?" Winter asked, out of breath and amazed to still be alive.

"I think so," Leven replied.

"Geth?" Winter said, looking in Leven's pocket.

He was not there.

"Where is he?" she asked.

"I have no idea. He was there yelling at me earlier."

They began to look around.

"Geth!" Winter shouted.

"Geth!" Leven copied.

They dropped onto their hands and knees and began searching the floor. Trash and debris were everywhere. People were walking over everything, trying to get out of the station or to their trains.

"He could be a million places," Winter cried.

"Just keep looking."

They looked everywhere Leven had been thrown or beaten upon. They checked the fountain and under the benches. Geth was nowhere. This was not a good thing, seeing how he was the only one who knew where the gateway was, and well, to be honest, they had become quite attached to the optimistic little toothpick.

"What should we do?" Winter asked.

Leven looked at her and sighed. "We have to do exactly what he would want us to," he answered. "We have no choice."

Winter's green eyes were sad. Leven stuck his hand out, and she placed hers in his. They walked together through the debris and subsiding chaos toward the platforms.

The stationmaster addressed the crowd and tried to make the disruption sound as though it was due to some new pipes that had recently been installed in the station's heating system. No one really believed that, but they all accepted it due to there being no other explanation. He announced they would quickly get the trains running on schedule.

"Did you get the tickets?" Leven asked.

"Of course," Winter replied.

"How much money do we have left?"

"It didn't cost us a thing," Winter grinned.

When they got to the platform their train was there and waiting. They showed their tickets, climbed on board, and found an empty compartment toward the end of the train. They pushed open the door and fell upon one of the seats with both exhaustion and relief.

"We did it," Winter whispered.

"So far," Leven added.

"What about Geth?"

"Fate will work it out," Leven said, trying to sound as though he believed it.

"We should have looked for him a bit longer," Winter moaned.

"We looked everywhere we could," Leven rationalized. "I know he'll show up."

Leven remembered how tired he was as his body gently reminded him by shutting down. Not only was he tired, but he had been pummeled by hundreds of shadows.

"Is it okay if I sleep now?" he pleaded.

"I guess so," Winter said, too exhausted herself to stay awake and watch him. "But if you hear clapping, join in."

A well-dressed man looked through the glass in the compartment door, then opened it. "Excuse me," he said, "but is this seat occupied?"

When Leven said no, the man nodded and sat down on the empty seat across from them. Leven and Winter were a bit saddened to share the compartment, but they were also too tired to really care.

It was lights out for both of them.

viii

Clover had really enjoyed driving a boat—so much in fact that when he got to the shore he decided to try out a car. He waited around on a busy street, looking for someone to leave their keys in their vehicle. Clover had always wanted to drive, but he knew it would be difficult due to his size. He was too short to reach the gas pedal and still see over the dashboard. So he borrowed a large stone from a rock garden, which he thought he might use to weigh down the accelerator. He planned to sit on the steering wheel and maneuver by twisting his body.

A man wearing a worried expression pulled to the curb and got out of his car with the engine still running. He took a stack of papers off the backseat and hurried up some stairs into a building. Clover hustled to the car and hopped in through the open window. He pulled the stone from his void and dropped the heavy rock on the gas pedal. The motor roared. He jumped up onto the steering wheel and craned his neck up so he could see through the windshield. If his friends back in Foo could have seen him, they would have been so jealous. Clover kicked the gear shift lever and the car popped into drive and shot off much faster than Clover had anticipated.

He had thought he would be able to handle the wheel so professionally he wouldn't need the brakes. He could see now he was probably wrong. The car flew wildly down the street, with people gaping at what looked like a vehicle driving itself. Pedestrians dived out of the way, and people on bicycles and automobiles swerved to avoid Clover's first-time attempt at driving. He threw his body weight to the left, and the steering wheel turned, sending the car into a tight spin around a corner. A policeman writing a parking ticket spotted the screeching vehicle and jumped on his scooter to give chase.

Clover straightened out the wheel and weaved his way between slower-moving cars—which happened to be all the other vehicles on the road. He was sweating and hanging on for dear life, with his toes wrapped tightly around the bottom of the steering wheel and his two hands gripping the top. The line of cars in front of him had slowed down, so he threw his weight to the right. The car bounced over the curb and flew up onto a walkway, scattering the tables in a sidewalk café. The bump caused Clover's belly to honk the horn.

Clover liked that. He moved his stomach in and out to warn those in front of him.

People were diving and jumping out of the way as he flew

honking down the walkway. His big blue eyes were as wide as saucers, and he was laughing giddily. Tires screeching, he turned a corner onto a less congested street. He flew down the road, beginning to wonder how he was ever going to stop. His plan had seemed so perfect, but in retrospect it had more than a few flaws.

Clover leaned to the right and directed the car onto the highway. He merged into the traffic and began to pull ahead of all the other slowpokes who were casually going eighty.

The traffic cop on the motor scooter had been left far behind, but seven speeding police cars were now on his tail.

Clover heard the wailing sirens and glanced behind him at the flashing lights and smiled. He honked the horn a couple of times just for fun and set his sights straight ahead and toward Leven.

ix

Winter woke Leven up by pulling at the hair on his arms. She had been awake for some time, worrying about Geth and Clover, and she wanted Leven to share her concern. Besides, they were only minutes away from their destination.

Leven didn't want to wake up. After going without sleep for so many days, the small amount of rest he had just gotten wasn't nearly enough to make him feel refreshed or even normal.

"What?" Leven said irritably.

Winter shushed him, pointing to their fellow passenger, asleep on the seat across from them.

"We're almost there," she whispered, "and we have no idea where to go."

"We'll wait at the station until Clover or Geth show up," Leven said groggily. "We can sleep on the benches there."

"We can't sleep," Winter complained. "Geth said we don't have time. We have to finish this or it's all over."

"Well, we can't go any farther without knowing where to go," Leven pointed out. "Isn't it Geth who's so big on fate? Well, let's see if he's right."

The sleeping passenger shifted in his seat and crossed his right leg.

"He could be anywhere now," Winter sighed. "He's probably still back at the train station. We shouldn't have left without him."

A slight buzzing noise sounded in the cabin, and Leven looked around for something to swat at. He couldn't see anything so he kept his hands to himself.

"It's not like I don't wish he was here," Leven said honestly. "I would feel much better about things if he and Clover were around."

Again something buzzed, and this time Winter heard it as well.

"Is there a fly in here?" she asked.

"I thought there was," Leven said, staring closely at the window and ceiling. As he was glancing around he noticed the sole of the sleeping passenger's right shoe. Near the center of the sole there was a flattened out gob of gum the man had stepped on. Leven would have thought nothing more of it, but the gum was wiggling just the slightest bit. Leven looked at Winter and pointed.

"Do you see that?" he whispered.

Winter leaned across the space between the seats. She could see a tiny sliver of wood sticking out of the gum stuck to the bottom of the sleeping man's shoe.

"No way," Leven whispered.

"I think it is," Winter said with excitement. "And he's trying to yell at us."

The train was pulling into Berchtesgaden.

"You've got to pull the gum off," Winter told Leven.

"But—"

"We're almost there," she said.

Leven got down on his knees and scooted closer to the man. He used his finger to poke lightly at the dirty gum. He put his fingernail beneath one of the edges and tried to peel it off, but it was stuck tightly to the sole. The sleeping man didn't seem to even notice. Leven boldly dug into the gum and pried at it. Nothing. It was still stuck, and the man hadn't stirred.

"You've got to pull harder," Winter whispered as if they were robbing a bank and Leven was trying to figure out the safe combination. "We're stopping."

Leven could feel the train slowing and knew that in a few moments the man would be awake and getting off. It was now or never. He seized the man's shoe with his left hand and pulled as hard as he could on the gum with his right.

No one could sleep through that.

The man woke up and hollered. Leven screamed too as the gum popped off of the shoe and into his hand. The man jumped to his feet. He glared down at Leven, who was still kneeling on the floor.

"What do you think you are doing?" he asked in English, taking Leven by the ear. His face was red and flustered. "Were you trying to steal my shoes?"

"No," Leven said quickly. "Honest, I—"

"I think we should talk to the authorities," the man huffed.

"No," Leven said, even louder. "I dropped my gum, and it got stuck to the bottom of your shoe." Leven held out the gross gob of chewed and stepped-on gum with the end of a toothpick sticking out. Little bits of grit and hair were mixed in the gum as well.

"You were retrieving your chewed gum?" the man asked indignantly, staring at the dirty gob in Leven's hand.

Leven looked at Winter and nodded slowly.

"Why?" the man asked.

"I wasn't finished with it," Leven said sheepishly.

"Really," the man smiled meanly. "Well, then, if you really weren't stealing my shoes, let's see you chew your gum."

Leven looked at the pink, already-been-chewed gum that had at one time been on the bottom of someone's shoe and was now in his hand. He could see the tip of Geth's head sticking out and wanted nothing less than to put it in his mouth.

"Just as I thought," the man barked, motioning to hail a conductor.

Leven had no choice. He popped the gum into his mouth.

Both Winter and the man were shocked. Both winced.

"Chew it," the man said, wanting to teach a life's lesson to a young man whom he perceived to be a thief.

Leven chewed slowly, making sure he didn't bite into Geth. The gum tasted like dirt and floor and mud, with a hint of cherry. His brown eyes didn't look happy.

"Yumm," Leven said weakly.

The man smiled. "Let this be a lesson to you."

He stepped out of the compartment as the train came to a complete stop. As soon as he was out of view, Leven spit the gum out onto the seat, gagging. Winter picked up the gooey wad and peeled it away from Geth, who was also gagging.

"That was disgusting," Leven and Geth said in unison.

Winter held Geth in her palm. He was dirty and covered with splotches of gum. He also had a new crooked bend in the middle, which made it difficult for him to stand completely straight.

"What happened?" Winter asked.

"I flew out of Leven's pocket as he was getting tackled by shadows. I tried to work my way back to one of you, but that clod . . ." he pointed after the man who was gone, "that clod stepped on me with his sticky shoes. I've been trying to get myself out of that gum for hours. My face was pressed into it so tight I couldn't even yell.

"Well," Winter smiled. "We're here."

Geth glanced out the window of the rail car and then back at Leven and Winter. He smiled. "We are, aren't we?"

"You didn't doubt fate, did you?" Leven asked.

"Not for a second," Geth answered. "Well, at least not for a *full* second."

Winter put Geth in her shirt pocket, and the three of them got off of the train, in Berchtesgaden, Germany.

X

Clover had a total of seventeen police cars behind him by the time he started to run out of gas. It had been a long, exhausting chase. No one had dared run the vehicle off the road because for one thing, it was driving itself rather well, and for another, the police feared it might have explosives on board.

As soon as the car began to slow down, the police cars circled and boxed it in. Clover threw his weight one last time and turned the car off the road and down a grassy embankment. The car rolled slowly to a stop. With guns drawn, the police flew out of their vehicles to come and investigate the car they had chased for so long. They threw open the doors, ready to pounce on whomever was inside.

Clover slipped unseen out of the car and walked between their legs and around their vehicles as they all talked and scratched their heads in confusion, all of them wondering how in the world the car could have driven itself.

Clover climbed into the open window of a vehicle whose driver had stopped to gawk. The driver was a thin man, wearing suspenders and smoking a pipe. As soon as the thin man realized there was nothing to look at, he put his gas pedal to the floor and drove

Clover the rest of the way across France and over the border into Germany.

When the thin man stopped just inside Germany to use a pay phone, Clover didn't waste any time. He secretly hitched a ride with a nice German couple and their new baby. That didn't last too long. The baby kept crying and keeping Clover awake. Clover appeared to the child so as to be a delightful, soothing surprise. Well, the child did like Clover. In fact, she held him and cooed. When the parents turned around to look at her and saw their child holding a furry, living creature, they needlessly panicked. The car swerved and rocked as the parents practiced their parental screaming skills. Disgusted with the noise, Clover climbed out through the half-open sunroof and jumped into the bed of a passing truck with an open back. He settled into a roll of insulation it was carrying and rode, somewhat peacefully, closer to Leven.

CHAPTER THIRTY

THE OCCIDENTAL TOURIST

L even liked Germany. At least the little bit of it he had seen. It was beautiful and green and vaguely reminded him of someplace he had been before. Berchtesgaden, however, was even prettier than the rest. It was a lovely town with quaint-looking buildings, beautiful flowers, and friendly people. Thousands of tourists filled the streets, and he could hear polka music coming from two different directions at once. There were a lot of men with moustaches walking around.

"I wouldn't mind getting something to eat," Leven said as they passed a gasthaus and the smell of cooked sausages and onions filled the air.

"No time," Geth insisted. "See that sun?" he pointed from Winter's pocket.

Both Leven and Winter nodded.

"When that sun goes down we have to be ready. If we

don't make it tonight, it will be too late."

"Too late?" Leven said in amazement. "Too late for what?"

"They have gotten through," Geth replied.

"Who's gotten through?" Leven said, so hungry he wasn't speaking clearly. "How could you know that?"

Geth smiled. "It's fate. Don't worry."

"So you're saying if we had not made it here right now we would have been out of luck?" Winter questioned.

Geth nodded.

"What if we hadn't found you on that shoe, or a boat hadn't picked us up, or—"

"What-ifs are for fools," Geth interrupted. "We are here because we are meant to be. Now let's hurry."

Leven was always tempted to point out how easy it was for Geth to say hurry. After all, he was riding along while they did all the walking. He also knew that Geth wasn't compelled to stop and get something to eat because, well, he had no digestive tract. And Winter wasn't about to help him fight for a meal break because she was still full from the cracker Clover had slipped her in the ocean.

Leven sighed and inhaled the aroma of cooking food as they walked along the tourist-packed street, heading toward the Konigsee, or the "King's Sea."

"So what do we do when we reach the Konigsee," Winter asked.

It was a silly question for Winter to ask. She knew from the pain in her head and the fear in her soul that the time was finally here to face Sabine and step into the gateway.

"We wait," Geth answered.

"Well, can't we stop here and wait and eat at the same time?" Leven begged.

Geth smiled as if Leven were joking, and it was obvious to Leven that he was going to have to take getting something to eat into his own hands. They were passing dozens of tourists, many of them eating as they strolled along the quaint streets. Leven spotted sausages and pretzels and ice cream. He decided to try to clear his mind in an effort to manipulate fate just enough to make one of those passersby offer him food. That way he could just keep on walking, and they would have lost no time.

He spotted a woman wearing a large hat, carrying a huge pretzel in her hand. He willed fate to have her reach out and give it to him. Instead, she patted him on the back, looking very surprised that she was doing so. Leven kept walking. He saw a man with a thick, delicious-looking sausage sandwich. It was made out of dark bread and had sauerkraut on it. Leven tried really hard to manipulate fate, but as they passed, the man just handed Leven his used napkin.

Leven tried one last time on a woman who was enjoying some bread and cheese. As she got closer, she smiled, made a fist, drew back her hand, and punched Leven on the chin.

She was as surprised as Leven was.

Leven staggered backward and tried to right himself. His brown eyes saw bleached white stars. Winter turned to see him stumbling and ran to his side.

"I am so sorry," his assailant said, displaying both her remorse and her American accent. "I have no idea what came over me."

Leven eyed her bread and cheese. "Is that mine?" he asked in fake confusion.

"Well, honey, actually . . ."

"I only remember being hungry, " Leven added.

"Well, you just help yourself," the woman said, handing him her food.

Leven smiled weakly as she walked off, shaking her head in disbelief, wondering with her friends about the strange thing she had just done.

"Way to use your gift," Winter scolded.

"I'm starving," Leven defended.

"That doesn't make it right," Winter insisted. "I could think the whole world besides us was ice and we could simply skate to the lake without interference, but that wouldn't be right."

"I can't skate," Leven admitted, taking a welcome bite of his newfound food.

"You know what I mean."

Leven smiled smugly at Winter, his bangs covering his right eye. "I won't do it any more," he chewed. "At least not today. Besides, I still haven't gotten the hang of it. If you hadn't noticed, I just got myself punched."

"Serves you right," Winter said nicely.

They reached the shore of their destination.

The Konigsee was a large, beautiful, blue-green lake surrounded by impressive, pine-covered mountains. It was a jewel in the lush German landscape and a favorite vacation spot for government dignitaries and military officers. On the far shore was St. Bartholomew's, a church that had stood for thousands of years. Day in and day out visitors came to take a boat ride across the lake.

When they reached the center of the lake the motor would be shut off, and absolute silence would descend over the scene. Then a solitary musician would stand on the deck of the craft and play his trumpet. The mountains encircling the lake produced an unbelievably clear and rich echo, which allowed the trumpeter to play a duet of sorts with himself. The performance never failed to move those who heard it. Even the most jaded individuals could not resist the serenity of the setting and the beauty of the music.

Years before, Leven's grandfather, Hector Thumps, had discovered the soothing effect music has on the planet. As he searched for a lake with a constant temperature, he had been delighted to discover the Konigsee and its remarkable mountain echoes. This extraordinary coming together of natural beauty and beautiful music created a mood similar to that a shooting star might stir up.

It was fate.

It was also the most beautiful place Leven and Winter had ever seen.

"So what do we wait for?" Leven asked, looking up at the mountains and taking in the entire view.

"We need to get on a boat," Geth instructed. "It will take us across the lake, and from there we can walk to where we need to go. You can both swim, I hope."

"No!" Leven quickly said.

"Not at all?" Winter questioned. "You swam in the ocean."

"That wasn't swimming," Lev insisted. "That was panicking."

"Well, you'll need to panic yourself down to the gateway," Geth said seriously. "We have no choice."

Leven looked at the huge lake and let the panic begin.

They bought tickets for the boat ride, and with the few Euros left over, Geth had Winter purchase a small pocket knife in case of an emergency. The price of the tickets and the knife added up to the exact amount of money they had left.

It felt sort of fateful.

They boarded the next boat and were soon on their way across the lake. The scenery was spectacular, but as the small boat glided across the green water Leven kept his eyes down, hoping to see the gateway. Unfortunately, the green water didn't reveal anything.

As advertised, halfway across the water the captain turned off the engine and the boat glided to a stop. The passengers quieted themselves and prepared for what was about to happen. It was so still, it was almost as if the entire planet were holding its breath.

An authentic-looking German with a long mustache and lederhosen stood on the deck of the boat and put a trumpet to his lips. He played, and the clear notes drifted across the water. As if answering back, the mountains replied in perfect tune.

The effect was so beautiful it gave Leven chills and caused Winter to tear up. It also left them speechless.

After a couple of songs, the boat started back up and carried everyone to the far shore where St. Bartholomew's stood. Leven and Winter got off and walked back behind the old church. The crowds weren't as dense as those on the other side of the lake, and as Leven, Winter, and Geth moved farther into the woods, the little group soon found itself quite alone.

"So, how does this work?" Leven asked Geth. "What do we do?"

"See those bushes?" Geth pointed to a clump of thick growth farther down the faint trail they were on.

They both nodded.

"We need to wait there until the last boat of the day makes its return trip. On the way back we will get into the water and wait. When the timing is right, we will swim underwater toward a very faint glow. That glow is the gateway. Swim in, touch the mismatched floor, and you will be in Foo."

"That's it?" Leven asked. "No secret knock or challenge?"

"That's it," Geth answered. "You have nothing to be afraid of. Actually, that's not really true. The water is near freezing. The multiple of seven is not always some balmy temperature. Your lungs probably have just enough capacity to make it down. If you don't make it into the gateway, you will most likely not pop back up alive. You can't stop swimming, understand?"

Leven took a moment to inventory his life. Being warned of your potential death by a toothpick can make a person quite reflective.

"What if the gateway is not working?" Leven asked. "What if we get down to it and it's out of order? Or what if the earth's no longer happy?"

"As long as we get in before the effect of the music fades, the gateway will work," Geth said. "If it were breakable it would have been destroyed by Antsel and me years ago. The gateway is unchangeable. It is a perfect creation made unbreakable by the will of your grandfather. It is also the one thing that can destroy Foo and eliminate all dreams. With no one in Foo to bring dreams to life, everyone here would be without hope. This existence would be dark and completely full of despair. Sabine has no idea what his selfish scheme will ultimately bring about."

"So I guess I can't back out now?" Winter asked.

"Back out?" Geth asked, surprised Winter would even say such a thing.

"Well," she said defensively, her head pounding, "I have no idea where we're going. Clover showed me some images, but . . . what if we swim through that gateway and it's worse than this?"

"It's not perfect there," Geth conceded. "It is filled with turmoil and confusion now, thanks to Sabine. But it is a place unlike any you have seen before. You belong there," Geth reminded her. "You chose to come here, but it was only with the promise that you could come back."

"I just wish I could know." Winter's green eyes darkened.

"Listen," Leven said, "I have no idea what's going on. A few weeks ago I was in school, worrying about my aunt's temper and Brick picking on me. Now, here I am, after crossing the world, listening to a toothpick tell me I had better swim fast enough or I'm dead. So, I'm a little confused. But the one thing I'm sure of is that I couldn't have done it without you," Leven said to Winter.

"If not for you, I would have been digested by a giant snake or drowned in an ocean. I wouldn't have even made it across the Oklahoma state border without you, Winter. I can't imagine what we'll find on the other side, but somehow I think it will be okay, if you're around."

Winter and Geth stared at Leven in astonishment.

"Are you okay?" Winter asked, reaching out to touch his forehead.

"Seriously," Geth added. "Maybe that cheese you ate was bad."

"Oh, knock it off," Leven said defensively. "See if I ever say anything nice again."

Winter smiled. "Thanks," she said, her face red. "I couldn't have done this without you and Clover . . . he should be here now."

"It's odd he hasn't caught up to us yet," Geth added.

"I wish we could wait a bit more," Leven said. He looked to the sky as the sun began to settle behind the nearby mountains. "It doesn't feel right to go without him."

"He'll make it back to Foo," Geth said confidently. "If he doesn't, then it is his design to remain here."

The three of them moved into the bushes Geth had indicated and made themselves comfortable on the ground. They were all silent and deep in thought about what lay ahead. Leven looked at everything around him with new eyes—eyes that understood he might never see any of this again.

"You okay?" he finally asked Winter.

"I've never been more scared in my life," she answered.

"Good, me neither," Leven smiled.

ii

Clover had no idea where fate was leading him. He was simply following the feeling inside himself. Sycophants are naturally drawn to their burns—there is a constant pull for them to return to those to whom they have been assigned.

The insulation truck had taken him quite a way. When it began going in a direction contrary to his feelings, Clover had abandoned the truck and hitched a ride in a tour bus filled with American senior citizens. As fate would have it, they were on their way to the Konigsee so they could take some pictures and prove to their friends back home that they were really living. The problem was, Clover felt they were going way too slow. He figured he would help them all out by squeezing in next to the driver's feet and pushing down on the gas pedal.

Clover had never heard such sustained, high-pitched screaming.

The bus flew as the driver frantically tried to slam on the brakes and stay on the road. Clover positioned himself so he could push the brake pedal up with his legs and hold the gas pedal down with his hands. The poor driver had no choice but to accept his fate and simply steer in an effort to keep the bus on the road.

It was a new model bus with a huge engine and lots of power. It sped down the autobahn at breakneck speed with everyone inside screaming and praying. An elderly gentleman with flowing white hair, wearing baggy shorts and dark knee socks, fought the g-forces and worked his way up the aisle of the bus, pulling himself forward by clinging to the seats.

"Stop this bus!" he yelled at the driver.

The driver was too occupied to reply. His main concern was trying to keep the bus on the road. The old man figured the driver just didn't understand English, so he got out his English-to-German dictionary and, while hanging on for dear life with his left hand, tried to look up the words with his right.

"Stopen die auto!"

The driver looked up at him as if he were crazy. "We're all going to die," the driver said in perfect English.

The old man turned back to the rest of the passengers and conveyed the message. Clover once again was amazed by the volume of noise the nice group of senior citizens was able to make.

As they barreled down the road, Clover grew jealous of the others, who were able to look out the window and see the passing scenery. He had grown quite fond of seeing the world fly by while driving himself earlier, and now he wanted to take just one look. When he took his weight off the gas pedal to squeeze out, the driver felt the bus slow and began frantically stomping and kicking at the pedals beneath him in hopes of stopping the vehicle. Caught in the fury of the attempt, Clover took quite a thrashing before he was able to crawl out from under the driver's feet and haul himself up onto the dashboard.

The driver was finally able to get the bus under control, and the passengers began to fan themselves and put their hands to their hearts instead of just screaming.

The bus came to a stop directly in front of a small sign that read: Berchtesgaden.

"That feels right," Clover said to himself. He waited for the driver to open the door and hopped off as if he didn't have a care in the world, happy they had made such good time.

iii

Leven and Winter could do nothing but wait. The last boat would not be leaving for an hour, and Leven was anxious and scared. Wanting to be alone for a moment, he left Winter and Geth in the trees and wandered back down the lakefront and to the small white church with the funny red roof.

St. Bartholomew church was hundreds of years old. It was a small, white cathedral, with big red onion-like domes on top of it. Originally, it had been used as a hunting lodge for great kings. Now, it was more of a photo opportunity for wealthy tourists. Leven wished his eyesight were clearer, but from what he could see he loved the look of St. Bartholomew against the lake and wished his life could be as peaceful as the scene before him. Going to Foo would seem much less of a sacrifice if the gateway had been in a barren desert or in the middle of a congested city.

Leven slipped into the dimly lit chapel and sat down on the back row of pews. A number of tourists wandered about, looking over everything and whispering. Leven turned from gazing at a family with two young kids and noticed a dark being sitting right next to him. He was so startled that he hollered out and jumped in his seat.

"Hello, Leven," the voice said, low and menacing. "*I've* been waiting for you."

Leven's heart was suddenly racing. It was not hard to recognize the rat-like features of Sabine. He looked just like his shadows, only bigger. There was also a dark aura around him.

"You're Sabine," he managed to say.

"Smart boy," Sabine's oily voice dripped. "But not smart enough to take the advice of *my* shadows and forget all this. Now look where you are."

A pair of tourists walked by, conversing loudly.

"Do you mind," Sabine glowered at them. "We're in a church."

The couple gave Sabine a strong look and walked away.

"How did you get here?" Leven asked, trying to keep his mind clear of Sabine's voice and thoughts. "Or are you just a shadow?"

"Oh, *I'm* quite real. *I* came here the same way all of Foo will soon arrive," Sabine said clearly. "Think of it, Leven. With Foo here, there will be nothing you can't do."

"That's impossible," Leven said. "You'll destroy everything."

"There is no impossible," Sabine snapped. "Geth and his self-righteous belief," he scoffed. "The dreams of man are not my concern. If you destroy that gateway, Leven, you will be destroying the possibility of perfect lives for everyone. Geth doesn't want you to know this. Geth wants Foo just as it is, so that he can rule over everyone."

Leven was silent as a few nearby tourists conversed quietly, examining some of the church artifacts. He could hear people outside and knew that life was going on as usual while he had to make decisions that would affect everyone.

Leven squinted. He could see the light from outside as it rested against the far wall. It was dimming quickly. Soon it would be time to swim.

"Think of it," Sabine twitched. "With Foo here, you will have it all. Geth wants to trap you, cut you off."

Sabine's words were not going unheard. Leven had many concerns and fears, and part of them were things Sabine was now addressing. It didn't feel totally right to destroy the gateway and trap himself in Foo forever. What if Sabine's plan were possible? What if the dreams of man were not dependent on Foo? Quite frankly, it scared the life out of Leven to think of destroying his only way back. His time here had not been charmed, but something inside him had given him hope that he could someday become more than he was. It was that hope and dream that had enabled him to go on each day. Leven couldn't let Sabine eliminate that belief for anyone else.

"There is no killing in Foo," Sabine said softly, as if he were sharing bad news. "Here, however, is a different story." A few more tourists filed in. "The moment you swim toward that gateway," Sabine continued, "*I* will kill you. *I* don't care if you have the great Geth with you or not," he mocked. "You touch that water, and *I* will kill you."

The church emptied a bit.

"It's not hard for you to stay alive," Sabine smiled enticingly. "Simply . . . don't swim."

Sabine stood up. "*I* know where the gateway is," he warned. "*I'll* be watching. You go into that water, and *I* will kill you and Winter."

In a sense Sabine was lying. He had no intention of letting Leven live. He contemplated taking care of the problem now, but the church was full of people: Sabine didn't want any further complications.

He smiled a wicked smile at Leven and drifted out.

Leven could hear a woman telling people in broken English that the last boat would be leaving soon and everyone needed to gather at the dock.

Leven slipped out of the church and back into the forest, Sabine watching his every move.

iv

It was October, and the day had been unseasonably warm, but Winter was unusually cold.

"Are you okay?" Geth asked her as the two sat on the ground beneath a couple of beautiful pine trees near the water's edge. A gentle, warm breeze descended on them, coloring the moment beautifully. Water lapped against the shore, and the reflection of the setting sun shimmered across the smooth water.

"I think so," Winter said. "Just frightened beyond belief." She took out the small pocket knife Geth had earlier instructed her to buy. She turned it over in her hand, looking at it with her green eyes.

"It's your home you'll be swimming toward," Geth said kindly. "You made me promise that you'd get back."

"I know," Winter smiled sadly. "At least that's what you've told me."

"I'm just keeping my promise," Geth teased.

"So will we make it?" Winter asked. "What if Leven can't swim fast enough?"

"Oh," Geth waved. "That's not the problem. The problem now is Sabine."

"Sabine?" she gasped.

"He's here," Geth said. "I knew he would get through. I could feel it earlier."

"Where is he?" Winter asked, not surprised in the least.

"Talking to Leven," he said without concern.

Winter stood up quickly. "Let's go," she said frantically.

"Sit down," Geth ordered nicely, patting the ground with his one little arm. "We've done all we can. It's now up to fate. Leven needs to be sure about what he is doing."

"How did you know Sabine is here?"

"We lithens travel by fate. It's important to know what road-blocks might be standing in our way. A soul as deep and dark as Sabine's is not easy to ignore," Geth answered. "Being from Foo, you probably felt him as well."

Winter was silent, her thoughts on so many things. She flipped the knife, turning it over in her hands.

Geth looked at Winter. "There is a little something I was wondering if you could help me with," he said. "I'm a bit embarrassed even to ask, but it seems as if fate moves me to do so."

Winter stared at him with a quizzical expression.

"I had you buy that knife for a reason." He cleared his little hole. "I was wondering if you might slice me another arm. If anything happens I would be much better off with two of them."

"Another arm?" Winter asked.

Geth looked pitiful.

"I guess I could," Winter said reluctantly.

"And could you sharpen my head?" Geth threw in.

"Sharpen your head?"

"It might come in handy," Geth shrugged.

Winter shook her own head. "You had me buy this to cut you up? Won't it hurt?" Winter asked.

"Just a bit," Geth said. "But I'd put up with a lot to have another arm."

"And a sharp head," Winter smiled at him.

Geth climbed up on a large boulder and lay down. Winter picked him up by the feet, and he turned his head to look away. "Are you sure?" she asked one last time.

He nodded.

She sliced slowly and calmly as Geth's body tightened in pain. The wood was hard and there wasn't much to work with. Winter feared she might cut right through. Geth bit down and looked away. Winter finished cutting, and Geth turned back. He moved his new arm and smiled weakly.

"Perfect," he said. "How about some fingers?"

Winter went to work on Geth's fingers and forehead. In a

short while Geth was a whole new toothpick and the sky was almost dark. Leven came through the trees with a concerned look in his eyes and the weight of two heavy worlds on his shoulders.

"So," Winter said. "Are you all right?"

"I'm fine," Leven waved.

"The last boat is all ready to set sail," she added, folding up the knife as Geth wiggled his new fingers.

"I know," Leven said sadly, still thinking of Sabine's last words.

Geth stretched and sprang off the rock and onto Leven. His new arm and fingers made the move considerably easier than it had been before. He flexed his tiny muscles and looked at Leven.

"You spoke to Sabine," Geth said almost reverently.

"How do you know?" Leven asked with shock.

"That's not important," Geth replied. "What matters now is what you believe."

Leven looked at Geth on his arm and then at Winter. Along with Clover, they were the only friends he had ever known. They had done nothing to cause him to disbelieve in himself, but his heart still ached to somehow know for sure that what he was about to do was right.

"I think I believe in you," Leven said. "I just hope I'm right."

"There will be none of that if Sabine gets his way," Geth said, referring to the destruction of hope.

Leven understood.

"Sabine said if I touch the water he will kill us," Leven said, his mind finally made up to do it.

"Sabine says a lot of things," Geth smiled, knowing that what

Leven had just uttered was a declaration of his resolve. "We'll get you to the gateway."

The bell of the last boat leaving sounded.

"I'll push you through the gateway if I have to," Winter added. "I know . . . ," Winter stopped what she was saying to rub her head. "I can hardly speak, my head hurts so . . ."

She would have said more, but she had been turned to ice.

She stood there baffled by her state. She thawed herself and looked over to see that Leven was solid ice. Geth dropped from Leven's frozen shoulder and down to Leven's feet. Winter thought for a second there had been a glitch in her own thoughts and that she had turned Leven and herself into ice by accident, but that thought evaporated quickly when she saw Sabine standing there.

"Sabine," she whispered.

"*I* forgot you were a nit," Sabine said to Winter, referring to her ability to thaw herself. "Where is Geth?" he demanded. "*I* heard him speaking."

Winter froze. Not because she was ice again, but because she realized Sabine didn't know what shape Geth was in. She felt pretty certain Geth's current size would not discourage Sabine, so she kept the truth to herself as she looked down and saw Geth standing behind Leven's frozen left foot.

"He's coming," Winter said, her head burning.

"Coming?" Sabine asked, looking around with concern.

Winter pictured him in ice and Sabine froze. She ran and touched Leven, who instantly thawed. She could hear the sound of the trumpet being played on the last boat of the day out in the middle of the lake. They needed to get into the water.

"Let's get out of here," she yelled to Leven as Sabine began to shake off the ice she had encased him in.

"Not so fast," Sabine sneered.

Leven and Winter turned to face him.

"So you've decided to ignore *me* again," Sabine seethed. "That's a decision you will not live to regret, Leven Thumps."

"We'll see about that," Geth shouted triumphantly.

Sabine looked around, suddenly scared. "Show yourself," he challenged, thinking that Geth was hiding somewhere in the trees.

"I'm right here," Geth answered.

Sabine directed his attention to Leven's sleeve, where Geth was clinging in all his toothpick glory.

"Geth?" Sabine questioned. "Geth? Surely the fates are playing with *me*," Sabine laughed scornfully. "*I* am up against a sliver of wood?"

Geth climbed up to Leven's shoulder and stood as triumphantly as a tiny piece of wood could. "You are up against *fate*."

"Fate?" Sabine scoffed. "You will never reach the gateway. That is your fate," he spat. The joy in his eyes over Geth's current state was very apparent. "Foo and reality will be one. And *I*," Sabine said pompously, "will rule them both."

"Flick me," Geth whispered into Leven's ear.

"What?" Leven whispered back.

"Flick me!"

Leven snatched Geth from his shoulder and flicked him as hard as he could toward Sabine. The little toothpick struck

Sabine in the left cheek with his newly sharpened head, piercing Sabine's skin and flying past him onto the ground beyond the dark figure. Sabine threw his hand to his face and obviously thought of Leven and Winter in ice because they were now just that. He tried to picture Geth in ice, too, but lithens are unaffected by nit tricks.

Winter defrosted and saw Sabine in white, frozen stiff. She held her thoughts there as Geth worked his way back over to Sabine. The concentration became too great. She turned from Sabine to Leven, touching his arms. Geth was already on the now defrosted Sabine. He didn't have much size, but he was creating a pretty good distraction by zipping over Sabine's body and jabbing him over and over. Sabine danced as he swatted with his hands and tried to grab hold of Geth.

The last rays of the sun were touching the edge of the lake. The earth would not remain in a good mood for much longer. Leven ran toward the water, knowing what he had to do. He was too slow, though, and Sabine turned him into ice again. It was like a vicious game of freeze tag, and Leven was always It.

Winter imagined not only Sabine as ice but the trees around him. They froze, and she moved as quickly as she could, slamming into a tall thin tree and breaking it down. It cracked and fell toward Sabine, who was now thawed and moving. Geth was keeping at Sabine just enough to distract him from repeatedly freezing Winter. Winter ran to Leven and touched his shoulder. He thawed in a running stride, heading for the water. As Leven's foot reached the edge of the water, Sabine froze him again. Now a solid chunk of ice, Leven fell forward into the water with a large splash.

"Lev!" Winter screamed before she was suddenly ice again.

Leven drifted out into the lake as Winter returned to form. She looked at Sabine with her eyes burning.

"You can't stop *me*," Sabine sneered at Winter. "You couldn't in Foo, and you can't now."

Images of her life in Foo began popping into her head like slides thrown onto a screen. She could see Sabine smiling. There was the girl with the long red hair. There was a strong-looking man with fire in his eyes.

The thought swept over her. This was not a new fight she was fighting. Her head cleared and her mind relaxed.

Winter shot ice from her being and froze Sabine. She thought hard and long, coating him over and over with thick layers. She wrapped him up until he was nothing but a giant block of ice, as stiff and frozen as his heart.

"It won't hold," Geth yelled.

"I know," Winter hollered back, "but I've got to get to Lev before he starts melting in the water."

Leven had drifted out quite a way from shore. His body bobbed up and down in the emerald green water. Winter turned to run but was ice again. Sabine was melted and at her already. She thawed and faced him once more. Geth was doing everything he could to be a distraction, but his attempt was thwarted by the sudden grip of Sabine.

Sabine smiled and looked at Winter. He glanced deliciously at the toothpick in his hand.

"The great Geth," Sabine sneered. "*I'd* prolong your death, but you being a lithen would simply accept the pain as fate."

Winter lunged forward and froze Sabine. She flicked Geth out of his hands and into the lake before Sabine could thaw and freeze her again. He then did just that and held her in his concentration until her will overpowered him and she was normal once more.

"This is pointless," Winter said, breathing hard. "Let us be."

"Impossible."

"That's not a word," Winter said as naturally as if she really knew it.

"Your precious Leven is melting," Sabine said, an evil smile flickering across his dark face. "Soon there will be no reason for our quarrel."

Winter thought the entire lake ice so as to preserve Leven, and it was.

"Impressive," Sabine hissed, looking out at the frozen body of water. He thought the mountains around them to be ice, and they were.

"Big deal," Winter said, changing the entire landscape around them into ice.

"I will not be outdone by a foolish child," Sabine seethed.

It was at that moment that Winter first saw movement up above Sabine and behind the trees. Sadly, it was too late for Clover to be of any help. Clover looked down from the top of a steep trail, wide-eyed and determined.

Sabine closed his eyes and froze the entire world.

Under his thoughts the whole planet and all that it had on it became solid ice. The earth groaned and the sky lit up with fuzzy stars and color as the planet wobbled. The ground creaked and shuddered as the wind howled painfully, the world crackling in pain.

"You can't defeat *me*!" Sabine roared.

Winter flashed back to the conflict in Foo. She could see Sabine and remembered the struggle she had fought there in her old home. She remembered having to run from Sabine and hide, so she could play the part in retrieving Leven that she was now playing.

Winter's evergreen eyes burned ice cold. The earth was screaming as it struggled to revolve as it was supposed to. The sky grew smeared and wavy. It was to humanity's advantage that Clover was not of this world. Being a sycophant, he was impossible to freeze, thus making him the only thing on the planet that wasn't solid ice. Winter shook herself from her thoughts and watched Clover leap onto the slick trail and slide quickly toward her and Sabine.

It was now or never.

"I'm done with all this," she said aloud, using words she had used before somewhere else. She thought it, and Sabine was ice. Her thoughts were more cold and concentrated than they had ever been.

It was perfect timing.

Before Sabine could return to form, Clover barreled into him from behind. His small amount of weight, combined with his speed, knocked Sabine over and sent him quickly to the ground, where the demon shattered into a thousand pieces of ice. Winter covered her head to avoid the storm, as bits of ice rained down everywhere. She stared at the spot where Sabine had been standing and marveled. She glanced down at Clover as he stood there, looking guilty.

"Oops," Clover said.

The earth creaked and groaned, as if it could not possibly make one more rotation. Winter quickly fell to her knees and touched the ground.

The world was green once more.

No history book has recorded the fact that at one point the entire earth was ice. But those who would argue that point were frozen as well and simply can't recall it. The doubt of anyone doesn't make it any less true. In fact, on those days when it's warm and you suddenly feel a chill, or a part of you feels cold, it's just your body remembering the time it experienced the sensation of being an ice cube.

"I really didn't mean to do that," Clover said, looking at the thousands of tiny pieces of Sabine. "I was just trying—"

"Don't worry about it," Winter spoke. "You may have just saved the world."

Clover smiled.

"So, can you swim?" she asked him.

"Came in second place in Sentinel Fields my senior year," Clover bragged.

Winter would have stood there congratulating him, but instead she took off running toward the lake. She flew into the water and almost lost her breath due to the coldness of it. She held her head above water and gasped for air. Leven was a good distance from the shore, coughing and thrashing. He had thawed upside down and with freezing water rushing into his nose and mouth. Winter swam to him and grabbed him under the right arm.

"We have to swim," Winter hollered at him. "Before it's too late."

"Where's Sabine?" Leven asked, confused, struggling to stay afloat.

"Gone."

"Gone?"

"It was an accident," Clover apologized, while swimming effortlessly up to Leven.

"Clover!" Leven cheered. "You're here."

"Of course," Clover smiled and spit, his forehead covered in goose bumps.

"We need Geth," Winter yelled.

"Right here," Geth answered, paddling over, his new arm working swimmingly.

"Toothpick," Clover said affectionately.

Geth smiled, swam to Clover, and climbed on. "We have to go now the sun is gone. Are you ready?" Geth asked Leven.

"No," Leven replied, smiling tightly and with chattering teeth. "I'm not sure I'll ever be. But I'll do it for the candy alone."

Clover smiled.

V

Sabine was no longer. Actually, he was no longer the personage he had once been. The shattered bits and remnants of who he was lay upon the still earth as the soil turned from ice back into its normal self. The tiny pieces of Sabine melted into the dirt and dripped down deep into the ground. He was now a countless number of shadowy bits. Every piece of him hissed and surged, scurrying through the dirt like a horrid stream of fluid black ants. He could feel the influence of Leven and Winter. They were still here, in the water and swimming toward the gateway. He had no form, but all was not lost. Every particle of him whispered and pushed forcefully under the earth and into the lake, breaking out from the soil and into the Konigsee. Like an explosion of deranged tadpoles he blew out into the water, swirling and pulsating. Leven was in the distance, swimming toward the gateway. Sabine collected every bit of himself into the shape of a rod and shot through the water like a torpedo toward Leven.

VI

Leven took a giant breath and swam down underwater. Geth had been right. The moment his head was below the surface he could see a faint light glowing in the distance. He pulled and kicked as he worked his way deeper and deeper. His lungs burned as a heavy anxiety smothered him. He turned to his side as if to try and resurface, but Winter was there pushing him downward. His chest felt like it was going to explode. He could see the gateway now, its corroded gray sides covered in rust and algae. It glowed bright and ominous. Winter swam by him and into the gateway. He watched her stand on the bottom of the box his grandfather had constructed and in an instant she was gone. Leven pushed forward in an effort to follow her, but before he could get there, his legs were struck by a streak of blackness.

The force of the blow propelled him away from the gateway and toward the surface. Leven spun like a rolling log as he twisted uncontrollably upward. Geth had warned him about not being able to make it back to the surface before his lungs gave out, but at the moment Leven wanted nothing other than to get some air. He was propelled at speeds he had not thought possible, forced upward by the impact of whatever had struck him near the gateway. Leven broke the surface of the water and shot twenty feet into the air. He made a terrific arc through the sky and splashed back down into the lake.

Leven kicked and thrashed, trying to right both his mind and his body. He had no idea what had just happened. Winter was gone and something had expelled him from the water.

Geth and Clover were nowhere to be seen.

Leven would have taken a few moments to seriously contemplate his state of affairs, but his earnest reflection was interrupted by something seizing him by his ankles and dragging him irresistibly down, back under the water. Leven screamed, and his body went rigid as it was hauled downward, deeper into the lake.

Leven willed his mind to concentrate. His eyes burned gold and he could suddenly see the recent past: there was Sabine's dark soul, each tiny fragment melting into the earth. Then Leven's mind showed him the present: millions of fragments of Sabine wrapped around his feet and dragging him to his death. His thoughts shifted, and he got a glimpse of the future: there he was, floating face down on the surface of the lake, his life over.

Never! Leven's mind screamed.

His eyes sizzled as he forced the vision of his death to reverse itself. He wrestled with fate and the future to will himself to live. The future was changing. Leven looked down at the millions of bits of Sabine and used his gift to manipulate them away from his ankles and into oblivion. With one incredibly strong thought, Leven blew Sabine's leftovers away from him. They were dispersed through the water like buckshot from a shotgun blast.

Leven had never felt his gift so strongly. He clawed at the water in an effort to get back to the top, but he was too deep. He would never reach the surface without air. His mind caught hold of fate, and the wind above the Konigsee formed itself into a giant vortex, revolving and boring its way down into the water, creating a funnel of air directly above him. The funnel picked Leven up, filling his lungs with air and spinning him out of the water and into the sky.

Leven was now thirty feet above the lake, twisting like a being in a blender. He might very well have been amazed, but his mind was too busy watching the pieces of Sabine gather and regroup. Like a thick black cloud, Sabine raced in from the north, surrounding the funnel and reaching in with thin, sharp limbs to slice and grab at him. Leven's mind raced with fear. He opened his eyes wide and manipulated the funnel cloud into lifting him higher.

The wind surged upward.

Sabine's remnants followed, swarming like black bees in the funnel around him. Every particle of Sabine hissed and screamed in confusion and hatred. Leven focused his thoughts, his eyes burned, and the tornado exploded, the wind hurling itself into the clouds and peppering them with Sabine's leftovers.

Leven dropped like a rock into the lake.

He hit the water headfirst and shot like a bullet down toward the glow. In an instant he could see the gateway. He twisted his body and plummeted straight toward it. There was no time for hesitation. He reached the gateway and stepped into the bottom of the box his grandfather had made.

Instantly the water disappeared, and Leven was lying on the wooden floor of a small room. He coughed and inhaled as deeply as possible. He couldn't seem to catch his breath. A single candle burned in the far corner. He looked to his left and there was Winter, smiling at him.

"I'm glad you made it," she said.

"Me, too," Geth added, jumping from a nearby table onto Winter's right shoulder.

Clover materialized next to both of them, his big blue eyes almost sparkling. "Welcome home, Lev," he said.

Leven was still breathing hard. He glanced around in amazement, wondering if what he saw was real. "So this is Foo?" he asked, realizing that as solid as everything looked, it did have a different appearance than what he had just left.

Leven got to his feet just as the door opened and a smiling Amelia Thumps stepped into the room.

"You made it," she praised. "I was afraid Sabine might have stopped you. I had no way to keep him from this room when he finally figured out the entrance."

"We made it," Winter smiled in amazement.

"Winter," Amelia said affectionately, taking her in her arms. "Foo has not been the same without you."

Winter's memory came rushing back. Her life in Foo was suddenly an actual memory she could recall. The pieces all fell together. She saw her childhood on earth. She saw where she had been standing when she was snatched and brought to Foo. She saw her home here in Foo and the people and friends she knew. She saw Geth as the king that he really was and Amelia as the kind and unknown defender of true Foo.

Amelia stepped from Winter to look closely at Leven.

"So this is the boy?" she asked Clover, eyeing Leven suspiciously. "Are you sure he's the one?"

"He is," said Clover. "We've seen him do all sorts of odd things."

"I've seen a lot of people do odd things. That doesn't mean they're the one."

"It's Leven," Geth spoke forcefully, ending any doubt.

"Geth?" Amelia asked, bowing slightly as she said it. "You're back?"

"I am," Geth answered.

"You're a little shorter than I remember," she smiled.

"Age has touched your memory," he laughed.

"Well, I must say this is a great day for Foo." Amelia turned to focus on Leven. "We've been waiting for you," she said kindly, opening her arms. "I've been waiting for you. You are my only family."

Leven yielded to her embrace, feeling for the first time in his existence the love of family. Despite all the doubt and confusion and fear he felt, it was right to be here. She held him at arms' length and looked into his eyes.

"I have something for you," she whispered, her voice quivering with emotion and her eyes shining.

Leven envisioned a watch or a photo or some treasured family heirloom. Instead she handed him a round, ceramic-looking pot with enough potch powder in it to blow up the entire house they were standing in.

"This looks like a bomb," Leven said nervously.

"It is," she smiled, patting him on the shoulder. "I've been saving it for years. You need to go back through the gateway with it. Just drop it in the gateway and stand on the crack. You'll be back here, and the gateway will be destroyed," she said casually.

Leven looked at the ceramic pot in his hands. It was red with a purple band spinning around it. On one side there was a one-inch nub sticking out. Above the nub there was a bit of unreadable writing.

"Hurry," Geth whispered.

Leven glanced at the gateway. The colors swirled and spun across the dirt. Leven looked again at the ball in his hands. He glanced at the others. It was one thing to have the courage to travel to Foo, but it was another thing completely to destroy the only exit he had.

"Hurry," Amelia said, echoing Geth's order. "There isn't—"

Amelia's warning was cut short by Clover's sudden scream. Everyone looked to the sycophant to find him pointing toward the gateway. Oozing out of the light were thousands of black dots. They hissed and cackled wickedly, swarming up out of the gateway like a thick virus. In an instant they were on Leven, clinging to him, entirely covering his body. Leven thrashed and stamped his feet, trying in vain to shake them off. Holding onto the explosive, his hands were useless.

Sabine was not done.

vii

Sabine had only one objective. If he could set off the explosive inside of Foo, Leven would be gone and the gateway would be safe from destruction. His thoughts were not clear as millions of crawling pieces of his once-self tried desperately to detonate the ball.

Winter tried to freeze Sabine, but there wasn't enough of him left for the spell to take. Clover leaped onto Leven's head and began kicking and swatting at the swarm of gnat-sized particles of black. The darkness covered Leven completely and then began to subside as every bit of Sabine swarmed over the ball, trying to make it explode. Sabine's remnants clung to the ball, beating it wildly. The detonator sank into the sphere, activating the explosives.

Clover yelped.

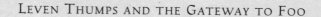

Leven dropped to his knees and dove headfirst into the gateway. His head was instantly in the lake, his legs still remaining and kicking in Foo as Winter tried to get hold of them. His mouth filled with frigid water, and the coldness was a vivid reminder of what he had so recently left. He glanced at the walls of the gateway and down at the floor. He could see the piece of sidewalk and road that didn't match up quite right—the very same spot his Grandfather Thumps had stood on when he started all this. Leven looked at the explosive as he hung upside down with only half his body visible. The ball was covered with what was left of Sabine, every particle of it vibrating frantically. Leven dropped the pot as a noise louder than any he had ever heard shattered his mind.

Darkness engulfed him.

CHAPTER THIRTY-ONE

Foo

Leven felt strange. His body was relaxed, settling like liquid on the floor. His ears were still ringing, and he couldn't see anything but black. He wiggled his fingers to see if he were still alive. He could feel the wood floor. He opened his eyes, surprised to see light. Winter was there smiling at him again.

"Are you okay?" she asked. "We pulled you back."

Leven looked up at Winter and at his grandmother. Clover was on the floor next to Geth. Leven glanced at the dirt of the gateway. There was no glow. Clover approached him and put his hand on his arm.

"Are you okay?"

"I've never been more scared in my life," he answered, getting to his feet, and repeating the words all of them had used at least once.

Winter hugged him as his grandmother did the same. Geth

was caught in the middle so he considered it to be fate and hugged Leven as well.

You may question the importance of what Leven did, but truth be told he made it possible for every dream to continue and every hope to go on—all without a single thanks from anyone.

As Clover cheered, a large gold platter slipped out from his void and clattered noisily onto the floor. Clover blushed and tried to pick it up quickly.

"Where'd you get that?" Winter asked.

"I, uh . . . I sort of borrowed it from those French guys who picked us up in the ocean," Clover said, looking at everyone guiltily. "Is that wrong? Because if someone would have told me that's wrong, I never would have taken it."

Leven smiled again, amazed at where his life had come to.

"All right then," Geth clapped. Of course it wasn't much of a clap, seeing how he had only two little sliver arms. But it was a pretty good click. "We've got to get going."

"Going?" Leven asked. "We're here."

"We've just started," Geth said seriously. "We must get to the Turrets of Foo, and you are the only person who can return me to my rightful state. Did I not mention that before?"

Leven did not smile.

"Sabine may be gone, but the division between good and evil grows. We have to stop those who would destroy Foo," Geth insisted. "Or all that we've done is in vain."

"So we're no better off?" Leven complained.

"Sabine's gone," Winter pointed out, "and the gateway is destroyed."

Leven didn't look as though he was impressed.

"I thought destroying the gateway was our mission," Leven questioned. "Didn't we—"

"Oh, it's just the beginning," Geth interrupted. "Maybe it would help if you take a look at what we'll be saving," Geth said. He jumped off Clover and onto Leven's shoulder.

Leven stood and moved out of the room and down the dark hall. The front door to Amelia's house opened without anyone touching it.

"How did—?" Leven asked.

"Doors know what to do here," Geth explained.

Leven stepped out of the house and into Foo and knew, without a doubt, that he was dreaming. He had never seen anything like what he now saw. Not only that, but he could see it clearly; his sight was perfect. Mountains and valleys and rivers and foliage filled his view, but they were nothing like those he had just left behind in reality. The sky was bright yellow near the ground and purple at its crown. Creatures he had never seen, and would have been unable to imagine, ran across prairies of long orange grass that blew in the wind. He could see incredible darkness to the north, and behind that darkness, thin pointed mountains that looked as if they were moving. A river of deep blue water spilled across his view, creating waterfalls in at least twenty places. The clouds were shaped differently, the air seemed to glisten, and if Leven wasn't completely wrong, he could have sworn he saw a person flying in the distance.

"Wow," he gasped.

"Not a bad view," his grandmother said, putting her hand on his shoulder. "But it's nothing compared to some of the other sights you'll see here."

"I can see everything so clearly," Leven whispered happily.

Geth cleared his wooden mouth. "Now what we must do is get to the other end," he said kindly. "Of course, that should be no big deal to you."

"Is Winter coming?" Leven asked, still looking out at the miracle landscape in front of him.

"Of course," Winter said.

"And Clover?"

"You are my burn," he replied, a gold goblet slipping out of his robe.

He blushed.

Leven took another long, clear look at his new home and his next journey.

"Can I sleep before we begin?" he pleaded.

"I think we can fit that in," Geth answered. "Heaven knows you're going to need to be rested."

Leven went back into Amelia's house and to a short couch that sat in front of a huge roaring fire. The fire was not only burning, it was also singing softly. The couch wasn't long enough to sleep on, but Leven didn't care. He lay down and stretched out his legs, and as he did so the sofa lengthened to accommodate him. He looked at the couch and then back at all those still standing there.

"Pretty cool," Leven admitted, closing his eyes as he said it.

"That's nothing," Amelia whispered, stepping up and laying a blanket over him.

Leven would have said thanks, but he was out cold.

Clover tisked affectionately. "That's my little human."

Geth smiled at Clover. "Keep trying."

The fire sang softly and the windows dimmed nicely as Leven experienced his first dream in a place where there was nothing but.

PRAISE FOR *LEVEN THUMPS* AND THE GATEWAY TO FOO

◆

A Texas Bluebonnet Master List Selection

Book Sense Winter 2006–2007 Children's Picks List

★ "Splendidly unpredictable plot twists. . . . [With] deliciously menacing monsters, equally delicious turns of phrase, and sly riffs on everything from pop music to Harry Potter, the author sends Leven Thumps and company on a long, strange trip, culminating in a literally explosive climax."
—*Kirkus Reviews*, starred review

"Excellent . . . palpable excitement and suspense. Kids and adults will enjoy this charming tale of good and evil."
—*Publishers Weekly*

"This rollicking, suavely told tale should captivate readers."
—*Bulletin of the Center for Children's Books*

LEVEN THUMPS

AND THE WHISPERED SECRET

◆

OBERT SKYE

ILLUSTRATED BY BEN SOWARDS

Aladdin Paperbacks

New York   London   Toronto   Sydney

LEVEN
THUMPS
AND THE WHISPERED
SECRET

OBERT SKYE

ILLUSTRATED BY BEN SOWARDS

*To the few who let me fall and then
offered me a way of redeeming myself.
May my words help the cause.*

LEVEN THUMPS
AND THE WHISPERED SECRET

CONTENTS

Contents

CONTENTS

GUARDED BORDER

PILLARS OF RANT

ICE CAVES

GREEN POND

SUN RIVER

MORFIT

FUNDRALS OF FOO

SWOLLEN FOREST

HARD BORDER

LIME SEA

DER

SENTINEL FIELDS

FISSURE GORGE

TERRITORY OF GETH

NITEON

CORK

UP
U
B — O
BACK   OVER
D
DOWN

VEIL SEA

THE LAND OF
FOO

SYCOPHANT RUN

TAKING CHARGE

Jamoon stood still, as stiff as a petrified plank in the dead of winter, the blood in his veins pulsing slowly. The air inside the cave felt brittle, like paper-thin glass that the slightest movement would crack and split. He closed his gray right eye and exhaled slowly, his frosty breath forming a foggy wreath around his robed head. In his right hand he held a long, wooden kilve, a weapon that harnessed power from dreams. He looked about but could see little in the darkness of the rocky cavern.

Still, Jamoon waited. He inhaled deeply, drawing the frozen fog back into his lungs.

"It's been hours," Jamoon complained. "Many hours."

Sabine and his shadows had left long ago to visit Amelia and to try to find the gateway. Jamoon had been ordered to remain in the cave and wait. He shifted from leg to leg and muttered to himself.

"Always second," he grumbled.

A Lore Coil had rippled over Jamoon hours before, filling his head with images and information. The explosion that had destroyed the gateway into Foo had created the Lore Coil—a wave of noise and images that radiated outward, traveling across Foo, feeding bits of information to anything it passed over. When the coil reached the borders of Foo, it would rebound and reverberate back to its epicenter, the clarity of its information weakening with each diminishing wave. Most inhabitants of Foo would not consciously perceive anything after the second pass—except for the Sochemists of Morfit, who spent their days listening for coils and debating the meaning of the information that continued to ripple across Foo.

Jamoon had detected the new Lore Coil on its first pass. He had heard the coil chattering about Leven Thumps, and Jamoon had seen an image of Winter. Jamoon had known Winter from before, and even though she appeared somewhat different in the static waves of the coil, there was no mistaking her green eyes. The coil had also spoken of Amelia Thumps and how she was now harboring Geth. The ripples of the Lore Coil hadn't clearly shown Geth's condition, but they seemed to indicate that he had somehow become small and vulnerable. Jamoon scowled, his half-heart filled with anger and fury. The hatred Sabine had felt for Geth was equally strong with Jamoon.

Jamoon had heard the waves of the Lore Coil exposing

Leven's condition, whispering that Leven and his band of friends had become susceptible to death. Leven had cheated fate by slipping into Foo through the gateway. Because of that, he could be killed.

That was good news. Unlike so many others who couldn't be killed in Foo, Leven, Winter, and Geth were vulnerable and could be eliminated.

"Foolish child," Jamoon said aloud, thinking of Leven.

The Lore Coil had also let Jamoon know that Sabine was still alive. Jamoon was both frightened and relieved by the news. He now stood still, dutifully awaiting his master's return.

Jamoon was a rant and very tall—well over six feet, with the right half of his body in the form of a strong and muscular human. His left side, however, was unstable, continually morphing into the shape of the dreams that someone in Reality might be experiencing. As a rant, Jamoon lacked the ability to resist or shape those dreams, and his constantly changing half was in perpetual conflict with his normal self. At the moment Jamoon's left-hand side had assumed the shape of a Brazilian soccer player, expertly dribbling a ball with that one foot. However, Jamoon's entire form was shrouded in a black robe, and the conflict he was experiencing was visible only in the constant gyrations underneath the thick fabric.

Jamoon was extremely uncomfortable, and as his right and left sides strained against each other, his body creaked in the frigid air. He shivered violently, the cold of the cave having seeped into the marrow of his bones.

His frosty breath ascended to the ceiling of the cave. "Come, Sabine," Jamoon whispered. "Where are you?"

In the distance a mournful howl sounded. It grew louder. Alarmed, Jamoon raised his kilve as if to fight. The noise became clearer, but the darkness kept it a mystery. Jamoon lifted his kilve higher and scratched its tip against the ceiling like a match. The friction made a shrill screech and caused the end of the kilve to glow. Jamoon quickly used the white-hot tip to draw a circle around himself on the floor of the cave for light. The completed arc glowed brightly, illuminating the walls and ceiling of the cave with pale images of old dreams that had been held in the kilve. In the light of the glowing circle Jamoon could see bits of black as they rippled across the ground. The blackness stopped outside the glowing circle, hissing and screaming as though tormented. Jamoon looked on in disbelief and shivered for a whole new reason. At his feet writhed the surviving pieces of Sabine.

"Master?" he questioned.

The black bits did not answer. The explosion of the gateway had blown Sabine apart, leaving nothing but a few hundred tiny specks of him in Foo. Those bits recoiled from the circle of light, back toward the entrance of the cave, compelling Jamoon to follow. Reluctantly, he stepped out of the light and dumbly obeyed, watching as the remains of Sabine snaked through the long, thick neck of the cave, weaving and sliding as though being controlled by some magnet below the soil.

Jamoon followed.

Sabine's dark remains exited the cave and swirled out into the open. The bright, square sun was just beginning to sink in Foo, and in the rapidly diminishing daylight, the surviving bits of Sabine were screeching angrily.

Outside the cave, just twenty feet away from its entrance, stood a fantrum tree whose branches were filled with nihil birds. The ugly fowls were frantically pecking at and devouring specks of old dreams. Those dreams had entered Foo, but upon leaving they had dusted the leaves and the ground surrounding the tree. The nihils were incredibly dirty birds. Black as rot, they did nothing but consume the residue of once-good dreams. They would peck feverishly at trees and soil until the branches were devoid of leaves and the ground was barren. Their call sounded remarkably like a wet cat being wrung out by someone with very large hands. As pestlike and insignificant as they were, this particular gathering of nihils was about to become something much more bothersome and significant.

The leftover bits of Sabine screamed and writhed on the ground, the noise attracting the attention of the nihils. Instantly, every last filthy bird swooped down and began to feast greedily upon the few remaining tidbits of Sabine.

Jamoon gaped in horror at the frenzied sight, his good right eye twitching uncontrollably.

"Foul!" the soccer half of him hollered.

Jamoon stamped at the ground and swung his kilve, but the nihils were not afraid. The birds simply scattered and immediately took to the sky, circling Jamoon in the dusky light of fading day. In a few moments all the nihils had finished eating and were soaring high overhead, their raucous calls creating an ugly din in the gathering darkness.

Jamoon looked to the soil but could see nothing remaining of Sabine. He shivered as the disappearing sun withdrew its warmth and the nihils continued to circle, swooping lower with each pass. Soon the birds were inches above Jamoon, hovering around his robed head. Jamoon looked up as the ugly birds began to falter in their flight, losing control of their wings and fluttering desperately. The birds belched and screamed in pain. Apparently they had eaten something that didn't agree with them.

The Sabine in them was taking a toll.

One by one and ten by ten the nihils plummeted to the ground, landing with dusty thuds. Jamoon covered his head as the flock of dead fowl rained around him. In a couple of minutes every last one of them had collapsed, heaped around Jamoon like a pile of matted fur.

Jamoon brushed one of the soiled carcasses off his head and shoulders. His breathing was heavy, and he could smell the stench of the dead nihils. He looked around.

"Sabine is dead," he whispered, and a thin smile appeared on the right side of his mouth.

The soil beneath the dead nihils hissed.

"Goal!" the left half of Jamoon yelled.

The soil hissed again, and the dead bodies of the nihils began to flutter and twitch. The spastic motion continued for a few moments, after which the dead birds began to rise. The nihils were very much expired, but thanks to their fermenting final meal, their dark bodies were moving.

Slowly at first, then more rapidly, hundreds of dead black birds rose from the ground. They beat their wings and took to the air, screaming and swirling in a dark cloud about Jamoon's head and hovering over him. There was no soul in them, but the final evil traces of Sabine caused their muscles and wings to still burn and react.

Jamoon pointed toward the birds and moved his right hand forward. The nihils moved as instructed. Jamoon lowered his hand, and the dead birds swooped to the ground and began to tear at the soil with their talons, furiously clawing at the earth.

Jamoon raised his hand, and the nihils rose and circled in a large black cloud behind him.

Jamoon liked the feeling of power. His right side smiled. Sabine was dead, but in his dying he had given Jamoon a powerful tool in the fight to merge Foo and Reality. Jamoon had the loyalty of the many armies of rants and those who fought to escape. Jamoon also possessed the secrets and traditions Sabine had instilled in him. He was a rant, but Sabine had shown Jamoon great things. Sabine had trusted him more than he trusted any other, and Foo knew this. Those in dark power would have no trouble aligning themselves with him. Jamoon could continue the battle to mesh his world with Reality, to take the power and gifts of Foo and rule the physical world, a world that wasn't even aware of Foo's existence or of the sacrifices of its inhabitants. Jamoon believed that if Foo and Reality were merged he would finally be whole.

"No longer second," Jamoon breathed.

Jamoon turned back toward the cave, motioning the dead nihils to follow. The hordes of tattered and filthy-looking birds obeyed his will and swirled about him. Their obedience gave Jamoon a feeling of great confidence and power. It was as if he were soaked in the wicked essence of Sabine.

Jamoon moved into the cave and down toward the deeper tunnels and caverns where the roven farms were. He needed to send the rovens to take care of Leven and Winter. He also needed to rally the Ring of Plague to help him find and destroy Geth.

The battle for Foo was far from over.

CHAPTER ONE

LET 'ER RIP

A thin, yellow light trickled through the window, lighting the room like a funeral parlor or like a restaurant wanting to hide its uncleanliness and save on electricity. Framed by the room's only window, a giant cube of sun melted in the purple sky and large, oval-shaped flocks of Tea birds cawed and whistled through the air as they returned to the Swollen Forest. In the distance, Morfit's highest mountain jutted above the horizon, its twin black peaks ringed by thinning patches of marsh-colored hazen, looking like two burnt fingers wrapped in dirty gauze.

Most residents in Foo were settling into their homes and hideaways, preparing to receive the incoming dreams night would bring. The air was quiet and dry, and the last whistle of the Tea birds faded. The trees had folded their branches and tucked their crowns down, like reprimanded soldiers who couldn't bear to look their commanding officer in the eye. As the landscape dimmed, Foo felt empty, showing no signs of life.

Amelia Thumps stood inside her home, gazing out the window at the darkening view of Foo's sleeping countryside. It was beautiful, and the evening felt as inviting as a warm bed after a long day. But Amelia knew it was not entirely peaceful. She could see there was no one about and nothing happening; still, she could sense something brewing on the horizon. She pushed her thick glasses up on her old, prunelike nose and sighed.

"So silent," she murmured to herself. "So quiet."

Amelia felt certain that if she were to sneeze, it would be heard as far away as Cork.

Amelia looked out the window with purpose. She had experienced enough in her life to know when things were about to change. She shook her head, wishing she could shake off the bits of dread in her heart.

"I'm too old for this," she muttered. "Much too old."

As Amelia stood gazing out the window, Leven was sleeping soundly a few feet away. The room was large, with clean, clay-tiled floors. Heavy, dark beams of wood spanned the ceiling, and the fire in the large stone fireplace was casting dancing shadows onto the walls. In the center of the room was a beautiful table that Hector Thumps had crafted many years before out of the wood of a fantrum tree. Amelia reached out and lovingly ran her hand along the edge of the table.

"Hector," she whispered, the touch of the wood reminding her of the husband she had lost so long ago.

Amelia sighed deeply and bent forward with her shoulders

slumped. Her old bones whined like ancient hinges on a heavy door.

Amelia looked at Leven.

She had always supported the dreams of mankind, but now she was having second thoughts. For the first time in a long while she felt that she had something she could lose.

Winter's soft snoring pulled Amelia from her thoughts. The young, wild-haired girl was sound asleep, lying on a long, feather-covered bench at the opposite end of the room. Amelia glanced again through the window and then turned back into the room, her face solemn and drawn, like a horse that had just learned the world was out of feed. She looked down at the thin sliver of wood lying on the large table. Stepping over, she bent down and poked it with her finger. The sliver awoke, blinked, and smiled up at her.

"A toothpick, huh?" Amelia said. "The great Geth now a needle of wood."

"I was as surprised as you are," Geth yawned. "Fate took me where it would."

Geth sat up and stretched his two thin arms. He flexed the tiny fingers Winter had carved for him and patted his pointed head. He blinked his eyes and looked down at the body and legs fate had given him. He was a toothpick, but he was here.

"It's not going to be easy," Amelia said sternly. "Getting you restored. You know, I hate to say it, but it might not be possible."

"Don't be foolish," Geth responded.

"Reprimand the young," Amelia said, waving him off. "I'll always speak my mind. The truth is, they will hate him like they hate you. The second Leven steps out of here he will have many enemies. The good cower in fear while the selfish move forward with the unraveling of Foo. And you will be sought after by many. Sabine might be gone, but Jamoon will never let you be restored to everything you were."

"We'll make it," Geth insisted. "You know the end. A person as stubborn as you would have nothing to do with this if you did not believe in the end."

Amelia was silent for a moment. Her eyes, looming large through the deep lenses of her heavy glasses, looked pitch black.

"They have been stealing gifts," she finally said.

"What?" Geth said, opening his small eyeholes as wide as he could.

"I have seen many who have had their gifts stolen," she whispered. "Sabine's desire was to transfer the gifts, but I don't think they have that part down yet. Some nits give their gifts up freely for the promise of being left alone."

"I don't believe it," Geth declared, his soul tightening.

"Believe it," Amelia said quietly. "There is talk of Winter having been involved with some of it during her studies with Sabine, years ago."

"Any help she gave Sabine was inadvertent. I know her soul," Geth said. "Look what she's done for Leven."

"I'm just reporting what I hear," Amelia said. "So, does Leven know about his . . . condition?"

"He has no idea," Geth replied.

"He will soon," Amelia said. "I think the destruction of the gateway created a Lore Coil. There is a great silence out there, as if a strong coil has passed over."

"Then we must travel fast," Geth said. "I have to get to the turrets and be restored."

"And Winter?"

Geth looked toward Winter as she slept. "She cannot be restored. Without Antsel, it's impossible."

"I never thought I'd hear you say that word," Amelia smiled. "Your time in Reality seems to have changed you." She looked at Geth closely. "You do seem different."

"I'm just as I was," he insisted mildly. "But I have to tell you . . ." Geth stopped talking and looked carefully around the room. "Clover?" he called softly. "Clover?"

Amelia looked about as well.

"Clover, I know you're here," Geth said, narrowing his eyes.

Clover appeared, red-faced and clinging to Amelia's arm. He was about twelve inches tall with gray hair all over his body except on his elbows, face, and knees. He wore a shimmering robe and a constant expression of mischief. His big blue eyes shone brightly in the dim light, and his leaflike ears fluttered softly. Leven was his burn, and he was a sycophant, one of the most important and magical things about Foo.

"I wasn't listening," Clover promised. "I thought I saw something on her shoulder." Clover brushed Amelia's sweater. "I'm sure it was just a bit of lint or something. I guess you're not big on housekeeping."

Geth and Amelia stared at him.

5

"Oh, all right," Clover admitted. "I heard you mention Antsel, and I couldn't help listening."

Geth smiled, then whispered, "Listen, we've got to get to the fire in the turrets. I must be restored. We can gain the advantage if all that was taken from me can be reclaimed. But if a Lore Coil has communicated our condition, we could be in for a challenge. We can only hope that Jamoon's forces misunderstand or don't receive the message. We cannot—"

Geth was interrupted by a loud wailing noise coming from outside. High above Amelia's home the sky screamed, sounding like every key of an organ being simultaneously pounded. Clover disappeared, and across the room Winter stirred slightly.

Pwwwwump! Skarrrrettt!

Something heavy fell onto the thatched roof, shaking the entire home.

Pwwwummp! Pwwwummp!

There was another thump and another thud and another bang. The noise was followed by the sound of violent scraping and scratching from above. Broken bits and pieces of the ceiling began to rain down. Winter awoke and sat up. The long-sleeved blue shirt and jeans she had on were covered in debris. Winter's green eyes were as wide as lily pads.

"What's that?" she cried, pointing at a huge hole in the ceiling where thick, leathery claws were scratching and ripping their way in. Winter looked at Leven, who remarkably was still sleeping on the couch.

"Lev!" she yelled. "Lev!"

The fire, which had only moments before been singing to Leven, began to echo Winter's scream like a trained parrot. "Lev! Lev! Lev!"

Other giant holes appeared all over the ceiling as numerous claws tore through the wooden roof. Amelia grabbed Geth from off the table.

"Looks like they've heard you're here," she said, shoving the great king behind her right ear. "We can't let them find you." She ran toward Leven, but a giant roven dropped down from the ceiling, landing in front of her and blocking her progress.

The roven was huge and hairy with wide copper wings. It had large, swirling eyes and a thick, hooked beak. Screaming at a decibel level unsafe for most eardrums, it grabbed Amelia's arm with its talons and tossed her aside. She landed in a heap on Leven.

Confused and still half asleep, Leven struggled to sit up as Amelia tried to lift herself off of him.

"What's happening?" Leven asked.

"The rovens are here," was Amelia's only reply.

Leven looked around, not certain if what he was seeing was real or a dream. He was new to Foo and still unsure of what to believe. The white T-shirt he had bought in France and his blue jeans were rumpled from the small amount of sleep he had gotten. He touched Amelia's couch with his hand, trying to convince himself he was awake.

Unfortunately, he was, and it was *raining* rovens.

The large, hairy beasts poured through the holes in the torn-up roof and ceiling by the dozens. They had different colors of hair and long, thick, talonlike fingers. They flapped their coppery wings and cawed like a murder of mutated crows. Some were roosting on Amelia's furnishings, while others surrounded Leven and Amelia on the couch, pressing their heavy bodies into them. Winter was on the opposite side of the room, boxed in a corner.

The fire was screaming.

A fine silt of wood and grass from the demolished roof filled the air. Winter counted the rovens and focused her glance as if to work her gift. Unfortunately, fate had other plans. A thick wooden beam dropped from the ceiling, knocking Winter in the back of the head and sending her sprawling onto the floor.

"Winter!" Leven yelled, as a roven seized him by the arm.

Amelia pushed through two big rovens, yelling, "Stop this!"

The rovens cawed menacingly as Amelia knelt down by Winter and checked for life. Winter was breathing, but she was out cold.

Amelia threw a frightened glance at Leven.

A few of the larger rovens leapt back up to the ceiling and began to bite and tear and pull at one of the biggest openings. Moments later they dropped down and backed away.

Leven was looking up at the opening, peering through it at the purple sky, when his view outward was suddenly obscured by the shadow and shape of a giant roven descending into the room. Leven had never seen a roven before, much less a roven of such massive size. The menacing creature was more than twice Leven's height, and its huge, copper wings grew directly from its shoulders

and along its gigantic arms. The wind from its thick wings swept through the room as the roven settled itself. Its entire body was covered with bright orange hair, and a pair of small, hooded, yellow eyes glared out from its fierce-looking face. The hair covering its body was so bright, it was hard to look at it directly. Braided around the roven, like a loose harness, were two thick, leathery bands that crossed in an X in front. The roven's chest was thick and wide like an ape's, but in every other point the creature resembled a mutated raven.

As the giant roven settled heavily onto the floor of the cottage, the other rovens in the room all lowered their heads in deference and spread their wings wide in a bow. The ugly leader opened its beaklike lips and emitted a triumphant bellow, then closed its huge mouth with a resounding clack.

The fire fainted.

Leven was shaking. He had stepped into Foo with the hope that things would be calm and safe. What he was staring at now was anything but.

"Look at my roof," Amelia demanded, talking to the rovens as if they were just a gang of bothersome kids who had cut across her prized lawn. "I'm not fixing that. And what have you done to Winter—"

The orange roven turned on Amelia and roared, distorting the old woman's lips, nostrils, and wrinkled forehead with the force of its cry.

Amelia pulled Winter into her lap.

The lead roven sniffed loudly. It beat its wings and turned to face Leven. It screeched in Leven's face, giving Leven a good whiff of what it had eaten earlier. Judging by the smell, that was something meaty and well past its expiration date.

The roven strutted around in a circle and flapped its wings. It peered under the table and behind furniture, as if searching for something. After a couple of minutes it turned back to Leven, roaring menacingly and covering Leven's face with spit.

Leven was too frightened to even wipe it off.

The orange roven bellowed again and flapped its mighty wings, signaling the rovens around it to move into action. Like robots they arranged themselves into two lines, one along either side of the large room, pushing any furniture out of the way and creating a barrier between Leven on one side and Amelia and Winter on the other. The speed with which they moved and the precision of their formation was amazing, and Leven watched in awe as each found its place and stood at attention. Those rovens who couldn't find a place in the room began to scratch and scream and push out into the open, extending the line outside the house.

Leven dashed from the couch and broke through the line of rovens. The big birds were too occupied with getting into formation to pay any attention to him. Leven knelt down by Amelia, who was sitting on the floor, holding the unconscious Winter in her lap.

"What are they doing?" Leven gasped, his body shaking. "There are so many."

"They're diggers," Amelia spat.

"This could be interesting," Geth whispered, speaking up from behind Amelia's ear.

Once they were all lined up, the rovens began to dig furiously at the ground. There were hundreds of them, and their sharp, leathery talons ripped through the flooring of Amelia's home and into the rich soil as easily as a child spooning a trench in a sand-box. Dirt flew everywhere as the rovens' talons spun violently. The trench they created was long and deep, and in a few moments most of them had dug so far down Leven couldn't see them.

The giant orange roven was still in the room, its yellow eyes trained on Leven and its wide copper wings stretched out as if to hide the chasm the rovens were creating. It glared at Leven, smil-ing as wickedly as its beaklike mouth would allow.

Leven needed his gift of seeing and manipulating the future to kick in. He tried to clear his mind and get an idea of what was happening. If he could see what was coming, he thought he might be able to manipulate it to his advantage. It was a nice idea, but it was too late. His eyes stayed brown. Besides, the dan-ger was now, not in the future, and there was nothing any of them could do about it.

Finally, the orange roven clamped its wings shut, stepped backward, and dropped down into the trench the others had dug.

All noise faded as the roven disappeared.

Leven looked at Winter. Her eyes were closed, and her breathing was shallow. Her blonde hair hung wildly around her pale face. Leven shook his head; he couldn't seem to focus his thoughts. He had entered Foo with the understanding that it would be a marvelous place filled with endless possibilities. He had thought the main challenge would be to get here. Now, as he looked around, he felt just the slightest bit misinformed.

The air remained still. For all the fuss and fanfare the rovens had made dropping in, it now seemed as though they had simply dug themselves into the earth and vanished.

Leven was amazed at the size of the trench they had created. It was as wide as the room and extended in both directions out either end of the house. Leven could see the large table that had once been in the middle of the room teetering on one edge of the gap.

Leven fell to his stomach and began to inch closer to the large trench the rovens had dug.

"Shouldn't we be running away instead of crawling toward it?" Clover asked, materializing on Leven's back as he crawled.

"I don't—" Leven reached the edge of the trench and stopped talking. Looking down, he groaned deeply.

There was no sign of any rovens, and the trench was so deep and so dark that Leven couldn't see the bottom. Clover jumped off Leven's back to stand beside him, and the two of them peered into the abyss. They looked to the left where the dark void stretched out as far as they could see. They looked to the right and could see no end of the trench in that direction, either. It reminded Leven of a thin, dark, evil version of some huge, ungrand canyon.

"This can't be good," Leven said breathlessly.

Clover leaned forward over the edge, staring into the darkness.

"Dumb birds," he spat. "I have half a mind to jump down there and sink my teeth into them. Who's going to clean up this mess?"

Amelia shifted Winter from her lap and crawled over next to Leven. She peered over the edge with Geth still behind her ear.

"Fascinating," Geth observed.

All of them gazed down into the endless dark.

"Maybe we should . . ." Leven began.

Leven wasn't going to say anything profound or offer up any real solution. He was simply going to suggest something like, "Maybe we should back up," or, "Maybe we should get away from the edge before anyone falls in." But, for all any of the others ever knew, he may have been about to say something that would have been wise and useful, an observation they could have used to buoy their spirits and work toward a hopeful solution and a plan of action.

Either way, it didn't make a difference.

Leven's words were interrupted by the guttural screeching of hundreds of rovens streaming up from the deep, dark crevice they had dug. The large fowls erupted from the darkness like a geyser of colorful, howling demons.

Leven, Clover, Amelia, and Geth didn't even have time to turn away before the rovens were right below them, latching onto the sides of the trench and clinging to the walls.

Leven spotted the huge orange roven. The beast's yellow eyes glowed with hate as it looked directly at Leven and screeched one last time. Then the wings upon the rovens' shoulders and arms began to shift and spin. They whirled together, creating a tremendous fan. Their spinning wings propelled them forward against the sides of the trench they were clinging to. The thrust of their wings was so great that the trench began to expand. It took Leven a moment to realize what they were doing, but before he could inform his friends, Geth hollered, "They're widening the rip!"

The ground groaned as it was being wrenched open, and Amelia's house began to splinter and break apart. Leven felt the soil crumbling beneath him as the walls of the trench collapsed and the ground began to slough off into the chasm. Leven and Amelia each grabbed one of Winter's hands and dragged her through a collapsing doorway into Amelia's small, ivy-covered kitchen.

The kitchen was made of stone, with rock counters and green, mossy growth on all the walls. A large window above a sink showed off the now-darkened landscape of Foo. As the house vibrated, the wooden bowls on the counter rattled to the counter's edge and fell to the floor with a resounding clump, and the kitchen walls began to buckle. Everything was out of focus and jiggling.

The fire in the fireplace regained its strength and began to scream in fear, wrapping itself around any beam or structure it could reach. As it screamed, it emitted fat puffs of smoke.

The large window above the sink blew inward, showering them in a storm of glass. Winter was still out, and the glass littered her hair like diamonds as Leven and Amelia held her up. The floor in the kitchen began to tip and slide toward the rovens' rip.

"We have to get out of here!" Leven yelled, dusting crystals of glass from his forearm and wishing the gateway were still accessible so they could simply return to Reality.

They turned to run, holding Winter's arms, but were stopped by the appearance of more rovens standing in formation behind the lead orange one. As Foo continued to shake, the rovens pushed into the kitchen. Fire lit the scene behind them, and Leven could taste the smoke and dust that hung in the air.

The lead roven looked directly at Leven and screeched.

Behind the rovens and through the kitchen door Leven could see what looked to be the entire landscape sliding violently into the gigantic rip the rovens had created. The fire screamed as part of it was dragged down into the trench.

The noise was deafening. Leven stumbled, trying to find his footing, barely able to stand due to the shaking of the ground.

"They can't kill us, right?" Leven yelled to Geth. "There's no killing in Foo?"

"There are things worse than death," Geth yelled back, offering no comfort whatsoever.

"Some wisdom!" Clover screamed from Leven's right shoulder.

"They're trying to suck us into the chasm they've created," Amelia yelled. "We'll wish we were dead if the gunt gets us."

Leven could think of few things worse than being trapped in the pit the rovens had just torn. And gunt? He didn't even want to know. Leven had spent so little time in Foo that his mind was not yet capable of imagining some of the brilliant and clever and amazing things Foo and its inhabitants could be capable of.

The orange roven threw its head back and flapped its huge

wings. It screeched like a heavy train throwing on all its brakes at once. The rovens beside it did the same. They shook and convulsed in an uneven dance, their wings spinning, their faces puckering in pain. Two seconds later the thick, colorful hair upon their bodies began to fall out in clumps. It dropped to the ground in patches and strips, exposing their white, naked bodies beneath. The hair piled heavily on the ground, surrounding their talons and creating colorful mounds all over the kitchen.

The lead roven continued to glare at Leven. It still seemed powerful, but it looked ashamed of its hairless body. It glanced away and quickly flapped upward through the now-missing ceiling and roof. The other rovens followed its example, pushing off the ground and out into the evening sky. The chasm outside the kitchen was still pulling everything down and under, growing larger every second.

"Watch out for the hair!" Geth warned. "If we're separated, get to the turrets."

Leven wanted to reach for Geth, but the piles of hair the rovens had shed began to swirl and rise, filling the air. Clover materialized, holding a comb. He threw the comb to Leven. Leven looked at the purple comb in his hand and wondered if his life could get any more confusing. He suddenly missed Burnt Culvert, Oklahoma. He missed his school and the normalcy of it. He even missed knowing that, as bad as tomorrow might be, he pretty much knew what was coming and had developed a way of coping with it.

The hair the rovens had shed was swarming now, forming a thick cloud that was swirling toward Leven like a tornado.

"Part it!" Clover screamed, waving his own comb in front of himself. "Part it!"

There was no time for that. The hair was flying through the air and crawling across the floor. Thick handfuls surrounded Leven, smothering his scream, dragging him to the ground, and rolling him toward the edge of the chasm. The cloud of swirling hair pushed up his pant legs and down his shirt, filling his ears and nose. He felt as though he were being rolled up in a giant sheet of hairy sandpaper. Out of his right eye he could see Winter, still helpless, being dragged across the ground by another cloud of hair. He knew that Geth and Amelia were most likely experiencing a similar fate.

Hair filled Leven's mouth and gagged him, smothering his terrified screams. He was powerless to resist. He was going over the edge. He tried to yell again, but it was too late.

The entire house was sliding into the expanding chasm. The fire had gone from screaming to running, grabbing at anything it could hold. A roven got in the way, and the fire twisted itself around its neck, choking the life out of it and setting its wings aflame.

The remaining bits of house gave in. Walls tumbled and folded into the dark void as the rip swallowed everything near its edge. The great chasm was now a mile wide and growing longer and wider with each second.

Leven kicked and screamed, but the hair dragging him was too strong. The funnel cloud of hair carried Leven over the chasm's edge and down into the dark void. The hair then released its grip, flying off into a thousand different directions. Leven grasped at the air with his hands, desperately reaching for anything to halt his fall.

Winter! Geth! Clover! he thought.

It was pointless. There was nothing secure for Leven to grab onto. Everything within his view was being sucked down into the horrific rip the rovens had created.

There was no light. Leven could feel broken sections of Amelia's home and the soil it had stood on tumbling past him as he fell. The dirt tore at him, twisting around his torso. Leven's head bounced off the side of the chasm, and he could feel blood running down his face. As he tumbled downward, his body contorted painfully. Leven could see flashes of fire, and a great rumble filled his ears.

Leven relaxed his body, realizing that there was nothing and no force strong enough to stop him from falling deeper and farther down the chasm. Fate had brought him to Foo, and now fate had tossed him to a very dark end. Leven's head again bounced off the side of the chasm, and his vision began to go black.

He couldn't help feeling incredibly misled.

CHAPTER TWO

WEDGIE

It's not easy starting something new. Few things are more intimidating than walking into a brand-new situation and having to make the best of it. Maybe your parents moved during your ninth-grade year and you had to make new friends in a foreign country where everyone spoke a different language from yours. That's uncomfortable, and, as any well-meaning adult might say, "a character-building experience." But what if you feel like you already have enough character, and you don't want to leave all your friends and go to a foreign country with different money and food and a big school where the other kids ignore you and make you wish you were a treasure chest or a dog bone or anything buried deep beneath the earth and out of sight? What then? Well, you do as your parents tell you, and hope you don't perish from too much character development.

Foo was not new to Geth, and yet here he was in a new situation where he would be fortunate to come out with just a little more character and not something far worse. Sure, he was not one to worry; he was, after all, a lithen who trusted fully in fate.

But something was different now.

Previously, Geth had been a tall, strong, formidable leader, feared and respected by most of the inhabitants of Foo. At present, however, he was a little less strong, a good bit less intimidating, and totally ignored by most people—which was understandable, seeing how no one pays much attention to a toothpick.

As the huge rip opened up, swallowing Amelia's house and everything in it, Geth had somehow managed to get stuck in the side of the crevasse. His frail little toothpick legs were embedded in the wall of the great trench. He closed his mouth and eyes as a torrent of dirt and debris tumbled past him.

He couldn't hear much above the roar of the avalanche of soil, but as the sound died just a bit, he felt the wall in which he was pinned slip and begin to descend in one giant slab.

Fate was having some fun.

Riding the toboggan of soil, Geth slid down into the dark chasm. Finally his descent slowed, and the wall of dirt he was stuck in came to a stop. Geth lay there on his back, looking up at the dim light at the opening of the crevasse, far above him.

A large, dark object was sliding down the wall toward him. For a moment, Geth figured it was a roven whose wings had been clipped in the chaos. But two seconds later, the heavy object landed on him, smothering him. Geth could tell by the smell of lintwood perfume that it was Amelia.

She was out cold and on top of him.

Geth could barely breathe. He would have been fine with waiting for fate to show how clever and wise it was, but he knew that what he most needed now was to get out from under Amelia and find Leven and Winter. He wriggled his arms and did his best to poke Amelia as she lay on top of him. It took a little effort, but on the fourth try he was able to give her a pretty good jab.

Amelia moaned.

Two more jabs, and she was fully conscious and moaning in complete sentences.

"That'd better be you, Geth," she warned. "And if it is, stop poking me!"

Amelia rolled off of Geth and felt carefully around on the dark ledge. Her right hand found the edge of the shelf while her left hand located Geth. She pinched him extra hard as she pulled on him and popped his legs out of the dirt.

"I suppose I deserved that," Geth said.

Amelia brushed him off the best she could in the dark.

"I think I have an amber stick," she remembered. Reaching into her pocket, she pulled out a wooden stick about three inches long. It was rough on the ends and smooth in the middle. She slid her fingers along the smooth center of it, massaging a small bit of oil from the wood onto the thumb and middle finger of her right hand. Then she snapped her fingers near one end of the stick and it lit up, crackling and spitting. She snapped her fingers at the other end, and it too burned. The light gradually drew into the center of the stick, causing the entire thing to glow while remaining cool to the touch. She held the stick out over the chasm and peered downward.

"Wow," she whispered.

The rip the rovens had created was gigantic, and things were still settling. Of course Geth and Amelia had no way of determining just how long it stretched or how deep it went, but they could detect a low, buzzing sound way up above them.

"Do you hear that?" Geth asked.

"Locusts," Amelia answered. "Jamoon is probably using them to inform the whole of Foo that he's after you."

"We've got to get out of here," Geth said.

"How?" Amelia complained. "We're trapped."

The ledge they had landed on was thin at one end, but there was room to move around on the other end. Amelia moved to the wider part and snuffed out the amber stick. Geth worked his way up to her right shoulder and patted her gently on her large, wrinkled earlobe. He was glad it was dark.

"I've never known you to give up," Geth said.

"Give up?" Amelia sniffled. "People give up when they have choices. We have no choice. The gunt will be here soon."

"Fate has fixed worse. Let's hope the message the locusts are delivering falls upon more friends than enemies," was Geth's only reply.

Amelia was a bit dumbfounded. "You've changed, Geth," she said softly. "Where's the fire you used to have? Where's your anger?"

"I don't know what you mean," Geth answered.

"The Geth that Antsel took from Foo all those years ago was considerably more hotheaded. Sabine took your life and your city and all you had worked for. Where's your resentment, your anger?"

Geth was silent; if he had had a brow it would have been furrowed. Amelia's words seemed to impact him. He couldn't see himself very well, but he looked at his arms and legs and wondered at what he had become.

Geth thought back to Reality. He remembered being a tree and the restraint he had used to contain himself. There had been many days when he had wanted badly to wrap a root around the necks of Leven's sort-of parents, Terry and Addy, and strangle them for being so cruel to Leven. He recalled too how he used to flex and thrust his roots violently under the soil for miles just to let off steam.

And he thought back to his life in Foo before any of this had begun. He could remember his mission and his hatred and disgust for Sabine and for what Sabine wanted to do to Foo. He could still remember Sabine capturing him, and the pain he felt as his soul was extracted and put into a seed. He had felt nothing but hate. But Geth felt none of that now. He had been reduced. His desire to stop what was happening was as strong as ever, but there was no anger in his heart—no hatred.

"Interesting," Geth whispered to himself. "I hadn't thought about it."

His thoughts were interrupted by a faint voice yelling in the distance. Geth jumped off Amelia's shoulder and inched to the lip of the ledge. Amelia was still sniffling.

"Shhh," Geth said gently. "I think I hear Winter."

Amelia caught her breath.

"Geth! Leven!" the voice sounded.

"You've got a bigger voice," Geth said with excitement to Amelia. "Yell out."

Amelia moved cautiously to the edge of the ledge and peered down into the darkness. "Winter?" she called.

Winter was somewhere below them. They couldn't see her, but her voice was just loud enough for them to make out what she was saying.

"Are you there?" she yelled from down below.

"We're here!" Amelia replied.

"And Leven?"

Amelia looked at Geth, wondering what to say.

"Tell her the truth, of course," Geth insisted.

"He's not here!" Amelia hollered.

"He must have fallen farther down," Winter called back. "I'm going after him."

"No!" Geth and Amelia shouted simultaneously.

Amelia relit her amber stick and peered over the edge. She still couldn't see Winter.

"I can see your light," Winter yelled. "I'm on a ledge below you."

Amelia dropped the amber stick off the ledge, and it drifted down like a falling star about three hundred feet and then stopped.

"Thank you," Winter called, picking up the glowing stick. She held it up and peered through the darkness at her surroundings. Although far below Geth and Amelia, she still was nowhere near the bottom of the chasm.

Glancing downward, Winter noticed a shaft of light rising from the darkness and shooting toward her. Winter was startled. The light was white and cylindrical and filled with floating circles of color and waves of blue. When it reached Winter, it stopped and leaned toward her. Winter stood still and speechless, waiting for it to touch her. She shivered with excitement.

It had been over thirteen years since Winter had enhanced a dream.

The shaft of light touched her under her chin and quickly spread through her, illuminating her entire being. All at once she was alive in the dream of someone in Reality. It felt so warm and safe and normal that Winter wanted to cry.

The dream belonged to a young girl in Africa—a young girl without a father, who had just lost her cat. Winter took the dream and amplified it by opening her mind. She moved the images around and took away any uncertainty and made it familiar for the young mind dreaming it. She gave the scenes within the dream an unusual hue and pushed the edges out to fit greater amounts of hope and imagination.

Winter felt so alive.

Peering over their ledge, Geth and Amelia could see the dream touch Winter. They watched Winter as she manipulated the light. The bright glow radiating from her body lit up the chasm and revealed a thin ridge that connected the ledge Geth and Amelia were on with Winter's platform below. Amelia didn't waste any time. She shoved Geth behind her ear and jumped down the ridge, sliding clumsily toward Winter, digging her heels in the dirt to keep her from plummeting all the way down. Small strings of soil reached out at her, slowing her down as she slid.

Winter manipulated the dream until it began to fade. Then she pushed the light out of her palms and sent what was left of the dream back into Reality.

As her mind was clearing, Winter felt some clods of dirt tumbling down from above. She lifted her amber stick up to see Amelia sliding toward her. More dirt rained down on Winter. Two seconds later, Amelia landed with a thud on the shelf of dirt next to Winter.

"Are you okay?" Winter asked, helping Amelia to her feet.

"Fine," Geth insisted, peering out from behind Amelia's lumpy ear. "But we'd better find a way out of here. The gunt will be coming soon."

"Gunt?" Winter asked, having no recollection of what that was.

"To fill the rip," Geth answered. "There are borders to Foo. The gunt makes it impossible to dig yourself out. And the last place you want to get stuck is in its path. Many souls have been caught in the glue and trapped forever."

"Then let's hurry," Winter said nervously.

"Hurry how?" Amelia asked, rubbing her sore backside.

"We need to get to the bottom," Geth replied. "Once we hit the floor, we can run until we reach the end of this rip."

"What if there is no end?" Winter asked.

"We'll let fate figure that out," Geth said.

Amelia took Winter's hand and scooted to the edge of the shelf. She sat down, wiggling her rear in the soil and tying up her skirt between her legs. Grateful she was wearing jeans, Winter sat next to Amelia, and Geth hopped up onto Winter and made his way to the front pocket of her shirt. It was a position he was very familiar with.

"So we just slide?" Winter asked, holding the glowing amber stick out in front of them and staring off into the darkness.

"The wall looks sloped," Geth said.

"The wall looks sloped," Amelia growled. "That's easy for you to say—it's not your rear you're riding on."

A mournful cry sounded from behind them, dull, but audible.

"The gunt is coming!" Geth said loudly.

Amelia pushed off the shelf and began sliding down the narrow ledge. Winter followed her lead. The ledge, made of clay, was wet from the many streams of water running up the sides, and Amelia and Winter quickly began to pick up speed on the slick surface. Long, fingerlike strands of dirt reached out from the wall of the chasm, attempting to slow them down as they raced. Amelia and Winter were moving too fast for the dirt to have much effect. It was a wild, uncontrollable ride that ended when Amelia's dress snagged on a protruding root, pulling her to a sudden stop. Winter slammed into Amelia's broad back.

The dull sound of gunt was no longer dull, but thundering

and crashing. Winter looked up behind them and could see thousands of white, froggish blobs showering down. The mushy white blobs meshed together and swelled, beginning to fill the chasm.

"Let's go!" Geth hollered. "It's coming."

"What do you think I'm trying to do?" Amelia shouted, tugging to free herself from the root.

She pulled at her dress, but it wouldn't give.

The gunt showered closer.

Amelia bent forward and with her old teeth tore at the cloth and bit herself free. Then she grasped Winter's ankles and pulled her with her as they began to slide again.

The gunt was upon them, racing after them so swiftly it created a tremendous wind, which whipped at Winter's hair.

"Go!" Geth yelled.

They weren't fast enough. A huge, sticky frog glob flew into Winter and pushed her from the ledge. Winter would have fallen all the way to the bottom, but the gunt caught her by the ankles, and she hung there upside down on the wall like a fly in a sticky trap. A two-foot-thick waterflight was running up the side of the chasm, making the area where Winter hung a muddy mess. Amelia reached out to try to free Winter.

That was a mistake. As soon as Amelia touched Winter's ankles, her hands were instantly caught in the white, sticky gunt. She had no choice but to hang onto Winter as millions of gunt balls continued to fill the entire rip in the soil. Gunt was also rising from the floor of the chasm and getting closer.

"This is not good!" Winter screamed, still dangling upside

down against the wall, water and mud washing over her and Amelia.

Straining to keep from falling out of Winter's upside-down pocket, Geth gazed out at the cascading wall of gunt. "I hope Leven's okay," he said.

"What?" Amelia panicked, glaring at the toothpick as if he were crazy. "We've got to do something! I didn't wait all these years to be buried by a pile of gunt."

"It's in the hands of fate," Geth said nonchalantly.

Amelia was dumbfounded. She too was a believer in the power of fate, but she knew something was not right with Geth. He was not the person he had been when he was first captured. Then he had been the lead token of the Council of Wonder, motivated by his hatred for anything that sought to destroy Foo. Now here he was rolling over, instead of actively willing fate to work for him.

But none of that mattered at the moment.

The gunt was at hand.

Packed together, like thick globs of egg white, billions of frog-shaped blobs of gunt advanced, pressed together, creating a river of sticky ooze that poured down the walls of the rip, rapidly expanding to fill the void.

Winter watched as a wall of gunt taller than any building or mountain she had ever seen inched steadily toward them.

She looked up at the thick stream of water flowing up the wall. She glanced at Amelia, who was still stuck to her ankles.

Then Winter closed her eyes and triggered her gift.

CHAPTER THREE

THORN IN THEIR SIDE

Tatum Manufacturing was a big, diversified company. Its managers had their figurative hands and literal money in hundreds of products and ideas. Chances were that in a week's time most people in North America had either sat on, eaten off, or passed by some product that Tatum had helped manufacture.

Geth, of course, was the result of their wood division. It was Tatum that had taken the chunk of him that had contained his heart and turned him into the toothpick he was now.

Geth was appropriately grateful.

The shape he had been shaved down into had made him easy for Leven and Winter to transport, and it had kept him small and out of the direct sight of Sabine.

Yes, Tatum had helped fate well. If questioned, Geth would have nothing but positive things to say about the company that had carved up his heart and spit him out looking like the sliver he was now. But Geth might have felt differently if he had known what else Tatum had done. You see, when the large chunk of tree that contained Geth's heart had been tossed into the blades and cut down in size, fate had kindly preserved enough of the great king's heart intact to keep him alive and enable him to guide Leven to Foo. But the monstrous blades of Tatum's wood division were not quite as skilled and precise as, say, the hands of a well-trained surgeon. In fact, they were less precise than the fins of a poorly trained circus seal. What those imprecise blades had done was put the majority of Geth into one toothpick. But those machines had also trimmed a tiny part of Geth and put it into a separate toothpick. That toothpick had been packaged and shipped from Burnt Culvert, Oklahoma, to North Carolina, while the toothpick known as Geth had stayed in Oklahoma.

And whereas Geth was a traditional-looking toothpick, the small piece of heart shaved from him ended up in a less conservative, specialty toothpick. That specialty toothpick was then packed into a box labeled "Ezra and Son's Extra Fancy Party Toothpicks." The marketing line on the label read: "Perfect for picking at even the most prestigious parties." The toothpicks in those packages were extra long, with fringed plastic purple tops.

Well, no sooner had that package of Ezra and Son's Extra Fancy Party Toothpicks been trucked across the country and delivered to a large grocery store in North Carolina than Charlie Pork had purchased the pack of toothpicks and carried them to the small sandwich shop he and his uncle Telly ran just off Interstate 40.

It was in that box of toothpicks that this small portion of Geth now lay. Of course, it was no longer Geth. Like a kidney that you might give to a friend in need, this vital part of Geth had been removed and now belonged to a toothpick all its own. And whereas the Geth we all know was a noble being whose every desire was for Foo and fate, this toothpick was different. This toothpick had received the dark part of Geth, and it harbored nothing but anger and hatred.

And confusion.

It was as confused and dark as any toothpick had ever been. Of course, it wasn't hard to be king of that heap, seeing that there are so few toothpicks who feel anything at all. But as it lay there in that box, the world dark, with thoughts of anger racing through its wooden head, it grew more and more hateful and anxious.

Thanks to a ding, or an imperfection, in the side of its top, the toothpick could hear. His hearing was a bit muffled due to his purple plastic top, but on more than one occasion he heard the name *Ezra*.

"Throw me that box of Ezra's," Charlie Pork yelled.

"This box of Ezra's?" the help yelled back.

"Them Ezra's."

The dark, angry, and confused toothpick had a name.

Ezra was taken out of the box along with a number of lifeless toothpicks and laid in a small tray near the soda fountain. He couldn't see this, but deduced it when he heard Charlie Pork say, "Put them toothpicks in that small tray next to the soda fountain."

Every once in a while Ezra would feel a hand reach into the tray, fumble around, and withdraw one of the toothpicks surrounding him.

Ezra knew his time would come. He would be picked, and when he was, he knew what he must do. That part of him that had been taken from him must pay for the horror he now had to suffer. Geth had forced Terry to chop down their tree. Now, thanks to Geth's thoughtless act, Ezra was incomplete and felt nothing but misery. He was being tortured and had been left with the bad end of the toothpick. Ezra knew of no one to blame besides the one who had gotten the good part of the deal—the one who had taken everything else and left him with nothing but anger. He would find that one and finish him off in a way that would clearly express just how upset and wronged Ezra was. Ezra had only one purpose, one desire—and whereas on a shopping list one item might mean a quick in and out at the grocery store, Ezra's one item was going to take some time and some very bad fate.

Geth must die.

ii

Tim Tuttle sat silently at his dining-room table. His body was still, but his mind was racing.

Tim was about as average as a person could be. Stick him in a photo with a thousand other people his age, and he would be the last one to stand out or be spotted. He did have two larger-than-usual ears, and his chin looked a bit like a turtle whose head

was constantly retracted, but those were his two most distinguishing features. Aside from that, his five-foot-ten stature, brown eyes, white teeth, regular nose, and all the other bits and pieces that make up a fairly normal thirty-nine-year-old man were unremarkable.

Tim Tuttle—an average man with an average job.

Tim had been a garbage man for over twenty years. Some might argue that he wasn't living up to his potential, but those arguing that should know that Tim loved his work. Why? Because it gave him the opportunity to think. He had all the time in the world to ponder. And, while collecting cans and dumping trash, Tim was always thinking. He had in fact thought of many great and marvelous things and had fabricated countless machines and toys from the discarded trash of others. But he had also pondered the meaning of life as he hoisted rotting vegetables into the bins, had formulated the answers to the world's most difficult riddles as he piled old newspapers into the trucks, and had found inner peace while hosing four-week-old egg salad off the curb.

Others, if they thought of him at all, might have thought him to be simply a garbage man with a sad life. In reality, Tim was more content and fulfilled than many of those who generated even the nicest trash. Tim had a beautiful wife, two great children, a comfortable home, *and* he had time to think.

But at the moment, Tim's thoughts were far from comfortable. His mind was completely focused on Winter Frore. It had been over a week since he or his wife, Wendy, had last seen

Winter, and Tim was more than worried—he was scared something horrific had happened to her. Winter was not their daughter, but they had loved her as though she were. She had been a part of their family, and the Tuttles had tried hard to make up for the horrible life Winter had at home with her mother, Janet Frore. The Tuttles lived a few houses down from the Frores, and they had always kept an eye on Winter.

It's not terribly unusual for a kind neighbor to be aware and watchful toward someone in need on their street. And the Tuttles were about as kind and solicitous as anyone. But there was a reason beyond the obvious for Tim's concern for Winter—a reason even Tim and his wonderful mind hadn't completely sorted out.

It had been almost thirteen years since an old woman had shown up on the Tuttles' doorstep and whispered a secret. Tim could still remember her face—wrinkled and lumpy. She wore a brown hood over her head and had a pair of horn-rimmed, thick glasses perched on her bulbous nose. She was slightly agitated, but determined in her whispering. At first Tim had not understood her, her speaking was so soft, but she had pulled him closer and whispered fiercely.

He had never forgotten what she said, nor had he repeated it.

When Winter was ten years old the old woman had once again shown up at his door. Tim had been stepping out to go to work, and there she was. Just as before, she had leaned in, whispered the secret, and forbidden Tim to tell another soul. And now Winter was missing.

"Are you okay?" Tim's wife, Wendy, asked, sitting down next

to him. "You look like you have the weight of the world on your shoulders."

Tim's heart began beating faster. Something wasn't right. His meal sat untouched upon the dining-room table in front of him. Steam rose softly from the sugared ham and the small, roasted red potatoes that circled it. There was salad and bread softer than most pillows. A long, thin bowl sat filled with dark gravy, and in two separate spots on the table there were dishes of butter and jam, waiting to be spread onto bread and consumed.

Tim's two sons, Darcy and Rochester, were sitting on the opposite side of the table. They both had dark blond hair, round noses, and very sad eyes.

"You're thinking of Winter, aren't you?" Wendy asked.

"She wouldn't just leave," Tim insisted. "I know she wouldn't. She's not that kind of child."

"If it meant she could get away from . . . that Janet woman, she might," Wendy said.

"She would tell us," Darcy cried. "She would tell us and say good-bye."

Tim looked at the faces of his two young boys and at Wendy.

"Maybe you should talk to Janet," Wendy suggested. "She's her mother. Find out what she knows."

"I don't think she'll talk to me," Tim said.

"You have to at least try," Wendy begged.

"You have to try, Dad," Darcy chimed in. "Winter's like our sister."

"She might be in trouble," Rochester added.

"I'm sure she's fine," Tim said, trying to comfort them. "But I'll tell you what." He stuck out his weak chin and tried to smile. "If it makes you feel better, I'll talk to her mother and to the police."

It was as if Tim Tuttle had just announced that there would be four Christmases this year. The other three faces lit up with hopeful smiles.

"And if they don't know anything, I'll try to find her myself," Tim threw in, knowing that Winter was too important to simply forget about. "But we have to believe that she is okay. We have to hope for the best. After all, she's a remarkable girl."

"I'll say she's remarkable," Rochester said. "She froze her whole class."

"Froze her class?" Tim asked in confusion.

Rochester's cheeks reddened and he glanced at his own knees.

"Froze her class?" Tim pressed.

"I don't know if it's true," Rochester finally admitted. "But some older kids were talking about how she froze her class—she turned them all into ice."

"Don't be silly," Wendy said, picking up her fork and stabbing a thin slice of meat. "They weren't speaking literally. How could someone freeze her class?"

Rochester shrugged and looked at Darcy.

"Last I heard it was impossible to freeze people," Tim tried to joke, his heart still racing. "Now, let's eat before this *meal* is frozen."

All of them ate with Winter on their minds.

CHAPTER FOUR

CHEW FOR YOUR LIFE

L even opened his eyes to find nothing but darkness. The slide to the bottom of the chasm had not been easy, and his head let him know it. It was throbbing. If not for the cold ground beneath his back, he would have had no idea which way was up. He closed his eyes, hoping that they would adjust to the darkness and that he would be able to make out something.

Nope.

He sat up and held his right hand in front of his face—he couldn't see any of it. The air was still and cool and smelled of damp dirt and mold. The sound of a few remaining dirt clods raining down from above made the darkness even more threatening.

"Boo!" Clover said from behind him.

Leven jumped three inches.

"Boy, someone's jumpy," Clover remarked casually. "That was some fall. You're lucky we slid the way we did. The soft, needy dirt kept picking at you, trying to slow down your fall. It helped some, but we're a long way from where we fell in. You probably would have even enjoyed the ride if you'd been conscious," Clover rambled on. "I wonder how deep we are now. We're obviously on the bottom, and my wrist is flaring up." Clover tisked. "I think it's swollen."

"So, what happened?" Leven asked, still in shock.

"It's an old injury, actually," Clover said. "I glued a lobb ball to my hand and threw it. I was trying to see if I could—"

"Not to your wrist," Leven said. "What happened up there?"

"Oh," Clover sniffed. "Well, those were rovens, and now we're miles below the surface of Foo."

"What are rovens?"

"I think they come from the medieval dreams period," Clover said. "Useless—they can't even manipulate dreams. Plus, they can be killed, and they let their hair do their dirty work for them. Don't mess with them, though—their talons are sharp as razors and can dig through anything. When they shed their feet or hands, or when they're killed, their talons are used as weapons."

Leven could feel Clover walking on the top of his head. He reached up and pulled him down. He wished Clover could see his eyes and in doing so realize how seriously confused he was.

"Where's Winter? And Geth?"

"Well, that's a good question." Clover cleared his throat. "I'll be honest with you. I have no idea. We slid a long way over. We could be miles away from them."

Leven stood and patted his arms and forehead, checking to

see if he was all there. Even though he had a cut on his head, a scrape on his right side, and a swollen ankle, he seemed otherwise okay. At least he was alive.

Well, sort of.

It's hard to feel alive when you find yourself in a place that only weeks before you didn't even know existed, miles below the surface, in a space so dark that death seems almost attractive if it brings with it the possibility of a little light.

"We've got to find Winter," Leven said, feeling lost without her. "Which way is out?"

"Up," Clover said, "but I think that might be a bit difficult. So our choices are that way," Clover turned Leven's head to look right, "or the opposite way."

Leven held his hands against the wall and walked sideways, feeling for any opening. There was no light, no gray, no contrast, only blackness.

Leven heard the sound of chewing, followed by the noise of blowing. Suddenly from out of nowhere there was light. Leven spun to find the source and spotted Clover standing on the ground with what looked like a glowing lightbulb sticking out of his mouth.

"What are—"

Before Leven could ask what Clover was doing, the lightbulb burst, and it was dark again.

"Holm on a sec," Clover chewed. He worked his mouth for a moment, then blew another bubble. As it grew it glowed, illuminating the area around him.

The light didn't do much to comfort Leven; it actually revealed in an awesome way just how dark and desperate a situation he was in.

"Wow," Leven whispered, looking around him. "We're in trouble."

The chasm was gigantic. Leven could see nothing but black dirt and darkness in all directions. Both walls of the chasm towered up beyond the light and seemed to extend forever. There was no sign of an opening. Leven could still hear the sound of dirt settling and water running up and down the walls in spots. The dirt in Foo vibrated, looking like great walls of staticky soil.

Clover's bubble burst, and they were plunged into darkness again.

"What is that stuff?" Leven asked, referring to the gum.

"Bubble bulbs," Clover chewed, his speech slurred. "I neva chew it 'cause it only comes in lemon flavor." Clover blew a big bubble and once again lit up the chasm. He handed Leven a piece of the gum. "Only one piece left after this."

Despite all the burns he had experienced at the hands of Clover's candies, Leven didn't hesitate; he put the piece in his mouth and began to chew. Clover was right: It was bitter, without even a hint of sweet. Leven grimaced. The gum was tough and tasted like the rind of an old lemon. Leven chewed for a bit more and then blew a bubble about the size of Clover's head.

It glowed brightly.

He turned, shining the light on everything around them. He could see bits of grass and deep gashes in the steep walls of the canyon. There were also roots and rocks sticking out of certain portions of the chasm walls and floor. In spots, water ran like thin ribbons up the walls. Leven put his right foot in front of his left and began walking along the floor of the chasm into the darkness, hoping there was a way out at the end.

Leven popped his bubble with his tongue. "So you think this will lead us somewhere?" he chewed.

Clover snapped. "Seems like a logical guess."

Leven blew. The new bubble was big but not quite as bright.

"Eventually the glow runs out," Clover lamented.

Leven's bubble burst.

"I'm not sure I made the right choice following you into Foo," Leven said. "Some paradise."

"Isn't it nice?" Clover replied, ignoring the sarcasm. "Wait till spring, everything is so much greener."

Leven wanted to point out the fact that they might not make it to spring, but he chose instead to light up the way. Clover glowed alongside him, two dimming bubbles making their way down the dark crevasse.

After a few minutes Leven stopped to check his swollen ankle and the cut on his head. The blood was dry, and there was no sign of new bleeding. Both the bubbles he and Clover were currently sporting popped.

"Looks like you'll live," Clover chewed supportively.

"I have to live," Leven said seriously. "Seeing how there's no killing in Foo. I might not understand everything here, but I'm pretty sure those rovens were trying to kill me."

"Phooey," Clover scoffed. "They didn't push you over the edge, it was their hair."

"So hair can kill?" Leven asked, dumbfounded.

"It can help," Clover replied. Both were still covered in darkness, having chosen not to blow. "Besides," Clover whispered, "you *can* be killed. Fate didn't bring you here, you snuck in."

"I was pushed in."

"Pushed, snuck, what's the difference?"

"So, I could have died falling into this?"

"Shhh. That's not something you want everyone to know."

"How do you know I can die?" Leven said, suddenly in shock.

"Your grandfather was killed," Clover said seriously. "He cheated fate and snuck back in, and it was sort of a surprise to everyone when it was discovered that he could be killed."

"Geth said my grandfather died, but not that he was *killed,*" Leven said desperately.

"You know Geth," Clover sighed. "He's always trying to rainbow up things. Here Geth is dying himself, and he's still trying to act like everything's great."

"Geth is dying?" Leven questioned, the surprise in his voice echoing off the chasm walls. "Where did you hear that?"

"He just told Amelia," Clover said. "Said unless he's taken to the flame in the turrets he won't last more than a couple of days."

"Am I the same way?" Leven panicked.

"No," Clover waved. "You're not a toothpick."

"We've got to get to the turrets," Leven said, ignoring Clover. "Geth will know what to do."

"Of course," Clover insisted. "If Geth isn't restored, then the battle to save Foo will be almost impossible. And as for you, you might be able to die, but I'm sure you'll live a long and full life."

"This is crazy. How am I even alive now?" Leven asked incredulously. "We fell such a long way."

"Like I said, you were lucky you slid down the side just right."

"So I'm the only one in Foo who can be killed?"

"There are a few other exceptions—Winter, Amelia, Geth, the rovens, siids, some rants, most vegetation, sheep—but aside from them, pretty much everybody else is indestructible. Of course, Sabine had creative ways to make accidents happen."

"I heard Amelia telling Geth how some here in Foo would hate me because I destroyed the gateway."

"Yeah, about that," Clover sniffed, "I wouldn't run for any sort of office at the moment. The votes might not be in your favor."

"Unbelievable," Leven sighed.

"Life," Clover sighed softly in return. "I think we'll look back on this—"

A gigantic sloshing noise sounded out from far behind them. The sloshing quickly became a gurgle, sounding as if the ground itself were gargling. Leven turned toward the sound and blew a bubble as fast as he could. There was nothing but black as far as he could see. The noise sounded again, this time louder.

"What is it?" Leven asked, suddenly shaking.

"Well, I'm not certain, but usually when the rovens rip the soil, gunt follows," Clover explained. "Normally they don't begin sealing the thing up so soon, but this is a big rip."

Clover did not sound like his usual fearless self.

Leven blew another bubble. It was large, but it was dim. The noise was getting closer, but Leven didn't turn to run. He needed to see to believe. He could feel a rising wind blowing on his face. Then in the far distance Leven saw a white glob smack the ground. Another large glob hit the wall, then another hit the opposite wall, splashing against the dirt like snowballs. There was one up high and two down low and three new ones at eye level. One smacked against the wall not too far from Leven; it looked less like a snowball and more like an albino frog. The gunt belched and then oozed into the wall, waiting for another of its kind to smack up against it and begin to seal the wound the rovens had created.

"We have to go," Clover insisted.

Leven's bubble wilted.

It was completely dark, but the sound of gunt smacking into the walls and floor of the chasm was almost deafening now. As the growing glob drew closer it was creating a terrific wind. The air pushed past Leven, blowing his hair and clothes. Leven quickly blew another bubble into the wind.

He half-wished he hadn't. The gunt blobs were everywhere, up the sides and piling up at the bottom of the rip. The large, white, froglike balls were wiggling and hissing and meshing together, creating a huge, undulating, sticky-looking mass that was filling up the bottom of the chasm and sticking to the walls. The mass was racing like a wave toward Leven and Clover.

The strong air popped Leven's bubble and pushed it back into his face. Leven turned and began running. He blew another bubble; the weak light lit up only ten paces in front of him. Clover blew too, but his gum was also wearing out.

Leven jumped over a huge hole in the floor of the rip. His gum popped, and he blew another bubble as quickly as he could, hoping he would be able to keep his footing as he ran. The guttural sound of the wall of gunt mounding up behind and rolling toward him was deafening. Like the sound of an approaching tornado.

Smlooooosh!

Leven felt something glom onto the heel of his right foot. It instantly stuck like cement, and Leven's forward motion wrenched his foot out of his shoe. He didn't stop to try to grab it, understanding for the first time just how sticky the white gunt was and how stuck he would be if it got hold of him entirely.

Both bubbles burst.

"We're not going to make it!" Leven screamed. "We don't even know where we're going!"

"Just blow!" Clover screamed.

Continuing to run, Clover and Leven blew as quickly as they could. The puny gum bulbs lit just two feet in front of them. The chasm took a turn, and Leven and Clover barely missed running into the wall. A large wad of gunt smacked into the back of Leven's left shoulder, throwing him off balance and up against the side of the chasm, pinning him to the dirt. Leven frantically tore at his shirt until he was able to rip away from the wall.

Leven kept running, but his bubble was out, and Clover's was wilting.

"Wasn't there another piece of this gum?" Leven yelled.

Clover was one step ahead of him, fishing in his void for the last piece of bubble bulb. "Here it is."

Leven felt Clover shove something in his mouth as he ran. It was a bigger piece than the last.

"I thought you said it only came in lemon!" Leven yelled, running and chewing as fast as he could. "This tastes like cheese."

Clover didn't say a word as he quickly checked his void. He pulled out the last piece of bubble bulb.

"Uh-oh," Clover replied.

Leven lurched forward two more steps. His stomach began to rumble and boil, generating huge bubbles of hot air that raced through his veins and into his hands and fingers and feet and toes. Clover stuck the last piece of bubble bulb into his own mouth and got a good look at what was happening.

Leven was quickly turning into an inflated, giant wad of goo.

Leven raised his hands to his forehead to feel what was going on. Both hands stuck to his head. As he tried to pull them away, they stretched like a piece of warm taffy. He tried to lift his feet from the ground, but they too stretched, stuck to the ground like a wad of chewed gum. Leven groaned and teetered as his body bent completely out of shape. He could feel his insides sticking together and swirling. He cast a wild, desperate look at Clover.

Clover's bubble wilted. "Sorry," Leven heard him say. "I thought I had thrown that candy away. They haven't made 'You

Be the Gum' in years. Ever since . . . well, I don't want to bother you with details, so let's just leave it at that."

Leven might have enjoyed the exchange he and Clover were having if, say, they had been back in Reality, sitting on a porch on a warm afternoon, watching the sprinklers and sipping a cool soda. But Leven was not sipping soda on a warm day. He was miles below the surface of Foo in a chasm ripped by rovens, being chased by roaring, gluelike frogs, and turning into a large piece of gum.

Leven's eyes burned gold. He was startled. His gift had seemed completely gone ever since he had entered Foo. But now he was feeling a sudden sense of relief and new strength, knowing that it was not gone. He could see the ocean of gunt closing in on them. He could see the fate they would suffer if caught in the seal. He could see the powerful wind the wave of gunt was creating in front of it as it undulated ever closer.

He could see exactly what he needed to do.

"Hold on," was what Leven wanted to yell to Clover. But his mouth stretched and sprang back like thick gum. He stretched his mouth again and through a tiny hole he hollered something that sounded like, "Muds pon!"

Luckily, Clover spoke gum, and he jumped onto Leven's shoulder.

Leven relaxed, and his torso began to expand like a giant gum bubble, growing and stretching to the size of a parachute. His cheeks filled out as well, giving him even more buoyancy. The wind created by the approaching mound of gunt blew him forward and helped him gain speed as he began to ascend.

The walls of the chasm were racing by them as if they were on a supersonic elevator. Leven could see some light now. The gunt was everywhere below them, rapidly filling in the rip. Luckily for Leven, his previous experience navigating across the ocean in Reality had given him a little practice with manipulating wind, and he was able to help fate push him faster up out of the canyon and toward the surface.

Leven couldn't see Clover, but he could hear him yelling, "Wheeeeeeee!"

They rose out of the chasm and were suddenly floating like a blimp over the ground. Below them, Leven could see the gunt continuing to pile up in the giant rip, and he developed a sudden urge to belch. As he did so, the air rushed out of him and he drifted to the ground.

Actually, "drifted" really isn't the most accurate word to use.

Leven's deflating body was propelled backward, swooping and diving, as if he were a balloon with all the air rushing out of it, and he ended up slamming into a large fantrum tree, where his gooey body stuck to the branches.

He was a complete mess—drooping and stretched in every direction. The condition was extremely painful and caused Leven's gumball eyes to see starlike bubbles. Clover wasn't helping the situation. He was horribly tangled in Leven's right arm and couldn't seem to get free. Leven tried to yell at him and help

Clover understand that even though the "You Be the Gum" had saved them, he still wasn't happy about his current state.

A weak "Waupsa donta" was all Leven could get out.

"You're welcome," Clover replied, not as fluent in gum as Leven had first thought.

Leven closed his eyes and passed out.

CHAPTER FIVE

AND THEN THERE WAS SORROW

W inter had experienced a number of uncomfortable things in her life. Like the time when she was ten and she was out playing in the woods with her sister, Autumn, and Autumn had dared her to swim in the river that ran behind their house. Winter didn't usually go for dares, but she felt her sister needed some showing up. So Winter jumped into the water and easily reached the other side. After she pulled herself up onto the bank, she looked back across the river and stuck her tongue out triumphantly.

Autumn yelled for Winter to swim back across, but Winter decided to mess with Autumn's mind a little more and ran off into the woods. She crossed the old train bridge and then followed an overgrown road at the bottom of a gully. Winter stopped where the road met up with a wide dirt lane. She was standing above the gap between the two paths where they didn't quite match up when she looked up. The temperature was a warm ninety-one degrees, and there in the early summer sky was a brilliant shooting star.

You can probably guess what happened next.

Winter was taken into Foo, snatched from her family and normal life at the young age of ten.

That had been an uncomfortable and confusing time for Winter.

Right now, however, Winter was every bit as uncomfortable as that, and then some. At the moment she could remember nothing of her previous lives. All she knew was that she was buried in gunt and was being smothered. The white stuff had oozed over and around them and hardened quickly, trapping Amelia, Winter, and Geth. The new gunt gave off a faint white glow, allowing them to see shapes and shadows.

Amelia had held her scarf over her face to create some breathing room, and Winter had pulled her shirt up over her head to do the same. Geth was pinned inside Winter's pocket, where he was also uncomfortable but not overly concerned. He merely wondered what fate would do next.

Their only hope was that at the very last second, Winter had frozen the stream of water flowing up the side of the chasm. The little waterflight was a couple of feet wide and about thirty inches thick. The gunt had been forced to form and harden around the shaft of ice.

The only problem was that Winter couldn't reach the ice to touch it and restore it to water. Well, that wasn't the only problem, but it was a big one.

Winter's voice was muffled under the layer of gunt. "If I can thaw the water, then we can try to climb up the shaft it created," she explained. "I just can't reach the water."

"Push your foot," Amelia hollered. "The gunt is thin there. If you can push through it, you should be able to reach the ice with your bare foot."

Winter pushed as hard as she could, and the coating of gunt cracked. Her right foot touched the ice and it instantly thawed.

Sure, Winter had achieved what she wanted, but she had actually made the situation much more urgent. Thawed water began to flow up into their space, fighting to steal every inch of air. Winter scrambled up into the tunnel the frozen water had created. She dug her fingers into the mud and pulled herself up through the rising water. The hole was like a flooded, crooked chimney with no light at the top. Winter held on to the sides of the shaft as a stream of mud and water cascaded up over her.

She looked down and reached for Amelia.

Amelia stretched her right hand up toward Winter, and Winter reached down as far as she could, but she could not quite touch Amelia's fingers.

"Reach!" Winter yelled desperately. "Reach!"

Amelia groaned and stretched her wrinkled hand upward.

"A little more!" Winter cried. "Just a little more!"

Amelia blinked her eyes, and as she opened them up she looked at Winter and curled her fingers inward and away.

"Amelia!" Winter yelled.

The water began to fill in even more, rising around Amelia

like a coiling snake. Winter could feel the gunt softening. Soon it would seal off the shaft the frozen water had created.

"Give me your hand!" Winter demanded.

"Do as she says," Geth ordered Amelia. "Grab her hand!"

Amelia's fingers opened just a bit and then closed to make a tight fist. Winter and Geth stared at her in despair.

"Go," Amelia said weakly. "Go. Climb before the gunt seals up this shaft."

"No!" Winter shouted. "Take my hand; I'll pull you up behind me."

Amelia blinked sadly.

"I won't leave you!" Winter cried, still desperately trying to reach down and grab Amelia. "We need you! Leven needs you!"

Winter watched Amelia's eyes briefly light up with the mention of Leven, but the happiness was quickly gone as the liquid rose up and around her neck. The old woman's thick glasses magnified the sadness in her eyes.

"Please go," Amelia pleaded with Winter. "Please. Find Leven and save Foo."

Geth jumped from Winter to Amelia and began pulling at the neck of the old woman's dress. "Come on," he demanded. "We need you. *Foo* needs you."

Amelia could only blink as the rising water covered her mouth and nose.

"No!" Winter cried out. "Stop her, Geth."

Amelia blinked her large, magnified eyes. She closed them and held her breath as water rose above her eyebrows.

"Help her, Geth!" Winter screamed. "Help her!"

Geth looked up at Winter. He was a toothpick, but it was apparent from his small eye holes knitted together that he knew hope was gone. Geth let go of the neck of Amelia's dress as the water floated him upward. "We have to climb before the gunt fills in," he declared.

"No," Winter sobbed. "We can't leave her."

But even as Winter whispered the words, she also knew it was too late. She looked down at Amelia, who was now completely submerged in the rising water. The last bit of air escaped from her nose and mouth, sending bubbles up. Despite the dire straits, Amelia looked almost peaceful.

Winter was sobbing, and Geth was bobbing in the rushing water. Never one to turn his back on fate, Geth jumped into a large bubble and rode it upward. As Geth rose, Amelia sank farther into the water. It looked as if she were encased in glass—a wrinkly old sleeping beauty that only a blind and desperate prince might kiss.

Winter could only cry. She hurt inside for herself, but even more, she hurt for Leven. Amelia was his only true family, and now she was gone. Winter wanted to curl up into a ball and let the gunt smother her, but instinct wouldn't let her. She began desperately clawing at the sides of the wet, muddy shaft, crying bitterly and inching her way to the top as the water pushed her up.

Her hands were bleeding and sore and she could no longer see much, due to the mud and tears filling her eyes and face. Sometimes clean water would clear her vision, but moments later her eyes would be packed with mud again. Her shoeless right foot was numb, and the gunt lining the shaft was growing sticky and making her progress almost impossible.

Just as she thought she could climb no farther, her hand reached the top of the chasm. Using her last bit of strength, she hauled herself out of the muddy shaft and over the lip of the chasm where she collapsed on the ground, crying.

Water sprayed up around her.

Geth was there waiting. He had tried to help pull her out, but being a toothpick, he wasn't much aid.

The gunt groaned and slurped as it wrapped its sticky self around Winter's remaining shoe and pulled it off. Winter jerked her leg away from the gooey mess and watched as her shoe became permanently enshrined in the gunt, the small, froglike bodies molding themselves into a continuous thick slab, their expressions and individual forms disappearing as they solidified.

The water stopped spraying.

Winter's shoe stuck partway out of the gunt, becoming a pathetic tombstone for Amelia.

Winter was a mess for more reasons than one. Her blonde hair, which had never been very manageable or neat, looked like a tangled nest of seaweed. She was wet and muddy, and both her shoes were gone. Her hands were raw and bloody and looked like a couple of cut-up beets.

Winter rolled over onto her back and cried some more. Amelia was gone. Leven was lost, and Foo was in turmoil. A wave of homesickness washed over her as she remembered Reality and what she and Leven had been through over the past few days. A couple of Winter's Foo memories also returned, but there were still some big gaps of gray forgetfulness in her brain.

She didn't know who she was.

Geth had the smarts to remain quiet and let Winter mourn.

The night was dark, with the purple sky pulsating. Stars rolled across the canopy like marbles on an invisible track. Occasionally two stars would collide, click, spark, and roll off in separate directions. It would have been soothing were it not for the situation they were in. Foo was beautiful, but even the landscape was wise enough to recognize this as a moment of mourning.

Finally, Winter rolled over onto her knees and crawled to the now sealed-off stream that had helped save their lives. She thrust her raw hands into the still water and rinsed them thoroughly, then splashed water onto her crying eyes. She was covered with mud. She worked on her hair and then her face and arms. She picked up Geth, dunked him in the water, and held him in the palm of her hand.

"I can't just leave her," Winter whimpered.

"She is with Hector," Geth said softly. "We can't let what she fought for fail."

"Is there even hope anymore?" Winter asked sadly. "Are we doing the right thing?"

"There is always hope," Geth answered. "We have secured that. Now it's up to us to make it stick. We must find Leven, and we must do it fast."

Geth had not told Winter about his condition, but he could feel himself hardening. He figured that at best he had two days before he would be nothing but a tiny piece of inanimate wood. His small body couldn't hold his soul much longer.

Winter tried to smile. She looked at Geth in her palm and could see traces of mud still on his head.

"Hold on," she said.

She dipped him back into the water and washed him off, then gazed for a moment at the reflection of the moon in the dark pool. She could see much more than just the moon.

Winter quickly turned around and saw twelve beings and twelve pairs of new eyes staring directly at her.

And, for the record, none of the eyes were smiling.

CHAPTER SIX

The Unlikely Cog

Dennis Wood slouched in his chair and sighed. The diner was empty except for him and an older couple quietly eating soup two booths down. Dennis was wearing a white, short-sleeved, button-up shirt and tan polyester slacks that required no ironing whatsoever. If for some odd reason you wanted to, you could take his pants, crumple them up, stomp all over them, and they would still shake right out, wrinkle free. Of course, what his pants possessed in ease of care, they lacked in style. Strung through the belt loops of those pants was a thin brown belt closed at the same hole that had closed it for the last ten years. Dennis had gained a pound three years before and lost one since then. He had on brown loafers with a wide Velcro closure above the tongue and was wearing a pair of his usual white socks. His digital watch showed thirteen hundred hours. It was set at military time because it made Dennis feel militaryish and a part of something he really wasn't nor would ever be.

Dennis had a big, white head. His light blond hair was thin and almost the same color as his skin. His hazel eyes were small and fuzzy, the pupils looking more like smashed raisins than perfect circles. He also had a pug nose and a tight mouth that opened only when food was coming in or when he had to reluctantly communicate with someone.

"What can I get you?" a middle-aged waitress asked as she

stepped up to the table and forced him into a small conversation.

Dennis tried to smile, but his expression more nearly resembled a grimace. Instead of speaking, he pointed to the item he wanted on the menu.

"Turkey sandwich?" the waitress asked.

"No mustard or onions," Dennis said apologetically.

"Right. And to drink?"

Dennis pointed to the word *milk* on the menu.

The waitress looked at him as if he were the sole reason she would never date again, took the menu from him, and walked away.

Dennis glanced around the cafe. He was seated next to a window, and through the glass he could see the building he had worked in for the last ten years. He could see the gold plaque attached to the corner of the building near the door. Dennis was too far away to make out the letters on the plaque, but he knew exactly what they said:

Snooker and Woe, Attorneys at Law.

Of course, Dennis was neither Snooker nor Woe, just Wood, Dennis O Wood, the janitor. The "O" didn't stand for anything. It was just an "O." His parents had felt he needed a middle initial, but lacked the creativity to come up with anything besides "O."

For ten years Dennis had cleaned the toilets and mopped the floors in the Snooker and Woe building. He had removed chewed gum from the outside sidewalk and cleaned every surface at least a thousand times. He had also emptied trash cans and ashtrays and passed many people in the halls, always without speaking to them.

For ten years.

And yet, just this morning, after Dennis had changed the toner in the copy machine, Jack Mortley, the man who had hired Dennis, the man who signed Dennis's checks, the man who had known him for ten years, had had to ask him his name before telling him there was a spill in the break room.

Ten years, and Jack still didn't know his name.

Dennis smoothed down the blond hairs covering his white head. He worked the knuckles of his hands into his eyes and rubbed. When he dropped his hands to the table, he was disappointed, but not at all surprised, to still be right where he was—having a late lunch, in a cheap diner, all by himself.

The waitress returned to his table and dropped off the sandwich and the milk.

"Enjoy," she said with little sincerity.

Dennis sniffed. He rotated the plate a half-turn and picked up the sandwich. It was limp at the sides, held together by a long toothpick with purple plastic fringe at the top. Dennis sighed and pulled the toothpick out of his sandwich. He would have simply set the toothpick aside and taken a bite—but, for some reason, as he held the toothpick between his fingers, he experienced a peculiar feeling.

He felt good.

And bad.

Dennis rolled the toothpick between his thumb and middle finger and watched the plastic purple fringe spin in circles. Then he set the toothpick down and took a bite of his sandwich.

The toothpick did what toothpicks do—it just lay there.

Dennis took another bite and looked through the window toward his workplace. He took a sip of milk, watching the toothpick out of the corner of his eye. There was something about it.

He set his glass down and picked the toothpick up again. He rolled it between his fingers. He switched hands and rolled it with the other. He scratched his pug nose and blinked.

He couldn't understand it.

He couldn't understand what he was feeling or if he was even feeling anything. He wondered if there might be a gas leak in the diner or if he was finally going loony from all the cleaning supplies and bleach he had breathed over the years.

The toothpick vibrated in Dennis's fingers.

Startled, Dennis dropped the toothpick into his glass. As he reached in to retrieve it, he tipped the glass over, and milk spilled out onto the table and ran off onto his easy-care tan pants.

Dennis didn't care. His pants were invincible.

He lifted the toothpick out of the puddle of milk, then stared at it as if it were a diamond ring or a gold coin he had spent years searching for. The old couple two booths down were caught up in their own conversation and as indifferent to the rest of the milk dripping down into his lap as Dennis was.

"Hey, hey," the waitress scolded, walking quickly up to the

table with a rag. "You could've used those napkins to stop it."

Dennis said nothing.

"If you stand up, I'll wipe the bench," she directed.

Dennis wriggled out of the booth and stood up, still holding the toothpick in his hand. He leaned over and reached for the handle of his briefcase. He didn't actually need a briefcase, but he thought it gave others the impression that he was more important than he actually was. He fished a ten-dollar bill out of his briefcase and put it down on a dry part of the table, dropped the toothpick into the case, snapped it shut, and walked out of the restaurant. Outside, Dennis hurriedly turned and headed toward the building with the gold plaque.

CHAPTER SEVEN

IT TURNS OUT THERE
ARE DUMB QUESTIONS

Leven had transformed from a large, sticky wad of gum, plastered in the branches of a tree, back to his normal self. But there were still bits of leaf and twig stuck to his clothes, up his nose, between his fingers and toes, and matted in his dark hair. A thin green twig was sticking out of the white streak in his hair, making it look like a misshapen dove carrying a tiny branch.

Clover busied himself helping Leven remove the larger pieces.

As he was pulling bits of debris off his clothes, Leven looked toward the chasm they had just blown out of. It was now completely filled with gunt and resembled a broad stripe of snow running through the landscape, with the deep purple sky giving it a kind of milky texture. In time, after the gunt had settled and lost its stickiness, some of it would be harvested like blubber and burned or used as cooking fuel. But most of the dense, spongy material would become covered with vegetation, providing nutrients for what was growing out of it.

"That was way too close," Leven said, referring to their escape from the flowing gunt.

Clover was earnestly chewing gum and didn't say anything.

"Are you still chewing that awful lightbulb stuff?"

Clover's hairless cheeks reddened, and he cleared his throat.

"What?" Leven asked. "Is that . . . wait, where did you get that gum?" Leven looked around himself.

"Well . . . I . . . I . . ." Clover stammered.

"Is that from me?" Leven panicked.

"I just wanted to see what flavor you were," Clover explained.

"What flavor?" Leven gasped, still frantically looking himself up and down for a missing chunk.

"It's not from you," Clover waved. "It was your shoe. I took a bite before you changed back."

Leven looked at the one shoe he was wearing. There was a large bite missing from the heel. Leven picked a speck of tree from his nose.

"So, who makes all this candy you have, anyway?" Leven asked. "I haven't seen a structure in Foo besides Amelia's place."

"I know," Clover complained. "Amelia really lived in the sticks. It's not good for people to be so isolated. I bet that's why she's so chatty."

"She seems okay," Leven said. "Now, about the candy, where do you get it?"

"The Eggmen," Clover said.

"The Eggmen?" Leven asked skeptically, brushing a large leaf out of his hair.

"They're pathetic warriors," Clover sighed. "Pathetic. I mean, talk about messy casualties. But they make terrific candy."

"And they use magic?" Leven asked, knowing of no other way to create candy that can turn its chewer into gum.

"No," Clover laughed. "Magic's not real. They use dreams. They live beneath the Devil's Spiral, and as the water from the Veil Sea runs through the massive canyon, it mixes with the dreams. It's quite a process. I'll take you there sometime."

"Devil's Spiral?"

"It's one of my favorite sites in Foo," Clover said. "The spiral eventually forces the water thousands of feet high and keeps the city of Cusp wet."

Clover began to sniff the air. "Do you smell that?" he asked.

"Smell what?" Leven asked.

"It smells like the tharms."

"Tharms? What are—" Leven stopped talking and put his hand to his right ear.

Something was moving nearby. Clover turned invisible.

"You're a great person to have around when things get tough," Leven whispered mockingly.

Leven looked behind himself. He could see nothing but darkness. The sound of chirping bugs filled the air. Leven turned back, and right in front of him was a grown man about Leven's height. Leven jumped. The man stood there scowling. He wore an orange robe and had long gray hair that hung down, partially covering his faded gray eyes. He was breathing like an angry bull and had his weathered hands on his hips.

"Leven?" he asked, in a deep, forced voice.

Leven nodded and backed up a step. "How do you know me?"

"The Lore Coil."

"What's—?"

"Where's Geth!" the personage demanded.

"We were separated," Leven answered.

"Perfect," the old man said sarcastically. "We . . . *I* need Geth."

Leven stood tall. "Who are you?"

"I'm . . . far . . . oh . . . ," he sniffed, scratching his head as if confused.

"Farrow?" Leven helped.

"That's it," the being said, relieved. "You need to follow us . . . me. You need to follow I, me. You lost Geth, but we'll find him. I think I know where he may be."

"Where?"

Farrow looked at Leven and wrinkled his brow. "Do all things from Reality ask so many boring questions?"

"Things?" Leven asked.

"*There's* a surprise," Farrow mocked. "Another question."

"Well, I'd like to know where we're headed."

"How 'bout I show you where we're going when we get there?" Farrow smiled unevenly.

"Last time I saw Geth, we were falling down a giant chasm. Do you think he might have escaped the gunt?" Leven asked.

"Too many questions. It would be best if you simply didn't talk," Farrow declared. He turned from Leven, using his bony hands to sweep his long gray bangs back behind his ears. "I said I, me, we'll find Geth. You're not a runner, are you?"

"I almost made the school track team a year ago," Leven answered naively, still picking bits of tree from off his arms.

Farrow growled. "No, is your *gift* running?"

"I don't think so," Leven replied.

"Good," Farrow said. "I hate trying to keep up."

Farrow twisted and began walking away. After ten steps, he turned to look back at Leven. "Aren't you coming?" he barked. "We'll have to walk and hope we find Geth before anyone . . . well, let's just hope we find Geth in time."

Leven looked to the sky as if there might be an answer written in stars. A huge yellow moon shifted, passing in front of a much smaller blue orb and hiding it. A ribbon of green light danced across the horizon.

"I only have one shoe," Leven hollered after the old man.

Farrow just kept walking.

Clover appeared and pulled a used shoe from his void. "I've been saving all the ones you grew out of," he whispered. "I can't believe you guys in Reality just throw these away."

Leven recognized his old shoe. It was from a year ago and had been well worn.

"Thanks," Leven said, taking the shoe. Hopping on one leg, he crammed his foot into it, then leaned down to lace it up. Shod, Leven took a few giant strides to catch up to Farrow. As he came up beside the grizzled old man, Farrow glanced at Leven and shook his head.

"Leven Thumps," he sneered, the tone of his voice turning cold. "'Look at me, I lived in Reality.' Then Geth abandons Foo and brings you back. His stone has been vacant far too long, if you ask us."

"Us?"

"Another boring question."

"Well, what do you mean by *his stone*?" Leven asked.

"That's not a question you should be asking," Farrow snapped, wobbling as he did so. "Try to remember who you are and who you are talking to."

"I was just curious because—"

Farrow wheeled to face Leven. His old gray eyes were swirling— and not the good kind of swirling like when you twist chocolate syrup into a dish of ice cream. No, the swirling in Farrow's eyes was more like the maddening kind of dizziness and confusion you feel right before you throw up or lose control of your emotions.

Farrow grabbed Leven by the neck of his shirt and steadied himself. His hands were old and rough and smelled rank.

"Curious?" Farrow rumbled, sounding like a different person than he had been moments before. "Curious gets you trapped in a seed and sent to Reality to wait while everyone else is left here to suffer and fight a losing battle."

"But I thought—" Leven tried to explain.

"You *thought*," Farrow spat. "I wish I had a medal to give you. Listen, Leven Thumps, the sooner you realize that you understand nothing, the better off you will be. Nothing is the same here as in Reality. All that you have known is now different. The air you are breathing is different. You think the sun will rise tomorrow?" Farrow challenged.

Leven nodded cautiously.

"Ha!" Farrow scoffed, letting go of Leven's shirt. He wobbled and grabbed onto Leven's sleeve. "The sun might rise tomorrow, and it might not. Maybe you'll grow older, and maybe not. Either way, you would be better off to forget what you know."

Leven's face burned red with frustration. "I know Geth would never—"

"Don't say Geth!" Farrow ordered. "He might be the heir, but he has done more to disrupt Foo than help. In my opinion this is no longer his battle. He should step down and leave the future to Morfit. I will help you find . . . Geth. But on the day that your need is met, I will feel nothing but pleasure as I turn and walk the opposite direction."

Farrow shook his head, let go of Leven, and flung the hood of his orange robe up. He twisted awkwardly again and began walking quickly down the path they were on.

"That guy should write greeting cards," Clover whispered softly into Leven's ear.

A low buzzing filled the air as bit bugs began moving into the night air from the branches of trees where they spent their days. Leven waved them away, irritated by their swarming. The bit bugs were ugly little things, nothing more than small bits of actual bugs that had escaped from dreams. Some were just legs, or antennae, or body segments, and they flew about erratically. Leven began walking again and after a few moments he had caught back up to Farrow.

"So we're heading to where Geth might be?" Leven asked.

Farrow stopped and looked at Leven with a scowl. "Who cuts your hair?" he snapped.

"What?" Leven questioned.

"Whoever did it, they did a bad job," Farrow said, starting to walk again.

Leven ran his fingers through his hair.

"Nice guy," Leven whispered to Clover. "This is ridiculous. We'd better be heading toward Geth. What time do you think it is, anyway?"

"What does that matter?" Clover asked. "Time is different here. No one ever really knows for sure."

"You don't keep track of time here?"

"Well, not like in Reality," Clover replied. "It's a bit more relaxed in Foo. Say you're enjoying a beautiful sunset, and you want it to last longer. Or it's three more days to Winsnicker Day, and you just can't wait, so you need time to speed up."

"Winsnicker Day?"

"One of my favorite days," Clover said happily. "There's a lot of skipping and decorations and singing about Professor Philip Winsnicker and his heroics."

"So when is Winsnicker Day?" Leven asked.

"It comes at a different time and day each year. I wish I had my schoolbook with the schedule. I hope I didn't lose it."

Leven shook his head, totally confused by his surroundings and the order of things in Foo. It was like nothing he had experienced in Reality, and he wondered if he might not be dreaming. But he still felt an urgency to find Geth.

"Well, even if time is working for us, we should be going faster," Leven said. "Do they have cars or airplanes here?"

Clover laughed. "Airplanes? Those big metal things that used to fly over your house in Oklahoma?"

Leven nodded.

"There are none of those things here," Clover said, as if surprised that Leven would even suggest such a thing. "No cars or airplanes, or anything made out of metal."

"You don't have metal here?" Leven asked.

"We do, but it's . . . well, sacred."

"Metal is sacred?" Leven laughed.

"That might not be the perfect word," Clover admitted, "but metal is something only those who occupy the Thirteen Stones are permitted to possess. It used to be that everyone used metal, but then there were abuses and trouble with it. All the great wars have been fought over metal."

"How does a realm with no killing have wars?" Leven asked.

"They fight blindfolded," Clover answered, as though it were the most natural thing that could be imagined.

"Seriously?"

"Both sides cover their eyes so that any strong blow is an accident."

"That's ridiculous," Leven scoffed. "You said Foo was a place of possibilities. But I keep hearing about more and more restrictions."

"The wonder and beauty are what we are fighting to restore," Clover explained. "The privilege of working with metal is not a restriction. It's an art that belongs only to the Council of Wonder."

Leven drew in a deep breath, wondering at what he was learning. He scanned the landscape and took a good look at where he was.

Despite its strangeness, Foo was absolutely beautiful. The green-tinted moon was smearing itself down toward the horizon and radiating long strands of light that wiggled like wet noodles up into the purple sky. Under that light, the white streak in Leven's hair had a phosphoric glow to it.

The trail Farrow was leading them down was dark and paved with narrow, rectangular stones. It looked like a billion sticks of multicolored gum had been used to lay it out.

Leven took everything in and breathed deeply again. Despite the surrounding beauty, Leven felt like he didn't belong here. He was scared to death and wished the gateway still existed. He wished that Winter and Geth and Amelia were back by his side— that they had not been separated. He wished he had more faith in fate and knew more clearly what part he was supposed to play.

Farrow had made no effort to shorten his stride, and he was now well ahead of them. Leven wasn't sure that Farrow had the answers, but he began trotting to catch up to the crotchety old man again.

"So what's this stone of Geth's?" Leven asked Clover, who had gone invisible again.

"His stone is part of the Thirteen Stones. He . . . actually, it might just be easier to show you." Clover suddenly appeared in front of Leven's face. He had his feet planted on the sides of Leven's neck and his hands were clutching Leven's ears. Clover had materialized many different times and many different ways, but he had never gotten into Leven's face before like he was now.

"What are you doing?" Leven asked, drawing his head back.

"Hold on," Clover said. "Watch my eyes."

"Can't you just—"

"Watch," Clover insisted.

Leven obeyed, and Clover closed his eyes. After a moment, wisps of gray fog began seeping out from the corners of his eyelids, and when Clover opened his eyes, a large cloud of fog drifted out and up. As the fog cleared, Clover's blue eyes glowed bright and then darkened. Patterns of dancing, colored light moved from Clover's right eye to his left, then disappeared.

In the blackness of the eyeballs, a map materialized with a legend that said Foo. Leven studied it. He could see that the land of Foo was all one mass. As he watched, a succession of brightly lit scenes burned up through the surface of the map. There were vivid images of people behaving strangely, fantastic landscapes, animals such as Leven had never imagined, and lots of colors and motion. Each little episode would appear for a moment, then dissolve as another took its place.

Leven could hear Clover's voice explaining: "What you're see-ing are dreams as they enter Foo."

Clover closed both eyes, and when he opened them again, Leven could see the towns and villages that were scattered across Foo. Clover blinked, and another image appeared. "These are scenes from Foo's past," he said.

Through a fine mist, Leven could see crowds of people com-ing out of their dwellings, gathering, then moving in waves toward the town of Cork. While he watched, one by one, large chunks of land broke off from the bottom of Foo and began drifting out into the Veil Sea toward the Wet Border. The images leapt from Clover's right eye to his left, and a moment later Leven could see a series of islands forming off the shore of Foo, located in the Veil Sea, near the Hidden Border. There were thirteen of them, and each had its own distinctive shape. As Leven watched, a large, hand-shaped section of Foo reached out toward the islands.

Leven pushed his right hand through his hair and rubbed his own eyes.

Clover began to speak, "Those thirteen islands have great control over what happens in Foo. The land reaching toward them is controlled by the collective will of the dreams of Reality and the desires of the inhabitants of Foo."

Clover blinked again, and Leven saw in Clover's eyes the image of an old man with a long beard, wearing a dark cloak. The man was breathing heavily, kneeling down, bent over, seeming to stare not just *at* but *into* the ground. As the man pulled a seed from his robe, Clover suddenly sneezed, and the image instantly faded. The little sycophant shook his head, and his eyes were back to normal.

"Excuse me," he said.

"Amazing," Leven whispered. "Is there anything you can't do?"

"Well, I can't juggle. And according to my fourth-grade teacher, I can't write poetry," Clover said disgustedly, letting go of Leven's ears. "What an elitist. So the word *buddy* doesn't exactly rhyme with *pretty*. I was expressing myself. I wish she could have—"

Leven cleared his throat. "Who was that old man, and what happens when he looks into the dirt?"

Clover didn't answer immediately. Instead he cleared his throat. When he did speak, he sounded choked up. "That was Antsel," he explained. "He could look into the ground and see everything, as if he were standing on a bluff and looking out into the open sky. A real soil seer can see much farther underground than anyone can see above. Antsel could see across the world, or most of Foo."

"What good does that do?" Leven asked.

"You'd be surprised," Clover said. "He saw where to plant Geth, and his gifts were such that he could see dreams even before they reached the surface of Foo."

Leven closed and opened his brown eyes slowly, revealing a small band of gold around his pupils. The band of gold flared and then cooled, blending into the brown.

"I haven't seen a dream yet," Leven admitted as though he were confessing a dark secret.

"That's not unusual," Clover said, jumping up onto Leven's left shoulder and patting him on the top of his head. "Some people never see them. For most, it takes a few weeks for the first ones to appear. And usually the first dreams that nits pick up on are ones coming in from relatives. But since you don't have any relatives, it might take you a bit longer. It will happen. One day you'll be walking and suddenly you'll see a shaft of light split through the soil. If you're close enough, it will attach to you and you'll begin to enhance it."

"Attach to me?"

"Through the soles of your feet or the underside of your chin—maybe up through your palms," Clover explained. "Don't worry, it won't hurt. It's quite remarkable."

"I'm not sure I believe that," Leven said. "More than a few of your stories have been wrong."

Leven tried to walk faster, but Farrow was still hundreds of feet ahead of him.

"So, where's the battle?" Leven asked Clover. "I've seen a number of odd things, but I see no war. Where's the great fight Geth talked about?"

"You'll see," Clover said. "The day will come when each of your questions will be answered. That day's just not now. Not everyone can be the Want."

"The Want?" Leven questioned.

"He occupies the thirteenth stone and is pretty important—big house, all kinds of power. He can see every dream that enters Foo. Some say it's made him a bit . . . well, eccentric."

"Every dream?" Leven scoffed.

"Every dream," Clover confirmed. "He alone possesses the power of the gifts. Some say he's mad from all the images he sees, but he's still the Want, and his power holds Foo together."

"So he's more powerful than Geth?"

"Of course," Clover laughed. "But Geth has been in his presence. That's not something most here could handle. I'm not really supposed to be telling you these things. I took a few liberties in Reality, but here sycophants are supposed to know their place and stay in it. So, it might be wise for you not to mention all this to Geth. The Thirteen Stones control everything here. Each member of the Council of Wonder occupies one of them. The largest is home to the Want. He used to visit other parts of Foo, but now he just remains there, watching and shifting dreams."

A giant, birdlike snake flithered overhead and hissed before settling into a thick patch of fantrum trees. Foo was unbelievable; Leven just wished he understood it better.

By now, Farrow had moved out of sight, and Leven jogged up the path looking for him. The fuzzy light from the moon dripped down, throwing dark shadows across the path from the fantrum trees that lined the way.

"Farrow?" Leven called, still not able to see him. "Farrow?"

There was no answer. A wind began to blow, rustling the leaves of the trees, softly at first but rapidly increasing in force. Soon the limbs were roaring with air and thrashing about wildly.

"Clover," Leven said. "Something feels wrong."

There was no answer.

"Clover?" Leven said a bit louder.

There was no sound but the howling of the wind in the trees.

"Farrow!" Leven shouted.

The moon shifted color from green to white, sizzling like a big Alka-Seltzer tablet. It glowed bright and then began to hiss and dim, and the wind suddenly quit blowing. Everything grew still and silent.

"Come on, Clover," Leven said nervously. "You have to be here."

"He's not," a voice said.

Leven turned to find Farrow standing only a couple of feet away. The old man stood with his arms crossed in front of him, the hood of his orange robe pulled up over his head. His eyes glowed a pale red.

"Where'd you—?" Leven began.

"Quiet!" Farrow ordered, his eyes pulsating.

Farrow uncrossed his arms and inserted two fingers of his right hand into his mouth. He created a high-pitched whistle that sounded out into the surrounding forest. Something began to rustle in the trees.

Leven looked around nervously. He glanced down at the trail in front of him and for a moment thought he saw Clover standing there, looking at him.

"Clover, thank—hey, you're not Clover."

Whatever it was, it was a few inches taller than Clover's twelve inches. The creature had stubby ears that resembled swollen corks, and where its tail should have been there was a third arm with a hand that it was using to scratch its forehead vigorously. Its face was square with a round, wrinkly nose and narrow eyes. It opened its tiny mouth and cooed at Leven. The creature rocked and bounced back and forth like a monkey.

Leven stepped back. Farrow whistled again, and a second creature slipped out from the trees and stood behind the other. It too scratched its forehead and began to rock. Soon they were cooing and bouncing in harmony. Two of them were far less cute than one. A third appeared at the side of the trail and also cooed, erasing any trace of cuteness.

"Clover," Leven whispered, "what are they?"

A fourth emerged from the dirt while a fifth and a sixth shimmied down a tree and stood behind Leven—all staring at him and cooing loudly.

"Seriously, Clover!" Leven said desperately. "Where are you?"

Three more dropped from the trees onto the path. Seven rolled in from behind. A dozen emerged from the forest—all of them cooing, their combined sound growing. Fifty of them pushed up from the side of the trail and joined the gathering. Some of them began to stand on the others' shoulders. Leven began to panic. Clover had clearly abandoned him, and the growing crowd was quickly closing in. The ugly creatures gave off a dirty, rank odor.

Leven closed his eyes and willed his gift to kick in.

Nothing.

"Farrow," Leven pleaded.

"Where is Geth?" Farrow barked.

"I have no idea. You said—"

"What does he look like? What form is he in?" Farrow pressed.

"What?" Leven answered, confused.

"The Lore Coil was short on description," Farrow growled. "The locusts the Sochemists sent out only described him as being small."

"He's not small," Leven lied. "And he will be here any moment."

Farrow looked around nervously and then stamped his feet in a rage. The hundreds of creatures surrounding Leven tightened their circle. And when a loud whistle sounded in the distance, Farrow smiled and whistled back.

"Tell me where Geth is!" Farrow raged.

"He's coming," Leven insisted, holding his chin out and staring Farrow down with his eyes. "You won't stop him."

"I brought you here to give you a chance," Farrow seethed. "But I can see now you are no good to us. You know nothing and should be buried."

Farrow began to tremble and shake. His lower half darkened and cracked, exposing the fake that he was. Like a cover being pulled off to expose a statue, Farrow, as Leven had known him, vanished. In his place were five of the little creatures stacked on top of each other like a totem pole. They squealed with delight, and the top one spoke.

"It's a first-impersonation quilt," he said, nodding down to the cloak they had been hiding under. "We tharms need them to disguise ourselves so we can make better first impressions. Our smell and shape seem to turn people off."

The five tharms that had once been Farrow hopped off each other and joined the hundreds of others pressing in on Leven.

"You should have given up Geth," they cooed in unison.

Another whistle sounded, and all the tharms jumped at once toward Leven. Instinctively, Leven sprang forward into the thickest gathering of them. He knocked over a half dozen before he was dragged to a stop by all of their tiny hands grabbing and holding him. Their third arms were particularly strong.

When Leven tried to scream, a couple of dozen little hands crammed his mouth into silence, and he was lifted off his feet. Hordes of the cooing creatures piled in under him, their tiny hands pinching and hoisting him higher. Then they took off running, holding Leven above them. Moving with surprising swiftness, they raced into the forest. Suspended on his back, Leven could see tree limbs flying over him, inches from his head and body. The pack of tharms pushed up a steep mountain not slowing in the least; in fact, they were gaining speed with each step, cooing madly like a million psychotic pigeons.

They crested a rocky mountain cap that was covered with a white, spongy fungus and rocketed down the backside, flying across the landscape. Leven was being held by a thousand hands, but he still bounced up and down with each movement and step. Leven's mind flashed back to his life in Oklahoma. He remembered the afternoons when he had tried to get home from school without the neighborhood ruffians Brick and Glen throwing rocks at him or running him over with their bikes. Leven had always run to get away, but now he was beginning to feel different. He could see the value in fighting for himself. As the tharms held him in their hands, running, Leven wanted desperately to act instead of being acted upon.

Leven's legs and arms burned as if they had fallen asleep and now blood was racing back into them like pins and needles.

Suddenly the creatures flipped him like a gangly pancake onto his stomach, so that he was being carried facedown and backwards. A great swarm of bit bugs hovered over the racing horde of tharms, their mass glowing brightly. The light from the bugs combined with the glowing bark of fantrum trees and a dim moon to give Leven more than enough light to see what was happening.

After a time, the strange escorts slowed, and Leven could see hundreds of other tharms standing in a circle around a large, dark hole in the ground. Each had all three of its arms raised above its head, fists full of soil.

The sight wasn't exactly comforting.

"Clover!" Leven screamed. "Winter! Geth! Anyone!"

It was no use. Nobody was going to help Leven. As they approached the hole, the tharms cooed in a great chorus, and the ones surrounding the hole parted to let the others through. The tharms carrying Leven stopped abruptly. They drew their arms back in sync and heaved Leven into the air over the hole.

Leven yelled, frantically grabbing for something to prevent his fall, then dropped like a rock into the hole. It was about seven feet deep, and in an instant he landed painfully in the bottom.

Immediately, the tharms began throwing handfuls of dirt in on top of him, pelting his whole body and quickly pinning him down. The clumps of soil clutched at Leven. Leven tried to stand, but the weight of the dirt was too much. He was being buried alive.

Leven's eyes burned gold. He tried to picture fate in a saving manner, but all he could see was the little bit of air around him in his hole—the same hole that was quickly filling up with dirt. Leven wanted to fight. He could see soft wind blowing through the trees of the forest. Leven manipulated the wind to snake through the dirt like a bionic worm and create a bubble of air around his body. The wind drew in and enveloped Leven like a bubble-wrapped mummy. Dirt continued to rain down. In a few moments Leven was entombed seven feet beneath the surface of the Swollen Forest, wrapped in thick, soft air.

Leven concentrated his thoughts to keep the air intact around him. The tharms were working like mad to fill in the hole, and the weight of the dirt piling up on top of it was overwhelming.

The air he had worked in began to heat up, and sweat poured into Leven's eyes. He trembled violently, fighting the very soil as it settled and acted upon him.

CHAPTER EIGHT

THE RING OF PLAGUE

Jamoon stood towering over Winter. There were eleven red-robed beings behind him. Winter had seen their eyes reflecting back at her from the puddle water she had been cleaning herself in after climbing up out of the gunt.

She stood to look directly at Jamoon.

Jamoon's thick black robe obscured all but his right eye, which was glaring. A bright red ring was embroidered on the cuff of both his sleeves, indicating Jamoon's status. Winter quickly pushed Geth up her sleeve as her heart rose to her throat.

A warm wind blew against her wet hair.

Jamoon's robe billowed, giving him a greater form than he already possessed. Winter would have been terrified just seeing Jamoon, but it was the robed figures with him that bothered her most. Eleven beings stood tall behind Jamoon—six on one side and five on the other. Each of them wore a scarlet cloak with a black band running around his lower sleeves. From a former memory, Winter knew who and what they were.

The whole of Foo knew who they were.

One of Sabine's most effective weapons of war had been his establishment of the two great Rings of Plague. Each Ring consisted of twelve nits, each possessing a different gift. Nits were people who were snatched from Reality by fate and brought to Foo, where each was given two things: a sycophant to help them cope with the shock, and a unique gift that they were expected to use in the work of enhancing dreams.

The gifts didn't come in nice red boxes with yellow bows. They were abilities that developed slowly and over time, based on the nits' needs and personalities. The gifts were ultimately bestowed by one of the Thirteen Stones in the Veil Sea.

Within each Ring of Plague Sabine had organized there was a complete assortment of powers: one to fight with ice, one to see through the soil, one to throw lightning, one to fly, one to fade, one to shrink, one to breathe fire, one to run like the wind, one to burrow, one to see through rock, one to levitate objects, and one to push and bind dreams.

Possessing all these gifts, the Rings could not be easily defeated. There was almost nothing they couldn't do or fend off. Under Sabine's direction, these Rings of Plague traveled across Foo, capturing any who would not join them in their quest to fuse Foo with Reality, and causing accidents to those who opposed them. A third of the inhabitants of Foo resisted Sabine's leadership, but most of those beings lived in Cusp or the beautiful, well-protected, and prosperous city of Cork. Now, the members of the Ring of Plague were looking to find a way to infiltrate these last few strongholds of resistance.

They had no mercy, only a quest.

And that quest was to achieve the ability to move freely between Foo and Reality. Having been originally snatched from Reality, the members of the Ring knew what they were missing and desired to go back, taking with them the gifts they now had. Like Sabine, they believed it was possible.

For all its power and determination, the Ring of Plague was not an invincible foe, however. With the help of Winter and others, Geth had defeated the first one years before. Using his ability to travel by fate, Geth had succeeded in capturing the twelve angry nits and now had those devoted followers of Sabine held captive in secret places throughout Foo. Only Geth and Antsel knew where they were being detained, but of course Antsel was now gone, which left the secret to Geth alone.

Enraged by Geth's disruption of the first Ring of Plague, Sabine was driven by an insatiable hatred of Geth, who as the head token of the Council of Wonder was the legitimate heir to the throne of Foo. Many years before, Sabine and his shadows had succeeded in capturing Geth and forcing his soul into the seed of a fantrum tree. But the rightful king of Foo had somehow escaped, and in some disguise was now back in Foo. If it was Geth's aim to pick off the members of the second Ring of Plague, Jamoon was determined to prevent it.

Winter was now confronted by Jamoon and eleven ominous

members of the second Ring of Plague. As a rant—an ungifted offspring of a nit and a cog—Jamoon was a being of such weak determination that he couldn't ever just manipulate a dream and move on. As with all rants, his left half was in a state of constant change, continually reflecting dreams coming into Foo from Reality. Even so, Jamoon had somehow risen to be Sabine's first in command and exercised some control over the members of the Ring.

Winter counted those there and realized that the Ring wasn't complete. She wondered what gift they were missing. Had she realized that the absent member was Sabine and his gift of freezing, she might have simply frozen them all and fled. Unfortunately, because of her fear and confusion, that fact didn't register.

Jamoon cleared his throat. "Hello, Winter," he said calmly, suppressing all surprise. "You have returned. I would not have recognized you were it not for your eyes."

Winter looked directly at him with her green eyes, fearing him, but having no clear understanding of who he really was.

"Where's Leven?" Jamoon asked.

Winter was silent.

"Where's Leven?" the eleven Ring members echoed in an ugly chorus, inching closer to the wild-haired girl.

Winter's skin crawled.

"How should I know?" she shouted, getting to her feet and trying to act brave. "Those stupid rovens knocked me out and split us up."

"And Geth?" Jamoon asked, as if he had only a casual interest. "Where is Geth?"

"Gone," Winter snapped, hoping they wouldn't search her. She pointed. "Look at the size of that chasm. He could be trapped anywhere in there."

The gunt had completely filled in the rip, but that didn't make the size any less spectacular. As far as anyone could see there was nothing but the dull shine off the gigantic river of gunt. It looked like a massive glacier that ran for miles.

"The rovens did an above-average job," Jamoon smiled. "And Geth was in there, you say?"

"I'm sure he was," Winter said sadly.

Jamoon and the members of the Ring hovering behind him began to hiss and shake, but whether they were registering frustration or joy, Winter couldn't tell.

"And the old woman?" Jamoon asked.

Winter's green eyes burned with hatred. She made a tight fist with each hand and could feel her fingernails digging into her palms, but she forced herself to take a deep breath and then release it. Gradually, the hatred in her eyes was replaced with sadness.

"She was trapped in the gunt," Winter answered defiantly.

"Then she is dead," Jamoon said sharply.

Winter was surprised by what Jamoon knew, but she forced herself to remain stone-faced and passive.

"Your eyes always could hide mountains," Jamoon sniffed. "But I can see that the Lore Coil did not sweep over you—

perhaps when it echoes back . . . For now, take comfort knowing that all of Foo knows of your mortal state. The Coil has been spotty on many things, but it spoke clearly about this. You are capable of dying. Reality, it seems, has made you vulnerable."

Winter's mind was racing, filled with impulses and synapses, frantically searching for some memory of what a Lore Coil was. The thought of everyone knowing that she and Leven could die was as frightening as any thought she had ever had.

As Winter was searching her mind, Jamoon tilted his head back slightly and clucked his tongue. Then he raised his arms, and the bottom half of his robe began to billow and sway.

Winter stared as bits of black seeped out from under his robe and rose into the air, where they separated, screaming and spitting and filling the sky. In just seconds, Jamoon and the Ring were surrounded by black, dead, yellow-eyed fowls. Jamoon motioned his arms forward, and the entire gathering of decaying nihils swooped toward Winter.

Winter froze them, but it didn't slow the dead birds in the least. Frozen they screamed even louder, hurling toward her like an aggressive ice storm. The nihils swirled about her like a frigid twister, violently whipping her hair, the beating of their wings sucking the air from her lungs. A single nihil landed on her shoulder, clinging to her with its ice-pick talons. The nihil pecked Winter sharply on the neck.

Winter felt the sharp beak penetrate her skin, sending frozen waves of dark emotion and fear throughout her body. Winter swatted and yelled, fighting the hundreds of other birds away. It was useless. Her vision pulsated like a dying star. She felt her knees buckling, and her mind and body were filled with thousands of dark and troubling thoughts.

As Winter sank to the ground, Jamoon lifted his arms and the nihils gathered into a cloud, then swooped down and disappeared up under his robe, as though they had been vacuumed up. As they did so, their hissing and screaming ceased, and silence descended over the scene.

In the darkness, Winter lay on the ground, her body twitching and shivering.

"Bring her," Jamoon ordered. "We will see what she remembers."

Two members of the Ring of Plague picked Winter up. Geth pushed up against Winter's wrist and scooted farther up her sleeve, hoping to remain undetected.

CHAPTER NINE

FRIENDS COME IN ALL SIZES, BUT USUALLY THEY ARE BIGGER THAN A TOOTHPICK

Dennis Wood didn't have his own office at Snooker and Woe, but he had discovered and claimed for his own a small, unused utility room—a closet, really—with a little window overlooking the street. Two years before, when the firm was throwing out some old furniture, Dennis had snuck a desk and a banged-up metal filing cabinet for himself and set them up in the closet. On the top of his desk was a cheap metal holder with a plastic strip embossed with the word *Janitor* on it. The name holder was the one thing he had been given by his boss. Dennis didn't view it as a gift; he viewed it as one more way for his employers to make sure he knew exactly what he was.

Dennis kept his cleaning supplies in one of the drawers of the filing cabinet and tools for building model toys in his desk drawers. He spent a lot of time at that desk pretending to think, assembling model planes, tanks, and cars. Sometimes he could waste an entire day just sitting there. It was a good day when nobody came looking for him to clean something or empty something else.

Of course, his time was never completely wasted. Dennis loved assembling his plastic or balsa-wood models—the more intricate, the better—and he would spend hours lost in the act of building. He wanted desperately to own a plane that could fly him away or a tank that could bust him out of where he was. But Dennis knew that would never happen, so instead he spent his money and time building what most of the world would call expensive toys.

Dennis wasn't building today.

For the last two hours Dennis had been sitting at his desk, staring at the toothpick he had come across during lunch. The toothpick felt warm and seemed to vibrate just a bit when he held it.

Dennis studied the sliver carefully, holding it underneath the thick magnifying glass he used for building models.

It was a long toothpick with a dark grain of wood running up and down one side. Just beneath the purple fringe top there looked to be the tiniest round knot, and above that to the side was a slight notch in the wood. The knot was no bigger than the tip of a dull pencil. Dennis reached for one of the X-Acto knives he kept in an empty mayonnaise jar on his desk and picked up the toothpick.

Dennis carefully poked the knot with the tip of the knife.

As he did so, the blade and the toothpick buzzed, causing

Dennis to jump and toss both to the ground. The X-Acto blade clanked loudly against the linoleum floor, while the toothpick bounced and rolled under the desk.

"I'm losing it," Dennis said to himself. "Losing it. My father was right."

Dennis's father, Chuck, had always been worried that his son, like him, would someday lose his mind, run away from his family, hide out in an abandoned building for a year, and eventually be committed to an asylum.

"A toothpick," Dennis muttered. "I got a sandwich and there was a toothpick in it. Lots of people get lots of sandwiches with toothpicks in them."

He tried to take his mind off the little sliver of wood lying beneath his desk, but it was nearly impossible.

"There's a toothpick on the floor," he mumbled. "So what?" A slight red crept into his cheeks, making his white head look like parts of it had been laundered in a load filled with red socks.

Dennis glanced at the small digital clock on his desk. The glowing numbers changed up one.

Dennis couldn't take it any longer.

Frantically, he pushed his chair back and fell to his knees, feeling under the desk for the toothpick. He found a washer, a paper clip, and an old fortune cookie slip. It read: "Dare to dream." Dennis remembered the day he had tossed that down. Not only was it not technically a true fortune, it was a painful reminder of his dreamless life. He tossed it aside again and pushed the desk back so as to be able to reach farther under.

He didn't know why, but he was desperate to find that tooth-pick. He groped around under the desk until his fingers brushed against the toothpick's purple top and he took hold of it and pulled it out. As he got up from the floor and settled onto his chair, he laid the toothpick on the blotter on his desk and stud-ied the little stick.

The toothpick vibrated.

"What the . . . ?" Dennis muttered, furrowing his brow. Two seconds later the toothpick vibrated once more and rolled to the side just a bit.

Dennis rubbed his eyes. He glanced around the little room, then fumbled through his top drawer and pulled out an even thinner X-Acto knife. Holding the toothpick beneath the magni-fying glass, he used the point of the knife to touch the tiny knot on the toothpick just below where the purple plastic top was attached.

The knife buzzed.

The hair on the back of Dennis's neck stood like the quills of a threatened porcupine. Dennis pushed the tip of the knife just slightly into the wood, and, like a miniscule cork being fired from a pent-up bottle of champagne, the tiny knot of wood popped out and shot up. It ricocheted off the magnifying lens and desk and into Dennis's right eye.

Screaming, Dennis dropped the knife and reached for his eye. But his concern for himself was short-lived as a much higher-pitched and more alarming scream sounded. Dennis let go of the toothpick to cover his ears. He looked around frantically. The noise seemed to be growing. He glanced at the tooth-pick, realizing that the tiny hole he had just opened was the source of the screaming. He pushed his index finger over the opening to shut it up.

The toothpick bit him.

Dennis drew back his hand and leaped up off the chair. The toothpick was still wailing. Panicking, Dennis reached for a broken stapler and slammed it down on the toothpick.

"Ahhhhhhhhh!" it wailed, much louder than one would expect something so small to do.

Someone outside the closet began banging on the door.

Dennis moved the stapler off the toothpick. He tore off a piece of Scotch tape from a dispenser on his desk and stuck it over the hole he had made, taping the toothpick to the desk and putting an abrupt end to the screaming. But beneath the tape, the toothpick was still vibrating madly.

The banging on the door stopped and someone yelled, "What's going on in there?" The door handle jiggled as whoever it was tried to make his way in. Dennis, of course, always made sure the door was locked. He had been interrupted too many times straightening staples or sorting pencils.

"Are you all right?" the voice asked with more disdain than sympathy.

"Fine," Dennis lied, noticing for the first time that the spot where the toothpick had bit him was bleeding. "I'm fine. The toner in the copy machine was leaking," he lied again. "There was a leak in the toner," he repeated, as if saying it twice would make it true.

Dennis tore off another piece of tape and secured the bottom half of the gyrating toothpick. The stapler he had hammered it with had done some damage. One end of the toothpick was slightly bent, and the tip had been split, creating what looked like tiny legs with a short, striped tail hanging down between them.

The vibrating ceased. Dennis just stared. He was trying desperately to make sense of what was happening but had no answers. He thought for a moment that he was simply dreaming, but that didn't seem likely because Dennis never dreamed. According to his father, this inability to dream was a family trait; the men in the Wood family didn't dream. When they closed their eyes at night they saw nothing but gray. Dennis had always wanted to doze off and see things in a way his sad life didn't offer, but it never happened. So he built models and pretended that he was someone else doing something altogether different from his actual activities.

Now, however, here he was, gaping at a toothpick taped to his desk and wondering if he really wanted to experience something different from what his days had always offered.

He decided he might.

After a few moments, Dennis peeled the tape off the top end of the toothpick to see if it would scream again.

Silence.

Dennis touched the purple, hairlike fringe and pulled back.

"Happy?" the toothpick whispered fiercely. "Captured Ezra, have you? Well, you've got me, now finish me off, coward!"

"What?" Dennis asked, confused.

"End it!" Ezra snarled. "But before you do, I want to see you. I want to see who cheated fate and did Ezra in. Slice me an eye."

"E . . . e . . . excuse me?" Dennis asked nervously, more than just a little unsettled by what was happening.

"An eye, you fool!"

"I can't cut you—"

"I demand to see!" Ezra screamed.

Dennis picked his X-Acto knife back up. He looked at the blade reflecting under the glow of the humming fluorescent light. There was perspiration on his forehead, and the palms of his hands were moist and cold.

"Do it!" Ezra yelled. "Slice me an eye!"

Dennis put the tip of the sharp blade against the toothpick. He had no real idea of what constituted proper feature arrangement for a toothpick, so he skimmed the edge of the knife across the base of the purple fringe and above the hole he was getting yelled at through. It was only a light cut, but it did the trick. The single horizontal cut opened just a bit and then fluttered due to the brightness of the light. The eye closed and the mouth sighed.

Dennis felt his own forehead to see if he was ill. "It's happened," he moaned. "I've lost my mind."

Dennis stood up and began pacing the small space. He grabbed a blue paper towel from a metal shelf and wiped his forehead and hair.

"Sit down," Ezra ordered.

Dennis sat.

"Listen," Ezra whispered, causing Dennis to lean in closer.

"All I want to be able to do . . ."

Ezra pushed himself up and out of the tape and sprang from the desk directly onto Dennis's forehead, where he bit down hard. Dennis screamed, swatting at Ezra as if he were a pesky fly. The blow knocked Ezra loose, and he landed on Dennis's left shoulder.

"Ahhhhhahhahh!" Ezra screamed just before sinking his mouth into Dennis's neck.

Dennis slapped his neck, trying to stop Ezra, but he was too slow. Ezra was now on top of his head, violently jumping up and down.

The banging on the door started again.

"What's going on in there?" a voice demanded. "Should we call someone?"

"I'm fine," Dennis yelled back, looking frantically around for Ezra.

"You're not fine!" Ezra screamed, diving from off a high metal shelf. "I will finish you!"

Dennis spun, accidentally

knocking over a large, open jar of rubber cement. The dark bottle rolled to the edge of the desk and dropped to the floor with an impressive *splack*. Rubber cement oozed out over the floor as Dennis batted the air like a six-year-old girl who has just seen a big, scary bumblebee.

Ezra dug into Dennis's right hand with his pointed tail, and Dennis pushed away, sending Ezra to the ground and into the spreading splotch of rubber cement. Ezra lay trapped on his back, more angry than ever, growling maniacally. He writhed in the sticky goo, screaming for Dennis's head.

"What's going on in there?" Dennis's coworkers outside the door yelled. "Open up right now!"

"Please stop screaming," Dennis whispered fiercely to Ezra. "I'll get you out, just stop screaming!"

Ezra closed his mouth hole for a second and stared Dennis down with his one eye. He opened his mouth and blew.

"You have thirty seconds," Ezra hissed.

"How do I know you won't just start biting me again?" Dennis asked.

"It's a chance you're going to—"

Ezra's threat was cut short by the sound of people slamming up against the door. Dennis's coworkers had lost all patience. They were working the doorknob with a screwdriver, trying to pop it open and find out what was happening inside Dennis's closet.

If this scene were in a comic book, you would have been able to see a tiny wooden lightbulb go on above Ezra's head. But this was not a comic book, so all Dennis saw was a slight mischievous smile from Ezra's mouth.

"You hate it here," Ezra said, giving voice to a secret that Dennis for years had been too afraid to admit.

Dennis nodded warily.

"You would do just about anything to get away from this place, wouldn't you?"

Again Dennis nodded, this time with more surety.

Ezra looked closely at Dennis. Ezra wasn't exactly coming from a position of strength. He was, after all, a party toothpick stuck to the floor with rubber cement. But he was exuding enough anger and rage to seem like a four-story-tall giant.

"Pull me out, and I'll take you with me," Ezra offered wickedly.

Dennis looked at Ezra like a fish that had been held from water for hours and was now being offered an entire lake.

"Take me where?" Dennis whispered.

"Foo," Ezra spat.

Dennis had no idea where Foo was, but he was fairly certain it wasn't located in the building he now cleaned, or in the city he had resided in for the last twenty-eight years.

Dennis reached for Ezra just as the door to the closet was finally forced open. He closed his hand around the toothpick and stood up to face those who had so rudely barged in.

"What is going on?" a short woman with big teeth and skinny legs demanded.

"Who were you screaming at?" asked Randall, the firm's newest partner.

"I'm sick," was all Dennis said.

He squeezed out the door, pushed into the hall, and ran toward the elevator. He rode twenty floors down to the lobby, where he walked quickly across the tile floor and out the front revolving door. It wasn't until he was three blocks away that he finally opened his fist and looked at the sticky toothpick in his hand.

Ezra growled.

"I'm sorry," Dennis apologized. "I didn't want anyone to see you."

"You have the spine of a used tissue," Ezra said meanly. "We could have taken them."

"You were stuck in glue," Dennis reasoned.

Ezra spat.

"You're a toothpick," Dennis added.

Ezra didn't like that. "Pig!" he shouted, jumping from Dennis's hand onto his forearm. He began rubbing himself against the hairy skin, giving Dennis one terrific burn.

Dennis blinked to stop himself from crying. On the basis of a promise from a very hostile toothpick, he had just walked out on the only job he had ever had, and now he had a wicked burn to go with the bite marks on his forehead.

Ezra scrambled up Dennis's arm and stopped on top of his shoulder. He was breathing as heavily as a toothpick could.

"Sorry," Dennis offered.

"Boy, I'll say," Ezra replied coldly. "If you're going to come with me, you have got to watch what you say. I might be what you see before you, but I will not always be."

That was too deep for Dennis.

"I need arms," Ezra insisted. "I'm not waiting for fate to mold me."

Dennis stared dumbly at him.

"Bite me," Ezra instructed.

Dennis felt like crying again. It's not easy, after all, to be insulted by anyone. It's even worse when you're being insulted by a small piece of wood that was once holding your sandwich together. Before Dennis could begin crying, however, Ezra worked himself up Dennis's face and forced his way into his mouth. It wasn't too hard, seeing as how Dennis was already in the process of dropping his jaw. After getting inside, Ezra stretched out across Dennis's front bottom teeth. He eyed the top teeth up above and then scooted over just a bit.

"Do it."

"Do uht?" Dennis asked, his mouth still hanging open.

"Bite me!" Ezra insisted.

Dennis gingerly closed his mouth.

Ezra hollered, "That's the worst biting I've ever seen. Bite, you baby!"

Dennis opened his mouth and chomped down hard.

This time Ezra screamed for an entirely different reason.

Dennis released, and Ezra called him a coward. Somewhat irritated by Ezra's bad attitude, Dennis ground his front teeth together. He could feel Ezra beginning to split in two. After grinding for a few moments, Dennis spat Ezra out onto the sidewalk.

Ezra bounced a couple of times and came to a stop. Glaring at Dennis with his single eye, he spat and growled. Dennis knelt down and instantly began to apologize.

"You are an emotional toddler," Ezra declared.

Dennis had never felt more confused in his life. And it is somewhat important to point out that Dennis had been plenty confused in his life. Like the time his mother told him she needed to go out for just a moment and then never came back. That was confusing. Or all the times his father would say he loved him and then would leave him for weeks to fend for himself. That was confusing too.

Now a toothpick had called him "an emotional toddler." That was also confusing.

Dennis reached to pick up Ezra but stopped when the tooth-pick ordered him to leave it alone. Dennis stared at the poor little thing as it writhed and moaned on the ground. Ezra's torso was wet and bent, thanks to the biting he had just endured. Ezra wriggled and yelled and took advantage of his soggy, chewed condition by painfully ripping a small strand of wood away from his side and forming an arm. The pain didn't slow him. He gasped as he struggled to rip a second appendage away from his body.

He succeeded, but the pain was too much. The tiny tooth-pick, which now had two arms, closed his only eye and passed out.

Dennis sat down on the curb and tenderly picked Ezra up. He laid the beat-up toothpick on his knee and folded a bit of his trousers over him. Ezra's damp purple-fringed top looked like an odd bug resting on his leg. Dennis shifted his position and leaned his back up against a huge Dumpster. As he looked at the battered little toothpick, Dennis couldn't help it. He began to cry. This time in earnest.

ii

The tiny chair just outside the classroom door was considerably less than comfortable. Tim Tuttle shifted in the seat and thought about just how he would phrase the questions he wanted to ask Winter's teacher. He wadded and tugged at the blue baseball cap he held in his hands. His heart was beating loudly.

After keeping Tim waiting another fifteen minutes, Mr. Bentwonder came to the door. He looked down the hall in both directions and let his eyes settle on Tim. Mr. Bentwonder sighed heavily, as if he had just solved every problem in the world and nobody had taken the time to thank him. He then blew his nose into a dirty handkerchief, shoved it into his pocket, and announced that he would see Tim now.

After they were seated in Mr. Bentwonder's office, Tim said, "Thank you so much for meeting with me."

"A teacher's time is a precious thing," Mr. Bentwonder breathed, his fat, mushy face jiggling as he spoke. "Now, how may I enlighten you?"

"I have a question about one of your students."

"You may have heard wonders about my intellect, but I'm afraid I can't read your mind," Mr. Bentwonder said, feigning modesty. "To which pupil are you referring?"

"I'm sorry," Tim said. "Her name is Winter. Winter Frore."

Mr. Bentwonder's face went from pink to pale in two seconds flat. He began to stammer and cough. He pulled his dirty handkerchief back out to cover his mouth, but that did nothing but leave his nose open to spray. He coughed so violently that Tim stood and started patting him on the back in support.

"Are you okay?" Tim asked.

Mr. Bentwonder brushed him away and tried to compose himself. He closed his eyes and patted his fat cheeks. "What about her?" he asked defensively. "She is no longer my pupil."

"What happened to her?" Tim asked.

"I've already told the police," Mr. Bentwonder sniffed. "It was the worst experience of my professional life."

"So she was expelled?"

"She would be if she walked in that door again," he said like a spoiled baby. "She put a spell on all of us."

"A spell?"

"On the entire class." He shook his head in disbelief. "One moment I'm filling their brains with information that might very well propel them to greatness, and the next thing I know the entire classroom is . . . frozen."

"Frozen?" Tim asked in disbelief and with a slight smirk.

"I know what you're thinking," Mr. Bentwonder said, shaking a finger at Tim. "Trust me, I understand science. I could have taught any number of subjects."

"I'm sure you could have."

"It *seemed* as though the room had turned to ice, but I'm

certain it was some sort of illusion. That witch," he growled. "Regardless, when I awoke from her trance, my tie had been cut in half, the principal was locked in a hall closet, and that brat was nowhere to be seen."

"Brat?" Tim asked. "And no one went after her?"

"Why should we?"

"Don't you have a responsibility to—?"

"I don't like your tone," Mr. Bentwonder said. "Who did you say you were, anyway?"

"I'm Winter's neighbor."

"Well, then, what business is this of yours?" Mr. Bentwonder asked testily.

"Don't you think—?"

"No, I don't think," Mr. Bentwonder interrupted. "And I will ask you to leave before I am compelled to use force."

"No need for that," Tim said, standing. "Thanks for your time."

Mr. Bentwonder blew his nose in response.

Tim Tuttle stepped into the hall and walked out the front door of the school. Nothing seemed to make sense.

"A frozen classroom," he said to himself. "How is it possible for a teacher to be hypnotized by a thirteen-year-old girl?"

Tim Tuttle pulled his baseball hat from his back pocket and put it on. He was more determined than ever to find Winter. He was also more curious than ever to find out exactly what had happened.

He stepped off the curb and headed to the Frore home.

CHAPTER TEN

ROYAL FLUSH

"Wake up, Winter," Geth whispered. "Wake up."

Winter could faintly hear his voice, but her head felt like a thick wad of throbbing clay.

"Are you okay?" Geth whispered. "You must wake up."

Winter had no idea where she was or if she would ever be able to open her eyes again. She was lying on something cold, and her hands were tied behind her and bound tightly to her body. A heavy shroud covered her from head to foot, and she was completely unable to move.

She moaned, her head full of cold, empty thoughts.

"Good girl," Geth said kindly. "Push the blackness out of your mind."

"But I can't open my eyes," Winter managed to mumble.

Geth smiled. "That's all right, there's nothing to see. Just relax."

"Where are we?" she groaned, licking at her dry lips.

"I'm not certain," Geth replied. "Something bit you, and Jamoon transported you here on the back of a roven."

Winter struggled against her bonds. "My wrists hurt," she complained.

"Of course," Geth said, patting her on the shoulder as she lay there. "They don't want you touching anything."

"Why don't they want me touching things?" Winter asked. "I don't need to touch things to freeze them," she added. "I only need to touch things to—"

It suddenly made sense—the cold against her back, her trapped and covered hands. Winter used everything inside of herself to force open her eyes.

She gasped.

She could barely see out of the slits in the mask, but she could tell that the entire room was solid ice and smaller than her height in all directions. The low ceiling was frozen, and crystals of ice drifted down from above, illuminated by a pulsating white light. Winter rolled her head from side to side. There were no windows or doors. The walls were solid sheets of ice, glistening in the dull light the crystals on the ceiling provided. In the corner was what looked to be a block of ice about the size of a bucket. There was a shallow basin on the top of the block and a small hole in the center of the basin.

"Sorry, but that's the rest room," Geth blushed.

"I don't know what good it will do me. With my hands

bound I can't use it anyway," Winter moaned. "How long till they take us out of here?"

"Well . . ." Geth cleared his wood hole. "They bring people here for one reason only. This place was Sabine's creation. He knew he couldn't kill, so he built this sadistic waiting room. He would keep his enemies here until they were weak enough for him to steal their souls and put them into an endless dark dream, or perhaps cram them into a fantrum seed."

"This is where he kept you?" Winter asked, feeling herself come awake even more.

"Yes," Geth answered. "It was three months before I was weak enough for him to extract my soul. You, however, are different." Geth closed his eyes as if overcome by thought.

"I understand. It's not a great feeling realizing the whole of Foo knows we're expendable," Winter lamented. "So a Lore Coil gave us away?"

"Yes, and it will probably drift back and forth for years, weakening with each pass. Some coils take hundreds of years to vanish completely. Even now, the air is filled with bits and pieces of conversations and events that have long since expired. Of course, most can't hear anything carried by the Lore Coil after a second or third pass. The Sochemists of Morfit can, but even they fight over what they think they've heard. There appears, however, to be no argument about our mortality."

"What about Lev?" Winter said quietly.

"Fate will tend him as it will us," Geth whispered.

"Hopefully he is well and headed for the turrets."

"So what'll we do?" Winter asked. "I can't even stretch out in here."

"Well, I hate to be the one to suggest it because then I've no one to blame but myself. But I could always find out where that toilet leads."

Winter turned her head as far as she could and looked toward the frozen stump.

"I would never have suggested that," she insisted, trying to smile.

"Fate's not always pretty," Geth sighed. "I'll get out and restore myself in the fire of the turrets. Then I can free you and alleviate your condition."

"My condition?" Winter tried to smile. "Oh, yeah, dying."

"Death is just a condition fate is forced to use at times," Geth said seriously.

"You're making me feel a lot better," Winter lied.

"Sorry," Geth said as nicely as he could. "You need to stay alive. Save your energy, because I don't remember this place serving meals."

"I'm already thirsty," Winter complained.

"Think of the bright side," Geth smiled. "There'll be less reason for you to use the facilities." And with that Geth took off running toward the block of ice in the corner. He flew across the floor, leaped into the air, and dove into the small hole, using the facilities in his own special way.

* * * *

ii

Major amusement parks would do well to study the pipes and drainage system of the caves that Geth was traveling down. It would make quite a ride—the Toilet of Terror. He first entered a long, steep pipe where he gained terrific speed before hurtling headlong into a succession of multiple bends and wickedly sharp turns that would have left a normal person breathless. After what seemed like hours, Geth shot out of a hole in the mountainside and into the Sun River. The river pulled Geth along for about a mile before he was able to work his way over to the bank and crawl out onto dry land.

Geth struggled for a time to catch his breath. Finally he stood and took a look around, surprised at how confused he was. He recognized the Sun River, but he wasn't sure at which point he had ended up. More of a concern, however, was that he had absolutely no idea where he had just come from. He would never be able to backtrack to find Winter. Geth knew Foo pretty well. He knew the places of breathtaking beauty and the places best avoided for fear of capture or danger. But he had no idea of the location of Sabine's ice caves. When he had first been captured and taken there, he had been in a drugged state. And when he had arrived with Winter a few hours ago, he had been tucked in the hem of her sleeve and so had seen nothing. Now, thanks to his wild ride through the pipes, Geth couldn't even begin to guess what direction he had just come from.

"Perfect," Geth said to himself. "Nothing like a challenge."

Geth dove back into the Sun River and swam quickly downstream. He paddled evenly and calmly. Stroke by stroke he raced through the water toward the Lime Sea, the strong current carrying him along at great speed.

By early afternoon, Geth was in the Lime Sea, paddling his way to shore. He hid in the water underneath the forest docks, waiting for someone or something traveling on through the Swollen Forest. Large, bloated mons swam in the water around him. Mons were disgustingly fat, fishlike creatures with large, wrinkled, pruny eyes and cellulite-coated bodies. They populated the Lime Sea and were considered a delicacy by the Waves of the Lime Sea. The mons would eat algae and weeds until they were so big they would explode; the Waves would then harvest and enjoy the carnage left behind. Everyone else in Foo found their remains to be too fatty, too tough, and too much like blown-up fish remnants to be at all appetizing. The mons sniffed at Geth, realized he was tasteless, and swam away.

Geth bobbed up and down, surprised at the level of concern he was feeling. After all, he was a lithen of the highest order, and it was completely out of character for him to be worried about *anything*.

His worry wasn't for Winter and her suffering and possible starvation, even though it didn't exactly bring him joy to think of her weakening in that coffin of ice.

He wasn't worried about Leven, either, even though the boy was a crucial player in what would happen in the battle to preserve Foo and completely restore the dreams of mankind.

He wasn't even worried about Clover. The little sycophant was amazingly resourceful and could no doubt take care of himself.

No, Geth's worry was for *himself.* As neat and compact and woody as a toothpick is, one's soul and heart can give it life for only so long. Geth had already beaten the odds by surviving the blades that had chewed him up as a chunk of tree. He had tempted fate by slipping from Foo and back. He suspected that his small body simply couldn't last too much longer, and Geth was beginning to experience worry—something no lithen had ever done. Geth suspected that if he were not restored to his former self within a couple of days, his heart would give out, and he would become nothing but a useless sliver of wood, good only for picking teeth and spearing cocktail weenies.

It was not a pleasant prospect.

Geth reached down and rubbed his left foot. Already he could feel the wood at his southernmost tip hardening.

"Interesting," he said, continually in awe of fate's working.

From beneath the docks he spotted a band of palehi, their faces reflecting the trauma of the many frightening things they had seen. The palehi were lean and short, with long, white hair pulled back in leather bands. They were usually shirtless, their arms marked in red stripes, each stripe representing a time they had successfully made it through the Swollen Forest. The palehi wore loose skirts that allowed their legs full range of motion, and their feet were wrapped with gunt-lined leather that was tied tightly at their ankles. They lived in the edges of the forest, and perpetual fear had bleached their skin a pale white.

Like the lithens, the palehi had been in Foo since the creation. But unlike the lithens, the palehi had never become a positive force in Foo. Following the wars, the palehi resisted ever taking sides again. However, for a price, the timid beings would escort anything that wished to travel through the Swollen Forest. They didn't guarantee they could safely get you where you were going, but they were as effective a way through as any.

Geth watched as a group of palehi tentatively circled a tall nit who was looking to traverse the forest. The nit had a fat sycophant on his right shoulder and was counting the red stripes on the arms of the palehi.

"You get me through the forest, and I'll make it worth your while, yes indeed, yes indeed. I'm very important, mind you," the nit said.

"I'm sure you are," one of the palehi responded. "Now, keep up and we should have no problem. Your name?"

"I like the name Francis, but unfortunately mine's Albert. Albert Welch," the nit replied. "I hold a position of great importance in Niteon."

The palehi looked unimpressed. One even smirked.

"I'm Simon," the lead palehi said to Albert. "Your sycophant's name?"

"Delph," Albert replied.

"We prefer not to see him," Simon said. "Sycophants only complicate things."

"Well," Delphinium huffed, "I know when I'm not wanted."

"That would be now," Simon said. "The last thing we need is some sycophant making things messier. If we don't see you, you can't interfere."

Delphinium glared and then disappeared.

Their white faces showing only fear, the palehi formed a circle around Albert. The tall nit straightened the felt hat on his head and buttoned his vest.

"Run quickly," Simon said to Albert. "We'll keep you circled."

Geth climbed out from beneath the docks as Simon was talking and ran as fast as his small legs would carry him. He scrambled onto the road, breathing hard in a dash to reach them. The palehi were beginning to move into the forest, and Geth's short legs made it almost impossible for him to catch up. Fortunately, *impossible* was a concept Geth had some trouble grasping. Geth lunged forward and snagged the right cuff of Albert's pants. He pulled himself up over the hem and into the cuff and settled in as Albert and the circle of palehi took off running into the forest.

CHAPTER ELEVEN

HERE AND FOUL

Clover hated the tharms. He had once had a run-in with them, when he was in his early fifties. It had been a dark night, and they had ambushed him, stealing him from off Antsel's shoulder and binding him in a silver dream sack that he couldn't work his way out of. Eventually Antsel had ransomed his release, and Clover had been set loose with a new love of freedom and a new dislike for the three-armed, foul-smelling, cork-eared miscreants.

Clover had hoped that single incident would be his one and only, but his hopes had now been dashed. He had just been sitting there, minding his own business, when suddenly and without warning he had been netted off Leven's head and whisked away with such speed that there was no way Leven could have known what had happened. And even though Clover was bound in a dream sack and hidden deep within a tharm's tunnel, he didn't fear the creatures or the place where they held him. What he feared was Leven thinking he had abandoned him.

Sycophants don't do well with feelings of having let their burns down.

The tunnel was dank, and the only light came from two burning torches, which were spaced about twenty feet from each other and stapled to the tunnel walls with thick, yellow rib bones of rovens. The torches illuminated a part of the tunnel that had been dug out to create a sort of room. That cavern had thirty or so silvery bags hanging from roots sticking down through the ceiling. All the bags hung still at the moment except for one that was rocking and twisting.

"Hello!" Clover hollered out from the bag. "Hello?" He knew from his previous experience that he was probably being held captive with other sycophants.

"No one's going to answer you," a voice yelled back.

"Good to know," Clover replied. "Where are we?"

"Who knows?" the voice answered. "Dirty tharms. They don't even give you a chance—snatching you when your back's turned."

"So where's your burn?" Clover asked.

"I've no idea," the voice said, breaking up a bit. "We had just come out of the Swollen Forest alive and were celebrating our success when I was snatched from off my burn's head. Poor Steven. I don't know what he'll do without me."

"They'll probably bury your burn," another sycophant said. "They've taken to burying nits these days."

Clover began to thrash around in his bag. If Leven was buried, the boy would suffocate. Clover had no time to hang around.

"I have to get out of here," Clover cried.

"How?" a few sycophants answered back, sounding confused.

"There has to be a way," Clover said, racking his brain.

All the other sycophants were dumbfounded. Sycophants did as their burns required. They were carefree, completely motivated by someone other than themselves telling them how to live their lives. For generations, sycophants had been snatched by the tharms and held captive until someone ransomed them. That was just how things were. "But—" one tried to argue.

"Stay if you want," Clover said. "But I'm in the mood for helping fate. Does anyone here have any matches?"

"This cannot be good," a high-pitched sycophant voice wailed.

"Matches or an amber stick," Clover clarified.

There was no answer, only the sound of some whimpering from the other bags.

"Fine," Clover shrugged.

He fished around in his void until he found a tin of I-Chews. He rubbed his finger over the wrapper, and the words on the label glowed. He read it out loud: "One piece will gently inflate your ego. Two pieces will cause excessive swelling. Three pieces or more, and you're asking for trouble."

Clover pried the lid off and poured every last piece into his mouth. The candy tasted like lint, and he could hardly chew, there were so many pieces. But as he chomped on it, the candy gradually liquefied and ran down his throat like syrup. He coughed and sputtered as he continued to chew.

"What are you doing?" a thin-voiced sycophant asked. "Are you all right?"

"I—" Clover would have answered, but he suddenly felt too self-important to address such common sycophants. His head began to swell, and the swelling was accompanied by a rapturous feeling of superiority that expanded as Clover's perfect body and ego continued to grow.

Clover looked at his arms as they rapidly enlarged. He smiled. They were, after all, such nice arms. The candy had him thinking of no one but himself.

"I am a rather gorgeous-looking sycophant," he observed smugly.

The swelling continued. Clover's eyes turned into puffy slits as his face bulged, making it difficult for him to see clearly. Clover felt some sadness over not being able to better look at himself. His body expanded, growing ever larger and filling up every inch of the dream sack he was hanging in.

His head was reaching beanbag-chair proportions.

His feet had grown to the size of watermelons.

The dream sack Clover was in was stretched to capacity, and it began to creak under the stress. Clover's ego was too big to hold. The sound of the dream sack stretching alarmed the other sycophants, and they yelped and moaned as they thrashed about in their sacks.

Clover swaggered in his bag. "Any football team would be pleased to have me," he bragged aloud.

Suddenly, there was a loud pop as Clover's dream sack burst, dropping him to the floor of the cavern. He bounced like a giant rubber ball. Freed from the sack, his ego and body continued to swell until he formed an almost perfect sphere.

"I must look quite spectacular," Clover said as he rocked back and forth. "Pity you're not able to see me," he yelled to the other bags still hanging.

"Get us out," the other sycophants yelled.

Clover would have replied, but a number of tharms who had been up on the surface had heard the popping of the sack. They now stood in the tunnel, staring with slack jaws, vigorously scratching their foreheads with the fingers on their third hands.

There was no time to lose. Clover rocked until he began rolling down the tunnel.

"Look at me!" he cheered for himself.

He bowled over three tharms and bounced and rolled down a side tunnel that had a steep decline.

Clover was finally able to pick up some real speed.

Tharms popped out from side tunnels and small caves along the way, all of them trying desperately to stop Clover. Their efforts were in vain. Clover plowed over all of them until he came to a long straightaway that leveled out, leading to a light at the end of the tunnel.

Clover smirked arrogantly as he shot out of the opening and rolled into the Swollen Forest. Hundreds of tharms burst from the tunnel behind him like an explosion of gangly rats hot on his tail. Despite wanting to allow everyone the pleasure of looking at him, Clover turned invisible. Thankfully there was still a little humble voice inside him that had its wits about it. Even though he was invisible, it was not hard for the tharms to follow the mangled trail of growth Clover was creating.

Gradually, the I-Chews began to wear off. After a few more positive thoughts and a number of spectacular tumbles, Clover's feet were back to normal. Moments later he was thin enough to maneuver easily through the thick growth of trees.

A few tharms were still pursuing him, but most had given up. Glancing behind him, Clover quickly pulled himself up into a fantrum tree and held his breath as those tharms still following ran right underneath him.

Clover congratulated himself as his body continued to contract. He wanted to rest and catch his breath, but he knew there was no time. If Leven had been buried, there wouldn't be a moment to spare.

Even so, with the effects of the candy still lingering, Clover had an urge to pull a mirror out of his void and admire himself.

"No," Clover said, fighting off his inner ego.

He dropped out of the tree and began running.

Leven was not far. He could feel it.

CHAPTER TWELVE

THE WEIGHT OF FATE

Sometimes it isn't easy to know what to think. Sometimes people experience or see things, and they have no idea what to make of them. Your friend tells you that you have to see a movie because it is the greatest thing ever filmed. So you get dragged to the theater, and it turns out to be a story about a girl who writes things in a journal and the journal becomes her friend. And there is even a scene where the actress dances with the journal, and the journal sings back. And when you walk out of the theater you not only doubt your friend's taste in movies, but you are beginning to doubt your choice of friends.

Sometimes it just isn't easy to know what to think.

Leven was experiencing one of those moments.

He was lying on his back, buried in the dark hole dug for him by the tharms, fighting desperately to manipulate fate enough to keep a protective suit of wind around him and maintain some breathing room. But the weight of the soil above him was growing too great, and the dirt was becoming increasingly aggressive. Particles of soil were pushing into the air bubble he had formed and filling his eyes and mouth. Even more concerning were the tree roots he could feel wrapping themselves around the outside of the bubble, acting as if they were preparing to get a grip and squeeze.

Leven rolled over inside the protective air and lay on his stomach. Sweat sprang from his skin and burst like tiny, wet fireworks in the confined space. The weight of the dirt at his feet had him pinned down and was compressing the air up toward his thighs, kneading and pinching his legs. Leven pushed up onto his elbows and focused his vision, concentrating his thoughts, straining to manipulate the wind he had drawn in.

More dirt closed in around his waist.

Leven didn't know how deep he was, but he strained upward. Each time he moved, more dirt filled in behind him, causing the wind wrapped around him to shrink and compress. Leven thought of Reality and the smothering he had often felt living with Addy and Terry. There had been more times than he could count when he had felt he was going to suffocate from their cruelty and neglect. Now, however, Addy and Terry were nowhere near, and Leven's fate was up to him. He took a deep breath, using up a big chunk of the precious wind. Leven refused to give up, tired of being acted upon. He pushed up with his palms. What little air remained was hot and stifling. It reminded him of being in the giant dirt snake that had swallowed him and Winter in Oklahoma.

By straining as hard as he could, he moved up slightly, but

more dirt beat down on his back. His head was pounding from the strain of manipulating the air around him and trying to resist the weight of the dirt holding him down.

Leven gritted his teeth and pushed up again, but it was no use. The weight of the soil was too much. The only air remaining was just that around his head and face.

Sweat was pouring off his forehead into his eyes. The air was diminishing, and his chest ached from trying to breathe. He could see no solution in his eyes, and his lungs were on fire. His thoughts began to go fuzzy, and resisting the blackness seemed pointless.

It's too hard, he thought to himself. *It would be easier to just go to sleep.*

Visions from his recent life flickered through his mind: Geth. Winter. Sabine. Amelia. Clover. Then his throat constricted as he felt his lungs begin to burst.

ii

Clover's heart was thumping so hard that it hurt his chest. He searched around frantically. There was no sign of Leven, but the little sycophant felt that he was in the right spot.

He looked down. The ground beneath him was dark and soft, as though it had been recently tilled, and there was a tall fantrum tree bedded in the loose soil. Clover could see the tops of its roots wriggling.

Clover knelt down and began digging. He thrust his tiny hands into the dirt and threw handfuls back over his head. He could sense

Leven beneath, and the fear he felt caused him to dig even faster. Despite feelings of confidence left over from the I-Chews, Clover knew that he alone was not enough to get Leven out.

He looked around, desperate for some help. There was nothing but trees and darkness. Clover dug some more, but the tharms had dug too deep a hole. Clover sighed, wiped his brow, and did the one thing he could think of.

He began whistling.

Sycophants have remarkable powers and the skills to do many things. They are loyal beyond measure, and their ability to make themselves invisible is as coveted as any gift in Foo.

On top of all that, the sycophants occupy the only uncharted bit of land in Foo—Sycophant Run—a place so mysterious and unknown that no one other than sycophants has ever been there. If an individual or creature were to attempt to reach Sycophant Run, they would be bombarded by the sycophant pawns, who guard its location zealously. Many have tried to reach their lands and learn of their ways and mysteries, but in a realm otherwise full of endless possibilities, invading Sycophant Run remains impossible.

But for all the wonderful and fantastical things that sycophants can do, there is one thing sycophants are sorry at.

They can't whistle.

Oh, they can make a whistling sound, but it is not pleasing in any way. Something about the lips they are blessed with produces a most horrible and discordant screech whenever they pucker up and blow.

Clover knew this and was counting on his whistle being more awful than ever before. As he blew through his lips forcefully, he rotated his head so as to throw the sound all around him, and the forest was filled with the awful screech and echo of Clover's whistling wail. It sounded like the desperate call of some poor creature suffering a violent death.

Clover's plan began to work almost immediately. As he whistled, he spotted a pair of tiny eyes flashing in the darkness between two distant trees. The eyes were filled with a look of concern.

Clover whistled louder.

More eyes, more concern.

Clover blew as though Leven's life depended on it. All around him more eyes appeared. The eyes moved tentatively toward Clover, curious about the suffering they were hearing.

There are a lot of mysterious and scary things about the Swollen Forest; it is not, for instance, a great place to picnic. But as in all of Foo, there are some wonderful things there as well. And some of the nicest things about the Swollen Forest are the Sympathetic Twill who live there. The timid creatures hide all day, but at night they busy themselves cleaning up leaves and mending tree branches that travelers might have broken. They also free sheep or animals caught in tall brush or thick bushes. The whole while they sniffle softly and reassure each other, patting one another sympathetically on the back. They are about knee-high and have large, lumpy heads and oversized feet. Their big heads are covered with wild, silver hair and house familiar faces with deep eyes and thick smile lines.

They aren't particularly brave, so they avoid threatening creatures, but the sound of a lone sycophant suffering by himself in an open field was impossible for them to ignore.

Dozens of sad-faced Twill shuffled out of the trees and cautiously surrounded Clover. One with an orange, knitted vest patted Clover lightly on the back and looked at him with great empathy. Another rubbed Clover's knee.

Clover pretended to cry. "My friend," he sniffled, pointing to the ground.

As if they understood, the Sympathetic Twill all began to dig. They plunged their hands deep into the writhing dirt, and in a matter of moments had excavated a good two feet.

Clover hopped down into the cleared area and continued digging. Dozens of hands made light work, and in a couple of minutes Clover's hands struck a small root. He pulled at it to clear the dirt away.

The root wiggled.

Clover stopped digging and clapped with excitement. All of the Sympathetic Twill began to sing for joy. It was only a finger, but Clover had a pretty good idea who was on the other end of it.

The finger moved slightly as Clover and the Twill continued to work. In a few seconds Leven's entire right arm was uncovered. Knowing that Leven desperately needed air, Clover dug as one possessed, hurling dirt out of the hole, heedless of the Sympathetic Twill he was peppering with soil. As Clover worked to clear the top of Leven's head, Leven used his own free arm to help.

"Don't die," Clover pleaded.

There was a muffled reply that became more audible as Clover uncovered Leven's face. As he cleared the dirt away, Clover could see Leven blinking his eyes.

Bawling with relief, Clover continued digging.

iii

Leven had felt the tug on his finger and figured it was some dead relative on the other side, trying to pull him into the next life. The thought made even more sense as a small circle of light began to show through. As the light became greater, Leven saw a face, and he had a different thought—either angels were hairy, or Clover was here to save him.

Leven's lungs burned so horribly he couldn't properly register what was going on. He blinked as the world opened back up to him. His head was now completely exposed in the round hole Clover and the Twill had dug. He instinctively gasped, desperately sucking in a breath of air. Leven scratched at the dirt with his free hand and was able to pull his other arm out and use it to help as well. Dozens of short, worried-looking Twill were digging like mad. Clover would dig with his hands and feet for a few moments, jump onto Leven's head, pat Leven, and then jump down and dig some more. A couple of Sympathetic Twill began to comb and smooth Leven's hair.

In a few minutes Leven was able to twist his waist. He threw his hands forward and tried to pull himself out of the hole. Everyone tugged and cheered him on.

"Almost there!" Clover yelled.

Leven pulled one more time and freed his lower body. For those looking on, it appeared that the soil was giving birth. Leven crawled out of the hole to level ground and collapsed on the soil. Clover let him cough and moan for about twelve seconds.

"Are you okay?" Clover asked, jumping on Leven's back.

"I think so," Leven spat, looking around. "Who are these guys?"

"Sympathetic Twill," Clover answered. "I couldn't dig you out fast enough, and they came to your rescue."

The Twill were gathered around Leven and Clover. Some were crying joyfully, and a few had their hands clasped above their hearts. All of them looked concerned but happy. A thin one with few teeth offered Leven a warm mug of what tasted like thick chocolate and two hot, buttery rolls dripping with jam.

"Thank you," Leven said, wiping dirt away from his mouth.

Leven ate every wonderful crumb and drank every delicious drop of chocolate. He handed the mug back and thanked them again.

The Sympathetic Twill all lined up, and one by one they hugged Leven or kissed him on the cheek. Then they slipped off into the woods and out of view.

"Where are they going?" Leven asked after the last one had patted his knee.

"Back into hiding," Clover answered.

Leven continued to breathe deeply, still trying to take in enough air to regain his strength.

"We really should go," Clover said, pulling on Leven's arm. "We have a goal to achieve."

"Just one second," Leven gasped, his chest still heaving. "I was buried. Remember?"

"You humans and the past," Clover said. "We need to keep moving."

Leven brushed his face, feeling the dirt on his skin. He knew that it was different from the dirt in Reality and that he was a long way from any home he had ever known, but he was alive.

"Where'd you disappear to?" Leven asked.

"The tharms bagged me. But I got away," Clover said, as if Leven might not have noticed. "It looks like I arrived just in time."

"I was working my way up," Leven said, brushing dirt from his hair.

"If you breathed through your fingers like the Waves you might have had a chance."

"Waves?"

"Of the Lime Sea," Clover answered. "But that's not important. The important thing is that I saved you, and you are lucky to know me."

The effects of the I-Chews hadn't completely worn off.

Leven smiled at Clover. "That's true. Are you okay?"

"I ate too much candy," Clover admitted.

Leven got to his feet, then reached down and scratched Clover on the head. He took another deep breath. "So where are we?"

"This is the Swollen Forest," Clover answered. "We were entering here when the tharms got you."

Leven looked around at the forest. "The trees are all bent," he said. "They almost seem angry."

The trees grew in odd directions. Some grew straight, but an equal number grew sideways or diagonally. Some were twisted into spirals, and some were bent into shapes or had grown into large knots. Most had branches that grew low on their trunks and stuck out like warped, greedy little hands and arms. Their bark was thick and deeply furrowed, and the tops grew together, the leaves forming a thick canopy that blocked out most of the light, shrouding the floor of the forest in even greater darkness.

The gnarled trees made Leven uneasy. He had always liked trees. Geth as a tree had been one of Leven's few comforts in life. But these trees were different—almost menacing.

"Why is it called the Swollen Forest?" Leven asked.

"The trees are constantly swelling and shifting," Clover explained. "At the heart of the forest, the trees are as big around as a building. I've seen one swell so big it burst. It's a lot more disgusting than you might think. All that sap and tree ligaments and . . . well, it's not pretty. As they swell, those around shift to give them more room. The forest reaches from the Guarded Border down to the Veil Sea."

Clover bent over and brushed some dirt out of the hair on

his ankles. As he straightened, his ears twitched. "It's an exciting place," he added. "Most people avoid it, but I've always liked it."

"What do you mean by that?"

"Well, for starters, there are many secrets buried in here. So don't go digging up things that you don't know what they are. I let out a secret years ago, and it's still haunting me. Luckily, it never really recognized me, and I've been able to keep it confused. I'll bet my trip to Reality really messed it up."

"You can bury secrets?"

"Of course," Clover answered. "People try to bury secrets in Reality, but here the secrets are literally buried. Weird things happen under the crust of our surface. There are also some amazing animals here."

"Animals?" Leven asked.

"They're not your soft, fluffy kinds of animals. The animals here are mostly dream mangled."

"What does that mean?"

"They're escaped bits and pieces of odd dreams. Have you ever dreamed you had a pony and then in that same dream your pony turned out to be a pig?" Clover looked to Leven as if for an answer.

"No," Leven said.

"Oh," Clover said, sounding a bit hurt. "Well, if you had, and if you had woken up before you should have, that pig-pony might very well have escaped your dream and been driven into the Swollen Forest."

Leven was silent.

"By *driven*, I don't mean that someone actually rode it here," Clover tried to clarify and fill the dead air simultaneously. "It was more figurative. Like the people of Cork chased it here because they didn't—"

"I understand the concept of driven."

"Good," Clover replied, as if he were a parent who had just escaped explaining something embarrassing to a child.

"So we are in a forest that is getting ready to burst, sitting on top of buried secrets, surrounded by mangled pigs?"

"And outlaws, and the sarus, and at least one siid," Clover added.

"Of course."

"This is one of the best places for them all to hide."

"So, can we get out of here?" Leven asked.

"If you want to," Clover said, looking around.

"Are all sycophants as helpful as you?" Leven asked sarcastically.

"I told you before, I'm not the best sycophant." Clover cleared his throat. "In fact, I'm probably one of the worst." The candy had completely worn off.

"I don't believe that for a second," Leven said honestly. "When I saw your face digging me out I was so relieved. Now, we need to do as Geth said and get to the turrets as fast as possible."

"Be careful," Clover warned, holding his finger in front of his mouth.

"About what?" Leven asked.

"Speaking a plan out loud can bring about thousands of difficulties," Clover whispered. "There are many in Foo who fight only to destroy the plans of any who dare to dream in ways contrary to their own. If they hear of yours, you could be in for it."

"Who would hear it out here?" Leven asked. "There's nothing but trees and dirt—"

Leven's thoughts were cut short as he tripped over a wriggling tree root that was slithering across the ground in front of him. Leven flew forward, sprawling with his right shoulder into a decaying, fallen tree trunk.

"Are you okay?" Clover asked.

"Fine," Leven said, embarrassed. He leaned against the tree as he tried to right himself, and the rotten tree moved. As it did so, a soft hissing sound came from the loose ground around its base.

"Can you hear that?" Leven asked.

"Yes," Clover said.

Leven pushed against the fallen tree a little harder, and the hissing grew louder.

"We should probably walk away," Clover cautioned.

Curious, Leven ignored Clover and leaned on the rotting tree even harder. It toppled over, exposing a large, flat, dirt-covered stone beneath its roots. Leven knelt down and brushed some of the dirt away. As he did so, the hissing increased.

Leven brushed some more dirt away, uncovering a row of large purple rings running across the top of the stone. The surface of the rock was warm, like the outside of an electric clothes dryer after it has been running for a while. Leven looked closely at the rock. Something was pulling him toward it.

When he touched one of the purple rings with his finger, the rock hummed.

"Leave it alone," Clover whispered. "It's probably hiding a secret."

"How do you know? What if it's someone? We can't just leave someone buried," Leven argued, remembering the fear and suffocation he had experienced when trapped underground.

"It's probably not a *someone,* it's a *something.* Now leave it alone," Clover said, beginning to panic and tugging on Leven's leg.

Leven ran his finger over the top of the boulder. His fingers snagged one of the purple rings. When he pulled on it, the boulder shifted slightly and the ground below it released a small, silvery wisp of steam. Leven pulled harder on the ring. The stone groaned and shook and then popped out from where it was lodged. Steam hissed up from where the stone had rested. Leven studied the indentation.

The dirt was packed, and there were tree roots running through it. And in the center of the depression was what looked like a round cap to some container.

"Just great," Clover moaned. "We need to get out of here."

Leven didn't listen. Instead, he leaned down and touched the cap with his fingers. It was solid and had a raised ridge across the top of it. He gripped it. He couldn't pull it out, but it turned easily.

"Don't!" Clover pleaded.

All Leven could think about was the suffocation he had felt. He couldn't let that happen to someone else. He turned the cap twice more and then lifted it from the ground. A burst of steam escaped from the wooden jar it covered. Leven peered into the jar and shivered, his brown eyes darkening.

"We should go," Clover begged.

The uneasiness was so strong Leven would have obeyed, but he was distracted by a golden glow he could see at the bottom of the jar. Leven reached for it and wrapped his hand around it. It was a metal handle of some sort. Leven turned it, and there was a loud clicking noise. When he tugged on it, the handle came loose, and he pulled it out of the jar. It wasn't gold, but it was a metal key, about the size of a pocketknife. The teeth of the key were ornate and the bottom of it was shaped in a swirling circular pattern. It was heavy and tarnished, but something inside Leven sensed that it was more important than it looked.

"What is that?" Clover asked.

"Nothing," Leven answered, closing his right hand around it.

"So, you're hiding nothing in your hand?" Clover asked.

"I think it's a key, but we should—"

Leven would have said more, but he was distracted by a reddish glow coming from the small hole the key's absence had created.

"Don't look at it," Clover commanded.

It was too late. Leven stared at the glow, hypnotized by its color. As he did so, the glow began to take shape and ooze up out of the lock.

Two fiery arms pushed out, squeezed from the lock like glowing putty. The arms were followed by a brilliant swatch of fire. Leven leaned back and then in. Around the edges of the flame were dozens of tiny sparks. As Leven watched, the sparks snapped and danced, morphing into a dozen glowing beings that cavorted around the edges of the larger body of fire continuing to rise out of the ground. It came up with a swoosh and towered over Leven, crackling and spitting tongues of flame.

"Get out of here!" Clover screamed. "Move!"

"What is—"

"Run!" Clover insisted. "You've released a secret and a bunch of decoys."

"What?"

"Run before any of them recognize you!" Clover screamed. "If they discover who you are, they will follow you the rest of your life."

"But shouldn't I—"

"Run!" Clover demanded. "I told you not to touch the dirt."

Leven shook his head, trying to pull himself out of the trance the fiery specter had cast.

"Run!" Clover ordered again.

Leven felt something on his face. He looked, cross-eyed, and there sitting on the bridge of his nose was a small, burning silhouette. The tiny being looked into Leven's eyes and glowed bright.

"I ate the last of the dub-rubble pie and blamed it on the neighbor boy," the small secret whispered. It smiled, looking greatly relieved, and then jumped from Leven's nose and dashed off into the forest.

"What was—?"

"Oh, you must have unearthed one huge secret," Clover moaned, his voice quavering. "When big secrets get buried, they generate a bunch of decoys in case someone unearths them one day. The little ones are trying to make you think it's no big deal to listen. We have got to get out of here!"

A wave of fear suddenly washed over Leven, so strong he felt as though he might throw up.

"Run!" Clover insisted.

Leven stood there, frozen in the light of the fiery secret. Clover grabbed a sharp stick from the ground and jabbed it as hard as he could into Leven's right thigh.

That did the trick.

"Ouch!" Leven blurted, grabbing his leg.

"Run!"

Leven took off running just as the liberated secret pulled itself erect, tilted back its head, and screamed.

CHAPTER THIRTEEN

LOOK BOTH WAYS BEFORE YOU CROSS THE STREET

Dennis looked at his trembling hands. As hard as he tried, he could not get them to stop shaking. He ran one through his thin hair and then sat on both of them, hoping that would keep them from twitching.

It didn't—now his whole body was shaking.

There was a faint banging coming from the inside of his filing cabinet, where Dennis's briefcase, wrapped in pillows and duct tape, was holding one very angry toothpick. Dennis's small, sad, dreamless life was being turned upside down, and he didn't know if he should scream for help or hide somewhere until it all went away.

Like a trained seal, Dennis had returned to the only place he knew—his work. Here in his closet he was safe for a moment. Sure, he had run out the day before, but nobody here had even given that a second thought. They figured it was just the way of the janitor. Now he was back, locked in his closet, and trying to understand what was happening and what to do next.

The muffled banging from inside the metal drawer continued.

Dennis took a quick assessment of his life. He had no family. No wife. No children. He had an apartment, but the window leaked, and the people upstairs were world-famous cloggers who would dance in their wooden shoes all night long. Once, Dennis had worked up the nerve to go and ask them if they could dance without their shoes. It had been a bad idea. The father had brought one of his wood-covered feet down onto Dennis's big right toe while yelling something about Dennis being a tyrant and trying to suppress art.

After that, the dancing intensified.

Dennis did have a little savings—a few hard-earned dollars he had put away. But he had no friends or future to spend it on. In fact, all Dennis had was a pillow-wrapped briefcase with a maniacal toothpick in it. He knew if he asked for help or understanding from his coworkers, they would simply have him locked up for mental instability and then go on about their business.

Dennis felt doomed. He glanced up at the single, small window in his "office" and could see only one solution. He climbed onto a folding chair and pushed open the base of the window. Noise from the city drifted up from the street and burst into the closet—the sounds of taxis honking and traffic flowing. It was twenty stories down to the street, but the sound of someone yelling at someone else could clearly be heard. Dennis stuck his head out the window. He was afraid of heights, and it made him dizzy just to look down. He quickly pulled his head back in and went to his filing cabinet, opened the drawer, and took out the pillow-wrapped briefcase.

For the moment, Ezra was quiet inside, and Dennis wondered if the toothpick knew what was coming. He ripped off the duct tape, unwrapped the pillow, and stared at the briefcase. He thought back to when he had purchased it. It had been his five-year anniversary at Snooker and Woe. He had heard and seen all the other associates there having parties and giving gifts to each other as each celebrated his or her fifth year of service.

But there had been nothing for Dennis.

So he had taken some money from his savings and walked down to the luggage store. There he had bought the third-least-expensive briefcase as a gift to himself. He had imagined someone asking him where he had gotten it, and him answering, "It was a gift for my fifth year."

But in all the years since, not a single person had shown even the slightest interest in Dennis or in the briefcase he always carried. The closest he had gotten to anyone saying anything was once in an overcrowded elevator when a woman told him to move his stupid briefcase because it was digging into her backside.

Dennis stared at the leather case one last time. He rubbed the smooth outside and sighed. Then he climbed back onto the chair and flung the briefcase out the window as hard as he could.

He watched it sail through the air and eventually come crashing down on the edge of a vacant lot, twenty floors below. The briefcase burst under the impact, sending bits and pieces flying everywhere over the empty block.

Dennis didn't know whether to sob or cheer. Fortunately for him, that was one more decision he didn't have to make, seeing how his thoughts were interrupted by a voice on his shoulder.

"Wow," Ezra growled appreciatively. "I didn't know you had that in you."

Startled, Dennis jumped, and as he came back down his right foot slipped off the folding chair and he toppled to the floor, slamming into his desk and banging his right cheek against the metal lamp. Blood shot out of his cheek like ketchup squeezed from a bottle. Dennis put his hand over the wound and struggled to his feet. Ezra hopped from his shoulder, where he had been standing, but Dennis couldn't see him.

"How'd you get out?" Dennis asked, scanning the room for the insolent toothpick.

"I worked my way through the latch," Ezra said, his voice coming from the direction of the highest shelf. "From there, pushing through the pillow was no problem. Looks like I got out just in time."

Dennis glanced toward the window.

"I . . . I didn't . . ." Dennis tried to explain.

"Don't explain yourself," Ezra commanded. "I'm proud of you, and for the first time."

Dennis was shocked. "Proud? I tried to kill you."

"You showed some backbone," Ezra growled again. "Sit down."

Dennis did as he was told.

Ezra jumped from the shelf onto the desk. He walked as close to Dennis as he could and looked him in the eyes.

"Listen," he whispered fiercely. "I might have been wrong. I mean, the way I've gone about this, but I need your help."

"My help?" Dennis questioned.

"There's someone I must find," Ezra spat. "I need you to take me there."

"Where? Who? Foo?" Dennis asked, still shaking and thinking back to what Ezra had told him earlier.

"Does it matter?" Ezra laughed scornfully. "What will you be leaving behind?"

"I can't just walk away from my job," Dennis reasoned.

"Fine," Ezra snorted. "Throw me out that window. I'll find someone else. I'll leave you here to your *cleaning*," he sneered. "I'd hate to take you away from *this*."

As uneasy as the toothpick made him, Dennis was smart enough to realize that Ezra was making a rather solid point. It would be no more pathetic to follow a toothpick somewhere than it would be to stay right where he was and wish for nothing more.

"Is it a certain city we're going to?" Dennis asked.

"We're?" Ezra growled.

"Do I need different clothes?"

"Do you *have* different clothes?" Ezra asked.

"Well, no."

"Listen," Ezra said irritably, hopping onto Dennis's shoulder. "We're going somewhere important. We are going to find the one who did this to me, and we are going to help him understand what he did. We are going to a place no map here knows of."

"Like Asia?" Dennis asked without thinking.

"Is Asia on maps?" Ezra howled.

"Well, I—"

"Hello! Are you in or not?"

"Will we ever be back?" Dennis questioned.

"No."

"I'll never see this again?" Dennis asked, motioning to his surroundings.

"Why would you want to?"

"Will it be dangerous?"

"Ahh, yes," Ezra smiled. "Very."

A feeling unlike any he had ever experienced washed over Dennis—a warm, thick, smothering feeling. The sensation swirled around and tugged at his soul with a strong emotional undertow. He bobbed a bit where he stood, letting the sensation soak him entirely.

"Do you know what you're doing? What if—" Dennis began to ask.

Ezra screamed at him. "What-ifs are worthless!" He threw his short, toothpick arms in the air. "You have no idea of what lies around you—this Reality and its lack of imagination! My world has already begun to seep in, thanks to those who have traveled back and forth to Foo."

Ezra touched the wall and smiled an evil, cold smile.

Dennis might have wondered what the smile was for, but his

wonder was interrupted by the building beginning to shake and wobble. Dennis could hear screams coming from outside his closet as the world jiggled. Cleaning supplies crashed in their metal drawer, exploding. Dennis could hear screaming through the window from the street down below. There was also a symphony of cars honking and careening into each other.

As the building continued to sway, Dennis looked out the window and saw the scenery moving. It was such an odd sensation that he had to hold onto his desk to remain standing.

The building of Snooker and Woe was moving—all twenty-four floors of it.

Its corners shifted in sync as the building literally "walked" across the street, blocking traffic and causing anyone within a mile's radius to stare in wonder. The entire city seemed to shake and wobble. Pipes beneath the building stretched and burst. Water and sparks shot everywhere, making the scene wet and smoky. Most people ran for their lives while a few fainted and a few others drew closer to take pictures. The building hoisted itself over the curb and up into the empty lot where the briefcase had landed earlier. Once cleared of the street, the building stopped moving.

As it settled it let out a gigantic, "Ahhhhh!"

Everyone inside the building and out screamed and hollered as they tried to comprehend what had just happened. What it looked like was that one of their city's skyscrapers had stood up, walked across the street, and sat down in a new spot.

"What happened?" Dennis asked breathlessly, backing up against the wall. "Did you do that?"

"You pathetic people and your lack of imaginations," Ezra scowled. "Thanks to the gateway, there are traces of Foo everywhere. Now, are you in?"

Dennis looked out the window at his new view. He heard things still trying to settle, and he could see the world from a different angle. It made him hungry to see even more.

"Where to first?" Dennis asked.

"The gateway," Ezra barked. "And hurry, you've already wasted too much time."

"The gateway?" Dennis questioned.

"Just get us to the train station," Ezra yelled. "I'll fill you in on the way."

Dennis stepped over the puddles of cleaning fluid that had leaked out onto the floor and moved into the hallway outside his closet.

"You might want to take the stairs," Ezra commanded. "I'm not sure the elevator's in the best shape."

Dennis took the stairs, four at a time.

ii

"Twelve thousand, four hundred and sixty-two dollars," the teller said. She was a pretty woman, with dark brown hair pulled tight up onto the top of her head and light green eyes that looked two-dimensional under the warm bank lights. "That's a lot of money," she smiled. "Good for you," she added, patting Dennis's hand.

"I've been saving for a while," Dennis blushed.

"Would you like an escort out?" she asked. "It's bank procedure to offer extra security to anyone making a large cash withdrawal."

"I . . . well . . ."

"No," Ezra whispered in his ear.

Ezra was tucked up behind the right side of the dark sunglasses Dennis was wearing.

"No," Dennis said loudly.

"Okay," she smiled. "Well, then, thank you for banking with Bindle County Bank." The pretty teller reached across the counter and pressed a sticker onto Dennis's chest. The sticker read: "I save a bundle banking at Bindle."

Dennis smoothed the sticker as if it were a precious gift given to him by a treasured friend. "Thanks," he said, feeling a little light-headed.

Ezra growled behind his ear. "Come on, lover boy. We don't have all day."

Dennis took his money and stuffed it into a small, red fanny pack he had purchased before coming into the bank.

"Outside," Ezra ordered.

Dennis zipped the fanny pack and walked outside. For a man with twelve thousand dollars in his hands, he seemed to have extremely low self-esteem. He walked more like a man with empty pockets and a fistful of debt.

"Where now?" Dennis asked.

"We need to get to Germany."

The thought was so absurd that Dennis hardly registered it. He stopped and scrunched his eyes and twitched his nose in an effort to compute what Ezra had just said.

"We need what?" he asked.

"We need to get to Germany," Ezra huffed. "And fast. There's a chance they haven't arrived there yet."

"Where? They?"

"Germany, you twit," Ezra spit in a rage. "And by *they*, I mean the ones who put me in this condition."

"Germany's across the world," Dennis whined. "And I don't have a passport."

"Well, then," Ezra said soothingly. "Why don't we just lie down here on the sidewalk and give up?" There was no soothing left in his voice. "I suppose the only people that ever go to Germany have passports."

"It's the law," Dennis pointed out.

"There's a new law," Ezra snapped. "Mine. What's the fastest way to get there?"

"Plane, I suppose," Dennis answered. "We could fly to the coast, but we'll need a passport to get across the ocean."

"There are other ways," Ezra insisted. "When you build one of your toy . . ."

"Models," Dennis corrected.

Ezra rolled his one eye. "Whatever," he grunted. "When you're missing a piece, what do you do, give up?"

Dennis was silent.

"You give up?" Ezra asked with disgust. "Well, this is not one of your toys. We will make it to Germany despite how many times fate tries to stop us."

"Fate?" Dennis asked.

If Ezra had had a tongue he would have stuck it out. "The power of Foo," he mocked. "Well, I think it's about time that I showed Geth what fate can do when placed in the right hands."

Dennis did not have a good feeling about things. "We're going to need some help," he pointed out. "I mean, a toothpick and me?"

"Help!" Ezra yelled. "Now, who in this sorry realm would be able to help someone like us?"

Dennis didn't answer.

iii

"And what business is that of yours?" Janet Frore asked Tim Tuttle, her eyes red from too much sleep and her skin white and pasty from too little sun. She was sitting on her ratty couch, wearing a nappy velvet red robe that was pulled together with a green rope of frayed material. Next to the couch was a large refrigerator that Janet had moved there shortly after she had lost her job at the post office. The refrigerator hummed softly as Tim shifted in the rough wicker chair Janet had reluctantly allowed him to have a seat in.

"We're just concerned," Tim said politely.

"You should waste your concern elsewhere," Janet insisted. "The child is not right."

"Excuse me?" Tim asked.

"Don't you collect trash?" Janet asked.

"I work for the waste management—"

"And don't you have your own kids?" she interrupted.

"Two boys, but I—"

"I'll tell you what . . . ," Janet slurred, smacking her dry lips. She interrupted her interruption to take a drink from the garden hose she had pulled in from the outside through a window. Water was cheaper than soda, and the hose allowed her to not have to move to quench her thirst.

Tim stared at her in disbelief as she shot water into her face. She looked like a bloated red fountain, water spraying in and out of her mouth.

Things got more than a little wet.

Tim jumped up and wiped some stray water from his face.

Janet kinked the hose. "Sit down!" she ordered.

Tim remained standing. He had had enough; besides, the seat he had been occupying was drenched. He thrust out his weak chin as far as possible to make it clear how determined he was.

"I'll tell you what," Janet continued. "Go raise those little boys of yours to be future trash collectors so that I can sleep comfortably, knowing my garbage will always be removed. And then, stay out of my business," she barked.

Tim's face burned red, not from embarrassment but from disgust. "Excuse me?" he said. "That is no way to talk."

"Oh," Janet jeered, "a man of principle."

Tim had no idea what she meant by that.

"Listen," Tim insisted, his mind racing. "I think the authorities need to get involved."

There was a flash of panic in Janet's eyes. The last thing she wanted was for more policemen to come snooping around, asking questions. Besides, Janet wanted to keep reaping the welfare benefits she received as a single mother.

"Hold on a moment," she snapped. "There's no reason for you to trouble yourself over the girl."

"Winter," Tim added, feeling that her name needed to be spoken.

"Whatever," Janet waved. "Don't get all panicked on me. She'll show up. The only friends she had were you and that nosey wife of yours. Where's she got to go?"

"My point exactly," Tim said. "She could be in trouble."

Janet snickered. "She's not in trouble. She always promised she'd run away. She's just keeping her word."

Janet Frore was a gigantic horse's behind. Sorry. It is unquestionably bad manners to talk poorly of others, but people like Janet make it hard to keep your words kind.

"I know she hoarded money," Janet added, opening the refrigerator near her and hauling out a long stick of pepperoni. Janet gnawed off a big bite and did Tim the great disservice of talking with her mouth full. "She'll come around when the money runs out," she splattered. "Now, if you don't mind, your large forehead is distracting."

Tim could take a hint.

CHAPTER FOURTEEN

THE SWOLLEN FOREST BEFORE THE TREES

The Swollen Forest was growing rapidly. Every day its borders expanded closer to the Sun River and the shores of the Veil Sea. If not for the Fissure Gorge blocking its way, it would have already overtaken Cork.

As big and beautiful as it could be, however, the Swollen Forest was not a good place. It was home to no cute elves or motherless deer that ran around smelling flowers with their rabbit friends. Likewise, you would never find a house made of candy there, or a young, naive, red-hooded girl skipping around with a basket. It was a dark, foreboding place, as unpleasant as a blind dentist informing you that all your fillings need to be dug out with a dull butter knife.

The Swollen Forest was home only to those who wished to stay hidden. Many a soul had wandered in and never wandered back out. The safest thing would be never to venture there, but if you did have to traverse it, your best strategy would be to travel fast. Travel through the Swollen Forest was best done with lighted torches and in company with a large group—or, better yet, encircled by a ring of palehi.

One of the things that made the journey so perilous was the dreams coming in from Reality. A dream would swoop in and latch onto any creature it could find. In that vulnerable moment, while frantically trying to manipulate and enhance the dream, the inhabitant of Foo might be pounced upon by any number of creatures, to be dragged off to be buried or sold or cleverly hidden for hundreds of years.

Albert had gone to Morfit as an agent of Cork. The tall nit operated one of the gatehouses on the edge of the land of Niteon and was concerned about the state of Foo and the conflicts that were raging. When the Lore Coil communicated that the gateway had been destroyed, it did not expressly say what had happened to Sabine or to Leven Thumps, the destroyer of the gateway. In an effort to learn the truth, Albert had gone to visit Morfit and was now on his way back to Niteon. To get there, he had to pass through the Swollen Forest, and he was understandably nervous. All he wanted was to get home and let someone else worry about Morfit's problems.

Albert and his escorts were now about halfway through the dark forest. The palehi were running swiftly, and as he struggled to keep up, Albert was totally unaware that there was a living toothpick riding in the cuff of his pants.

They were all breathing hard, and their legs were tired. The palehi's straggly hair was drenched with sweat and hung down over their eyes, making it hard for them to see clearly. So far the band of runners had successfully managed to avoid any incoming dreams, but fear of what might happen if they stopped kept them moving quickly.

Albert was especially short on breath, and he was gasping as he asked the lead palehi, "How much farther, Simon?"

"We are closing in on halfway," Simon replied.

"Has the forest been quiet lately?" Albert asked.

Simon stared at Albert as if he were crazy.

"What I mean is, have there been any new . . . problems?" Albert clarified, his lungs burning. "Those Lore Coils can wreak havoc on normalcy."

Simon didn't answer immediately, but finally he said a single word: "Jamoon."

"Jamoon?" Albert asked.

"He has new power."

"Power?" Albert gasped, stumbling over a large boulder and struggling to keep up. "What kind of power?"

Simon wasn't exactly a great communicator, and Albert had difficulty making sense of his reply.

"Shadowy nihils surround him, and their bite can rot the mind. He is searching for those who slipped through, and his birds have a powerful effect on those who do not have the right answers. Some of his victims have been found wandering without purpose, looking for shade dark enough to hide them forever."

"I say," Albert panted, wiping sweat from his eyes.

"The Lore Coil spoke of Sabine," Simon added.

Albert shivered. Hanging on to keep from being bounced out of Albert's pant cuff, Geth put his small hand to his ear.

"You think Sabine has something to do with this?" Albert asked.

"Perhaps with the nihils. But Jamoon, they say, is acting under the influence of something unknown, much as Sabine was. Regardless, Jamoon will find Geth or destroy Foo trying," Simon said. "Everything up is down. The poison of Jamoon and Morfit is too strong to ignore."

Simon shivered, turned his head from Albert, and picked up the pace. Albert struggled to keep up, while Geth strained to hear over the sound of running feet on the forest floor.

"Morfit is gigantic," Albert said. "There are more regrets than ever. And all sorts of beings walking around with silly looks and concerns upon their faces."

"Go back to Niteon and forget," Simon said. "Cork is blessed not to know how tainted the rest of Foo has become."

Running at a smooth, even pace, Simon was still talking in riddles. "I'll tell you this," he said, "the Children of the Sewn can't frame the darkness fast enough. Their walls are filled with dark images—so much gray. Many in Foo won't step out of their homes for fear the Ring of Plague will steal their gifts."

Albert's ears burned at the mention of stolen gifts. Simon also had Geth's attention.

"Stealing gifts?" Albert sputtered, his breathing and stride both uneven. "Impossible."

"Believe as you will," Simon said indifferently.

"But what about—" Albert started to say.

"Watch out!" Simon yelled, throwing out an arm to stop Albert.

Simon's warning was too late. A thick, yellow dream rose up through the floor of the forest and trapped Albert, flowing up around him like a glass tube. Albert looked out at Simon, but the lead palehi was unable to help him. All that he and the rest of the palehi could do was surround Albert and the dream he was caught in and wait.

Albert frantically worked with the vision. It was a long, detailed dream that belonged to a math professor back in Reality. The professor was consumed with a certain complex problem and was dreaming about a possible solution. Albert tried to manipulate the details of the dream to resolve the man's frustration so that he could simply take a deep breath and awake refreshed, but the dream was too intense and long.

In the darkness of the surrounding forest a low moaning and clicking noise sounded. Absorbed in the dream, Albert couldn't hear it, but the palehi could, and they glanced about wildly.

The sound grew louder.

"Sarus!" one of the palehi yelled. "Sarus!"

The palehi began to tremble and run in place.

"Stay!" Simon commanded. "He will pay. He will pay!"

"Payment means nothing if we are suffering in a gaze!" another palehi yelled, bolting off into the trees. His departure was like a bullet from a starting pistol at a marathon. Except for Simon, all the palehi raced after him. Only Simon remained, standing there staring at Albert stuck in the dream.

Albert could see the palehi fleeing, but the dream he was working in would not end. He began manipulating things in such a way that the professor having the dream would be confused and wake up. Albert threw in a vision of a clown, a little red wagon, the professor's first-grade teacher, and a scene played by garbage men. In Reality, the professor tossed and turned as the unrelated and implausible images filled his mind. But he was tenacious and didn't give up.

The moaning and clicking grew louder. Now, even Simon was panicked. He turned toward the moaning sound, then back at Albert.

"Sorry," he mouthed. "I can't take sides."

Simon turned and ran as fast as he could in the opposite direction, leaving Albert on his own.

Of course, Albert wasn't completely alone. Geth stood tall in the cuff of Albert's pants, peering out, curious what the outcome of this would be. He could feel Albert thrashing about, frantically trying to put to bed the dream he was working on. Geth could also clearly hear the sound of what was coming in the woods. He knew the noise, and he knew the sarus were at hand. He wasn't at all surprised that the palehi had fled.

The thunderous clicking was deafening now, and Albert was sweating, madly moving things around in the dream. In desperation, he threw in a vision of the professor's ex-wife, and the terrified professor awoke instantly, ending the dream.

Albert was free, but it was too late.

CHAPTER FIFTEEN

ICY RECEPTION

There are lots of wonderful places that most of us might like to visit someday. The beaches of Costa del Sol seem like a good place to go. Maybe you'd like to see the Grand Canyon or the pyramids of Egypt or the world's biggest ball of yarn.

Then, there are the places you would rather not go—a tax collectors' convention, a sewage treatment plant, or maybe the home of someone who keeps spiders as pets and insists on taking them out of their cages and making you hold them.

You could also add the ice caves in the Mediania Mountains of Foo to that list of undesirable destinations.

At the moment, those ice caves were home to Winter Frore, who was being held captive there, encased in an icy coffin. After Geth had escaped, the room had gradually grown smaller until Winter was lying on her back, not even able to lie entirely flat, and her whole body was screaming out in pain.

Winter's stomach growled. Her throat was parched, and her body was running out of energy. She had no idea how long Geth had been gone or if it was morning or night. She missed Leven and Clover and Amelia and Geth. She wanted desperately for Leven to appear and tell her everything was going to be all right.

Winter didn't know how much longer she could last. In her cramped condition, she felt like a seed that desperately wanted to grow but was wrapped in cellophane.

She was also confused. When she had stepped back into Foo, her head had begun to fill with memories and images of the life she had known before going to Reality. Now, however, those memories were beginning to fade. They were like a wave that had pushed onto shore, but the ocean was now receding. All she could clearly remember was her life in Reality. She also remembered Leven, but what they were fighting for was fuzzy. If they had some cause, she could not remember what it was.

"Hello?" she hollered out in a panic, as if she might forget who she was if she didn't act quickly. "Hello!"

Through the narrow slits in her mask, she stared at the icy ceiling above her.

"Please, Jamoon," she yelled. "I'm ready to talk."

There was no reply.

"Please!"

A loud click sounded, followed by the creaking of breaking ice. The ceiling and walls began to slowly move outward.

Winter's heart beat with hope.

After a few moments, Winter actually had enough room to

stretch out. Her legs and back and neck rejoiced in the movement. There was some ferocious tingling as her blood rushed back into veins and muscles, but the pain was almost glorious.

The ice continued to groan and creak, and in a few minutes the room was back to the size it had once been.

A tall, narrow door opened, revealing a short rant standing in the doorway. He wore a dark blue cloak and a hood that covered everything but his right eye. Winter could tell from his height that he was not Jamoon. She couldn't see all of him at once because of her mask, but she could see from his stance that his left side was that of a model. Somewhere in Reality some young girl was dreaming of becoming a runway model.

"If you freeze me, we will draw the walls in even tighter," the rant warned her.

"I won't freeze you," Winter promised.

"Follow me," he commanded. "But remember there are eyes watching."

Winter tried to roll over and stand, but the shroud held her down, and she was too weak.

"I can't get up," she said. "My legs . . ."

The rant grunted irritably. He stepped into the room and lifted the shroud off Winter but left the hood in place and her hands tied. He took hold of her left shoulder with his right hand in a grip so strong that Winter feared he might break her collarbone. But despite the pain, she kept quiet, not willing to acknowledge his strength.

He yanked her to her feet, and she wobbled like a newborn

colt. Her right leg was okay, but her left one gave out, and she found herself back on the floor.

"Is this a trick?" the rant barked.

"I can't walk," Winter insisted. "My legs have been cramped up."

The rant seized her by the shoulder again and hauled her up. "Prisoners like you are more trouble than they're worth," he growled.

"I'm . . ."

"Sorry," he finished for her. "Very sorry, indeed. I know all about you, nit. And a weak apology is not going to make right all the trouble you've caused. Jamoon will finish Sabine's work, and you will be nothing but a memory a few misguided souls will be forced to recall."

Winter held her tongue. She was not used to rants talking so boldly to her. Despite her loss of memory, she knew that in the social order of Foo, rants certainly had no place talking down to nits. Rants were of less importance than cogs, and cogs were looked down upon by most nits. The only reason rants were so loyal to Sabine was that they were weak and easy to control. It always baffled Winter that not a single rant could see the truth—the truth being that a merger of Foo with Reality would be an end to every rant. In Reality their dream-halves would die and they would cease to exist. Sabine had filled their heads with the lie that their bodies would be restored.

"What's my motivation for this photo shoot?" the model half of the rant asked. "Be quiet," its other side ordered.

It was difficult, but Winter followed the rant down an icy hallway. The hood obscured her vision, and she felt pain with each step. But there was also a better range of motion and movement for her legs and arms, and as they went along, she tried to see and memorize as much as she could of the layout of the caves.

There were portraits on the frozen walls—some beautiful, some ugly—all of them coated with patterns of frost. They passed a picture of a man standing over something, a jagged metal sword in his hand. Winter looked away. The floor was also frozen, and there were no windows anywhere.

The hallway made a turn, and Winter slipped on the uneven floor. With her hands still bound, she had no way to stop herself from falling.

"Get up," the rant ordered.

Winter tried to stand but lost her footing again.

"I think I hurt my shoulder when—"

The rant grabbed her by the sore shoulder and pulled her up with one quick jerk. Winter saw stars.

"In here," the rant directed, pushing Winter through a low doorway into a warm room.

Through the slits of her mask, Winter could see Jamoon seated behind a large wooden desk at the far end of the room. There was a fire humming in the fireplace behind him, and the floor was covered with thick, furry animal hides.

Jamoon looked up, his right eye glaring at Winter.

"She said she wants to talk," the rant informed Jamoon.

"Good," Jamoon replied, laying aside a thick scroll he had

been looking at. "It doesn't take long for the ice rooms to break a soul."

Winter commanded her mind to stop being so jumpy and confused, but it only halfway obeyed. The rant pushed her farther into the room, hurting her sore shoulder again.

Winter winced and couldn't help whimpering.

"The lighting in here is awful," the model half of the rant complained. "If I come off looking pale . . ."

"Leave us!" Jamoon ordered, annoyed.

The rant bowed and backed out of the room, his model half whining about the shoes she was forced to wear.

Jamoon stepped over to Winter and lifted his hand toward her.

"Get away from me," Winter demanded, shrinking from his touch.

Jamoon ignored her and unhooked her hood, pulling it off to expose Winter's head.

Winter looked around. The room was filled with heavy pieces of furniture, and its walls were mossy. The fireplace and mantel were large and ornate, and thick patches of black nihils clung to the ceiling, fluttering like bats.

"Why am I here?" Winter challenged. A long strand of her blonde hair stuck to her lip, and she spat it out.

"Winter," Jamoon said, walking around her. "You don't look like the Winter I used to know. Do you remember me?"

"I know you're Jamoon," Winter answered.

"And?"

"That's all I can remember," Winter replied honestly. "My

visions of Foo are fading. I can only remember Reality."

Winter felt odd being so truthful, but she couldn't see any advantage in creating lies. She had lived such a solitary existence in Reality—few friends and only the coldest communication from her fake mother, Janet.

Jamoon stepped closer to Winter and leaned down so that his mouth was only inches away from her face. She could smell the bad breath coming from whoever was currently occupying his left side.

"You remember nothing of the . . . plan?" he whispered, withdrawing just a bit.

The dead nihils on the ceiling screeched.

"Plan?" Winter whispered back, feeling as if discretion were needed.

She could see only Jamoon's right eye, but he used that eye to stare deeply into both of hers. He was looking for something, but Winter's green eyes were too hard to read.

"Morfit holds the answer for you," Jamoon growled softly.

Jamoon straightened. His right side was under control, but the left side of his body flailed about wildly. Somewhere in Reality, someone was beginning a new dream. There was a sucking noise, like a big wad of wet clay being expelled from a glass tube. The noise was followed by deep breathing, and Jamoon's left side collapsed beneath his robe. He now looked like half a person standing on just one leg with a deflated left half. He hopped over and sat down behind his wooden desk.

Winter tried hard not to stare.

There was a faint croaking sound, and Winter made the assumption that half of Jamoon was a frog at the moment. She was glad he was robed; the uneven matchup would have been almost impossible not to laugh at.

Jamoon leaned back in his furry chair, trying hard to balance his unequal self. He now smelled wet and mossy. On his desk was a mug of hot liquid. He picked it up and took a sip.

"What of Morfit?" Winter asked.

"Morfit was necessary to the plan," Jamoon said hoarsely.

"And I was a part of it?" Winter asked. "How could that be?"

"You don't understand," Jamoon snapped. He paused and lifted his right hand, pulling the hood of his cloak even tighter. Only his right eye showed. "We were in this together. You implemented it. Don't you remember?"

The pain in Winter's shoulder was mild compared to the sock in the gut she felt on hearing Jamoon's words. "In this together?" she whispered. "How could that be? Who am I?"

There was a sharp knock on the door, and Jamoon quickly stood. The wide wooden door opened, and a hooded messenger announced, "The Sochemists have sent word."

Jamoon glanced at Winter. With his right hand he quickly pulled her mask back over her head and sealed it.

"I have a few things I need to take care of in Morfit," he said. "You'll be returned to your cell."

Winter stared as Jamoon left the room. "Who *am* I?" she whispered again.

CHAPTER SIXTEEN

BLACKNESS GATHERS

Berchtesgaden is a beautiful little German village filled with interesting locals whom tourists enjoy watching. There are quaint cobblestone streets lined with Alpine-style houses that, with their black exterior beams and white walls, look like life-sized cuckoo clocks. And as with cuckoo clocks, every so often a door or window opens and a German maiden steps out and waters blindingly red flowers in a flower box or enjoys a smoke from her pipe.

The buildings alone are a visual treasure, but add a lake of magical beauty right next to the village, and surround those uniquely green waters with an emerald forest towered over by spectacular, snowcapped mountains, and, well . . . there are not words to describe it. Poets have tried, but all have come short of capturing its true enchantment. The village of Berchtesgaden and the nearby lake called Konigsee are two of the greatest photo opportunities Mother Nature has ever put together.

But Mother Nature had to be a little concerned about what had been happening lately in the picturesque setting. It had begun a couple of days before, when the locals had awakened to find hundreds of fish floating on the green surface of the Konigsee. The fish appeared to be dead, but when the townsfolk began to scoop them up, they realized that they were still alive. They were just limp and listless.

The lake water was tested, but there was no indication of conditions that would cause fish to suddenly give up swimming and decide to float on the surface. Besides, there were still plenty of fish swimming in normal fashion in the lake. The locals cleared the lake of those floating on top and continued on as if nothing were the matter.

But, the next morning, there were more floating fish.

The residents of the Konigsee area were baffled.

What they didn't understand was that the mysterious under-water explosion that most of them hadn't seen or heard had blasted Sabine into hundreds of bits. A lot of those bits had perished; others, still stunned from the blast, were alive but too sluggish to escape the mouths of hungry fish swimming by. To the fish, the residue of Sabine looked like nice little treats. But after ingesting particles of Sabine, the poor fish became despondent—so much so that they simply stopped swimming and floated to the top to await their deaths.

As those listless fish were being hoisted on board the boats, bits of Sabine oozed out of their mouths and slipped away.

All day and night long, tiny flecks of black worked their way out of the water and oozed on shore. Some attached themselves to boats and rode up to the docks. Some clung to the outsides of fish being hauled out, and a few grabbed hold of any tourist who had the nerve to stick a finger in the water to see how cold it was. Each of the surviving bits migrated to a spot behind a weathered shed. There they waited until all had gathered.

When the gathering was complete, the bits merged into a mass the size of a soccer ball. Moaning softly, it lay on the ground like a giant, black, pulsating amoeba.

Sabine was not finished.

He could feel his incompleteness. He was aware that the best of him—or, more appropriately, the worst of him—had been destroyed. But he sensed that a part of him had survived, not only in Reality but also in Foo. His plan to mesh the two realms had not been completely thwarted—not yet, anyway.

He would need some help. He could feel that somewhere in Reality there was something else from Foo—something or someone who had made it out of the gateway. Sabine willed his residue to form a shape that the wind and the elements could manipulate more easily, flattening out into a thin, black sail. He was but a shadow of his former self: His edges were tattered, his two thin arms were hard to control, and his face was nothing but a couple of eyes above a white, oozing slit, but it was a start.

Sabine moaned, and the wind scattered in fear. He hissed, and the ground trembled.

He was exultant. His dream was not yet over. There was an ocean to cross and someone he desperately needed to find.

He billowed, letting the wind lift him up and away toward the west. Riding a strong current, he sped along, hissing like a black bullet through the sky, heading directly toward America.

CHAPTER SEVENTEEN

BUGGED

Leven maneuvered between two exceptionally thick fantrum trees and jumped over a hole the size of his old twin bed. His breathing was hard and labored. Clover clung to his neck screaming about how much better the immediate situation would be had Leven actually listened to him and left the humming dirt alone. Now a handful of confusing secrets were tracking him.

"Sorry," Leven said as he ran. "Do you think they're still following us?"

"If any saw you, they are," Clover replied sternly. "Secrets don't give up."

Leven scrambled up a small hill and ducked behind a pink bush that was shaped sort of like a squatty camel.

"I can't run any farther," Leven wheezed. "Let me catch my breath."

Clover materialized on Leven's head. He was shading his eyes with his hand, peering over the bush for any sign of what Leven had just dug up.

"You might be lucky," Clover said, turning invisible again. "I'm not sure the big secret saw you."

"I hope you're—"

Leven stopped talking. There on his nose was another small burning secret. Before Leven knew what was happening, the secret made eye contact.

"I didn't wash my hands before making that bread you're eating," the small secret admitted. The secret laughed joyfully and wiped its brow, looking relieved after having confessed. It then dimmed and took off running away from Leven and Clover.

Leven ducked farther behind the bush, hoping no other secrets could see him.

"What do we do?" he asked Clover.

"Stay hidden."

"The secrets don't seem very dangerous," Leven pointed out.

"That's exactly what they want you to think," Clover explained. "They're trying to lull you into a false sense of security so that when the real secret catches up to you, you won't run away."

"How many little ones are—?"

The bush they were behind began to shake. Leven stared at it. The bush then spit, hunched its back, and walked off, looking more like a camel, and leaving Leven and Clover crouching there exposed.

"I thought that was a bush," Leven said, moving to hide behind some trees.

"It is," Clover said. "Our bushes, like our clouds, have a

tendency to become what you imagine them to be. You must have thought that looked like a camel."

"I did."

"Well, then, it's your fault it walked off," Clover said. "It's probably looking for water."

A loud, deep scream pierced the sky from behind them. Leven turned to face the noise.

"I don't think I like this forest," Leven complained.

"Shhhh," Clover whispered.

The screaming sounded again.

"What is it?" Leven asked.

Clover let just his hands become visible. Both hands opened and spread.

"I have no idea, but I think it's wise to run from screaming things. It could just be a tree or rock, trying to trick us into helping. Then when we get there, whack." Clover smacked both his hands together.

There was another long scream, followed by the sound of moaning and a clicking noise. Leven could think of few things he would enjoy more than turning and getting away from the sound, but he couldn't just leave someone in danger. Despite what he knew was right, he was still a little surprised to find himself actually running toward the noise.

"I hope you know what you're doing," Clover said, hanging onto Leven's neck.

"So do I," Leven replied.

The screams sounded desperate. There were hollow pockets

of noise around each, like feedback from a hot microphone.

Leven plowed through a patch of shrubs, searching for the source of the cries. In the distance he saw a man hovering a few inches above the ground, seemingly caught in a large shaft of light. Surrounding the shaft of light was a thick swarm of millions of flying bugs. The bugs surrounded the man like a gigantic cloud of dirty exhaust. Several palehi were shrieking and running in various directions off into the woods.

"That's Albert Welch," Clover hollered into Leven's ear. "I know his mother's sycophant quite well. We used to go—"

"That's great," Leven interrupted. "What's he doing?"

"A dream has him," Clover yelled. "When the dream fades, the sarus will take him captive."

Leven had no idea what was happening, but he found himself unable to stand still. He picked up a large, dead tree limb. As he gripped the end of it, the bark seemed to mold around his fist.

"What are you doing?" Clover asked.

"I'm not sure," Leven answered.

Leven held the stick above his head and ran toward the shaft of light and the circling cloud of insects. Before he could reach the man, the dream apparently ended and the shaft of light dissolved, leaving Albert free to be attacked.

Being a nit, Albert was blessed with the gift to be able to see below the surface. He fell to his knees and pressed his face into the soil, looking for any cave or underground spot where he could hide and be protected. His gift did him little good. The sarus swarmed beneath him and began to lift him off the ground.

Leven hollered and shouted. He waved his stick and swatted at the cloud of sarus. The sarus dropped Albert and turned all their attention to Leven.

The sarus clicked and moaned even louder as they turned. Leven waved his stick at them and tumbled onto his back. The tiny, buglike animals buzzed in chaotic victory. They poured down upon Leven like a thick wave of fleshy pebbles, clicking and moaning.

Flapping their dusty wings in unison, the bugs crawled up under Leven's shirt and penetrated his nose and ears. Leven was instantly unrecognizable. In only a moment, the swarming sarus covered him completely and were piling on top of each other, causing Leven to look like a lumpy green mummy.

Then the biting began.

The sarus bit down on any spot they could find. Their dull teeth pinched Leven like tightly wired clothespins. When Leven screamed, the sarus entered his mouth, muffled his cry, and streamed like beads down Leven's throat and into his lungs.

He began retching and choking, spitting out sarus by the hundreds. He could feel their tiny mouths clamping down on his hair and his clothes and on any exposed skin. The pain was intense, but Leven didn't dare open his mouth to holler again.

With a hold on him, the sarus began to lift Leven from the ground. Their wings beating in a whir, the sarus climbed into the air, carrying Leven back toward the shelter of the forest. Leven kicked and struggled, but the sarus had him and were not about to let go.

ii

Albert quickly got to his feet and hid himself behind a bush that looked like a large rock. As he peered over the top of the bush, Albert felt something sharp jab him in the ankle. The stabbing sensation then moved up his right arm, and before he could swat away whatever it was, Albert saw a toothpick standing on his shoulder.

The toothpick cried, "Hold on, Leven!" and jumped from Albert's shoulder, running after the swarm of sarus.

Albert rubbed his eyes. He bent over and picked up a handful of stones. From behind the bush, Albert began throwing the stones at the sarus. His sycophant, Delphinium, reappeared.

"What are you doing?" Delphinium screamed.

"Helping," Albert argued.

"Well, knock it off," Delphinium insisted. "How am I to keep you safe if you keep trying to help people?"

"Good point," Albert said, dropping his stones and running for safety. "I'm far too important for this."

iii

Geth followed the swarm as fast as he could. He gasped at the number of sarus covering Leven—there were millions. He knew fate would not be as kind to Leven here in Foo as it had been in Reality, but fate *had* helped Geth find Leven again. That had to be a good sign.

What wasn't a good sign was that Geth could feel his feet and legs hardening, and the hardening was making it difficult to run.

Geth hopped onto a tree stump and gazed into the distance toward where Leven was now being levitated by the sarus higher and farther away. Geth whistled, just as a large single sarus was flying past him. The sarus immediately turned and attacked Geth, knocking him from the stump. The two of them rolled across the ground, Geth administering blows with his small sliver arms, and the sarus trying desperately to take a bite out of Geth. Finally, the sarus used its pincers to grab Geth's toothpick head. The agitated bug then shot up into the air holding Geth. Geth twisted and tried to pull free, but the sarus wouldn't have it, flying even faster and higher. Geth thrust the top of his sharpened head into the belly of the sarus, and the bug exploded in a puff of dust, leaving Geth alone in the sky.

Screaming like a teakettle venting its frustration, Geth tucked his arms in and dove directly toward Leven. He aimed for a fistful of sarus covering Leven's right shoulder. Geth's sharp head skewered three of them perfectly, and they were pulverized, evaporating in a puff of dust that drifted toward the ground. The sarus could be caught, or smashed, or stabbed, but they would always just turn to dust, which pollinated the other sarus and kept their kind multiplying by the hundreds.

Geth threw out his right arm and grabbed hold of Leven's left shoulder. The sarus swarmed, and Geth began going at them with his legs and arms. They squealed like tiny winged pigs as he punctured one after another, each victim turning to dust.

Leven was struggling as hard as he could, swinging and kicking as he was lifted higher into the air. The sarus continued to fill his mouth. Gasping for breath, Leven retched and bucked wildly in the air.

A thick, dirty sarus buzzed in as Geth lost his grip and fell to the ground. Geth stood quickly and tilted his head toward the flapping menace. The sarus flew into the tip of Geth, cutting its wing and slapping down against the ground like a hand against water. Ten more flew down into Geth. He fought them off with the tip of his head and twisted, throwing himself onto the back of a particularly large one. The sarus he was straddling rocked and twisted upside down in an attempt to throw Geth. But Geth grabbed hold of the two thick strands of hair that grew out of the sarus's head like antennas. Gripping them tightly, he was able to control the sarus he was now riding. He pulled the hairs back, and the sarus raced straight toward Leven. Hundreds of other sarus saw what was happening and swooped in to knock Geth off the back of their comrade. Geth wouldn't have it, and by pulling and pushing the two hairs he maneuvered brilliantly around all the incoming sarus and back to Leven.

Geth flew around Leven's head, down the length of his body, and beneath him as Leven floated in midair. There were very few exposed spots on Leven. The sarus had their mouths clamped down on his skin and clothing and were lifting and flying Leven as a team.

A huge sarus flew directly into Geth's path, causing a miniature head-on collision. Geth flew off the back of the sarus he was on and shot down the length of Leven and up against Leven's ankle, where he blew through some biting sarus and scratched up against the skin. The tip of his head twisted just a bit, and Geth became caught in Leven's sock.

The sarus didn't notice. They just shifted and continued to bite down on Leven, their wings beating, lifting him higher and higher.

The swarm finally began to descend into the forest and beneath the trees. There the sarus on Leven thinned just a bit, and he could see out of his right eye again. The air was dark and smelled of wet, musty wood.

As they descended farther, Leven was suddenly plunged into water. The swarm was lowering him into a huge vat that had been fashioned from the hollowed-out trunk of a very large tree. The water pushed up past his waist and chest. The sarus who had been biting onto his lower half released their hold and spread across the top of the water like a thick oil slick. It was nice to have them off him, but being lowered down into water was not exactly something that Leven liked. He was not a strong swimmer, as he had proven when it came time to dive to the gateway.

As Leven's chin hit the water, the remaining sarus on him released their mouths. Leven bobbed almost softly in the sarus-covered water; he spat a few stray sarus from his mouth and wiped his brown eyes with his hands while dog-paddling to stay afloat. The entire watery surface was covered in millions of moss-looking sarus, dipping themselves in the water and washing the taste of Leven from their mouths.

Leven didn't feel sorry for them in the least.

The vat was round and about twenty feet in diameter. Leven had no idea how deep it was, but he couldn't feel the bottom. All around the vat were gigantic trees with thick trunks, many as big around as the vat he was in.

Very little light fell from above, due to the canopy of trees, but the rim of the vat glowed as if painted fluorescent. The glow was strong and lit up everything in the area. Leven had no idea what the sarus wanted from him or what he should do. He could see over the rim of the vat and into the trees. In front of a few trees were tall piles of thin sticks, stacked like teepees without material covering them.

Something poked Leven on the ankle, and he kicked frantically to defend himself. As he flailed in the water, the sarus moved back, creating a clear circle around him. Leven was making so much noise that he barely heard Geth whisper into his ear.

"Don't say anything, but I'm right here."

"G—" Leven stopped himself from saying Geth's name, but nothing could have prevented his smile or held back the wave of relief Leven felt just knowing Geth was around. "How did you—?"

"Don't let them know I'm here," Geth whispered. "They have excellent hearing. You need to talk to them."

"To the bugs?"

"Shhh," Geth warned.

Leven could feel Geth slide back behind his right ear.

"Talk to them?" Leven said to himself, looking at the thick, fuzzy patches of sarus that covered every bit of water except for the small circle around him.

Leven cleared his throat.

"Hello?" he called out.

The sarus seemed to collectively shiver in the water.

"Who are you?" Leven asked.

They were silent. In fact, the entire forest seemed silent. Leven had not seen too terribly much of Foo, but so far what he had seen had either been deathly still or deathly loud. Leven wasn't sure which he preferred.

"Where am I?"

The sarus vibrated, making the water shimmy. It took a second, but Leven began to realize that the vibration was actually sounding something out.

"We have you, Leven," the water vibrated, sounding like a shaky train whistle with a deep echo. "The water has you."

"Who's we? And how do you know my name?" Leven asked.

"The sarus," they vibrated. "We have you. That is enough."

The vibration stopped, and in a couple of moments it was completely quiet again. Leven turned himself in the water. His head bobbed just a bit and water entered his mouth and nose. Leven blew out and looked over the rim of the vat and into the forest.

"What now?" Leven whispered to Geth. "Are they going to just leave me here?"

"Who are you talking to?" the sarus vibrated.

"No one," Leven lied. "I was just thinking."

"Thinking?" the sarus questioned. "You have nothing to think about. We have you, and you will remain here forever."

"Forever?" Leven asked, slightly panicked.

"Not forever," the water vibrated. "Eventually, the seed will swell and you will die."

"Seed?" Leven asked.

"Your death will have purpose beyond the reward," was their only reply, and as far as replies go it wasn't terribly comforting.

"I don't understand," Leven said, scared.

"You are Leven?"

"Yes," Leven answered hesitantly.

"Then Jamoon will reward us for your demise," the sarus vibrated. "And this seed shall grow strong from your gifts."

Leven's legs and arms were growing tired from treading water. His thighs burned so badly he was surprised to look down and see that they weren't actually on fire.

"I can't swim forever," Leven complained. "Can't you just let me lie on the ground forever? I'll hold the seed or whatever."

The water vibrated madly. "We know what you nits are capable of if you lie on the ground."

Leven thought of his Grandfather Hector. He had lain on the ground of Foo and eventually, thanks to his brain chemistry and his willpower, had convinced himself to disbelieve in Foo and return to Reality.

"The water is a constant reminder that you are still here," the sarus buzzed. "No more questions."

The sarus vibrated and began to lift off the water's surface.

They swarmed and moved out from over the water and above the piles of dry sticks stacked in front of the trees. They dropped onto the sticks, buzzing around them. The sticks began to click and rise, the sarus swarming on each piece of wood. Leven could see that the piles of wood were actually pieces hooked together. The sarus perched and clustered on the wood, standing it up and creating what looked to be a disjointed stick man that stood about five feet high. They walked stiffly toward the vat, clicking and spitting.

A fist-sized cluster of sarus zoomed through the air and swooped to the ground. They picked up a small object and flew over Leven's head. They dropped the object, and Leven heard the tiny splash.

The sarus stick man bent over and picked up a long pole.

He . . . it . . . they . . . whatever . . . lifted the stick up above the vat and brought it down, whacking Leven on the head. It was so sudden and unexpected that Leven didn't have time to react.

Leven saw stars swirling around his head, and his eyes were white with pain. He reached to the top of his head and felt the gigantic goose egg that was already beginning to grow.

"What was that?" Leven said loudly.

"They can't answer you," Geth whispered back, still behind Leven's right ear. "They can only speak with the water. They probably didn't mean to hit you; they're just incredibly clumsy on their sticks."

Geth was right. The stick came down toward Leven two more times, but it looked more like they were trying to knock something other than Leven with it. Eventually, after Leven had been smacked two more times and the sarus had thrown the pole down at least two dozen times, the stick connected with a notch in the rim of the vat. The second it connected there was a great whooshing sound as a massive, circular wood cover clamped shut over the top of the vat.

Leven and Geth were trapped.

With the cover closed, the vat resembled a giant wooden egg. The sarus danced clumsily around the container, hitting it with sticks. The sticks caused the water inside to swish and splash around.

"What do we do?" Leven asked Geth, swimming from the center of the vat to one of its sides.

Though the vat was closed, there was still enough fluorescent green light to make it perfectly clear just how doomed they were.

"This is interesting," Geth said, sounding a bit less optimistic than he usually did.

"What'll they do to us?" Leven asked.

"Nothing," Geth answered. "We're in a gaze. The sarus use them to nourish fantrum seeds. That was a seed they dropped in here. Eventually it will swell so large it will crush you and use your body and soul as nutrients. With your gifts you could help create a gigantic tree. When the seed cracks the gaze, it then drops down into the hole beneath, and a tree grows." Geth moved from Leven's right ear over to his left.

"Of course, we won't last more than a couple of days in here," he went on. "You'll drown, and I'll harden to the point of death long before the seed swells. It's only a matter of days before I'm done."

"If we do get out, do we have time to get you to the turrets?" Geth was silent.

Leven wouldn't have it. He found a small ridge where the top and bottom halves of the gaze met. It was enough of a ridge that he could hold on and not have to keep treading. Water continued to slosh as the sarus outside pounded the gaze.

"What are they doing?" Leven asked.

"Keeping the water moving," Geth answered. "They don't want you to forget you are experiencing this. They'll stop in a moment, but they'll come back and beat it at least once a day for as long as you live."

"We have to find a way out," Leven said with determination. "Where's Winter?"

Geth considered telling Leven she was just fine, but he knew they needed to deal in truth, not lies. "They've captured her."

"What?" Leven asked, losing his grip and splashing in the water. He grabbed the ridge again and steadied himself. "Who captured her?"

"Jamoon," Geth said solemnly.

"And you just left her?" Leven accused Geth.

"I am no good to anyone if I don't get to the turrets," Geth explained softly.

"Clover!" Leven said, remembering his sycophant. "Clover can help get us out of here. Clover!" His voice sounded hollow in the closed vat.

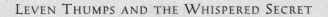

There was no answer.

"Was he with you near the trail?" Geth asked.

Leven nodded, and Geth wiggled with the movement of his head.

"He would have known to stay quiet and get out," Geth said, still trying to sound hopeful. "I'm sure he's working from the outside right now, trying to get to us."

The beating of the sticks against the gaze stopped. The sarus were done for the day. After the echoes of the beating faded it was shockingly quiet once again.

Leven began to search the gaze for any possible way out.

iv

There were a few things about Reality that Clover was beginning to miss—the casual pace of life being one of the biggest. It just seemed as if he'd had so much more free time in Reality. Leven's entire life had been slow, and Clover had needed to do very little to keep up with him. But ever since the day Clover had revealed himself to Leven, it had been almost nonstop running and rescuing.

Clover missed his "me time."

It used to be that he could watch Leven fall asleep and then spend the night out in Burnt Culvert, looking for rocks or interesting trash. He would always know that when he returned to the porch, Leven would still be there asleep. Now, however, it seemed that every time they turned around, something huge happened.

Clover didn't mind the adventure, but he was looking forward to the day when things would settle down a bit.

Today, unfortunately, was not that day.

Clover had tried to warn Leven against helping Albert, but Leven had too much hero in him to let Albert just stand there and be captured by the sarus. Now, thanks to Leven's big heart, the sarus had him instead of Albert.

Clover shivered, clinging to a tree branch high above the gaze Leven was imprisoned in. He watched the sarus dance around the gaze, beating it with their sticks, making sure Leven was fully aware of the elements around him.

As the sarus stopped their beating and retreated from the gaze, they moved directly below Clover and began to abandon the sticks they were controlling. The sarus would vibrate, and the stick skeletons they were clinging to would rattle, slide out from under them, and click up against the ground in a pile. The thousands of sarus who had controlled each stick would then fly off into the forest to find other victims to keep in other gazes.

Clover watched quietly.

In a matter of minutes the sarus were all gone, and Clover was alone in the tree, looking at the still gaze below him.

He shivered again.

Clover was not a big fan of the sarus. Years before, when Antsel had been working his way through the forest to rescue a lithen who had been buried here, he had stumbled into a cloud of sarus. They had attacked Antsel, and Clover had tried to help fight them off. It was a silly thing for Clover to even try, seeing how Antsel's gifts made him amply able to take care of himself. The sarus had swarmed Clover and forced their way into his mouth and nose and even into the void he had on the front of his robe. Fortunately, Antsel and Clover eventually got away. Clover was able to spit and blow the sarus from his mouth and nose, but it took him years to get all of them out of his void. In fact, the last one he had pulled out had been in Reality.

Clover shivered a third time.

He was not about to show himself to the little pests. They would certainly cram and hide themselves in his void so that every time he reached in to get something he would be attacked. So he stayed invisible and hidden until the time was right for him to rescue Leven.

The time now looked right.

Clover jumped down from the tree and onto the gaze. The giant vat swayed just a bit under his weight. Remaining invisible, he yelled, "Leven!"

There was no answer. Clover banged on the top of the gaze, but he couldn't hear anything from inside. The gaze was too thick.

Clover crawled around on the rounded lid, looking for something that would open the vat. He had watched the sarus beat it closed, but now he couldn't find a single notch or lever or crack to open the thing up.

"My little yolk," Clover said sadly, knowing that Leven would not approve of the nickname, but using it anyway because he knew Leven couldn't hear. "Hold on. I'll get you out."

Leven didn't reply because Leven didn't hear.

Something whispered from the nearby woods. Clover looked around nervously. The noise was thin and garbled, but it seemed to penetrate Clover's skin, wrap around his bones, and shake him.

It was not a good feeling.

The whisper rustled again, and Clover knew that the secret Leven had accidentally let loose in the woods was still searching for them.

It was not a good secret. Clover could feel that in his bones.

Clover leapt from off the gaze and back up into the trees. He dug his feet into the bark of a tree and sprang through the air to a tree farther down the way. Then he stopped for a second to think.

"Yes," he said to himself, having thought of a possible solution. "Of course, it could be dangerous." Clover shrugged, as if the danger were something for someone else to worry about. He pushed off a branch and ran in great leaps toward the center of the Swollen Forest.

He had a burn to rescue, and a secret to save him from, and he could think of only one creature that might be able to help on both accounts.

"Why not?" Clover clicked. "He owes me."

CHAPTER EIGHTEEN

THE ONCE-PERFECT
BALANCE OF FOO

C lover found a particularly thick grove of fantrum trees. He climbed to the top of the tallest one and rested on its leafy crown. His ears fluttered. He reached into his void and pulled out what looked to be a small rock. That small rock was actually a duft, a unique object that came in very handy for locating something lost. The duft was white with a ring of red running around it. In the center of it was a small black smudge. Clover pressed one of his fingers into the smudge.

The duft began to purr. Clover used his finger and thumb to spread the small smudge around. Like clay, it moved and spread easily. Unlike clay, it purred and shivered.

Clover twisted the duft with both hands, and the duft quickly expanded to the size of a large dinner plate. Then Clover spat on the duft and rubbed the spit around with the hem of his robe. In a few moments the surface of the duft began to shine. Clover lifted it up so that it faced the square sun.

The purring intensified.

The duft began to glow and pulsate with what sounded like a strong heartbeat. Clover smiled, pulled it down into his lap, and looked at its glowing surface. With one of his fingers he began to draw on the shiny duft. He drew thick, bumpy horns on a long, bloated body. He drew large teeth and a gigantic, split, tongue-like tail. He drew deep, swirling eyes and stony, hoofed feet. Clover even sketched two little creatures hanging off the beast's ears. When he was done drawing, the duft was still glowing slightly. Clover looked at the likeness and smiled again.

"Not bad," he said to himself.

Clover folded the edges of the duft back into itself, covering the drawing he had just created and bringing the duft closer to its original form. Clover worked and massaged it until it was a ball again.

The purring died down, and slowly a thin, red line curled around the circumference of the duft, until it looked almost exactly how it had appeared when Clover had first pulled it out.

"Perfect," Clover said. "Well, almost, just one last thing."

He took his fingernail and scraped out the initials "C.E." on the bottom of the duft. Holding the duft in his hand, Clover lifted his arm to the sky, swirled his wrist around a few times, and then threw the duft as hard as he could in an upward direction.

The duft whizzed through the air, flying up. It arched and

began to turn back and over. For a moment it appeared as if it were losing speed, but suddenly it shot off over the Swollen Forest like a bullet.

Clover took off after it, jumping from tree to tree like a lemur trying to outrun a forest fire. The duft was traveling too fast to follow closely, but each time Clover thought he had lost it, the duft would circle back, show itself, and turn in a different direction.

Clover threw himself up against the crown of a thin, pink fantrum tree. The top of the tree bent forward under Clover's weight, snapped back, and then violently sprang forward, catapulting Clover in the direction of the duft.

The purple sky lightened, causing the duft to be almost invisible. It would have been impossible to spot if not for the glowing red band spinning around it.

"Slow down," Clover screamed as he hurtled through the air, the wind and his speed causing his cheeks to ripple. "Sloooow dooooown!!"

Thick flocks of Tea birds lofted up, under, and around Clover. Screeching, they scattered about him, bothered by someone other than themselves flying through the air. A few pecked at Clover as he flew by. Clover covered his eyes and tucked himself into a ball. He bowled through the birds, the force from the tree that had flung him propelling him farther still.

Clover was closing in on the duft. He stretched his fingers and reached out to grab hold of it. His grip didn't slow the duft in the least. It simply dragged Clover up and through the air.

Clover screamed.

The duft changed course, pitching and spinning to the ground like a one-winged bird and taking Clover with it.

Clover let go and clutched a tree branch. He pushed off down toward the direction the duft had taken. The duft zipped out of sight, screaming as it neared its target.

Clover aimed for the noise.

Clover tore through the thick upper branches of tightly packed fantrum trees. He skidded down and around the trunks. He tried to grip anything that would slow him down, but his hands kept slipping off the bark. Clover slammed suddenly into the ground and rolled to a stop near a moss-covered boulder.

Clover shook his head and brushed the dirt out of the hair on his arms and legs. As usual, he wished someone other than himself had been there to witness what he had just been through.

The noise of wood snapping sounded from behind.

Clover disappeared, letting his eyes alone materialize. He glanced toward the noise.

"Hello?" Clover whispered.

Another branch snapped.

Clover backed up and scanned the area for the duft. The forest was dark, thanks to the thick trees. The only light came from the heavy blanket of kindle moss that covered most of the forest ground. It glowed lightly, giving the space beneath the tree canopy a cavelike feel. Clover spotted the small band of red shining a few yards away.

"There you are," he said happily, forgetting the noise he had just heard. "I know you only work once," Clover continued, moving toward the duft, "but I'd like to keep you for my scrapbook."

Clover reached the duft just as the red band dimmed to nothing. He bent down and touched the duft.

It was warm.

"So where is he?" Clover asked.

The duft just sat there on the ground. With only his eyes showing, Clover looked around, wondering if the duft hadn't worked.

"You were supposed to lead me to a siid," Clover sighed. "It's pretty unprofessional of you not to do your job." Clover leaned over and picked up the duft. "How can I be expected to—"

Something snorted right in front of Clover, startling him and spraying him with a coating of sticky goo. He couldn't see the source of the snort, but he had his suspicions—a siid.

Clover could still remember Antsel's eighth-grade oral report on the mysterious siids. Antsel had stood near the Education Trough in the classroom, dispensing words that filled the trough out of which the younger, less-educated students fed. Clover could see Antsel clearly in his head. He could see the words tumbling out of his mouth and into the trough:

"The siids were created to balance the weight of Foo," Antsel had begun. "There were seven originally, all of them spread out over the entire realm of Foo. The siids also possess the power to kill, overriding the usual invulnerability of the inhabitants of Foo. Most of the time they remain hidden, happy to be ignored, but as their stomachs become empty, they are forced to leave their hiding places and devour, say, half a village, or an entire class of school students who are too engrossed in their studies to simply look up, scream, and run for their lives."

Clover smiled, remembering how Antsel had paused at that point to create a greater dramatic effect. Antsel then continued:

"After years of siid problems, the citizens of Cusp decided they were tired of living in fear, so they captured a siid in an effort to restore peace. They bound the siid and imprisoned it on the edge of Cusp above the Veil Sea. Their thought was that other siids would see what they were capable of and leave them alone. What they didn't understand, however, was that since the siids possessed the power to kill, they also had the power to die. They fed on villagers and other creatures because they needed to live. They also needed to be a certain size because their weight stabilized Foo.

"After being put on display, the siid they had captured eventually died of starvation, and its rotting body was dumped into the Veil Sea. The people of Cusp were amazed and empowered by what they had done. They had destroyed a siid.

"The other six siids were then sought for game. Two more were killed, and the remaining four went into hiding. Two are rumored to be living in the Swollen Forest, and the other two are thought to be somewhere in the mountains above Fté. Together they help Foo maintain some balance. It's not unusual to feel Foo move when one of the siids is up and wandering about."

Clover was still proud of the A grade Antsel had gotten on his report.

Another snort sounded. It drew Clover out of his thoughts about Antsel. The snort also showered Clover with another wave of sticky spit. He stepped back a few inches and made his eyes disappear. He felt it was better to be heard and not seen.

"Easy," Clover nervously said to the dark. "If you're what I think you are, then I need you."

Another snort. Another torrential wave of goo.

"A warning would be nice," Clover tisked, wiping thick saliva from his face. "Or perhaps you could turn your head when you do that."

Another snort.

The space was dark, without kindle moss or light of any kind. And then the siid opened its glowing eyes.

Clover half wished for the dark again. The beast stepped out of the gloom, looking very much like a gigantic version of the drawing Clover had sketched. The siid lunged at Clover, its heavy hooves tearing at the ground and sending a shower of dirt flying. Clover was invisible, but the siid could smell him. The beast opened its gigantic mouth and clamped its jaw shut over Clover, trapping him inside its mouth.

Clover relaxed and, acting on instinct, began to rub himself against the siid's rough tongue, giving the siid a good taste of what it had inside. Clover knew that the siids learned by licking; he only hoped the beast would remember him. Or at least recognize that he was a sycophant and not digestible.

The giant siid flung its head and rolled Clover around in its mouth. The creature then drew its snout in like an accordion and thrust it back out, shooting Clover from its mouth to roll into the dirt.

The siid roared.

Clover stood and became visible again. He wiped at some of the wet slime on his fur and looked up at the siid.

"I'm glad you remember me," Clover said.

The siid roared again, communicating with Clover its unhappiness at being disturbed. Two small creatures dangled from the siid's ears. They were called waxels; all the siids had them. The waxels hung off the siids' ears, cleaning the beasts and arguing with one another. At the moment the two waxels were arguing about how impolite and disgusting Tea birds could be.

Clover ignored the waxels; he had come for the siid. He also knew that the siids liked motion.

"Sorry to bother you," Clover said, swaying to make his point. "But I have some friends who are dying, and you seemed like the only hope to save them."

To appease the beast further, Clover shook his right leg and shimmied a bit.

The siid roared a third time, giving Clover the go-ahead to climb aboard, and the little sycophant didn't hesitate.

CHAPTER NINETEEN

AISLE SEATS ARE BETTER

Desperate times call for desperate measures. That's a saying, or a bit of advice, or a catchphrase, or a string of words used to confuse people less intelligent than you. In any case, it means: Life is tough, so you'd better fight hard—or something like that.

Dennis Wood had never been more confused in his entire life, and he had no idea how to fight hard. At the moment he could barely breathe. He was thirty-two thousand feet above the earth, flying toward New York. The plane ticket had cost him six hundred and twenty-five dollars.

Dennis had never flown before. He had built thousands of toy planes and had often imagined himself swooping through the air, shooting enemies and destroying anything in his path. But playing with model airplanes was a far cry from riding in the real thing.

Ezra was hiding out in Dennis's fanny pack. It was hard for the aggressive toothpick to remain quiet. It was not in Ezra's personality to stay hidden away. He had bitten Dennis's fingers each time Dennis had unzipped the pocket to check on him. Ezra was a pain, but considering that what he really wanted was to scream at the passengers and poke the pilots, he was actually behaving halfway decently.

Dennis looked out the window and took stock of his life. He could see nothing but the top of the airplane's right wing surrounded by white clouds, and he wondered what had caused him to do something so out of character. He had withdrawn his life savings, quit his job, and here he was traveling across the world—all under the direction of a toothpick he had found in his sandwich.

When he thought about it that way, he felt even more thickheaded than usual, and he was suddenly glad his father and mother had died years before. He knew they would have been beyond disappointed with what he had become and what he was doing now.

Dennis glanced out the window again and gasped. He rubbed his eyes in astonishment. Emerging from the white clouds and keeping pace with the plane was an inky-black shadow that in some strange way looked like a man. The billowing form had long, thin arms and a pair of white eyes that were turned on Dennis, staring at him intently. At first the shadow was floating on the wind, but then it settled on top of the wing, spreading itself out like a puddle of black paint.

Dennis blinked and pressed his face to the window. When the blackness suddenly rippled up against the window, Dennis gasped and reared back, leaning into the man sitting next to him. The man had previously been drinking and was now sound asleep.

"Excuse me," Dennis said, shaking the man's shoulder.

The man grunted and opened his eyes.

"Do you see that?" Dennis asked, wide-eyed, pointing at the window.

Sleepily, the man leaned across Dennis to look where he was pointing. Just then the black form swirled into a ball and pressed its white eyes up against Dennis's window. The large man shrieked in terror and recoiled, attracting the attention of all the other passengers.

A flight attendant came quickly to his seat. "Sir," she said sternly, "you will need to calm—"

"Look!" he slurred, gesturing toward the window.

The flight attendant looked, but there was nothing but white clouds.

"What is it?" she asked.

"There was something black," he spit. "This guy saw it too."

Dennis just sat there like a post, staring straight ahead. He didn't shake his head or nod in any fashion.

"Listen," the flight attendant reprimanded the agitated man, "you are making the other passengers uneasy. Any more outbursts from you, and you will be arrested at landing."

"But . . ."

She let her eyes show him how serious she was. His hand trembling, the large man reached for what was left of his drink and finished it off in one swallow, then laid his head back on his seat, eyes wide open, and breathed heavily.

Nervously, Dennis glanced back out the window. There was nothing but the top of the wing and clouds.

ii

Sabine moved along the bottom of the wing, fighting the slipstream of air, searching for an opening to get in. He could feel that whatever had been touched by Foo was inside this plane. He hissed, the sound mingling with the rush of air under the wing. "In," he whispered violently. "In."

On the back edge of the wings there was a tiny seam between the wing and one of its flaps. Sabine arranged himself into a long, black thread. He pushed through the small seam and, like fishing line being reeled in, coiled up into the plane. He threaded himself through the wing. He found a pinpoint of room next to some wires leading into the fuselage of the plane and moved himself into the inner body of the 747.

"In," he whispered. "I'm in."

Sabine slipped in under the service quarter door and traced the lighting track that ran along the carpeted aisle of the plane. The front end of him glowed white with two small eyes. The rest of him was as black and thin as the devil's dental floss. Sabine hated that he was no longer the person he had once been, but his ability to change shape to suit his need was a half-decent consolation prize.

He inched across the floor, letting himself feel where to go.

He still didn't know exactly who he was after, but he could sense that what he was looking for was here. Someone on the plane had been touched by Foo.

Sabine twisted around the ankles of a tall, skinny woman with short hair. She was not it. He swirled around the ankles of the man next to her. Not only was he not it, but he needed to change his socks.

One by one, Sabine made his way around the ankles of everyone there.

Nothing.

Nothing.

Nothing.

Something.

Sabine wrapped himself around the ankles of a pale man with ugly shoes in row seventeen. It was clear that this man had not been to Foo, but he possessed something that had.

Sabine's whole stringlike being crackled, causing at least two passengers to glance around as if they had heard something. Sabine slithered up Dennis's leg and along the tightly buckled seat belt. Dennis, still looking intently out the window, was unaware of what was happening right in his lap.

Sabine pulled the toggle back with his tiny mouth and slithered into the fanny pack. To anyone looking on it would appear that there was simply a very long black string hanging out of Dennis's fanny pack. Sabine could see Ezra lying there on a big wad of money. Ezra turned.

As quickly as a snake's tongue, Sabine shot out and around

Ezra, wrapping himself tightly around the toothpick. Ezra tried to fight back, but Sabine had him sewn up. He cautiously pulled at Ezra, slipping him out of the fanny pack and pulling him down the carpeted aisle. Ezra clawed at the carpet and tried to fight back. It was no use; Sabine carefully dragged him all the way to the rear of the plane. There he pulled Ezra under the service door and into the service area. Sabine drew in his long string to create a more sinister and ghostlike shape. He hissed, staring intently at Ezra as he clenched him in his thin, shadowy hands.

"You've been to Foo," Sabine moaned.

Ezra couldn't answer due to Sabine's grip over his mouth.

"You," Sabine hissed. "You." He moved his shadowy fingers away from the top of Ezra.

"You're a real brain," Ezra spat. "You? You who?"

"Geth," Sabine whispered in fear.

"Geth?" Ezra whispered back. "I'm not Geth," he growled. "We are no longer one. He betrayed me."

"Be still," Sabine commanded, relaxing his grip just a bit.

The purple plastic fringe on Ezra's top rippled. He blinked his one eye and then jumped up and began to stab Sabine. Sabine reached out, trying to get hold of Ezra, but the tiny toothpick was too quick. Ezra bounced off the walls of the plane, screaming threats about what he would do to Sabine. The purple fringe on top of Ezra was flailing wildly and created a zipping noise as he whizzed around the cabin. Sabine was too slow to catch Ezra. He thinned into a string again and shot toward the vent he had slipped through earlier.

"No, you don't!" Ezra screamed.

He grabbed the end of Sabine as he tried to slip away. Sabine pulled and wiggled out of the service area and into the innards of the plane. He pushed out into the wing again and slithered out the same seam he had entered. Ezra was still holding tightly to the end of Sabine back in the plane.

The air outside the plane was violent and tore at Sabine, whipping him around like the loose string he was. The open air expanded Sabine's form into a thick rope. Sabine flapped up against the wing, while inside, Ezra held onto the tail end of him, refusing to let go. Ezra was as angry as any toothpick had ever been, furious over the thin string of Sabine trying to get away.

iii

Dennis looked out of the window for the hundredth time. There was nothing but white clouds.

"You did see that?" he asked the drunken man, referencing the sight they had seen earlier.

"I see a lot of things," he replied. "I don't trust my eyes anymore."

Dennis turned from the man and remembered Ezra. Surprised to find the pack unzipped, he reached in, half expecting his fingers to be bitten and half disappointed when it didn't happen. Dennis sorted through the few objects in the fanny pack, searching for a spot of purple.

There was none.

Dennis leaned forward and looked down at his feet. No purple. He glanced around the plane, wondering where Ezra could be and if he should be nervous about his absence.

As he turned to look out the window, he saw something flapping around like a long black rope, the end of it glowing white.

Dennis screamed. He couldn't help it. He had been holding it in, and like a bad bit of air it had popped out of his throat at the most inopportune time. His scream caused Mr. Drunk to scream, and Mr. Drunk's scream set off the rest of the passengers as one by one they looked out the windows and realized that something quite concerning and out of the ordinary was going on.

Little did they know Sabine was just getting started.

Dennis wished he had taken a train.

iv

Tim Tuttle stared at Terry Graph in awe, but not in the good kind of awe. This was not like when you are fortunate enough to witness a huge meteor racing across the sky and slamming into the ground. Nor was this the kind of awe that hits when you are driving across the country and there on the side of the road you spot a restaurant in the shape of a hot dog. This was the kind of awe you feel when you realize you have the great misfortune of standing there right in front of the ugliest, most stubborn, most cold-hearted person on earth.

"So you don't know where he is?" Tim asked.

"He's not even my blood."

"But—"

"But yourself," Terry snipped. "That boy was forced upon us. He was lucky we had the generous spirit to put up with him for so long."

As I mentioned, Tim was in awe.

"Addy," Terry yelled back into the apartment. "Come tell this fool what that dumb boy did."

Addy made her way to the door while Terry receded into the interior of the apartment.

Tim had been fortunate enough to pick up on the trail of Winter. After he had left Janet Frore's house, he had considered all the possibilities of where Winter could have gone and had concluded that she had most likely traveled by bus. Besides hitch-hiking, there was really no other way out of town.

Tim knew that if Winter had stayed around, she would have hidden out with him and his wife. They would have been happy to hide her. So, figuring that she must have fled the area, the bus seemed like the most likely mode of travel. Unfortunately, no one at the bus station was much help. One ticket lady seemed to remember selling a ticket to a minor, but she couldn't remember where that ticket had been to. Tim had been discouraged until a couple who were getting off a bus overheard him asking questions and told him they remembered meeting a nice girl with blonde hair when they were leaving the week before. It was entirely fortuitous. The couple debated with each other for a moment before they agreed on the fact that she had been heading to Oklahoma to visit her grandmother.

"Sure it wasn't Texas to see her grandfather?" the man said.

"Certain," the woman answered.

Tim took the first bus he could get to Oklahoma. After asking a dozen bus station employees and four taxi drivers, Tim had been fortunate enough to find a cabdriver who remembered dropping Winter off at a school in Burnt Culvert, Oklahoma.

"Home of the Fighting Ashes," he had said.

That same taxi driver took Tim to Sterling Thoughts Middle School. There Tim found hundreds of kids who were willing to tell him all about the strange girl who had come to their school and frozen its two biggest bullies. The children had even pointed out Brick and Glen, who now spent their lunch breaks standing against the wall, shaking like nervous Todd. The students then added a new depth to Tim's search by informing him that Winter had run off with a strange kid with a white streak in his hair, a boy named Leven Thumps.

At the public library, Tim had not found a single Thumps in the phone book, but he did find a Thumps in the newspaper. It seemed that not too many days before, the home of one Terry and Addy Graph and their adopted son, Leven Thumps, had been frozen and destroyed, lifted into the air and dropped to the ground. It wasn't too hard from there to find where Addy and Terry were now living.

Tim half wished he had never found them. They were awful people and reminded Tim a great deal of Janet Frore.

"Addy, tell him about that brat," Terry demanded. They had never invited Tim in, so he just stood there on their doorstep.

Addy Graph stepped up. She was a large woman with a big forehead and messy hair. The apartment Terry and she were living in was a disaster. Tim couldn't see the whole thing from the door, but what he could see was awful. It looked like something a trash dump might throw up if things like trash dumps were capable of having the flu. There were dishes and litter all over. Leven had always been the one to do the cleaning; in his absence, Addy and Terry did nothing.

"I'll tell you what that selfish boy did," Addy spat. "He picked up our house and smashed it into a million—"

"Billion!" Terry yelled from inside.

" . . . a billion pieces," Addy said. "My sister dies in childbirth and leaves me a burden like that? What's this world coming to?"

"This isn't the America my father fought for!" Terry yelled.

"So do you know where he went?" Tim asked.

"How would I know?" Addy barked. "If I knew where he was, I'd have him over my knee administering the punishment he has due."

"I need to find him," Tim added.

"Why's that?" Terry asked, stepping back up to the door.

"I think he could be in trouble."

"Trouble?" Terry snarled. "Trouble?"

Terry was beside himself. Not literally. This story would be that much more painful if there were two Terrys, able to stand next to each other and simultaneously curse Leven.

But Terry felt he had been cursed since the day Leven had been brought home from the hospital and he and his wife had been forced to take care of the kid. Leven had made Terry's life miserable. Leven was always hanging around, eating their food, sitting on their furniture, and talking without being asked to. Life with Leven had been hard for Terry.

So imagine how surprised Terry had been to discover that with Leven gone, things were even worse.

Shortly after Leven had walked out, things had gotten weird. Addy had thrown a fit and insisted that Terry find work. She had also stolen Terry's drinking money. And, as if a dry throat and the prospect of having to find a job weren't bad enough, the tree outside had snuck up on Terry through the toilet.

Those now seemed like the good old days, seeing as how Terry had subsequently lost his entire house. It had been lifted up by the roots of the dead tree he had hacked down, frozen, and then dropped. The house had shattered against the earth, sounding like a million ceramic golf balls being dumped off the Empire State Building. In the end there was no chunk bigger than a stick of kindling left. That night Terry had stood there dumbfounded, confused, and scared. Sure, it wasn't far from his normal state of dumbfounded, confused, and *angry*, but the fear sparked something in him. It twisted and turned until the fear was more of a burning *hatred* for the kid he had been forced to take in all those years before.

That trailer home had been all that Terry had. Yes, there was Addy, but Addy's value was depreciating faster than the mobile home had been. Now Terry had nothing. The house had not even been insured.

The hatred grew.

As the hard, dark thoughts filled his head, Terry began to realize something. It was almost as if for the first time in his life he could see something he needed to accomplish. He could feel and think and spit nothing but hatred for Leven. The kid had to be *somewhere*. An ungrateful fourteen-year-old boy with no money can't just disappear off the face of the earth.

That would be impossible.

"Last we heard, some church in Maine claims to have spotted the boy," Terry spat. "I was going to call them, but I lost the number."

"Maine?" Tim asked excitedly.

"It's in Canada someplace," Terry snipped.

Tim didn't correct him. "Thanks," he said. "If I find him, I'll let you know."

"Oh, goody," Terry slurred. "Did you hear that, Addy? He'll let us know. Well, you better. I got a score to settle with that brat."

Terry slammed the door, ending the conversation.

CHAPTER TWENTY

SEPARATED AT BITE

It was so silent. Leven could hear himself breathing, but nothing else. He repositioned his hold on the narrow rim inside the vat. He and Geth had been soaking in the gaze for hours, and Leven had little or no doubt that his body could now outwrinkle any raisin around. His entire being felt like a massive bruise.

"We've got to get out," Leven urged.

"Only the seed can set us free," Geth said solemnly. "They build each gaze as an intricate puzzle. A series of blows with wood in certain spots closes the gaze. And only the growth of the seed opens it back up."

"So this is it?" Leven asked. "We're done for?"

"We'll see what fate has in mind," Geth said.

"Maybe Winter will come for us," Leven suggested, more to himself than anyone else.

"Actually," Geth said, "Winter has her own problems. By the time she might find us it will be too late."

"What about Amelia?"

Geth was silent.

"She's trapped too?" Leven asked.

Geth was still silent. "I'm afraid she was caught in the gunt," he finally answered, knowing Leven deserved to know. "Winter tried to save her, but it was no use."

"She's dead?" Leven asked sadly.

His eyes burned momentarily and then cooled.

"Are you sure?" Leven added.

"I'm sorry."

Leven had barely known his Grandmother Amelia, but she had been his only real family. He had nobody else, and the knowledge that he was the single remaining Thumps was as painful as learning of Amelia's passing.

"She was so kind," Leven whispered.

"And important to Foo," Geth added.

Leven hated the rovens. He hated everything that was happening. He hated the selfish and dark dreams of Reality that had helped give beings like Sabine power. Leven wiped water from his eyes.

Geth patted Leven on the shoulder.

"I want to get out and see where she died," Leven insisted.

"Then we must hope that fate has us favorably in its sight."

"Amelia wouldn't want us to give up," Leven said. "At least Clover is out there; he can help. That's something."

"That's true," Geth replied. "But it will take more than a single sycophant to save us from this gaze."

"You don't know Clover," Leven said. "He won't stop until we're free."

"We'll see what fate has in mind," Geth agreed with excitement, even as his tiny body was hardening further. "This is always my—"

Geth was interrupted by a terrific screech that pierced the air. Leven shook, and Geth grabbed onto a lock of Leven's hair right below the white patch. The screech continued, and in the faint glow Leven could see rows of pointed, white objects piercing the sides of the gaze. The container began to vibrate, and Leven lost his grip and floated toward the center of the vat. The agitated water splashed into his eyes and up his nose. He sputtered and wiped his face and could see the dots growing larger and beginning to look like white wedges pushing through the wood.

"What's happening?" Leven yelled.

"I have no idea," Geth yelled back, water sloshing everywhere. "But I think those are teeth!"

Leven looked closely and realized Geth was right. The small white mountains were huge teeth, penetrating the gaze. From the pattern of the teeth it was obvious something gigantic was biting down.

There was a horrific wrenching noise as the gaze was lifted. It began to shake violently, rattling Leven and Geth around like beans in a child's toy. Water sloshed up Leven's nose. His head

banged against the walls of the gaze. Then, like lightning striking, his gift kicked in.

Leven's eyes burned gold. His mind reeled as streaks of blinding light flashed through his head, popping like the flashbulbs
from a thousand cameras. Leven could see himself in the water as
the powerful jaws of the beast holding them finally came together
and bit off the entire top of the gaze. Leven could also see himself caught in the teeth of the beast.

He couldn't let that happen.

Leven shook off his thoughts and glanced around as he was
being sloshed about in the water. The light from his eyes lit the
inside of the gaze in a brilliant manner.

"What do you see?" Geth yelled.

"We're about to be eaten," Leven yelled, "unless we duck!"

As much as he hated the water, Leven dove below the surface. Fighting to stay submerged, he opened his eyelids and looked up. His eyes shone, and he could see Geth a few feet above him, floating on top of the water. Leven reached up with his right hand. Just as his fingers were about to close around Geth, the beast's bite cracked the shell of the gaze, and his mighty teeth clamped together like a tightly wound bear trap. Leven closed his hand, whipping it back just as the creature's jaw closed. Water rushed into Leven's mouth and nose. He gagged and swallowed huge fists of liquid as he struggled to breathe. The bottom half of the gaze broke away and the vat tipped onto its side, pouring Leven and the water out in one humongous wave.

The beast screamed.

Leven tried to catch his breath as his chest burned and heaved. He spit and moaned, gasping for air.

The beast screamed again.

Leven scrambled from the broken gaze and opened his fist to set Geth free, but Geth was not there. Frantically, Leven patted his body, searching for Geth. He could feel nothing but the key still in his pocket.

The beast screamed even louder, as if bothered by Leven's ignoring him. Leven looked up to get his first real glimpse of his assailant.

It would not be lying to say that Leven suddenly longed for the peace and quiet of being trapped in the gaze forever. Towering over Leven was one of the seven siids—the fifth one, to be exact.

A hundred avalands would have been less threatening.

The siid stood on four thick, meaty legs, each capped off with a hoof the size of a small hill. Its legs were wrapped in twisted vines and strands of old rope that looked to grow from the belly of the beast. The siid's body was long and wide, like that of a bloated whale. The creature's skin was pockmarked and scarred. There were spikes sticking out of its back and circling down under its body and around its hind side. The head of the beast was round, with a square mouth and long, twisted ears that looked like fleshy braids. Clinging to the end of each ear was a small, monkeylike waxel. One was red, the other yellow.

The siid's green-burning eyes were as large as its bottomless nostrils. On its shoulders were two mushy humps, and behind those humps were two long, leathery arms that were tearing at the ground with pointed claws, scooping up water with flat thumbs and carrying it up into the creature's mouth. At the far end of the beast was a thick tail split down the middle like a forked tongue. Both bits of tail whipped at the air, slapping and cracking in a circular motion.

Leven tried to catch his breath, but the sight before him stole every ounce of air his lungs had held. His throat burned painfully as air rushed out of his mouth. Leven closed his eyes and tried to calm himself—and to control his gift.

There was nothing but fear.

The siid lifted its head and breathed in, sucking broken tree limbs and loose dirt up from the ground. They stuck to the siid's nose as if it were a vacuum, and when the beast blew out, debris and saliva flew everywhere.

Leven could feel his knees weakening as he tried to decide what to do.

The beast opened its gigantic mouth and roared, sending noise and wind circling madly, like a small tornado. Caught in the wind, Leven stood there shaking, easy prey for the siid. The beast moved forward and with one swoop picked up Leven in its gigantic mouth.

Leven could feel the monster's mouth clamped tight against him. He half expected to hear the sound of himself being crushed but couldn't feel any teeth tearing into him. The siid reached into its own mouth and took hold of Leven's head with one arm and Leven's feet with the other. It turned Leven in its mouth, licking him with its thick, beanbag-looking tongue. Leven felt like a buttery ear of corn. He wanted to scream, but he also longed to keep his mouth shut so as to prevent a better taste of tongue.

After rotating Leven a few more times, the beast let him roll out of its mouth onto the ground. Leven lay there spitting and coughing. He felt his arms and legs and realized that he was still intact.

The siid stood right above him and snorted.

Leven looked around at the night. There was no one in sight. No sarus, no Geth, just the broken gaze and a creature as big as a mountain.

Leven was astonished to hear someone talking to him.

"Did I come through or what?" Clover asked, invisible but nearby.

"Clover?" Leven looked around in disbelief.

"How many times am I going to have to save your life?" Clover asked proudly.

"You did *that*?" Leven asked, looking up at the siid.

"It was no big deal," Clover said, blushing so strongly that his two red cheeks materialized momentarily and then disappeared. "He owed me. Plus, I promised him a fresh fantrum seed and gaze water. Siids prefer water that's been sitting around."

Leven got to his feet, his legs as wobbly as wet noodles. He could feel Clover helping to steady him.

"Thanks," Leven said honestly, still not comfortable standing so close to the siid.

Clover whistled and materialized. The siid quickly whipped its tail around and picked up Leven with one half of the fork and Clover with the other.

"Don't worry," Clover said. "It'll get us out of the forest."

"I can't leave without Geth," Leven insisted, struggling in the fleshy fork of the siid's tail. He broke free and began feeling the ground around him, calling, "Geth!"

Clover bounced around doing the same.

"Where was he last?" Clover asked, smiling.

"He was in the gaze," Leven lamented. "I tried to grab him, but he got away. We have to find him."

"He's not here," said Clover, pointing out the obvious. "He was probably caught in the runoff. I'm sure he's in the Waz River by now. He'll float to Fissure Gorge."

"Geth!" Leven yelled, his chest burning with pain for his misplaced friend.

The forest began to moan. The sarus were returning.

"We need to get out of here," Clover said urgently. "Geth is a master at making it back. Besides, he told us if we were split up to get to the turrets."

"Geth!" Leven yelled one last time.

In the trees there was a sweeping whisper. As Leven turned his head, a small, burning secret burst from the trees and sprang onto the bridge of his nose.

Clover spotted it and yelled, "Don't look at it!"

Leven shut his eyes and tried to bat the secret off his nose. The secret wouldn't have it. It pushed up on Leven's eyelids, forcing Leven to open his eyes. Leven had no choice. He looked at the secret, and it smiled.

"I embezzled from my boss," the secret whispered. Then it clapped its tiny, fiery hands and dashed away.

"The secrets are getting more serious," Clover said. "We have to get out of here."

"But Geth . . ."

Clover wasn't listening. He gave his pathetic imitation of a whistle, and the siid picked Leven and him up again with its tail. Clover semi-whistled a second time, and the huge beast began to step quickly. Foo rocked as the siid pushed forward. The scales on its body clicked and rubbed in an awkward rhythm as the two monkeylike creatures hanging on its ears continued to argue with one another. Apparently the red one really felt it was the yellow one's turn to clean the siid. Their high-pitched screaming cut through the air and reminded Leven of brakes squealing on a car.

"This is the way to travel," Clover said, excited. "We should make up some time."

Leven could think of little besides Amelia and Geth and the time they didn't have.

"Now's probably not a good time to complain about you not ever really thanking me for bringing you here, is it?" Clover asked.

"I don't think so," Leven answered sullenly.

"That's okay," Clover said. "We can talk about it later."

Leven closed his eyes and tried to see the future—nothing.

"Come on, Geth," he whispered. "Come on."

The siid ran.

Leven didn't feel so well.

CHAPTER TWENTY-ONE

BE CAREFUL WHERE YOU STEP

Janet Frore wasn't comfortable. Ever since the dumb man with the dumb forehead and dumb hair had come by, Janet had been bothered.

"What business does he have worrying about the girl?" Janet whined. "Besides, I did everything I could for Winter, and if she runs off it's no concern of mine," she tried to convince herself. "I should add up how much that child has cost me. I'm sure the total would be astounding."

Janet didn't stand much. She stood up for things like moving from the couch to the bed, going to the rest room, walking out to get the mail, or driving to the grocery store. Other than that, she sat on the couch, eating and thinking nasty things about everyone she knew, had known, or would someday meet.

Today, however, was mail day, and Janet was in for some standing.

Janet liked to let the mail build up for a few days and then gather it all in a plastic sack. Normally she would venture out in midafternoon, but thanks to a terribly engaging soap opera, Janet had been unable to pull herself away from the TV and get the mail at an earlier hour.

So, here it was, eight o'clock at night, and Janet was suddenly feeling an unusual burst of energy. She decided to use that energy to go for the mail.

Janet hefted herself from the couch, rising like a fat wad of dough in a hot oven. She pushed up and onto her two poor legs. She gave her lower limbs a few moments to adjust to the shock, then began to shuffle out of the room.

Janet stopped at the front door to catch her breath. She had decided to shed her robe and was now wearing a yellow house-coat with a row of red flowers stitched around the bottom hem and along the sleeves and neck. Of course the flowers didn't stand out half as much as all the food stains she had dribbled down the front. Janet cleared her throat and choked a bit on some food that was still sitting in there. She ran her puffy fingers through her long, thinning hair and reached for the doorknob.

She pulled, and the world around her came leaking in.

Janet could see the night sky. She could see the lights on in the neighbors' homes. She listened to the streetlights buzzing and took in the sound of a softball game being played down the way. It had been so long since Janet had stepped out at night that she had almost forgotten how it was.

She looked down at the walkway. It was littered with rolled-up newspapers that she had never taken the time to come out and collect.

She stepped onto the walkway and began to journey down toward the mailbox. A light wind blew through her hair and around her body. The smell of fresh-cut grass filled her nostrils.

Janet stopped in her tracks. There was something about being there, covered in night and a veil of stars. There was a celebration in the wind and a sense of nature in the sounds around her. For a brief and fleeting moment, Janet almost regretted how much of life she was missing.

"Dumb nature," she muttered, shaking the feeling off.

Three young boys appeared, riding down the street on their bikes, their laughter and talk filling the air. They pedaled near Janet's house; upon spotting her, the tallest one yelled out, "Hey, look at that whale in a dress!"

They all laughed and continued on past.

Without even thinking about it, Janet reached down and grabbed one of the rolled-up newspapers she had been too lazy to gather up. She flung it as hard as she could, knocking the tallest boy in the back of the head. His bike wobbled, and he crashed into the curb. He rolled over and looked back at Janet.

"Serves you right," she barked as she stood on the edge of her walkway where it haphazardly met up with the city's sidewalk. "You need to—"

Janet stopped talking due to the appearance of a shooting star streaking across the black, fuzzy sky. She looked up at the celestial miracle and watched it fade in the distance. The temperature was a perfect sixty-three degrees. She wasn't standing directly over the mismatched sidewalk, but there was a bit of her hanging over the line, a bit that might not have been there had she spent the last few months of her life doing something besides sitting and eating. Fate snatched a wisp of her, and although she had no understanding of what had transpired, she could feel that something about her had changed.

"I need to stop getting up," she complained, shaking her head.

Janet collected her mail, shuffled back inside, slammed the door, and locked it tight.

CHAPTER TWENTY-TWO

THE SPIRITED HITCHHIKER

To Leven, the Swollen Forest was nothing but a confusing maze of trees and terror. Noises he had never heard and could not identify seemed to sound at every turn and from every patch of darkness.

It didn't exactly help that he was racing through the place twisted into the tail of the fifth siid, with a whispering secret stalking him. Or that he was beginning to feel ill.

"How do we know he's not just taking us somewhere to eat us?" Leven yelled to Clover.

"I guess we really don't," Clover yelled back. "He promised he would take us to the far bridge, but I've heard stories about what a hard time the siids have keeping their promises."

"That's great," Leven complained. "So you talked to him?"

"Well, it wasn't so much talking as it was—"

"Telepathy?" Leven guessed, thinking about a movie he

had seen once where a bear talked to a horse with its mind.

"No," Clover answered. "It was more like swaying."

"You talked to him by *swaying*?" Leven asked.

"I hope that's what we were doing," Clover said, suddenly embarrassed. "Let's just consider it a good sign that he hasn't eaten us yet."

"Perfect," Leven said sarcastically.

The siid moaned. A round, furry creature with big ears and a number of legs ran in front of it. With one smooth motion the siid dipped its head and scooped up the poor creature. The beast chewed and crunched on its victim as it continued running. The sound was a bit distressing.

"This is not good," Leven hollered. "I don't feel well."

Crunch!

"What else can we do?" Clover hollered back. "It's a jarring ride, but we'll get there."

There was a sickening squishing sound as the siid swallowed. The squishing sound was followed by a soft popping noise coming from across a distant field. That noise was followed by a long, drawn-out scream. Leven quickly turned his head. Up ahead, a middle-aged man was standing there next to some trees, screaming.

"What's he doing?" Leven yelled to Clover.

"It looks like fate just brought him here," Clover replied.

"You mean he just stepped into Foo?"

"I think," Clover said. "If the sycophants come then we'll know for sure."

No sooner had Clover said it than dozens of little Clover-like creatures began to appear on and around the man. Some were red and some were black as well as gray and yellow. Some were fat, but most were thin, and all of them were wearing small, shimmering robes. Sycophants dropped in from above and sprang up and out of the trees, all of them complimenting and yelling flattering things at the poor soul who had just stepped in. There were so many they muffled his screaming. The man swatted and screamed with even greater force as the sycophants kicked and scratched at one another, fighting over who would get to claim the new recruit as their burn.

"Pick me, pick me!"

"He's mine!"

"I burn for him!"

The conflicts became increasingly violent, and hundreds of sycophants backed off, letting only the most determined fight it out. In a few moments one sycophant stood triumphant on top of the screaming man's head.

The man batted and swung at the larger sycophant as the rest of the sycophants booed and hissed. Those who had lost began to disappear or slunk off dejectedly. The winner instantly started to console and comfort the screaming man.

"You're okay. I've got you now. You've entered Foo, that's all."

It was an awkward thing for Leven to watch. He turned his head away from the scene as the siid continued to lumber through the forest.

"What an awful jolt that must be. I feel sorry for that poor guy," Leven said after they were far away from him.

"What do you mean?" Clover asked naively. "He got a syco-phant."

"And an entirely new life."

"He'll get used—"

"Where will his sycophant take him?" Leven asked.

"Probably to Cusp, or, if he's lucky, to Cork," Clover said. "He'll be safe and happy there. It is the most wonderful—"

"Why doesn't Winter have a sycophant?" Leven interrupted.

Clover was silent.

"Does she?" Leven asked.

Clover shivered.

"Well?"

"Lilly," Clover whispered.

"Lilly?" Leven questioned. "She has a sycophant named Lilly?"

"She did," Clover answered. "She had to let her go when she returned to Reality as a baby. It was the Want's decision."

"Can't she get her back?"

"No right-minded sycophant would ever take back a burn who had let it go," Clover said passionately. "Especially Lilly. When Winter was first snatched into Foo, she was immediately assailed and piled on by dozens of sycophants, just like that guy. All the sycophants were arguing and fighting over who would claim her as their burn. In the end a white sycophant named Lilly won."

Clover sort of sighed.

"Lilly was an exceptional sycophant," he went on. "She

worked patiently with Winter, trying to make her feel at home and safe. She told her the things she needed to know and helped Winter recognize and cultivate her nit gift of being able to freeze things. Lilly was as devoted to Winter as any sycophant has ever been. She loved Winter, and under Lilly's guidance, Winter became one of the most outspoken and truest defenders of Foo. When Antsel proposed the idea of Winter returning to Reality as an infant to help Foo, Winter agreed. But it meant giving up Lilly."

The siid groaned and picked up speed.

"Lilly took the separation very hard. She was completely crushed. To her, saving Foo wasn't half as important as being with Winter. When Winter cut Lilly loose and stopped being her burn, Lilly wailed and mourned and lost all sense of who she was or why she would even want to live."

"So does Lilly have another burn now?"

"I don't know," Clover said. "I suppose . . ." Clover stopped talking as the siid came to a jarring halt, the ground pushing up in front of them like a huge wave as the beast settled.

"What's happening?" Leven asked.

"Either we're here, or we're in trouble."

The siid unwound its tail and with a gentle lob tossed Leven and Clover to the ground. It turned, breathed in, and blew gunk all over them and then turned back into the forest, leaving Leven and Clover alone. The ground rumbled as the great beast moved away.

Clover smiled and said sheepishly, "That's actually the third time it's helped me. It has the worst memory, and keeps on forgetting we're already even."

"You'd better hope it never remembers," Leven said.

"It'll never remember," Clover waved. "Now, the waxels on its ears might."

"So, where are we?" Leven asked, changing the subject and wiping the last bit of spit from his eyes.

"Right where the siid swayed it would set us," Clover answered. "The first bridge is just over that ridge. It will lead us to the turret trailhead."

"Let's go," Leven urged, holding his hands to his queasy stomach.

Leven squeezed between two large bushes that reminded him of a gate. He then began running between the trees, searching for the best direction to go and feeling like a kid looking for a hiding place during a competitive game of hide-and-seek.

Leven stopped at the edge of a purple stream. The large rocks in the water were shifting and moving about like stone turtles. Just across the stream, behind the trees, someone or something was crying.

"What's that?" Leven asked.

"It could be a trap," Clover said casually. "Sometimes unburied secrets will trick their victims into coming to them."

"I don't think this is that," Leven said. "It sounds almost human."

The sobbing did sound human—and scared. Leven had never cried quite like that, but there had been many times in his life when he had wanted nothing but to wail like the voice he could now hear.

A cloud of shimmering orange bugs flew across Leven's view. Leven waved them away and looked to the distance. He was somewhere he had never known existed, and the haunting sound of someone in pain was too much for him to turn away from.

"I can't ignore that," Leven whispered.

"It's your future," Clover shrugged, turning invisible and hopping up on Leven's head.

Leven waded through the water toward a dark patch of trees where the noise was coming from.

"Hello?" Leven called out.

The crying stopped.

"Are you all right?"

"Who are you?" a strong, suspicious female voice shouted back.

"It doesn't matter," Leven insisted. "But if I can help . . ."

"Where am I?" the voice cried.

"In the forest," Leven answered, still unable to see who was speaking.

"These trees aren't normal," the voice said. "I've never seen the things I'm seeing now. I'm not right." There was a long pause followed by another, "Where am I?"

"In Foo," Leven answered.

There was more sobbing and then silence.

"I can help," Leven added. "There's a bridge just over there."

Leven's assurance did little good, seeing how she couldn't really see him or where he was pointing.

"I don't belong here," she cried. "I'm not whole."

"Come with me," Leven said forcefully, surprised to find strength in his voice.

There was silence for a few moments. Then a whisp in the form of Janet Frore emerged from the forest like a ghost.

"We can help," Leven offered.

Janet simply cried.

Neither Leven nor Janet had any idea who the other was.

CHAPTER TWENTY-THREE

WASHED AWAY

It's not hard to doubt yourself. Many people have encountered miraculous things, only to talk themselves out of believing what they have seen. Millions who have witnessed unusual events and actions have later allowed others to convince them that they didn't see what they actually saw.

Sometimes our minds are out to get us.

Winter was in just such a state. She was back in her icy chamber, lying on her back, covered again by the mask and shroud, with her hands tied behind her body. Her wrists and hands ached from being tied so tightly, and her brain buzzed with the knowledge that as long as her hands were covered she couldn't touch her surroundings and thaw anything.

She also had absolutely no idea what to believe. She thought she knew who she was, but Jamoon had messed with her thinking. She wanted so desperately to see Leven. She knew that he would know what to do. She wished for Clover to suddenly appear, or for Geth to yell out that he was back and that he would take care of things.

Winter was worried about her mind. It felt as if someone had stuck a hand into her head and was now peeling away her thoughts and recollections. Winter couldn't remember anything about who Jamoon was. She had no idea whose side he was on or if she was on that side along with him. She shouldn't have been surprised. When she had been reverted to a baby so as to return to Reality and help Leven, she had known that she was probably giving up all her other memories.

Under her shroud, she thought about the small, makeshift toilet that Geth had escaped through and realized how next to impossible it was that he could somehow rescue her.

Still, she had to have hope.

Winter's brow furrowed, her long, white-blonde hair hanging down under her mask and covering her right eye. She blew out, trying to move her hair from in front of her face, but the mask made it useless. She got painfully to her feet and twisted her body, trying to see her bound hands. She couldn't see them at all. She moved to the corner, away from where the door opening was, and stood so that she could see her hands in the reflection of the icy wall. With the mask over her head, it wasn't a perfect glimpse, but Winter could see what was binding them.

"What fools," she whispered. "Why did I not think of that before?" Winter smiled as her stomach growled and her mind prepared a course of action.

She moved to the far wall and stood with her head down and her shoulders slumped.

"I need to speak to Jamoon," Winter pleaded to the walls.

"It's late," a voice echoed back. "Jamoon is in Morfit."

"I have no idea of time," Winter replied. "And if Jamoon is not here, let me speak with that sickly rant. I know he'll want to hear what I have to say."

There was a long, pregnant pause as the guard digested what she was saying. She could almost hear him imagining the reward Jamoon would give him if he were to deliver a talking prisoner. Of course, Jamoon would be equally unhappy if she had nothing to offer and the guard had interrupted him for no reason.

"Well?" Winter said impatiently.

There was the noise of cracking ice followed by a slit of light that shone through the wall, exposing the exit. The crack in the ice expanded, and there stood a single rant. He was wearing the traditional black robe. He was tall on his right side and lumpy on his left. Winter couldn't even guess what the left half of him was at the moment. In his right hand he held a long, wooden kilve.

"If you—"

One could argue for days about what the guard had intended to say. Perhaps he was going to say, "If you want, I'll carry you." Or maybe he was going to say, "If you find a pair of prescription reading glasses, they're mine." Of course, both of those possibilities seem unlikely, seeing how he was a rather aggressive rant who didn't like to do extra work and had perfect vision.

What he was about to say will most likely never be known

because as he began to speak, Winter froze his right side while simultaneously freezing the covering on her hands. She hurled herself against the icy wall, shattering the frozen rope and cloth that had been keeping her hands bound.

With her hands free, Winter touched and thawed the rant's kilve. She snatched the staff from the guard as she stepped around him and began running down the icy hall. The kilve was long and wooden and painted with the ashes of dark dreams. The pointed end was sharp, with its edges so finely sanded they could have slit the throat of a roven. The other end was as blunt as a steel fist. Kilves were an effective weapon for beating your enemy or for utterly destroying incoming dreams. Winter could feel the evil this particular kilve had been a part of.

She shuddered and kept running.

Looking out through the slits of the mask, Winter tried to remember the little bit she knew of the place, but everything was ice and there seemed to be hundreds of hallways heading hundreds of directions. Most of the ice was smooth and reflective. Winter felt as if she were in a house of mirrors, with her reflection looking back at her from all angles.

Winter raced down a wide corridor, shaking her arms to get the blood flowing back in her wrists and hands. Her shoulder hurt from the beating it had previously taken. An angry shout behind her rang out.

They were coming.

Two large rants appeared in front of her, running toward her as if they knew of nothing else worthwhile in life. Winter thought of them as ice. Their dreamlike sides writhed and complained, trying to support the weight of their now-frozen right halves. Winter dashed between them and pushed them to the side.

The footsteps and shouts behind her grew louder.

Winter ran as fast as she could, her heart and head pounding like wet shoes tumbling in an electric clothes dryer.

"Stop her!" a thunderous voice screamed.

Winter touched the wall with her right hand as she ran. Instantly the structure thawed, turning into a wall of water, which collapsed in a terrific wave. She threw the kilve to her other hand and touched the wall on her left as she ran. It too became a gigantic wave of water. Winter could see the entire fortress behind her beginning to thaw, the water rising, picking her up, and carrying her down the hallways as it melted. She put her arms out in front of her and let the giant wave hurl her away from her pursuers. She could hear their screams fading behind her.

Winter raced with the wall of water down a steep set of stairs, out into and across a brick courtyard, and into another hallway. Ahead of her she could see a gigantic stained-glass window. The image was of the Want working with metal. It was a beautiful piece of art, but Winter knew it was her or the window. She extended her arms and held the blunt end of the kilve out in front of her.

The kilve shattered the glass with the water following right behind to wash the bits away. The room behind the window was huge, and as the water dispersed and ran off in a thousand directions, Winter settled to the floor and gently washed up against the brick fireplace.

She pulled herself up onto her hands and knees, her hair hanging down inside her mask like a bunch of wet spaghetti noodles. Winter had had enough. She jabbed the pointed end of the kilve into the seal of the mask and ripped it open. Winter threw off the mask.

She frantically looked up and back.

It appeared that no one had made it as far as she had. Winter worked herself out of the loose bodysuit she had been shrouded in, exposing the outfit she had been wearing when she had stepped back into Foo. Winter knelt and bit at the wrist of her right sleeve. There was already a small opening in the cuff thanks to Geth having hidden there. Winter pulled out a small length of elastic. She bit at her other sleeve and pulled out another small piece. She flipped her hair back and grabbed a handful on the right side. She twisted the elastic around it, creating a long, wet pigtail, then did the same to her left side.

Winter sighed. It was heaven to have her hair out of her eyes at last.

She was searching around for an exit when a voice spoke out, startling her.

"You look much younger than the Winter Jamoon spoke of."

Winter jumped in shock and took a defensive stance with the kilve. Hidden in the shadows near the edge of the fireplace was the small, disgusting rant. He stepped closer and coughed. As the light hit him, she could clearly see his red right eye.

"I told Jamoon you would try to escape," he said knowingly. "Jamoon is too slow to listen to me."

"Well, now that we both understand what I'm doing, I'll be going," Winter said with determination.

"Wait," the rant said, coughing and waving his right hand impatiently. "You still don't remember your part? Jamoon said you would remember and help us."

"I don't know what you're talking about," Winter said, her own soul wriggling uncomfortably.

The rant's right eye burned.

"Just let me leave," Winter bargained. "When I remember what you're talking about, you'll be the first to know."

"I can't let that happen," he growled. "You will die before you get—" He stopped talking due to his left half beginning to bubble and hiss.

As much as Winter wanted to know what the rant had to say about Jamoon, she knew she needed to act fast. Rants were weakest when they were shifting. It was a dirty play, but she was not about to lose the opportunity.

Winter drew back and swung the kilve with as much strength as she had. The stick struck the sickly rant in the right shoulder, and he collapsed like a pile of stacked cards, screaming as he hit the ground.

"Stop!" he cried, his body still adjusting.

Winter was out the door and into the mountains before the rant could say another thing.

CHAPTER TWENTY-FOUR

I'm on the Top of the Whirled

S ome people like to fly. You may have met such a person. Perhaps he was a tall guy in a red hat who sat next to you. And maybe he went on and on about what a miraculous thing flying is, and how it's the second safest form of travel, elevators being the first. But even a person like that would have a hard time finding the joy in flying in a plane that had thin, sinister black strands whipping around the wings and slapping against the windows.

Let's just say the passengers of flight 7229 were concerned— meaning they were screaming and fanning themselves and making deals with their Maker for him to save their lives.

Dennis Wood was still buckled in his seat, nervously watching the long, black cords of Sabine whipping around the plane. Dennis had never really thought about dying, but he began to wonder if this wasn't his time. He looked around at all the crying and screaming people and thought, *At least I'm not alone.*

Outside the plane, the string of Sabine fought valiantly, trying to pull away from Ezra and regain a position of strength. Neither Sabine nor Ezra was making much headway. It was hard for Ezra to destroy someone who was really already dead. And in turn it was fairly difficult for Sabine to get away from such a determined toothpick.

"Let me go," Sabine hissed from both ends.

"Never!" Ezra yelled, still holding on to the tail end inside the plane.

Sabine whispered to himself. "The clouds," he spat. "The hazen."

In Foo the clouds were called hazen and took their shapes from the imaginations of the inhabitants. Sabine felt it was time to wake up the clouds of Reality. With the end of him outside of the plane, Sabine twisted himself into a loop, stretched up, and lassoed the clouds. He tightened his loop, and all at once the clouds turned a burning orange color. As the clouds changed color, lightning began to strike.

Once.

Twice.

Fifty times.

The clouds were no longer just clouds, they were hazen, and they were desperate to prove their difference. Sabine imagined them as violent beasts.

The plane bumped up and down like a jerking seesaw.

The captain came on the intercom. He sounded as if he couldn't decide whether to cry or scream. He nervously announced that they would be climbing higher to find smoother, safer air. Most passengers wished he had announced that they would be flying lower to find safer *ground*. The announcement failed to comfort any of them, seeing how the very clouds around them were beginning to take shape and attack the plane.

Dennis was sweating. The thick clouds were gaining color and form. Like gigantic marshmallows they brushed up against the plane. They smeared across the windows and left a pale, glue-like residue.

Seven passengers and one flight attendant passed out, which caused the rest to begin pulling their hair and rocking violently. A short man, who looked like a lima bean in a suit thanks to his green face and squat body, began tearing at his seat, searching frantically for a parachute.

Dennis pressed his face to his window. It looked like the earth was coming apart, the unraveling beginning in the air. A few of the clouds had thick, burning faces and long, billowing arms that were anything but cute. Dennis remembered as a child lying in a park looking up at the clouds. Back then he had seen the shapes of toy boats and horses. Now, however, the clouds looked horrible, huge and evil.

The plane rocked and twisted as the clouds grabbed hold of it. The four engines struggled and whined as one very large hazen pushed against the plane going forward.

The captain flipped desperately through his book trying to find any sort of instruction for handling rabid clouds.

"Anything?" the copilot yelled.

"No," the captain yelled back frantically. "But there is a section for taking notes."

A sinister hazen moved in front of the plane. Its eyes looked like pieces of white-hot charcoal, and its mouth looked like a meteor crater. It opened its mouth wider, and the plane flew right into it. All the lights in the aircraft flickered and dimmed as the plane turned upside down. Those who had long ago given up obeying the seat-belt sign dropped to the ceiling and then back to their seats as the plane turned back over. Four thick clouds wrapped themselves around the wings and pushed the plane forward and down.

Dennis wiped his forehead and bit his tongue. It felt as if they were traveling just over the speed of life.

"Ezra!" Dennis yelled.

Ezra didn't hear Dennis, but if he had he would have been angry about him even asking for help when Ezra had his own troubles to deal with.

As the plane rocketed toward the ground, all the passengers gave up hope of ever living through such an ordeal. A number of people sat back in their seats and let their lives flash before their eyes, while others screamed until their lungs were raw, then collapsed in fear and exhaustion.

Dennis unbuckled his seat belt and stood. He looked down at the bank sticker on his shirt and at his unwrinkled pants. For some reason that seemed to comfort him. His outfit felt like a uniform, like he was a part of something. The plane rocked to the north, and Dennis flew into a young lady whose face was the color of a honeydew melon.

"Sorry!" Dennis screamed.

She looked at him as if he were crazy.

The plane tilted forward even further. Three of the overhead bins popped open, and bags exploded and rained down on passengers.

Outside, the hazen were fighting over the plane. Dennis's stomach lurched. He needed a bathroom, and he held onto the seats as he worked his way toward the rear of the plane. He leaned over far enough to look out a window. Despite all the clouds wrapped around the plane, there were a few holes where he could see the ground.

It wasn't far away. At the speed they were traveling, they would hit the ground in a few minutes.

The plane suddenly flew sideways, and Dennis lost his footing. He fell to his knees and began clawing his way toward the bathroom. Passengers and luggage burst into the aisle. When he reached the rear of the plane he could hear a high-pitched screaming. He stepped away from the bathroom door and pushed open the service door. Still feeling sick, he moved into the very back of the plane. There, up near the ceiling, was Ezra, twisted into and holding onto a thin strand of something black.

"Help me pull!" Ezra screamed, his small voice barely audible over the screams of the passengers and the roar of the engines.

"Let go!" Dennis screamed back. "The plane's going to crash!"

The black cord Ezra was clinging to sizzled and hissed.

"Let go!" Dennis shouted, grabbing onto Ezra and trying to pull him off Sabine. "Please!" Dennis begged. "Please."

Ezra swore, made a rather harsh remark about Dennis not

being a man, and let go. Sabine slithered out.

Almost instantly the hazen stopped pounding, and the plane began to level out. Dennis could hear a more hopeful chorus of screams from out front.

"You fool! He's from Foo," Ezra screamed at Dennis. "I shouldn't have let him go. He can get us back."

Ezra's purple top was writhing and swirling.

"Only if we're alive," Dennis reasoned.

Dennis grabbed Ezra and shoved him into the fanny pack. He walked back out front. Everyone was still screaming, seeing how the plane was still moving rapidly toward the ground. Dennis looked out and hoped that he was right about letting go of the black string and keeping them alive.

The thick, orange hazen began to cluster under the plane, pushing upward as the plane hurled toward the earth. Dennis could see trees and mountains rising up. The clouds pushed some more, and the plane slowed. Several wet hazen wadded themselves up and crawled into the engines. The engines coughed and stopped, allowing the hazen to slow the plane to a complete stop about fifty feet above the ground.

It is quite a sensation to be sitting in a huge metal plane, hovering above a busy freeway being held up by a ring of clouds. The cars below came to a screeching stop, frantically trying to get or stay out from beneath the hovering plane.

Then, as if to make a point, the hazen flipped the floating plane one last time and set it down gently on its top in the middle of Interstate 40.

ii

Tim Tuttle looked at his surroundings and wondered exactly what year it was. The home he was sitting in looked as though it had not been touched or updated since 1952. A large portrait of a young girl holding a bundle of wheat hung over a small fireplace that was fronted with a rock facade. The carpet underfoot was yellow shag, with wide wear patterns that ran the entire length of the room. In one corner there was a birdcage with a single tiny, sickly sounding, orange bird in it. Every couple of seconds it would try to chirp, but the sound was more like a wet cough. In the other corner, two small desks faced a green chalkboard. Written on the chalkboard was a list of difficult-looking spelling words. The desks were occupied at the moment—one by a girl with a blonde bob who looked about ten and the other one by a boy with a buzzed head who looked around twelve.

Tim was sitting on a short couch with a huge rose pattern print. He was in the home of John and Margo Hunch. Thanks to Terry's tip about Maine, Tim had made the trip out there to see if he could get one step closer to finding Winter and the boy named Leven with whom she was said to be traveling.

Tim had spent the morning at the public library looking for information.

Luckily for him, it had not been very long since Winter and Leven had been through Maine, and the story of a boy and girl driving a car off into the ocean was not hard to find. Most of the stories talked about Cape Porpoise, and most mentioned a woman by the name of Margo Hunch as the last person to talk to the boy, at a church barbecue. Leven and Winter had run off after Margo had asked too many questions about who they were. A number of people had chased after them but, according to the story, the two kids had stolen a car and driven it off a wharf into the Atlantic Ocean.

Tim had come to the Hunch home hoping to find some answers. Margo had welcomed him in and then run off to get him something to drink. She came back into the room and handed Tim a teacup filled with lemon-flavored water. Tim took a sip and set the cup down.

"Delicious," he lied. "So, Margo, you talked to these children?"

"Mrs. Hunch," she corrected. "And just the boy. The lemon helps with the digestive tract," she added, pointing to the cup of water she had served up, and settling into her own seat.

"Oh," Tim said, confused. "Thank you. Well, what did they say?"

"Not much. I didn't recognize them so I walked up to the boy. I thought, *New faces, let's welcome them in.* Anyhow, I . . ."

Her daughter, sitting at her desk, raised her hand.

"Yes, Florence?" Mrs. Hunch said.

"What's the capital of Norway?" Florence asked.

"If I told you, that'd be cheating," Mrs. Hunch sang. "But I'll give you a hint: Norway is often referred to as the Land of the Midnight Sun."

Florence didn't look all that grateful for the help.

"So," Mrs. Hunch continued, "I was fascinated with a white streak of hair the boy had. I was only showing interest in him, and I think he got offended. But I had seen a report on him on TV about how he supposedly ruined his parents' house."

Her son's hand went up.

"Yes, George."

"Can I use the bathroom?"

Mrs. Hunch was silent.

"*May* I use the bathroom?" George corrected himself.

Mrs. Hunch picked up a small egg timer that was sitting on the end table near her. She flipped it over, and the sand began to run down. "Be back before the last grain," she said, giving permission.

George raced off to the bathroom.

"You've got quite a system here," Tim said, referring to her home-schooled children.

Mrs. Hunch sighed. "It's not always easy. But if you knew what goes on in some public schools."

The last grain of sand dropped in the egg timer just as the sound of the toilet flushing was heard. George came racing back into the room and frantically slid into his desk. He looked at the egg timer and sighed.

"Two paragraphs on why soil erosion is less of a problem than the government says it is," Mrs. Hunch said, handing out George's punishment for taking too long.

"But—" George tried to argue.

"Three paragraphs," Mrs. Hunch said.

George slumped in his seat.

"Well, I can see you're busy," Tim said, standing. "I won't take any more of your time. Just one last question, though."

Mrs. Hunch looked perplexed by the thought of a question being asked without a hand being raised first.

"The newspapers all say that the children drove the car right off into the ocean," Tim said.

"That's actually not a question," she pointed out, "but from what I hear, that's what happened."

"And the car just sank?"

"It hit some ice, or rocks," she said. "It was very cloudy, so nobody got a perfect look at where they fell in."

"Have they found it? The car," Tim clarified.

"Not that I've heard," she said sadly. "What a terrible tragedy. Those poor little hoodlums. I'll try to make their lives count by using them as an example in my teaching."

Tim just looked at her.

"A bad example," she specified.

Florence raised her hand and asked her mother if she could build a working volcano for her science project. Mrs. Hunch nixed the idea and suggested instead that she paint the back porch.

As Tim stepped out the front door he asked, "How far is it to the spot where they drove into the ocean?"

"Two miles that way," she pointed. "There's a small flower shop just before the turnoff."

Tim thanked her and made his way to his rented car.

iii

The ocean looked gigantic. The sky was clear and blue. Tim had driven past the flower shop to the end of the wharf. He had then gotten out and searched for signs of a car flying off. At the end of the dock he found the exact spot where the car had gone into the water. The skid marks from the police car that had been chasing Leven and Winter were thick and dark.

"Where are you?" Tim asked the air.

The newspapers had all reported about how the authorities had searched the ocean for the sunken car but found no sign of it. Some speculated that it may have floated for a few moments and then been pushed farther out to sea by an especially strong current. None of that made sense. Tim knew there had to be more to the story.

He knew that Winter was still alive.

Tim kept thinking back to the old woman who had twice stood on his doorstep so many years before. He thought about what she had told him and wondered if what was happening now had anything to do with the secret she had shared.

Regardless, Tim knew he couldn't give up. Winter was somewhere, and even if the trail had grown cold here at the edge of the Atlantic Ocean, he couldn't stop looking. He turned and headed toward town and back to the public library, his heart practically bursting in his chest.

CHAPTER TWENTY-FIVE

BRIDGE TO NITEON

L even had never seen a whisp before. Of course, he had never seen rovens or sarus or siids or tharms or Foo either. But there was something about the whisp that was sadder than all the things he had seen so far. A whisp was a person, but it was an incomplete person. Sometimes those in Reality are not properly lined up on a mismatched sidewalk or lane, so fate snatches only a wisp of them into Foo. Such an occurrence leaves the person in Reality feeling as if he or she is missing something or not all there, and it creates a whisp in Foo—an incomplete being that can't touch or feel and has no physical capacities.

A great sorrow radiated from the whisp Leven was looking at. It was clear she knew she was not whole and seemed to understand that she never would be again.

"Where am I?" Janet asked.

"Foo," Leven answered.

She was a large woman with a wrinkled face and dirty, unkempt hair. She looked like a pale prune in tight slippers and a yellow housedress.

"What's the matter with me?" she cried.

"You're a whisp," Clover said, materializing on top of Leven's head.

Janet jumped back three feet and put her hand to her mouth. She had been startled by Clover, but she was terrified by the fact that when she threw her hand to her mouth, it went right through her head.

"I'm a ghost," she whimpered, looking closely at her hands.

Clover laughed. "Ghosts aren't real. You must not have been lined up right for Foo to snatch you completely. So, it took a little of your essence and left you mostly whole in Reality."

Janet reached out and tried to touch Leven. Her hand went right through his shoulder. In the last green light of dusk Leven could see tears streaking down her face.

"Am I dead?" she asked.

"No," Leven said, trying to calm her and wondering how he could explain a place he still didn't fully understand. "This is Foo. We'll get you some help, but we need to hurry."

Janet just cried, but she followed behind as Leven began to walk. Clover pointed out the direction, and Leven made his way around some thick, knotty trees and through a patch of gigantic, oval-shaped boulders.

The trees behind them whispered. The whispering sounded confused, as if searching for a direction.

"This place is creepy. Let's get out of here," Leven said, walking faster.

The trees opened up, and there was the entry to the first bridge. The bridge spanned Fissure Gorge, which was enormous. The far side looked miles away. As wide as the gorge was, it was over twice as deep, and its depths were pitch black, except for a thin line of orange running along the very bottom. The orange ribbon glowed and pulsated, sending up currents of warm air.

The whispering of the trees could still be heard, hissing throughout the forest like a snake in search of food.

"The secret's not going to give up, is it?" Leven said in a hushed voice.

"Let's hope that it stays in the trees and doesn't cross the gorge," Clover said, his voice indicating that he was holding onto Leven's right leg. "Most secrets don't dare expose themselves in the open like that. And it will never enter Cork."

Leven reached the opening of the bridge. There was a large brick arch spanning the entrance. On the left side of the arch was a small stone building with a crooked chimney jutting out of its thatched roof. A door opened in the guardhouse, and a gigantic bird stepped out. The bird was as tall as Leven and wore a blue jacket and glasses. His feet looked white under the moonlight.

"You wish to cross?" he asked.

"We're on our way to Niteon," Leven said.

"Is that whisp yours?" he chirped.

Leven turned and looked at Janet. "She was lost in the forest," he said. "After we get to the turrets, we'll take her to Cork."

"Are you aware of the war?" the bird asked suspiciously, walking around Leven.

"I am," Leven answered, begrudging the time they were wasting standing there, "if you are talking about the war Sabine started."

The bird nodded and stepped back. "I wish you well," it said.

Leven nodded back and moved toward the bridge. He was stopped by the excited clamor of the bird.

"What are you doing?" the bird squawked.

"I was going to cross," Leven said, confused.

"Without flattering it?"

"Excuse me?"

"The bridge," the bird said with disgust. "Have you never crossed before?"

"No . . ." Leven began.

The bird sighed, which actually sounded like a very long whistle. "See those rocks over there?" The bird pointed to a number of rocks jutting out from the near side of the gorge.

Leven could see the rocks. He could also see numerous other rocks sticking out into the gorge. Some actually extended out over the gorge a number of feet. Some were only a few inches long.

"Those are young bridges," the bird explained. "The stones on this side get curious to know what it's like on the other side. So they shift and stretch and grow until they either give up or connect with another bunch of curious stones reaching to get here from the other side."

"You *grow* your bridges?" Leven asked in disbelief.

"They grow themselves," the bird chirped. "It is a miraculous thing when they actually meet and a new bridge is created. Of course, once the two sides meet, they realize there really is nothing great on the other side, and they become indifferent. They sit there until someone tries to cross. Then they simply fall apart and drop into the gorge."

"So if we cross, they'll fall?" Leven asked incredulously.

"If you don't flatter them, they will," the bird replied in a tone that suggested Leven was far from brilliant.

"Flatter them?"

"Tell them they're doing a good job. You know," the bird said. "We must preserve the bridge."

"So I talk to the bridge?" Leven laughed.

"And you'd better be convincing. Otherwise the bridge is destroyed and you're caught in the air of the gorge or you drop to burn forever in the glow." The sentinel bird stopped talking to dig under his right wing with his beak. "Sorry," he apologized, "I'm trying to kick the bird in me, be a bit more dignified. But let me say this, even if you did make it back out of the gorge after you fell, there would be so many angry about the loss of another bridge that you would wish you were dead."

Leven glanced at the bridge, then looked again at the gorge. It seemed deeper than any sky Leven had ever gazed up into.

"I'm doing this for Foo," he said to himself, only just beginning to feel the power and purpose such a place as Foo really held.

"So, I just . . . *flatter* it?" he asked.

"Yes, and you'd better sound sincere," the bird whispered.

Leven stepped up to the very edge of the bridge and cleared his throat. His stomach was even more uneasy. He looked out over the gorge. It was so wide he couldn't clearly see the other side. By now the night was fully upon them and the moon shone bright. The moon's light was like white syrup being drizzled slowly over the entire scene. The light was so dense that bits dripped from the sides of the bridge and dropped in zigzag lines into Fissure Gorge.

"How come the moonlight doesn't drip straight down?" Leven asked Clover.

"The gorge is filled with soft and hard air that makes up a maze of sorts," Clover answered. "If you were to fall off into it you might just as easily fall to the side or diagonally, or down, or even up. The air never stays the same. The heat at the bottom belches, and as the warm air rises, the composition of air within the gorge changes. Things that fall into the gorge can sometimes be suspended in the air for years and never reach the bottom. I had a friend who threw a pout in there years ago, and last I heard it was still screaming and falling in one direction or another. People and animals have fallen in and eventually died of old age, trapped in the air, their decaying bodies floating around until they're gone."

"That's pleasant," Leven said.

"I know." Clover pointed. "See how the moonlight slides and drops so beautifully?"

"So if we fall in, the air will catch us before we hit the bottom?"

"More like *trap* you," Clover said. "There are things worse than 'splat.'"

Leven looked into the gorge and watched streaks of moonlight sliding back and forth and up and down like erratic shooting stars.

"We'd better hurry," Clover reminded him.

Leven cleared his throat again and began talking to the bridge.

"Hello."

He waited a moment for the red in his cheeks to subside.

"We would very much like to travel across such a fine-looking bridge," Leven continued, glancing at the sentinel bird for approval. The bird nodded as if impressed.

"I've been on other bridges," Leven said, more earnestly, "but none were as impressive or beautiful."

The bridge seemed to shiver.

"I really would enjoy the journey across you," Leven said. "I can't wait to reach the other side and tell everyone what an outstanding job you do."

The bridge really shivered, and the bird practically beamed.

"I think that will do it," the bird whispered, nodding happily.

Leven glanced at Janet and then down at his feet. He touched the edge of the bridge with his toe and quickly pulled his foot back. He shrugged his shoulders, closed his eyes, and took a tentative step out. He had no desire to fall into the gorge, but he would have no way of knowing if his flattery had worked until he started across.

The bridge was still shivering.

Leven took another hesitant step. The bridge was holding up. Leven looked back at the bird and waved.

"Good-bye! I am off to enjoy the beauty and strength of this marvelous bridge," Leven said loudly for good measure.

The bridge liked that.

Leven walked cautiously but with purpose, deliberately placing each step. He wanted to run, but he had no idea how the bridge would respond to that. He also made the mistake of looking down. It was a long drop. The thin, iridescent ribbon of light at the bottom looked miles away and glowed like molten lava. Leven proceeded carefully.

After about thirty feet Janet spoke up.

"How come you're whole?" she asked as she floated behind him. It sounded like a question she had been longing to ask for some time.

"Whole?"

"Not like me," she said.

"You're a whisp," Leven answered, not fully understanding things himself. "Most of you is still in Reality. Just a tiny, wisplike part of you is here."

"So is it because I lived a horrible life?" Janet asked. "Is this what happens to bad people?"

"What?"

"I know I was a hard person," she said defiantly. "My mother always said I wouldn't make it to heaven. Now look at me. I am nothing but air. I didn't even love my own child, and now she's gone."

"I'm sure she's okay," Leven said indifferently, concentrating on getting across the bridge.

"She left me," Janet said, "because of who I was."

"Life's a long time," Leven said, walking as quickly as he could and wondering if he was making any sense. "I never thought I'd be here because I didn't know here existed. Now I'm racing against time to save a toothpick just to be able to live in a place where I'm still not convinced I belong. It's the same for you, except you're still who you were in Reality as well."

Janet's eyes began to leak again. "That frightens me almost as much as being here," she said. "Few people get to step away from themselves to look at who they really are."

Leven didn't answer. Moonlight poured over him and ran down his left side. He could feel the sensation of it and marveled at the complexity and beauty of Foo. Two stars streaking across the sky crashed into each other and sent sparks flying everywhere. Leven thought he heard the moon sigh.

A small, burning secret raced up from behind Leven and drifted up his leg. Before Leven noticed, it was perched on his nose and staring him in the eyes.

"I had a lifelong crush on Sally Teon," the secret giggled as it danced on Leven's nose.

Leven swatted it away. The small secret happily flew off into the night.

"I thought you said it wouldn't follow us," Leven whispered.

"That was just another decoy secret," Clover replied from on top of Leven's head, still invisible. "The big one won't expose itself."

"What are you talking about?" Janet asked, not having seen the tiny secret.

"Nothing," Leven said, looking in the direction the secret had run.

"So, can I affect what I'm like in Reality?" Janet asked. "I mean, can I help change myself in the condition I'm in?"

"I don't know," Leven answered. "But it's probably not too late to try."

For a second Janet's eyes showed hope, but that hope was quickly drowned by more tears. Clover materialized and offered Janet a tissue from his void. She reached for it, and they were both reminded of her limitations.

"Sorry," Clover said, feeling bad about offering it. "When I see a person crying, I just naturally . . . and, well, I forgot you weren't really a person but a . . . I mean, people come in all shapes and sizes and well . . . I wonder what it would feel like to be invisible right now."

Clover disappeared hastily while Janet continued to cry and drift along behind Leven. He walked steadily across the gorge, his feet kicking up the moonlight wherever he stepped. Light flashed like sparks around his shoes.

After a time, Clover reappeared on the top of Leven's head. The sycophant commented on how much he preferred being carried to walking himself. Leven smiled and reached up and scratched him behind his ear.

Leven could clearly see the other side now. He slowed and looked around him. For the thousandth time in so few days he was amazed at where he was. The bridge across the gorge reminded him a little of the ice highway that he and Winter had driven on while crossing the Atlantic Ocean.

The glow at the bottom of Fissure Gorge belched, and warm air raced up, sending the streaks of moonlight shooting back into the sky.

"Why are we slowing?" Janet asked.

"Yeah," Clover added, "I don't want this bridge to change its mind about holding together."

"It really is beautiful here," Leven said. "I can't wait to see Cork and the other parts."

Leven kicked up a puddle of moonlight as he picked up his pace. He waved the moonlight away as if it were a batch of bubbles.

"Beautiful?" Janet scoffed. "Don't be stupid. I think you have—" She stopped herself, realizing that she needed help, not more enemies. "I suppose if you squint it's not awful," she tried.

Clover squinted and looked at Janet as if she were daft. There was a light wind, and Janet drifted over just a bit. She tried to grab Leven's arm for support, but she had that pesky lack-of-substance problem still going on.

"Just let the wind go through you," Clover advised.

Trying to do so, Janet drifted back a few feet and then began moving forward again.

Sitting on Leven's shoulder, Clover spoke softly into Leven's ear. "So, now that we're out here, why don't you show me what you dug up?"

"What?" Leven replied, playing innocent but knowing perfectly well that Clover was referring to the metal key he had found when he was digging up the secret.

"I saw that key," Clover explained. "You pulled it out before the secret."

Leven wanted to show Clover the key, but he didn't want anyone to take it away before he understood what it was.

"If it's made of metal, it needs to be reported," Clover warned.

"Really?" Leven asked. He thought back to when he had been ten and had attended a baseball game in Oklahoma. Terry had won two free tickets in a radio contest. Terry didn't want to take Leven, but Addy had screamed and yelled at him about how important it was that Leven have a positive male role model so that he didn't grow up and come back and steal from them.

The afternoon had been nice—the weather had been warm, the game exciting, and Terry had sat two sections away from Leven. Then, in the sixth inning, as a soda vendor was walking up the stairs near Leven, a foul ball flew up and hit the vendor in the back of the head.

The poor guy collapsed, his drinks bouncing and rolling all over. One can of soda fell into Leven's lap, and he quickly slipped it under his seat. The vendor was dazed, but after he shook it off he began collecting his sodas. He wasn't sure, because of the blow to his head, but he thought he was missing three. Leven's face burned red as he nudged the cold soda beneath his seat with his toe. He wanted to give it back, but he had only tasted soda a couple of times in his life, and he was so thirsty. After the vendor asked four more times, however, Leven sheepishly pulled out the soda and pretended that he had just found it.

His hope was that the vendor would let him keep it. The vendor didn't. In fact, he didn't even say thanks. The imagined taste of what Leven had missed was still strong in his mouth.

Now he was afraid that if he showed Clover the key, Clover might make him give it up. Clover smiled and held out his hand.

Leven sighed. He reached into his pocket and pulled out the key. It was a golden color, and as a bit of moonlight touched it, the key glistened. Reluctantly, Leven set it in Clover's palm.

"Beautiful," Clover whispered. "It's definitely metal."

Leven held out his hand, and Clover hesitantly gave him the key back.

"Hold on," Clover said, reaching into his void. He pulled out a thin string of leather. "Put the key on this," Clover explained. "Then you can keep it around your neck and you won't lose it."

Leven took the leather string and threaded it through the key. He tied a square knot and slipped the key and band over his head. Leven pulled on the neck of his shirt, and the key slipped down, hidden beneath.

"What was that?" Janet demanded. "What are you doing?"

"Nothing," Clover insisted. "Drift over there."

Janet did as she was told. Clover disappeared, and Leven touched his T-shirt to make sure the key was still there.

"Be careful who you tell," Clover whispered.

"I will," Leven said, rubbing his chest.

"Are you okay?" Clover asked.

Leven didn't answer, but something wasn't right.

CHAPTER TWENTY-SIX

ENTERING MORFIT

It was considerably warmer than Winter usually preferred it. She was also much hungrier than she had been in a long time. Winter half wished for the filler crisp Clover had given her at sea. Her stomach felt like an empty cavern filled with nothing but wind.

Jamoon had not fed her in captivity, and the only food she had been able to find in the hours since she had escaped were some young bickerwicks growing at the base of a sweaty fantrum tree. Not all fantrum trees are created equal, mind you. Some thrive well in the cold, others do better in the blistering heat, and some do all right in either. Unfortunately for the trees, however, they usually don't get to choose where they're planted. So, those poor fantrum trees who are stuck in a hot place when they prefer the cold will sweat a lot. And wherever there is fantrum sweat, there are bickerwicks.

Bickerwicks grow in clusters around the base of sweaty trees, and as they grow and begin to crawl they emit a chilling zap that keeps the trees cold. Bickerwicks are small, orange, and egg-shaped. They are spongy and have a marshmallow taste, but they are also cranky and make such a fuss as you chew that a person can tolerate only a few of them at a time. In her state of hunger, however, Winter had eaten more than just a few.

She was now regretting it.

Gulping them down as fast as she had, she had failed to chew them thoroughly. Winter could still hear them yelling and fighting with each other from inside her stomach. She willed her digestive system to hurry up and digest them.

Her stomach rumbled.

Winter skirted past a flock of mud-covered little men who were building a large wooden vat, and through a prairie filled with temperamental holes that kept opening and then snapping shut at her. Without the bodysuit she had been shrouded in, her feet were bare. Winter found a couple of thick fantrum leaves and, using strips of kindle moss for laces, fashioned herself a pair of makeshift shoes.

They were far from fashionable, but they fit.

Winter had no clear idea where she had been held captive, so she simply headed downhill.

After about an hour she spotted the top of Morfit in the far distance. The peaks were covered by a large, lazy gathering of thick, orange hazen.

"Morfit," Winter whispered in awe. From what Jamoon had

said, perhaps that was where she would find the pieces of the puzzle that would show her who she really was.

Winter proceeded with caution, having no idea who she would encounter or who was on her side. In fact, she wasn't sure what side she was on any longer. She wished she could just find Leven and Geth and have them help her sort things out. Winter kept her eye on the top of Morfit and pressed forward, hoping to find a clue there.

Two hours later, Winter could see the base of Morfit at the end of the road she was on. As always, beings from all over Foo were walking toward Morfit, carrying boulders that represented their guilt or sorrow or sin. After arriving, they would set their rocks in place and walk away without their burdens.

Winter couldn't believe how huge Morfit was. Her memory of it was vague, but she couldn't recall it being nearly this humongous. It sat there like an entire mountain range, its base thick and as wide as a large lake. It was different shades of black, causing it to look as if it were covered in bruises of varied intensity. There were smaller mounds in front of larger mounds and larger mounds circling a massive center peak higher than the rest. At the top of the peak was a lone tower that looked tiny and millions of miles away. All over Morfit there were holes and caves and archways—thousands of openings in the great black mountain. The size and darkness of the place were overwhelming.

"We have to be losing," she whispered to herself. "Unless I'm on the bad side," she amended, "in which case it looks like we're doing okay."

A high, crumbling brick wall surrounded Morfit. It wrapped around the entire mountain, resembling a fat, decaying worm with moldy growth between its segments. There were four entrances—one on each side of the towering mountain. Outside the wall were round lumps of earth, houses to rants and cogs who had not yet proven their loyalty to the point of Morfit granting them a place to live.

Winter emerged from the woods, breaking from the forest near the entrance at the back of Morfit. Two huge rants stood near the gate. Both held thick kilves and were carefully checking those passing through the gate. Winter watched one of the rant guards stop a traveler and pull back the traveler's hood to look at his face. They appeared to be searching for someone. The thought made Winter happy, knowing that if they were still looking, Geth and Leven were probably still free.

"I need in," she whispered to herself.

Winter looked at the ends of her hair and at her arms.

"This won't do," she said. "They'll spot me instantly." She slipped back into the forest, looking for a wen nest. Winter's memory was filled with holes, but she had recollections of many small bits of Foo and the people and creatures who occupied the realm. Wens were common birds who laid eggs that were good for only one thing—throwing. So many dreams coming into Foo involved people throwing or smashing things, and the wens were a result of that. They laid eggs that were filled with nothing but color, perfect for young kids to steal and throw at things.

Winter, however, had another use in mind. She climbed seven trees before she found one. A large wen with a pink puffy face, a green pointed beak, and no feathers except on her behind, was sitting in the nest. The wen saw Winter and sighed. She mumbled and then grudgingly moved her plush behind to reveal a nest full of white eggs covered in black diamonds.

"Perfect," Winter said.

Winter rubbed each egg with her palm, and as she did so the black diamonds changed color. Winter pulled out the three eggs that had shown red diamonds.

The wen, who had been watching, sighed again.

"Work all day just so you can throw things," the wen complained.

"Excuse me?" Winter asked.

"I didn't say anything," the wen lied.

Winter didn't feel the least bit bad stealing eggs from the wen. She knew the strange birds didn't lay eggs to create other birds. Most wen eggs were used to torture and vandalize the Children of the Sewn who lived in the roots of the Red Grove. Winter was simply taking the eggs for a more dignified use.

Winter jumped from the tree and crouched back behind a boulder. She smashed the first egg against the top of her head.

Deep red dye bled down her hair.

She pushed the thick dye back from her forehead and smoothed it into the two pigtails she had created. Then Winter cracked the other two eggs on the sides of her head and massaged the red dye deep into her white-blonde hair. It was messy, but it was working. In a few minutes, Winter had brilliantly red hair.

It still wasn't enough of a disguise.

Winter washed her hands off in a small stream and worked herself back out to the trail. A couple of people passed her, each carrying rocks to drop off. Behind them a single cog in a black cloak was making his way down the path, carrying a rock in his cold blue hands. He was mumbling something about how he would never lie to his wife again once he set that rock down.

Winter stepped out in front of him, holding her kilve in her right hand.

"Ah!" the cog screamed, his orange forehead wrinkling.

"Heading to Morfit?" Winter asked.

"Yes," he said.

"Drop your burden and cover it with your cloak," Winter insisted, waving the kilve.

"But I need—"

"The rules have changed," she snapped. "Drop it here!"

"But—"

Winter didn't want to, but she swung her kilve and struck the cog behind his right knee. His leg buckled, and he fell to the ground, dropping his rock. He struggled to get to his feet. Winter thrust her kilve down, pinning the back of his robe to the ground. The poor cog pulled and screamed his way out of his cloak, then took off running as fast as he could, yelling something about his wife and waving his blue hands in the air.

"It's so much easier when they just obey," Winter said, wondering where she had learned to use a kilve like that.

She slipped the cloak on and pulled the hood up over her head. Then she picked up the rock, held it in front of her, and began to shuffle toward Morfit, moaning. A small shadow passed over her. Winter looked up. Way overhead she saw the sickly rant she had left in the ice cave. He was riding on the back of a large roven. The roven screamed and swooped toward Morfit.

Winter pulled her hood even tighter around her head, hoping not to be spotted.

Near the gate she met up with two other travelers and tried to make it look as if she were moving with them. One was carrying a rock; the other had a bundle of fabric. Winter could clearly see the rants that were guarding the door—both were as tall as the actual gate. One rant stopped the nit carrying the fabric.

"Business, or the result of pleasure?" the rant questioned, bending down.

"I'm to see the Council of Whisps," the nit said.

The rant laughed. "The Council is gone."

"Gone?" the nit panicked. "My cause was up for review. I've brought them fabric. When will they be back?"

"Never," the other rant growled.

The poor nit just stood there, looking as though his life was over. "What's happening?" Winter heard him whisper to himself as she shuffled past.

"Stop!" the taller rant commanded Winter.

"Business, or the result of pleasure?" he demanded.

"Business," Winter said. "I have dreams to trade."

"Where did you get that?" he asked, referring to the kilve she carried.

"It was given to me by a rant much bigger than you," she said with authority. "Now, may I pass? Or would you like to explain to him why I was held up?"

Rants were not great under pressure.

"On your way," he waved.

Winter walked through the gate. Her heart felt like it was in her throat, as if with one good cough she could expel it. She moved farther into Morfit and stopped to compose herself.

Winter knew she shouldn't be here; if Jamoon spotted her, there would be more trouble. But she wanted to know what Morfit held for her and what Jamoon meant by her knowing the plan. She needed to see if she could discover who she really was. She tossed aside the rock she was carrying and listened to it hiss and groan as it became part of the mountain.

Winter worked her way through the lower slums of Morfit where those who were frightened by light lived.

"Hello, pretty," someone yelled out to Winter.

She kept going as if she hadn't heard. He moved toward her to better make his point, and Winter pictured him in ice.

She climbed up a long, dark, twisted spiral of stone stairs. From heights all over Morfit water fell in thick streams and misty veils, the water originating in the many springs Morfit had been built around. At the top of the stairs was a round pit filled with the bones of sheep. The bones rattled as a large rat scurried through them, searching for some small scrap of leftover meat. The rat hissed at Winter and called her a spy.

Winter moved on.

She made her way along a narrow, jagged ledge that led to an archway opening up into the grand chambers. All around her were the sounds of laughter and fighting. Winter couldn't remember Morfit being this dirty or this dark.

Above the base of Morfit was a large, roofed courtyard, ringed by small rock caves and burning torches. Gathered in that chamber were hundreds of dark-cloaked rants. Winter pulled her hood more closely around her head and entered, working her way along the back wall of the courtyard, keeping to the shadows cast by the torches.

Amazed by the vastness of the gathering, Winter began counting. She stopped at around four hundred, estimating that there must be at least two thousand rants packed into the hall. Each was standing still, as if awaiting something or someone.

Then those gathered began to chant rhythmically:

"Whole again once more."

"Whole again forever."

"Whole again with power."

"Whole again."

"Whole again."

Winter could feel the darkness in the words. Swaying in unison, the gathered beings chanted louder, the words taking form as they mixed with the torchlight. Winter could see letters and meanings rising above the chanting crowd.

"Whole again once more."

"Whole again forever."

"Whole again with power."

"Whole again!"

"Whole again!"

"Whole again!"

Winter put her hand to her heart and was surprised to find how fast it was racing. The words of the chant sizzled like drops of water in a hot pan—each word dancing on the surface and hissing into nothing but steam.

"Whole again!"

"Whole again!"

Suddenly the chanting stopped. As the words drifted downward, settling on the heads of those in attendance like ash, a tall, dark-robed figure ascended to a podium and raised his right hand.

It was Jamoon.

He stood at the front of the gathering. The bottom half of his robe billowed and swayed, filled with shadowy nihils. Every few seconds a couple of the dead birds would slip out, only to turn and work themselves back beneath his robe.

At his appearance, the crowd fell silent.

"The Sochemists have studied the Lore Coil," Jamoon declared. "They speak of bits of Sabine still in Reality—pieces that will work to create another gateway."

The crowd murmured.

"Shortly they will rebuild what was destroyed," Jamoon shouted, his voice ringing through the hall. "When the gateway

is reconstructed we will have complete access and will be made whole. Our armies gather at the Guarded Border waiting to spread the message of Morfit to all parts of Foo."

"What of Geth?" a short rant near the front yelled.

Jamoon's right eye burned.

"Geth will be found," Jamoon seethed. "That is why we are gathered. You are to search every bit of Foo, until you have recovered him and Leven. Dig up the gunt, tear down the trees, bury any who stand in your way, but find them—and when you do, kill them instantly. Their dead bodies are all the proof I need. They cannot be allowed to live."

Winter opened her mouth to gasp. Unfortunately, portions of the bickerwicks in her stomach were still fighting with each other, and their bickering could be heard.

"You digest!"

"No, you! I was here second."

A couple of rants in front of Winter turned to see what the fuss was.

"Who are you?" one asked.

"I . . ." Winter tried to answer.

It was no use. Half the crowd had now turned and was staring at her.

"It's the girl!" one yelled.

The hall erupted with angry cries. Even from where she was, Winter could see Jamoon begin to smile. Winter turned and ran toward the entryway. Three rants stepped in front of her, and she froze them. They fell against each other and became wedged in the opening. Winter quickly turned and bolted for another entrance.

"Seize her!" Jamoon yelled.

Winter looked back at the crowd of rants and froze them all—all of them half frozen, their other halves struggling and complaining about having to hold the frozen part up. The room was now full of a variety of half-dreams complaining. Even Jamoon was stiff, but as he stood there, Winter could see the dead, decaying nihils beginning to seep out from under his frozen robe. At first there were just a few, but in a couple of seconds there were whole flocks of them, out and racing toward her. She was not about to freeze them, fearing them more as ice than as simply dead.

Winter ran as fast as she could, slipping out of the archway and leaping up a stone stairwell. Behind her she could hear the shrill caw and hiss of the rank nihils overtaking her. Winter reached the top of the stairs to find a locked door. She pictured the wooden doorknob as ice and it froze. She then slammed the blunt end of the kilve into the knob, and it shattered into a million pieces.

"Thank you," the door sighed, happy about being set free.

The nihils were getting closer, their caws filling her head with fear.

Winter pushed the thankful wooden door open and stepped into the room behind it, then quickly closed it and leaned against it, breathing hard.

The nihils were in the stairwell outside the door.

Winter moved a large chair up against the door, but her

efforts were in vain. The black nihils began pulsing through the now-gaping knob hole like a geyser of oil. They flowed through the knob hole and under the small gap beneath the door, screaming and hissing like a cold, biting wind.

Winter did a little screaming of her own.

The nihils swarmed around her, biting and scratching her with their beaks and talons. Winter waved the kilve at them, but it was useless. As they closed about her, she had difficulty breathing and could see her vision fading. In a matter of moments she was unconscious and lying in a helpless heap on the floor.

The nihils turned and flew out of the room. They swept back down the stairs and over the half-frozen crowd. When they reached Jamoon they circled him tightly, warming him with their movements.

Jamoon soon thawed and headed up to Winter.

CHAPTER TWENTY-SEVEN

SNAPPED

The media had no idea what to make of it—a full-sized plane landing upside down in the middle of a busy freeway with no fatalities? Baffling. The only injuries reported were some scrapes and bruises and two broken arms, both belonging to the same person.

Some who witnessed the incredible episode claimed that fiery, demon clouds had softly set the plane down. Those who reported the story refused to even humor such a silly account. Regardless, traffic along Interstate 40 was backed up for hundreds of miles as everyone scratched their heads and wondered just how to move an *upside-down* 747.

Dennis sat on the edge of the freeway next to a number of other stunned passengers. He had a small, blue, airline blanket wrapped around his shoulders and was drinking some bottled water that a Red Cross volunteer had handed him. He really had no idea what had happened, but he was pretty sure he had something to do with it. He figured it would be best not to point that out to others.

After everyone had been evacuated from the plane, Dennis had noticed a small patch of black moving behind some foliage off to the side of the road. He watched it glide from one tree to another, almost as if it were stalking him. He could see it even now, lying beneath a large bush.

Dennis unzipped the fanny pack and looked down at Ezra.

"Did we do this?" Dennis whispered.

"We helped," Ezra said, jumping out of the fanny pack and up onto Dennis's shoulder.

"What is that blackness?" Dennis asked, motioning with his head to the bush at the bottom of the embankment.

"Not exactly sure," Ezra said. "But it's from Foo like me. It tried to talk to me—called me *Geth*," Ezra spat.

Dennis put his head in his hands and sighed. "I should never have ordered a sandwich."

The black shadow wriggled beneath the bush down below as trucks and cars drove by, people gawking and honking at the plane up above.

"Follow me," Ezra said to Dennis.

Ezra jumped from Dennis's shoulder and dropped down the side of the tree-lined embankment.

"I don't think we're supposed to . . ." Dennis slapped his forehead. "Ahhh," he gasped, stumbling over the guardrail and rolling awkwardly down the embankment after Ezra.

As usual, nobody noticed Dennis.

When he stopped rolling, Dennis scrambled to his feet and ducked behind some trees near the bush where the black spot was lying. The blackness fluttered away, moving deeper into the growth, with Ezra right on its tail. Dennis limped along after them, rubbing his sore knees and elbows. In a few minutes they had moved into a forest, far enough away from the freeway that they could barely hear the noise of the traffic. To Dennis it felt as if they were miles away from civilization.

The black shadow stopped, hovering above a decaying tree that lay sprawled out on the forest floor.

"Who *are* you?" Ezra yelled.

The blackness pulsated and whipped itself into a more ghost-like form. It had two small hands, tiny eyes, and an oozing mouth.

"Who are *you*?" it hissed. "You've been touched by Foo."

"'Touched,' my ankle," Ezra raged. "I've been cheated by Geth. He lives, complete and free, while I am nothing but anger."

"Geth," Sabine hissed.

"We are heading to the gateway to make things right," Ezra sneered. "If you wish, you can be my servant."

Sabine laughed wickedly. "You fool," he hissed. "The gateway is gone."

Dennis knew Ezra well enough to know that he was going to have to hold him back. He grabbed onto Ezra's legs and tiny tail as the furious toothpick swung with his arms and swore, trying to get at Sabine. Dennis could feel the anger raging through Ezra. It seemed to bleed out of the toothpick and into Dennis's blood. The sensation was almost overpowering.

"Fool?" Ezra seethed at Sabine. "I'll show you who the fool is."

Sabine withdrew a couple of feet.

"Listen," Dennis said, trying to calm things down and to understand the rage he himself was beginning to feel. "I think . . ." he stopped to soak in the rage. He opened and closed his eyes slowly. "I think . . ."

"Who are you?" Sabine hissed, drifting up to Dennis. "Who are you?"

"I'm Dennis," he answered, his body trembling with gathering anger.

"He's nobody!" Ezra yelled, his purple tassel writhing like a nest of snakes.

"Nobody?" Dennis whispered, his head beginning to pound.

"Nobody!" Ezra screamed. "I'm only using him to get me to the gateway."

Dennis couldn't remember feeling more agitated.

In the far distance the sound of sirens screamed. Dennis looked down at Ezra. He was holding the angry toothpick between his thumb and finger, and he studied the little monster's ugly face. It was contorted with rage and hatred. Dennis fed off the anger. He thought of all the times his father had been disappointed in him. He thought of how his mother had always wished he were taller or smarter. He thought about his employers and how they had always dismissed him as a nobody.

He knew they weren't even aware that he had left. And he thought of what he was doing. Sure, it was a ridiculous quest, but it was a purpose.

The anger Dennis felt was so strong he couldn't stop shaking. He looked down again at Ezra, who was still screaming.

"Nobody!" Ezra repeated. "Didn't you hear me? I said—"

Dennis couldn't help himself. He grabbed the top of Ezra and in one angry motion bent him in half. It was so sudden and unexpected that Ezra had no time to react.

Dennis stared at the bent toothpick. Ezra's upper half was connected to his lower half by only a thin splinter of wood. The top half of Ezra stared up at Dennis in total shock.

"You . . ." Ezra sputtered. "I . . ."

Dennis looked at Ezra in his palm and felt no pity. In the distance the sirens grew louder.

"I'll be making the decisions now," Dennis seethed, a look of determination on his face such as he had never had before.

Stunned into silence, Ezra blinked weakly, and Sabine withdrew a couple of inches.

Dennis looked up, his eyes red and wet, his blood filled with anger.

"Dennis," Sabine hissed.

Dennis reached out with such surety that Sabine didn't even flinch. He grabbed Sabine and twisted him around his forearm like a thick rope. Sabine responded by spreading up and around Dennis's shoulders, forming a ragged, black cloak. Sabine's eyes and mouth lay two-dimensionally at the neck of the cloak.

"I've never dreamed before," Dennis said angrily.

"I can fix that," Sabine hissed.

"I want to see this Foo," Dennis demanded.

"Of course," Sabine hissed. "Of course, Darrin."

Dennis turned and lowered his head so that Sabine's white eyes were directly in view of his. "My name is *Dennis,*" he spat angrily.

"Of course," Sabine hissed.

"Listen . . ." Ezra weakly begged.

Dennis wasn't in the mood to listen. He stuffed Ezra's broken body into the fanny pack, Ezra moaning the whole time. Then, straightening his wrinkle-proof pants and wearing Sabine as a tattered, open cloak, Dennis stood tall and puffed out his chest. He smoothed the sticker the bank teller had placed on his chest, viciously zipped up his fanny pack, and stomped farther into the woods, leaving behind the scene of the accident and the person he once was.

Dennis felt invincible.

ii

Tim Tuttle was slightly nervous about flying. Normally, he wouldn't have given it a second thought, but the strange story he had just heard about a plane landing upside down on a freeway was making him a bit uneasy.

Uneasy but determined.

People were also talking about the twenty-four-story office

building in North Carolina that had simply gotten up from the corner it was on and "walked" to the opposite side of the street. A plane landing upside down, a building changing location: nobody had a logical explanation for either event. Some thought it was the result of earthquakes and tornadoes, but the problem with that theory was that there was no other indication that any earthquake or tornado had actually occurred. One television network reported that these incidents were illusions staged by a clever magician who was trying to make a name for himself. They retracted their story a couple of hours later.

The world seemed like a crazy place. What made Tim most uneasy was that in the very back of his mind he couldn't help but think that all these things were somehow connected to what Winter was going through.

Before his flight, Tim had spent the day at the library, researching newspaper stories from around the world. If it was true, and Winter did have some way of freezing things or hypnotizing people, there certainly had to be an article documenting something odd going on somewhere. And Tim figured that if that odd thing had something to do with ice, then he might be back on the trail.

Unfortunately, the newspapers were full of odd people and odd events. But nothing he had found had any obvious connection to Winter or Leven or ice.

There was one brief article, buried in a London newspaper, describing a bizarre incident that had taken place in a Munich, Germany, train station a few days previous. According to the report, something had turned the station into a chaotic mess, with travelers being hurled around or lifted up by unidentified assailants. Blame was tentatively placed on a malfunctioning new heating system at the station, but nobody who had been there bought into that at all.

There were quotes from passengers who had lived through the ordeal. Tim would have thought it was simply another odd story, except for the last quote from a Frau Dent. She had said: "A young boy and girl started clapping, and for some reason that seemed to help settle things down."

There was no mention of ice, but the young boy and girl stood out. Tim had printed the article and stared at it for hours, thinking. When he called his wife, Wendy, to tell her what he had found, she encouraged him to do what he thought best.

"I've always wanted to go to Germany," Tim said, "and my passport's current from that convention of the International Waste and Litter Society last year in Nottingham."

"Then go find her," Wendy urged.

So, Tim was now on a plane crossing the Atlantic Ocean, wondering what in the world he would find when he landed in Germany. Winter had meant a lot to his family, but this quest was more than that. For the very first time he was truly beginning to understand just how important Winter was. The secret the old lady had whispered to him was finally beginning to make sense—sort of.

"She holds the seventh key, but does not know it. Watch her carefully."

Tim turned off his overhead light and pulled his ball cap down over his eyes. He needed sleep, and he had a feeling this might be his last chance to get some for a while.

"Seventh key," he whispered as he drifted off, wondering how he could *watch* Winter when he still had no idea where she was.

CHAPTER TWENTY-EIGHT

SIGNS O' THE TIME

By the time Leven and Clover and Janet reached the other side of Fissure Gorge, Janet had stopped crying, Leven's stomach hurt worse than ever, and Clover had tried more times than you can count to convince Leven to let him take care of the key. On the Niteon side there was a giant stone wall running along the entire length of the gorge, protecting Niteon from who knows what. Leven stepped off the bridge, through an opening in the wall, and onto solid ground.

"You're a beauty. I'll tell the world about you!" Leven yelled back to the bridge as he walked away.

The sentry bird on the Niteon side was less kind, ordering Leven to move on and stop talking to the bridge.

"They can sense insincerity," the big bird chirped, thinking Leven was being sarcastic.

Leven moved away from the gorge and into Niteon. He

could see nothing but a moonlit landscape. There were small hills and beautiful trees dotting and accentuating everything he could see. A broad stone path, with stone arches randomly stretching over it, ran far enough into the distance that Leven couldn't see the end of it. The only structure in sight was the giant bird's guardhouse.

"So, why do birds guard the bridge?" Leven asked Clover as they passed beneath two stone arches and onto the path leading to Cork.

"What else would birds do?" Clover asked, confused.

Leven shrugged. It didn't feel right to go farther without Geth. In Leven's mind there was no way Geth could have gotten in front of them, and it made sense to wait a bit for him.

He mentioned his concern to Clover.

"You're forgetting that Geth could have traveled in a number of ways," Clover said. "He could have found a sarus and ridden on top of it the whole way. Or he could be traveling on the back of a roven, or maybe he hitched a ride with a Sympathetic Twill and has taken one of the other bridges. You watch. When we get to the turrets, he'll be there."

"You're right," Leven said, knowing he needed to just focus on their goal of reaching the turrets and let fate do the rest.

Leven motioned for Janet to follow him and began walking quickly toward the turrets. In the distance there was a thick, lumpy patch of black horizon, darker than the night.

"What's that darkness over there?" Leven asked, pointing toward a gigantic, cystlike growth in the sky. Even in the darkness of the night it stood out, looking like a mushy black hole. It was in the opposite direction of the fire shooting up from the turrets. The blackness looked too substantive to actually be hovering in the air.

"It's not good," Clover said.

"Then what is it?"

"Bad," Clover suggested, sounding as though he wasn't all that impressed with Leven's level of knowledge.

"I understand opposites," Leven said, frustrated.

"We used to have the most spectacular sunrises," Clover said, leading into an explanation. "It's been many years, but we in Foo used to wake to find the marvelous dreams of mankind painting our world brilliant colors. Like a kaleidoscope. Sure, there were always spots and lines of black, and mornings of great darkness, but mankind was ultimately moving forward and dreamed of being better. There were some who were selfish, but now . . .

"That blackness is the result of sick dreams. The Children of the Sewn can't frame the dark dreams fast enough. And the museum expansion where they hang and store the dreams has been caught up in bureaucratic red tape for years. But, if they can frame a rotten dream, then it is less likely to spread and grow. Whereas the good dreams, when properly framed, are much easier to focus in on and achieve—their frames expand. But as I was saying, the Children of the Sewn are behind in both areas."

"Children of the Sewn?" Leven asked.

"They have the gift of framing the dreams of mankind."

"You can't frame dreams," Janet spoke up, making it obvious that she had been listening in. "Dreams are just your brain trying to sort out all the garbage life throws at you."

Clover made himself visible. "Excuse me?" he asked.

"I saw it on a TV special," Janet said with less enthusiasm. "It's just your brain trying to organize the junk you see during the day. I'm pretty sure that's what's happening to me now."

Clover shook his head.

"This can't be real," Janet said. "I can't even touch you."

"It wouldn't be appropriate anyhow," Clover pointed out.

"I can't eat. I can't even sit," Janet complained. "And I can feel I'm somewhere else. Somewhere, someone just needs to wake me up."

"Sorry," Clover said unsympathetically. "You are very much awake, both here and in Reality. The sooner you understand that, the better off you'll be."

Janet looked at Leven as if he might have something to add.

Leven shrugged. "I don't know much more than you," he said. "But I do know that despite things looking different here, I can feel it's real."

Janet didn't argue, but she did begin crying again.

"Women," Clover said, disappearing.

Leven and Clover and Janet picked up their pace, running along a narrower, worn stone path that bordered the brink of the gorge. Every few hundred feet the path in front of them would suddenly lift up, move to the right or to the left, and then drop down again, creating a new trail in a new direction. The fourth time the path did that, Leven began to question if they were going the right way.

"We are," Clover insisted. "Just stay on the path."

"But it keeps changing," Leven said, his breathing labored.

"It'll make up its mind eventually," Clover said. "No path wants to just lie there. It's trying to provide you the best journey."

"That's nice and all, but we need to get there."

"We will."

"Isn't there a normal path?"

Leven was going to argue the point further, but the path in front of them had heard Leven and was insulted by his ingratitude. It no longer wanted to go to the trouble of providing an interesting journey. So the path picked itself up, rose fifty feet into the air, and then slammed down, making a straight line through some trees and right to the turrets.

"Happy?" Clover asked.

"Thrilled," Leven answered, running even faster down the trail and toward the flame.

Leven's concern for Geth kept him going. But he was tiring. Gradually, his running turned to jogging and the jogging turned to walking and the walking led him eventually right up the front steps of a house that sat at the entrance to the turrets. The house was four stories tall with an ivy-covered porch that wrapped all the way around the ground floor. The roof was made of wood shingles that looked dry enough to spontaneously combust. There was a wide front door that was painted blue and had a fat wooden doorknob on it. On the wall next to the door was a sign that said:

HOURS: 8–8

In back of the house, a tall wooden fence ran for miles in either direction. Leven could see the high, distant flames of the turrets. They were still many miles off, beyond the fence.

"What is this place?" Leven asked, wiping sweat from his forehead and pointing to the old home.

"The gatehouse entrance to the turrets," Clover replied.

"Entrance?"

Clover read the sign. "Gates open at eight."

"We can't wait for the gates to open!" Leven insisted. "Geth needs our help!"

Leven stepped onto the porch with Clover and tried the handle of the front door. It was locked. He looked back at Janet, who was still standing on the path. Leven moved to a large window under the porch and pressed his face to the glass. Inside he could see shelf after shelf, each lined with books. A couple of the books slid off their shelves and began to approach the window. Two opened and pressed themselves up against the glass, showing off their pages. Leven jumped back.

"Books are so vain," Clover said. "Always wanting everyone to know their story. If they think for a second that you don't know what is inside of them, they'll strut around showing off their stuff forever."

Another book slammed up against the glass, trying to get Leven to look at it. It was opened up to a page with a painting of a boat on the Lime Sea.

Leven moved away from the window and back over to the door. He knocked and listened for any response. Something inside banged and rattled. A few seconds later the doorknob turned, and the door opened.

Leven recognized the man instantly. It was Albert, the same gentleman he had helped rescue from the forest. Albert gave no indication that he recognized Leven. Beyond Albert, inside the house, Leven could see a fat sycophant resting in a chair with its feet dangling in a bucket.

"Gates open at nine," Albert instructed.

"The sign says eight," Clover said.

"Well, what do signs know? Gates open at nine."

A couple of books had moved out of the library and were now trying to get out the front door to present themselves to Leven. Albert kicked them back with his foot.

"We have to get to the turrets," Leven begged. "We need to meet someone."

"Well, meet them in front of here," Albert insisted. "There is no one inside, and no one will be allowed inside until the gates open at ten."

"You said nine," Leven pointed out.

"That doesn't sound like something I would say," Albert claimed, kicking another book. "Gates open at ten."

Albert slammed the door.

Leven walked to the edge of the ivy-covered porch and looked around the house at the tall fence behind it, then stepped off the porch and walked toward it. He reached out to stick his hand through the slats, but as he reached, the fence shifted to block him. Leven scooted over and tried to reach again. Again the fence moved to keep him from even reaching through.

"Do you think we can climb over it?" Leven asked Clover.

"No way," Clover said. "This fence would swat you down every time you tried. We'll have to wait here."

Leven was going to argue the point a bit more, but he spotted a thick patch of soft-looking green grass growing beneath some tall trees.

"I don't know about both of you," Leven said, "but if we have to wait, I could really use some sleep and maybe some food. My stomach feels awful."

Clover materialized and handed Leven a filler crisp. "Just nibble it. It'll fill you right up."

"Thanks," Leven said.

"So what about me?" Clover asked.

"What *about* you?" Leven said, kneeling down on the soft turf.

"I'm not actually tired, and you know how much trouble I can get in with a couple of hours of unsupervised time. And in the dark, even."

"Janet will watch you," Leven mumbled, lying down on the soft green grass and closing his eyes. "Gates open at ten. Hopefully."

Clover looked at Leven and tisked. He looked up at Janet, who had begun crying again.

"Wanna play a game or something?" he asked.

She just stood there.

"Come on," Clover finally said, "follow me."

Janet followed Clover into the trees.

ii

The moonlight rested upon the secret's shoulders like a thick dusting of dandruff. A light wind caused the dandruff to swirl. The very tip of the secret's feet still burned orange from the heat of the soil; the rest of it had cooled nicely and was practically invisible to the naked eye. It swatted a few pesky decoy secrets away from its head.

It breathed.

It then exhaled a torrent of soft whispers and low murmurings. The secret stepped lightly across the ground. It had braved crossing the bridge and was now moving down the same path Leven had traveled earlier.

It sought the soul who had dug it up.

It had not gotten a complete look at who had set it free, but it had seen the eyes, and that should be enough. The secret shivered. It could still feel the hands of the nit who had buried it so many years before. It could also feel the fear and the anxiety the nit had placed deep in the soil along with it.

The secret expanded and then contracted. It wanted so deeply to let go of what it was holding inside. Even in its state, it knew it held a secret that many would kill to hear.

It reached the turret's gatehouse.

For some reason it was frightened of the sycophant and was relieved to see no sign of it. But there beneath the trees by the fence lay a tall boy sleeping.

The secret moved closer, making no more sound than a pair of bare feet walking in long grass.

The secret whispered, hoping the boy would stir and open his eyes slightly.

The boy moaned and rolled over, his closed eyes pressing into the grass.

The secret whispered louder.

It was no use; the boy was sound asleep.

The secret moved behind the trees. It would wait.

CHAPTER TWENTY-NINE

THROWING FEAR

Winter could feel her hands beneath her chin and her knees pushed up against her chest as she sat curled up in a ball on the dirt floor. She opened her eyes, but couldn't see much more than she had been able to with them closed. She straightened her back and moved into a kneeling position. The soil around her knees crunched and crackled. Her head felt thick and littered with streaks of darkness that the bite of the rotting nihils had left behind. Winter was covered in leftover bits from the decaying birds—a claw here, a beak there, and two eyeballs caught in the hem of her shirt.

As her green eyes adjusted to the dark, Winter looked around the room she was in, taking in every inch. The room was huge, with white, tile-covered walls and a domed ceiling. At the center of the dome was a small opening that created a skylight of sorts. A circle of moonlight was dripping in, and Winter could hear the sound of wind building.

Jamoon stood at the edge of the moonlight near a table filled with steaming food. Winter had forgotten how hungry she was. In the corner of the room was Jamoon's roven. The roven rocked sideways, clicking its lips. Jamoon ripped off a big piece of meat from a platter on the table and threw it to the roven.

Winter thought about diving toward the food, but instead she worked her way up onto her feet and dusted off her knees and palms. She touched her sore shoulder and winced. The last thing she could remember was running from Jamoon's nihils.

Jamoon smiled. Of course, it wasn't the kind of smile you would see on a four-year-old in a family portrait; it was more like the kind of smile a wicked darkness would smile after it had successfully destroyed everything good that had ever existed. Jamoon was still wearing his robe, and the dream he had stepped into Morfit with was of a body builder. His left side was ripped and strong. Most rants would never leave Morfit if they were lucky enough to get such a useful left half. The body-builder side matched some of the natural strength and size Jamoon's right side enjoyed. The bottom of Jamoon's robe billowed.

"Do you not recognize this room?" Jamoon asked tauntingly.

Before Winter could answer there was a knock on the door and a cog entered, carrying a small board with a dream film over it. The blue-handed cog showed the board to Jamoon.

Winter looked around again. The room *was* familiar to her. She tried to force her mind to remember.

Jamoon handed the board back to the cog.

"Well," Jamoon said, "there is still some uncertainty, but the Sochemists feel that your beloved Geth is dead."

Winter's stomach lurched.

"They are still debating it," Jamoon went on. "But in time, they will come to an agreement."

"He can't be dead," Winter insisted.

"I can bench-press my own weight," the body-building side of Jamoon bragged.

Winter stayed quiet.

"Send the locusts," Jamoon instructed the cog, ignoring his other half. "Transmit a message from the Sochemists. Let all of Foo know we have Winter. That should bring the boy here."

"As you wish," the cog said, backing out of the room and closing the door behind him.

"Geth is not dead," Winter asserted.

"Perhaps," Jamoon said. "The Sochemists will sort it out."

"Just because they say it doesn't make it so."

"You have no understanding of the politics of Morfit."

Winter pictured Geth in her mind. She thought she could feel he still lived. But her head was so full of dark and depressing thoughts she wasn't sure if it was a false hope.

"You helped create this room," Jamoon said, bringing the subject back to where it had been before the cog had entered. "You thought you were helping Foo, when in reality you were forwarding Sabine's plan. Now look at you: alone, and possessing the blessed ability to die."

Winter closed her green eyes. Her hands were trembling. She

let her fear race through the open ceiling and out into the night air, trying to picture Leven wherever he was.

"You really don't remember any of this, do you?" Jamoon laughed wickedly.

"I remember," Winter lied, not wanting to give Jamoon the satisfaction of being right.

"I don't believe you do."

Winter was silent.

"If you do, then where's the key?" he demanded.

Winter had absolutely no idea what Jamoon was talking about, but she decided to stick with lying.

"Wouldn't you like to know," she snapped, raising her green eyes to meet Jamoon's single exposed one.

"Toy with us and Leven dies," Jamoon said. "Of course, he will die anyway. The Lore Coil has made one thing perfectly clear: Leven is mortal. There are many who will smile at his death."

Winter couldn't allow such talk. She thought of Jamoon's right side as ice. Nothing happened. She focused her green eyes. Still nothing.

Jamoon laughed. "Surprised? Your gift is useless in this room. The Want himself has touched these walls. With his touch he took away the ability for any who stand in here to exercise their gifts. Crazy fool."

Winter could feel the panic rising in her throat like sour mush. Fear shot off her and into the air. All Winter could think of was Leven.

"No gift and the ability to die." Jamoon stepped closer. "You betrayed us once before. Now you will pay for it."

Jamoon seized Winter by the wrists.

"Somebody spot me," his left side demanded.

Jamoon twisted Winter and threw her to the ground like wet garbage. The nihils beneath his robe poured out. Winter screamed, and once again her fear shot off from her, through the window, and into the night air.

"I am only letting you live so in case Geth does still exist I can use you as a bargaining chip," Jamoon sneered. "But, I don't have to keep you alive *and well*—how about just *alive,* and how about *just barely?*"

The nihils fluttered and screamed, darting around the room like black pulses of light.

Winter, still on the ground, crawled to get away. She was too slow, and there was nowhere to go. The nihils flowed beneath her like water and lifted her into the air as Jamoon stepped closer. His right eye burned with rage.

Another bolt of fear shot off of Winter and out through the window. *Leven,* Winter pleaded, her heart trembling.

Leven.

CHAPTER THIRTY

EGYPTIAN SILK

Dennis looked at himself in the hotel mirror. He moved the disposable razor over his scalp, removing the last bit of hair from his head. He was ready to be someone else. He toweled off the remaining bits of shaving cream and took another good look at himself. He was surprised to see himself smiling. It made sense, seeing how he had never been happier. He had also never been more sinister. As a general rule, sinisterism is usually not that happy a thing, but Dennis was so new to it, he couldn't properly interpret his feelings. He dried off the top of his bald head and looked back at Sabine.

Sabine was sprawled out on the second bed in the hotel, looking like a ghostly black towel. All the lights were turned off, aside from the small one in the bathroom. Sabine preferred the dark. Dennis had worn him in as a robe, and now Sabine was trying to feel sinister despite the elegant, thousand-thread-count sheets he was lying on. Luckily for every wicked cause he was a part of, he was perfectly sinister, whether sleeping on satin or in soil.

Dennis had no answers as to what his future held, but he and Sabine felt that heading toward the spot where the gateway had been located was as good a move as any. With Dennis's help it might be possible to build a new and better gateway. Dennis picked up the fanny pack and pulled out the crippled body of Ezra. He looked at what he now saw as the pathetic little tyrant and wondered where he would be now if he had ordered a piece of pizza instead of the sandwich Ezra had been in.

"Need to look at what you did?" Ezra seethed, his speech weak and airy. "Broke a defenseless toothpick in half."

Dennis pinched Ezra tightly. There was still some feeling of anger and hatred in the sliver of wood, but Dennis knew that most of the passionate hatred the toothpick had once housed had been transferred to himself.

"You don't know what you're getting yourself into," Ezra coughed weakly. "You don't have the stomach. You gutless—"

Dennis didn't let him finish. He jammed Ezra back into the fanny pack and zipped it up.

"No stomach?" Dennis said to himself. "We'll see."

He splashed water on his face and approached Sabine, who was still sprawled out on the bed.

"I want to know what Foo is," Dennis said.

"Why?" Sabine hissed from his small mouth at his far corner.

"How can I build a gateway without knowing where it leads to?"

"Foo is paradise," Sabine seethed. "A paradise that is being withheld from people like you."

"That doesn't seem fair," Dennis said, trying to sound bold. "And this gateway?"

"It will be the hope of millions," Sabine lied. "You will be a hero to millions."

Dennis liked that.

"And what about this Geth that Ezra spoke about?"

Sabine hissed and then breathed in very slowly. "Don't think of Geth," he demanded. "He will be dead before you get there. My other half will see to that."

"And that's a good thing?" Dennis asked.

"That's a perfect thing," Sabine hissed. "One less wall to knock down before we can have it all."

Dennis liked that too.

Dennis flicked off the bathroom light and climbed into the other bed. They had an early flight to catch. Dennis slept soundly in his white shirt with the bank sticker and his wrinkle-proof pants—getting ready for whatever lay ahead.

ii

Tim didn't understand a word of German. People wearing felt hats and drab clothes just stared at him as he walked down the street, trying to figure out where he was. He had taken a taxi from the airport, but the cabbie had dropped him off at the wrong spot, insisting that he was where he had asked to be.

Tim was confused. He needed the train station, but all he could see were houses and a few small businesses. He stepped into a tiny delicatessen and bought a bit of cheese and bread with some of the money he had exchanged at the airport.

"Excuse me," Tim tried. "Train station?"

The owner of the shop looked at him as if he had just let a pack of monkeys loose in his store.

"Trains?" Tim said again.

The owner wiped his hands on his apron and pointed to the west. "You go," he insisted.

Tim couldn't tell if he was being instructed to leave or given directions.

"Thank you," Tim said, backing out. "Guten Tag," he added, trying to be gracious.

The German shopkeeper just shook his head.

Tim walked down the street in the direction he had been pointed. Germany was so green and beautiful, with honest-looking people. He couldn't believe he was here. If someone had asked him two weeks before where he would be today, he never would have guessed.

Tim was happy collecting trash. Now here he was halfway across the world, working off a hunch to find Winter and a boy named Leven. As with the trash he collected, he couldn't wait to figure out the story behind what remained.

After walking two miles, Tim found the train station. He walked in and looked around as if the answer might be right there.

It wasn't.

Instead, there were rows of wooden benches in the middle of the depot and people walking back and forth trying to catch trains that would take them someplace they would stay until they went someplace else.

Tim walked through the crowd and up to the ticket window. Behind the glass sat a skinny woman with braided hair and crooked white teeth. She smiled, which took Tim by surprise.

"Do you speak English?" Tim asked, smiling back.

"A bit," she said, still smiling.

"I read about the situation that happened here a couple of days ago," he tried. "People flying around." Tim waved his arms in the air as if to demonstrate.

Her smile left.

"Were you here?" he asked.

"No," she said solemnly. "But Herr Wondra." She pointed to a ticket window four glass panels down. "He was here."

"Thanks," Tim said.

He slipped four windows down and found himself facing a man with no smile.

"Do you speak English?" Tim asked.

"Of course," he answered curtly.

"You were here during the incident?" Tim asked. "When people were flying around?"

Again with the arms.

The German man sniffed. "I was," he said sharply. "This is a result," he added, lifting up his right arm to show off a cast. "I hurt it flying through the ice."

"Ice?" Tim asked, the hairs on the back of his neck dancing like a bunch of uncoordinated teenagers.

"Glass," the man corrected. "I flew through the glass."

"Not ice?" Tim questioned.

"Some of the glass may have . . . melted," he finally admitted, looking around as if concerned that others would overhear. "I flew through this glass," he said confidentially, pointing toward the pane of glass he was behind at the moment. "The glass, it . . . broke, and I fell on my arm. I was scared to be getting up. That I might get cut . . ." He paused to see if Tim understood.

Tim nodded, "Of course."

"But it wasn't glass," he continued. "There was water everywhere and the glass was melting. I took one day off," he said shamefacedly.

"Only one?" Tim said sympathetically.

The ticket master liked that. "I've never missed another day in my life," he declared proudly.

"So it was the heater that caused all the mess?" Tim asked.

"Certainly not," the man said, sticking out his strong German chin. "No heater could do that."

"So what happened?"

The ticket agent looked as though he were thinking, but he

obviously already had the story down. "It began while I was in pursuit of a young American."

"Girl or boy?" Tim asked.

"Girl," he said, as if proud of his memory. "She was in tears and wanting to travel to Berchtesgaden. I remember, because I have spent many weeks there."

"What did she look like?" Tim asked, trying to stay calm.

"Wild, blonde hair," he sniffed. "Young. Stubborn, of course."

"Of course," Tim said, his pulse racing. "And this Berchtesgaden . . . ?" he prompted.

"Proof that God prefers Germany," the ticket agent said proudly.

"Did she go there?" Tim asked.

"How should I know?" the agent said suspiciously. Suddenly he was far less friendly than he had been. "Why all the questions?" he asked.

"No reason."

"Are you traveling somewhere?" the agent asked, switching to a professional tone. "If not, please step aside."

"Actually," Tim said, "I would like a ticket to this Berchtesgaden place."

The ticket agent didn't smile. It was apparent from his eyes that he was suspicious and concerned about all he had said. He straightened himself and brushed back the sides of his hair, as if physically regaining his composure.

"Your papers, please," he finally said.

Tim handed the man his passport, happy to oblige.

CHAPTER THIRTY-ONE

CHOOSING A PATH

Leven wasn't dreaming—which wasn't too surprising, seeing as how he was in Foo and dreams there are more common among those who are awake. But, even though he was not dreaming, he was most definitely sleeping. The soft bed of grass he was lying on in front of the turrets' gatehouse was enjoying his company, and it swayed gently, rocking him as he slumbered. A couple of large mushrooms wandered over to give his head a decent place to rest. A little-known fact of Foo is that all fungi are incredibly friendly and love to be of service when they can.

If it had not been for the pain in his stomach, Leven couldn't have been more comfortable. At the moment, he was sleeping facedown on the grass, his forehead resting on the spongy mushrooms.

Small wits, tattered pieces of old dreams with a bit of life still left in them, watched over Leven. The wits liked to hide in trees, disguised as odd-looking leaves. They would pluck off the large fantrum leaves to make space for themselves in the trees. The plucked leaves from the nearby trees had drifted down and covered Leven in his sleep. He was so camouflaged that when Clover came back looking for him, he didn't spot him right off. Luckily, Leven gave himself away by his contented snoring.

Clover leaned over Leven and gently shook him.

"Leven," he said softly. "Leven, wake up."

Leven barely stirred.

"Leven," Clover said casually, "that whisp woman's in trouble."

Leven's eyes flew open, and he sat up. He looked at Clover, blinking. He shook his head and tried to pull his thoughts together.

"Janet's in trouble?" he asked, still confused by sleep.

"Oh, Janet. That's right," Clover laughed. "I keep wanting to call her Pam."

Leven rubbed his eyes and stood. "Is she in trouble?"

"Here's the thing," Clover said, clearing his throat. "Someone I know wanted to sleep, and so as to not bother you I decided to show Whispy a game I used to play. I never thought anyone would take her."

"She's been taken?" Leven said. "By who?"

"I don't know." Clover tried to cry. When he could see Leven wasn't buying it, he knocked it off. "They had horns and outdated hair. Oh, and they were dressed in fire."

"Fire?" Leven asked.

"Their skin was burning and they were wailing. Probably

because of their hair," Clover said. "They told Janet to follow them, and she did."

Leven was fully awake now. He looked about wildly. "We need to find her. Do you know where they were going?"

"My guess is to the gorge, or the Guarded Border, or the Lime Sea."

Leven put his head in his hands and sighed. "What game were you playing, anyway?" he asked.

Clover was quiet for a moment. "Rotscotch?" he finally said tentatively.

"Rotscotch? How do you play that?"

"I don't want to bore you with the details," Clover waved. "Let's just say it's really fun and involves decay and jumping."

Leven gave Clover a serious look.

"All right," Clover sighed. "It wasn't really so much a game as me wanting her to dig up something for me to eat."

"She can't dig," Leven pointed out.

"Tell me about it," he said. "She was a lousy player. I ended up having to do most of the work. But as I was digging around some trees, I accidentally dug up some things I shouldn't have—some bad thoughts," Clover whispered. "Judging by their hair, I'd say they'd been buried there since the early seventies."

Thanks to Terry, Leven's step-guardian, Clover had watched a lot of TV while in Reality. When Leven was sleeping or doing chores, Clover would slip up by Terry and watch whatever was on. Consequently, Clover knew quite a bit about American culture, popular history, and old hairstyles.

"We need to find her," Leven said.

"She'll be all right," Clover insisted. "She's a whisp. She can drift off whenever she wants, and they can't do a thing about it."

"So why did you wake me up?" Leven complained.

"Gates open in five minutes," Clover said casually.

Leven suddenly remembered why they were here. "Geth didn't come, did he?" he asked, glancing around.

"Not yet," Clover said, as though it were just a matter of time.

Leven's stomach lurched again. "Why is it still so dark?" he asked, turning to face the sun.

The sun was covered by a stippled black cloud.

"Maybe it's going to rain," Clover said.

"I don't think those are rain clouds," Leven said, watching the dark, grainy splotches move closer.

"Well, then what—" Clover stopped talking and his pointed ears began to twitch, to better listen to the distant buzzing in the air.

As the cloud drifted closer, it began breaking apart. Long ribbons of darkness hurtled down from the cloud like stringy, wet noodles. To avoid the approaching storm, Leven and Clover hurried up onto the porch of the gatehouse, taking cover under its roof.

The cloud moved overhead, showing off its belly. It was a cloud, but not in the normal sense. Leven could now see that the darkness was caused by a dense swarm of locusts. All at once thousands descended, flying wildly, filling the air with the buzz of their wings.

Leven leaped for the knob on the gatehouse door, but it was locked. Locusts in plaguelike proportions whipped and tore across the sky in a boiling mass.

"What are they?" Leven yelled above the din.

"Locusts!" Clover shouted. "They communicate news from Morfit."

The locusts began to settle, roosting on any rail or structure they could find. As soon as they landed, they dried up into small husks. Leven looked beyond the porch, and as far as he could see there was nothing but a blanket of light brown, dead locusts covering the ground. He took a step, and the husks beneath his feet disintegrated into a fine dust that drifted in the air, carrying in it the words of an unspoken message.

"There is little life left in Winter. She draws her last breath at the top of Morfit. When the morning arrives she will be no more. Neither the Waves of the Lime Sea nor the Want can prevent what will soon happen when the Ring returns."

For the first time in his life, Leven understood the adage, "No news is good news."

Winter was in trouble.

"What does it say?" Clover asked, refusing to touch any of the locusts.

"Winter's in trouble," Leven said. "We'll have to hope fate gets Geth here because we've got to get to Morfit, and fast. I've seen people fly here in Foo. How is that possible?"

"Only with the help of dreams, unless it's your gift," Clover said.

Leven shook his head, knowing those were not possibilities.

"There has to be another way besides simply running there," Leven said to himself, pacing the porch and rubbing his uneasy stomach. Desperate for a solution, Leven closed his eyes. When he opened them back up they were burning gold.

Leven looked around, light from his eyes sweeping the porch like a searchlight. He saw nothing but the images in his head. Stars streaked across his view. He saw strange, red-cloaked beings reading the locusts and hopping onto the backs of huge, lizard-looking creatures and racing across the ground. Leven shook his head and stared at Clover. His eyes were luminous.

"Wow," Clover said, "you must really see a clear view of fate."

"I saw some red-robed beings riding on giant lizards," Leven said. "They were heading our direction."

"The lizards are probably onicks," Clover said. "I don't—"

"Are onicks fast?" Leven interrupted.

"Not many things are faster," Clover said. "And they're loyal only to the rider on their back."

"Do you have any rope in your void?" Leven asked urgently.

Clover looked at Leven like he was crazy for even questioning.

"Get it out fast," Leven said. "And give it to me."

"All right!" Clover cheered, reaching into his void. "This should be fun."

Leven dashed off the porch and down the stairs, pulverizing thousands more of the dry locusts as he did so. He ran toward the edge of the locust-covered lawn. Clover was following behind him, yelling something about how real friends fill friends in.

"I'll tell you in a second," Leven shouted back, continuing to run. His stomach lurched and he stumbled a couple of steps before he could get his stride back.

The path they were on shifted, and Leven followed the new direction to the edge of a grove of trees. Beyond the trees was a broad, open valley. Leven could see for miles. The ground was covered in every direction with dried locusts, and in the far distance Leven could see the string of riders coming his way. Leven's chest now burned, and he stepped back, remaining hidden in the trees. His stomach bubbled.

"Is that what you saw?" Clover asked, handing Leven a coil of white rope.

Leven let the rope uncoil. On each end was a pink, plastic handle with pink tassels.

Leven rolled his eyes. "Is this the only rope you have?" He was having a difficult time breathing. "It's a jump rope, and it's pink."

Clover's face was its own special shade of red. "Um . . . it belonged to my sister," he tried. "And it's all I have. Are you okay?"

"I'm fine," said Leven, his face turning pale. He tightened his grasp on the end of the jump rope.

Leven peered out of the trees at the riders, who were still a long way off. Even so, the red-robed beings looked huge.

Another small decoy secret hopped out from behind a tree and flitted in front of Leven.

"Look out!" Clover yelled.

Leven saw it too late. The secret grabbed onto Leven's nose, looked him in the eyes, and spoke: "I took the last life jacket on the sinking boat."

The secret laughed and laughed and then floated away.

"It must have followed you across the gorge," Clover said. "We should get out of here before the big one finds you."

Leven held the jump rope in his hands and hoped what he had manipulated in his head a few minutes earlier would come to pass. He could see the red-cloaked beings more clearly now. There were eleven of them, each clinging to the back of a huge lizard. The lizards had flat, iguana-like heads and long, lean bodies, with thin, spiky tails. All the lizards' legs were a blur, and the scaly beasts were running single file, moving at an astonishing speed, on a path that led right past the grove where Leven was hiding.

"Who are they?" Leven asked, willing his stomach to settle.

"Like I said, they're onicks, and you don't—"

"Not the lizards. The riders. Who are they?" Leven pressed.

"They are members of one of Sabine's Rings of Plague," Clover answered. "They must have been searching for you and Geth. The locusts have probably asked for them to return."

"So they're bad?" Leven asked.

"The worst," Clover replied, turning invisible. "Listen, Leven, maybe we should give up on getting to Morfit."

"What?" Leven asked, shocked, putting his hand to his mouth to hold back a burp.

"The Ring is dangerous," Clover said. "We should get to Cork. We'll be safe there. That is the job of a sycophant, keeping his burn mentally stable and safe."

Leven didn't reply. He knew they were not too far from Cork. He also knew that Cork was paradise, untouched by the wickedness of Sabine's plan. Cork was supposedly the most peaceful place in Foo.

The onicks and their riders were getting closer.

Leven thought about eating real food in Cork and getting some real sleep. He thought about resting and feeling better away from fear and the secret that was stalking him. He thought of Geth and hoped that somehow fate would help him and Winter.

"What do you think?" Clover asked. "Let the riders go, and we'll get to Cork. It's too dangerous out here. Winter's tough, and Geth will be fine."

Leven looked at Clover with disappointed eyes. "No way," he said. "Cork would be nothing without Winter and Geth."

Clover smiled. "I was hoping you'd say that. I was just trying to be a real sycophant."

"I could never—" Leven's stomach cramped up. He bent over and reached for his throat, his face was as white as bleached cotton.

"Are you sure you're okay?" Clover asked.

"I . . ." Leven gagged. "My stomach . . . and my throat . . ."

Leven leaned over, holding his stomach with one hand and his throat with the other.

The onicks were getting closer.

"Seriously," Clover said, "are you all right?"

Leven answered by opening his mouth and projecting a stream of white foam. The foam ran from his mouth and puddled on the ground. Leven instantly felt better. He put his hands on his knees and breathed in deeply. His throat had quit burning, and his stomach no longer ached. He wiped his mouth and then his forehead.

"Did you eat too much filler crisp?" Clover asked.

"I guess so, but I only had—" Leven stopped talking because something in the white foam was wiggling.

"What's that?" Clover asked.

Leven looked at the foam on the ground. Clover leaned in close and smiled. He turned back to Leven.

"I told you Geth would find us," Clover said proudly, pulling Geth from the goo.

Geth was shuddering, spitting, and wiping foam off himself.

"How?" Leven asked, completely amazed. He took Geth from Clover. "You were in my stomach?"

"You swallowed me when that beast bit open the gaze," Geth sputtered. "I tried to climb out, but I couldn't do it. After you ate that filler crisp, I ran around for hours, working the contents of your stomach into a lather."

"I'm so sorry," Leven said.

"Fate's not always attractive," Geth admitted.

"Apparently, sometimes it's disgusting," Clover added.

The approaching onicks could now be heard, breathing hard, their scaly feet making a loud scratching sound on the stones of the path.

Geth looked out between the trees and saw the red-robed riders.

"The Ring of Plague," he whispered in awe. "The Ring is here, now?"

"Um, the turrets are back that way," Clover pointed out.

"But the Ring," Geth said excitedly, hope flowing back into him.

"We were going to hop on one of those lizards and try to save Winter," Leven explained. "But shouldn't we get you to the turrets first?"

Geth wiped the last bit of froth off of himself. He was still hardening and could feel himself growing closer to being nothing but a dead sliver of wood. But Geth understood fate. And it simply felt too fateful to have been thrown up just as the Ring of Plague was arriving. Geth had defeated the other Ring, and to die helping Leven knock off the last remaining one was just too significant to ignore. Plus, Geth cared for Winter too much to think only of himself.

"Leven," Geth said boldly, "this is your decision. You are an offing, and it's time you began trusting fate. It will be much harder to defeat the last Ring if we let them get to Morfit."

"But you're dying," Leven reasoned.

"What is death if not everyone's fate?" Geth said calmly. "I'm a lithen. I don't think now is the time to start making decisions based solely on my own understanding. And you, you are an offing who has made it through the Swollen Forest, escaped a gaze, survived a roven's rip, and traveled unharmed over Fissure Gorge."

The sound of the thundering onicks was growing louder.

"You are the grandson of Hector Thumps and essential to Foo and the dreams of all mankind," Geth continued. "And now fate has put you right here, right now, with the Ring approaching. Can you not feel the fate?"

Clover looked at Leven with anticipation, recognizing the importance of Geth's words.

"You are Leven Thumps," Geth said solemnly.

The onicks were almost there.

Leven closed his eyes. He could feel fate settling over him. He knew it would take some time to get Geth to the turrets despite how close they now were. He knew that Winter was in need and that the Ring of Plague had to be stopped. But he believed that fate had set him right where he was and that it was up to him to seal that fate and work on the Ring. He hoped time would stretch to accommodate everything.

"I've got a lizard to catch," Leven said, swinging the end of the jump rope and feeling much better with an empty stomach.

"Fantastic," Geth cheered, even as his body hardened further.

Leven smiled, happy just to have Geth back with them. Not that he had truly been gone, but it was nicer to have him out of his stomach and visibly along for the ride.

The onicks had arrived. They began racing by, just outside the trees Leven and Geth and Clover were hiding in. The onicks were amazing creatures. Their eyes were thin, blue slits, and their skin was green, streaked with red and pink that seemed to bleed backward in the wind as they hurtled along.

On the back of each thundering lizard rode a single being. All of the riders were wearing long, red robes with black rings around the cuffs.

" . . . eight, nine, ten," Leven counted to himself.

Leven leaped from behind the tree and whipped his rope toward the last rider and its onick.

Leven was one off.

The rope curled around the tenth rider, the pink handle whacking him in the face. Leven yanked as hard as he could, and the rider flew backward off his onick and into the eleventh and last rider behind him. Both riders came hurtling toward Leven. He dodged out of their way and ran toward the two riderless onicks, which had stopped, confused over losing their passengers. Leven jumped on one and whistled as loudly as he could.

It didn't move.

Clover materialized and slapped the confused lizard on the behind.

The onick took off racing down the path just as the two riders who had been knocked off staggered to their feet and began to compose themselves. Geth worked his way into the pocket on the front of Leven's T-shirt.

"This is much better," Geth shouted, feeling some life returning to him. It seemed as if Foo was suddenly filling up with hope.

Leven sped after those in the lead, who had not seen what had happened in the rear. He fit so perfectly on the lizard's back, it was almost as if it had been made for him. The huge beast had large shoulder blades that rose up, and Leven tucked his head behind them to lessen any wind resistance. With its aerodynamically shaped head, the onick whizzed along at a breathtaking speed, drawing ever closer to the red-robed riders in front.

Leven was trying to decide what to do next when Clover screamed, "Watch out behind you!"

Leven looked back and spotted the two riders he had pulled off. They were riding double on the other onick and coming up quickly behind him. They pulled next to Leven, and the one on the back reached for him, his red robe flapping like flames. Leven lashed out with his foot, but the rider grabbed it and wouldn't let go. Leven kicked until he lost a shoe, and the assailant flew off the onick and onto the ground.

"You have a hard time keeping your shoes on!" Clover yelled.

Leven would have said something in reply, but he was too astonished. The fallen rider had dived into the soil and was beginning to burrow after him. The mound of dirt was speeding toward him. It was not a comfortable sight.

Leven dug his knees into his ride and pleaded with it to speed up. The rider racing next to him tried to reach out and finish the job that his now burrowing passenger had been unable to accomplish. Leven leaned to his right, and the onick veered in that direction, racing off the path and into a thick field of cork and ivy.

Leven's mounted pursuer was still right on his tail, both onicks thundering across the ground. The rider pulled close to Leven and, grabbing Leven's shoulder, dragged himself onto Leven's ride. As they wrestled for control of the racing lizard, the

rider's hood blew back and Leven could see the face of his assailant. He looked quite normal, like a math teacher or a doctor. His eyes, however, looked like they belonged to someone who made a habit of harming others.

"You have no idea what you are tampering with!" the rider yelled. "The Ring of Plague cannot be defeated!"

Leven's onick had reached a thick growth of trees and was now wildly dodging through them. Leven's heart raced with fear. He was having to fight to keep himself from pulling away and riding off somewhere safe. Leven closed his eyes and let fate settle over him again. He opened his eyes back up and threw his weight against the hooded foe, causing him to lose his balance and teeter to one side of the speeding onick. The cloaked assailant tried to right himself but suddenly disappeared when he was clipped by a passing tree trunk and violently snatched away.

"Nice move!" Clover cheered.

Leven's right hand burned. It began to glow red and swell.

"My hand," Leven yelled. "It's glowing."

"Interesting," Geth said.

"Yeah, real interesting. But keep riding," Clover urged. "We have to keep moving."

Leven steered with his knees, turning his onick in a wide circle back through the trees and toward the path they had detoured from. When they broke from the trees, the ground in front of them suddenly erupted as the burrowing rider Leven had kicked off earlier popped up right in front of the plunging onick. Getting into the spirit of things, Leven's mount didn't miss a beat. It lowered its head and ran directly into the hapless being. The impact sent the astonished rider spinning into the air and out of the way.

Then Leven's *left* hand began to burn, and a redness began to creep up his arms. Leven could feel the burning, but his mind was calm, as if it had been expecting this to happen.

"What's happening?" Leven hollered.

"You're changing," Geth shouted back. "Offings grow by experience, not time!"

Leven looked away from his hands and spotted the riders up ahead. They were kicking dirt up as they sped over the top of a tall hill and down toward the valley before the gorge. Leven didn't have time to trail behind them. Winter was in trouble.

"Come on," Leven yelled at his ride. "We can't let them beat you."

He found that onicks have a rather competitive spirit. His onick suddenly accelerated. He had picked one fast lizard.

Leven counted the riders in front of him.

There were nine.

Leven raced up alongside the last one in line and steered his ride into the side of the thundering beast. The unexpected bump unseated the rider, who went flying. The rider came down hard, bounced twice, then landed on his feet, sprinting after Leven.

"Looks like we've got a runner!" Clover screamed.

Leven looked back.

"He's huge," Leven said. "He's twice my size."

"Well, then you'll have to hit him twice as hard," Geth

observed. "Think of Winter and remember who you are!"

Leven's arms burned red.

The runner could barely match the speed of Leven's onick, but as he got close he reached out and grabbed a handful of Leven's shirt, trying to pull Leven off or pull himself up onto the racing onick. Before he could do either, Leven flexed, elbowing the runner in the jaw. The runner's teeth popped out like popcorn. He lost his grip and dropped to the ground, wounded and out of the chase.

Leven wiped his forehead as his chest and torso began to burn and swell like his arms. The swelling wasn't painful, and it seemed to give him strength. He thumped his heels against the sides of his ride.

"Come on!" he commanded.

His onick responded. Under Leven's urging, it raced in behind the next victim, and with a swing of its head it was able to send the rider tumbling off into the dirt.

Leven's right foot burned as images of his life in Reality began to crowd his head. He could see Addy and Terry and all the misery they had put him through. He could feel those experiences making him stronger now.

"Get 'em!" Leven shouted to his onick.

The beast surged ahead and easily toppled the next rider with its head.

Leven's onick would have gotten a third rider if the cloaked being hadn't turned and spotted them. This rider was big and had a square face with one terrific eyebrow and twice that many moles. He looked at Leven with an expression of surprise. Then he opened his mouth and blew out a terrific blast of flame.

Leven could feel the fire licking at his own eyebrows and part of his torn shirt. The heat also entered Leven's nose and throat, but it only stoked the burning in his chest and caused his body to grow stronger.

The fire-breathing rider leaned back and blew flame at Leven's onick. The speeding lizard veered to avoid the blast, and Leven lost hold for a moment but gripped the onick with his heels. He regained his seat and urged his ride forward. As it pulled ahead of the fire-breathing rider, Leven's onick flicked its tail, catching the fire-breather by surprise and causing him to do a rather spectacular flip into the air before slamming into the ground far behind them.

"Wow!" Clover said, impressed.

"I didn't expect the fire," Leven admitted.

"Tell me about it," Clover said, a small tuft of hair above his eyes smoldering.

"Are you okay?" Leven asked as his onick thundered closer to those still ahead of them.

"Fine," Clover lied, his leathery forehead dripping with sweat. "It's you I'm worried about."

"Me?"

"You're changing," Clover said with awe. "Look at your hands and your shoulders. I've never seen it happen so fast or so strong. Something big must be coming."

Leven tried to look at himself the best he could. He could see his hands and his feet; more important, he could feel the change.

"Worry about that later," Geth directed. "We have five more riders to take care of."

Leven dug his heels into the lizard, and the onick's tongue shot out. Leven jabbed with his heels again, and once more the beast's orange tongue leapt from its mouth and then recoiled. The onick's tongue was at least four feet long and moved with lightning speed. It was bumpy and coated with thick, sticky-looking mucus.

The tongue gave Leven an idea. He moved in behind the next rider and dug his heels into his ride. His onick's sticky tongue shot out and wrapped around the left wrist of the rider in front. As the tongue retracted, it pulled the rider off. Leven watched the poor nit land on the side of the path and tumble down a steep incline.

Leven rubbed his lizard behind the ear. It turned and tried to bite him. Apparently his ride wasn't doing this for him. As Leven was rubbing the onick he noticed that his hand, while not burning red any longer, now looked larger than it had only moments before.

"Yeah, yeah, nice hands—now stop admiring yourself and get those other riders," Clover yelled out from on top of Leven's head.

Leven's cheeks burned red for a different reason as he sped up to the next rider and watched his onick use his tongue to pull the rider off. The rider was momentarily suspended in the grip of the tongue, and he glared at Leven. He had a blue face with red lines running horizontally across it, like a bloody barcode. Leven blinked, and the rider was gone.

Leven looked around nervously. His head felt foggy, as if he were in a dream.

"Where did he go?" Leven yelled.

"He's still there," Geth hollered.

Leven looked and was surprised to see a miniature version of the same rider there on the tip of his onick's tongue. He looked like a small action figure. Before the onick could retract its tongue, the small rider ran along the bumpy surface and jumped onto the onick's head, where he stood glaring at Leven defiantly.

"Let me handle this one," Clover said, jumping onto the head of the onick and grabbing the miniature rider in his hands.

The rider returned to his normal size, and Clover found himself holding onto the rider's ankle. The rider kicked his leg, sending Clover into the air behind Leven just as the onick tossed its head, sending the rider careening to the corklike soil.

"Clover!" Leven yelled as his onick raced on.

"Right here," Clover responded, scrambling up the onick's tail as they continued to fly across the ground.

Leven's heart was racing as his entire body seemed to enlarge. He sped up alongside the next victim. The rider looked at Leven in shock; he had been blissfully unaware of anything going on behind him. He waved his hand, and Leven's body began to lift off the onick. Leven grasped the shoulder blades of his onick in a desperate attempt to stay on.

"What's happening?" Leven panicked.

"He's levitating you," Geth answered.

Leven's still-burning feet were pointing straight up in the air, making him look as if he were doing a handstand on the shoulder of the onick. The rider caused Leven to sway from side to side, trying to force him to release his grip on the onick. Leven's fingers were burning again as he dug into the skin of the beast. The onick didn't really appreciate that. It twisted and bucked, whipping Leven's legs into the rider who was levitating him.

Before the rider could react, Leven's onick followed up the kick by flicking out its tail, catching the rider just under his chin.

The levitator flew farther than any of the other victims Leven had knocked off previously, landing with a dull thud in a field thick with temperamental holes.

There were only two riders left in front of them, and they were rapidly nearing Fissure Gorge, still at breakneck speed.

Leven could feel his legs growing longer, not by inches and feet but by centimeters. The white strip in his hair glowed like a lit bulb. Once again he could see scenes and bits from his life in Reality. He could see Terry and Addy screaming at him and telling him that he would never be what he wanted to be because that was impossible. Resentment burned inside of Leven, like a gasoline-marinated lump of coal that had just touched a lighted match.

Leven also saw his neighbors who had ignored him and his peers who had made fun of him, and he felt nothing but pity for them. He wished they could see how their behavior had contributed to making him who he was. Leven's entire body burned as if on fire.

Leven let the feeling wash over him as he raced closer to the gorge. He began trying to think up compliments he could yell at the bridge.

Leven's onick moved up and bit the tail of the onick in front of him. It didn't do any damage, but it did cause the rider to turn and spot Leven. Instead of turning to fight, however, the riders ahead picked up speed, racing even faster toward the gorge. Leven was concerned: They seemed off course for meeting up with the bridge. In fact, they were heading straight for the wall that bordered the edge of the gorge.

Leven tried to turn the head of his onick, but the lizard wouldn't have it, going after the two in front of it with its tongue.

"Whoa!" Leven yelled. "Turn!"

The giant lizard wasn't listening, and the wall bordering the edge of the gorge was rapidly drawing near. The two onicks in front of Leven ran faster, showing no signs of slowing. Leven tried his best to concentrate to manipulate the outcome, but all he could get his eyes to do was burn gold while his soul rose up into his throat.

The riders in front of him reached the wall and, without slowing, their onicks leapt over it and out of sight.

"Stop!" Leven screamed at his own ride. He thought about jumping off, but it was too late.

His lizard reached the wall and sprang over it and out into the void above the gorge. Leven allowed himself to scream as he held tightly to his doomed ride. With his eyes closed, he heard the wind whistling against something. He opened his eyes to see wide, dark, leather wings extending out of each side of the onick. The beast had suddenly slowed and was drifting down, still following the two in front of it, which were also moving in what felt like slow motion.

Clover materialized. "Don't let go!" he screamed, his voice strangely loud in the sudden quiet. He was holding tightly onto Leven's arm and staring down into the depths of the gorge.

"I wasn't planning to!" Leven said, also speaking needlessly loudly in the now-quiet air.

The onick he was on was swimming slowly through the air toward the two in front of it, its giant wings acting as fins. The two onicks split, one drifting up and one gliding down. Leven's lizard aimed for the high one. It floated up and circled slowly, using its sticky tongue to send the other onick into a slow roll. It unseated the rider, who flailed about with his arms as he floated down.

Leven watched as the rider slowly descended through the air, down into the gorge. Halfway down, he hit hard air and began to drift in a different direction, becoming trapped in the maze of air. Leven held on even tighter to his ride, not wanting to experience the same fate.

Out of nowhere, lightning ripped through the air, illuminating the gorge like a violent bug zapper. The strike missed Leven by a few feet, but his onick screeched and used its wings to swim higher. The rider Leven had just unseated apparently had the gift of lightning, and though trapped in the maze of air, he began firing bolts as he drifted up, then down, then sideways.

The ribbon of lava at the bottom of Fissure Gorge belched, and a warm wind wafted up, lifting Leven's onick and its passengers even higher and scattering the new lightning that was now shimmering continuously. The uneven air in the gorge caused the jagged bolts to sizzle in all directions.

From below, the only remaining rider ascended toward Leven, urging his onick up. The two lizards screamed at each other as Leven tried to maneuver his out of the way.

He couldn't completely avoid the beast, and as it passed Leven's ride, there was a terrible ripping noise followed by a hideous scream—his onick had lost its tail. It turned in the air to face its assailant, crying like a wounded bird.

The last rider made a slow, wide turn and came back directly at Leven. As the two onicks collided, they thrust out their tongues and grabbed hold of one another, slowly twisting in the air, like two alligators wrestling.

Neither onick would let go of the other's tongue, and the struggle made it almost impossible for their wings to get the air they needed underneath them. They were all drifting down, surrounded by shimmering lightning.

Wide-eyed, and clinging desperately to the back of his enraged onick, Leven watched as Clover swam through the air and onto the head of the last rider. Clover pushed back the hood of the rider's cloak, grabbed a huge handful of his hair, and pulled on it as though he were a farmer trying to harvest the world's most stubborn beet. The rider's eyes watered as he frantically reached up, causing his onick to twist and lose more air.

The rider grabbed Clover by the throat and squeezed as hard as he could. Clover's eyes bulged as he tore at the rider's hands. Leven didn't think about how useless it was for the rider to try to kill Clover; he just reacted.

The rider was large, with a huge frame and thick, black hair. If it had been weeks before and Leven had been in Reality, he wouldn't even have dreamed of confronting someone like that. But it was not weeks before, and Leven was mounted on a winged lizard, floating miles above the ground, with burning fists, watching someone hurting Clover.

Leven drew back his right hand and swung. The air parted to allow his fist to travel the distance to the rider's jaw. A terrific crack sounded, and the rider twisted sideways and floated off his lizard. The poor beast released its tongue and descended belly up toward the bottom of the gorge, desperately struggling to get some air beneath its flailing wings.

"Not bad," Geth remarked.

Released from the rider's grip, Clover caught an updraft and drifted up. Leven pulled up on the head of his onick and urged him toward Clover. Leven's onick swam through the air beautifully, and Leven blinked, suddenly realizing that he could see the soft outline of the different layers of air. He navigated in and through them as he made his way steadily toward Clover. Lightning continued to lick at everything—at the walls of the gorge, the clouds, and at the air around Leven.

Leven dodged a thick bolt. He swooped gracefully beneath Clover and reached out his hand, surprised to see Clover smiling widely, his cheeks glowing. As the onick continued to rise, Clover took Leven's hand and swung onto the onick right behind him.

The ribbon of lava at the bottom of the gorge belched once more.

Leven and Clover were lifted up as a thick scratch of lightning flashed next to them.

"You're not done yet," Geth warned.

"What?"

"That last one may be onick-less, but he's flying after us."

Leven dug his knees into his lizard as the last member of the Ring flew through the void toward them. He grasped Leven and turned him, wrapping his arms around Leven's burning chest. The being was incredibly strong, and he was squeezing the air from Leven's lungs, forcing his life out.

"You fool," he hissed into Leven's ear. "You have damaged the Ring."

Leven couldn't respond due to his lack of breath and his impending doom.

The last rider gasped in sudden realization. He wrenched Leven's head around and stared fiercely into his eyes.

"You are Leven," he seethed. "I've found Leven."

Leven would have asked *his* name—but again, the dying thing.

"You can die," the hooded assailant hissed joyfully. He tightened his hold, bleeding every last drop of breath from Leven's lungs.

Leven willed his gift to kick in, but there was nothing, and his vision began to go black as lightning continued to flash everywhere.

"Not so fast," Geth ordered.

Geth was out of Leven's shirt pocket and standing on the rider's arm that was wrapped around Leven's neck.

"What?" the rider cursed. "What . . . who are you?"

"I can't believe you've forgotten me, Sam," Geth said boldly.

"Geth?" Sam said in disbelief. "Geth?"

Sam released his grip on Leven just a bit, and Leven gasped for air, realizing that he could now see the maze of air in the gorge almost perfectly. His offing eyes were completely adjusting to Foo. In fact, Leven's amazing eyes could read the air so well that he could see a solution to the brute holding him. Leven lightly nudged the onick he was on with his right heel. The beast drifted over and down as Sam turned his attention to the bold little toothpick.

"The great Geth," Sam laughed. "We've been searching everywhere for you, and now I see you are too insignificant to be a concern."

"The least bit of good can put a hole in a mountain of evil," Geth said wisely.

Sam laughed, having no idea how literally Geth was speaking. Geth leaped up and came down as hard as he could with his legs pointed. Geth pierced Sam's forearm, causing Sam to yell and momentarily release his hold on Leven. Geth pulled himself from out of Sam's arm and grabbed hold of the white in Leven's hair.

Leven knew it was now or never. He kicked his onick in the

ribs and it bucked, propelling Sam straight up into a strong current of air. Leven then navigated the onick through the clear patches, swimming through air and crashing lightning toward the top of the gorge.

"He can still fly," Clover pointed out as they were rising.

"If he can work his way out of the air," Leven replied.

Leven had propelled Sam into a thick, complicated maze of air. Clover looked back to see Sam flailing about in slow motion, desperately trying to find his way out of a maze he couldn't see.

"Brilliant," Geth said. "He could be stuck in that air for years."

"I couldn't have done it without you," Leven said.

Clover cleared his throat.

"And you, of course," Leven added.

"Could you see the air?" Geth asked in disbelief.

Leven nodded.

"Amazing."

A gigantic bolt of lightning flashed from below, just missing Leven's feet.

"We should get out of here," Clover said needlessly.

Leven dug his heels into the onick, guiding the beast upward through the maze of air.

Fissure Gorge belched again, helping to push Leven and Clover into the open sky above the gorge.

The cool air felt wonderful on Leven's face.

"Back!" Leven commanded the onick.

The onick instantly agreed, flying them safely to the other side of the gorge and one step closer to Winter.

"You were smart to follow fate," Geth said.

Leven only smiled.

Once above land, the tireless onick glided to the ground, retracted its wings, and began running again at its familiar astonishing speed. Leven couldn't resist patting the beast on its head. Once again it snapped at him.

"Some people never learn," Clover shouted, so as to be heard above the rush of air. "The onicks are loyal to the passengers on their backs, but they don't like to be reminded that they've helped someone out."

"What an amazing creature," Leven yelled back.

With that, Leven tucked his head behind the onick's shoulder blades as they raced toward Morfit.

The afternoon was deepening. Purple sky pushed against the yellow horizon, giving the world of Foo a thick green cast. A milky stream of whisps passed in front of the dipping sun and caused the entire scene to shimmer. Leven thought of Janet and hoped she was all right.

"How much farther?" Leven asked Geth, raising his voice above the swish of the passing air.

"We've got a bit of a ride still," Geth answered. "But we should be able to see the tip of Morfit soon."

"I hope Winter's all right," Leven yelled.

"You know, this all could be a trap," Clover pointed out.

"I'm sure it is," Leven said quickly. "But we'll let fate take care of that."

Geth smiled.

"Besides," Leven added, "we have—"

Leven was unable to finish what he was saying, due to a heavy jolt of energy ripping through the air and striking him squarely in the chest. The impact sizzled, sending pain to every inch of his body and causing the key hanging beneath his shirt to burn his skin. The shock went through Leven and into the onick. The beast's legs were knocked out from under it, and it began to roll, throwing Leven off and even farther down the road.

Dirt and pebbles rained down as they both skidded to a stop. Dazed, Leven coughed and spat as he pushed himself into a sitting position. The poor onick got to its feet, shaken and limping.

Clover tried to comfort Leven as he sat on the ground.

"What happened?" Clover asked.

"I don't . . ."

Again Leven was cut off, an invisible bolt of energy tearing through the air and slamming into his back. Leven was thrown forward ten feet and landed on his face on the ground.

"What's going on?" Geth yelled.

Before Leven could answer, he was struck again, this time directly in the heart. Leven clutched his chest, moaning and writhing in pain on his back on the ground. Clover came to him.

"I don't know what you—" the little sycophant began.

Leven opened his eyes, shutting Clover up. Never had Leven's eyes burned so gold. It looked as if fire were leaping from them.

Clover reared back.

"Wow," Geth whispered.

Although she was not there, all of a sudden Leven could see

Winter. Her face was pressed flat against a dirt floor. There was darkness all around, and she was screaming.

Leven got to his feet and looked in the direction of Morfit. With clenched fists and his eyes ablaze, he began to viciously manipulate fate.

Clover's knees were shaking from the intensity of Leven's actions. The sky pulsated, beating out the light for the day, while Leven's gaze stretched farther into the dusk. Leven raised his hands and closed his eyes.

"Winter," he whispered fiercely, seeing her in his mind. He could also see a tall, hooded, two-sided being standing over her.

Leven held out his arms and directed his energy toward Morfit.

CHAPTER THIRTY-TWO

STOLEN

Jamoon pushed Winter to the ground with his right arm, relishing the delight of being seemingly unbeatable—as long as Winter was without her gift.

"Give up," he hissed.

Winter reached out at Jamoon and scratched his arm until she drew blood. He screamed angrily and let her go. While Jamoon was looking at the scratch marks, the decaying nihils circled around him, waiting for their next order.

With Jamoon distracted, Winter glanced around the room. She spotted the kilve she had once carried. It was leaning up against the wall, and she dashed across the room and grabbed it. In one swift motion she turned and struck Jamoon on the right shoulder with the heavy staff. Jamoon dropped to one knee, and his dark nihils began to screech.

Winter wheeled toward the door. The roven in the corner

stretched its wings, blocking the exit, and the nihils swarmed around her, pecking at her skin with their beaks. The pain drove Winter to her knees.

Jamoon was back up. He parted the nihils and grabbed Winter by one of her pigtails. He pulled and his grip stretched every feature on Winter's face and made it hard for her to breathe.

Jamoon mocked her as she struggled. "Not much of a fighter without your gift," he sneered. "How wonderful it is that now you can die."

"What about the plan?" Winter gasped, hoping to catch Jamoon off guard by being honest.

"What plan?" Jamoon asked, glaring into her green eyes.

"The one you whispered about to me in the ice caves."

"You mean *your* plan?" he asked coolly.

"My plan?" Winter choked.

"You really can't remember, can you?" Jamoon laughed. "Look around you. Doesn't this room mean anything to you?"

Winter looked around, confused. "No."

Jamoon's grip tightened. "You were so different then. Young, but not as young, and so willing to help make Foo a better place. Fool."

"I don't understand," Winter gasped.

"Don't you remember what you did up here? The experiments, the use of metal? You walked right into it. So willing to break the rules in an effort to help the common cog—such an idealist. Those poor souls who have no gift," Jamoon taunted. "And you just wanted to find a way to give them one. That's when you dreamed up this room."

Winter winced as Jamoon pulled even harder on her hair. The nihils chirped sadistically as the candles on the wall increased their flame, brightly lighting the room. Winter looked closer at her surroundings. The walls were white and tiled. Along two of the walls were large ceramic hooks. Beneath the hooks were tables covered in sheets made from white feathers. Behind Jamoon, there was a mechanical-looking contraption.

The machine looked familiar.

"It's such a sad thing when a nit dies," Jamoon went on. "Such a sad, sad thing—a life and a gift gone for good. Fewer dreams can be enhanced in a powerful way. Yet, even when dying nits wish to transfer their gifts, they can't. Or should I say, they *couldn't.*"

"So you're extracting gifts?" Winter gasped.

"Unsuccessfully, until we found you," Jamoon laughed.

Winter began to cry as small bits and pieces of what had actually happened came back to her.

"You had just the right brain to solve such a complex and taboo problem," Jamoon exulted. "You wanted so desperately to help, and Sabine was happy to let you. You figured out how to do everything we needed. With the ability to possess multiple gifts, we could conquer Reality easily. Of course, we needed the gateway to get there, and its destruction was a depressing blow. But, thanks to your *fate* and what remains of Sabine, I believe we have hands working in Reality to rebuild the gateway. There is only one person who can ruin things now."

"The Want?" Winter guessed sadly, fear almost suffocating her.

"That fool," Jamoon hissed angrily. "What good is he to us, now that we can take and, soon, bestow gifts?"

"Then—" Winter stopped herself, suddenly realizing that the one they needed to stop was Leven.

"Who can rebuild the gateway?" Winter asked, sure that Jamoon was bluffing.

"With enough pain and persuasion we are confident Leven and you will show us everything," Jamoon spat. "Of course, you'll be much easier to work with once we've removed that bothersome gift of yours."

Jamoon moved closer to the odd metal machine, dragging Winter with him by her hair.

Winter's heart was thumping like a flat tire on a spinning rim. She looked down and was surprised to see it was still in her chest.

"Leven," she whispered.

"Leven," Jamoon scoffed. "He can't help you now."

Jamoon forced Winter to sit and strapped her right wrist to the machine. Fear was everywhere now, swirling around the room like a sticky twister and mixing with the flapping nihils. Ignoring her whimpering cries, Jamoon strapped down Winter's left wrist. While Winter thrashed and screamed, Jamoon secured her left leg.

But as he reached for her other leg, a thick bolt of blue shot down through the skylight and struck Jamoon in the right shoulder. Jamoon flew across the room and slammed into the wall. He hit it so hard, the wall cracked and broken tiles rained to the floor. Dazed, Jamoon shook his head and weakly tried to stand. With his nihils circling him, ready to inflict further pain on Winter, he looked wildly around the room.

"What was that?" Jamoon demanded.

Winter was silent.

"You'll pay for that," he said, figuring the attack to be a work of Winter. His eyes narrowed in anger. "What was that trick you just pulled?" he demanded.

Winter had no idea what had struck Jamoon, but as she looked fearfully at his angry face, another bolt of blue streaked in from the skylight—this one striking him squarely on the chin. Jamoon was lifted four feet into the air and then dropped to the ground in a heap. Dazed, he looked up from where he had fallen and growled.

The nihils swooped down and began to tear into Winter. As she screamed and thrashed, Jamoon staggered to his feet and lurched over to the machine.

"Let's end your tricks!" Jamoon raged, strapping down her remaining foot.

The birds lifted off of Winter as Jamoon reached over and hit the switch on the side of the machine.

Light flashed and Winter was out.

ii

After having fought with Jamoon from a distance, Leven turned to glance at Clover and Geth. Clover looked like a new bride who has just discovered she has married a monster. His blue eyes were wide with fear, and his leathery little mouth was hanging open.

"What?" Leven asked defensively.

"You were either fighting something," Clover said, "or you were doing some really awkward dance."

"I saw a large cloaked being," Leven explained. "Both halves of him didn't match."

"It was probably Jamoon," Geth deduced. "He's a rant. Rants can't just manipulate a dream and move on. Half of each rant remains in a dreamlike state."

"Jamoon," Leven whispered, looking down at his hands.

Clover shook his head in disbelief. "He had Winter?" he asked.

"Is she okay?" Geth asked.

"No," Leven said. "I couldn't completely control my thoughts. But I think I knocked Jamoon down a couple of times."

Clover's jaw dropped again. "You actually manipulated fate from a distance?"

"I don't know," Leven admitted. "It was more like my actions here affected what was happening there. What does that mean?"

"It means that I have one heck of a burn," Clover said proudly. "As an offing you shouldn't be able to do that. Isn't that right, Geth?"

Geth didn't answer.

"So what *am* I?" Leven asked, talking more to himself than to anyone else. He had felt so different ever since his fight against the Ring of Plague. He could see things more clearly, and it felt as though his heart had expanded to fill his entire body. His eyes were burning gold at the moment, but there was no vision behind them. When he shook his head, the gold remained.

It felt like the first day of summer, when school is finally out and days and days of freedom stretch out before you. It felt like he was somebody else—somebody stronger and unafraid. He couldn't remember ever having been scared or hurt, and he could see hope and possibility in things as insignificant and insecure as himself. He felt as if he were made of putty and someone had shoved their thumb under his ribcage and pushed him taller. Even the horizon looked to be at a different level. He looked at his feet to see if he was wearing platform shoes. He wasn't, but the high-water pants he was sporting were even higher on him.

"What's happened to me?" Leven asked, this time wanting an answer.

"We need to get you to the Want," Geth said, hopping onto Leven's shoulder. "You are definitely Hector's relative."

"First things first," Leven replied. "How are you doing, Geth? Can you hold on? If you're all right, I think we had better go help Winter."

"Don't worry about me," the battered little toothpick said. He could feel himself hardening even more, but he didn't want to admit it. "I think you're right. Winter is the one we need to concentrate on."

Leven tucked Geth behind his ear and jumped back onto the onick. He took his seat behind its shoulder blades and was surprised to find the fit different from before. The broad back felt somehow smaller.

After making sure Clover was also aboard, Leven dug his heels into the onick, and the quick beast took off, racing toward Morfit.

CHAPTER THIRTY-THREE

ECHOES OF THE BLAST

The world is full of people who like to bring people down. I know of at least two. You can probably think of more than that.

Then there are those people who are helpful and constructive and like to reach down and help others up. Those people are way better than the first kind and very much in the minority.

Tim Tuttle was that second kind of person. He had spent his entire life thinking well of others and helping where he could. He had a lovely family, and though his job was menial, he had the brain of a genius.

He also hadn't traveled much, and when he got off the train in Berchtesgaden, Germany, he was blown away by the spectacular scenery. "Who knew Mother Nature was so big on green?" he said in awe.

As the train pulled away, Tim began walking down toward

the Konigsee. It was early morning and there were very few tourists out. A couple of old men were working with brooms up and down the street, cleaning gutters and walkways, and a tiny car passed by, delivering firewood.

As Tim strolled toward the lake, he admired the clean shops and stores along the way. A woman with matted hair and short arms wheeled a case full of bread in front of him on her way to her shop.

"Excuse me," Tim shouted after her.

She turned.

"For sale?" Tim asked, pointing to the bread and holding out some money.

She looked bothered, but not bothered enough to pass up money. Tim bought two small loaves and thanked her in German.

She wasn't all that impressed.

Tim tore into the bread and was so involved in eating it as he arrived at the lake that he almost stepped off the dock and into the water.

He stopped himself just in time. He looked up, and his jaw dropped. His bread fell out of his mouth and onto the ground— instantly four ducks raced for it. The Konigsee was the most beautiful sight Tim had ever seen.

You may have read in books that one spot or another is the most beautiful place on earth. Well, those books are lying, *unless* they are talking about the Konigsee. Surrounded by tall, snow-capped mountains and forests of gorgeous pines, the valley where the Konigsee rests is breathtaking. The green water and the pristine setting would make even Zeus look into the price of real estate there.

"I'm not in Iowa anymore," Tim said honestly.

At the dock Tim purchased a ticket and climbed onto a boat going across the lake. There were only three other tourists on board, so Tim stretched his legs up onto the seats next to him. Halfway across the lake the boat stopped and shut off its engine. A stocky German man in leather shorts stood on the front of the boat and began to play a trumpet. The ring of majestic mountains surrounding the lake created a beautiful echo that accompanied the trumpeter.

Tim couldn't sit still. He stood and turned around, taking in the entire scene. A German boy with a thin mustache and white, freckled skin who helped run the boat noticed the look on Tim's face.

"Spectacular, isn't it?" he said in almost perfect English. There was obviously something about the outfit Tim was wearing that gave away the fact that he was an American.

"It feels like my eyes can't properly describe it to my brain," Tim smiled.

The German boy grinned.

"I'd never heard of this place before," Tim said.

"Most people are more aware that Hitler died nearby," the boy said, sticking his chin out. "Such a beautiful place to be marred by such evil. You are from the States?" he asked, changing the subject.

"Yes, Iowa."

The boy didn't know what Iowa was, but he nodded his head. "Here on business?"

"I think I'm here to see this," Tim said, motioning to the lake and its surroundings. "And, I'm looking for someone—a young boy and girl."

Again the boy smiled. "There are lots of boys and girls that come here."

"It would have been a couple of days ago," Tim clarified.

"I wasn't working," the boy apologized. "I wish I had been. I would not have missed the explosion."

"Explosion?" Tim asked anxiously.

"Booosh," he said with excitement. "It was after sunset, and an explosion went off under the water," he explained. "Some think it was an earthquake, but my mate was here, and said it was no earthquake."

"Was anyone hurt?"

"No," the boy waved. "A number of fish have died. But, I tell you, earthquakes don't usually kill fish."

"Did they investigate?" Tim asked, the hair on the back of his neck standing up again.

"I'm not sure I understand," the boy said.

"Did anyone search underwater, or try to find out what it was?"

"It's pretty hard to see anything under this water," the boy said, referring to the beautiful green color that hid everything below.

Tim looked over the side of the boat and down into the

water. The surface was a milky emerald green. There could have been anything hidden down there.

"The authorities thought it could have been a terrorist, or some trick," the boy went on. "But I know of no reason why someone would want to do that here. Maybe it was Hitler turning over in his grave," he tried to joke.

Tim laughed politely, since he was one of the nice kind of people previously mentioned. He looked down into the water again.

Tim needed to think. He also needed something else to eat.

The boat started back up and continued traveling to the distant side of the lake.

ii

The Munich Germany Airport was as busy as any place Dennis Wood had ever been. People pushed forward like determined mice with no maze and a straight shot to cheese, and the overhead speakers kept shouting instructions in German. The old Dennis would have been intimidated, but the new Dennis was not.

As Dennis walked through the airport, people moved out of his way. He stood tall, stone-faced, and dark. He wore Sabine like a robe over his shoulders, soaking in the blackness with each step he took.

He reached a small glass booth with a large, uniformed man sitting inside. The man's girth was almost more than the glass booth could accommodate, making it look as if the entire thing might burst at any moment. The uniformed man had a short forehead and a wide, moist nose with a sweaty little mustache beneath it.

"Your passport, please," he asked, his jowls jiggling.

Dennis handed him his driver's license. The man looked at it as if it were a joke. As he looked up, however, bits and pieces of Sabine floated like black lint off of Dennis and into the official's ears. Dennis could see the flecks actually moving around in the whites of the man's eyes.

"Business or pleasure, Mister Dennis?" the man asked, his voice sounding as if he were in a slight trance.

"Business," Dennis answered.

The guard looked Dennis up and down. He stared at his bald head. "Your hair color?" he asked, following his routine and not realizing he wasn't holding an actual passport.

"Blond . . . when I have any," Dennis answered.

"And your age?"

"Thirty-one," Dennis sniffed.

"And the business you are on?"

"I'm here to rebuild something," he said, frustrated. "Now can I go?"

"One moment," the guard waved uncomfortably, which was a struggle, seeing how he had so little extra room in his booth. "What is the company you are with?"

Dennis said the only thing he could think of: "Gateway."

"They make a fine computer," the guard sniffed, stamping

the front of Dennis's driver's license as if it were a passport. "Enjoy your stay, Mister Dennis. Next."

He handed Dennis the stamped card.

Dennis walked away fuming. He was tempted to correct the guard about his name, but he let it go—for now. Someday, however, the entire world would get it right and fear the presence and power of Dennis Wood.

iii

Wearing Sabine as a black, tattered robe with an ugly hood, Dennis stepped off the bus in Berchtesgaden. He pushed back the hood, and the October sun danced off his bald head.

"This is it?" Dennis asked, referring to their location.

"It is," his robe hissed.

"I want to see the spot."

Dennis walked with purpose toward the lake. Wearing Sabine had given him great confidence. It had also helped him understand what was happening. As a cloak, Sabine had seeped information into Dennis. The seepage had left dark, tattoolike marks all over Dennis's skin. Sabine had told him of Foo. He had told him of the gateway, and he had promised Dennis great power and endless dreams if he helped Sabine return.

Dennis had never dreamed before, and the mere thought drove him mad with ambition. He trusted Sabine. And he reveled in the blackness that had entered his life. He could see that there would be things to stop him or impede his progress, but none of those things overshadowed the fact that if he held on, Dennis would be able to escape his past and, for the first time in his life, dream powerful dreams.

"How'd he do it?" Dennis asked Sabine as he walked. "How did he build a gateway here? More importantly, how will we?"

"We will work at night," Sabine buzzed. "We must secure materials."

Dennis looked around as he got closer to the lake. He couldn't see anyplace nearby to get the kind of materials they would need. "We'll need a car to get the supplies," Dennis said. "It could take some time."

"We don't have time," Sabine seethed.

Dennis couldn't wait to dream, but he was also thirsty from traveling. He crossed the street and entered a dimly lit gasthaus where a few patrons were drinking and eating fish. The walls were lined with decorative china plates and beer steins. The floorboards were wood and worn from years of thirsty people walking across them. Dennis walked past the tables and booths and took a seat on a stool at the long wooden bar. There was a lone man, wearing a blue baseball cap, sitting on the stool next to him. Dennis waved at the waiter and ordered a drink.

"We shouldn't delay," Sabine hissed silently and directly into Dennis's skin.

"I just need a drink," Dennis whispered aloud. "Don't worry. I'll work as fast as I can," he said irritably.

The man in the ball cap on the neighboring stool heard

Dennis talking and thought he was addressing him.

"Excuse me?" the ball-capped American said nicely. "Were you saying something?"

"No," Dennis snapped. He was about to follow that "No" with something along the lines of, "Mind your own business" or, "Why would I be talking to someone like you?" but Sabine burned into his neck, sending a signal to hold his tongue.

The bartender delivered Dennis's drink, and Dennis took a gigantic swallow and then belched. "Sorry," he said to his neighbor. "I was thirsty."

"No problem," the ball-capped patron said kindly. "Are you from America?"

"Yes," Dennis answered, getting signals from Sabine to play along.

"What state?"

"North Carolina, actually," Dennis answered.

Sabine fluttered and rolled. There was something about the American that made him burn. It was clear that this man had not been to Foo, but it was as if he had been in contact with someone who had. Weary of Dennis's poor communication skills, Sabine decided to take over the conversation.

"Where are *you* from?" Sabine hissed out of Dennis's mouth. Both the American and Dennis looked surprised. "I mean, where are you from?" Sabine said, in a lower and softer tone and with an almost comical voice.

"I'm from Iowa," the American said, looking at Dennis with confusion. "My name's Tim. Tim Tuttle."

Tim stuck out his hand, and Dennis shook it.

"Why are you here?" Sabine said, using Dennis's mouth again.

Tim smiled awkwardly. "I'm looking for a couple of kids," he said.

Tim was the kind of person who usually thought the best of others. Most anyone who sat next to Dennis would have thought him to be a creepy jerk at best. Tim, on the other hand, saw Dennis as just a dim-witted oddball, and felt compelled to talk to him.

"Kids?" Sabine hissed hungrily out of Dennis's mouth.

"Are you okay?" Tim asked, tilting his head to study Dennis's face.

"Fine, fine," Dennis lied. "I've just got a wicked cold," he recovered. Sabine burned through Dennis's skin, commanding him to let Sabine do the talking. "You're looking for kids, you say," Sabine prompted.

"A young girl and boy," Tim said seriously. "But this is the end of the trail at the moment."

"Are they in trouble?" Sabine asked.

"I think so," Tim answered. "But I'm not sure I even know that."

Sabine's pulse quickened. He loved to take advantage of fate when it was working in his favor, and an extra person like Tim would make the work of building a new gateway much easier. Fate was such a fool.

"Leven," Sabine said out of Dennis's lips.

Tim spat his drink out, getting the bartender wet.

"Excuse me?" he said, wiping his mouth. "What did you say?"

"You're looking for Leven and Winter," Sabine said matter-of-factly.

Tim's mouth dropped to the floor, and his eyes gave the decorative plates lining the wall some competition for saucer size. "You know them?" Tim asked.

"I believe we are working for the same thing," Sabine said through Dennis, trying to keep his voice light and as un-sinister-sounding as possible.

"How do you know them?" Tim asked, so excited that he didn't let his great brain take a moment to analyze the bad vibes coming from Dennis.

Dennis stood and motioned for Tim to follow him. "I've got a lot to tell you."

"I can't believe this," Tim said with excitement, following Dennis to a corner booth. "Are they okay?" he asked.

"I believe so," Sabine hissed out of Dennis.

"Thank goodness," Tim said, taking a seat, the smile on his face impossible to suppress. "I've been so worried."

"We've all been worried," Dennis hissed.

Tim was too excited to see the danger sitting right before him.

CHAPTER THIRTY-FOUR

DOOR NUMBER ONE

The onick slowed as the base of Morfit came into view. It was dark by now, but thousands of small, glowing lights twinkled from all over the mountain. Leven could see people and creatures trudging toward the base, carrying rocks of various sizes in their hands. Leven guided the onick behind a row of short, orange-colored trees and hopped off.

"Will it wait for us?" Leven asked Clover, referring to the onick.

"If no one else jumps on its back," Clover answered. "Onicks are loyal only to those who are on top."

"Maybe we should hide it or something," Leven suggested. "It could come in handy later."

Clover was already fishing around in his void. He pulled out a thin wooden jar with a small lever on the top. It looked a bit like an old-fashioned can of aerosol spray. Clover read the label and smiled. "Doesn't expire for another twenty-two years."

He sprayed a shot of air at the onick. The air created what looked like a hole in the poor creature.

"Wow!" Leven said. "What is that stuff?"

"An attempt by the citizens of Cusp to be more like the syco-phants," Clover said haughtily. "It can make you invisible, but it's very sticky and uncomfortable. Plus, it takes hours to wash off. Not to mention the bugs that get stuck in it." Clover tisked. "Everyone wants to be us."

Clover began to spray the onick all over. The poor beast didn't mind because he didn't know what was happening. In a few moments nothing remained visible but a bit of rope tying him to the fantrum tree.

"Hurry," Leven said, as Clover was putting the finishing touches on his masterpiece. "We need to get in there."

"I'm almost done," Clover said, turning toward Leven. As he did so, he accidentally sprayed the lower half of Leven's left arm.

Leven just stared at his lack of limb. His arm looked as though it had been cut off just below the sleeve of his T-shirt.

"Oops," Clover said, just as the can sputtered out the last of its contents.

"Perfect," Leven complained.

"Sorry," Clover tried. "But don't worry. It'll wash off even-tually."

Leven looked down. It was the oddest sensation not to see his arm and hand there. He brought his hand up to his face and touched his nose. As he pulled away he noticed a slight stickiness on his invisible fingertips.

"I'm sure this will help," Leven said sarcastically.

"Mister Sunshine," Clover beamed happily. "That's the attitude."

Leven was tempted to use his invisible hand in an unkind fashion. Instead, he said, "No 'Mister Sunshine.' Let's just find Winter so we can take care of Geth."

Leven stepped away from the fantrum tree and began moving toward Morfit. Clover followed close behind after leaving a vapor stick beneath the tree. He had cracked the vapor stick, and a horrible smell was now lofting through the air. The noxious fumes made Leven light-headed.

"That'll keep people away from our onick."

"I'm not sure I want to go back now," Leven said, pinching his nose with his visible hand. "That's awful."

Clover would have responded, but he was having a hard time breathing himself. Leaves on trees began to droop as small bushes and plants curled up or threw dirt on themselves to escape the stench. Leven and Clover could hear the poor, invisible onick gag, pass out, and fall against the ground. Due to the odor, however, neither ran back to help it. It wasn't until they were a good three hundred feet away that they could safely breathe again.

"I'm not going back there," Leven insisted. "I've never smelled anything that bad before."

"It was a strong stick," Clover agreed. "But the smell will fade."

"Wait a second," Leven said. "Where's Geth? I thought you had him."

"I did," Clover said ashamedly.

"Well, where is he?"

"He was riding on my back," Clover explained. "I was afraid he might blow away. Plus, he started lecturing me about some of the things I've been doing. I'm sorry, but I'm my own person, unless of course you want me not to be."

"Clover, where is Geth?"

"Don't worry, I just put him in my void."

Clover started fishing around in his void for Geth. He pulled out a sticky popsicle stick.

"Nope, that's not him," Clover said. "What if it was? That would be so weird."

Leven shook his head.

Clover put his hand back in the void and pulled out a post-card with the state of Oklahoma drawn on the front.

"Nope."

He pulled out a leaf shaped like a kitten, a plastic spoon whittled into a plastic knife, an apple core, a temporary tattoo of a butterfly, a dry spaghetti noodle, a live moth, and a dead fish before he finally found Geth. Clover pulled him out and held him in his palm.

"Here he is," Clover announced.

Leven had never seen Geth looking frightened before.

"Don't *ever* put me back in there," Geth whispered fiercely. "Ever. Please."

Leven picked up Geth and put him in his shirt pocket. "Sorry."

Geth clung to Leven.

Leven moved to the edge of the trees and near a wide dirt path. He could see a number of people shuffling toward Morfit. Most held stones in their hands and wore robes of some sort. Leven looked down at his pathetic outfit. The flood pants and his torn shirt he had bought in France were about as uncool as anything he had ever seen. Clover had fished another old sneaker out of his void, so Leven now was wearing two shoes, though they didn't match.

"Shouldn't I be wearing a robe or something?" Leven asked.

"We don't have one," Clover pointed out. "But you might want to pick up a rock and look sorry about it," the sycophant instructed.

"A rock?"

"Morfit is built by the stones of everyone's shortcomings," Geth said. "Bringing and leaving rocks frees you of your guilt. Toss a rock and it meshes with the mountain, growing up or out, depending on your throw. Morfit was once a sacred place that had something to do with the power Fissure Gorge produces. Now it's nothing but a huge, dark reminder of how far we've come."

Leven looked up at Morfit, towering high overhead. "So, any rock will do?"

"Any rock," Clover concurred.

Leven bent over and grabbed a large stone from the ground, holding it in his one visible and one invisible hand.

"Wow," Clover said dramatically. "You must have done something awful."

"You said 'any rock,'" Leven pointed out defensively.

"Still," Clover resounded.

Leven ignored Clover and tried to look distraught.

"Are you going to be okay?" Clover whispered.

"You said to act guilty," Leven reminded him.

"Well, you're pretty convincing," Clover said suspiciously. "Now we need to do something about your eyes."

"What about my eyes?" Leven said.

"They're still burning gold," Geth answered.

Scattered about the ground were small puddles of water. Leven leaned over one of the puddles and looked at his reflection. Leven's eyes *were* burning gold, despite the fact that there was no vision in his head. Leven, however, was more taken aback by how much older he looked. The white streak in his hair was brighter and more prominent, and his face looked less like a child's.

"I look—"

"Here," Clover interrupted, rummaging around in his void. "Take this."

Clover handed Leven a black gumball.

"I'm not eating anything you give me out of there, without some explanation."

"That takes some of the fun out of it," Clover said, "but if you must know, it's a Pigment-o."

"And?"

"It should help disguise your eyes."

"How?"

"It changes your eye color," Clover said briskly. "Now take it so we can go find Winter."

"It'll change my eye color?"

Clover crossed his heart.

Leven stuck the black ball into his mouth and chewed. Surprisingly, it tasted like real gum. Leven chewed quickly, stretching and pulling the gum in his mouth.

"So?" Leven asked, wondering when something would actually happen.

"Now blow a bubble," Clover instructed.

Leven blew a great big bubble. The gum pushed out beautifully, creating a perfect sphere. Leven kept blowing and the bubble grew even greater, dwarfing the size of his head.

Leven blew more, and the bubble popped.

Instinctively, Leven closed his eyes as it burst, and when he opened them back up he was surprised to find he wasn't covered in the remains of his popped bubble. Not only was there no trace of gum on his face, but it was no longer in his mouth. Leven looked around on the ground, but there was no sign of any chewed gum. It was as if it had disappeared completely.

"Where'd it go?" Leven asked Clover.

"It didn't go anywhere," Clover said. "As it popped outside it also popped in you."

"Popped in me? So my eyes are black?" Leven asked.

Clover looked closely at Leven. "Yes . . . yes they are."

Leven leaned over the puddle again.

He had thought he looked different *before*. There, staring back at him, was some person with light gray skin, black lips, completely black hair except for one gray streak, black eyes, and black freckles. Leven dropped his rock and lifted his one visible hand to his face, noticing that his fingernails were as black as night. He looked like a poster boy for Goth coal miners.

Geth tried to look sympathetic, but he was still too spooked about spending time in Clover's void. Leven felt his own face and grumbled.

"It wears off," Clover insisted.

"So when you crossed your heart and said it would change my eye color, you left out a few things," Leven accused.

"I was going to say more but, again, where's the fun in that?"

Leven shook his head.

"I could have given you pink," Clover said defensively.

"I suppose I should be happy then," Leven joked.

"See, Mister—"

Leven stopped Clover with his dark eyes.

"Right," Clover said. "Maybe we should just go."

Leven smiled weakly, retrieved his stone, and began walking forward. They soon joined others on the path who were carrying stones and making their way closer to the mountain of Morfit.

The wall surrounding Morfit was impressive in size but not in condition. Everything in Foo looked as if it had been built hundreds of years ago and had been crumbling ever since.

The gate Leven was moving toward was manned by four tall rants in orange robes. One was currently turned away from the travelers coming in. The way he was shaking and buzzing, it was obvious he was taking on the shape of a dream and trying to hide from the eyes of others looking on. Leven stared at all the rants in amazement.

"Business, or the result of pleasure?" one of the rants asked Leven.

"I've got a stone to place," Leven answered.

The rant grabbed Leven by the shoulder. "Where's your arm?" he growled, glancing at Leven's invisible limb.

"I lost it in Reality," Leven answered.

The rant looked at Leven's dark eyes and skin, then impatiently waved him through the gate.

Leven stayed silent until he was well within the walls.

"So, they *are* looking for you," Clover whispered from the top of Leven's head. "You're lucky I thought to spray your arm."

"I'm pretty fortunate," Leven joked, slipping close to the base of Morfit and moving cautiously around those souls who were dropping or throwing their stones. The air was filled with the click and scratch of clattering rocks.

Morfit was as imposing as any mountain, town, structure, or person Leven had ever seen. He would have felt less threatened with Terry standing over him, tearing into him as he had so many times before. Up close, Morfit was like a jigsaw puzzle that had been haphazardly put together—rocks and bricks and materials of all kinds had been fused into one massive maze and mountain.

Around its base was a fringe of thick, dry moss and steep trails leading upward that penitents could climb to deposit their stones. The sound of clicking rock was everywhere, along with harsh laughter and agonized screaming.

"I'm not sure I like this place," Leven whispered.

"The wise stay away," Geth whispered back.

The dark night sky seemed to mesh with Morfit, but the burning lights scattered across it gave its shape some definition. From where Leven stood he could see thousands of dimly lit holes and dwellings stacked upon each other. In the circle of each light there were people or beings, talking or fighting or eating.

"Why would anyone come here?" Leven whispered. "It feels horrible."

"Morfit has long been a place of deceit and blackness," Geth answered. "Since the early days of Foo, people have gathered here to argue about the fairness of such a place as Foo and how they can govern a world with so much instability and possibility.

Morfit is also a safe place to get away from dreams, seeing how they can't penetrate the mountain. Rants stay in their current form when they step in. Some rants stay here for years because they like the other half they are currently entertaining."

A stone door flew open near the base of Morfit, and a thick swarm of whisps streamed out, giving the appearance that Morfit was exhaling. The whisp swarm dipped and swooped into the dark night and disappeared.

The stone door snapped shut.

Leven could see a row of small shops, each offering to sell bags for carrying stones. Next to the shops were mounds and mounds of straw for sale, to feed the assorted beasts that transported so many to Morfit.

"The rest of Foo is so beautiful," Leven whispered. "This place even *feels* ugly."

"The dark dreams of men and those who controlled Sabine and probably now control Jamoon have great strength in Morfit," Geth said.

"Who controlled Sabine?" Leven asked.

Geth didn't answer, due to a large group of rants coming their way. The rants all wore robes and were holding kilves that glimmered under the moonlight.

"We have to get out of here," Geth whispered. "Don't let them see you."

Leven spotted a small door. Above the door was a stone head with stone wings behind it. The stone head had a glowing ring in its mouth. Leven stepped up to the door and pushed it open with his hands—his invisible one leaving a sticky residue on the door. Inside was a narrow, dark hallway that sloped upward. Lining the wall were yellow claws, each holding a blue-burning candle. The lights ran along both sides and stretched on for what looked like miles. Leven felt like a plane coming in for a landing.

"Where are we going?" Clover whispered.

"Go up," Geth said.

The lights on the wall seemed to draw them in. Leven looked down and could see bits of feather and bone littering the dirt floor. The walls of the chamber were constructed of uneven stone, with the claw-held candles protruding every ten feet. In each claw was a fat, blue, glowing candle that whispered in insecure fear as it burned.

"Look away."

"Let me burn."

"I'm trying."

Leven ignored them all, moving deeper into the belly of Morfit. There were no doors or windows or alternate chambers. Leven turned and realized that the candles gave the illusion of multiple directions. After he had gone a few feet, Leven had no idea where he had come from or where he was going. And, most distressingly, he could no longer feel the pull of Winter's fear.

"This isn't right," Leven whispered to Clover.

"That's true, we're going left."

"No, something is foul."

"Sorry," Clover apologized. "I may have held onto the vapor stick a little bit longer than I should have."

Leven wasn't listening. He turned and began to make his way in the other direction. The candles were singing a different tune now.

"Wrong way," they mocked.

"Turn around."

"Lost?"

Leven spun and looked behind him. It appeared to be one long tunnel, stretching endlessly in both directions. But he couldn't tell if he was heading out or in. Even the floor was confusing. It seemed to slant in both directions.

Clover sounded nervous. "Just pick a direction and go."

The candle flames had turned vicious now, calling out names so unpleasant it would be wrong to repeat them here.

"Run!" Clover yelled.

Leven took off running in the direction he had committed to, not knowing whether he was heading in or out.

As Leven ran past them, the candles began spitting small wads of blue flame at Leven. He felt one land in his hair. Clover yelped in alarm, appeared, and began violently slapping Leven's head in an effort to put out the flame. The candles were shooting so many little torches around, it looked as though Leven were running through a shower of fireworks. A ball of flame fell into his right front pocket and started his pants on fire. Leven beat on his pocket and put the flame out.

"We're not going to make it," Leven screamed.

"Make it *where*?" Clover asked, so confused by what was going on and where they were heading he couldn't think straight. "I think I'm going to be sick."

Leven thought that would add perfectly to the situation. The language coming out of the candles was now so vulgar that Clover was tempted to stop and ask them if their mothers knew they spoke like that. But seeing how candles don't have mothers, and Clover was scared for Leven's life and trying to hold his lunch down, he refrained.

"There's a door!" Leven yelled.

They reached a large, wooden door; it swung open upon Leven's touch. He ran through it, turned, and slammed it, pushing his back up against it, shutting out the candles and their taunting. A few sparks sputtered through the keyhole and then died down.

"What was that?" Leven asked, breathing hard.

"Some people's candles," Clover huffed disgustedly, trying to catch his own breath.

Leven looked around the room they were now in. It was hexagon-shaped with a high, domed ceiling. The walls were covered with large rugs that kept changing the patterns that were woven into them. In the center of the room was a huge, open fire pit. The flame was silent, but flickered gracefully in the warm air. Small furry balls that looked like circular mice rolled around on the floor, to and from the fire, stealing tiny bits of flame, which they carried out of the room through small holes at the base of the walls.

"Is this a good room or a bad room?" Leven asked Clover.

"I don't know, but the fire has better manners than the stuff we just left," Clover responded.

"Well, I'll tell you something I'm *not* doing," Leven breathed. "I'm not going back out that door."

Leven stepped away from the door and began to walk around the room, looking closely at the floor and walls. The small furry balls scattered from in front of him. He looked up and could see an opening where the smoke from the fire was able to rise and exit the room. He couldn't see another door, but the rugs were covering a fair portion of the walls of the six-sided room.

Clover jumped from off Leven's head and onto the floor.

"Who lives in Morfit?" Leven asked, as he examined the rugs.

"Anyone who has the stomach for it," Geth answered. "And a lot of children."

"Children?" Leven questioned.

"Of course," Geth said. "Children who step into Foo had better hope they enter in Niteon or near Cusp. If not, they are usually rounded up and brought here for education. Some of the highest levels of Morfit are used for keeping and teaching children."

"What are they taught?" Leven asked, the idea of children living in such a dark place feeling perverse and depressing.

"They are taught to manipulate dreams in a way that is pleasing to those in power."

"Like Sabine?" Leven asked.

"Exactly," Geth said.

"Do you think we could fit through that hole?" Leven asked, pointing toward the opening in the ceiling.

Clover smiled.

He climbed into Leven's hands and pulled his hairy ears

down over his head, making it look as though he were wearing a swim cap.

"What are you doing?" Leven smiled.

"Throw me," Clover said, nodding upward.

"I was thinking of tying these rugs together and climbing out," Leven explained.

"There isn't time," Clover insisted. "Besides, how would you tie them together? Now, throw me."

Leven shrugged and held Clover in his two hands that looked like one. Leven pumped his arms and threw Clover as hard as he could up toward the opening. Clover missed the hole by at least three feet, slamming his head against the ceiling and falling back to the floor with a thud.

Leven hurried to his side and kneeled down next to him. "I am so sorry," he said, picking Clover up.

"Don't worry about it, Winter," Clover slurred, calling Leven the wrong name while looking at him. "Hey, did you always have stars flying around your head?" he asked dizzily.

"Great," Leven said, shifting Clover in his hands. "Let's try to tie the rugs."

"No," Clover waved, shaking the cobwebs out of his head. "Maybe I'll see if the fire is strong enough to climb."

"Climb?"

Clover leapt up and jumped above the fire. Instead of falling, he hovered in mid-smoke. Then he grabbed onto the smoke and began to climb the warm air. There was barely enough smoke to hold Clover, but he eventually made it all the way to the hole.

"Why didn't you do that in the first place?" Leven yelled up.

"I didn't think the fire was strong enough to hold me," Clover yelled back.

"Should I try to climb it?" Leven asked.

"No, you're too heavy. Let me find something to throw down to you."

Leven waited a few minutes before he heard the sound of something loud scraping against the ceiling. A few moments later there was a large stick being lowered down. The wooden pole was long, with thick, twisted, bulging knots on it every two feet. It was cold and wet, but long enough to reach from the floor to the ceiling.

Leven wasted no time scaling the stick and climbing up through the hole. It reminded him of the stiff ropes he'd been forced to climb in gym class.

"Good job," Geth said as he reached the top.

"Where'd you find that stick?" Leven asked as he stood.

"It was over behind that rock partition," Clover explained. "I think they use it to push things through their pipes."

Leven wished he hadn't asked.

"Let's go," Leven said, reaching out for Clover.

Clover looked at Leven's hands and ewwed. "No offense," Clover said, hopping onto Leven's back.

"None taken," Leven replied, wiping his damp hands on his high-water pants.

"Where to now?" Clover asked.

"Up," Leven answered.

CHAPTER THIRTY-FIVE

THE FUEL OF FEELINGS

Leven climbed the stairs three at a time. He could feel the pull of Winter again; she was somewhere up above them.

Leven climbed the stairs four at a time.

He reached another floor and ran down a hallway with open arches toward another flight of stairs.

"Do you know this place?" Leven asked Geth, the lighter streak in his hair glowing from the moonlight that seeped through the arched window.

"Yes," Geth said. "Behind that wall is a staircase. They must have Winter in the Want's room at the top. But walk softly—the council room for the Sochemists is at the head of the stairs."

"The Sochemists?" Leven asked.

"They do nothing but interpret and argue over information any Lore Coil might still be passing. They never agree on the warped and incomplete things they hear, but Foo takes their interpretations seriously."

Leven moved down the open hallway and toward the stairs. Soon he could hear voices coming from the room next to them.

"I'm telling you. He is alive and well," a voice yelled.

"Ridiculous," a different voice yelled back.

A third voice responded loudly, "The coil said nothing about him being well. Maybe you should open your ears next time, Fadium."

"Oh, you haven't heard a coil correctly in years!" he argued back.

Leven tiptoed past the door to the Sochemists' room and then began running up the stairs, taking them three at a time. After the equivalent of five floors the stairwell ended, opening into a small alcove off a long hall. The alcove was dimly lit with candles that hummed softly, and the walls were lined with large paintings depicting the first age of Foo. Leven looked at the pictures and could feel emotion over each scene.

"It was a dark time," Geth said, sensing his interest in a picture of a large group of men and beasts gathered on a field.

"I can see metal," Leven said, touching the picture. He withdrew his hand quickly, not liking the uneasy feelings the painting generated.

"Of course," Geth said, "before the great battles, metal was widely used. Now metal only exists in dreams or on the Thirteen Stones."

Leven moved farther down the hall and stopped at a gigantic

mural that depicted a great battle. All the combatants were depicted wearing blindfolds. Leven touched the mural and shuddered from the pain it produced. He pulled his hands away.

"They fought blindfolded so that the killing wasn't intentional and death could occur," Geth explained softly. "Those days were as dark as the ones we have yet to go through."

The candles began to weep.

There were paintings of the mangled bodies of Eggmen scattered along the shores of the Lime Sea. Next to that picture was one of the Waves of the Lime Sea retreating to guard Alder.

"Is there any hope?" Leven asked reverently.

"Of course," Geth insisted. "There must be for you and Winter—for all those around us, and for those in Reality. Few understand how connected we all are, or how our happiness comes as much from the experiences of others as it does from our own."

Leven continued to move down the hall. He wanted to run away, but the paintings seemed to draw him in.

"What is this place we are standing in now?" he asked.

"A forgotten arm of the school," Geth said with disgust. "For many years they taught history here. Now it is nothing but an unused museum of things we would like to forget, but will soon remember as we do them all over again. Winter was taught here."

"She was?"

"Sabine himself picked her to lead his noble cause," Geth said sarcastically. "I now believe that he tricked her into finding a way to steal gifts."

"Jamoon can steal gifts?"

"That's what Sabine was trying to do when I was put into a seed," Geth said. "From what I could make of the Lore Coil, they were successful."

Leven came to a stone staircase. The stairs were so infrequently used that they moaned beneath his weight as he climbed them.

Leven stopped and closed his eyes. He turned to Geth and shook his head. "I've been feeling Winter's fear pulling me closer," he said. "Now I can feel nothing."

"Let's hope we're not too late," was Geth's only reply.

Things didn't feel all that hopeful.

CHAPTER THIRTY-SIX

OPENING YOUR EYES

Leven was spent. His short time in Foo had been exhausting. And now he had climbed so many stairs his legs were burning with pain. The path to the top of Morfit was winding, dark, and endless.

Outside, a strong wind had begun to howl in and around the mountain.

Morfit rumbled.

"What's that noise?" Leven asked.

"It's getting ready to rain," Clover answered.

Lightning flashed outside and tiny bits of white light glimmered, for an instant making the room look like a disco. Two seconds later, thunder boomed.

Thunder in Reality is pretty straightforward—it grumbles and fades. In Foo, however, the thunder roars awful and insulting words.

"Did it say something?" Leven asked.

"Just ignore it," Clover said.

Lightning flashed again, and thunder roared its vulgar response.

"That's harsh," Leven said, having heard something in relation to his IQ. "Is it talking to me?"

"Everyone hears something different," Clover said. "Keep going."

"What do you hear?" Leven asked.

"Oh, it loves to call me fat," Clover mocked. "It knows that bothers me."

More lightning and thunder.

"Hey, I'm the perfect weight for my height!" Clover yelled back.

"I thought you said to ignore it," Leven said, though the thunder was making him feel less than capable himself by commenting on his complexion.

Clover grunted.

"How much higher?" Leven asked. "And where is everyone? We haven't passed a soul."

"Nobody climbs this high," Clover shivered. "Bad things happen at the top of Morfit."

"Bad things?"

"Unspeakable things," Geth added.

Lightning struck again and thunder sounded.

"Oh, yeah?" Clover hollered, shaking his fist. "Say that to my face!"

"What kind of unspeakable things?" Leven asked, genuinely

concerned. "I mean, it might be a good idea to know what we're walking into."

"I've heard they've found a way to dispose of people," Clover said. "It's even rumored that they know the secret of sycophants."

"What secret?" Leven asked.

"How to get rid of us," Clover shivered.

"I thought nobody knew—" Leven stopped talking so as to better read what he was seeing. Up the stairs, a few feet from where he stood, was a closed door with weak, white light spilling out from underneath it.

"That's it," Geth whispered weakly. "The White Room."

Lightning flashed, followed by another wave of rude thunder.

"I'm not sure I can do this," Leven admitted, feeling tired and spent. "What if Winter's . . ."

"Don't even think it," Geth said. "You can do this. Foo needs you. You'll soon understand that the future belongs to those who believe in the beauty and power of their dreams. This is for so much more than you can now comprehend. Remember that feeling of fate."

Clover patted Leven on the shoulder.

Leven closed his eyes. He had changed, and he just needed his mind to believe it. Moving up the last couple of stairs, Leven reached out and took hold of the door handle. He held it in his hand for just a moment and then pulled it down.

Without a sound, the door slowly opened. Inside the room, a cylinder of bright light shone from the ceiling. Within it, lying on the floor, was a girl with red hair.

Leven blinked and looked more carefully. Then he leapt into the room and ran to her side. He knelt beside Winter and lifted her head into his lap with his invisible hand. She was covered in blood, and her clothes had been ripped to shreds.

"Winter," Leven whispered. "Winter."

She didn't respond.

"Is she alive?" Clover asked.

"She's breathing," Leven said, pushing her hair back from her face. "But just barely."

Leven glanced around the room. The walls and ceiling were lined with white tile. There were hooks along the walls and small, feather-covered tables beneath the hooks. In the middle of the room sat a machine. It was large, with a black leather seat and tall, thin metal handles that turned out like scythes. A thick chain lay near a footrest, and there were iron clamps where someone's hands would go. A blue splotch of light crawled up and down the handlebars like a fat caterpillar. Next to the machine stood a black-robed being Leven had never actually met, but one he had fought before.

Jamoon said nothing but simply stood there, using his lone right eye to glare at Leven. Next to Jamoon was the large roven that had helped destroy Amelia's house. The roven was still mostly hairless, although there were spots where new hair was beginning to grow in.

Leven wasn't happy to see either of them, but he was even less thrilled about what else was in the room.

Up near the ceiling, thousands of black nihils were circling.

Their beaks were silent, but their wings rustled ominously.

Leven's body began to burn with anger. He gently lowered Winter to the floor and stood tall. He no longer felt fourteen. He felt as though he had lived two lifetimes in the short while he had spent in Foo. He looked to be missing an arm, but he felt complete. He felt like he was back in school, confronting the bullies—only this time he faced something much more sinister.

"Look how ripped my abs are," Jamoon's body-building side bragged.

Jamoon sneered at his own left side and pulled his robe closed.

"What have you done to Winter?" Leven demanded.

Jamoon cackled. "It seems she was stronger than I had anticipated. She's alive—for the moment. Something I won't be able to say about you soon."

Jamoon gestured, and the nihils descended violently upon Leven. They pressed him to the ground, pecking at his closed eyes and body. Leven yelled, trying to swat them off, but there were too many to resist. Geth worked himself out of Leven's pocket and tried to skewer the nihils with his pointed head. But before he could do so, one of the nihils clamped its beak down on Geth. It shook him violently, then rose from the fluttering pile and flapped to Jamoon.

Jamoon smiled, reaching out to pinch Geth between his fingers.

"Enough!" Jamoon ordered his birds. "I have what I want."

The nihils stopped fluttering and pecking but continued to

hold Leven down with their tiny talons. Leven looked at Jamoon.

"The great Geth," Jamoon laughed, holding Geth in front of his face. "Your fate has certainly put you in a pathetic state."

"You know nothing of fate," Geth said calmly, feeling the final bits of his small body hardening. "You can't win."

"Can't I?" Jamoon seethed.

"Give him back," Leven demanded. "I'm the one you want."

Jamoon looked at Leven and dropped Geth to the floor. Before Leven could even register what was happening, Jamoon lifted his right leg and brought the heel of his boot down hard on Geth.

"No!" Leven screamed, willing his gift to come to him so he could do something. "Leave him alone!"

The nihils were still holding Leven down.

"How sweet," Jamoon hissed. "How touching. You care for a toothpick. We will find a way to merge Foo and we will take the gifts of every nit to use as we please in Reality. And there is nothing Geth"—Jamoon stomped his foot again—"or you can do about it. The dreams of mankind may die, but ours will be fulfilled."

Jamoon's birds closed around Leven's neck and squeezed.

Jamoon raised his foot and slammed it down again. Geth screamed out. Leven fought against the nihils' hold, but there were too many of them.

"Good-bye, Geth," Jamoon chortled. "As for you, Leven, you have no power in this room. Your gift is useless here. And soon, we will have it permanently. It appears that Winter was the perfect draw."

Thunder struck.

Leven's head felt full of tar, every thought sticking to the next. Leven had understood Jamoon's taunt about him having no gift in this room, but he could feel his abilities percolating beneath his skin and about to erupt.

Jamoon moved toward Leven. He waved the nihils out of the way and yanked Leven to his feet, then dragged him toward the machine in the middle of the room.

Winter stirred. Her eyes blinked as she lay on the floor and watched what was happening.

"No," she whispered. "Clover, are you here?"

Clover appeared on the floor by Winter. He tried to comfort her by petting her hair as she watched Leven being hauled away.

"Pull the switch," she whispered to Clover, "before Jamoon ties him in the seat."

Clover glanced at the machine and spotted the large blue switch on the side. He had no idea what it did, but he wasn't about to second-guess Winter. He jumped up and raced across the room. Jamoon was about to place Leven into the machine's seat when Clover reached the switch and hit it as hard as he could.

There was a loud pop, and a jolt of energy blew into the wall, cracking a large section of tile. Light rained down like confetti, swirling around the machine. In the unexpected flash, Jamoon let go of Leven and staggered back as wind began to push in through the broken tile.

Clover appeared, smiling as the air whipped past him. Jamoon spotted him and hit him with the backside of his right hand, sending Clover flying into the wall.

"No!" Leven yelled.

Leven closed his eyes and let fate settle over him. He then looked up, his eyes beginning to burn.

"It's about time," he said to himself.

His body shook and his muscles rolled, like a monstrous wave rising up from the sea to crash on a shore. Leven looked down at the one hand that wasn't invisible. His gray skin and black fingernails on his visible arm were trembling like coins on an active train track. Light shot from his fingertips and burst from his skin. The light in his eyes began to swirl like a tornado of fire, dispelling the black brought on by Clover's Pigment-o and shining across the room like spotlights.

Leven turned and moved toward Jamoon, and Jamoon gasped at Leven's glowing eyes.

"Your gift works?" he hissed. "Impossible!"

"Impossible is not a word," Leven said, echoing Geth's frequent saying.

Leven pointed his right hand at the cowering Jamoon, and light flashed from his fingers, striking Jamoon in his chest and hurling him across the room into the far wall.

Leven stared in disbelief at his own hands, surprised at what he could do. Then, remembering Amelia, he turned his attention to the roven. The great bird screeched and spread its mighty wings. It quickly shed the small amount of hair on its body, which fell to the floor and gathered itself into a dirty mass that surged through the air at Leven. Leven let his eyes burn, staring intensely at the hair as it rushed toward him. Every strand caught fire under his gaze, creating a fiery net that disintegrated in a shower of sparks.

Ashamed, the roven covered its naked body with its wings and turned away.

The nihils screamed and swooped wildly above everyone.

Leven closed his eyes and began to manipulate and draw in any existing wind he could envision. Air raced in through the hole in the ceiling and the crack in the wall, filling the room with noise and swirling currents, which suddenly reversed themselves, rushing back through the hole, creating a giant vacuum.

Leven opened his eyes to see Jamoon and his roven clinging desperately to anything that would hold them down. But the suction was too strong. It dragged Jamoon across the floor as the roven dug in with its claws and remained standing in shame in the shadows.

With a glance, Leven directed the wind away from Winter as she lay there nearly lifeless on the floor.

The vacuum gathered the nihils into the center of the room, sucking them into a swirling mass, suspended above the floor.

Satisfied that he had them under control, Leven stood in front of them as the terrible wind held them there.

Leven lifted his hands and stared at the decaying birds in awe. He had come a long way from the trailer park in Burnt Culvert. He was also a different person from the one who had stepped through the gateway with such doubt and lack of confidence. He finally understood Geth's insistence that "Impossible is not a word."

The wind tore in and out of the room, morphing and manipulating the nihils until their blackness took on a new form. The ragged form of Sabine stared at Leven with its tiny white eyes, the wind still holding it captive.

"Leven," the dead black mass hissed. "Foolish boy."

Leven's eyes burned.

The light was too great; the blackness that was Sabine seethed and writhed as the glory of Leven's stare caused him to wither and shrink. Leven closed his eyes and then opened them quickly. A fantastic flash of light shot out, exposing every inch of the room and rippling out into Foo.

There was one final, horrific scream, interrupted by a loud pop as the nihils and who they really were vanished for good.

On the far side of the room, Jamoon worked himself to his feet.

"You have ruined everything," he screamed. "You have stolen our chance to be whole."

"You're wrong," Leven said calmly, closing his eyes to suck the wind back out of the room.

Jamoon struggled to keep himself from being lifted off the floor. It was no use. Debris swirled around the room like a whirlwind, and like a black spaghetti noodle, Jamoon was suddenly sucked up through the opening.

"Leven . . ." he screamed one final time. "I've only got two percent body fat," his left side added.

The wind and lightning were beating against the tower. Leven could feel the walls vibrating and the floor swaying. It felt as though the top of Morfit wouldn't hold for much longer.

Leven hurried to Winter and lifted her up. She leaned against him, struggling for breath, but finally spoke. For some odd reason he envisioned her saying his name. Instead she whispered, "Geth."

Leven looked around frantically, worried that the poor toothpick had been swept up by the wind.

"Don't worry," Clover hollered, appearing on the left of Winter. "I picked up Toothpick as soon as I could." Clover opened his right hand to reveal Geth lying there. He wasn't moving, but Leven didn't have time to do more than grab Geth and stick him to the still-tacky skin of his invisible arm.

"Thank you, Clover," Winter whispered, smiling weakly. "I'm glad you're okay."

"Frozen," Clover smiled back, giving her another nickname. "I'm fine. Jamoon can't really harm me."

The tower groaned and rocked under the battering of the howling wind.

Leven cast a warning eye on Jamoon's roven and gestured for him to come. The shame-filled bird screeched, remaining right where it was.

"They're not like the onicks," Clover yelled above the noise of the storm. "He's loyal to Jamoon even though he's gone."

Leven looked around frantically as if there might be another solution to their dilemma.

"We have to get Geth to the turrets now!" Leven hollered. "If not, it will be too late for him!"

Clover shrugged his shoulders and strode across the room

toward the roven. The roven looked down at Clover and cocked its head in confusion. Clover swung his right foot and kicked the roven as hard as he could in the leg. The surprised beast opened its beak and screeched. It was just the reaction Clover was hoping for.

Clover leaped up and crammed himself into the giant beast's mouth. The roven choked and staggered around as Clover worked his way down its throat. In a few seconds Clover had taken some control of the roven's body. He walked awkwardly over to Leven.

"Are you sure about this?" Leven yelled.

The Cloven nodded.

Leven hoisted Winter onto the roven's back, then climbed up behind her. He wrapped his legs under the belly of the bird and held onto Winter.

"Fly!" Leven yelled.

The Cloven leaped from the floor and up through the sky-light, out into the dark and stormy sky.

Leven held Winter tight, and she turned her head to him. "Destroy the tower," she said weakly.

"What?" Leven screamed.

"Destroy the tower," she repeated, and fell unconscious again.

Leven looked back at the tower. Knowing that Winter probably wouldn't ask him to do something just for fun, he concentrated his thoughts, manipulating all the wind in the area to gather at this exact spot. He opened his eyes and the wind obeyed, hurtling like a giant wave toward Morfit. The tower swayed but didn't fall.

Still determined, Leven thought of his life in Reality and of the time he had chased two bullies away by manipulating lightning. Leven looked at all the light in the sky and closed his eyes to focus its force. When he opened his eyes, lightning converged from every direction, every bolt simultaneously striking the tower.

That did the trick.

The tower exploded, sending a shower of rocks and debris hundreds of feet into the air.

The Cloven screeched.

"Fly!" Leven hollered again.

The beast flapped its great wings, soaring ever higher.

Leven pulled Geth from off of his sticky arm and looked at his friend in his hand.

"Geth," Leven screamed.

Geth's mouth moved slightly, and Leven leaned in to hear what he was trying to say.

"You did it," Geth gasped.

"I'm not done yet," Leven said, tucking Geth into his pocket and commanding Clover to pick up his speed.

Clover threaded his way through the rain and lightning, his wings beating hard against the stormy air. Winter stirred, but remained out cold as Leven closed his eyes and attempted to see the future. He wanted to see if Geth would survive until they could get him to the flame. He wanted to know if Winter would be okay and where they would all be tomorrow and if they would be safe. But all he could see was confusion and rain playing to the sound of insulting thunder.

Clover made a sharp turn and sped up. As he did so, the key Leven had had tied on a leather string around his neck flew out of his shirt collar. Leven caught it and pushed it back into his shirt as quickly as he could.

Clover put the roven into a steep, diving turn. As he did so, the clouds opened up, and Leven caught a glimpse of Fissure Gorge far below them. The bottom of the gorge looked a million miles away.

In the distance Leven could also see the flames from the turrets.

"Faster!" Leven ordered.

The Cloven beat its mighty wings, then tucked them in, aiming for the pillar of flame.

As they drew closer, Leven could see that the fire was burning in the center of a formation of twelve stone turrets. Each turret was at least fifty feet high and covered with thick purple vines. Near the top of each tower was an opening big enough for a person to stand in, and the fire caused the inner side of each turret to glow orange. Surrounding the turrets was a large circular river. In the far distance, Leven could see the gatehouse and the fence he had slept near.

"Hold on, Geth," Leven said. "We're going down."

If there was a trace of life left in Geth, it didn't show. His features were as still as petrified wood. Leven wouldn't have it; clenching Geth in his palm, he hollered at Clover to fly into the flame.

Clover did as he was told.

The Cloven's giant wings glowed as he entered and hovered in the flame. Leven secured Winter under the braided harness and then he dropped off the beast, with Geth in his palm, down into the fire.

Clover flew off, leaving Leven hovering hundreds of feet above the ground, held up by the strength of the flame.

The fire licked at him, but it did not burn. Leven opened his palm just enough to see Geth.

"You can't die!" Leven yelled. "You are a lithen, and the last heir to Foo. You are Geth," Leven screamed. "You can't die. I need you!"

Leven let go of Geth and watched as he seemed to float in the flame. In a moment the fire caught onto him and ignited his whole body. Leven was tempted to reach out and grab Geth back, but he knew that this was the only chance.

In a few seconds Geth was gone, nothing but light ashes drifting down through the flame.

Leven closed his eyes and let the fire wrap around him and lower him closer to the ground. Leven was descending, as if in a fiery elevator. Remarkably, there was heat, but he didn't burn, and as he got closer to the heart of the flame, it seemed to thicken and absorb his fall. In a few moments Leven was low enough to jump from the flame to the ground.

He stood to the side and watched as the flame slowly diminished and was finally sucked with a swoosh back into the soil until another day. All that remained was a pile of white-hot coals.

There was no Geth.

Leven was pulled from his thoughts by the screams and cries of Clover in the form of a roven. He landed near Leven, and Winter weakly slid off his back and into Leven's arms. Leven held her, propping her up.

"Where's Geth?" she asked sadly, looking at Leven as if she had never seen him before.

"The fire consumed him," Leven said, confused. "Is that what's supposed to happen?"

Winter blinked, barely able to stand. Leven closed his glowing eyes and let the feeling of hope and possibility that Geth had always preached settle over him. Leven's mind was strangely calm. He somehow felt this was a beginning, not an end.

The Cloven screeched, and Leven opened his eyes.

A cluster of red, glowing embers was drifting down through the last wisps of rising smoke.

Leven and Winter stepped back and watched as the embers settled onto the coals, which began to stir and swirl. There was a flash of light, and as it dimmed, Leven could see shapes forming. There were feet and legs and suddenly there were arms. The light returned, shimmering around the body as it came into complete form.

There, standing in the coals, was a man.

"Geth?" Leven whispered, amazed that what he now saw had once been a toothpick.

Geth stepped from the coals and dusted himself off.

Geth was taller than Leven by a foot, and he was smiling

warmly. His blue eyes positively glowed with life. He was wearing a dark green robe over a black suit of leather, and his hair was dark blond and long.

Leven had never seen a more intimidating being. Though

Geth was a man, *beautiful* was the word that came to mind.

"Geth," Winter whispered.

"This feels a lot better," Geth smiled. "Much, much better."

He stepped closer and took both Leven and Winter in his arms.

"You did it," Geth said.

Winter was crying, Leven was trying not to, and Geth was lifting them both, his heart filled with hope again.

Clover tried to walk the roven closer, but he was losing control of the beast's body. Clover popped his head out of the roven's mouth and smiled at Geth.

"You're taller than I remembered," Clover said.

The roven coughed, propelling Clover out of its mouth and onto the ground. The angry beast shook its ugly head, screeched defiantly, and then flew away just as the ground below Leven, Geth, and Winter began to tremble and roll.

The sound of rushing water and splintering wood filled the air. In the darkness, buildings began to rise from the earth all around them. Small homes and shops popped up from the ground like structural mushrooms.

Leven took Winter's hand and steadied himself as the soil folded open and walls formed around them. A ceiling closed itself over all of them, and an old woman was there standing by an oven.

"What's happening?" Leven asked.

"The flame is restoring all that was lost," Geth said. "In a matter of minutes the fight for Foo will be closer to where it was before Sabine cursed me. What you see now is the City of Geth and all who occupied it at the time of Sabine's curse."

"The City of Geth?" Leven said proudly.

Geth just smiled, while through the windows Leven could see home after home popping back up. Leven's heart swelled so large he was afraid it was going to burst and mess up the whole scene. He looked at Winter and saw she was crying.

"Unbelievable," he said, smiling.

Winter could barely stand, but she leaned on Leven and smiled back. She couldn't believe how different Leven looked. He was taller, and looked at least a couple of years older.

Windows and walls continued to form around them as the City of Geth worked its way back to what it once was. People popped up from nowhere, unaware that they had been trapped in a static state. The old woman by the oven simply continued cooking, oblivious to any memory of having been anywhere but right there over the last while.

Geth led Leven, Winter, and Clover out of the house that had formed around them and down to the road. Legions of regal-looking soldiers marched in the streets.

"Amazing," Winter said. "Look, Lev, everything's so lovely."

A bright sun was just rising, illuminating trees and gardens of beautiful flowers, sparkling with morning dew. Cobblestone streets formed, lined with quaint cottages and impressive public buildings. Leven could see the silhouettes of a thousand homes and buildings rising from the ground.

Geth looked down at Leven and Winter. Clover appeared on Leven's shoulder. He had a big grin on his face.

"Remember when you were a toothpick?" Clover asked.

Geth laughed and rested his hand on Leven's shoulder.

Leven had never felt happier.

CHAPTER THIRTY-SEVEN

THE CONSTRUCTION BEGINS

Tim pulled the last of the lumber out of the rented truck. Then, together, he and Dennis carried the building materials around the gasthaus and to a small abandoned barn not too far from the lake's shore. Tim was still trying to digest the story Dennis had told him earlier.

Foo?

Gateway?

Impossible!

Tim would have walked away from it all, simply thinking Dennis was crazy, but Dennis had known about Leven and seemed convinced a new gateway could be created. Plus, Dennis had shown Tim an angry, bent-in-half, talking toothpick. Tim now figured anything was possible.

Tim and Dennis had traveled to the nearest town and purchased a number of supplies to build a box that they would then place in the water to travel to an unknown destination hidden in everyone's brain. It was hard to believe, but Tim could think of no other explanation for some of the things he had seen and learned.

They stacked the wood up against the barn wall. Tim looked up at the night stars and then glanced down at Dennis, wondering why in the world he was putting so much trust in such an odd individual.

Dennis had on his tattered black robe and his wrinkle-proof pants. On the front of the robe he had placed his bank sticker. Dennis stood as if the entire ensemble made him invincible—his bald head shining under the light of the moon.

"So we build a box, fix it to the lake floor, and swim in?" Tim asked. "That's it?"

Dennis looked confused. Luckily for him, he was wearing Sabine. Sabine hissed up through Dennis's skin and out his mouth.

"We'll need a mismatched piece of ground," he breathed, trying hard to be civil, but sounding like an angry kitten.

Dennis began to writhe and scream. His black robe fluttered and whipped wildly about him. Dennis fell to the ground and lay there perfectly still. Sabine could feel that the last essence of him in Foo was no longer.

After a few moments, Dennis opened his eyes to find Tim hovering over him anxiously. "Are you okay?" he asked, reaching to help Dennis up.

"Fine," Sabine said out of Dennis. Dennis added a small hand wave to make it more convincing.

"So where do we find a mismatched piece of ground?" Tim asked.

Again Dennis looked confused.

Tim filled the silence himself.

"I guess we'll just build the box and worry about that when we get to it," he said enthusiastically.

"Excellent," Dennis hissed.

"I guess it's not too late to get started tonight," Tim added.

Dennis smiled and fought the urge to throw his head back and laugh wickedly. He won the battle with himself by placing his right hand over his mouth and pretending to cough.

Tim picked up a hammer.

CHAPTER THIRTY-EIGHT

THE CALM

Leven had never seen so much food. The large table in the center of the room was covered with meat-filled platters and deep dishes of whipped roots and potatoes. Gravy boats drifted among the islands of bread, filled to the rim with dark, savory sauces. Carrots the size of small, closed umbrellas, sprinkled with parsley, lay stacked like wood in a large dish, butter melting slowly over them.

The aromas were delicious.

Leven looked around the table in the immense dining hall of Geth's magnificent castle. Next to him sat Winter. The red had faded from her blonde hair, and she had her green eyes open and on full display as she took in the delectable sights and delightful smells.

Leven took her hand and squeezed it. "You okay?" he asked.

Winter smiled, pushing her hair behind her ears.

It was miraculous that she was even alive. Sadly, her gift had been stolen. It was a terrible thing for a nit to lose her gift, and Leven knew it would take some time before Winter was truly healed. He had already promised her that he would do whatever he could to get her gift back.

Leven looked past Winter to Geth. Geth was busy making up for all the food he had been denied as a toothpick.

Leven laughed, watching him.

He thought of the feelings he had for the small toothpick and the joy he had experienced at being able to see Geth as he really was. Foo felt safer with Geth and his city restored.

Geth had promised Leven he could have a couple of days to rest, but after that they would be leaving Niteon and heading to Lith. Geth felt it was time for Leven to meet the Want.

"Are you getting enough?" Leven asked Geth.

"No," Geth answered, with a full mouth.

"You might want to use your old self to clean your teeth when you're done eating," Clover said from across the table.

In the last couple of days Clover had thought up, and used, every toothpick joke imaginable.

"Have I used that one before?" Clover asked.

"Yes," they all answered.

Next to Clover was an empty chair. It reminded Leven of Amelia. He had known her for such a short while, but he felt like less of a person with her now gone. He hoped wherever she was, she was with Hector and happy. He wanted her to know that as he fought for Foo he wouldn't let her down. She would always be in his heart.

Leven also thought of the whisp he and Clover had found in the woods. In a small way he could relate to her. She had been snatched from everything she knew and put down in a place she had never even dreamed of. He had already talked to Geth about trying to find her. It was another one of the things they had to accomplish.

Jamoon had not been found. He was assumed dead, since his falling had been an accident of sorts. Already the Sochemists had sent out two waves of locusts informing the residents of Foo that all was well and Morfit was still in control.

Geth had been monitoring incoming dreams and trying to figure out if there was any truth to the rumor that someone in Reality was constructing a new gateway. Geth felt the chances were slim, but knew it was possible, if the one constructing it had the right brain. Geth had also reported that so many of the dreams coming into Foo at the moment were showing signs of changes in Reality—buildings moving, planes landing upside down, and huge dirt avalands showing up all over. It seemed as if Reality was showing the first signs of the war it didn't yet know about.

Leven looked down at himself. He touched his new black shirt and could feel the key hanging beneath it. He had still not shown it to Geth or Winter, but he and Clover had studied it for hours. Clover had said over and over that it was probably just a useless key and that Leven should just give it to him to throw away. Leven wasn't falling for it. He didn't know exactly what it was, but he knew he'd be wise to hold on to it.

He had no idea just how right he was.

Leven looked at Geth and Winter and Clover and the empty chair. The sight and smell of food filled his senses to the point where he thought they might burst.

Leven stood and struck his glass with his wooden spoon. All eyes turned to him.

"Just a few weeks ago, I was in Oklahoma, wishing my life was more interesting," Leven said, smiling at each of his friends. "Thanks for making it so full."

Each raised his or her glass, and Geth smiled. "Hear, hear!" he shouted.

Outside of Geth's castle the purple night sky pulsated and the stars cheered.

AFTERWORD

THE WHISPERED SECRET

Moonlight flooded the room like a heavenly night-light. Leven had never been in a more comfortable bed. Outside his half-opened window the leaves of a cluster of fantrum trees rustled softly in the dark breeze. The trees closest to his window tapped against the top of the glass, as if summoning Leven to sneak out.

Leven wasn't going anywhere except to sleep.

Leven could smell the sweet air flowing in through the window and dancing around the room. The gold glow from his eyes made the black ribbons of breeze visible.

The night felt somehow different. Leven figured it was because Clover wasn't around. Clover had been begging for the last couple of days for Leven to let him return to untie the onick and to go to the tharms' cave and free all the captured sycophants. Clover had insisted that it would take no more than a day, and that if he went invisibly and alone he could be in and out with no problem. Leven had told Clover he could do whatever he wanted, but that wasn't good enough. So, Clover kept on begging. Finally, Leven had *insisted* that Clover go.

Now Leven wished he hadn't agreed.

Leven pulled his thick blanket up and closed his eyes. The breeze outside moaned softly. Leven fluffed up his pillows and repositioned his head. He looked down the length of the bed to where his feet were. He didn't remember ever sleeping in a really comfortable bed. The single bed on the porch where Terry and Addy had stuck him was lumpy and narrow, and the bridge Leven and Winter had slept under was even worse. Now, here he was, these last few days sleeping in a bed bigger than himself with a mattress that could give marshmallows pointers.

Leven sighed, and for a moment life seemed good.

It's funny how fleeting those moments can be.

Sleep settled over Leven like new snow as a soft whisper blew into the room through the half-opened window. The whisper moaned, swooping around the room like an undisciplined tornado.

Leven's tired eyes blinked open, and he looked toward the window as a thick patch of night sky began crawling in. It would have been impossible to see if not for the light color of the walls. The image reminded Leven of the air in Fissure Gorge.

Leven sat up.

Once through the window, the patch stood and slunk along the wall as if it were hiding. But the small amount of moonlight gave it definition.

"What are—"

Leven stopped talking because the whispered secret was tip-toeing closer, unaware that Leven could see it.

Leven was foolish not to act.

The secret stepped closer and stared Leven directly in the eyes. He had been recognized.

Any calm Leven had previously felt was now gone. The secret lunged at Leven, knocking him in the chest and sending him flying backward off the bed. The secret banged in and out of his ears and through his brain like a metal stake.

Leven grabbed at his head and screamed in pain.

He tried to fight it, but there was nothing to grab. He knocked a water basin from a small table and sent it crashing to the floor. The once-buried secret moved off Leven and howled joyfully. Then it whipped around the room and began to slip out the window.

Leven sat there trembling.

Suddenly the door to his room opened, and there stood Geth. He looked around the room and spotted the secret slipping out. Without saying anything, Geth lunged for the window and grabbed hold of the secret's feet. The whispering secret hissed and kicked itself free, pushing all the way out of the house.

Empty-handed, Geth turned to Leven.

"Are you okay?"

"I think so," Leven replied, still shaken by the experience.

"You released a secret?" Geth demanded.

"By accident," Leven said. "I dug it up in the forest, days ago."

"Has it been following you?" Geth panicked.

"Clover had been keeping an eye on it," Leven said in a daze and feeling more frightened than he ever had before. "I didn't realize what it really was."

"What was it hiding?" Geth demanded. "What did it tell you?"

"I can't say," Leven said. He was trembling all over. "I can't tell you."

"Of course you can," Geth insisted. "The whole of Foo will know in a matter of days. Once a secret informs the soul who dug it up, it's under no obligation to keep it to itself. And a secret that strong will tell anyone who will listen."

Leven stood in a panic. "We have to find Clover," he insisted. "Now!"

"Why?" Geth asked.

"Because," Leven moaned, "in a few hours all of Foo is going to know how to get rid of sycophants."

"Sit," Geth insisted, pushing Leven's shoulders down. "You know how sycophants die?"

"I think so. We have to find Clover."

"You couldn't possibly know," Geth said. "That secret is untouchable. It can't get out. If sycophants could be killed, then their lands could be captured. And their lands hide some of the most important tools in Foo."

"Then what was that secret?" Leven asked, still shaking and pointing toward the window it had escaped through.

"It must have been a decoy," Geth said calmly.

"How can you tell?"

"The real secret is locked by key," Geth said. "There's no way it could get out unless you had used the key."

Leven's face went pale. He reached down his shirt and withdrew the key that had been hanging around his neck.

Not since Geth had been pulled from Clover's void had he looked so frightened. Geth touched the key carefully.

"How?"

"It was an accident," Leven said. "We were in the forest."

"The Want must be told," Geth declared. "Tonight."

"And we have to find Clover."

Geth looked down at Leven. "Of course," he said.

Leven stood and glanced at the soft bed he was leaving. It didn't matter; he could think of nothing but Clover. Leven threw on his dark robe and let his eyes burn gold.

He had a secret to stop.

WHO'S WHO IN FOO

LEVEN THUMPS

Leven is fourteen years old and is the grandson of Hector Thumps, the builder of the gateway. Leven originally knew nothing of Foo or of his heritage. He eventually discovered his true identity: He is an offing who can see and manipulate the future. Leven's brown eyes burn gold whenever his gift kicks in.

WINTER FRORE

Winter is thirteen, with white-blonde hair and deep evergreen eyes. Her pale skin and willowy clothes give her the appearance of a shy spirit. Like Sabine, she is a nit and has the ability to freeze whatever she wishes. She was born in Foo, but her thoughts and memories of her previous life are gone. Winter struggles just to figure out what her purpose is.

GETH

Geth has existed for hundreds of years. In Foo he was one of the strongest and most respected beings, a powerful lithen. Geth is the head token of the Council of Wonder and the heir to the throne of Foo. Eternally optimistic, Geth is also the most outspoken against the wishes of Sabine. To silence Geth, Sabine trapped Geth's soul in the seed of a fantrum tree and left him for the birds. Fate rescued Geth, and in the dying hands of his loyal friend Antsel he was taken through the gateway, out of Foo, and planted in Reality. He was brought back to Foo by Leven and Winter.

SABINE (SUH-BINE´)

Sabine is the darkest and most selfish being in Foo. Snatched from Reality at the age of nine, he is now a nit with the ability to freeze whatever he wishes. Sabine thirsts to rebuild the gateway because he believes if he can move freely between Foo and Reality he can rule them both. So evil and selfish are his desires that the very shadows he casts seek to flee him, giving him the ability to send his dark castoffs down through the dreams of men so he can view and mess with Reality.

ANTSEL

Antsel was an aged member of the Council of Wonder. He was fiercely devoted to the philosophy of Foo and to preserving the dreams of men. He was Geth's greatest supporter, and he was deeply loyal to the Council. Snatched from Reality many years ago, he was a nit who had the ability to see perfectly underground. He was a true Foo-fighter who perished for the cause.

CLOVER ERNEST

Clover is a sycophant from Foo assigned to look after Leven. He is about twelve inches tall and furry all over except for his face, knees, and elbows. He wears a shimmering robe that renders him completely invisible if the hood is up. He is incredibly curious and mischievous to a fault. His previous burn was Antsel.

JAMOON

Jamoon is Sabine's right-hand man as well as a rant. Because he is a rant, half of his body is unstable, transformed continually into the form of the dreams being entertained by humans. He is totally obedient to Sabine's wishes. Jamoon believes Sabine's promise that if he and his kind can get into Reality, the rants' unusual condition will be healed.

HECTOR THUMPS

Hector Thumps is Leven's grandfather and the creator of the gateway. When fate snatched him into Foo, he fought to find a way back to the girl he loved in Reality. His quest nearly drove him mad.

AMELIA THUMPS

Amelia is the woman Hector Thumps married after he returned to Foo a second time. She is Leven's grandmother and lives between Morfit and the Fundrals of Foo. She was the protector of the gateway to Foo.

TIM TUTTLE

Tim is a garbage man and a kindly neighbor of Winter. In Reality, Tim and his wife, Wendy, looked after Winter after being instructed to do so by Amelia. When Winter goes missing, Tim sets out to find her.

DENNIS WOOD

Dennis is a janitor whom fate has picked to carry out a great task. He leads a lonely life and has never dreamed.

JANET FRORE

Janet is a woman who believes she is Winter's mother but has no concern that Winter is missing. She has spent her life caring only for herself.

TERRY AND ADDY GRAPH

Terry and Addy were Leven's horrible-care givers in Reality.

THE ORDER OF THINGS

CHILDREN OF THE SEWN

The Children of the Sewn live beneath and amongst the roots of the Red Grove. They are patched together from dreams and imaginations. They are the only framers in Foo. Their task is to frame the strong dreams so that they can be focused on and achieved, and to frame the darkest dreams so that they are contained and stopped.

COGS

Cogs are the ungifted offspring of nits. They possess no great single talent, yet they can manipulate and enhance dreams.

EGGMEN

The Eggmen live beneath the Devil's Spiral and are master candy makers. They are egg-shaped and fragile, but dedicated believers in Foo.

FISSURE GORGE

Fissure Gorge is a terrific gorge that runs from the top of Foo to the Veil Sea. At its base is a burning, iridescent glow that creates a great mist when it meets with the sea. The heat also shifts and changes the hard, mazelike air that fills the gorge.

GIFTS

There are twelve gifts in Foo. Every nit can take on a single gift to help him or her enhance dreams. The gifts are:

See through soil
Run like the wind
Freeze things
Breathe fire
Levitate objects
Burrow
See through stone
Shrink
Throw lightning
Fade in and out
Push and bind dreams
Fly

LITHENS (LIE´-THUNS)

Lithens were the original dwellers of Foo, placed in the realm by fate. They are committed to the sacred task of preserving the true Foo. Lithens live and travel by fate, and they fear almost nothing. They are honest and are believed to be incorruptible. Geth is a lithen.

LORE COIL

Lore Coils are created when something of great passion or energy happens in Foo. The energy drifts out in a growing circle across Foo, giving information or showing static-like images to those it passes over. When the Lore Coil reaches the borders of Foo, it bounces back to where it came from. It can bounce back and forth for many years. Most do not hear it after the second pass.

NIHILS (NILLS)

Nihils are black scavenger birds that pick at the leaves and bark of trees, searching for and eating small bits of leftover dreams that have settled in the trees. They are aggressive and a nuisance.

NITS

Niteons—or nits, as they are referred to—are humans who were once on earth and were brought to Foo by fate. Nits are the working class of Foo. They are the most stable and the best dream enhancers. Each is given a powerful gift soon after he or she arrives in Foo. A number of nits can control fire or water or ice. Some can see in the pitch dark or walk through walls and rock. Some can levitate and change shape. Nits are usually loyal and honest. Both Winter Frore and Sabine are nits.

OFFINGS

Offings are rare and powerful. Unlike others who might be given only one gift, offings can see and manipulate the future as well as learn other gifts. Offings are the most trusted confidants of the Want. Leven Thumps is an offing.

PALEHI (PALE´-HIE)

The palehi are a group of beings who refuse to take sides.

They escort people through the Swollen Forest. They are pale from all the frightening things they have seen. Their arms are marked with stripes that keep count of how many trips through the forest they have made.

RANTS

Rants are nit offspring that are born with too little character to successfully manipulate dreams. They are constantly in a state of instability and chaos. As dreams catch them, half of their bodies become the image of what someone in Reality is dreaming at the moment. Rants are usually dressed in long robes to hide their odd, unstable forms. Jamoon is a rant.

RINGS OF PLAGUE

The Rings of Plague were created by Sabine. There were originally two, but Geth defeated one of them. The remaining Ring consists of eleven nits plus Sabine, each possessing one of the different gifts of Foo. Collectively having all the gifts, they are a threat to most.

ROVENS

Rovens are large, colorful, winged creatures that are raised in large farms in the dark caves beneath Morfit. They are used for transportation and are sought after because of their unbreakable talons. Unlike most in Foo, rovens can be killed. They are fierce diggers and can create rips in the very soil of Foo. When they shed their hair, it can live for a short while. They often shed their hair and let it do their dirty work.

SARUS

The sarus are thick, fuzzy bugs who can fly. They swarm their victims and carry them off by biting down and lifting as a group. They can communicate only through the vibration of water. They are in control of the gaze and in charge of creating gigantic trees.

SIIDS

There were originally seven siids—humongous, mountain-sized beasts whose weight helped balance the landscape of Foo. Siids have the gift of killing and in turn can be killed. Years ago some siids were hunted and killed off, and now many in Foo feel that the unbalance and darkening of Foo are somehow connected to their absence.

SOCHEMISTS

The Sochemists of Morfit are a group of twenty-four aged beings who listen for Lore Coils and explain what they hear. They are constantly fighting over what they believe they have heard. They communicate what they know to the rest of Foo by using locusts.

SYCOPHANTS (SICK´-O-FUNTS)

Sycophants are assigned to serve those who are snatched into

Foo. Their job is to help those new residents of Foo understand and adjust to a whole different existence. They spend their entire lives serving the people to whom they are assigned, called their "burns." There is only one way for sycophants to die, but nobody aside from the sycophants knows what that is.

THARMS

Tharms are short, smelly creatures who populate the Swollen Forest. They have a third arm where a tail would be. They are mysterious and love to capture and bury things in the forest. They also like to ransom those they have caught for favors.

THE TURRETS

The turrets of Foo are a large circle of stone turrets that surround a mile-high pillar of restoring flame. The turrets sit on a large area of Niteon and are surrounded by a high fence. The main way to the flame is through the gatehouse that sits miles away.

THE WANT

The Want is the virtually unseen but constantly felt sage of Foo. He lives on the island of Lith and can see every dream that comes in. He is prophetic and a bit mad from all the visions he has had.

THE WAVES OF THE LIME SEA

The Waves of the Lime Sea are a mysterious and misunderstood group of beings who guard the island of Alder. Their loyalty is to the oldest tree that grows on the island.

WHISPS

Whisps are the sad images of beings who were only partially snatched from Reality into Foo. They have no physical bodies, but they can think and reason. They are sought after for their ideas, but miserable because they can't feel or touch anything.

